# VOICE

## OF THE

# FALCONER

# VOICE

## OF THE

# FALCONER

DAVID BLIXT

Published by
Sordelet Ink

English language excerpts of Dante Alighieri's L'INFERNO, PURGATORIO, and PARADISO that appear in this novel are from, or adapted from translations of each text by Robert Hollander and Jean Hollander (Doubleday).

English language excerpts of THE BALLAD OF VERONA by Manuello Guido are from, or adapted from, a translation by Rita Severi.

# Voice of the Falconer

First Edition by Sordelet Ink
Cover by David Blixt
Maps by Jill Blixt

ISBN-13: 978-0615783154
ISBN-10: 0615783155

www.davidblixt.com

Printed in U.S.A
Published by Sordelet Ink

IN MEMORIAM

JIM POSANTE
(1946 – 2008)

PAGE HAMILTON HEARN
(1960 – 2008)

WILL SCHUTZ
(1962 – 2009)

ARTISTS – MENTORS – FRIENDS

"Time is for dragonflies and angels. The former live too little
and the latter live too long."

— *James Thurber*

For Janice, Dashiell, & Evelyn ~

Signifying everything

# CONTENTS

# DRAMATIS PERSONAE

♦ a character recorded by history     ◊ a character from Shakespeare

## *Della Scala Family of Verona*

♦    FRANCESCO 'CANGRANDE' DELLA SCALA – Ruler of Verona, Imperial Vicar of the Trevisian Mark (Verona, Vicenza, Padua, & Treviso)

♦    GIOVANNA DA SVEVIA – Cangrande's wife, Paride's aunt

♦    FEDERIGO DELLA SCALA – Cangrande's cousin

♦    ALBERTO II DELLA SCALA – Cangrande's nephew, brother of Mastino

♦    MASTINO II DELLA SCALA – Cangrande's nephew, brother of Alberto

♦    VERDE DELLA SCALA – Cangrande's niece, sister of Alberto & Mastino

♦    CATERINA DELLA SCALA – Cangrande's niece, sister of Alberto & Mastino

♦    ALBUINA DELLA SCALA – Cangrande's niece, sister of Alberto & Mastino

♦ /◊    FRANCESCO 'CESCO' DELLA SCALA – Cangrande's heir, a bastard, b. 1314

◊    PARIDE DELLA SCALA – son of Cecchino della Scala, b. 1315

xi

## Nogarola Family of Vicanza

- ANTONIO NOGAROLA – Vicentine nobleman, elder brother to Bailardino

- BAILARDINO NOGAROLA – Lord of Vicenza, husband to Cangrande's sister, Katerina

- KATERINA DELLA SCALA – sister to Cangrande, wife of Bailardino

  BAILARDETTO 'DETTO' NOGAROLA – elder son of Bailardino and Katerina, b. 1315

◊ VALENTINO NOGAROLA – younger son of Bailardino and Katerina, b. 1317

## Alaghieri Family of Florence

- PIETRO ALAGHIERI – Dante's heir, lawyer, knight of Verona, steward of Ravenna

- JACOPO 'POCO' ALAGHIERI – Dante's youngest son

- ANTONIA ALAGHIERI – Dante's daughter, taking holy vows as Suor Beatrice

## Carrara Family of Padua

- MARSILIO DA CARRARA – Lord of Padua, cousin of Gianozza Montecchio

- NICCOLO DA CARRARA – cousin of Marsilio, brother to Ubertino

- UBERTINO DA CARRARA – cousin of Marsilio, brother to Niccolo

- CUNIZZA DA CARRARA – sister of Marsilio

## *Montecchio Family of Verona*

◊ ROMEO MARIOTTO MONTECCHIO – Lord of Montecchio, father to Romeo

◊ GIANOZZA DELLA BELLA – Mariotto's wife, cousin to Carrara, mother to Romeo

◊ ROMEO MARIOTTO MONTECCHIO II – son of Mariotto and Gianozza, b. 1321

AURELIA MONTECCHIO – sister to Mariotto, wife of Benvenito Lenoti

BENVENITO LENOTI – knight of Verona, husband to Aurelia Montecchio

◊ BENVOLIO LENOTI – son of Benvenito and Aurelia, b. 1319

## *Capulletto Family of Verona*

◊ ANTONIO CAPULLETTO – Lord of the Capulletti family, born in Capua

◊ ARNALDO CAPULLETTO – uncle of Antonio

◊ TESSA GUARINI – wife of Antonio, mother of Giulietta, b. 1313

◊ THEOBALDO 'THIBAULT' CAPULLETTO – nephew of Antonio, b. 1315

◊ GIULIETTA CAPULLETTO – daughter of Antonio and Tessa, b. 1325

xiii

# Supporting Characters

ABBESS VERDIANA – Benedictine abbess in charge of Santa Maria in Organo in Verona

♦ ALBERTINO MUSSATO – Paduan historian-poet

◊ ANDRIOLO DA VERONA – Capulletto's chief groom, husband to Angelica

◊ ANGELICA DA VERONA – Tessa and Thibault's Nurse, wife to Andriolo

AVENTINO FRACASTORO – Personal physician to Cangrande

◊ BAPTISTA MINOLA – Paduan noble, father of Katerina and Bianca

♦ BERNARDO ERVARI – knight of Verona, member of the Anziani

♦ BISHOP FRANCIS – Franciscan Bishop, leader of Veronese spiritual growth

◊ FRA LORENZO – Franciscan friar with family in France

♦ FRANCESCO DANDOLO – Venetian nobleman

♦ GUGLIELMO CASTELBARCO – Veronese noble, Cangrande's Armourer

♦ GUGLIELMO CASTELBARCO II – Castelbarco's son

GUISEPPE MORSICATO – Nogarola family doctor, living in Ravenna

HORTENSO & PETRUCHIO II BONAVENTURA – twin sons of Katerina and Petruchio

◊ KATERINA BONAVENTURA – Paduan born heiress, daughter of Baptista Minola

♦     MANOELLA GUIDEO – Cangrande's Master of Revels

MASSIMILIANO DA VILLAFRANCA – Constable of Cangrande's palace

♦     NICCOLO DA LOZZO – Paduan-born knight, changed sides to join Cangrande

NIKLAS FUCHS – German-born campanion to Mastino della Scala

♦     PASSERINO BONACCOLSI – Podestà of Mantua, ally to Cangrande

◊     PETRUCHIO BONAVENTURA – Veronese noble, married to Katerina

◊     SHALAKH – A Jew, Venetian money-lender, father of Jessica

THARWAT AL-DHAAMIN – Moorish master astrologer, called the Arūs

TULLIO D'ISOLA – aged steward, Grand Butler to Cangrande

ZILIBERTO DELL'ANGELO – Cangrande's Master of the Hunt

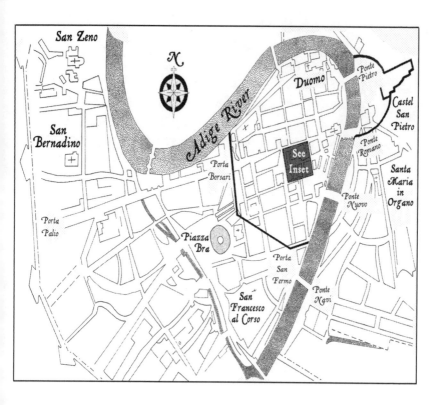

 The City of Verona

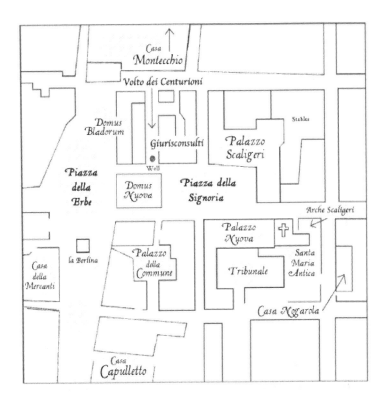

Casa
Montecchio

Volto dei Centurioni

Domus
Bladorum

Giurisconsulti

Palazzo
Scaligeri

Stables

Piazza
della
Erbe

Well

Domus
Nuova

Piazza della
Signoria

Arche Scaligeri

la Berlina

Palazzo
della
Commune

Palazzo
Nuova

Tribunale

Santa
Maria
Antica

Casa
della
Mercanti

Casa Nogarola

Casa
Capulletto

# Piazza della Signoria
## 1325

Northern Italy

Adige

Lago di Garda

Rivole

Vicenza

Treviso

Illasi

Montecchio

Venice

San Bonifacio

Padua

Verona

Cremona

Adige River

Calvatone

Mantua

Po River

Bologna

Ravenna

40 Miles

Lucca

Florence

Pisa

Arno River

Wretched me who loved a sparrow-hawk
I loved him so much that I'll die from it:
At the sound of the bird call he was obedient,
And in no way did I feed him too much.

Now he's ascended to new heights,
Much higher than he ever used to –
Next he's seated in a garden
And another has him in her power.

My hawk, that I nourished,
I made him carry a golden bell,
For I was the boldest at hunting –

Now you're as free as the sea,
Having broken your bands, escaping
When you were caught in your own hunt.

- Anonymous late 13th century Poetess

...O, for a falconer's voice
to lure this tassle-gentle back again!

- Juliet
*Romeo & Juliet*, act II scene ii

# PROLOGUE

*Verona*
*Friday, 12 July*
*1325*

## "THE GREYHOUND IS DEAD!"

The news spread quickly, an inferno of desperate tidings. The great man had been traveling in haste to Vicenza – always it was Vicenza! – to head off yet another Paduan attack when he had taken suddenly ill and died.

All over Italy, Guelphs rejoiced the demise of their nemesis. Cities embraced or conquered by him looked around at a world reshaped and wondered what would befall.

Within an hour of the news' arrival in Verona, the inevitable crowd had congregated outside the Scaliger palace in the Piazza della Signoria, hundreds of men staring upwards for a sign, a signal. A savior.

On the north side of that same piazza, in the Giurisconsulti, the fourteen-member city council shouted in fierce debate. "Why not hold free elections?"

"Because we have no idea who will step into the void!"

"The people will only vote for a della Scala!"

"Then we have to decide which family members should be allowed to run."

There were pitifully few choices. The ideal candidate, Cecchino della Scala, was dead, killed in a tournament mishap last February. There remained three nominees, none suitable, none of age.

"Damn fool! Never saw past his own delusions of grandeur, never took the elementary precaution of making a will!"

"Especially after Ponte Corbo, you'd have thought—"

"Shut your mouths, the pair of you," snapped Guglielmo da Castelbarco the elder, a senior member of this council. "We have work."

"Yes," agreed Bernardo Ervari, an efficient functionary and Castelbarco's friend. "First we must confirm his death. I've sent couriers and priests. The next thing we need to do—"

"—is contact his wife, in Munich," finished a tough, broad-shouldered fellow with wine-stains on his doublet. New to the council, his suggestion was met with covert smiles. Petruchio Bonaventura was a man known for his wife as much as himself.

Castelbarco nodded as though that had been his intent. In truth, there was another message to send first, one he alone could write. For his fellows were mistaken. There *was* a will.

"Actually, Bonaventura, I say we let her live in blissful ignorance." When heads turned his way, the short-statured knight called Nico da Lozzo opened his hands. "Fut! We all know what she'll say. But Paride's only ten years old, there's no chance the people will accept him."

"The people will accept whomever we tell them to," observed a clean-shaven man in the miter of a Bishop and the cassock of a Franciscan.

Castelbarco tested those waters. "You'd nominate a child, your Excellency? The Church would endorse one so young?"

"It's a more palatable option than—"

"Even knowing," interjected Nico da Lozzo pointedly, "who would be pulling his strings?"

Out of the ensuing uneasy silence, the ruddy-faced Petruchio Bonaventura suddenly laughed through his unkempt beard. "At least the bride-thief and the cradle-robber aren't here to add to our dilemma. I for one can do without the bickering."

Their chuckles of agreement were suddenly drowned out by a roar that shook the walls. Bolting from their stools, the Anziani of Verona raced outside, praying it was all a mistake, hoping against hope to see the Greyhound restored to life.

Instead they reached the steps outside to discover the question of succession unpalatably resolved for them.

On the balcony of the new Scaliger palace stood three men, each as different as family resemblance allowed. The first was a whippet-thin man of middle years and middle height. Federigo della Scala, grandnephew to the first Scaliger to rule the city, was shaking his knobby hands above his head as if he had just won the Palio, the summer sun highlighting the silver in his hair.

The second man, only eighteen years old, was by far the largest of the trio. Oft mocked for his shambling gait, he was nevertheless well liked thanks to his liberal purse and generous smile. Alberto della Scala, called

Alblivious by those who knew him.

The third man atop the Palazzo Nuova stood apart from his cousin and brother, right at the lip of the balcony. He didn't wave, didn't smile. Darker of hair than the others, his face owned a handsome leanness. Flashing in the late afternoon sun, his eyes were a blue so dark as to be mistaken for black. Named for the first Scaligeri ruler, he looked down from the palace built by his namesake that was now, by the power of the people's cheers, his.

Mastino della Scala. Sixteen years old last month. No one mocked him. Not ever.

The Greyhound was dead.

Long live the Mastiff.

# I

# Vex Not His Ghost

# ONE

*Ravenna*
*Saturday, 13 July*
*1325*

JUST AS GIOTTO was ambivalent about his O – what could be simpler? – so the stars regarded the boy. But far below their winks and capricious tricks of fate, mortal men made the grave error of taking him at face value.

Corrado certainly did. In a side room of the church of the *Frati Minori*, he was standing with his back to the door, measuring a stone slab with his forearm, when a voice said, "He was shorter than that."

Corrado jumped and spun round, sweat breaking across his brow. But the intruder was just a boy, hardly as high as Corrado's breastbone. Backlit by the slanting sun, a few golden curls among the chestnut caught the light.

"Laid out, he measured at five feet, six inches, but he stooped, so he seemed even shorter. That is what you're trying to decide, isn't it?" The boy strolled into the mausoleum, and Corrado saw with disgust that the lad was comely, too pretty by half. But those eyes… They were unsettling, dancing green flecked with gold, a pale blue ring around them. Full of mirth, full of mischief.

Corrado shook a fist. "Beat it, brat, or I'll beat you."

Shrugging, the imp smiled, his mouth curling like an artist's afterthought. The angelic perfection was marred only by a small scar beside the right eye. "Only trying to help. He was my grandfather, you see."

*Oh damn.* Corrado had been told there were relatives living in the city, but hadn't expected them to come visiting the body in the middle of the day. He stepped forward, fist high. "I said get out of it!"

Skipping backward on his heels, the boy laughed as if Corrado were a motley fool dancing for his amusement. "As you wish." With a sweeping bow the boy vanished back into the sunlight, whistling as he went.

Listening as the whistle slowly faded, Corrado wiped the sweat from his eyes and muttered a blasphemous curse. Best get this done and go. Church parishioners were hard at prayer or gossip, and most of the friars were engaged in tedious holy affairs. But the little bastard could tattle, bringing his elders back with awkward questions.

Still, the boy's information had been helpful. Knowing the size of the body, Corrado simply measured the slab covering the sarcophagus as two-thirds the thickness of his forearm. That done, he could do the calculations back at the inn.

Crossing beneath the side chapel's huge wrought-iron candelabra, Corrado retreated into the church proper. To ward off suspicion he genuflected and pretended to pray. The Franciscans in their silly hoods went about their business, paying no attention to another scruffy pilgrim. A minute later he was out the door, dropping a copper coin into the devotion box as he passed. He was a satisfied man. The tomb was easily reached, and accessible only from the main church, not through the monastery.

Which was a stroke of luck, as he'd been hired to rob it.

♦    ◊    ♦

Taking care not to be followed, Corrado made his way to the Red Griffin Inn. Two miles outside the city walls, it was sparsely populated, with just a few men drinking on the ground floor, and no women except for a fat old wench with arms the size of tree-trunks who brought the ale and threw out any troublemakers.

Four armed men sat with their backs to the far wall. One pretended to doze, the other three diced on a scarred wooden table. They didn't signal to him, but each one caught his ostentatious rubbing of his nose. The job was on.

Corrado ordered a stoup of wine, then ascended the side stairs to the inn's finest room and knocked.

"*Entra!*"

The room was well-appointed, with heavy tapestries and large windows. The windows were thrown wide to admit the midday sun, the bright light illuminating dust motes floating on the hot, still air. The heat was oppressive, and even in the street there was no movement to the air. Inside, it was almost unbearable.

The room's occupant was sprawled on a chair and foot-stool by a window. Fully dressed in a fine doublet, light shirt, expensive hose, and tall leather boots, he was reading from some book and eating olives from a bowl. His sole concession to the heat was a hand-fan, very like a lady's.

As Corrado closed the door behind him, the man kicked the footstool across, transferring his feet to the windowsill. "You sweat like a pig, man. Or is it something else? Tell me you weren't seen."

Sitting, Corrado decided not to mention the child. "No."

"Good." Dipping into the olives again, the fellow made no offer to share. "Your report?"

"The slab is six and a half feet long, two and a half wide, and eight inches deep. It looks to be fitted, which means an extension inside, probably another two or three inches. It needs all six of us."

The dandy spat a pit out the open window and daintily wiped his lips. "Five, you mean."

"You're not coming?"

The question was evidently amusing. "Do I look like a hired hand?"

Corrado scratched his head. "I'm not sure we can do it with less. Can I—?"

"May I." The correction was casual, automatic.

"May I—?"

"No. No local involvement. Five will have to do."

Corrado watched the dandy suck down another olive, thinking how absurdly simple it would be to kill him. He wouldn't be able to show his face in Tuscany again, but he'd be free. He could take the four men downstairs and build a band of highwaymen – maybe up by Verona, where the Alps forced travelers to a single path. Or else Spain. There was always a need for Italian soldiers in places like Aragon or Portugal. All it would take…

Pretending to think, Corrado rose and began to pace. "That means there's no one can keep watch – it'll take all of us to lift the damn thing. No way to keep the friars from ringing the bells if they find us out."

"Cut the bell-rope before you begin." Relaxed, the dandy fanned himself and thumbed a page of his book.

"Aye, that's a start." Pausing behind the dandy, Corrado drew a misericordia from his tall boot. Eyes on the dandy's exposed neck, Corrado took two quick steps forward…

He was pelted by small wet objects, then something hard. There was a twist of his wrist, his knees buckled, and a moment later he was flat on his back, his knife no longer in his hand but pressed against his throat. The dandy had a boot-heel against his arm, and was grinding his knee into Corrado's sternum.

"Corrado, Corrado. You've already incurred a death sentence. Why try for two?"

Corrado gasped. "I – I didn't —"

Somehow the fan was still in the man's left hand. It cracked across Corrado's cheek. "Of course you did. I'm surprised it took you so long. You're not the quickest hound in the pack, are you? You're released from prison and imminent hanging with me as your only watcher. If you remove me, you're free. Now, how hard is that?" The knife didn't waver as the dandy put more weight down on his chest. Instinctively Corrado sat up, causing the knife at his throat to draw a trickle of blood. "But you must remember, dear sweet Corrado, that you are not as swift as a cat, nor do you have sharp teeth for gnashing. You are a simple rat, with a skill for skulking. Whereas my nature leans far more towards the feline. And like a cat, I can play with my food before or after killing it. At the moment, I need your skills. But not so much that another offence will be tolerated. Understood?"

Vomit in his throat, tears in his eyes, Corrado didn't move a muscle. "Yes."

"Excellent." The dandy rose, dropping the knife to the floor. Gulping down air, Corrado doubled over, clutching himself.

Retrieving his book and clucking his tongue over having bent the pages, the dandy returned to his perch by the window. Turning the chair upright, he settled his feet again on the sill. "Gather your disciples, and prepare yourself to teach them the only lesson you know, my wormtailed – if not friend, shall I say at least comrade? For we are comrades, *a fin, fin et demi*. Tonight the very trade that condemned you shall give you life. Pray do not vomit on the floor, I just had the girl in to sweep."

Corrado touched his bleeding neck and pulled himself upright, his feet crushing the strewn olives into the floorboards. His breath easing, he plucked up the knife and crept from the room. At the door he turned. "Where will you be, my lord, when we're through?"

"Here, or out. Never fear. Our arrangement is solid. If you are successful, you shall receive the letters of pardon and be free to die again another day. Now leave me to suffer this unbearable heat. Oh, and Corrado – could you send the girl in? I'm out of olives."

As Corrado departed, the dandy took a moment to adjust the open window – the window that marked this as the best room in the inn. Glass was so much more useful than mere shutters. It was a heartbreaking blow to the dandy that fifty or so years earlier the Syrians had sold their secrets to Venice and not his own city. The whole of Italy was clamoring for glass vessels and baubles. What a monopoly the Venetians were building!

The maker of this particularly crude window had not been Venetian. The beech wood ash and the sand were improperly mixed, with many large imperfections where the artisan had blown too hard or too soft. But it was sufficient to provide a reflection. Poor simple Corrado had chosen the exact wrong place to stand when he drew his knife.

The girl entered with a fresh bowl, and the dandy watched that same reflection as the girl bent over to clean up the squashed olives on the floor. She had splendid hips, and he imagined that backside of hers was as tasty as a peach. He thought he might call upon her later – or rather, insist that she call upon him. A fine diversion while Corrado plied his trade.

The girl departed and he returned to his book, a rather poor collection of poems. Just as he was losing himself in the second stanza, something in one of the bubbling imperfections caught his eye. Something moving on the rooftop further along the inn. Probably a bird.

Some minutes later, as he stood and stretched, he glanced out the window and noted the serving girl he fancied chatting with a child. He watched, amused, as they talked earnestly for several minutes. He could have leaned out the window to hear, but it was nothing of consequence.

# TWO

CORRADO WAITED for the final Benedictine observance before setting out, using the time to make sure his men were well-oiled for the work at hand. It took a queer man to be a grave robber, and Corrado was the only one among them who'd been convicted of that particular crime.

It was only a week since he'd been slated to hang from a gibbet for violating a rich man's grave – it was a rule of his profession not to pay attention to names. Not only could it engender sympathy for some widow or child, it was bad for the imagination.

Caught, he'd taken a fierce beating before being dragged in front of a consul who judged him guilty as sin. Which Corrado couldn't argue, since they'd turned out his pockets to find the dead man's rings, fingers and all. He'd begged quite shamelessly for his life, unabashedly offering his services to the city if only they would spare him. Deaf to his pleas, they'd beaten him again and thrown him in with murderers and heretics, who had cheerfully continued the beating. His profession lacked esteem in the eyes of more accomplished villains.

Then, an hour before the dawn of his slated death, he had been taken from his cell to a carriage with covered windows and transported to a house overlooking the Arno. Manhandled through the door and thrust down among the straw rushes of the foyer, he'd looked up to see the dandy sauntering towards him.

"This is a grave-robber? Really? I would have thought he'd been leaner. Perhaps stout of stomach, stout of heart. Can you speak?"

Corrado had mumbled something and the man had laughed,

unleashing a further string of jibes. After an eternity of empty talking, the dandy had smiled and ordered Corrado to his feet. "Like the emperors of old, I have the power to grant life or mete out death. And, like that first Caesar, I am given to rash clemency. But, like Pompey, I must have a little something in return. You don't have a daughter, do you?"

Corrado blinked and stammered that he hadn't, that he knew of.

"Pity. Then it must be a father. No no, not your father, or even mine. No, I am looking for a surrogate father, and you are uniquely suited to bring me one. I have a particular fellow in mind. Oh, do stop trembling and listen, don't ruin my fun – I'm playing Caesar! I need a less-than-living fellow delivered into my hands. If you do this minor deed for me, I might be able to have your regrettable sentence lifted. Well, I'm fibbing a bit – I've already had it lifted by a special decree. I have stored the document neatly away. No one knows of it save me and the Anziani, and the city elders aren't likely to raise a fuss if I let you go to your arranged marriage to a hempen wife. However, if you aid me in this little task, I'll gladly hand the thing over and we can smell the last of each other. What do you say?"

Corrado had had trouble following the fellow's jaunting talk. "You want me to steal a body for you, and you'll let me go?"

"What a mind! What a prodigy! In a dozen years he'll be reading and writing at the level of a trained monkey! What do you say?"

What else but yes? He'd chosen four other men from the prison, strong hands eager for freedom – not men who had beaten him, which was a pleasant revenge.

Learning whose body he was to steal, Corrado had felt a shiver of fear. But with his neck at stake, he now led his company of cut-throats and fiends to the walls of the city, guarded by a single man with a torch. Seeing no armour and only what weapons a man might carry on a lonely road, the town porter let them in.

Corrado led them to the handcart he had stashed in town. It bore picks, iron crows, and a storm lantern. Pulling on hoods so they resembled friars of the Frati Minori, they set out towards the churchyard. It was a perfect night for grave-robbing, moonless and so cloudy that even the stars would not reveal the trespassers.

As it was between the hours of observance, the friars of San Lorenzo were all hopefully asleep. Corrado wanted none lingering in the church, as he had no desire to raise a hand against a holy man. But without the corpse there was no freedom, only the end of a rope to make corpses of them all. One dead body for five live ones. The trade was more than fair, so woe to anyone who tried to stop them.

One by one they slipped into the church, glancing down the darkened nave towards the altar. One of the robbers knelt to cross himself, but the others stopped him, thinking it unwise to draw the Lord's attention.

Padding on cat's feet, Corrado led them into the side chapel. Inside he set the shuttered lantern on the floor and lifted two metal wings just enough to illuminate the marble sarcophagus. He glanced around, but all was the same as it had been that afternoon – save that the candelabra overhead was now covered with a tarp. Odd. But who knew why friars did anything?

Crossing to the stone slab, he lifted his iron bar and sidled it under the lip of the heavy lid. The other felons joined him, and they began to heave.

Corrado began to sweat. Not from the warm night or the exertion, or even fear of discovery. He had serious misgivings about desecrating this particular grave. Under any normal circumstance he wouldn't have dared. In life this was a man who had consorted with demons. Unearthing his bones was a sure invitation to do the same, or worse.

They'd been at work for two minutes, scraping and grunting, when one of them said, "Did you hear that?"

All five froze, listening intently for the patter of sandaled feet. But the church was silent.

Corrado turned to the man who'd spoken. "What did you hear?"

"It – it sounded like – like a voice."

"Where?"

"In here!"

Corrado scowled. "Nerves. Everybody gets that way, first time. Now push. The sooner he's out and in the cart, the sooner we'll be gone."

They started again with their tools.

"Who's in here, anyway?" asked a dark-haired murderer as he pushed and wheedled the end of his iron crow.

"Doesn't matter." Corrado swiped at the sweat in his eyes. He didn't want them knowing. It was bad enough that he knew.

"Must be damn important, to buy us our freedom."

One man stopped, staring at Corrado suspiciously. "He's not a saint, is he?"

"No," grunted Corrado. "Far from it. Now be silent." His nerves were on end and their chatter wasn't helping.

He was just pushing down on the iron crow when a voice, clear as glass, said, *"Cianfa dove fia rimaso?"*

This time they all heard it. One robber raised his crow to strike. "Who's that?"

*"Cianfa dove fia rimaso?!"* The question echoed around the small chamber.

"It's not outside," hissed another robber. "Where's it coming from?"

He was answered by a chuckle that frightened them more than the bodiless voice. One man's shaking hands were no longer able to hold his crow. It clattered to the floor. "You heard that!"

Corrado was utterly still, trying not to feel the hairs standing on his forearms and neck. This wasn't imagination. There really was a voice!

"Who is it?" demanded the convict who'd crossed himself. Snatching up the shuttered lantern, he moved it close to the inscription chiseled in the marble. Corrado knew he should stop the man, but he felt unable to move.

The convicts all clustered around the tomb, kneeling or bending close to read. One of them spoke the words aloud. *"Theologus Dantes, nullius dogmatis expers quod foveat claro philosophia sinu."*

In the close light Corrado saw their widening eyes and tried to forestall their fear. "He was just a –"

"Fiend!" One felon backed away from the inscription as if it had begun to glow with infernal fire. Another closed the seal on the night by saying the poet's name aloud.

"Dante!"

From out of the darkness came a rattling of chains, followed by a whispered voice. *"Si?"*

There was no discussion, no consideration of noose or gallows. The lantern was dropped as all five hardened criminals turned and high-tailed it into the night. Corrado was in the lead, praying harder than he had ever done. He ran clear out of the city, ran until his legs could no longer carry him. A week later he would take ship for Spain, still convinced that his steps were dogged by the undead poet who had seen the shape of Hell.

Had he witnessed what happened next he would have been even more certain that the devil had stepped into the world of men. As the fallen lantern cast its light upwards, a shadow on the ceiling moved.

Then the macabre became mundane. The tarp over the huge candelabra shifted and a figure unfurled itself to dangle in midair. There was the smallest scuffle as two feet touched down on the stone floor.

"Cesco?" came a voice from somewhere up above.

"Just a minute." The lantern was set to rights, and the storm shutters were opened wide to illuminate the whole chapel. "Let there be light."

A second boy dropped to earth, and the two youths grinned at each other. Dressed alike in dark shirts, hose, and hoods, they were as different as two youths could be. One was big for his age, his size only promising to increase now he had reached his double-digit years. He took after his father, a cheerful barrel-chested hulk of a man, and several lords had inquired after having him as their squire in three years time. Like his father, and his father's father, fidelity ran through the veins of Bailardetto da Nogarola.

Sadly for the hopeful lords of the Feltro, Detto's loyalty was already pledged. No oath to a knight – or even a king – could bind Bailardetto as tightly as friendship bound him to the angelic imp at his side.

Despite his whole thirteen-month seniority, Cesco was shorter than Detto. He moved with liquid grace, appearing at times almost bone-less. Restless, never still, it was as if he was endowed with such a surplus of energy that he would combust if it wasn't spent. His golden-edged chestnut hair fell perpetually over his eyes, and he gazed from behind this veil like a tiger through tall grass. Encountering him that morning, Corrado had noticed the colour of those eyes – green, with the pale ring of blue about them. Vibrant and unsettling.

Detto idly picked up a fallen crow while Cesco sauntered over to the marble slab covering the poet's final resting-place. It was scraped in several places, and the boy traced the pock-marks with his fingertips. "Sorry, O theologian. I should have stopped them sooner. But I hope you enjoyed the show!"

"Sorry I laughed, Cesco," said Detto. "I ruined it."

"Ruined? It was inspired! They thought it was demonic. But now we have to hurry."

Detto picked up the lantern. "Where, home?"

The boy called Cesco shrugged. "You can if you want. But I have a cat whose tail needs pulling." In answer to Detto's puzzled glance, he said, "Somewhere out there, beyond the city walls, a man waits for a gruesome delivery. I want to tell him it won't be coming."

Any other ten year-old might have been trepidatious at the pros-pect of facing a full-grown adult who trucked with grave-robbers. But Detto's faith was unshakeable. "Lead on!"

Closing the lantern, they exited the church under the cover of darkness and skipped down the shadowy street.

Behind them one of the shadows shifted to trail along in their wake.

◆      ◊      ◆

The dandy waited in his room, annoyed. The girl was late. He'd arranged with the inn-keeper's wife that the girl should be sent to his chamber before midnight, giving him enough time to mount her then have her bathe him before Corrado and his cronies returned. She hadn't yet arrived, and his temper was fraying.

"Which only bodes ill for you, my dear," he said to the empty room. A single candle glowed near the bed upon which he sat impatiently. Perhaps she had refused? But no, he'd paid so much that they would beat her if she disobeyed. In fact, if she didn't arrive with a black eye, he determined to give her one himself. Perhaps two – symmetry in all things pleased him.

A sound caught his attention. Focused as he was on the door, it took him a moment to realize it had come from the window. And again. *What on earth—?* He crossed to the window, but recoiled a fraction as a third pebble whanged off the thick bubbled glass. Moving swiftly, he threw open the window and peered out into the night.

A beefy lad was standing there, readying another stone. "Stop that this instant!"

The black-haired boy looked instantly chastened. "Isn't that Luigi's room?"

"No," came the dandy's angry reply, "nor do I know of this Luigi of whom you speak. I will, however, talk to the proprietor and make certain your hide is tanned past enduring!"

The boy looked for a moment over the dandy's head, then gave him the fig and ran. Already in a mood, the dandy stalked away from the open window and began to pace. He now had a reason to speak with the owner. He would demand satisfaction for being disturbed, and then quietly speak of his patience in waiting for his 'bath'. The girl would be sent – though now there was hardly time for both the lovemaking and the bath. One would have to be done quickly, or not at all. A fastidiously clean man, he usually would have set the pleasures of the flesh aside, or at least made quick work of them, in order to be washed. In his present state, however, he was grimly certain which would be dispensed with.

There was a knock on the door and a timid girl's voice said, *"Signore?"*

Taking in a satisfied breath, he settled his face in an unpleasant smile. *"Si. "*

"I am here for – for your bath, *signore*," came the shamed whisper.

He crossed back to the bed. "Then come in and get on with it."

The door swung wide and the girl looked about the room like a hare entering a fox's den.

Seeing her empty hands he said, "Where's the water?"

"I – I thought – I mean..."

"You thought what?"

Her discomfort was delicious. "I thought you wanted – that I was supposed to – that is –"

"That I wanted what?"

The girl pushed the door shut and flushed an even darker shade of crimson. "That you wanted me to – to – p-pleasure you," she finished, humiliated and frightened.

"Whatever gave you that idea?"

Now she was confused. "My mistress said —"

He walked nearer, circling her while she bowed her head under his stare. "Your mistress is obviously dense. If I expected to be pleasured, I would have asked for a handsomer girl. You're not much to look at, really. What's your name?"

"Emilia," she answered in a whisper.

"A plain name for a plain thing. Hard to imagine any man bedding a girl so bony and hang-dog. Can you smile? Let me see your teeth. No, haven't even got good teeth. Probably won't be a tooth in your head this time next year – if you're still alive at all, that is."

She was ready to cry now, hardly able to stand, she was shaking so hard. "I should go—"

"Yes you should." He watched until her fingers were on the handle of the door. "Of course, I don't know what you're going to tell your employer. I gather she thought I wanted you to – ah, *pleasure* me. What a phrase. She very well may ask me in the morning. Now, as I am nothing if not an honest man, what shall I say but that you left without even trying? Oh, I'll tell her all about how you came, and cried, and squeaked like a mouse, then scurried away. But I don't think she'll appreciate that poor effort – do you?"

Her hand hovered by the door handle. "I thought you didn't want me."

"I don't. Not at all. You are perhaps the most worthless piece of woman-flesh it has ever been my misfortune to behold. I don't suppose you have a suitor? You do? His name? Ah, well, reticence is your strong suit, isn't it? Not a quick-witted man, I should think. And what would he think if he were to discover that you had come into a guest's room late at night to bathe him, but hadn't brought the water? Are you so dim-witted that – what was his name?"

"Dom," she said, a look of utter horror spilling over her features.

"Would Dom accept such forgetfulness at face value? Or might he think that you wished to be here? I would never tell him, no, but it is a rather amusing story, don't you think? I might regale the other guests over breakfast, and he might hear, and then what would he think? What *could* he think?"

"Please, no," she said, advancing on him with her hands out.

"That would be devastating, would it? Though, now that I think of it, it would be entirely another matter if we were to actually have some sort of congress. Then the tale loses all its humour. I mean, look at you – I could hardly brag about my conquest, could I? No, it would only show me up for a desperate man with poor taste and no morals."

"Please," she said again, though at the point she was so bewildered that she wasn't even certain what she was pleading for.

"And it would also stand you in good stead with your employer." He sighed wearily. "Very well. If I must." He began to unlace his doublet. "Though don't expect payment as well. You are asking quite a lot from me as it is."

"Please," she said again. "No lights."

He threw his doublet aside. "I quite agree. Bad enough that I have to feel the bag of bones, I shouldn't have to look at it." He removed his shirt so that she could gaze at his splendor, then leaned over to blow out the candle. The window stood open, but without moon or stars the night was black as pitch, both without and within. He heard a rustle of her clothing as he doffed his boots, letting them fall loudly to the floor. He laid his hose neatly on the edge of the bed before sitting on the lumpy mattress. The linens were all his own – he did not intend to bring lice home with him. They even bore his initials, heavily embroidered. His naked skin could feel the embroidery as he slid himself to a comfortable position and waited for the girl to join him.

There was curious sound, a soft thump as if she had jumped. Then the weight in the bed shifted as a second, lighter form joined him. "You'd best be moist. If you make me do any work, you'll regret it." He reached out a hand and was surprised to feel cloth under his fingers. "You should have taken it off. Now I'll have to rip it from you."

"Don't be so eager," was the cool reply. "You may want some energy later."

The voice was high, but unmistakably masculine. The dandy started to sit up, only to feel a knife at his throat. "Cianfa, Cianfa, you've already incurred a beating. Why try for two?"

A series of thoughts flashed like lightning through his head. He didn't know the voice, though he could tell it was young – how young? – and cultured, carrying the same edge of scorn that Cianfa himself had spent years cultivating. And the speaker knew his name! How? He was registered under a false one.

Even the cadence of the words themselves were familiar. It took him a moment to recall saying something like it this afternoon to his hired felon. He managed to keep his surprise hidden as he said, "You're not Corrado."

"The importunate grave-robber will not be returning to you – this night or ever, I fear." The knife-holder addressed the girl, still hidden in the darkness. "You may depart, my reluctant Iphigenia. This won't take long."

A shuffle of feet, then the door opened. The momentary light from the hall revealed his assailant's form, if not his face. A mere child!

Cianfa tensed his muscles to toss the imp across the room. At once the knife flicked. The dandy took a sharp breath as blood trickled down his cheek.

"Predictable, wouldn't you say? You could possibly – *possibly* – outmuscle me in a fair match. But what in this sinful world is fair? Surely not our mortal coil, a fact you are more than capable of conveying, if not understanding."

"You're remarkably well-spoken for a murderous infant," observed Cianfa.

"*Grazie.* You're not ineloquent yourself, for a foppish despoiler of graves and hymens."

In spite of the knife at his neck, Cianfa couldn't help a laugh. "If you were old enough to shave you'd know I have to kill you for that."

"Just for that? O, let me give you better cause!" As the boy laughed, the knife's point did not waver, informing Cianfa that the laugh was as calculated as the words. "Regarding my tender years, well, the immortal gods alone have neither age nor death. All other things almighty Time disquiets. Perhaps I can practice my razor on your neck, and shave a few years off a rather miserable life."

Cianfa took his time framing a reply. "Boy, if you don't intend to murder me here in my bed, I can't really see how you're going to escape."

"No?"

"The moment you move, I'll be at your heels."

"Baying like the ravenous three-headed hound, I'm sure. Are you advising me to murder you, sir? It seems rather against your interests."

"I doubt you could stomach it – killing a man."

"It's true that I've never yet taken a life. But the only way your death would sour my belly was if I were forced to eat my kill. Still, I'm really only here to convey a message. What happens after is of no consequence." Cianfa snorted. "Does that amuse you?"

"I must confess, yes. To throw away a life with so many years ahead of it in order to pass on a message seems – rash."

Without moving the dagger's point, the boy somehow conveyed the hint of a shrug. "My own affair."

"Just harbour no illusions. Youth or no, I'll have your guts out and made into lute strings."

The boy laughed. "A fitting end for my poor guts! But I have no illusions regarding your morality. After hearing such a wooing scene as that, I marvel I haven't felt your tail whipping about the bed."

"I only bring it out for formal occasions." Cianfa's right hand was moving imperceptibly towards his pillow and the small paring knife under it. His fingers grasped hold of it and in a single move he beat the threatening blade away with one hand and slashed with the other.

He thought he'd made contact with the little bastard's flesh but he couldn't be sure, the imp acted so fast, rolling backwards and away in the darkness. Now he was somewhere in the room, unmoving.

The naked man crept slowly from the bed's straw, hideously aware of every noise he made. He held the tiny dagger before him, questing. No one on his side of the room. The blood dripping down his cheek had reached his chin, and he felt a drop on his naked chest. He wished for clothes, for his sword. He wished he had a torch that he could burn this wretched inn to the ground.

*If I open the door, I'll have light enough to find this little shit.* To do that, he had to cross the path of the open window. But there was no moon, hardly any light at all. He wouldn't be exposed for more than the length of a breath.

As he passed the window, Cianfa felt a sudden pain in his shoulder. His legs collapsed as he was knocked away from the window, his knife clattering across the floor. The crash his body made was nothing to the oaths that passed his lips as his left hand found the shaft of an arrow protruding from his shoulder.

In an instant the boy was kneeling over him, dagger at the ready. "My, my. I withdraw my earlier compliments. You have the tongue of a sailor, if not morals so lofty. I think my guardians would find your tutelage repellent, so I shall deliver my message and be gone." This time the jaunty words didn't entirely conceal the anger in the young voice.

Blinking, the naked dandy bit his lips. "Cowardly little catamite!"

"Little, I confess. But cowardly? I am not the one threatening the life of a bare-faced babe. As for the last, if you're making an offer –" Cianfa squirmed as his genitals were gripped. "– no, your dimensions are not something that would arouse my least interest. Perhaps if I were younger..."

Cianfa thrashed and felt the sick sensation of a knee to his testicles. At the same moment the knife's tip found the soft skin beneath his eye. Cianfa held very still. "You can't do this to me," he breathed.

"Oh, you can dish it but not drink it?" The boy's anger was gone as swift as it had come. All that remained was the mockery. "Sad, sad Cianfa. What would the Guild think if they saw you now? Would your family come to bail you out again? Or does failure mean exile this time?"

Through the pain, Cianfa felt a real fear. *How does he know who I am?*

"You have a long night ahead of you so I will be brief. My message is in two parts. The first is this – do not trifle with the poet's remains, or you will find yourself living a Hell worse than that he gave your namesake.

If he is moved, the name of Donati will be so ruined that Heliostratus' fate will seem kind. Please inform all your Florentine friends of the same. *Firenze* disowned him. *Firenze* may not have him back."

The child drew suddenly back, releasing Cianfa Donati's eye from the tip of the blade and his groin from the diminutive knee. Cianfa curled into a ball and tried not to whimper.

"The second part of my message is even simpler. When you've had enough, say 'I am a sore and sorry ass,' and it will end."

Sick to his stomach and rubbing the bloody flesh beneath his eye, Cianfa gasped. "Enough of what?"

In answer, the boy whistled. At once the door opened. The hallway light framed a massive man with hands that could bend horseshoes.

"Cianfa Donati, meet Dom. Dom, Signor Donati. No doubt Dom has been having a word with his sweet Emilia and would like some pointers in dealing with the fairer sex. By prior agreement the discussion will involve no arms, but rather the lofty discourse of knuckles, elbows, fingers, knees, and toes. I told him you were nothing if not chivalric, and he has agreed to end the debate when you have spoken those seven magical words." Tucking the dagger into his belt, the child lifted himself onto the windowsill, preparing to depart the way he had come. "Oh, Dom – don't touch his shoulder. It wouldn't be sporting."

"It's not his shoulder I'll be touching." The man entered, followed by the girl Emilia bearing a candle. The better for Dom the blacksmith to work by. She closed the door to the hall behind her as Dom cracked his knuckles and flexed his hands.

Recoiling, Cianfa Donati dragged his eyes to the child poised languidly on the window-ledge. Curly locks veiled eyes so bright they were almost feverish. There was a small coin hanging by a thong around the boy's neck that caught the candlelight. Above it Cianfa saw a trickle of blood and felt a fleeting moment of satisfaction.

Tracing Donati's eyes, the liquid youth daubed at the blood and licked his finger. "Ah! *The weakness of little children's limbs is innocent, not their souls.* And Cianfa – no thoughts of reprisals, please! Not even to the girl. Else I'll have to reveal to the city elders of both Ravenna and Florence that you have conspired to free convicted felons in order to desecrate holy ground and remove a noble man from his final rest. Death, and immortal damnation to boot. Now, I bid you good-night. And remember, 'I am a sore and sorry ass!'" A leap, a gentle roll onto the roof, and the boy was gone, leaving the retreating Cianfa to the open arms of Dom.

# THREE

OUT ACROSS THE ROOF a shadow was waiting, crouched low. Cesco danced over the clay rooftop tiles and said in fluent Arabic, "Ah, mine own keeper. Whither I goest, thou goest. How annoying," he added in Italian.

"Who is he?" The shadow's voice rasped painfully.

Ignoring the question, the boy indicated the small bird-bow, barely visible in the dark. "'Twas quite a shot, from stable-top. How didst thou know thy bolt would pass me by?"

"Thou art too small to be concerned about, little dancer. Who is he?"

Cesco's answer was tart. "A man of limited skill with whom I could have dealt myself."

"A quick temper is a quick grave."

This last rumble was in Greek. The boy chose to remain in Arabic. "As I am small yet always seen, so thou art large and nigh invisible. Yet thou truly canst not guide whom thou lovest."

The archer rose from his crouch, expanding and unfurling like a dark banner up and up to his full height. He wore European clothes, but battered and careworn, as if he were a servant. Doubtless he had finer clothes than these, but Cesco had never seen them. The servant guise was an important one, for if he wore his native dress, or clothes too fine, he could quite possibly end up needing no clothes at all. Damned or saved, the dead need no garments, for there was no shame in death. Shame was for those living who could not see beyond the skin to the man within.

For the archer's skin was dark – darker than most of his race, though not quite African dark. He was a Moor.

Following the boy to the edge of the roof, the archer dutifully recited the end of the boy's quotation. "But God guideth whom he will; and He best knoweth those who yield to guidance." His voice sounded like a rusty sword scraping the bottom of a well, painful and hollow, but deep. The unexplained bubbled scars around his throat spoke to the cause.

Cesco laughed. "*Cave ab homine unius libri!*" With that he shimmied over the edge and dropped to the ground.

"*Et mors ultima ratio,*" answered the Moor, turning to find a more discreet way down.

As Cesco rejoined the earthbound, Detto popped up from behind a water barrel. "Did it work?"

Cesco clapped his friend on the shoulder. "You played your part brilliantly! If he'd kept that window closed, I'd've been sunk, and that poor girl would have had a rough time."

Preening at the praise, Detto was still a little resentful. "I wish I could have gone in."

"No, you don't." The broken voice of the Moor made Detto jump. Whirling around, he pointed an accusing finger. "What's *he* doing here?"

Cesco pulled a face. "He's been following us ever since we slipped out of the house. He was even in the back of the church, watching."

Detto looked up at the shadowy figure whose skin was barely lighter than the night with a resentful mixture of awe and fear. "How does he *do* that?"

"Well, in the dark you can only see his eyes. And his teeth, if he's smiling. He's like a cat."

The Moor bowed from the waist. "Knowing your love of cats, I take that as a compliment."

There was a cry of pain from the inn's best room, and Cesco pointed. "Like our friend up there, it's cat and mouse that I enjoy. Not that he's enjoying it now. Come, shall we go?"

He set out back towards the city proper, via a disused postern gate the boys had discovered. As they strolled, Detto said, "Now will you tell me what this was all about?"

"Some men were trying to steal Papa Dante's bones."

"I figured that much. Who were they?"

"Florentines." Cesco was busily thumbing his own blood off the image of Mercury on the coin hanging from his neck. He never took it off, calling it his luck.

Detto walked on for a bit, thinking. "I suppose they wanted to ruin his grave for all the nasty things he said about them."

"That was definitely part of it, but I think that they wanted something more."

"What?"

"They want the poet's bones buried in Florence, to their greater glory," said the Moor from behind them.

Detto looked to Cesco for confirmation. "But that doesn't make sense! They exiled him!"

Cesco picked up a loose stone and sent it skipping down the dusty roadway. "As his fame grows, so does their shame. Today they want everyone to remember he was Florentine. As our shadow here says, it's to their greater glory. Besides, they'd hate to miss out on the fare of the pilgrims who are currently staying in Ravenna to see his demi-sainted bones."

"Oh." Detto's brow furrowed. "So who was the man at the inn?"

The answer sought in vain by the Moor was now freely given to Detto. "His name is Cianfa Donati, the great-nephew of the Cianfa Donati that Dante saw in the seventh bolgia of Hell's eighth ring."

"And who was *he?*"

"Tsk. You should read more. In life, he was a Florentine cattle thief and shop-breaker. In death, he gave God the fig." Cesco made the rude hand gesture, his thumb between his middle and ring fingers. "This Cianfa is cut of the same cloth. He hired those men, thieves and killers all."

"*Cianfa dove fia rimaso?*" repeated Detto.

"A line from *L'Inferno.* I doubt they'll ever get the joke."

"Surely he would, though," the Moor rumbled in Arabic. "Doth he know whom thou art?"

Cesco was scornful. "No, mine ebony monster. I went unto him in Cupid's robes, with thou as Hephaestus."

As the Moor made a sound that could have been a grunt or a laugh, they came to a gap in a wall. Detto slipped under, and Cesco barely had to duck at all, but it was amazing to see how easily the Moor followed. For all his years (he had to be nearer sixty than fifty) he was as spry as he was silent.

As they passed into a beam of light from an open casement, Detto spied the blood trickling down Cesco's neck. "You're hurt!"

Cesco touched two fingers against his chin and drew them away. "A scratch!" He lapped the blood off his fingers and glanced at the Moor, who merely tossed the boy a pocket-cloth as he said in Arabic, "Marry, 'tis enough."

"It surely is," replied Cesco.

Detto whined. "Speak a language I know!"

"So *learn!*"

The two boys joked and re-enacted portions of the evening as they ambled through the sleepy city streets. Once they tried to lose their keeper by ducking through another wall gap far too small for him. When they halted to catch their breath a mile on, he was nowhere to be seen. But the moment they started off again, Cesco laughed and invited the Moor to emerge from the shadows and join them. When the Moor appeared, Detto muttered in Cesco's ear, "How does he *do* that?"

"I'm hoping he'll show me," Cesco whispered back.

"Mreow," said the Moor, which sent Cesco into paroxysms of laughter.

Even Detto couldn't help giggling. "What are we doing tomorrow?"

"Tomorrow we see if a pig can fly," answered Cesco, wiping an eye and daubing his chin again. The bleeding had stopped. "Failing that, we'll tie old man Morsicato's beard into such a knot that even the Gordians will die from envy."

"Who are the Gordians? Do we get to trick them too?"

Cesco shook his head. "It's been done."

The Moor remained silent, letting youth enjoy itself. If he read the stars aright, this might well be their last Ravennese adventure together. Mars and Mercury shared the same house as the Sun. Something was about to change.

"Will they be mad?" he heard Detto ask.

"I can't imagine why. We had our shepherd to guide us home."

Detto eyed their shepherd warily. They'd known each other for all the years of his life, but Detto's father had never stinted in expressing his ill-wishes for the Moor. The son had inherited the father's mistrust, but Cesco trusted the Moor, which created an impossible contradiction for poor Detto. Cesco was never wrong, not about people.

"But I'm sure they'll find some reason to be mad anyway," Cesco continued with a shrug. "From the sound of it, they have the searchers out. Or else it's a midnight festival."

From a distance it certainly looked like a festival. At first they took the flickering light to be firebrands and metal-caged lanterns on the end of poles. Could the household really be so worried as to be searching for them in droves?

The closer they drew to their abode, the greater the light – far too great. There were frantic cries, shouts of panic, crowds of men organized into teams with buckets and leather bags in hand. A pair of double lines led to both the nearest fountain and well, the sea being just distant enough to be impractical.

A building was burning, the monstrous illumination blotting out the stars that were just breaking through the clouds.

Detto stood rooted to the spot. "Cesco, that's…"

"Our house!" All amusement was gone in an instant. Sprinting forward, Cesco made to run into the flaming house down the road. The Moor was after him a moment later, wrapping him about the waist and lifting him off his feet to keep him back.

"Let me go! *Let me go!* My poems! My lute! Everything I've ever composed! My whole life —"

"— is already up in smoke," rasped the Moor, fighting the boy's mad struggles. "If I let go, you will be too."

"Devil take you, Tharwat, let me go!"

The Moor turned Cesco around roughly and slapped his face, hard. "Stop! Cesco, stop! Breathe. Listen. Nothing that has been created cannot be created again, better. You carry your art in you. Within the blaze are only the physical manifestations. Let them go."

"Not just mine! Don't you realize – *his* words! In *his* own hand! The only copy!"

The Moor nodded. "That is a terrible loss. But the work exists in a thousand copies by now. Breathe, and reason."

Furious tears pooling in his eyes, Cesco's lower lip trembled for several moments. Then he fell limp. "You're right."

Wary lest it be a ploy, the Moor set the youth's feet back on the cobblestones. "Fight the fire, but do so wisely. Not even you, little dancer, can run between flames."

Cesco threw the Moor a sour glance before running to join the nearest line, throwing water so furiously at first that he spilled more than he conveyed. It was a wonder to the Moor, who knew the boy so well. Cesco's hatred of fire was only slightly less than his loathing of cats, both rooted in unrecollected experiences.

After a moment of looking for the house's master, the Moor took a place near the flames. Recognizing him as a servant in the burning house, he was accepted by the Ravennese. As he reached for the first leather bucket, a distant corner of his mind inquired, *Why this house? Why now?* But he set those questions aside as he grabbed, heaved, passed back, grabbed, heaved, passed back.

The flames were tremendous, and the cause of saving the house was already lost. The main task now was to keep the fire from spreading to houses on either side. In that, the citizens of Ravenna were moderately successful. Dawn found two singed yet whole edifices flanking the smouldering hulk that for eight years Cesco had called home.

By then none of the house's inhabitants were to be found. They had vanished in the smoke-filled, flickering night.

◆     ◇     ◆

Some hours before that dawn, during an exhausted pause, the Moor had discovered the house's owner, likewise resting. Ser Pietro Alaghieri's head of fine brown hair was blowing free, his face sooty and tired. Twenty-seven years old, in recent years he had begun to look more like his father – his face had thinned a bit, making it appear longer. He didn't own his father's beak of a nose, but the solid jaw was the same, and the full lips. The three parallel scars on his forehead were always more visible when he was flushed. His large brown eyes streamed water, though from smoke or tears it was impossible to tell. His twin hounds ranged alongside of him, tails low, whimpering as they looked at their former abode.

When the Moor approached, one hound snuffed his hand. "They were with me."

"I know. I found them a couple minutes ago and sent them to the convent, under guard." Pietro's voice was so hoarse from shouting and breathing smoke, he sounded almost like the Moor. "So tell me, Tharwat, where the Devil had they gone this time?"

Tharwat al-Dhaamin explained in remarkably few words. At the end, Pietro shook his head. "Donati? Antonia knows him, I think. My mother certainly did. He was a cad even then. Damn. So, what did Cesco do to him? Do I want to know? Did he ever endanger Detto?" At the Moor's grimace, Pietro snorted. "I shouldn't have asked. Where one goes, the other follows."

Tharwat patted the nearest of the skittish hounds. "To his credit, he kept Detto's role in the last act to a bit part."

Pietro's wry smile showed he appreciated the Moor's choice of words. "He *is* a trifle theatrical." Tharwat raised an eyebrow. "All right, more than a trifle. Still, we were very lucky they weren't in their room. I was in a fire as a boy." He shook his head, suppressing a shiver at the memory.

"I did not know that."

"When they sentenced my father to exile they looted and burned our house. We escaped, but with nothing. If not for my mother's relations, we would have starved."

"I am very sorry." The Moor looked at the flames still licking the sky. "Do we know how this began?"

"No. But it was no accident. Can you see to read?"

Kneeling, the Moor blinked repeatedly to clear his eyes, then studied the screw of paper Pietro handed him, unjumbling the coded characters and their various meanings. All at once the meaning revealed itself. Tharwat felt his breath catch. "You are correct. This was deliberately done. To delay us? To kill? Do we know who?"

"No, just why. Someone knows."

"Why not attack before now?"

"Because the person behind this had nothing to gain. Until now. That really only leaves one option."

Perhaps the Moor's thinking apparatus had been smothered by the smoke. But, of course, Pietro had already had hours to parse the meaning of the news. "Which came first, the fire or the note?"

"The note. Castelbarco sent the courier pell-mell for Bologna. It reached me this afternoon. I rode like the Devil to get here and found the house already burning. Virgil and Cato were frantic, weren't you boys?" Pietro patted the dogs vigourously.

A few Ravennese stopped by to offer their condolences. Pietro thanked them. Most had not done so, whispering that this was his punishment by God for his sins.

When the well-wishers were gone, Tharwat said, "It is regrettable that your studies have been interrupted yet again."

"It's always something. Besides, it looks as though my unruly charge is about to be taken off my hands for good." Taking the message back into his possession, Pietro loosed a sour laugh. "The arsonist and the courier probably passed each other on the way here."

"Cesco has a cut on his chin from his adventures this evening. The doctor should look to it."

"He's treating burns at the moment, with Esta's help. Damn, it's tempting to say the hell with the house and get horses and go. But people will wonder —"

"Let them. Follow your instincts. At best this was a delaying tactic, at worst attempted murder."

"Or a destruction of documents," said Pietro, reminding the Moor of all that had been in the house. Years of writing. His father's writing. All the originals, in his father's own hand – gone. That alone was an immeasurable loss. Still, the strong-box with the most valuable papers might have survived. There was one paper in particular they would need now.

"In any event, if we delay we are handing the enemy a gift."

"Unless the road is watched. This might be to spook us out of the covert into open ground."

"Does it matter?"

"No." Pietro massaged the muscles above his right knee, working to ease the stiffness from an old wound. "Look – there's Novello's steward, bringing men." Guido Novello da Polenta was the lord of Ravenna, and a long-time admirer of Pietro's father. "Novello won't be far behind. I'll talk to him, explain. The time for secrets is past. He'll help, maybe loan us some soldiers. He's a good friend. And he feels guilty about me already." Pietro's voice was full of sadness. Despite his recent troubles, Ravenna had been good to him. Now he had to leave.

The Moor rose. "I will find the doctor and his wife and send them to the convent to prepare the children. I myself will remain until the fire cools and see if the document survived."

"Don't bother." Pietro smiled for the first time. "Even if the strong-box is intact, the paper won't be in it."

The Moor paused, then nodded in approval. "You trust no one."

"A lesson hard learned."

"A valuable one. Let me add to your worries – you said only one person stood to gain from the fire. I can name at least three." Walking away, the Moor left Pietro to run through the names of their enemies. It was a long list, and inconclusive.

# FOUR

SER GIUSEPPE MORSICATO, once doctor-barber to princes and armies, now a glorified nursemaid to two willful brats, climbed the steps to the Church of Santo Stefano degli Ulivi, the house of Dominican nuns right in the heart of the city. It was an hour before Lauds and he'd sent Esta home to pack his traveling bag. That had been an argument. Then he'd told her not to wait for him but to return to salving the burns of the firefighters. That had been an argument. In another week it was the anniversary of their marriage, and he was going to Verona, alive or dead, without her. That had been an argument. He'd won two battles, and only lost the important one. This night showed every sign of not working out well for him. *At least it wasn't my house that burned.*

Reaching the massive door he rang the bell as softly as he could. After a wait the panel slid open and the porter stuck his head out. He was an old man, half blind and toothless, unable to leer, much less threaten the virtue of the women he and his brother guarded. "Whozzit?"

"It's me, Adamo. Morsicato. I'm looking for Suor Beatrice."

"My my my!" chuckled the porter. "Another visitor! Come to take the children off our hands? The Abbess won't be pleased. She's gotten them out of that Godless house at last!"

Morsicato could hear female voices murmuring in the yard beyond the door. "Adamo, let me in. I need to speak with Suor Beatrice."

"Is her brother with you? He's not welcome in a house of God," added the porter acidly.

"No, Ser Alaghieri is back fighting the fire."

"Ser Alaghieri! What did he do to deserve knighting? This fire is God's vengeance, says I. Serves him right, says I! The Abbess thinks so, too!"

It took a further five minutes of wrangling before Morsicato was allowed to enter. Within, all was as he expected. In a city largely built around timber, fire was the most dreaded of calamities. The sisters of Santo Stefano were busily preparing their cloister to shelter any injured or dispossessed people – any not bearing the name Pietro Alaghieri. Christian charity only extended to Christians.

Properly dressed even at this hour, the nuns scurried from store rooms to guest rooms, the more level-headed among them preparing salves. Morsicato ran a professional eye over their preparations and grunted with something like approval. Then he asked Adamo's brother, also old but by no means as feeble or cantankerous, to guide him to Suor Beatrice and the children. "This way, *dottore*."

They passed the stair to the Dormitory, the lines of trestle beds with only one door, beside which the Abbess nightly slept like a cat. The old girl was no fool. Indeed, rumour said that in her youth she had played the fool with clergy and the laity alike, and knew too well what went on behind closed doors. That was why there were no doors whatsoever in the Convent of Santo Stefano dell'Ulivi of Ravenna.

Suor Beatrice was in the Scriptorium with the boys. Detto was fast asleep on a pallet. Cesco lay with his eyes closed. But that meant nothing.

"Suora," murmured the doctor, voice low.

Suor Beatrice got to her feet at once, looking him over. Morsicato realized he must look a sight. His beard, usually neatly forked, was a mass of bristles with layers of ash and soot among the black hair. His bald scalp was covered in smudges from wiping his hand over it. With another woman, even a nun, he would have felt self-conscious. But he'd known this girl since before she'd taken her vows. She had a practical streak that would make Zeno the Philosopher proud. Her greeting demonstrated that quality. "Can anything be saved?"

He shook his head. Lips thin, she ushered him in. Once sure that an older nun was present to chaperone, Adamo's brother went off to inform the Abbess of the doctor's arrival. Morsicato hoped it would provoke no great interest. He was a frequent visitor, often called in when there was a patient beyond the sisters' powers.

Suor Beatrice brought the doctor to the table bearing a bowl of sooty water and some rags she had used to clean the boys. Mopping at his face, she asked, "Is anyone badly hurt?"

"Not that we know of. Ahh, thank you." He bowed his head so

she could scrub at him. "No, everyone's accounted for. But Pietro's lost his records of the benefice, I think."

"Oh no!" groaned Suor Beatrice. "It will make his reinstatement that much harder."

"Yes. And other papers were lost – some belonging to your father."

Born Antonia Alaghieri, the twenty-three year old novice called Suor Beatrice trembled very slightly, her worst fears realized. But she was her father's daughter. She shed no tear, busying herself with cleaning the doctor's face.

Morsicato looked past her at the Scriptorium. In the daylight hours the sisters worked here, laboriously creating blackish-brown ink from tree-sap. He was still surprised that the girl had chosen the Dominicans. It was the Benedictine Rule that suited Suor Beatrice to the ground. *Ora et labora* – 'pray and work.' But perhaps the reputation of this particular convent had attracted her. Which is to say, it wasn't a whorehouse.

No, this particular abbey was run more like a well-drilled military company. The sisters in the convent had many duties, never any time for idleness. From the moment Antonia Alaghieri had set foot within the cloister, her talents were seized upon by the Abbess, a lady far too shrewd to miss what a lucrative skill the young novitiate brought with her. For years Antonia had been in charge of the production and distribution of her father's works. Suor Beatrice was the obvious candidate to provide a new source of income for the abbey – the making of books. Of course, the content of the books made here were substantially different. Writing of Heaven and Hell, indeed! Hardly fit for Christian eyes.

The workshop in the abbey was not a grand enterprise such as she had been used to in Florence and Verona. Still, Antonia was allowed to employ an illustrator from the city, and two of the older sisters whose backs were no longer strong came three times a week to aid in the scraping of parchment. Each new book was a commission from some wealthy noble, endowing the house with tremendous riches in return for a personalized bible, complete with a family tree.

Suor Beatrice was a diligent worker. When she was not at prayer or at meals she could be found in her little room with lamps, a brazier, and her inks. Yes, the cloister suited the girl more than anyone thought. Morsicato knew her only regret was her reduced contact with her brother and his charge.

Finishing with the doctor, she reached over to stroke Cesco's damp curling hair. In repose the dimple beside his eye was more pronounced, as if when waking he could will the tiny scar away. There was a rude bandage on the boy's chin that Morsicato would have to replace in the morning. It would insult the girl to do it now.

Idly, Morsicato lifted a vellum parchment from the table. By the light he saw the illuminator's drawing, and read beside it Antonia's own fine script: *He shall return no more to his house, neither shall his place know him any more.* Apt. In more ways than one.

"There's more news than the house, I'm afraid," said Morsicato softly, darting a glance at the older nun. "Pietro got the message tonight."

Deliberately cryptic, he hoped the girl would follow his meaning. It wasn't so much to deceive the chaperone nun, who could have no conceivable interest in their affairs beyond simple gossip. But Morsicato suspected Cesco was feigning sleep, and the doctor owned strong feelings about letting the boy know too much, even at this late date.

Fortunately the girl was quick as a whip. "From the Feltro?"

The doctor nodded. "He's gone. Word came tonight."

"So the fire..?"

"Probably. Your brother says you know what we require. I have no idea what he meant by that."

Antonia leaned back, staring at the doctor without actually seeing him. Then she turned to the other nun. "Sister Adela, could you find Mother Abbess and see if she is free? I need to speak to her on a matter of some importance."

Obviously conflicted, Sister Adela went to fetch the abbess. The instant her footfalls were lost in the cacophony outside, Antonia wrenched Morsicato to his feet. "Help me!" Grabbing an awl used for scraping parchment clean, she rushed to the back of the Scriptorium.

Morsicato followed and knelt beside her as she jammed the awl into a crack between the flagstones. "Lift it," she urged him. "Hurry!"

Morsicato obediently heaved upwards. The flat stone groaned without giving more than an inch. "They patched the floor last year, and I didn't want to…" She pushed awkwardly down on the awl, adding her weight.

At last Morsicato realized what they were about. He glanced over his shoulder. The door was empty, but he thought he could see a pair of eyes hidden by curls watching them intently. *Damn the boy.*

The doctor told Antonia to go intercept the abbess when she came. As she obeyed, he shifted his position to strain at the awl, levering the slab upwards inch by inch.

Their timing was fortuitous. The doctor heard Suor Beatrice greeting her mistress just beyond the door. Pietro's sister used an overloud welcome, while the Abbess spoke in lower tones. "The children are well?"

"Over-tired after all the excitement, that's all," replied Suor

Beatrice. "They're sleeping now. Doctor Morsicato is looking after them."

"I heard the doctor had come. I thought he would be helping prepare the salves." She sounded disapproving.

The awl slipped. Morsicato swore under his breath.

"I'm sure he will," said Suor Beatrice. "He wanted to look at the boys first. But he brought me news. There has been a death in the family." A careful lie. She hadn't said whose family.

"Your brother?" asked the Abbess at once.

"No, no. A distant relation. But it requires a journey to see to his affairs. I must leave tonight."

There was a pause in which the doctor was certain the noise he was making would bring the old harpy down upon him. But when the Abbess spoke her suspicions were clearly directed elsewhere. "Your brother's house burns down, and a death in the family? An unfortunate night for the house of Alaghieri. But I doubt it requires you to break your vow to this house."

One last heave, the sound of stone grinding stone. Morsicato shifted the slab, revealing a small crevice beneath. Within lay a long tube, sealed at both ends. The doctor plucked it out and quickly stuffed it up the sleeve of his gown. Replacing the stone as best he could, he stood and turned.

The boy was standing at his elbow, just out of the light. "What is it?"

"You could have helped," whispered the doctor tartly. "Go back to bed."

"It looked like —"

"Nothing. Get back in bed."

"Why, when we're leaving so soon?" But Cesco did go back to the bed and lay down. Closing his eyes, this time it looked as though he might try to sleep. *Infuriating imp!*

Outside the Scriptorium, the argument was gaining heat. Though Antonia would never be deliberately insolent to her superior, there were two or three subjects she could be obstinate about. The Abbess had hit upon one.

"No, you may not go. I forbid you to have contact with your brother as long as he is outside of God's view."

"Mother Abbess, surely it cannot be a sin to refuse to over-tax the people of Ravenna. Charity is a Christian act."

"Excommunicate is excommunicate. And look at his household. I shudder to think what those boys learn at the knee of that heathen devil. Surely these unfortunate family events are a sign. And now they are under my roof, they will be made good Christians again."

"I'm afraid both boys must leave with me. They have been summoned as well. As you say, there is trouble in my family, and we are all needed to set things right. I swear to you, before God, it is only for the children that I ask your leave."

A pregnant pause. Then the Abbess sniffed. "You've not yet taken your final vows. You are free to go wherever you wish. Now, if you'll allow us, the sisters and I have duties to attend to."

That was ominous. Morsicato didn't want Antonia to be as unwelcome in this convent as her brother was. Brushing himself off, he stepped into the hallway. "Mother Abbess," he said, bending into a deep bow. "A troubled evening."

She dipped in return. "Indeed. Pray God that the fire does not spread."

"It is in God's hands. But we are fortunate that you are here. I saw the salves your charges were preparing – excellent. Now, may I have a word with you? In private?"

"I have much to do."

"Then I shall accompany you. Suor Beatrice can look after the boys." He escorted the Abbess back to the main yard, speaking *sotto voce* as they went. "Mother, I will be brief. I need Suor Beatrice to accompany me to Vicenza. We – she, her brother, and I – are all charged with the safety of the children currently in your care. In short, we do not believe that the fire was an accident. As long as they are under your roof, they bring danger to this house."

The Abbess was genuinely shocked. "Who would harm children? Even ones as notorious as those two?"

Morsicato put on a grim face. "Bailardetto's father is an important man with many enemies. We must take him back to where he can be safe. And of course young Cesco must come as well. You know they are inseparable."

She looked at him skeptically. "And you need a nun to join you? What, to bear holy arms?"

Morsicato chuckled. "No, alas, or else we could take Father Stefano. He has some skill in war, I hear. No, we need Suor Beatrice to bear witness to a document. It is a complicated legal matter, I won't bother to…"

The Abbess stopped in her tracks. "That's three stories. A death in the family, the children's safety, and now some legal quibble. Which is it?"

"All three, lady," answered Morsicato tiredly. "All three. The death caused the legal mess, and has led to danger for the children. She will not be gone long. But it is vital to the children that she goes."

There followed an extended pause, and Morsicato admired her skill in creating it. She was waiting for him to fill the voids, give her more information. He merely waited, immune to that particular trick – his wife did it far better. Finally the Abbess sent him back to inform Suor Beatrice that she was permitted to travel with Ser Dottore Morsicato – *not* her brother! – and remain absent until the boys were safe, both in body and spirit. Suor Beatrice was to make a vow to that effect. But first the Abbess made Morsicato check over the salves.

Returning to the Scriptorium, he passed a whispered conversation with Antonia. She began by thanking him, then proceeded to speculate on what might await them in the north until a certain rigidity in Cesco's posture made him wave her to silence.

"Gather your things," he said, passing her the sealed tube. "We leave before dawn."

# FIVE

THE SAME RISING SUN that found Pietro Alaghieri's house a smouldering wreckage also cast its light on the great palace that now belonged to Mastino della Scala, which he was now strutting through. Strutting was the word, for he was dressed in a multicoloured doublet that looked like a peacock in full plume. This, when the other members of his family were dressed in the white of mourning.

Room after room, Mastino gave orders crisply and efficiently, if without grace. "Remove this, replace this, have this delivered to Alberto's rooms. Send this as a gift to the Pope, this to the Emperor, that to Robert of Naples." All this had clearly been laid out in Mastino's mind for a long time, and the satisfaction he took in seeing it finally come to pass was manifest.

Among Mastino's retinue was Guglielmo da Castelbarco, at a loss why he was required to witness these changes, which had little to do with the running of the city government. But the number of tiny barbed comments, toss-away jests, and shrewd glances quickly informed him that he was here to be put in his place. Castelbarco found himself the butt of a half-dozen jokes to the other minor lords, the licker-fish that had attached themselves to the new Lord of Verona like leeches.

When they came to the library, Mastino waved his hands at the shelves of books and pigeonholes of scrolls. "This all has to go."

"Why?" asked Castelbarco baldly.

Mastino threw open the shutters and looked down into the street, waving at the crowd. "My brother needs an office. Co-captains we may be, but we can't be expected to share everything." A smirk. "If you want it to stay, perhaps you could convince the Anziani to build my brother a public palace of his own."

Castelbarco demurred, pointing out deferentially that there was no money for such an enterprise because, of course, all the city's funds were already engaged in military matters.

"Then this will all have to go," repeated Mastino with a grand smile. "Won't it?"

"Perhaps Alblivious will learn to read." This sarcastic comment emanated from Niklas Fuchs, Mastino's close companion, just arriving.

Where Mastino had found Fuchs was a subject of some debate within the Anziani. Though his accent was heavily German, his birth-place was unknown, as was his family. Fuchs was a tall man, lean but solid, with an enviable reputation in the lists. Jousting had made Fuchs wealthy, so unlike Mastino's other companions, he was not in search of favours. Rather, he and the Mastiff were kindred spirits.

Fuchs' remark caused Mastino to burst with guffaws, though Castelbarco thought perhaps he laughed a trifle too much. The gate having been opened, others threw out comments denigrating Mastino's older brother, making up in insolence what they lacked in wit.

"What news from Serravalle?" Mastino's elder sister was married to Rizardo de Camino, the titular lord of that city. When he'd come to power just a year earlier, Rizardo had contemplated changing sides and joining the Guelphs. The Scaliger had quashed that idea, hard. Mastino wanted to be sure that with the old dog dead, Rizardo had no intent of trying it again.

"Your sister has him cowed," reported Fuchs. "He's pledging his loyalty."

"He'd better." Mastino's eyes rested on a merlin, blindfolded and tethered to his perch. The former owner of this palace had loved his hunting animals, and every room housed at least one of his fabled three hundred hunting birds.

Reaching out a hand, Mastino caressed the bird's beak. He hadn't noticed it wasn't corded shut. The bird let out an angry caw and snapped. Mastino jerked his hand away, but not swiftly enough to avoid losing an inch of flesh from the palm of his hand.

"Damn!" Cradling his injury, he looked around in vain for the Master of the Hunt, responsible for the menagerie. "Tell Ziliberto to have that animal destroyed. And clear this room out."

The Grand Butler of the palace, Tullio d'Isola, had visibly aged over the past two days. "What shall we do with the books?"

"Burn them." Accepting a cloth from Fuchs, Mastino pressed it against his bleeding palm. "Or sell them. Makes no difference to me. But get them out of here. Today." He stalked from the room, trailed by Fuchs and the rest of the leeches.

Castelbarco decided to remain behind as the Grand Butler sank heavily upon a box-stool. "We haven't even buried him!"

Castelbarco laid a sympathetic hand on the elderly retainer's shoulder. "Everything changes. Where's his brother?"

"With Signor Alaghieri," sniffed d'Isola. The disapproval was manifest. Castelbarco could hardly disagree. If Alberto della Scala was with Jacopo Alaghieri, it meant he was surrounded by whores and empty flagons. "A pity Jacopo di Dante doesn't take after his father."

"Or his brother," added d'Isola wistfully.

Castelbarco plucked a scroll from a hole and glanced at the title. "*Ecerinis.*"

D'Isola nodded. "Maestro Mussato's play."

"I've never read it, but I hear it's stirring."

"It was excellently written." The aged Grand Butler hesitated. "It excoriates the Capitano in the person of Ezzelino the Tyrant."

"How he must have loved that." Grimacing, Castelbarco tucked it back into its cubby. "You seem to have many copies."

"The Capitano bought all he could. I believe he intended to destroy them, but the poetry was such that he couldn't bring himself to do it. Instead he hid them here."

"A shame." Castelbarco scanned the shelves. "There are so many treasures in this room. Letters from poets, statesmen – popes, even!"

"More than you know. Of late he's been collecting the works of the old Romans. Snapping them up sight unseen. No one knows what's in this library – plays, letters, histories. None of it has been catalogued. He never found the time…"

Guglielmo stood straighter. "Then we can't possibly let this library be lost."

"But who would risk Mastino's displeasure by taking it?"

Castelbarco's impulse was to do just that, but the young bastard would make him pay dearly, one way or another. He offered another solution. "Send it to the friars at the Chapter Library." Possibly the oldest library in Europe, the library at the great Duomo of Verona was originally a Roman *scriptorium*. There the friars kept original copies of Justinian's Codes and the Institutiones of Caius. Scholars flocked from the corners of the earth to study the library's contents. "Tell them it's a donation from their new Capitano. If we give them to the Church, there's no way he can protest without soiling the gloss of his new title."

Tullio smiled in relief. "I will do just that. Lord Castelbarco, when do you plan to read the will?"

Not many men knew there was a will. But of course the Grand Butler would. "We have to wait for the delegation from Venice to arrive, and Madonna Giovanna ought to be here as well. At the end of the week, probably." Castelbarco added, "I want him laid to rest first. Lord Bonaccolsi is bringing the body home."

With that sobering thought, they girded themselves to follow and hear the rest of the Mastiff's dispositions.

◆    ◊    ◆

At that moment the clutch of riders from Ravenna were already an hour into their journey, the hot summer sun hanging over their shoulders. A troop of horsemen rode before and behind them, a gift from the lord Guido Novello. Some had served in campaigns with Ser Alaghieri and wondered if the midnight fire had been an attack. Certainly their presence hinted as much. They had not been told, as Novello had, who it was they were truly protecting.

The core of the party was made up of Pietro and his sister, Cesco and Detto, the Moor, and Morsicato and his wife. The presence of Esta da Ferrara *in* Morsicato was a surprise to Pietro, but it was a battle the doctor had lost and Pietro had been too exhausted to relitigate.

They traveled without servants. Pietro had left his household staff behind to salvage what they could of his life. Although he believed them honest, he'd been duped by a clever servant once before. One in a long list of betrayals.

As unusual as their party was, it was easily explained. Anyone who stopped to look would think Detto and Cesco were Pietro's pages, al-Dhaamin his servant. For this reason Cesco and Detto rode before Pietro, with the Moor clad in Pietro's livery just behind him, leading spare horses.

The twin greyhounds Cato and Virgil ran along with them, helping to keep straying mounts in line. The five knowing adults did the same for the boys. They were afraid that this pair would gallop off on one of their ill-timed larks.

So far there had been nothing untoward. Detto was all curiosity about their destination, but Cesco seemed entirely unconcerned. Before leaving the convent, he had wet his eyelashes and stuck out his lip to one of the sisters, wailing his lost possessions. As a result he carried an old lute, which he strummed absently as he sat his saddle.

They rode the whole morning before encountering another party on the road. A noble woman in an open carriage, with only a driver and an escort of two men-at-arms. The carriage was moving slowly in the opposite direction and seemed no threat, yet it had Pietro's thumb pricking. As he trotted past the conveyance, Pietro glanced inside and was rewarded with a view of a mass of curly red hair and an ample bosom. The woman nodded gravely. Pietro bowed from the saddle and passed on. He was happy when they were out of sight again.

He'd noticed Antonia and Esta looking at the carriage with longing. "If there were any way we could wait for a carriage, we would," he told them.

"We'll manage, Ser Alaghieri." Esta was a large woman, almost as broad in the shoulder as her husband, but her chest could not be described as a barrel. It was more apt to say robust.

Antonia nodded. "If you need to rush ahead, go. Morsicato can stay with us."

Pietro shook his head. "We don't know what kind of welcome we'll get, and I can't have us exhausted when we arrive. We all ride together." He glanced at Cesco's back. "Besides, we have to figure out how to tell him."

"He's too young!" Esta knew the secret, only because it was impossible that she not know.

"In body, perhaps," remarked Antonia with a slight smile. "In guile, he's positively ancient."

Aware he was being talked about, Cesco dropped back to ride between Antonia and the doctor. "So, Auntie, tell us – have you joined your brother and given up God?"

Antonia winced, though Pietro did not react – he was used to being baited. "You're a beast, Cesco. You should apologize."

He blinked innocently. "Whatever for?"

Morsicato went on the attack. "For the scare you gave us, you little whoreson. Disappearing last night."

"I just wanted to see if any life still crept through your carcass, piss-guzzler."

"Hmph. Honestly, I'm surprised you weren't blamed for the fire. And yes, I heard about that business with Donati. You're lucky you came off so well. What eleven year-old gets knife wounds? Your uncle Pietro never got knife wounds at your age!"

"He didn't know what he was missing."

Detto dropped back as well, rallying to his friend's defence. "You should be thanking him!"

"For almost getting killed?" asked Pietro lightly.

Cesco looked across Antonia to Pietro. "You would prefer someone stole your father's body?"

"Not at all. I would have preferred you tell me what was in the wind, so I could have had them all arrested."

"Where's the fun in that?"

"And how do you think I'd feel if you were hurt?"

"But I'm fine!" To demonstrate his fitness, Cesco tossed the lute to Detto and flipped over in his saddle to stand on his head. Around Ravenna the boy was famous for his horse-tricks.

The doctor was unimpressed. "Stop that this instant. Be serious."

Cesco obediently rolled back over, retrieved the lute, and started strumming again. "I will when you sing some new song. I've heard this one all my life. A chorus of 'Don't do this, don't do that!' Is it any wonder if I strike a few discords?"

Pietro took a deep breath. "Cesco, I need you to listen. There are important things happening."

Detto looked sulky. "I don't see why *I'm* being sent home."

"You're not," said Cesco, his fingers finding a jaunty tune. "I am."

The Alaghieri siblings exchanged a look. Esta shook her head. "You told him? He's too young!"

"That is for the stars to say," observed the Moor from behind them all. "His chart did say he would not be long lived."

Morsicato leaned in his saddle to take his wife's hand. "Dear, it's simple. If we do not move now, time will run out. At the moment we have the advantage of confusion. If we wait even a month, someone else will take the reins. It's harder to mount a horse that already has a rider in the saddle. Pietro's message says it has already begun."

Cesco plucked a few low strings, adding a musically dark emphasis to the doctor's words.

"What message? Whose chart? Who's going to die?" Detto cast a worried look at Cesco. He knew of Tharwat's skill at astrology. It was one of the things his father hated about the Moor.

"Bailardetto, be quiet for just a moment." Antonia spoke with the authority she had gained when she'd taken the name Suor Beatrice.

"But you're talking about Cesco as if he wasn't here! Doesn't he have a say?"

"They're getting there." Cesco palmed the lutestrings to stop their vibrations. "Right now the generals want their troops in order. But if Madonna Esta thinks I'm not ready, she's wrong. I've been waiting for this day all my life."

Pietro laughed deliberately. It was one of the best tactics when the boy became over-dramatic. "All your life? How old are you now? Sixty? Seventy?"

"I'm acutely aware of my age, thank you. In fact, I was discussing it with Signor Donati just last night. But just because you all were still in swaddling clothes at my age doesn't mean I can't handle myself. I know a hawk from a hound."

At this turn of phrase, Antonia and Pietro wore matching frowns. Morsicato said, "What do you know?"

The eyes he turned on them were pools of verdant innocence. "I know – nothing. Nothing at all." He began to strum again, and his words came as lyrics:

> *Great books have I conn'd by the score, dear sir,*
> *And learned hist'ry might reach this sore chin,*
> *Masters of oratory I've done proud, sir,*
> *With barbs to turn your blood to gruel so thin,*
> *But about myself? I know not a whit!*

> *Chamate, and how neglected kings may die,*
> *Now in me lies the root of war's great art,*
> *– what , dear Nuncle, was I not meant to see? –*
> *And with sword in hand can I part a heart,*
> *Yet about myself, I cannot tell you shit!*

The nearby guards were laughing. Esta frowned at the vulgarity, but the rest were listening intently.

> *I know medicine, doctor, just a touch,*
> *Enough to see a heart that's out of home.*
> *I can speak four tongues, though that's not much,*
> *Since our Moorish friend is a walking tome,*
> *But ask about poor me, every tongue is bit!*

> *O, teach him to harp with his nails sharp,*
> *That is how you make a man of many parts!*
> *As steeped in knowing as I can ever be,*
> *Yet woefully, wonderfully ignorant –*
> *About me. About me.*

Grinning, Cesco let the cord play out. The nearby guards applauded, and Cesco bowed to them before turning back to his minders. "But I am free to guess. Tell me, Donna Esta, what's my name?"

The doctor's wife looked startled. "What's your – why, it's Cesco. Cesco."

"Yes, that's what you all call me. But what, Madonna Morsicato, is my baptismal name?"

Flustered, Esta hesitated. Morsicato supplied the answer. "Pierfrancesco Alaghieri."

Throwing back his head, the boy laughed theatrically. "Oh, that didn't sound rehearsed! I hope you never have to lie to a patient, doctor, because you're terrible at it. And your wife goes to the truth before she remembers to lie."

Esta flushed. "You say that as if it were a bad thing."

"An honest woman is a wonderful thing to know," winked Cesco. The lasciviousness was quite crude in one so young. "Still, the ability to lie when it is required is a handy skill. Even after all this time, you have to think about it, your mind spinning like the wheels of a water-clock, searching for the right lie."

"What lie?" demanded Detto. "Cesco, what are you talking about?"

"I'm talking about my name. My station. My life. It's all a lie." He looked deliberately at Pietro. "Isn't it, Nuncle?"

Pietro and the Moor shared a long, considering gaze. Finally Tharwat shrugged. "This might be the best way."

Pietro considered, then opened his hands in invitation. "Tell us, nephew, what you've deduced. We'll judge if you're ready."

Trotting ahead, Cesco flipped around to sit his saddle backwards, facing them all. Enjoying himself greatly, he was unknowingly giving a perfect imitation of someone the knight, the astrologer, and the doctor knew all too well. "Well, to start, I'm not your nephew. That's the first untruth."

"Untruth," said Pietro wryly. "How delicate."

"Yes," said Morsicato. "He's not exactly calling us liars."

"Tell me I'm wrong." He addressed Detto. "The story we've been told is that I am Ser Alaghieri's nephew, the orphaned son of his older brother, Giovanni, who drowned the year I was born."

Detto frowned. "That's right. You are."

"I'm not, actually." Cesco brushed the curtain of curling hair from his eyes. "As attractive as it would be to be Dante Alaghieri's grandson, there must be some other explanation for my being raised in Ravenna. I would guess that I was fostered out to protect me from something."

Detto was breathless, his brow knit in anger at being lied to. "Protect you from what?"

"I don't know, exactly." Cesco's eyes flicked among his guardians. "But it's plain sense. I've been surrounded by bright if unorthodox men, all geniuses in their way – except for Uncle Jacopo, who's as dumb as a box of rocks."

He might have expected Antonia and Pietro to laugh at the insult to their absent sibling. But they were listening as intently as Detto and the mounted soldiers. Knight, nun, astrologer, and doctor had spent many nights over bread and wine, debating how much of the story the boy believed. Now they were finding out. "Go on," said Pietro.

"I've received a superlative education – numbers and letters, history and geography. I've been taught everything from languages to warfare by some of the finest teachers Ravenna has to offer, while my mind was broadened by the dear auntie novitiate here, and grandfather Dante, the greatest poet of the age."

Pietro opened his hands. "I hear nothing yet of why you're not an Alaghieri."

Cesco leaned back in his saddle, folding his hands behind his head and stretching out his legs as if relaxing. "It's like this – if I were your nephew, that would explain you, Uncle Jacopo, Aunt Antonia and Grandfather Dante. But what about the doctor here?"

Morsicato shrugged. "A doctor has to practice somewhere."

"Ah, but I've seen how you dress wounds! What is a battle-hardened knight-physician doing in a little rural city with no serious ties to any faction, Guelph or Ghibelline? Your wife complains hourly about being stuck in this backwater hole. You adore her, so why not move away?"

"You tell me," growled Morsicato.

Instead of answering, Cesco pivoted to face the Moor. "Then there's the Arūs, our Moorish astrologer. Why is he here?"

Tharwat remained silent. It was Pietro who spoke. "Why shouldn't he be? He's my friend."

"Not your servant, though. The Ravennese may buy the tale that he's your slave, but he owes you no bondage I've ever seen. Why, then, has he never left, despite all the harassment the locals give him?"

"I like seaside living," said the Moor, his voice rasping.

Cesco turned to Detto. "Have you noticed that they never let me out of their sight if they can help it? If I'm out, either Pietro or Tharwat is always around. And when we traveled to Florence, Nuncle Pietro hired forty armed guards to go with us."

Antonia's reply was sharp. "There's a price on his head. The Neri faction, including the Donati whose nose you tweaked last night—"

"It wasn't his *nose* I tweaked."

"— were only letting him return to take care of our mother's estate. They could have changed their mind at any time."

"But then why didn't they go with him? They stayed with me wherever I was."

Pietro answered that. "You're a child. I'm a man, and a knight. I can protect myself."

Storm-clouds threatened Cesco's mood for a moment. "How did you get that limp, then, or those neat little scars on your face?"

"The limp I got at the first Battle of Vicenza, just as you've been told. These," Pietro brushed his forehead scars with a gloved finger, "I got from a cat."

"A very large cat," added Morsicato with a dark chuckle.

Cesco pulled a face. "Fine, don't tell me. I'm still right about you two never letting me get off by myself."

"You sneak off often enough."

"Always with my Shadow. So there's some danger looming over me. I figured that out long before now. In fact, I knew it even before I started breaking your codes."

Antonia went rigid and the doctor took in a sharp breath. Pietro and Tharwat said nothing. Esta and Detto both asked the obvious question, and at the same time. "Codes?"

"Codes." The boy's satisfaction was manifest. "Ser Alaghieri and his friends are spies for someone of great importance in the Ghibelline cause. The messages come in all forms, by all means. Yet you rarely send messages yourself. So you are the clearing house for secret communications."

"Spies?!" Detto was laughing until he saw the faces of the adults around him. "Really?" They had all just risen in his estimation. Whereas Esta was staring accusingly at her husband, and Pietro was feeling the dark glares of the soldiers, who now suspected him of some dark arts. This might end badly for them all.

"Alas, nothing so dramatic," said Pietro, voice bored. "The doctor, Tharwat, and I have friends in far-off places. With the full knowledge and cooperation of the lord of Ravenna, we occasionally receive bits of news and pass them on to important people."

"Bits of news that arrive in secret, in code," added Cesco.

"Information is valuable."

"My point exactly."

Pietro's gaze narrowed. "So instead of leaving well enough alone, you decided to spy against your own family. How clever. How loyal. How *mature*."

Cesco waved this off. "That's your father talking. You'd have done the same."

"Actually, no. Did you learn anything of interest?"

"About the grain supplies in Spain, quite a lot. About the iron mines north of Erfurt, even more. About the truce between Robert the Bruce and Edward II, and the secret communications that led to the

Pope recognizing the Bruce as king of Scotland, everything. About the accession of Muhammad-bin-Tughluk, a little. About who my father and mother are, not a jot or tittle."

Pietro listened as the child recited a litany of secret communications compromised, knowing that Tharwat was engaged in the same exercise, mentally cataloging which codes were too easily deciphered. He actually felt a perverse pride in the boy for finding them out – a pride tempered by the frustration of tethering him to the ground. "If there's no hint that we've been lying to you – and I've yet to hear anything that sounds like real evidence and not another of your flights of fancy – then what on Earth leads you to think you are anything more or less than you've been told?"

"Spoken like the great lawyer you are destined to be!" Now it was Cesco's eyes that narrowed. "Fact: you are raising me not to be a poet or a lawyer, but to have knowledge of warfare, medicine, law, philosophy, art – all the qualities needed to be not just a knight, but a great nobleman or prince. Fact: you try to guard me in a way that speaks of some great danger. Fact: you three have cast aside great careers to take care of me. And most damning fact of all: you never tell me about my father – not even his date of death. Now why would that be if my father was, forgive me, a long-dead and forgotten Alaghieri of no weight? No, I say that I am the son of someone famous, someone important, someone who ordered you to stay with me until I was sent for."

A long silence ensued. Then Pietro couldn't help himself – he burst into laughter. Morsicato joined him, then Antonia, and even Tharwat smiled.

Nothing took the wind from the boy's sails like being laughed at. Jaw tightening, he glared at them. "Tell me I'm wrong!"

"Do you have any idea how absurd you sound? It's the secret dream of every unhappy child in the world. 'I'm some great king's son, and when I'm old enough he'll send for me and save me from this boring, humdrum life!'" The soldiers were laughing too, and Pietro pressed on. "Maybe we were raising you that way because we want the world to be open to you, Dante's only grandson. Maybe we guard you because you get into so much trouble. Maybe we've cast off our great careers because we're happy in our lives, and wealthy enough not to care. And maybe we don't talk about my elder brother because we hardly knew him, and have nothing nice to say." He appealed to the soldiers. "The wild imaginings of children – honestly!"

Detto looked angrily at Pietro. "He says you've all been lying to him his whole life. Tell him the truth. Now."

Morsicato smiled. "We'd better."

"Yes," replied Antonia. "Or else Bailardetto will have us in stocks and screws."

Detto was ready to give them a hot answer, but Cesco forestalled him. "Don't bother. They have to tell us soon. Something's happened. The letter Nuncle Pietro has tucked in his sleeve is some kind of news. He came racing from Bologna to share it with us, only to find his house on fire. It's why we're not staying to fix things in Ravenna. That's over. Wherever we're going, they have to tell us the truth before we get there."

"Maybe. But if we're going to reach your castle in the sky, we have to pick up the pace. Captain Martino? Let's ride harder. Amusing as this has been, we've slowed to a crawl." Pietro clicked his tongue and his horse trotted forward. The soldiers all obeyed and soon they were moving along at a brisk clip once more.

Pietro pushed his mount's pace just a little bit harder to ride alongside the fuming Cesco. Reaching into his sleeve, he withdrew the coded letter he'd shown Tharwat the night before. He wondered how Cesco had even known about it. "Here, clever puppy. Cut your teeth on this."

Cesco snatched up the single sheet and devoured the contents. The eyes that came up were wide with delight. "I haven't seen this code before."

"When you break it, we'll talk more."

"So I'm right."

Voice so soft it was almost lost in the clatter of hooves, Pietro said, "Not about everything, little man."

"But about this?" insisted Cesco excitedly.

Pietro felt a huge grief spreading through his chest. "Yes. Yes you are."

# SIX

THEY WERE FORCED to suspend their conversation in any case. The advance party had stopped at a crossroads ahead. Arriving, Pietro could see the road was heavily beaten. Men and horses. Lots of horses.

The captain of Novello's men-at-arms rode over. "An army, Ser Alaghieri. Traveling fast."

Pietro dismounted at once. "Anyone in sight?"

"No, sir. But they say the marks are unmistakable. At least two hundred mounted. The Lord knows how many foot. And in a hurry," added Martino.

Tharwat dismounted and knelt, looking at the tracks. "The mounted left the foot to lag behind."

"Vicenza," guessed Morsicato. "The Paduans have marched on Vicenza again."

"Father!" Bailardetto sawed the reins of his mount as three sets of hands restrained him. "They're besieging my father!"

"Actually," said the Moor, "I believe they were retreating."

A quick study of the crossroads proved him correct. There were traces of a heavily laden army heading north for Vicenza, but those were old. The freshest marks, made within the last day, were definitely pointed south. Without their wagons. Almost in wonder, Captain Martino said, "They left their siege machines behind?"

Pietro softly addressed al-Dhaamin, choosing his words carefully. "If they heard the news, why wouldn't they press the attack?"

The Moor's face was blank. "I don't know."

Detto punched a fist into the air. "My father beat them back!"

Pietro glanced at the Moor, who shrugged. "It's possible."

"Why not?" asked Cesco. "After all, Nuncle Pietro beat back a whole Paduan army single-handed."

Detto eyed Pietro skeptically. "He did?"

Pietro ignored them, his mind elsewhere. "Tharwat. Could you..?"

The Moor nodded. Passing the reins of the spare mounts to a soldier, he stepped lightly into his saddle and kicked his horse into a gallop north. If Novello's men took umbrage, Pietro ignored it. He would trust al-Dhaamin's survey more than a whole troop of explorers.

They waited at the crossroads, eating a cold meal and making water. Cesco was uncharacteristically pliable. Eating, answering Detto's questions, teasing the dogs, all the time his eyes were somewhere in the aether. Puzzling out the code was evidently consuming his store of excess energy. A blessing.

After a long conversation with his wife, Morsicato crossed to Pietro's side. "Everything all right?" asked Pietro.

"I have some serious explaining to do when we get home. Do yourself a favour, son. Don't get married. Or if you do, make sure she speaks a different language." Pietro suppressed a grin as the doctor watched their charge. "An apt solution, giving him the message."

"His love of puzzles." Pietro pulled a hunk of cheese from his saddlebag and began unwrapping it. "I decided to make it work for us."

Morsicato took an offered corner of cheese. "It's his flaw. One of them."

"To be unable to say no to a challenge? I know."

"No one better." With that shared smile, Morsicato returned to his wife, leaving Pietro to sit beside a tree and eat his bread, cheese, and grapes in peace.

That, given enough time, the boy would crack it, neither man doubted. Hopefully then he would feel that he had earned the truth within it. In that way the challenge fit the pattern of testing and tempering that had begun eleven years before in Vicenza, and refined seven years ago by the very capable hands of Pietro's father.

*Father...* By himself for the first time since the fire, Pietro let himself feel the merest tinge of his impending loss. His eyes welled at once, and he quickly tucked those emotions away. A dragonfly upon the water, he'd barely touched them and they'd nearly swallowed him whole.

Pietro had never dreamed when he took responsibility for raising Cesco that this day would actually come. And never, never, had he dreamed it would be so soon. *Too soon...* Esta was right, in a way. It was too soon. Far too soon.

Not too soon for Cesco, who might well be ready. No, it was too soon for Pietro to let him go.

◆          ◇          ◆

Eight years ago, at the tender age of twenty, Pietro had found himself charged with raising a three year-old boy. Terrified, upon arriving in Ravenna he had turned to his sister for guidance. She'd stared back at him as if he'd grown a second head. "What makes you think I know the first thing about babies?"

"You're a girl," had been Pietro's simplistic reply. She'd laughed and informed him that, as she was more concerned with father's affairs and intended someday to join a nunnery, she had never had much truck with children. "Find a nurse."

Dante was no help either, having been absent for almost all his own children's youth. Tharwat, so capable in so many fields, was as ignorant as Pietro. And the doctor could tend childhood maladies, but couldn't cope with this brilliant and infuriating boy.

So it had fallen to Pietro to be the father-figure. Pietro, who'd always had a strained relationship with his own brilliant, caustic father.

An obvious prodigy, Cesco was ostracized by the children of Ravenna almost from the first. Three years old, he'd gone out to play in the street and rushed back to his new home beaten, nose bloodied, scrapes on his hands and knees, bruises all over from a kicking.

As Morsicato tended the injuries, Pietro had demanded, "How did it start?"

Little Cesco sniffled blood mixed with snot and tears. "I didn't punch first." Which wasn't quite an answer. When Pietro repeated the question, Cesco had shrugged.

"Were you showing off?"

"No!" A hard look had made the boy revise his answer. "Jus' talking."

"What about? What kind of talk?"

"Nothing. Honest! Jus' talk!"

Cesco had never given a satisfactory answer. Not that Pietro needed one. It was all too easy to imagine the scene: Cesco walking up to a group of the town's boys – older boys, as Cesco would see them as equals, worthy of his camaraderie. Pietro imagined the cast of Cesco's gait, the wryness of his grin. So superior, so coy, so clever, using big words to tease them. What the words were didn't matter, it was how those words were spoken.

Civilization never extended to children. Like animals, children perceived so much that adults glossed over, and were merciless in exacting revenge for slights. They may not have had the words for how Cesco made them feel. But he made them uneasy. He made them feel small. So they had made him feel the same way.

"No one likes a know-it-all," Pietro had said.

"Me either," was the three year-old's testy reply. "Ow! Here, doctor, lemme do tha'!"

The next day Cesco had slipped out of the house against orders. Within minutes he returned home, running full out, a pack of kids on his heels. Pietro had been correct, these boys were almost twice Cesco's size. But this time, it was two of the older boys who bore bloody noses. Cesco darted into the house and stayed there for days, avoiding the rocks that were thrown into open windows whenever he passed by.

Over time he won the admiration of a few Ravennese boys through sheer daring. At around age five he became the leader of a small crew that wandered the city during their free hours. Which began a new and more frustrating era of his childhood. Cesco's sense of dangerous fun started getting him into trouble. Races, wars with sticks, petty thefts – these were common activities for young boys. But Cesco was soon escalating their deeds, making what was playful into games for mortal stakes. Miraculously, none of the boys died. But there were injuries – Lord, the injuries! Cesco had had his share, but they were nothing compared to the litany of broken bones and lost blood belonging to the other boys. Before he turned six years old, the town's parents had decided he was a bad influence. There were deputations to the Alaghieri household, threatening action if 'that boy' went uncontrolled and unpunished.

With his few playmates cut off from him, he had turned to adults. But the only adults who had time for him were his own family, the doctor and his wife, or the Moor. And these adults were always poking, prodding, urging him to funnel his energies into some productive vein. Pietro was as guilty of this as anyone.

It was Dante who had tasked the boy hardest. Ignoring Cesco's existence in the early years, somewhere along the way Pietro's father had decided that the boy was interesting. They played word games, then chess, then started creating riddles and puzzles of philosophy and religion that would have made the scholars at Bologna blench. Dante's writing slowed, much to everyone's despair, but it couldn't be denied that in Cesco the poet had found a foil, a goad, a butt for his jokes and a hone for his wit. They had driven each other mad, but couldn't resist the other's company.

Dante's sudden death four years ago had been a blow of colossal proportions – the only time Pietro had ever seen Cesco at a loss. Not so much weeping as howling, gnashing, tearing. For the first time Pietro was frightened at the depth of emotion within the boy who was always so controlled, so sarcastic, so glib. It reinforced how terribly lonely the boy must feel.

*Thank God for Detto.* Three times a year, Bailardetto Nogarola was sent by his parents to live in Ravenna, acting as a page for Pietro. But Pietro neglected the training of his page, allowing him instead to be the friend Cesco so desperately needed. And Pietro had to admit, Cesco probably had more to teach Detto than he would ever learn as a mere page.

Of course, natural worrier that he was, Pietro fretted for Detto as well. Was he doomed to a life as a tag-along? Would he ever grow into his own man? For that was Pietro's measure of a man – did he belong to himself? Or was he another man's creature? Having spent most of his life in the shadow of two remarkable men, Pietro valued independence above all else. It was a lesson he had imparted to Cesco. *Perhaps too well.*

Even with Detto as his companion for weeks at a time, Cesco must have felt isolated growing up. Ignored and shut out by his peers, talked down to by strangers, forced to perform for adults he knew. Because, as much as they wanted to be his friends, Pietro and his fellow tutors were all too aware of the future that lay before Cesco, and the need to prepare him for it.

They just hadn't expected it to come so soon.

♦    ◊    ♦

Morsicato returned to sit beside Pietro. "I've been banished. But I've got wine." He passed over the stone bottle. "How long do you think he's known?"

"I think he's always suspected, but never been sure enough to ask until now."

"Well, we always worried how he'd take it. It looks like we needn't have bothered." Morsicato mopped his forehead and stole another hunk of cheese. "He's devious. Like his father."

Pietro shook his head. "His father didn't have us."

"Still, do you ever worry?"

"No." The answer was a little too firm to have the ring of truth. "Worrying will only add grey to your beard." He indicated the mouthful of hair the doctor was chewing along with his cheese. "See?"

That elicited a chuckle. "Aren't none of us getting any younger."

Pietro put his cheese away and stood to rub down his sweating horse. "Be thankful. Now we can watch the whole world go grey trying to rein him in."

He was echoing an old debate, one that Pietro, the doctor, and the

Moor had shared over many bottles of wine through the last decade. Did you shape genius, or did genius shape you? Sometimes, in the early years, Pietro's father had descended upon them and proclaimed opinions made of granite. "Genius is the gift of God, and cannot be bred or altered. You cannot steer an ocean." *Well,* thought Pietro, *if anyone had known...*

Antonia and Esta approached, walking gingerly. Both were already saddle-sore. "Where are we spending the night?" asked Suor Beatrice. Her pleading tone almost made her brother laugh. Antonia Alaghieri never pleaded with anyone.

"Before now, I was thinking Vicenza, before. We'll have to see what shape the world has taken. It might not be safe."

Esta was still annoyed that she had not been part of the inner circle of 'spies.' Evidently Antonia had explained, softening her attitude towards Pietro – Morsicato was clearly still *persona non grata.* To Pietro she made polite conversation. "I'm so sorry about your house. But you haven't been living there much lately. Are you sorry to leave Bologna?"

Pietro hadn't even thought about *that* loss yet. He tried to make it sound trifling. "I've learned about everything I want to know. I just kept putting off the examinations. But really, it's been no fun at all since Petrarch left."

"Who?"

Antonia answered. "My brother's French friend, Monsieur Petrarca."

"She only calls him French out of spite," objected Pietro. "He's as Florentine as she is."

"His family followed the pope to Avignon," said Suor Beatrice, "the place father called —"

"— *la puttana* of France," finished Pietro. "I know. Trust me, I know."

In frustration Esta repeated, "*Who* is he?"

"Francesco Petrarca. Son of a papal clerk whose father has more ambition than understanding. Petrarch wants to be a poet, his father demands he study law. We've had many discussions over merging the two, and becoming a modern day Cicero. But, sad to say, Petrarch has no interest whatsoever in the law. Even with me tutoring him, he didn't do well."

Antonia smiled at this last, new fact. "Oh-ho! Is that why he left Bologna?"

"His father is ill," said Pietro gravely, chastening his little sister. "He's returned to Avignon to await the inevitable, which will set him free to become whatever he wants." *A condition that could be said about Cesco. And me, too.* "Still, I am sorry. He's the best friend I made there, other than the professors. If I had listened to Mari I would have been friends with him much sooner." He was referring to Mariotto Montecchio, an old friend from Verona. "They knew each other in Avignon. Mari even wrote to me about him, years ago."

Cesco was lying on his back, staring at the small screw of paper. Now he suddenly made a raspberry noise, crammed the note into his boot, and sat up. He looked at Detto, who was standing under a tree whistling to a small finch. The finch fluttered to the lowest branch then, after cocking its head, hopped down onto Detto's outstretched finger.

"How do you *do* that?" demanded Cesco.

"Do what?" asked Detto, secretly pleased. The truth was that animals loved him. He had a kind of animal magic that calmed any beast and made them trust him implicitly. It was a skill Tharwat also possessed, though to a lesser degree. Oddly, this simple ability made Cesco insanely jealous.

As he demonstrated now by drawing his sword. "Care to try?"

Grinning, Detto cast the finch back into the air and unsheathed his own weapon. "I'll try not to take off your head."

For the journey, Tharwat had fitted the boys out with blades very like the old Roman gladius – short, wide thrusting weapons with wicked tips. Though Bailardetto was looking to outstrip his friend in growth in spite of Cesco's year head-start, they were neither of them a size where they could wield a longsword. Nevertheless Tharwat, Pietro, and Morsicato had each taken turns teaching them swordplay, first with stick, then staff, now with blade. It was an accelerated training, since both were quite adept. The adults had suspected it was a skill they would need, and the boys were encouraged to spar whenever they had the opportunity.

"Go off a ways," Pietro told them. "You'll frighten the horses."

"Not to mention," taunted the doctor loudly to their backs, "the very real possibility that they'll kill one of the animals by mistake."

Both boys grabbed bucklers, too, the fist-sized round shields used to beat away an opponent's thrust. Thus armed, they prepared to spar. The hounds barked excitedly, accustomed to what was coming. Soon the air was ringing with their shouts and the clangs of their blades. Novello's soldiers started making discreet wagers.

Still brushing his horse, Pietro paused to watch the mock duel. Detto was already shaping up to be a fine fighter. His feet were wide-spread, his stance was low, his knees bent, just the way his father had taught him. He was well-balanced and the power of his arm was amazing for one so young. In ten years he would be one of the strongest swords in Lombardy.

Like the obverse of a coin, Cesco made no concession to form or practicality. He stood upright, his legs relaxed and too close together.

He let his buckler hang, unmindful. His sword, too, he left low, until it whipped up to strike. He had speed and grace. Detto struck methodically, but Cesco was never there, dancing away while slicing a light cut at his partner's buckler. Slash, ting. Slash, ting. Detto feinted and feinted again, yet wherever his true blow fell, Cesco was never under it.

The fight was not uneven. Often Cesco became trapped by his own cleverness and his buckler would come winging up to block a thrust he'd mistimed. His own attacks were beaten aside with power from Detto's surging parries. As they clashed, they traded insults as well as blows, quickly developing a rhythm of verbal patter and shrieking metal.

Watching their play, Morsicato grunted. "They're good. Though Cesco could use a refresher in the basics."

"Would do no good," observed Pietro.

Antonia had never seen them spar before. "Isn't it dangerous?"

"They're good for each other," said Pietro. "Detto is learning that speed is as important as strength, and Cesco is finding that, every now and then, a little discipline is a good thing."

"No, I mean isn't it dangerous if someone sees them? Or hears them," she added after a particularly loud yelp from Cesco. Detto had stabbed for his face and barely missed. Esta gasped and several soldiers said 'ooo'.

"They're fulfilling their training as pages." Pietro spoke distractedly, having just spied Tharwat returning. Gone just over an hour, the Moor reined in and dropped from his saddle. Although his horse was lathered, his complete ease made everyone release a collective breath.

"There is no army, Paduan or Vicentine, between us and Quartesolo. There are traces of a second army chasing this one, traveling by another road to head them off. And there are marks of a smaller party that was forced to move by the armies."

Pietro didn't like that last, but made up his mind. "We continue on to Vicenza." There was a peal of laughter behind him, and he pointed at the warring boys. "We need them to stop so we can get moving."

They called but were ignored. The boys were in high spirits, and so far the hits were even. When Pietro let out his most insistent bellow, Cesco flipped his sword into the air and gave the fig over his shoulder before catching the hilt and lunging again.

"That little bastard!" The soldiers' muted laughter kindled Pietro's indignation.

Tharwat reached over his saddle and lifted a powerful bird-bow from his tack. It was already strung, so he fitted an arrow into the groove between his first and second fingers. "Shall we get their attention?"

Grinning, Pietro lifted a similar bow from his own gear. The bow was not an approved instrument of war. Only crossbows were holy weapons, and Pietro had cause to loathe those fiendish contraptions. In recent years the Moor had been teaching Pietro how to hunt with the bow, and slowly Pietro's aim had improved. Besides, he was already an excommunicant, and Tharwat a heathen Moor. Hell already awaited them both. So why not carry bows?

Pietro nocked an arrow. "That weeping pine?" He used his chin to indicate the tree, a good ten yards past the boys.

The feathers on the Moor's shaft stood out, having been taken from a mallard duck. "The trunk."

"The large knot near the split branch. It'll sail just over their heads."

"And the winner?"

"The loser has to answer any question from the boy."

Morsicato clapped Pietro's shoulder. "I hope you have your answers worked out, my boy."

Pietro thanked the doctor for his encouragement. "Do you want a piece of this?"

"No, thank you. I've seen Tharwat shoot."

So had Pietro, but he'd been practicing at the butts behind his house and thought he might actually have a chance this time.

In unison they raised their bows and counted three. Released, the shafts sliced the air with a thin whistle, meant to crease the space above the combatants.

Just at the moment of release, Detto lunged for his partner's leg. Cesco should have jumped back from Detto's oncoming attack, but instead he spun around Detto's near side, away from the blow, and swept Detto's legs out from under him. Then he sat down as the thin dark streaks passed well overhead and smacked into the tree.

Cesco rolled over and sat on Detto's chest, sword held lazily near his partner's neck. "You should cry foul. There was interference."

In another moment they were trotting over. "Nuncle Pietro, you should really know better. After all, alone among us, you've actually been skewered." The thin smile creased further. "Where was that, again?"

"You know where."

"Ah yes! At the Battle of Vicenza, you said. The first or second?"

Pietro didn't bother to respond, since the answer was already known.

"Where was my father, then?" demanded Detto.

"Away," answered Pietro. "Your uncle Antonio was in charge."

"Which means *La Donna* was the real guiding light." *La Donna* was Cesco's name for Detto's mother – The Lady. He'd only met her a handful of times since coming to Ravenna, and hadn't seen her at all in two years. It was a mark of how she had touched his life that he could discern so accurately a truth from a battle almost as old as he was.

Detto looked a little sad at the mention of his mother, and Cesco immediately turned the talk back to the battle, demanding that Pietro relive it. As they mounted and began the trek north Pietro did just that, though he omitted a few important details. He didn't mention Montecchio or Capulletto by name, saying only that he'd ridden into battle with 'two friends.' Hardly an appropriate sobriquet these days.

There was one name, however, that Pietro could hardly fail to leave out. He wondered if that had really been Cesco's goal.

The tale told, the boys lagged behind to discuss warfare in general and Tharwat drew up next to Pietro. "My arrow was truer."

"Mine had the inner track."

"It's certainly lovely to think so. So who answers the question from the boy?"

"One each, do you think?"

Al-Dhaamin nodded. "He earned it, the little fool."

"He saw us," said Pietro, "and made a show of being missed."

"Worse. He goaded his friend into the attack."

"So he could play the hero. Idiot. I like how Cesco acted as if he saved Detto's life."

"They were in no danger."

"I know it, and you know it. And Cesco knows it. But he likes to be the hero."

"Even when there is no danger."

"And yet," admitted Pietro, "when they moved, I could feel my heart stop in my chest."

"Mine was in my throat."

It was easy when one met the Moor to think that he had no emotions at all, that whatever had so scarred his flesh had also rendered him senseless internally. His harsh voice rarely carried any inflection, even now. But eight years with their joint charge had drawn the two men into a kind of intimacy that neither had looked for, and both valued.

Cesco cantered up on Pietro's other side. "So who won?"

"I did," said both Tharwat and Pietro in unison. Pietro added, "Next time we'll spare ourselves the effort and aim right at your head."

"You mean you weren't? I only moved because I know what poor shots you both are. The safest way to avoid being hit is to stand where you're aiming."

"Give me the fig again and you won't find anywhere to hide." Pietro stretched out to ruffle the boy's wild hair.

Cesco ducked away, trying to fix his unruly hair. "So who won, really?"

"You, I suppose. You've earned two questions, one from each of us."

Cesco reared back in mock surprise. "That's two more than I thought I'd get. I'll have to think of something to ask. By the by, it's astrology."

Pietro took some water from a skin. "What is?"

The boy produced the crumpled screw of paper from inside his boot. "This code. It has to do with the stars."

Pietro turned to Detto. "Two hours since he first laid eyes on it, and that's as far as he's gotten. I'm unimpressed."

"I'd like to see anyone else do better."

"Nobody else has your advantages," Pietro retorted. "Who could have helped me with that code? The list is short – father, sister, brother, doctor, and astrologer. Hmm. Astrologer. Perhaps it has to do with the stars!"

"Sarcasm doesn't suit you, Nuncle," said Cesco. "In fact, the pursuit of irony is a poor suit of armour for those of weak wit."

This was a trick Pietro knew well. Cesco often retreated into word-play. Pietro snapped his fingers. "A week's wit spent at once, then. If sarcasm ill-suits me, then deliberate obtuseness suits you even less," he said, paraphrasing an oft-repeated chastisement of his father's. "Use what you have. You've handicapped yourself by starting from scratch, as if you know nothing of the men who devised it."

"I know so little of anything, how could I do less?" Cesco held out the paper. "Clearly this author knows little of astrology, as that layer is of the most basic kind. The date on the paper was three days past – the sun was just into the ninth house then. The moon formed a trine with Mercury, but that's been missed. Written in the second hour of the day, when Venus reigns. Scorpio ascendant, and Jupiter was in Cancer, and the eighth..."

"Yes, yes, you've been well tutored. Even a parrot can recite Virgil."

"I'd rather be a dancing monkey," said Cesco, slipping to hang sideways in the saddle and scratch his armpit. "That way I could earn my keep. Chireep!"

"What a pleasant change that would be."

Still hanging, the boy's smile turned nasty. "You're just upset that you missed me."

Pietro spurred his mount. "That, at least, is true."

# SEVEN

## Verona

TULIO D'ISOLA entered the palace's private chamber just as Mastino was lecturing his brother Alberto. Two years Mastino's elder, Alblivious was forever innocent and guileless. This caused his ambitious sibling more problems than it solved. Alberto's latest gaffe was in letting slip Mastino's intention of holding back the pay of Verona's mercenary army for a month to furnish himself with a fine processional parade.

"...you damned fool, yes it's a problem! Our uncle relied on the mercenaries more and more, calling on his own knights less often. So until things settle down, we're going to need these greedy bastards—" Mid-diatribe, Mastino rounded on the Grand Butler, turning his ire from one victim to another without breaking rhythm. "If my uncle hasn't returned from the dead, you'd best turn right back around! I have no time for bric-a-brac and petty complaints!"

Having known Mastino man and boy these sixteen years, d'Isola was no way startled by this greeting. "My Lords Capitano," he began, tweaking Mastino's nose with the joint-captainship, "there is a delegation arrived within the city requesting an audience. A delegation from Venice."

Hands braced on the table before him, Mastino stilled. "Did they give their names?"

"The leader of their party is Ambassador Francesco Dandolo."

Mastino hissed through his teeth. Alberto looked a blank. "Is he someone important?"

Ignoring his brother, Mastino pressed d'Isola. "Where, do you think?"

"I believe the Domus Nuova would be best for an official visit of state," replied the Grand Butler.

"Call my man, have the proper clothes prepared. We shall receive Ambassador Dandolo in – three hours. Let him stew."

D'Isola bowed. "As you think best."

♦    ◊    ♦

### The Road to Vicenza

Despite the Moor's assurances, it was a wary ride, with Novello's men continually scanning the horizon for an ambush. But as the sun began to descend, Detto was able to doze, held upright in his saddle between Morsicato and Esta. Tharwat was scouting ahead, and Antonia was too focused on staying upright to fear an attack. "I'm not made for riding," she said through a clenched jaw.

Whereas Cesco was. He fidgeted, slipping one foot out of his stirrup and wrapping it around the saddle's pommel. His restlessness had nothing at all to do with unseen dangers. Finally he ranged himself alongside Pietro. "Two questions?"

"That was the wager."

"The Arūs isn't here. Do you mind receiving them both?"

"Let loose."

"Poor choice of words, considering the contest." Cesco paused, considering. "Tell me – have you ever been in love?"

Pietro's mind balked like a horse hit on the head with a warhammer. "What?"

The eyes were less green than blue at this moment. *A traitor to the core.* "My first question. Have you ever been in love?"

"That's your question? You don't want to know about your father?"

Cesco pointed an accusing finger. "Oh-ho! So it's my *pater* who matters, not my *mater*? Thank you. But I'll find out soon enough. No, I want to know why you've never married. I know you've had offers, good ones."

"I – hmm. Perhaps I'm not the marrying kind."

"Nonsense! You're positively made for a family life! But that was an evasion. You said you'd answer anything."

"So I did." Pietro felt a tightness in his chest, and had to take a deep breath before answering. "I did love once. An older woman."

"So what was the problem? Too large an age difference?"

"No. She was married to a man I liked."

"Hah! And because you liked him, you didn't try anything." Cesco applauded slowly, shaking his head. "Courtly Love. The mournful sigh from afar! I know Grandfather Dante fell into that trap, but I didn't think you were such a fool!"

"Oh, I'm a bigger fool than you imagine."

Hearing the bitterness, Cesco grew more interested. "So what happened?"

Pietro's gaze was far away. "She wasn't what I thought she was."

"The failure of all great loves."

That remark brought Pietro back. "And what do you know of great loves? Have you fallen for some false idol?"

Cesco made a face, proving that at least in this, he was an average eleven year-old. "Not me! Men make fools of themselves for women, even in literature. I've always wondered if Lancelot was happy once he and Guinevere ran off together. Pleasure for a month, perhaps two. But it had to start to pall. The reality of her couldn't have matched his dreams. Within a year I'll bet he was lusting after someone else. The only time love can truly last forever is if they both die before they get to know each other." Cesco's brow furrowed. "But that makes sense, about you. I've always wondered why you didn't marry. You're smarter than I gave you credit for," he added.

"Why thank you," said Pietro dryly. "Your second question?"

Cesco swung his leg back around and found his stirrup. "On second thought, I think I'll save it for my Shadow."

◆    ◊    ◆

Very soon they passed Quartesolo. As they approached the city they passed abandoned war machines – trebuchets, ladders, the makings of a siege-tower – all heaped by the side of the road, forgotten. Within a half-hour they were crossing the bridge to Vicenza, a city none but Morsicato and Detto had set foot in for eight long years.

At once they noticed the outskirts were marred by the detritus of a great fire. Awake now, Detto looked anxiously at the charred walls of his birthplace. Pietro assured him that there were no signs of a battle.

The city guards were on them before they reached the gate in the great wall. Morsicato rode to greet them. Pietro remained among Novello's men. If he'd come with banners unfurled and the train that was his due, Ser Pietro Alaghieri would doubtless have been accorded a hero's welcome. But it was not Pietro's intent to invite attention until he knew how the ground lay. Morsicato had once been the private physician to Donna Nogarola. When questioned he said simply that they were returning the elder son of Bailardino to his father in this time of distress.

The armed men were for the boy's protection.

The garrison visibly relaxed and the doctor passed some words with them, gaining the news he repeated to Pietro moments later, *sotto voce*. "They know he's dead. The fire was accidental, and seems to be why he was rushing here – even though there's a truce, Padua could hardly resist such a chance. On the way here, he just died. Once they heard he was gone, they expected the city to fall in days. But the Paduans never arrived. They're mystified as to why."

"Who was leading the Paduan army?"

"Your old friend, of course."

The title was ironic. Marsilio de Carrara was hardly Pietro's friend. Three times they had met in battle, and each time Pietro had somehow stumbled away not only alive but bearing the laurels. After the death of his noble uncle, Carrara had taken up the running of Padua. Recent accounts said his younger relatives were terrorizing the city, leaving the blame squarely at Carrara's door. Those rumours filled Pietro with a warm glow.

Passing under the gate, Pietro saw that years had brought little change to Vicenza. In spite of the fires it had suffered through a decade of intermittent siege, the city was rebuilding in the same old way – wood, not stone. The decimated structures would be recreated just as they had always been. Some lessons took hard learning.

Happily, the Nogarola palace was intact. Technically it belonged to the entire Nogarola clan, but Detto's uncle chose to live on the estate outside the city. A crossbow hit had festered, costing him an arm. Though he still occasionally rode into battle with a shield strapped to his body, Antonio da Nogarola was no longer fit to lead his family's fortunes.

That honour fell to Detto's father. Bailardino da Nogarola was a bear-like man with a genial temperament. The palace belonged to him, but Bail was often away on matters of state and war. With Detto so often in Ravenna, and Detto's brother Valentino spending much time with his one-armed uncle, the only permanent resident of the palace was Bail's wife – *La Donna*, as Cesco called her. The whole of the top floor was given over to the care of Detto's mother, and for two years she had never ventured from it.

Dismounting, Cesco stared at the palace doors with a concentrated frown. "I know this place."

"You should," answered Morsicato. "You spent your first couple of years here."

Detto's head-stutter was comical. "But – this is *my* house!"

"All in the fullness of time." The Moor was gazing around the street. "Let the grooms take the horses and let's get inside."

"Yes, all of us, inside," said, Pietro ushering them towards the shaded entryway.

Though fortified outside, the interior of the three-story building was built in the old Roman style, with a central garden and balconies looking down into it. It was eerie for Pietro to be back here. The proudest memories of his life were alive in this building. As were the worst.

Cesco walked slowly, staring in utter bemusement. "I've been here..." Suddenly he bolted around a corner into the inner courtyard, Detto in his wake.

"Stay inside the palace!" The Nogarola guards were chuckling, and Pietro gave them a boys-will-be-boys shrug. "Tharwat, Morsicato, can you make sure they don't slip off to the markets or something?"

The Moor was already moving in a light run. Morsicato bussed his wife's cheek before he stalked off, refusing to run, muttering as he went. "Put a leash on him, teach him to heel..."

The steward arrived, greeting Pietro and the women warmly. Antonia had only ever been to the palace once, but the steward remembered Esta and Pietro well. "The master is away, Ser Alaghieri, as well you can imagine."

"Chasing Paduans or on his way to Verona?"

"The former, I believe. He hoped to catch them while they were still on this side of the border."

"Thank Heaven they didn't reach the city," said Esta.

"Indeed, madam. We thank God for it with every breath. With the Greyhound gone—"

"Yes," said Pietro briskly. "Just so. Now, if you could arrange some refreshment and show the ladies to the baths. I believe they could use a rest after our long ride. I have to thank our companions and send word back to Lord Novello that we arrived safely."

"Of course, Ser Alaghieri. Shall I unpack your baggage in the guest suite?"

"Thank you, but we're not staying more than a night or two." As the steward gave orders to his waiting staff, Pietro touched his shoulder lightly. "That last is not to be published. Just let people know that Detto has come to be with his father in this time of crisis."

No stranger to intrigue, he. "Shall I say that business requires you to travel back to Ravenna as soon as the lady is rested."

"That's just right. And please send a messenger to Lord Nogarola to inform him I've arrived with Detto."

"Immediately. Do you wish to see his lady wife?"

From the moment he saw the city walls, Pietro had been steeling himself to do just that. "If it is convenient."

Minutes later he was climbing the stairs to the top floor of the palace, listening to Novello's soldiers clatter away on the street outside. As he reached the second floor he paused beside a door that led to the roof. Banishing evil memories, Pietro allowed himself to be directed down the corridor to the *chatelaine's* chamber. "This is the door." The steward knocked, then opened the heavy wooden portal without pause. She was expecting him. Bracing himself, Pietro stepped within.

The room smelled too sweet, a peculiar mixture of humanity, drugs, and incense that indicated a sickroom. The rays of the setting sun slanted through shuttered windows. Once there had been thin and delicate curtains in this room, but shutters were better to block out light. Light was no longer this lady's friend.

In the unwanted illumination of the open door, Pietro saw an elderly woman sitting beside a massive bed, a book in hand. In the bed a second figure was propped with pillows, her hands folded in her lap. There was just light enough to show that the beautiful chestnut hair had developed streaks of grey. There was just light enough to see the skin sagging on one side of her face. There was just light enough to see the fire of intelligence and passion still blazing in her eyes.

"Ser Pietro Alaghieri," slurred Katerina della Scala slowly. "Tell me – how is my boy?"

# EIGHT

*Verona*

"MY LORD AMBASSADOR," said Mastino, rising to kiss the Venetian on both cheeks. Dandolo was equally demonstrative to both brothers before settling into the chair set for him. Notably, the chairs of state were set at the same level as his own. Cangrande had always met with Venetians from up on the dais. It was meant as flattery, and taken as weakness.

"A sad time." Dandolo voice was heavy with diplomatic grief. For himself, he couldn't have been much troubled by Cangrande's passing.

"Indeed," answered Mastino. "He went before his time."

"We must not question the wisdom of God's plan. Perhaps it was Fate that put you in that chair. If so, you must shoulder the burden. To aid you, I have a gift." He waved to a servant by the door, and the object was placed in Mastino's hands.

It was a silver globe engraved with all the constellations. Though he didn't much care for astrology, Mastino made a show of admiring it. "Thank you."

"A trifle. No great man should be without a guide to the stars. Your uncle once employed a most remarkable man, an astrologer. Ignazzio, that was his name. Whatever became of him?"

"If I'm remembering the man you mean, he also met an untimely fate. In a foreign land."

"A shame. He was a singular astrologer – practical, if you can call any astrologer that. And he had an apprentice, a Moor that served as his bodyguard. Do you know where *he* is now?"

"I do not," said Mastino apologetically. "I've never had time for dabbling in mysticism. But if it interests you, I will make inquiries."

"You are very kind."

Mastino passed several more compliments with the Venetian, admiring the smooth and disarming way the older man behaved. He seemed bored by everything. Mastino tried to act the same. If he remembered it, he made no reference to the last pope's nickname for this particular Dandolo.

On the other hand, he was ready to lob the gifted silver orb at his brother's head. As joint-captain, Alberto had to be present, but he apparently couldn't even take a lesson three hours old. When Dandolo made the subtle, genteel allusion to Verona's tariffs on Venetian land exports, Alberto bluntly offered to lower them. Mastino revised that sentiment at once, mentioning their ongoing mourning for their dear late uncle who had been such a good friend to Venice as well as Verona. "Rest assured, my lord ambassador, when we are past our grief, we'll do whatever we are able for our good friends and neighbours."

"Oh, I would not presume to intrude state matters upon you at such a time. It would be inexcusable. Though, if I may be candid, Lord Mastino – you are not what I expected. A sixteen year-old, thrust into power, one might expect posturing or incivility, stemming from insecurity. You show none of that. The office of Capitano seems to suit you."

A smile cracked Mastino's veneer of boredom. "Or perhaps I suit it."

"Perhaps that is indeed the answer."

"Yet I *am* young, and have much to learn. Especially from august councilors like yourself."

Alberto was still a few words behind, focusing on something Dandolo had said. "If you aren't here to discuss matters of state, then why are you here at all?"

The ambassador had not said the office suited Alblivious. But Dandolo was a skilled statesman, and not everyone he dealt with was a cultured game-player. "Why, for the reading of the will. We are often asked to arbitrate in these matters, and in such a case as this, it is best to have an impartial party as witness."

"Is there a will?" asked Mastino, feeling a slight prickling sensation. "Do you know its contents?"

Dandolo rose, preparing to take his leave. "I have absolutely no knowledge of what it might contain. But there is certain to be one. Your uncle was a man of surprising parts. Venice is quite interested in hearing his final wishes."

*Damn.* Maybe he should have handed over the trade rights at once. "Lord Ambassador, if you have some warning, the whole of Verona will be in your debt."

"Sadly, Lord Mastino, I have no direct knowledge of your uncle's will. I refuse to speculate as to whom it might have been entrusted. This is, after all, an internal Veronese matter." He paused, then lowered his voice. "Though I will offer this word of advice. This office does suit you. If I were in your shoes, I would be certain no one was in a position, legal or otherwise, to take it away from me."

Mastino rose to take Dandolo's hand. "Thank you, lord ambassador, for your advice. I appreciate it. Truly."

Satisfied, the Venetian departed for his lavish rented house a block away. Alberto began to talk before the door was even closed, but Mastino sent him off to join that fool Jacopo Alaghieri. Alone, he sat thinking for a long time. Then he called for d'Isola. "Send for Guglielmo da Castelbarco."

◆ ◊ ◆

## Vicenza, the Nogarola Palace

Cesco emerged into an open atrium filled with flowers and statuary, a single tall fountain at the center. Atop the flowing fountain, three stone women poured water into the basin.

"This is the garden!" said Detto. "I used to play here when I was little."

"Me too," murmured Cesco in wonderment, his eyes roaming the columns and shrubs. "I've dreamed of this garden – and this fountain!" Running his fingers over the fountain's lip, his hands paused just out of sight. He laughed in astonishment.

"What is it?"

"Nothing." Cesco leapt up onto the fountain's lip and performed a series of spinning steps along the edge, occasionally dipping his foot into the water.

Normally Detto would have followed, but this once he remained earth-bound, a look of hard concentration etched across his face. Cesco paused. "Am I defiling your sacred home?"

"What? No, no. It's just – Cesco, are we brothers?"

"To the death."

"No, I mean are we *brothers*?"

Dropping to sit on the fountain's edge, Cesco pursed his lips. "I think we'd know it."

"I wish we were. Not like stupid Valentino."

"Why not, then?" Producing a knife from his sopping boot, Cesco made a small cut on his palm. Grasping the meaning, Detto did the same then clasped Cesco's hand. For a moment their blood mingled. Then

Cesco doubled over in mock pain. "O, it burns, it burns!"

Detto gave Cesco the fig, looking quickly around afterwards to see if any adults were watching. Turning back to Cesco, his face clouded. "Aren't you mad at them? They *lied* to you."

Cesco put his hand in the fountain and watched his blood make a small cloud. "Very mad. But not for the reason you think. They lied to protect me, I see that. I'm mad because they thought I couldn't figure it out. I mean, really, I – look out!"

Cesco rolled deliberately into the water, and Detto immediately splashed down beside him. Peering out over the fountain's lip, Detto hissed, "What?"

"He's found us." Cesco pointed to where the Moor stood behind some gauzy curtains, watching them.

"He's not the only one," said Detto, as a little boy of seven years came thundering into the atrium from an inner chamber.

"Detto!" shouted Valentino, Detto's little brother. "Detto, where are you? They said you were back! Detto! Where are you?"

Cesco pressed his mouth close to Detto's ear. "He looks awfully dry, doesn't he?"

Grinning, Detto flexed his shoulders. "He does."

Waiting until their prey drew near, they pounced.

Their splashes and screams echoed up the open atrium, through the shuttered windows into the room where Pietro was standing, the weight of a hundred years on his shoulders. "*Bongiorno*, Madonna."

"You must pardon me if I don't rise." The words were slow and slurred, emerging as they did from only one side of her mouth.

"How is it?"

"There is progress." The last syllable gave Donna Katerina tremendous difficulty. She raised her left arm a fraction. It was doubly injured – first horrible burns, then the stroke. She had taken to wearing a glove of supple leather stitched all the way to her elbow. "As for the rest, I endure. But what brings you? Surely not a romantic visit. Though my husband *is* away, I am not so alluring."

Her disingenuousness did not amuse, but still Pietro smiled. "Your beauty is merely more delicate now, my lady." That made her laugh, which in turn made her cough. The nurse leaned in with a bowl of water for her to sip. As she drank, Pietro slipped to her other side to sit on a vacant stool. After her mouth had been wiped dry, she turned her head to him. "Your sense of humour is coming along nicely."

"With Cesco in my house, how could it not?"

The intelligent blue eyes flashed, and Pietro saw the ugly thing living in her mind, closer to the surface than it had ever been. The stroke had weakened her defenses. Or else she had ceased to care about dissembling in front of him.

"He's here." It wasn't a question.

"Downstairs," said Pietro, wondering if she had truly failed to hear the noise from below. "Would you like to see him?"

Again the hunger leapt to the fore, but this time it dueled with her pride. Clearly she longed to see him, but had no desire to be seen *by* him – not in her present state. "Perhaps. But first tell me everything. My husband reads me your letters, and Detto's, but there is still two years worth of growing I have missed."

"Time is a little short."

"Nonsense. Bailardino isn't here. You and he can make your war plans when he returns."

"War plans?"

The lady smiled for the first time, and Pietro perceived why she had refrained from it. The right side of her face curled into life while the left remained sagged, turning that smile into a twisted grimace. Her smile was now more lop-sided than Pietro's, though his was natural, hers enforced. "You haven't heard? Mastino has taken over the palace, with both his brother and cousin Federigo at his back. They won't be shifted without force of arms. And by now my beloved sister-in-law is surely on her way. So many claimants."

Unwelcome news, but not entirely unexpected. "Your husband will support Cesco?"

"As will da Lozzo and Castelbarco, and probably Bonaventura. You must bring in Montecchio and Capulletto."

"One or the other," said Pietro bitterly. "If one joins, the other will oppose us to the death."

"You underestimate their loyalty to you. Now, tell me about my boy."

Glancing at the nurse, Pietro realized that secrecy no longer mattered. He began with the recent business with Cianfa Donati, then moved on to other tales: the impromptu trip to Venice, the incident with the shipwright, the ill-fated bear-baiting. All tales of Cesco's flamboyance, his genius and daring. He did not mention the nightmares, nor the long hours staring at the same page of a book. He left out the nervous recurring illness that Morsicato attributed only to "an excess of energy in so small a frame." He omitted the bouts of tears, or the sudden flights of meaningless rage that could overtake the boy.

He concluded with the boy's own analysis of his parentage, the inadvertent clues he had pounced upon. Her answer was a wry look. "Did you really think we'd fool him?"

"I only wonder he hasn't guessed it all," said Pietro ruefully. That reminded him, and he bowed his head. "Lady, I am sorry for your loss."

Katerina was less grave in acknowledgement. "Not so great a loss as you might think. He has not been the man you knew. Though perhaps you find that gratifying."

Side-stepping the barb, Pietro plowed on. "Lady, I need to know who Cesco's mother is. She must be sent for."

Donna Katerina's eyes became veiled. "I think the more pertinent question is, who is his father? Don't you think he wants that answered?"

Pietro had no desire to play these games. "Who is the lady Maria? Where is she?"

The sound she produced could have been a laboured breath, or else a soulfelt sigh. "How boring you've become, Pietro." His name as she pronounced it sounded like the Spanish *Pedro*. "She has already been summoned. Though I do not know if she will come." Donna Katerina had trouble swallowing, and her nurse came forward again to give her water.

When she was well, Pietro said, "Would you like to see him now?" She made a minute shake of her head. "Tonight. When he is asleep."

"What about Detto?"

"I'll see him soon enough. When Cesco is in power, Detto will come to visit."

"Your son is turning into a fine young man."

"I know. His brother is much the same. They are Bailardino's, through and through." She arched her right eyebrow. "Doubtless you think that a good thing?"

Pietro was saved from answering by a shout of laughter from the atrium. "Is that them?" Pietro told her it was. She considered for a moment. "Perhaps I *will* see them. If you don't find it too distasteful."

It was a long process. Picking her up was difficult because of his weak leg. Eventually he had her in his arms and carried her through the door to the gallery above the atrium.

Looking down, Pietro saw that Detto and Cesco had been joined by Katerina's other son, Valentino. They were playing some game which involved Cesco touching every pillar in the gallery in sequence, all the while singing and dodging the attacks of the other two. On a bench far below sat the doctor, sipping a goblet of wine and watching thoughtfully. Off to one side, unobtrusive, stood Tharwat, half his attention on their boyish antics, half looking for threats.

Her right arm about Pietro's neck, Katerina watched without change of expression. But Pietro felt a tremble run through her. He tried not to tremble himself. In all the years he had known her, they had never been this close. Unwilling, he breathed in her scent. Lavender. How could he have forgotten?

It was a relief when the lady's husband came pounding up the stairs, still covered in dust from the road. "How now! Out of bed!" His dark hair had thinned and his bristly beard was shot through with salt, but in every other respect Bailardino was a man in his prime. "Alaghieri! They told me downstairs! A welcome face in a troubled time."

"It is a holiday," said Katerina. "All our prodigals have returned to us."

"Just as welcome as that first Prodigal," said Bailardino, lifting his wife gently from Pietro's arms. "Light as a sparrow, just like the day we met. D'you want to go down? A spell in the garden might do you good."

"I am tired. I think I need to rest."

Instantly contrite, her husband at once carried her back to her bed. Pietro remained by the railing, watching the youthful sport below with unseeing eyes. After a time the door behind him shut and Bailardino drew near. "Thought you'd arrive tomorrow at the earliest."

"A small but determined party. Detto's doing well."

This brightened the warrior's face. "I swear, I don't know how I survived a life without children. They make everything make sense!" He shot Pietro a happy grin. "When are you going to settle down, boy?"

"When this is all over, maybe." He nodded at the closed door. "She seems well."

Bailardino released a weighty sigh. "Kind of you to say, lad, but we both know you're lying. She should have recovered more than this. Walking by now, they say, and no slur."

"How do the doctors explain it?"

"What they always say. '*An imbalance in the humours.*' Not that I find it so damned humourous."

"Morsicato's with us. He'll help."

"I'm just happy that her brother's death hasn't caused a second stroke."

"She does seem to be taking it well."

"Better than me." Bailardino ran his meaty hands through his wispy hair, then cuffed Pietro's shoulder. "I'm sure she was glad to see you, though! She's always had a soft spot for you. Come, let's talk of more pleasant things – like the war we're going to bring to that little shit! How much do you know?"

Pietro quickly recounted their journey. In return, Bailardino gave him the news from Verona. "Mastino has taken over the palaces. He's wooing the younger courtiers and flattering the elder statesmen – those he values, at any rate. Castelbarco is immune, but worried. And Venice has sent Francesco Dandolo to treat with him."

"The one that Pope Clement called—?"

"The same."

"That's not necessarily bad," observed Pietro. "Our resident astrologer is on cordial terms with him. What about Alberto?"

Bailardino snorted. "Alblivious? Like a faithful dog, he does what his brother tells him. He's so likeable that Mastino's using him to soothe the people."

"That's not good."

"Worse than you know." Bail hesitated, then blurted out, "Your brother's with him. Making it seem as if your family supports Mastino."

"Poco?" Mouth agape, Pietro shook his head. "The idiot. He knows! He damn-well *knows!*"

"Probably thinks he's being clever, spying for you."

"Instead he's doing more harm than good. As usual." Pietro was torn between laughter and rage. With Poco that was normal.

Bailardino shrugged. "In the meantime, I've been summoned to swear my loyalty to the new joint-captains. The messenger found me on the road. Now that the Paduan army has drawn off, Mastino has ordered – ordered! – me to come to Verona without delay and kneel before him in the Piazza della Signoria. Show my family's 'continuing bond of loyalty to the Scaligeri.'" His distaste was palpable. "A Nogarola, told to kneel before someone other than a pope or a emperor? I knelt to the Greyhound, but that was my choice. He never demanded it."

"Twenty to one it's for Dandolo's benefit," said Pietro.

"No wager." Suddenly Bailardino's bearded face broke into a thin smile. "There's one ray of sunshine. Cousin Federigo was charged with reorganizing the army and he's made a right mess of it. By all accounts they're close to mutiny."

"In just three days? How did he manage that?"

"He flogged a dozen men and stopped the pay of Otto the Burgundian's whole company. I also hear rumours of an entire month's wages delayed so that Mastino can have a lavish parade." He grinned at his impromptu rhyme. "There. As good as your old man!"

Pietro's mind raced ahead. "That *is* good news. If the army comes to us, it'll be seen as a sign that they take Cesco as the true heir. Will they follow a boy they don't know?"

"The Greyhound's son? They'll follow him to the end of the Earth and beyond."

Pietro asked about the Paduan army. Bail said he didn't know why, after setting out to take advantage of Vicenza's recent fire, they had turned back. "You'd think his death would have spurred them on!"

"Count your blessings." As they trudged down the main staircase to the ground level, Pietro added, "By the way, Cesco doesn't yet know who his father was."

Bailardino's expression questioned Pietro's sanity. "Don't you think it's time he learned?"

"I do. But let me do this my own way."

Reaching the atrium, Bailardino shrugged. "I could never manage him. From the time he started walking he's always gotten the better of me."

They passed through gauzy curtains into the central garden. The game came to an abrupt end as Detto ran into his father's bone-crushing hug. "Hello, my little man! Where have you been gadding? Look at you! All grown up!"

Detto disengaged to drag Cesco forward. "Father, this is—"

"Oh, I know that imp well. Hardly grown since I last saw him. Hello there, *dottore!*" Seeing the Moor, Bail's cheerfulness vanished. "Astrologer."

Al-Dhaamin bowed in the Italian style. "My lord."

Ignoring their cool greetings, Pietro seated his weary legs on the bench beside Morsicato. He gestured towards the younger boy. "Bail, are you going to introduce us?"

"Oh, damn me, you've never met? Valentino, this is a dear friend to our family, Ser Pietro Alaghieri, also known as Pietro di Dante. A good friend of your mother's and mine."

Young Valentino performed a neat little bow, and Pietro complimented him for it. Seven years old and already he looked like his father and brother, if thinner. His eyes held a worrisome echo of his mother's acuity. But only an echo.

When the other introductions were finished, Valentino ran back to Detto, who cuffed him genially on the ear. They were about to resume their game when Pietro clapped his hands together. "Boys, come here. It's time."

"Finally!" cried Detto.

"Time for what?" demanded Valentino.

"Time to listen," said Bailardino.

"In a moment!" Cesco ignored Pietro's summons, leaping instead up to the fountain and clinging to the shape of Melpomene, the muse with the sword. From somewhere he produced an inkwell and a quill and, using the muse's arm as his desk, scratched a quick word on the back of the coded paper.

Pietro waited for him to finish. "Very well. What have you deciphered?"

Cesco lazily turned over the paper and read. " '*He is dead. Come quickly. The little dog is already moving.*'" He glanced up, a pupil taking his final examination. "That's right, isn't it?"

"Just about." Their best code, broken in less than a day by an eleven year-old boy. A boy Pietro had reared. He could take pride in that, at least.

Valentino glanced at his brother. "What was that?"

"Not now, Val," growled Detto.

Cesco swung around to perch on the statue's outstretched arm. "So, the dead man. Is that my father? Or someone threatening me."

Pietro considered a soft answer, then decided against it. "Your father."

Nodding, Cesco flipped over the muse's arm to hang upside-down from his knees, waving the paper to dry the ink. "I'm the only heir, then?"

Bailardino snorted. "Would that you were."

Swaying back and forth, Cesco's inverted eyebrows arched. "*The little dog?*"

Tharwat spoke. "A literal translation. There's more to the name."

"I imagine so." Swinging out, Cesco flipped in midair and landed upright like an acrobat. "First, take this." He handed Pietro the slip of paper, folded so that the coded side was facing out. "Now, tell me about my dearly departed sire."

Bailardino frowned. "A little respect, boy."

Cutting across off Cesco's inevitable retort, Pietro said, "Your father was a great man. A powerful man. When you were a child there were several attempts on your life. Because of that, he was forced to foster you out – first to Bailardino here, then to me. Our hope was that when you came of age you could return to take your place at his side. But three days ago he died unexpectedly, which has changed everything."

Valentino turned to his father. "But papa, the only one who died this week was Uncle Francesco." Detto gasped, turning to stare at his brother. Valentino retreated in confusion. "What? What?"

"Uncle Francesco's dead?" Detto was some time picking up his jaw. Then he made the connection and gasped again. "Cesco's his son?"

"And who, exactly, is this noteworthy Uncle Francesco?" Before anyone could answer, Cesco clapped a hand to his forehead. "Oh! You mean Francesco della Scala, known as Cangrande, the Great Hound of Verona. Grandfather Dante's patron, brother to Detto and Val's mother, the man who knighted Nuncle Pietro, *il Capitano di Verona*, *Dux Bellorum*, and Vicar of the Trevisian Mark. *Il Veltro*. The Greyhound. Is it him you mean?"

"The same." Only Tharwat noticed that Pietro winced at that last title. But only he had been looking.

Superbly pleased with himself, Cesco was leaning against the fountain. "I seem to have heard of him once or twice." He grinned at Pietro and raised his eyebrows. Only then did Pietro glance down at the little note Cesco had returned to him. Unfolding it, he read in Cesco's neat practiced script:

> *Cane Grande della Scala, lord of Verona.*

Cesco's eyes flickered back and forth between the adults. "So what's my name? My *real* name, I mean."

That gave Pietro a moment's pause. He didn't actually know the boy's true name, the name he'd been given at birth. Instead he gave a carefully worded answer. "You were baptized Francesco in the church of Santa Maria Antica in Verona. I was there. So was Bail."

"And my mother?" Seeing the blank look on the adult faces, Cesco cracked a light grin. "Ah. A bastard, is that it? *Il veltro del Veltro,*" he punned. *Veltro* meant both *greyhound* and *bastard*. "And my father, the noble Capitano, is dead?"

"That's what this message says."

"So I go from one orphaned life to another. We believe this message?" he added, rather wisely, Pietro thought.

"There are seven people living who know that code – four of them live in Ravenna, two more here." Pietro nodded at Bailardino. "Only one of them is in Verona."

"Not Jacopo!" cried Cesco in mock dismay. Pietro, Bailardino, and Morsicato all chuckled. Tharwat said nothing.

"No, Jacopo is not involved in our little side business."

"Thank the Lord. A secret in Jacopo's head will be all over the Rialto in an hour."

"While a secret in your head will go unspoken for a lifetime," observed the Moor.

"Well, at least until it's useful. Scala," said Cesco, rolling the name around on his tongue. "Della Scala. I think I remember… there was a night, it was dark. There were torches, lots of people shouting. They were chanting it. Scala." His eyes came back into focus. "Did that happen? It wasn't a dream?"

Pietro nodded, secretly pleased Cesco had held on to that memory. "That happened. But now isn't the time for that story. We must brief you on the history of the city, our potential allies and enemies – everything you're going to need to know. Then we have decisions to make."

Bailardino leaned close to Pietro. "Now?"

"Sand is slipping away every second."

Bail laughed as he gestured at the children. "Damn silly gathering for a war conference."

The Moor's voice rumbled softly. "It is their war."

# NINE

FOOD WAS ORDERED as four men and three children sat in the atrium, talking through the political landscape as it stood. For Cesco's benefit, Pietro began by describing Mastino and Alberto. "But those two are not the only claimants to the Scaligeri line. We have Detto and Val here, of course."

Cesco faced Detto. "Best two out of three falls." Detto laughed and Val looked anxious, wondering if Cesco was serious.

Pietro ignored the interruption. "Then there's Paride della Scala, a year or so younger than you. He's Cangrande's great-nephew. His father, Cecchino della Scala, would have been the perfect one to take Cangrande's place. But fortunately for you, he died earlier this year."

Cesco adopted a solemn air. "An ill-omened year for us Scaligeri. But if we're concerned about the people welcoming a whelp like me – and I take it that we are – why should we worry about a boy who's even younger?"

Morsicato's forked beard positively bristled. "Because of who is behind him."

"His aunt, Cangrande's wife." Pietro acknowledged Cesco's despairing expression. "I know, it's confusing. Cangrande and his oldest brother, Bartolomeo, married sisters. Giovanna da Svevia and her sister are the great-granddaughters of Emperor Frederick II. That makes little Paride Giovanna's nephew twice over, and a potential heir to the Holy Roman Empire."

"My, what a tangled web I've fallen into! So this lady wants to set up young Paride as the ruler of Verona as the first step towards conquering the world. Pitting him against me, the fruit of her husband's philandering. That might make for an awkward family reunion. Should I send flowers?"

"It's worse than you know," growled Morsicato. "She tried to have you killed when you were a baby. That's why Pietro took you in, to protect you from her."

The doctor stared defiantly at Pietro and Bail, daring them to contradict him. His knowledge of this particular secret was the true cause of his exile in Ravenna, and he was savagely pleased to finally expose the lady, righting a wrong he had endured for eight long years.

What Morsicato didn't know was that Giovanna hadn't been the only person to order an attempt on Cesco's life. The very first attack on the boy had been planned by the crippled lady in the room above them, the first move in a chess match to bring Cesco within her sphere of influence.

It had been foretold that Katerina would raise the great man Cesco was destined to be. Everything hinged on that prophecy and the star-charts that accompanied it. People had died, wars had been won and lost, all because Cangrande and his sister had been determined to play their parts in some oracular dance. Pietro's own life had been at risk many times, as had Cesco's. It was the thing that had driven Pietro from Verona, determined to shelter the child from this madness as long as he could.

Both the prophecy and the fact that Donna Katerina had ordered killers to attack the baby Cesco were secrets shared only by Pietro, Tharwat, and the lady upstairs. Cangrande had known, but Cangrande was dead.

Hearing the doctor's statement, Valentino was both excited and horrified. "Auntie Giovanna tried to kill Cesco?"

"I never liked her," said Detto at once.

"Yes, you did! She gave you sweets!" protested Val, igniting an argument between the brothers that their father had to put a stop to.

The steward arrived to say supper was ready. Dutifully the pack of them trooped off to the dining hall where a fine meal was laid out. Antonia was waiting for them – Esta, it seemed, had gone to begin airing out their home in the city. Bail dismissed his staff for the evening, ordering a posting of guards to be certain they weren't overheard.

Pietro waited until the eight of them were alone before resuming the conversation. "Antonia, we were running through the names of Cesco's rivals. Mastino, Alberto, and we just came to Paride and his loving aunt. Yes, boys, it's true what the doctor says. Donna Giovanna tried to have Cesco killed on several occasions. But more than that. To get rid of him, she ordered the death of my father, my self, and Detto's mother."

"Mother?" said Detto and Val together.

Bailardino was frowning. "Don't frighten them too much."

Pietro was unapologetic. "They need to know the stakes."

Reluctantly, Bailardino nodded. "Then they'd best they hear it from me. Lads, you've often asked how your mother got those burns on her arm." He quickly told the story of the burning carriage, how Donna Katerina had rushed inside to rescue the three year-old Cesco from death. "She was pregnant with you, Val, at the time. You might not even be here."

A horrified silence. Then Cesco said, "Why am I not burned then?"

Pietro gave him a half-apologetic look. "She didn't know you'd already escaped on your own."

"So it's my fault," said Cesco blankly.

"No, it's not." Pietro was emphatic.

Val was staring at his father. "I've seen you be nice to her! She tried to kill me, to kill mommy, and you were nice to her!"

Bailardino took his younger son in his arms and pointed at Cesco. "To protect him. And all of us. Otherwise she might have figured out he was still alive. Instead, we let everyone think he died in the carriage."

Val threw an ugly look Cesco's way, but Cesco was too busy parsing the situation to notice. "She sounds like someone I want to get to know – if briefly. Do I have any more murderous relations?"

"Just the normal kind. There's Detto and Val's mother, upstairs," said Pietro, his insides roiling. "Though she isn't well enough to receive you at the moment. She's the last of her generation. There were five, three brothers and two sisters. All gone now, save Katerina."

"It's no wonder they're all dead, with such a formidable list of enemies! Though admittedly most are from within the family. How very wise, to keep enemies so close. You mentioned that Mastino has three sisters. Are there any other familial names of note?"

"One," said Tharwat. When Pietro shot him a curious glance, he added, "Pathino."

"Ah." Pietro seemed dubious. "Gregorio Pathino. Though I doubt he's still using that name."

Cesco rubbed his hands together. "Ooh! He sounds a man of many parts. Tell me more."

Pietro shrugged. "He's Cangrande's bastard brother, and he's convinced he's got a great destiny. The only way to achieve it, though, is to remove members of his family. He tried kidnapping you twice. He's the cause of that scar beside your eye."

"You told me I fell!"

"I lied. I do that sometimes." Hearing himself, Pietro didn't like who he was sounding like. He took a different tack. "Pathino was threatening to blind you, and his knife slipped. Honestly, Tharwat, I don't see him as a part of this. Pathino's claim isn't helped by Cesco's death. Besides, he's labouring under a curse, he refuses to take the life of his kinsman. He takes it seriously. Trust me, I know."

The Moor did not respond. Cesco said, "Very gallant of him. I suppose my dimple was a loving buss. Do I have any friends at all, or is it just we three boys against the world?"

"We have friends. Powerful friends, and good men." Pietro began listing names: Guglielmo da Castelbarco, Nico da Lozzo, Mariotto Montecchio, Antonio Capulletto, Petruchio da Bonaventura, and a dozen other influential men of Verona. Still holding Val in his lap, Bailardino chimed in, speaking of the dispositions of the armies in the region, the various wars brewing, most notably the one currently raging with nearby Padua.

Passerino Bonaccolsi's name came up, and Bailardino confessed that no one knew where Verona's close ally, the Lord of Mantua, was at the present time. "He was with Cangrande – in fact, it was he who sent us word the Greyhound had died."

"Where is he now?"

"Bearing the body back to Verona."

Here was a question plaguing Pietro. "How did he die?"

The answer did nothing to quiet his nerves. "Passerino mentioned an illness, but some people are saying it was poison. The only thing anyone seems sure of is that he's dead." Bailardino's voice was thick, and Pietro remembered that Cangrande had been raised in this household. It must have been like losing an exceptionally gifted foster-son. *How I'd feel if I lost Cesco.*

The food remained untouched as the discussion carried on. The younger children were mostly quiet. Though Detto and Valentino knew most of the men mentioned, they had never been privy to such adult assessments of faults and skills. Already their worlds had been shaken by so many revelations.

Through it all Cesco sat perched in the large carved chair, sometimes sprawled, sometimes sitting with his feet up and his arms wrapped about his knees – he was not built to sit still or comfortably. Occasionally he posed a question, simple clarifications. The rest of the time he made absent comments, filling the air while he absorbed the information presented him.

The Moor waited until Pietro and Bailardino had spent themselves before speaking. "One thing not yet mentioned is the fire last night."

Bailardino's head came up. "What fire?"

"My house," said Pietro. "Arson. It had to be an attempt on Cesco. But, fortunately, he and Detto were – out." Pietro frowned as Cesco shot him a winning smile.

Bailardino was furious – his son had been in danger. "Mastino!"

Morsicato raised the obvious objection. "How would he know about Cesco?"

"There's only one way," said Pietro, gritting his teeth. "Poco."

Bailardino and Morsicato turned to stare. Antonia spoke up, a pleading note in her voice. "You don't think our own brother —"

"Antonia, we've always laughed at how bad he is with secrets. This is the big one. I'm willing to bet a year of my life that the moment Cangrande was dead, Poco was blabbing everything he knows to Alblivious. Which is as good as telling Mastino to his face. I think our brother has gone to the enemy."

Morsicato shook his head. "I'll wager your one year against five of mine that it was Giovanna. We already know arson is not beyond her."

Pietro shook his head. "Mastino is in her way as well. He would have been poisoned or stabbed already. Why remove Cesco when there are so many other obstacles in Paride's way?"

"Unless she planned to have Mastino blamed for Cesco's death," mused the doctor. That thought gave Pietro pause. It certainly sounded like a Scaligeri stratagem.

They returned to the atrium, carrying the wine with them. It was time to discuss plans. Morsicato immediately voiced his opinion that they should remain in Vicenza, amass support from the safety of the Nogarola palace. Pietro disagreed. "We'd be ceding the battlefield from the start." Bailardino concurred. As the doctor lapsed into a sulky silence, Pietro said, "So the question is how we enter Verona."

Bailardino was certain. "At the head of an army. What choice do we have?"

"We could go in as we are – the boy, the Moor, the doctor, and myself."

"And me!" cried Bailardino, Detto, and Val all at once. It was worth a chuckle, despite the tension. Like father, like sons.

"What about the women?" asked Morsicato uneasily. "Esta will stay behind, but..?" He glanced sideways.

"Thank you for remembering me," said Antonia tartly. Pietro had to smile – he hadn't heard that tone from her since she'd left for the nunnery. "I'm coming too. I swore an oath."

Pietro shook his head. "Bad enough we have to take Cesco into danger. If I thought for a second the city would declare for him sight-unseen, I'd leave him here with you."

"You could try," observed Cesco.

Pietro carried on, gazing at his sister. "You should remain here."

Jaw set in an all-too-familiar jut, Antonia looked just like their father. "Should. Won't."

Pietro turned to the other men at the table for support. The Moor merely shrugged. "You may attempt to keep her from coming. You may even succeed, if you're willing to employ force against a woman."

"Fine." Pietro let the matter rest for the moment. "The question stands – at the head of an army, or alone and unheralded?"

The doctor scrubbed his bald pate. "Alone? You'd be mad. Mastino will have us all whisked off and murdered. What could we gain?"

"The element of surprise."

"It *is* just what Cangrande would have done," observed Tharwat.

Silence followed that remark. Pietro knew his own thoughts, and he tried to weigh the reactions of the others. The doctor thought any march to Verona was too dangerous. Bailardino wouldn't be comfortable without an army at his back. Tharwat seemed to lean towards the surprise entrance, though that was harder to guess. Antonia was stubbornly determined to be with them, whatever course they chose. Valentino was just excited to be here. Detto looked pensive. And the center of their enterprise? Cesco was playing with a blade of grass, his whole attention on tying it into a knot.

"What about you, Francesco? What do you think?"

The boy looked up. "You mean I have a say?"

"Oh God, no!" cried the doctor. "You're asking him if he wants to be straightforward and dull, or sneaky and dramatic. That's like asking fire if it wants to burn in a hearth or consume a city! He'll choose to go down in a blaze of glory!"

Cesco wiggled his eyebrows under his fell of curling hair. "How colourful, doctor! We'll make a poet of you yet. But as to burning calmly or being a raging inferno – why not both?" The boy spoke for just a few minutes.

"See, *Ser Dottore*?" said Pietro when the boy had finished. "He likes to surprise us as well as our enemies."

"Damned clever!" Bailardino ruffled Cesco's hair. "I'll send a message to Mastino tonight, asking for an escort. Hopefully he'll send Alberto."

"And I'll send instructions to Castelbarco," said Pietro. There was no question now. The boy's plan was sound, and everyone had a part to play. If Bailardino looked slightly bewildered, the other adults merely gazed on in knowing satisfaction.

The group broke up. Morsicato ascended the stairs to look in on the lady of the house, and Bailardino went off to arrange for messengers to Verona. Antonia was deputed to take the boys to their rooms for rest against the morrow.

At the curtains Cesco turned and fixed both Pietro and Tharwat. "Don't talk about me behind my back."

"We wouldn't dream of it."

The child studied them both and his face grew grave. "Just tell me what I'm supposed to be, and I can be it." With that, he disappeared through the door.

When he was gone, Pietro took a drink of watered wine. "Did your hackles rise when he mentioned *Il Veltro*?" He spoke softly. In a Scaligeri household, walls had ears.

"As if someone had stepped upon my grave."

"I for one thank God he's dead. Mastino and Giovanna both to deal with is bad enough. *That* rivalry would have killed one of them."

"You heard him. He suspects we've held something back."

"He's right, of course. Damn him. But how could we tell him? Look what it did to Cangrande."

"Then we are agreed."

Pietro shook his head. "One more secret to keep."

The Moor moved off to watch the boys through the night, leaving Pietro alone with his thoughts.

*I'm just like Cangrande, playing games.*

*But his game is played*, said an internal voice that sounded much like his father. *A new game begins tomorrow.*

Yet Pietro was uneasy. It was a game that Cangrande set the pieces for.

# II

# FROM BEYOND THE GRAVE

# TEN

*Verona*
*Monday, 15 July*
*1325*

THE APPROACH OF AN ARMED party set bells ringing, calling citizen defenders to join their professional counterparts on the ramparts. Tools were abandoned in the fields as men and women fled for the sheltering protection of Verona's walls. Before the banners were even visible, the whole of Verona knew they were being descended upon.

A dozen fancies poured in a thousand ears, some dismissed, some believed. Whispers said it was the Paduans striking while Verona was vulnerable. Others dared hope that it was their lord restored to life, returning to take the reins of their frightened city. At dawn the new co-captain Alberto della Scala had been seen riding out of the city, accompanied by his boon companion, Jacopo Alaghieri. To gather the army? To flee the city? To take a holiday? No one knew.

When the Nogarola eagle came into view, the populace breathed a collective sigh of relief. All was well. Bailardino Nogarola was a stalwart friend of Verona. The citizens returned to their fields or their wares, leaving the formal opening of the gates to the professionals.

In his son's manor on the city's north side, Guglielmo da Castelbarco completed his preparations. For the last twelve hours he had eluded Mastino's repeated summons by staying with friends and relations, nowhere longer than an hour or two. At midnight he'd received written instructions from Ser Alaghieri. Reading the note over again, he wondered if Alaghieri knew what the devil he was about. The young man had more than average sense, but the instructions smacked of foolhardiness. Still, there was nothing to do but issue his invitations and hope that

Alaghieri, ironically a Knight of the Mastiff, was not baiting the bear too close.

In Cangrande's palace, Tullio d'Isola mentally framed his resignation as he assisted Mastino to dress. The co-captain had chosen light armour for the occasion, as befitted a public audience with a friendly general before an emissary of Venice. His polished cuirass gleamed whenever it touched the light.

But the young Mastiff waved away his usual helmet. "I want the Houndshelm."

With a severe bow, Tullio retracted Mastino's gilt nightmare and walked to where Cangrande's formal helmet rested on a T-shaped frame. Made of steel skinned with gold, the Houndshelm fitted entirely over the head in the German fashion, having no cheek pieces to open. The face-plate came to a point at the chin, above which there were holes about the mouth and nose for breathing. One long slit ran across the eyes, creating an inhuman visage.

What made the helmet famous was the massive snarling hound's head that crowned the wearer, silver wings extending from the sides. A display of wealth and power, with a nod to myth and prophecy.

Tullio's late master had once disdained such displays. Cangrande's original helmet had been plain steel, with that same hound's head looking far more ferocious for its lack of ornamentation. But his master's tastes had changed these last few years. Only the fascination for the greyhound remained the same.

Holding it in his aged hands, Tullio found himself unable to place the helm on Mastino's head. They stood for several strained seconds before Niklas Fuchs stepped in and took the great, awe-filled mantle from Tullio's reluctant fingers and ceremoniously lowered it into place.

"Heavy," grunted Mastino, fingers deftly working the chinstraps.

"As is all authority, my lord." Fuchs' accent betrayed his origin on the far side of the Alps. "But it suits you."

The worst part, Tullio saw, was that this was true. The helmet might have been made for Mastino. Not so magnificent as the helmet's last owner, but proportioned as one's thoughts would wish a man. Well-formed, with fine shoulders, sturdy legs, and long strong fingers, he cut a fine figure as he crossed to the balcony and prepared to receive Bailardino Nogarola's oath of fealty.

Ever since the first great della Scala had been murdered in the company of Bailardino's father, the stars of the two families had been intertwined. The place of the murders was visible from the balcony, an alley on the corner the Piazza della Signoria, called the *Volto dei Centurioni*. The two men had been surrounded and stabbed multiple times, their bodies quickly concealed in an old well, scant feet away. The motive was the revival of a long dead ideal, the Veronese Commune, but all that resulted was the election of another della Scala. There was no lever on earth that could remove this family from Verona.

The cheering in the streets grew louder as the Nogarola party appeared. Mastino emerged into the sunlight and the two lords hailed each other, Nogarola on his horse, the young Scaliger standing on the palace's small front balcony in sparkling splendor. The populace went wild.

But even as the ovation continued, those with politic savvy realized something was amiss. Nogarola, under his battle-scarred helmet, hadn't moved to bow, and certainly not to kneel.

Nogarola himself seemed diminished, smaller than his old boisterous self, even under the unseasonable cloak. The keener-eyed of the Anziani noticed the absence of Mastino's brother, who had ridden out that morning to meet Nogarola on the road. Moreover, where was Guglielmo da Castelbarco? Occasion demanded his presence.

The cheering died, and still Nogarola did not dismount. Awkward silence became agonizing tension. Even the crowd began to feel it.

Finally Mastino spoke. "Cousin Nogarola, welcome to Verona! We have seen so much history together, our two families and our two cities, that a bond exists between us greater than nationality, civic pride, or blood! It is only fitting that as the wheel turns, we renew our pledges to each other…" He continued on, his address aimed more at the citizens than Nogarola. It wasn't their first taste of his oratory – he'd spoken from this very balcony two days earlier. He was not his uncle, not witty, nor wry, nor ribald. Mastino was plain-spoken, invoking Verona's great past and greater destiny, drawing the crowd into a surge of patriotism.

As he concluded, the masses turned their expectant eyes on Nogarola.

Who remained on his horse.

Had it been Cangrande facing this quiet insolence, he would have made a jest. Mastino's dignity was not so secure. In growing anger, he snapped his fingers at his men escorting Nogarola. Instantly the reins of Nogarola's horse were seized and they started to lead him away. The crowd muttered, uncertain and not a little angry.

But the sudden movement of his horse seemed to spur Nogarola, who raised his head and shouted, "Nephew, I fear you mistake!"

Mastino stood stiffly upright. "I? Mistake?"

"Yes! You mistake both yourself, and me!" A gloved right hand came up, the helmet was removed. The rider's stature and odd immobility was instantly explained. This was not Bailardino. Instead the man in the saddle was Antonio Nogarola, his missing arm disguised by the bulky cloak. "I'm afraid my brother had business elsewhere. He asked me to pay our family's respects in his stead."

Short of lying on his deathbed, there was no possible excuse for Bailardino's absence that was not an insult. Mastino opened his mouth to rage, accuse, curse, but Fuchs quickly stepped close and whispered in his ear. Mastino nodded, causing the Houndshelm to bob. "We've heard your city has been sorely tried once more. Is he chasing Paduans? Fighting the fire?"

"The Paduans never attacked, so the truce still stands," responded Antonio Nogarola. "And I have the pleasure to report that the fire is contained and Vicenza is once more hale and whole!"

Mastino leaned away from the murmuring Fuchs. "Your news is welcome, uncle! We look forward to entertaining all our friends here for many years to come. Join us, let us drink to your recent victory!"

Antonio Nogarola shook his head of whitened hair. "I have promised my brother to wait here for him, so that we might, together, swear loyalty to the true heir of Cangrande!" He was staring at the eye-slit of the Houndshelm, a grim smile on his face.

From his place behind Mastino, Tullio d'Isola wondered what was happening. Everyone around him seemed equally confused. And still no sign of Castelbarco — nor, he noted, of Petruchio Bonaventura and Nico da Lozzo.

*Where had they all gotten to? What was happening?*

♦    ◊    ♦

Riding down the road a mile outside the city, Petruchio da Bonaventura was demanding answers to those very questions. "Castelbarco, where the hell are we going? What the devil is going on?"

"We're off to see a friend," was all the answer Castelbarco would give.

"Probably found a new whore and wants to show her off," said Nico da Lozzo. Petruchio laughed heartily at the unlikeliness of the thought. Ten years of married life had hardly dimmed Petruchio's spirit, though it had added pounds to his body and caused his long brown hair to be mixed with strands of pure white. He was broader now than he'd been on his wedding day, but his eyes still danced, and his domestic arrangement was still the envious gossip of Verona and Padua both.

Nico da Lozzo, the short and wiry Paduan defector, remained lean of face and outspoken in opinion. In that, he and Petruchio were well matched. Practical, energetic, loyal, and high-spirited. The perfect conspirators for this insane enterprise.

They were drawing closer to the camp holding the main contingent of Verona's army when they saw a small band of soldiers under the flag of the Nogarola eagle. Scenting mischief, Petruchio said, "What the hell?"

"Isn't he in Verona, kneeling to the little shit?" voiced Nico.

"Clearly not," said Castelbarco. "He's here to meet us instead. And with him some familiar faces."

Petruchio exchanged a smile with Nico. "It's mutiny, then."

"About damn time," said da Lozzo genially.

Castelbarco released an inward breath of relief. No, they weren't fools. They'd divined his purpose and were not averse to it.

In moments they were being hailed by Bailardino, riding out to greet them. Behind him came a young knight in fine Veronese armour, helmet obscuring his face. The three conspirators greeted Bail warmly, already making jokes about their newfound treason. Then Nico jutted his chin at the knight. "Who's your friend?"

"What, don't you recognize the scoring?" said the helmeted knight, touching the dents in the armour. "After all, you were there when I got them."

Mid-dismount, Nico da Lozzo goggled. "It can't be – Alaghieri?"

Removing his helmet, Pietro slid down to embrace Nico. He then faced Petruchio Bonaventura, whom he didn't know nearly as well, despite having seen the man's wife naked. They were acquainted mostly by reputation and minor tragedy. Clasping arms, Pietro felt the strength of the man's gregarious grip.

"Don't tell me we're going to topple the della Scala family in favour of Dante's son? A fine idea, but I doubt the masses would allow it. Unless he has his father's way with words."

"Well, we can't nominate you," retorted Nico. "Your wife runs your household. Would *she* like the job?"

"Kate, Capitano? Not that she couldn't do it, but I beg you not to suggest it to her. She'll get ideas."

Castelbarco took control. "I obviously don't have to broach the topic of treason – it's all too clear that's what we're about."

"One man's treason is another man's patriotism," said Nico.

"Says the professional traitor," laughed Pietro. Nico had changed his colours before now.

"His pragmatism trumps his patriotism every time," agreed Petruchio.

Taking no umbrage, Nico shrugged. "I am a simple man with simple pleasures. Are we killing the bastard?"

"Who said anything about killing Mastino?" said Bailardino. "We're merely out looking after his army for him. It's why we've come – to get the army on our side."

"It shouldn't be too hard," said Petruchio, "with all Federigo's blundering. But even with a Nogarola in the lead, will they follow us?"

"He *is* a della Scala by marriage," Nico pointed out. "We could use that."

"We won't have to," said Bailardino. "We already have a della Scala."

Both Petruchio and Nico turned to study the group assembled nearby. They spotted some gregarious boys with a Moorish soldier standing behind them. Then they noticed with whom the boys were talking. Petruchio started. "Alberto? We're going to pit Alblivious against his brother?"

"Dear God, no!" asserted Bail with a laugh.

"Who, then? Not Paride?" Nico was squinting at the boys.

Pietro waved to the Moor, who said something. In response, one of the youths clambered up into a saddle and rode over. Watching the boy approach, Castelbarco leaned close and whispered in Pietro's ear. "I have to admit, after all this time, I'm curious." Pietro just shook his head.

Arriving, the boy grinned down on them. "Alberto's nice enough, Nuncle. I'm ashamed we're using him like this. But I think I'll recover." He turned to the newcomers. "Welcome to our uprising. My name is Cesco, and I'm your leader." It was said with a verbal wink that made both Petruchio and Nico laugh aloud.

Castelbarco was studying the youth, and Cesco said, "Do I have a blemish, my lord? I'm a little young for it, I thought. Or perhaps I've grown a second head. That's the trouble with the della Scala clan, I hear – like the Hydra, cut off one head and two grow in its place."

Castelbarco inclined his head. "I'm measuring you against an over-active imagination."

The boy hopped lightly down from his saddle. "Blessed Mary! I'm sure I fall horribly short. You must be Lord Castelbarco." He delivered a bow of exceeding gravity.

"Wait!" said Nico, just catching on. "Cesco – *Francesco?* Little Francesco, the bas – I mean... but – you're dead!"

"Ah, a soul of eloquence and perspicacity. Tell me your name, sir, that I might kiss the sole of your boot and swear to follow you solely throughout the world."

"N– Nico," the martial ex-Paduan stuttered.

Stifling laughter, Pietro intervened. "Cesco, this is —"

"Nicolo da Lozzo!" cried Cesco, as if it were a name he'd known all his life. "Of course! I trust you won't mind turning your coat again, in a good cause."

Nico was confounded. "Is this a good cause?"

"How should I know? I'm just a child. And you must be Lord Bonaventura, he of the willful wife! How does she fare in this time of trouble?"

Petruchio scowled at Pietro. "He's a bit scrawny, don't you think? Why don't we strangle him and put one of my boys in his stead?"

"You're welcome to try," offered Pietro.

"Yes." Cesco's left hand rested on the hilt of his short sword. "I may be little, but I'm a bastard of a fighter."

Castelbarco was already appreciating the boy's style. In just a few moments he had touched on all the objections that could be raised to him – his age, his size, his questionable heritage – and turned them deftly on their heads. He'd certainly charmed both Lozzo and Bonaventura. No, imagination fell far short of this boy.

Nico slapped his hands together. "Oh-ho! I take it, Pietro, that this is why you've been holed up in a sleepy backwater like Ravenna?"

"I like Ravenna." Pietro sounded a little defensive.

"So much that you let yourself get excommunicated rather than tax them. Fool." Nico shook his head in mock admonishment, then grew serious. "I smell the Capitano's hand at the back of this."

Castelbarco nodded. "Your nose doesn't fail you."

Petruchio rounded on him. "You knew?"

"I had to know. I am the executor of his will. He gave me instructions as to its implementation. Why do you think the will hasn't been read out yet?"

"I wondered," said Petruchio. "Has Mastino been after you to see it?"

"Strangely enough, not until last night," said Castelbarco. "But no one even knew if there was one."

"Probably in fear of a surprise like this one," mused Nico.

"Mark Antony and Octavian," said Cesco brightly. "Does that make me an emperor-in-training?"

"I bet he suspected Paride's name in the place of honour," added Petruchio.

"The time for secrets is behind us." Pietro briskly described how matters stood.

Bonaventura stroked his whiskered chin. "So you think, what, you'll show him to the troops, tell them he's Cangrande's brat, and they'll march to his defense?"

"That's about it," admitted Pietro.

"I prefer bastard to brat," added Cesco seriously. "Or love child."

More colourful."

"*Il Veltro's veltro*," said Nico.

"That joke's been made."

"He's young," said Petruchio.

"Cangrande was knighted at six," countered Bailardino.

"Meaning I am not teething, but rather long in the tooth," said Cesco. "So, my dear new friends, will you breathe with us?" In answer to their blank stares, he explained, "Conspiracy. It comes from the Latin, *to breathe together.*"

Nico grunted. "I will, if you promise Verona won't turn into a schoolroom."

"I make no promises. That way I never break them."

"Very wise." And, astonishingly, Nico gave the boy a leg. Petruchio did the same. They weren't kneeling, but these two grown knights were giving this strip of a boy a formal bow. Castelbarco began to hope they might survive the day. "Let's get moving. There's much to do."

Remounted, Nico fell in alongside Pietro. "How are you keeping Alblivious so docile?"

"I sent Poco a note, saying this was Mastino's idea for a grand show."

"Alberto has no idea who the boy really is?"

"He says not," said Pietro dubiously, sending a dark look in Poco's direction. He still suspected his brother of revealing all to Mastino and Alberto.

"Our happy hostage," laughed Petruchio.

"Our oblivious hostage. But not for much longer. He's about to learn the truth, along with Verona's army."

"A rude awakening."

"Very."

Riding in the rear of the company, Castelbarco reflected that they had cleared the first hurdle – the boy had gained the allegiance of two of the great men of Verona. The next hurdle was the army. And then came the city itself.

There was no turning back. They were committed.

# ELEVEN

*Verona*

AN HOUR AFTER Antonio Nogarola's arrival, the warning bells rang out again. This time the friendly banners brought no sigh of relief. Civil war loomed on the horizon. Everyone foresaw the glow of Verona in cinders.

Yet the city gates still opened, for at the forefront of the army were some of Verona's most famous faces – Alberto della Scala, Castelbarco, Nico da Lozzo, Petruchio Bonaventura, and Jacopo Alaghieri. At their center rode Bailardino Nogarola, clearly visible as he waved to the masses just as if nothing at all were amiss.

Helmeted and riding behind Bailardino, Pietro Alaghieri entered Verona for the first time in ten years. He wasn't entirely certain what he should feel. Joy? Nostalgia? Remorse? Excitement? All at once, probably. Instead he felt a strange vindication. Also very alive.

The man beside him began to shift. Pietro murmured, "Remember. Be still and you'll live. Raise a fuss, you'll be hunted down by your own men."

The eyes of Federigo della Scala held daggers, but he said nothing. He couldn't. Under the helmet his mouth was gagged, and a draped cloak hid the bonds on his wrists.

Alberto had needed no such precautions. A simple threat of violence bought acquiescence. Poco, too. He hadn't been happy to see his brother, and had vehemently denied Pietro's accusations of revealing Cesco's identity to Mastino. Well, Pietro could deal with his little brother later.

*If we're all still living.*

They rode through the city until they reached the Piazza della Signoria. The crowd parted to admit them, and they passed under La Costa, the monstrous bone that legend said belonged to a dragon or some other ancient beast that the city had united to defeat in battle.

Pietro allowed himself a nostalgic glance at the Domus Bladorum, the guest lodging he'd shared with his father and brother a decade ago. He was startled to find the window occupied, and astonished when he recognized the man within. Francesco Dandolo, ambassador and nobleman of Venice! The handsome patrician face was a bit more creased, which only added to his gravity. *I hope he enjoys the show!*

Across the square, Mastino stood upon the balcony Cangrande had used for grand orations. Just big enough for one man to occupy, it served as an excellent podium.

Bailardino nodded to his brother, still sitting atop his horse in the square, then lifted his chin to address his nephew. "Mastino della Scala! I, Bailardino da Nogarola, Lord of Vicenza by the grace of your honoured uncle Cangrande della Scala, have come to hear the reading of his will. And I vow that, in this place and at such time as it has been read, I shall swear my allegiance to his true heir!"

"Sadly, my lord, there is no will." Mastino's voice was full of remorse. He must have spied his brother and the helmeted Federigo at Bailardino's back, but to his credit he retained his composure. "My uncle died unexpectedly, without making direct provision for the future. But we, his surviving heirs, have joined together to avoid any threat of bloodshed and strife, to create a new government based on his spoken wishes."

"There is a will!" This shout came from Castelbarco, edging his mount a step forward. He turned to a citizen, apparently a random choice, but in reality one of Castelbarco's clients, told to be present today. "Sirrah, would you please cross to that well?" He was pointing to the disused stone basin at the corner of the square, in the alley called the *Volto dei Centurioni*. The spot where, years ago, Mastino's namesake had been murdered. The well was thought to be cursed.

The crowd parted to create a path for the obedient citizen. Castelbarco continued issuing instructions. "Uncover the well, please, and raise the bucket."

Mastino spoke out. "This is madness! Citizens, you are being tricked. Disperse!"

If ever there was a futile order, this was it. The theatricality of the moment had every citizen within earshot riveted.

While the man plied the chain, Pietro had a long moment in which to sweat. Castelbarco had taken a terrible risk leaving the will in such a public place. How could he know that the well would go unused, in spite of the prohibitive signs? But it *was* cursed, and the Veronese were particularly superstitious.

Mastino was talking with someone inside the door behind him. Pietro glanced around, looking for Tharwat. The Moor was nowhere in sight. A hopeful sign.

The bucket finally reached the top of the chain. Eager citizens peered in. "It's empty!"

Full of expectation, the crowd released a disappointed breath. But Castelbarco was unperturbed. "Is there a chain attached to the bottom of the bucket?"

There was. The excitement was like the charged air before a storm. The chain hauled up, a small iron box appeared. It was clasped with a series of three locks, and the engraved ladder of the Scaligeri seal was clear on the box's front.

Mastino pointed, shouting loudly. "Bring that to me!"

Something flashed in Castelbarco's hand. "Why, my lord, when I have the keys?"

Overt animosity was growing. Castelbarco's man removed the chain from the box and carried it through a field of expectant faces to where Castelbarco sat atop his fine steed. There were impatient mutterings as he worked the locks, each with a separate key. Finally the lid fell back and an oilskin was removed. From out of the waterproof casing Castelbarco produced a scroll-tube just like the one Morsicato had taken from the floor of the abbey in Ravenna. Castelbarco held it high.

"As Cangrande's executor, I call upon these men to witness the mark of the Scaliger's sigil on the case, and here again upon the wax." Castelbarco held out the scroll-tube to nearby citizens, who could later be called upon to testify that the seal was valid. He then held the scroll out to Lozzo and Bonaventura, to Alberto and the helmeted Federigo. When the bound man started to shake his head Pietro stabbed his long spurs into Federigo's leg, making the elder della Scala stiffen sharply. To those watching, it appeared to be a nod.

Mastino was shouting again. "A lie! There is no will! Guards, arrest those men!" But no guard could reach them through the crowd of soldiers that instantly stood to attention facing outwards, protecting the inner circle of nobility. Not Bailardino's men – these were the soldiers of Verona. Who, it was suddenly understood, did not support Mastino.

"I open the seal, and again I call upon those men present to verify that the wax on the parchment bears the ladder, the eagle, and the hound." Again it was passed about, though this time it did not go before Federigo. Even Alberto della Scala agreed that the seal was valid.

Castelbarco broke the seal, unfurled the parchment, and began to read: "*In the name of God, Amen. Francesco della Scala, Cangrande, of Verona, to be buried in Santa Maria Antica, my soul bequeathed to God.*" There followed the traditional bequests to churches and holy orders in their varied and extremely generous forms. "*To my great-nephew Paride, grandson of my lamented brother Bartolomeo, one tenth of my fortune and my castle at Pescheria, to be paid in the year of his majority.*"

Pietro watched Mastino's reaction to that. There was a slight relaxing, but nothing more. He was a Scaliger, he kept his thoughts to himself. *It should be the family motto.*

Castelbarco continued: "*To my two nephews by my beloved sister Katerina and her husband the noble Bailardino da Nogarola, those christened Bailardetto and Valentino, one twentieth of my liquid wealth and my castles at Schio and Illasi, to be bestowed the year of their respective majorities.*" There followed several more minor relations, all men, some legitimate and some not, to whom he left gold or silver, but no land. Often one of his favourite horses, hawks, or hounds accompanied the bequest. Federigo della Scala was among these names and the crowd noted his apparent lack of interest in his good fortune.

Cangrande's wife Giovanna was dealt with lavishly. Then the will reached his sibling. "*To my beloved sister Katerina I bestow my favourite riding crop and my personal copy of the play Ecerinis, with revisions by the author, Albertino Mussato. To my brother-in-law Bailardino I leave his pick of my hawks and a sum ten times Katerina's dowry, in recompense of services rendered to my family, and my everlasting thanks to a friend.*"

Listening to the words beneath the words, Pietro resisted smiling at this final wry jab Cangrande had given his sister, the last gasp of an antagonism that now stretched beyond the grave.

More minor bequests here and there. Most names Pietro recognized – Passerino Bonaccolsi and Nico da Lozzo made out rather well. But as yet the vast bulk of Cangrande's wealth was left untouched. A few unknown names came up, and it was generally assumed that these were Cangrande's low bastards, littered about the Feltro – two boys and four girls. These, though, were just the ones he acknowledged. There were undoubtedly many more.

Two names were as yet remarkable by their absence. They remained unspoken until Castelbarco reached the second-to-last paragraph.

"*To my brother Alboino's first son, my cherished nephew Alberto, I do bequeath an annuity of seven thousand gold florins, one-third of my remaining hounds, and the entire contents of my wine cellar.*"

A roar of laughter as all eyes turned to see Alberto blush. In spite of his current predicament, he grinned widely. He thought it as funny as they, and the crowd loved him all the more for it.

"*To his sisters, my nieces Albuina, Verde, and Caterina…*" A fine sum for each girl, leaving them even greater heiresses than they already were. Verde was married long since, but Caterina was just fourteen, Albuina a year younger, both being raised in a distant convent. This new wealth would make them the most sought-after brides in Lombardy.

Castelbarco now reached the name that all had waited to hear. "*To my nephew Mastino…*" Several heads turned to watch the man in the Houndshelm, expecting him to receive an incredible bounty. "*…to him I bequeath my castles at Valdagno and Badia, two-tenths of my entire fortune, and my second-best sword, in the knowledge that he will always be ready to raise it to Verona's greater glory.*"

A massive intake of breath became a rumbling mutter. High on the balcony, Mastino did not move a muscle.

Castelbarco held up a hand, but had to wait for a full two minutes before the noise dimmed enough for him to be heard. In his best carrying voice he read aloud the last bequest. "*To my acknowledged heir bearing my own name, Francesco della Scala, raised in the custody of Ser Pietro Alaghieri, Knight of the Mastiff, I leave the residue of my wealth and all my remaining lands and bastions, as well as all my hereditary titles and rights. To him I hand my best sword, and with it the standard of the della Scala line, and crave all my clients and followers to do him honour and serve him well, all to the greater glory of God and His garden on Earth, Verona. Amen.*"

Shock beyond measure. The crowd erupted, babbling, shouting, exclaiming their amazement. Some were laughing – their beloved Capitano had played one last trick on them!

"Mastino della Scala!" Castelbarco shouted, repeating the name until his voice could carry up to the balcony. "Mastino della Scala! Do you acknowledge this to be the testament of your uncle, our lord Cangrande, *il Capitano di Verona*, and will you abide by the terms of his will?"

Face invisible under the Houndshelm, Mastino said, "Where is this heir?"

Heads turned expectantly, first to Castelbarco, then gazing around at the assembled knights for a charismatic giant in whom could be seen the figure of his sire. But there was no sign. "He is safe, and within the walls of this city. He awaits your pleasure."

Mastino threw up his hands in a show of amazement. "Does he hide? If he is who you say he is, I am his kin – he has nothing to fear from me! He claims to be the heir of Cangrande della Scala, and yet he cowers behind scribbled words and armed men? Is that the way the heir of the Greyhound honours his father?"

"We are here to represent him, lord." It was a feeble answer. Though the heir's representatives included several great men, it was significant to all present that this purported heir was not here in person.

Sensing another shift in the crowd, Mastino leaned forward on the railing. "I refute your claims! This is a feeble attempt to wrest control of the city from the rightful leaders, elected by the people, for the people! How dare you make unsubstantiated claims, throw the city into chaos during this time of unrest and bereavement! Paduans march on our cities! We are besieged on all sides, and while you prate and scheme, Verona will fall! How dare you? Have you no civic pride?"

It was a good show, the beginning of an excellent speech. Pietro had to put an end to it. Standing in his stirrups, he threw off his helmet. "Mastino della Scala! What do you know of civic pride? Down here are men who have fought and bled to preserve this city! Where are your wounds? What scars do you bear from battles in Verona's name? I, Pietro Alaghieri, Knight of the True Mastiff, that first Scaliger who fought for this city, demand an answer!"

Again the mob was all aflutter, this time in admiration. Excommunication be damned, Ser Alaghieri was a true Veronese hero. When he had been Mastino's age he'd taken a near-crippling wound in the city's service. And he was right about Veronese heroes! Antonio Nogarola had lost his arm that same day. Bailardino had fought in the front lines of every major battle of the last twenty years, Castelbarco not far behind. Both bore the scars to prove it. Whereas young Mastino had yet to win a name as a soldier.

Seizing the initiative, Pietro pressed on. "Your blessed uncle, my friend, the Lord of Verona, placed a child in my care eight years ago, charging me to raise him and prepare him for his duty, away from envious eyes and secret plots." This deliberately stirred memories of attempts on the child's life, one in this very square. "I bring with me a document written in the Scaliger's own hand, fixed with his own seal, testifying that the child I have raised is blood of his blood, his sole legal heir!"

The Mastiff snarled. "And where is this pretty baby? How well could you have raised this mythical child if he refuses to come and claim his right? Perhaps, Ser Alaghieri, you have switched the boy for one of your own!"

Pietro fixed his eyes on Mastino. "Your uncle placed his trust in me, in Lord Nogarola, and Lord Castelbarco. It is significant that he did not enlighten you. Perhaps you should be less free with your tongue."

It was an incredible insult. Duels had been fought over far, far less. But Mastino's heated response was lost in a sudden thunderous applause. The sound came from the Giurisconsulti, the building in which most of the legal wrangling in the city took place. All heads turned as the doors were thrown wide and Verona's City Council, the Anziani, minus only five members, came roaring out into the square. In their midst was Antonia Alaghieri.

"And what is this?" demanded Mastino in a mockingly beleaguered voice. "Some new claimant? Is there a great-aunt who wants to be Capitano?"

Those that heard him laughed. But the majority of citizens watched as the representative of Verona's wise men stood on the steps and raised his hands for silence. "We city elders have listened to the reading of the will, and studied another document placed in our possession." Bernardo Ervari held up a small twist of paper. "We have authenticated it, and now we call upon you all to bear witness to our judgment. The youth placed in the care of Ser Alaghieri and his family is, indeed, the heir of Cangrande!"

Pietro watched as Mastino digested their ploy. While they had wrangled in front of the crowd, Cesco's *bona fides* had been verified by the Anziani, called into secret session by Castelbarco's friend, Bernardo Ervari. With the Veronese army, the Vicentine army, several nobles, and the whole of the Anziani behind him, Cesco's faction had in an hour created a base of power that would be hard to crack.

Hard, but not impossible. There was still that most powerful of deciding bodies – the public. Mastino took a steadying breath, then launched his attack. "So the Anziani wish to support a child, a mere boy who bears a regal name he has not earned. Ser Alaghieri speaks of blood shed for Verona. This invisible heir, this child, has not seen Verona with his eyes since he was in swaddling clothes! What kind of loyalty could he have to this city, our city? He is no Veronese!"

"Of course not!" agreed a youthful voice. "You are so right! What kind of loyalty could I have to Verona, this canker on the arse of Italia!"

Pietro gasped along with the rest of the crowd as they traced the sound of this new voice to its owner. The boy was lounging casually on the steps of the Giurisconsulti. "I want nothing to do with this godless city of whores, thieves, and sodomites!" he declared, throwing a hideous wink in Pietro's direction.

*O dear God, but I hate that boy.*

# TWELVE

CASTELBARCO'S TEETH were clenched as he whispered, "I take it this wasn't part of the plan."

Pietro could only shake his head. "I should have known that Cesco wouldn't stick to any arrangement. Even his own."

"We're all dead men," moaned Bail *sotto voce.*

They may as well have spoken aloud. All attention was focused on the boy, who now made a rude face and continued, pitching his voice high to carry through the square. "I am proud not to be Veronese! If what I see before me is evidence of the true spirit of Verona, I'm relieved I wasn't raised here. If you, the citizens of this pestilent blight of Lombardy, can be swayed by words – mere words, paltry, hollow, meaningless words – then this is indeed the foulest pit of Creation, worthy of Dante's Inferno! How dare you! You have all knelt to this man." From the foot of the steps, Cesco pointed to Mastino, high above across the square. "You've sworn to follow him for all your days! How dare you contemplate a change of allegiance? Is he a will-maker's ape? Is a Veronese's oath so scorned, so worthless, that it melts away with the slightest gust of wind?"

Moving to high ground, he halted on the top step of the Giurisconsulti. "I am a child, untested, unknown. This great lord, so many years my senior, has taken up the mantle of my sire – and where was I? Suckling at my nurse's teat!"

There was a single laugh from someone in the crowd. Cesco pointed to the amused man, egging him on. "Yes, I'm a baby – indeed, I am what *he* called me, a pretty baby! Perhaps I have a taste for boys – since

I'm surely not old enough to like women!" The laughter began to spread. "No, if you are able to set aside your faith in one leader and exchange him for another on the basis of mere words — *words!* — then Verona is not the city I was taught she was!"

Cesco turned in a slow circle, peering at the buildings. "What a strange place! Is Verona a horse that, in mid-charge, changes the rider in the saddle? O fickle bastion of pride, where is the honour in that?" He suddenly spied Castelbarco and company. "How dare you, you elders of the city, how dare you raise a hand to put a weak child in the place of the noble and magnificent Mastiff? Do you wish to control the city — and the city's money! — by using a mere babe to your foul ends? Am I your Paduan *bardassa*, your butt-boy, that you can hold me up and use me to hoodwink the good people of this city into reneging on their chosen oaths?"

Cesco bounded down the steps and into the crowd. The people parted, confused, listening, unsure what was happening. "The great Mastino is quite correct! I *am* a child! How do you know that I am the true son of your beloved Lord of Verona? What proof have you seen?" He threw up his hands. "NONE! None at all! You have heard only words! Pretty words, fine words, but only words words words! They prove nothing! Perhaps I have my father's eye, perhaps his chin — but he was a great man, a warrior of great renown! Now, he might have earned his fame at a younger age than I — for as you all know and I learned only this morning, he was knighted at the age of six. But how could you see that man in me? Puny me, a weakling, short for my age, not able even to carry a man's sword!" Cesco shook his head of chestnut curls, the blonde streaks catching the midday sun. "No, citizens of Verona, I say NO! Whatever they tell you, do not be deceived! Whatever they say, do not believe them! If you, the citizens of this august city, allow yourselves to be swayed by words, then you are nothing but whores and fools who follow a promise of a primrose bed! How could *I*, a child, lead *you*, the people of a great and noble city, a city destined to be the grandest of all the world, a city that will bring about a new age of man!"

All at once the people began cheering. Breathless, Pietro was startled into a smile. Base and noble alike were grinning. Completely aware now that they were being played upon, it was so well done they could not bring themselves to object.

Suddenly Pietro saw Tharwat. The Moor had appeared on the far end of the street, his height catching Pietro's attention. He raised his left hand. The sinister hand. The signal that Cangrande's wife Giovanna was in the city. Cesco was in danger.

But they couldn't whisk him away now! *Damn!* Pietro started scanning the crowd of jubilant faces for something, anything that posed a threat.

But the only threat was Mastino, who sensed he was losing his grip on the masses. "Cousin Francesco! I hear what you say, and I applaud you for not letting yourself become the tool of these avaricious men! Truly, Scaligeri blood must run through your veins! Come up here, cousin, let us embrace!"

Alone in a wide circle made by the crowd, Cesco bowed his head. "You do me too much honour, my lord! You call me cousin, but you must know – all of you must know – I was born on the wrong side of the blanket! Yes, perhaps Cangrande was my father, but my mother is unknown – even to me! Who knows, in the hot night after some battle, what woman was brought to his tents to ease his tense mind? Perhaps she was a common whore. Or worse, a Paduan!" Peals of laughter. "No, great one, I dare not contaminate you with the filth of my birth!"

Mastino was grim, having to play through this farce. "Filth? You say you are the son of the great Cangrande, yet you dare call our late lord, my beloved uncle, filth!"

Cesco's ashamed head bowed even lower. "I claim to be no such thing! It is these men, these wicked men, who try to abuse the great people of Verona into believing that I am what I am not! Until yesterday I was told I was the nephew of Ser Alaghieri! All my life I have been lied to! Never was I told the truth of my heritage, never even told my true name! Now that I stand here before you, I cannot claim the great mantle they place upon my shoulders! I am not worthy!" He spun about and held out a demanding hand to Castelbarco. "Let me see this so-called will!"

Castelbarco blinked twice. He'd listened to the boy in horror, wondering if the child's antics were going to get him torn to pieces by an angry mob. Now he knew he would be lynched if he did not hand the paper over to this monstrous infant.

Receiving it, Cesco made a show of reading the will. Suddenly he let loose a cry of surprise. Running through the crowd, he leapt up onto the lip of the well in the *Volto dei Centurioni* where he waved the paper over his head. "They lie! My lord, my friends, they *lie!*"

The crowd reared in shock, none moreso than the conspirators, chilled in spite of the sun directly overhead.

"They lie to you, my lord," Cesco called to Mastino, now on the far side of the square opposite him. "And to you, *cives Veronae!* All of you! They lie!"

Mastino managed to not play along. But he didn't have to. Cries of 'what lie?' and 'read the will!' were taken up from all quarters as eight hundred citizens pressed to hear, with more outside the square demanding to know what was happening.

Cesco waved the paper again. "There is another bequest! Oh, that I were Veronese! But they don't want you to know it, friends! They don't want you to hear it! They're afraid that, if you remembered your love of him, you might tear them to pieces for their cupidity! If you remembered how much my father loved you, how deep went his civic pride, you could not tolerate these avaricious men who try to fob off a mere child on you!"

"Read it!" came the cry from ten score voices at once. "Read it!"

"I cannot!" There were tears on his face, his voice cracked. "How can I? I am not worthy! They say I am his son, but you don't know me! Even I don't know who I am! They tell you who I am, but those are just words! But *these* words, these here, they are direct from the great man! Only a great man could possibly have written this last bequest! Oh, if only I'd known him! Father!" Throwing his head up to the sky, Cesco's whole body shook as if filled with great emotion, tears pouring down his face.

*This is the performance of a lifetime!* thought Pietro in chagrin. *We should have charged admission. What Verona may have gained, the stage has lost. Now we can only hope that he can lead the herds to where they need to go without over-playing his role.*

Mastino was shouting, but over the thunder of the masses he could not be heard. The whole crowd was chanting, bleating, urging Cesco to read the last bequest. "Read the will! Read the will!"

Holding the parchment out away from his body, as if begging someone else to take up this burden, he finally raised his hands in surrender. "If you insist! But brace yourselves, citizens of Verona. If you are the men I believe you to be, this will break your hearts!" He raised the parchment to eye-level. "*And to the people of Verona, that glorious jewel in the crown of Italy, I bequeath a further tenth of my fortune to be distributed to every man of woman born, and endow a yearly festival of sports and games to honour the city of my birth, whose humble and faithful son I have always been.*" Lowering the paper, he made a show of gazing at the mob. "You see? *This* was the man! *This* was Verona's true son! *This* was Cangrande! This was the Greyhound!!"

With a secret smile, Pietro did some quick math and came up with eleven-tenths. But the crowd didn't waste time on such trivialities. They erupted, surging forward. Cesco was plucked off the lip of the well and handed from body to body, carried along over the heads of the crowd in a joyful processional that ended at the front steps of Cangrande's palace, directly below the balcony upon which Mastino still stood, utterly flummoxed. "Sca-*la!* Sca-*la!* Sca-*la!*" they roared. No longer for Mastino. Their chants were for Cangrande's heir, this magnificent child who championed the common citizen, the tragic boy who had been lied to all his life, the boy almost twice as old as Cangrande had been when he'd earned his knighthood.

"Holy Christ," murmured Castelbarco in genuine prayer as he watched in wonder. Pietro felt the same astonishment, but with an inner glow of pride. In minutes this eleven year-old had turned a suspicious and angry crowd into a cheering, jubilant throng of supporters.

Yet when the crowd set him down, something in Cesco's expression made Pietro start. Still smiling and waving, he wore look of puzzlement on his face. Pietro saw Cesco's hand lift to pluck at his collar, his movement swift as if swatting a fly.

Immediately Pietro swung out of the saddle towards the boy, but Cesco held up his free hand to halt him. Taking this as an indication that he was about to speak again, the crowd stilled.

"For the love you have for the city, the love you bore my father and the love you have for the noble Mastino, please – let these questions raised today be answered by wiser heads than mine." Cesco stepped out of the shadow of the palace and, looking straight up, addressed the Mastiff. "O cousin, we must discover the truth of this matter! Shall we retire indoors to discuss these lies and this marvelous truth?"

Under the Houndshelm, Mastino shook his head. "But, my little friend, I fear – I fear for my life! These men who have brought you, they have suborned the army! As you say, men who yesterday swore faith to me now serve your masters! If I open the doors, will they stop until they have slain me and all my loyal followers?"

Cesco's next move was so swift that no one had time to react. Plucking a knife from the belt of someone in the crowd, he sliced the flesh between his shoulder and his neck. Dropping the blade, he squeezed the wound, wincing in real pain as the crimson liquid spilled forth. "See, cousin! I bleed! I would sooner see my own life-force spilled here and now than let them harm one hair on your head! But your fear is no cowardice, I am sure! If you like, let me in alone. I shall place myself in your power, and let the people see the amity between us!"

Pietro was horrified by both the sudden violence and the dangerous suggestion. He was even more surprised at Mastino's response. "Youth is fragile. What if some mischance befell you? How could I quell the masses? They would suspect me of having done away with you and my life will be forfeit! No, little one, let us meet tomorrow when cooler heads have prevailed and we can untangle the knots your sponsors have woven!"

Cesco bowed his head in reverence. "I am but a child and have not the wisdom of your years. I shall retire to my uncle Bailardino's house. Meanwhile, talk to them, cousin! Talk to the people of Verona! Make them see sense! For, in spite of all good will, this great city cannot have two masters!" Cesco turned to where Pietro was hovering. "Ser Alaghieri, will you escort me from this place? I have caused enough trouble today!"

The crowd begged him to stay, hands plucked at him, a cloth came forward to staunch the blood flowing from his neck. Pietro touched the boy's exposed flesh and was horrified to discover, despite his dappling of sweat, how chilled he was. Was it the sun? The performance? The old nervous illness? Pietro glanced around for Tharwat, but the Moor had disappeared.

Soldiers made a path for them back to Pietro's horse. Before they could start, Cesco stumbled. "Lo," he called out as Pietro lifted him, "I swoon! Remember, all of you – the only blood that should be spilled here today is mine! Not Mastino's! Never his! He is an honourable kinsman to my great father!"

Lifting Cesco into the saddle, Pietro had to hold him in place as they exited the square by the easiest route – past the church of Santa Maria Antica, and so to the street behind the square, heading towards the river.

Bailardino's house was just a few yards from the gate to Mastino's palace. Lifting Cesco down from the saddle, Pietro had to fight the throng to get him to the door. Cesco waved and smiled all the while, though Pietro noted that he only waved with one hand. The other seemed to be cupped around something.

Pietro got the door closed behind him. "You little bastard. That was amazing. Though a little melodramatic at the end."

"I had no choice," murmured Cesco just loud enough for Pietro to hear. "Our enemies don't waste any time."

"What do you mean?"

Cesco daubed the cloth at the self-inflicted wound where his neck met his shoulder. "Well, I don't want to unduly alarm you, Nuncle," he said, smiling crookedly, "but I believe I've been poisoned."

# THIRTEEN

THE SUN WAS JUST SETTING as a furtive group of men tapped on the massive doors of the Casa Capulletto on the *via Cappello*. These men represented influential merchant guilds and banking houses in Verona. They and their colleagues had divided themselves into three parties to seek out certain important Veronese and sound their support for the new faction that had come upon the scene.

The tall doors swung wide and the servants, told to expect such a deputation, ushered the guests quickly in, sealing the portal behind them. The emissaries followed an arched brick passage through to an enclosed garden wide enough for a hundred men.

It seemed the yard was already appointed to make them comfortable. But a quick glance around told them these were the preparations for some great soiree as yet unenjoyed. For nine years the Capulletti had thrown magnificent feasts to celebrate the day of San Bonaventura – an ironic name for a saint, in light of the title's present owner and his slightly mad wife. Today was the feast day, tonight the night when all the best and wealthiest of Verona (with one pointed exception) were to have come here to show a fine masculine leg or a lovely feminine bosom.

Instead the doors were shut against the mob, the city braced for civil war.

The guests were greeted by the lady of the house, her station evident by the ring of keys hanging over her distended waistline. If their errand had not been so urgent, their target so influential, they might have smiled up their sleeves at the sight of this tiny thing with her swollen belly welcoming them in her role as *chatelaine*. She offered refreshment and asked them to wait, as the master of the house was concluding a previous appointment.

In truth, Antonio Capulletto had no other appointment. But he owned a knack for maintaining a hold on his clientele. After judging the right interval, he appeared through the doors that led, not into his house, but to his office along the opposite courtyard wall. Hobbling along in his wake was an elderly blood relative, Arnaldo, a spent force, present out of respect.

Without acknowledging his wife, the master of the house slapped his hands together loudly. "How now, my friends! What news this is! My house was in the midst of preparing the food for tonight, and now – well, we're in quite a stew ourselves, aren't we?"

Just then a fair haired boy ran the length of a balcony above. All unseen, he skidded to a halt to listen as old men spoke their fears.

"...a disaster!"

"...civil war..."

"...untried youth, not even a man..."

"...won the crowd in a matter of minutes..."

"...wonder what the Venetian envoy thought..."

One merchant sliced through to the heart of the matter. "What are you going to do?"

Capulletto waited until he had their undivided attention. "Pietro Alaghieri is one of the most honourable men I've ever met. He once did me a great service, and I have no doubt he is in the right. I intend to put all my resources behind him."

The voices began clamouring immediately, asking "Is that wise?" and "Shouldn't we have a foot in both camps?"

Capulletto waved their objections aside, doggedly declaring his support for Pietro's faction. "You're all probably right. Prudence mandates overtures to both parties. But not here, not now. I support Alaghieri to the death, and beyond."

"Montecchio is saying the same thing," someone said, mentioning the unmentionable.

Capulletto blinked, sandy brows furrowing slowly. Then, like a snapping oyster, his bearded jaw clamped shut. He spoke through gritted teeth. "You sent to treat with him as well." His Capuan accent had never quite lost its rustic roughness, and in anger became more pronounced.

To their credit they blenched but did not buckle. Antony took a turn about the garden, biceps visibly flexing. He was a broad, mighty man able to use his size to his advantage both on the battlefield and in the market place.

Finally he came to a halt. "It isn't Pietro's fault that he attracts licker-fish like the horse-thief. In fact, it shows what an honest man Alaghieri is — *everyone* wants to support him. What I said stands. Besides, will any of us will thrive in a city ruled by Mastino della Scala?" That set off another hot debate, weighing the unknown Scaligeri heir against the known, unpalatable nephew.

Above all the heated voices, the fair-haired boy wore a sour expression. Theobaldo Capulletto despised his uncle with a passion unhealthy in one so young. He watched now as the ancient fool (twenty-eight years old!) prattled on to his guests about his friendship to this knight Alaghieri.

Theobaldo's eyes strayed, as they always did, to Tessa. Dear, dear Tessa. She was trying to smile and be a good hostess, in spite of her discomfort. Once so lively, now timid, terrified of the swelling in her twelve year-old belly.

While his uncle Antony declaimed, Theobaldo sauntered insouciantly down two flights of stairs to the ground floor. Easing himself through one of the two doors, he crept to where his aunt-by-marriage stood, well back from the gathering of men. His fingers brushed her shoulder.

Tessa knew who it was without looking. Her hand crept around her back and stole into Theobaldo's. It was a fleeting embrace, just enough to bring tears to both the pregnant girl and the ten year-old boy she'd once been meant to wed.

"He won't even notice," said Theobaldo, loud and clear. Sure enough, the beefy master of the house didn't raise his head from his conference.

Tessa slowly stepped back and back into the shade of the long balcony that ran around the third floor of the house. Slipping through one of the two doors leading into the house proper, she fled up the stairs as fast as her swollen ankles could carry her, Theobaldo right behind, their hands clasped tight.

They came to rest in a shadowy spot on the balcony where they pressed close together and watched the happenings below. "Who's right?" asked Tessa in Theobaldo's ear.

He knelt beside her. "Whoever the right person is, he'll side with the one against him."

She touched his hair, sad for the bitterness in his tone, sad for his fate, sad for her own. "Oh, Thibault."

Thibault. No one called him that anymore. It was his mother's version of his baptismal name, but that Germanic lady was dead from trying to give Thibault a brother. His father had used it lovingly, respectfully, but Luigi Capulletto had died after a bad fall from a horse during a hunt. Orphaned at six, Thibault had passed into the hands of his uncle and grandfather. Thibault remembered Ludo Capulletto as a fat, vicious old man with nothing but scorn for Thibault's dead father; a diseased carcass who rarely stirred from his bed, and then only to work with Uncle Antonio and the lawyers to steal away Thibault's rightful inheritance. At the time, Thibault hadn't understood or cared about the money and the lands draining from his end of the hourglass. He knew only that he was alone in the world. His sole comfort came from the two ladies of his nursery.

The first was his nursemaid, Angelica, a short plump woman full of laughter and mockery whose gigantic husband doted on her charge, able to toss little Thibault into the air and catch him one handed – his other hand was usually down his wife's dress. Their own little boy had been still-born, and so from the time Thibault was an infant all her milk and their combined kindness had been for him alone.

The other was Tessa. Betrothed to each other since before Thibault was born, they'd been raised together to be as much sister and brother as bride and groom. He had pulled her hair, she had teased and tickled him, they'd sung and played nursery games under Angelica's delighted care. Despite her thirteen month advantage of age, young Thibault had surpassed Tessa in height and strength by the time he was seven, and every-one commented on what splendid children they would have – him with his ice-blonde hair, her with those delicate features and deep blue eyes.

Even now his insides quivered as he recalled a day two years before when she'd taken his hand like this and led him to a sunny room on the highest floor where no other houses could see in. Their nurse was off 'making fun' with her husband, Andriolo, and they were alone.

Dropping his hand, Tessa had closed the door, then crossed the room to stand in a sunbeam. Blushing, she'd said, "You're to be my husband."

"I know that." Thibault had been anxious to get back to the nurs-ery and his toy Trojan Horse. So intent he was on returning to finish the battle, he hadn't immediately noticed what she was doing. The laces of her child's bodice were loose, and in a deft move it lay on the floor. He'd watched, feeling his blood beating all through him, his face and neck turning scarlet. Tessa had reached down and, gripping the hem of her shift, pulled it up over her head. She wasn't wearing small clothes, and her young boy's body was bare and bold before him.

"What are you doing?" He was awkwardly aware of an impulse to do *something*. What, he had no idea. He'd seen her naked a hundred times when they were small, though now Angelica saw fit to separate them on bath-day. There was something different in seeing her like this. It felt wrong, and exciting.

"You're going to be my husband," she said again, and though she had clearly rehearsed this speech her voice shook and her hands clasped in front of her, a belated modesty. "You know what Nurse and Andriolo are doing. That's what husbands do with their wives." She hesitated. "Do you want to try?"

He did. He very much did. They spent a breathless hour looking at each other, tentatively touching and recoiling, not sure what to do or what should be happening. Whenever their skin met there was a flush and a tingling in them both, and they laughed shyly and pulled away. The sun warmed them as they tried to behave as adults did, with no concept or model to copy but Angelica and Andriolo, whose rough play they couldn't duplicate.

Frustrated, Thibault had at last begun to cry. "I don't know what to do!" His tears had made him even more ashamed.

She'd pulled his head to her breast, suddenly a sister again. "There's all the time in the world. When we're married, then we'll know."

"I want to be married now!"

"So do I, my Thibault," she'd said. "So do I."

Then the door had opened and Angelica had surprised them. Her face flushing first in astonishment, then in mirth, she had cried, "Oh my! You little devils! Is this what you do when I'm off at my wifely duties?" Bolting up, the two children had thrown on their clothes, Thibault running so fast from the room he never knew what excuse Tessa had made.

For weeks afterwards Angelica had teased and embarrassed them with knowing comments in front of her husband. But she never told Uncle Antonio. Thibault and Tessa themselves never talked of it, but from then on whenever Thibault looked at Tessa there was a stirring that hinted at what married life would be like.

Then all at once their engagement was shattered. Like everything else in Thibault's life, Uncle Antony had taken what was rightfully his. Remembering that wretched marriage day, with Tessa's wedding veil hiding the persuasive bruises from her father's fists, Thibault felt a cold rage. He didn't blame her, of course – her unwillingness was as clear as glass. He didn't even truly blame the girl's parents, who had seized a sudden chance to elevate their daughter by marrying her to the head of the household.

No, Thibault's rage was reserved for his uncle, who had done this for the same reason he did everything: to hurt Thibault. In the worst day of his young life, Thibault had been forced to watch, helpless, as his wife married his uncle. It made Thibault's flesh creep to imagine his uncle seeing Tessa's skin, touching it… Worse, to think that the knowledge denied Thibault had been bestowed instead on his usurping uncle. As it clearly had. Within the first month Tessa had become pregnant.

Angelica was delighted since she too was with child, and so could again be nurse in the Capulletti home. Early on, he had mentioned to Tessa the possibility of losing the baby – perhaps if she fell on it? But she said it was better this way. "As long as I'm pregnant, he won't touch me." So in a perverse way Thibault came to love the child inside her, who kept her from his uncle's bed.

Holding Tessa's hand, he felt her squirm. "What is it?"

"The baby," she said sourly, face pained. "She's active." Unlike Thibault, Tessa was not fond of the uncomfortable daughter within her. Angelica was sure that it was a girl, and no one even thought to argue. Though missing several teeth and with breath that could kill a horse, the nurse was never wrong about such things. It gave Thibault pleasure to think that his uncle's first child would be a girl, not an heir. He was determined not to be displaced so easily.

Tessa shifted, easing her ankles. Looking at the worried men below, she asked, "What's happening?"

"Another faction has arrived to take the Greyhound's place."

"Are they going to fight?"

"Let's hope so. Maybe there'll be a battle in the forum and he'll be killed," said Thibault, nodding to his uncle.

Tessa shied away. "Don't say that. God wouldn't like you to wish for a death. Even his."

"I hate him." It was bald fact. The Sun rises in the East. Flowers bloom in the Spring. Thibault hated his uncle. "I'll do whatever it takes to ruin him."

She stroked his hair again, a gesture he found almost unbearable. Almost. "I was looking forward to the feast," she said with a sigh. "My first as lady of the house."

Thibault stiffened. She *wants* to be lady of the house? She was *proud* of that title? "He's lucky. I was going to spoil it for him. Somehow."

Perhaps she realized she had wounded him, for she whispered, "We both know whose lady I should be, and whose house I should be lady of."

"Yes." Thibault relented, relaxing against her.

The conference in the orchard below ended, and the emissaries prepared to depart with their host. Without even looking for his child-bride to bid her farewell, Antony Capulletto ordered his sword and gambeson. Then, throwing on an over-tunic to hide the quilted armour, he strode with the others through the bricked arch and out into the street, leaving his nephew and wife to console each other in the shadows of the balcony.

# FOURTEEN

SUMMONED TO THE HOUSE on the *via da Santa Maria*,
Antonia found it aflutter with activity. Identifying herself, she was urgently
conveyed up the stairs. It was an unfamiliar house to her. Clean and spare,
it still bore the mark of Katerina Nogarola, despite her prolonged absence.

Antonia opened the indicated door, ready with a flushed smile of
praise for Cesco's magnificent, if flamboyant, performance in the piazza.
But the scene that met her drained all colour from her face.

Stripped to the waist, Cesco was sprawled on a daybed, propped
upright by several bolsters. Morsicato knelt beside him, the doctor's
head close to the boy's chest. Detto and Val sat ashen-faced and silent,
watching.

Antonia started forward, only to be restrained by her brother. Pietro
had been leaning on the wall beside the door. His fine armour removed,
he wore just a loose shirt and his only affectation, the short trousers that
hid the puckered scar on his thigh. His face was stricken, teary, dread-filled.
"What's wrong?"

"Someone in the crowd pricked him with a needle." Pietro's voice
was a vacant murmur. "Poison."

"Merciful Lord," she whispered, instantly crossing herself and
starting to pray. Her prayer was interrupted, however, when the doctor
leaned back. Seeing blood all around the doctor's lips, she gasped.

Cesco loosed a smile in her direction. "Vampiric, isn't he? But
please, continue your intercession on my behalf. Just in case the doctor's
methods are too late."

Antonia finished her prayer. Then in her most efficient tone she said, "What can I do?"

"Prayer is the only thing. You see what modern medicine is. *Leave us put our trust in God and He will see us through.*" He followed with a phrase of something flowery in Arabic that Antonia could not make out. Pietro, however, winced.

Morsicato spit heavily into a basin. "Until we know what it was, we can only do some basic things. We sent for Fracastoro, and leeches are on their way from the apothecary—"

"Along with his whole shop," added Cesco.

"Stop talking," ordered the doctor, wiping his face and washing his mouth out with heated wine. "Conserve your strength."

Cesco twisted to face Detto and Valentino. "In other words, I'm irritating him. Nothing worse than a loquacious corpse." Detto made a show of smiling. Valentino was huddled close to his brother, eyes wide.

Ignoring his impatient patient, Morsicato pressed leaves into the open knife-wound. "Antonia, lads, come here. Each of you take a limb and rub it. Boys, take his feet. Lady, please sit here and take his hand. Pietro, take the other. Now rub gently, keep his humours flowing."

"Rubbies. I'm like a puppy!" said Cesco. "Is this medical, or are you just trying to distract me so I don't talk myself to death?"

"It's a stimulant of sorts. An old witch once told me that she kept a poisoned man alive by keeping his blood flowing in just this way."

Cesco's eyes were limpid and unfocused, unnaturally bright. "A witch? Did she put a curse on you? Is that how you lost your hair?"

"I'll get her to put a curse on your tongue so that it shrivels to a crisp," retorted the doctor in spite of himself.

"Don't waste your silver. It may happen yet."

"How did this happen?" asked Antonia, rubbing at Cesco's clammy and cold skin. "I didn't see anything."

Cesco shrugged, still smiling. "A hand clapped my shoulder in the crowd, harder than need be, just hard enough to disguise the needle jabbing me." He winced and the smile became fixed, determined.

"Bastards," growled Detto, a horrible whimper in the back of his voice. He looked as bloodless as his friend, but far more frightened.

"I found the needle and plucked it out – the good doctor has it in his urine jar over there." Cesco pointed vaguely to a trestle table where all of Morsicato's tools had been hurriedly laid out.

"He cut himself to release the tainted blood," said Morsicato. "Probably saved his life."

"A compliment from the doctor. I must be in real peril." Cesco shivered and closed his eyes. "I also did it to let my enemies know that I was aware of their tactics. Whichever of them did this."

"I bet it was Mastino," said Detto.

"Or Giovanna," said Pietro. "She's back in the city."

Antonia knew why her brother was adding to Cesco's worries. The boy liked nothing more than a challenge. If they kept him thinking, he might have a better chance.

"Either way," replied Cesco, "it explains why Mastino wouldn't let me in. He recognized my self-mutilation for what it was. I'm sure he'll agree to the meeting tomorrow – he expects me to be dead by then. He's really quite capable," laughed Cesco, shivering again. "Whoever did this, the plan was enacted quickly, with a minimum of fuss. I'd hate to die before I see if it works."

"You're not going to die," said Pietro, rubbing the small hand vigourously. "It's not in the stars."

"You sound like my Shadow."

Antonia raised her head in an unspoken question. Pietro answered her aloud. "Not here. I assume he saw who it was, and is tracking him."

"For revenge?"

Cesco shook his head slightly. "Baldy here has to know what the poison was. I imagine the Arūs presently has my would-be murderer in a locked room somewhere and is beating the living daylights out of him for an answer."

"I wish I could be the one to do it," said Detto fiercely.

Cesco playfully kicked at his friend – or tried to. His leg hardly twitched. "I promise I'll get myself poisoned again someday, and you can be the one to save me." Detto looked like he might cry, but bravely bit back his sob and kept rubbing Cesco's right foot.

The amused patient turned back to Antonia. "You see, the only other way to know what the poison was is to wait and see what form it takes – what symptoms I have." He swallowed. "Like all the spit that's in my mouth."

The doctor produced a little clay bowl. "Spit into this. Don't swallow it." Cesco obeyed, and the doctor stepped away, reappearing with a jug and a shallow cup, which he handed to Antonia. "Each time he spits, make him drink this."

"Is it wine?" asked Cesco hopefully.

"Water and vinegar." Cesco made a face and a rude sound, then coughed. Antonia realized he had been getting progressively worse since she entered the room – his pupils had dilated to twice their normal size, making his eyes look black, not green.

"Doctor," said Pietro hesitantly, "I don't want to leave him, but there are things that have to be done. I mean, nothing's more important, but…"

"But just in case I do survive to see the sun," said Cesco, "it would be good to put me on Verona's throne as well. Go. Tell my noble supporters what's happening – and inform them to prepare to flee if I do expire. Give them my thanks." His words were becoming thick. He raised his head to spit again into the bowl, wincing as he did so.

Morsicato and Pietro stepped away to confer. With a last look at the patient, Pietro exited. As the doctor returned, Cesco said, "I think you should know, *medicus meus*, my head hurts."

"Where?" None of Morsicato's usual gruffness or cynicism was evident by look or tone. He seemed calm, detached – a fact that frightened Antonia more than anything else.

Cesco considered. "All over, but distinctly in the back. And my jaw. My jaw is going numb. I don't know how much longer I can talk." When the doctor took up the boy's free arm to start rubbing, Cesco clucked his tongue. "What, no rebuke? No cutting remark? I'm appalled. Am I to die without that razor-like wit biting me to the last? You could have said, 'A blessing on us all,' or, 'Tell me when you can't.' Something! I refuse to die without at least practicing my cunning."

"Idiot boy." Up close the doctor's eyes were damp, but his voice was clear. "You were supposed to stay with the Anziani, not be carried through the throng. You were lucky not to get a knife in the ribs."

Cesco's laugh was a feeble wheeze. "I beg to discuss your definition of luck."

◆    ◊    ◆

Downstairs, Pietro was giving instructions to Bailardino's servants, specifically ordering them not to tell anyone of the young master's illness.

"My lord," said one, "there have been several callers. Ser Capulletto and Ser Montecchio have both sent pages, each asking for a few minutes of your time. The guildsmen are lurking in the streets at the back of the house, asking to know what the young master's policies will be —"

Pietro cut across him. "We don't have time for any of them, so do your best to politely brush them off. Meantime we have to find some way of communicating with the Giurisconsulti that won't be traced. I suppose the Anziani are in council with Bailardino and the rest?"

"Yes, and they, too, have requested your presence —"

Pietro waved a hand in annoyance. "Tell them I'm greeting old friends, and tell the callers I'm with the Anziani. That'll buy us an hour or two. Then have whoever you send to the City Council whisper in Bail's ear – no, his absence would be talked about. Have his brother join us. Move!"

Pietro was scribbling down notes to order his thoughts – one of his father's habits – when Fracastoro arrived. The famous doctor immediately started to ask about the rumours he'd heard about a coup, about ten years of mystery and intrigue. Pietro interrupted him harshly. "There's no time. Cangrande's heir has been poisoned, we don't know what kind, we're trying to find out. He's upstairs, with Morsicato."

Fracastoro became professional. "Was the poison ingested?"

"He was stung with something barbed. A needle."

The elderly physician to three Scaligeri lords said no more but lifted the hem of his gonella and raced up the stairs, his urine glass thumping against his chest. Pietro watched him go, hoping this man would carry a miraculous cure with him, fearing he would be as helpless as Morsicato.

*It's your fault,* said the judging voice of Dante that still lived inside Pietro's mind. *You should have been with him the whole time. You should have had more guards around him. You should have known!*

Pietro returned to his scribblings, trying desperately to engage his mind in the many necessary tasks at hand. All he wanted was to be upstairs holding that boy's hand. *No, I want to be wherever Tharwat is, beating the living Christ out of the poisoner.* But his sense of duty to his friends as well as his ward made him write out plans and contingencies. If Cesco didn't die, there were a hundred things that had to be looked after.

*And if he does?* Hating himself for even considering the possibility, Pietro knew he owed it to his friends to see that none of them were hanged or beheaded for his folly. For his father's voice spoke true: This mess was entirely his own fault.

◆　◊　◆

Upstairs, the two doctors removed themselves to the table of instruments to confer. "The wound at his neck?" asked Fracastoro.

"He did that himself, to stop the poison."

"Smart lad. Do you have this needle?"

From the tools Morsicato grasped a pair of tweezers and carefully lifted the deadly instrument from the phial on the trestle. Fracastoro sniffed at it. "Foul. You've ordered leeches?"

"Should be here any minute."

"Well, it can't be a simple poison, it's working too fast."

"A compound," agreed Morsicato. "You think we should bleed him?"

"I do. But not too much – we must keep him awake. If he sleeps, we lose him. We need to know what kind of poison was used."

"That's being attended to," said Morsicato grimly.

By the bed, Antonia lifted Cesco's sweat-sopped head. "What did you think you were doing?"

"A crowd – enjoys spectacle, auntie. I gave them one." He paused while Antonia poured some more liquid down his throat. "Euch! Foul

FROM BEYOND THE GRAVE

stuff. I think the doctor's – trying to poison me. But anyway, auntie – grandfather used to say that people are contrary by nature. So I knew that if I told them why – I couldn't be their Capitano, they would immediately start arguing why I should."

"And you added that last piece to the will," said Antonia. "If they accepted that was genuine, they had to accept that you were, too."

"I'm not sure they thought it through that far," admitted Cesco feebly, "but it certainly made me into their champion."

"You're brilliant," said Detto admiringly.

"Mmm. My light seems to be fading."

Morsicato approached. "Antonia, girl, move aside. We're going to bleed him."

"Thirsty again, doctor?" asked Cesco. No one laughed. Antonia stood away as the bearded man placed yet another bowl by the bed and laid a cloth over Cesco's arm. He then used a lancet to pierce Cesco's vein. Val looked away, but Detto did not.

Suddenly there was a thunder of feet on the stairs outside, and the door burst open. Pietro held himself upright in the doorframe. "Doctors – Tharwat's back."

Cesco grinned. "Always knew you were – faking that leg wound."

Morsicato looked to his fellow doctor. "Will you take over? This will be the news we were waiting for."

As Fracastoro took up the lancet and cloth, Pietro said, "Bring a bandage." With a fearful look at Cesco, he turned and retreated back down the stairs, leaning on the wall for support. Running up the stairs had clearly hurt. Morsicato exited as well, closing the door behind him.

Cesco blinked and coughed, but was unable to spit the excess of bile in his mouth. "I guess – we'll soon know," he mumbled.

"Be still, child," said Antonia, moving around him to rub his other arm.

Val leaned over towards his brother and whispered, "What's wrong with Ser Alaghieri's leg?"

"An old wound. He got it the same day uncle Antonio lost his arm. He can't run well."

"Our own Achilles," muttered Cesco. "I wonder, then, who that makes me?"

◆     ◊     ◆

At the bottom of the stairs the Moor was leaning against the wall, one arm hanging loosely at his side. He and Pietro were talking in quick short bursts.

"Dead?"

"No, but he won't escape. I have his bag of weapons."

"Good. But—?" Pietro gestured at the Moor's arm.

"A knife. Unvenomed," said al-Dhaamin. "I hope."

"Is it bad?"

"Hardly anything. A waste of time binding it."

"Did he have a name for us?"

"Nothing definitive. We will question him further. I thought it more important to return with details of this foul, hideous venom."

Pietro's flesh crawled. Whatever the poison was, if it was enough to turn the Moor's stomach, it was no ordinary concoction.

Morsicato arrived, and Pietro moved aside so the doctor could cut away the sleeve to start dressing the Moor's arm. "What did you learn?"

Tharwat didn't waste any words in telling everything he had learned about the ingredients of the poison.

"Dear Christ," murmured Pietro.

"This man says this mixture was left sealed in a container in a dung heap for two weeks, and doused with sesame oil to bind it. A large dose would kill a grown man within a day, perhaps two."

"He's not a grown man, he's a child!" raged Pietro. Hearing the note of pleading in his voice, he wondered to whom it was directed.

Tharwat was grim. "Let us pray the dose was small."

Pietro turned to the doctor. "What can you do?"

"Nothing more until the herbs arrive. If he'd swallowed it, we could force him to vomit it up, but as he was stung, it's already in his blood. That's both good and bad. It means it's affecting him faster, but it's also less potent. Poison ingested is the most destructive. There."

Finished working on the Moor, the doctor felt a leather bag pressed into his hand. "The man's tools," said Tharwat. "Nothing's broken."

"Thank you." Morsicato started up the stairs, but paused to look back. "The man's not dead?"

"No."

"Pity."

♦     ◊     ♦

Waiting, Fracastoro snapped his fingers. "Has he tried olive oil yet?"

Surprised, Antonia answered, "What? No – no, I don't think so."

"It's worth a try. Valentino, go down to the kitchens and ask for a goodly amount of olive oil." The lad left the room gratefully.

Eyes closed, Cesco said, "Are you going to cook me? I'd prefer a good basting…"

"Olive oil can be used to draw out toxins in the blood," explained

Fracastoro. "We'll make a few small cuts in your feet and your other arm and soak them in it."

"At least I'll smell better," said Cesco. "My breath is – foul."

Fracastoro leaned forward to sniff. It was familiar, the smell. "Hellebore," he muttered.

The door opened and Morsicato returned. Motioning Fracastoro close, he started to relate the nature of the venom.

Suddenly Cesco opened his eyes. "I want to hear."

"No, you don't," said Morsicato firmly.

Cesco sat feebly forward. He was trying not to shiver, but it had grown beyond his power to hide it. "I want to hear."

Pursing his lips, Morsicato said, "You were poisoned with a combination of venoms. It began with the body of a mouse stung to death by scorpions, then ground to powder and mixed with black hellebore, poppy seeds, and eel brains. At least, that's the Moor was told."

"Then it's the – truth," said Cesco, falling back and closing his eyes. His breathing was laboured. "The poisoner would be – too scared to lie."

"I can attest to the hellebore," said Fracastoro in a soft tone. "Smell his breath."

Morsicato did, wrinkling his nose. "How do you feel now? Is there anything new?"

"It feels – it feels as if someone has – nailed a piece of wood between my heart and lungs."

"That's the scorpion venom. Lie still now. We have to confer."

The two doctors stepped to the trestle table and spoke in low whispers, discussing and even arguing back and forth until a servant announced the arrival of the apothecary, his cart in tow.

Now began the real work: the leeching, the bleeding, the continual rubbing of the limbs, the sweet-smelling compresses. Cesco's feet and arms, with small cuts in them, were laid in bowls of olive oil, and he was force-fed crushed herbs and vinegar through a mouth that was now almost entirely swollen shut. Cesco made two more morbid jokes before he lost all consciousness of his surroundings. From then on he was adrift in a world of feverish imaginings and wrenching pain.

The first scream came from nowhere. He was lying stiff and still when all at once he opened his mouth and released a noise so inhuman that everyone recoiled. They had to bind his hands because he started to beat them against the bed's edges, knocking away the bloody olive oil.

He was never a good sleeper, plagued by evil dreams. But this night Cesco lived the nightmares with his sightless eyes open.

# FIFTEEN

BAILARDINO'S BROTHER spent the early part of the night shuttling back and forth between the Giurisconsulti and the house across from Santa Maria Antica – an awkward trek, for he had to pass directly beneath the palace where Mastino had barricaded himself. The news he brought was neither exciting nor surprising. The City Council had been up all night treating – through intermediaries – with Mastino, who was playing a delaying game.

*He knows,* thought Pietro. *He knows, and he's waiting to see.*

At midnight Bailardino arrived. He was greeted first by servants, then by an exhausted Pietro. "How is he?"

"Still alive," said Pietro dubiously. The screaming had stopped. Pietro hadn't thought it possible, but the silence was worse.

Bailardino beckoned Pietro into his study, where he closed the door before collapsing into a chair. "Is it as bad as Antonio says?"

"Worse. He stopped breathing twenty minutes ago, so the doctors tried something drastic. They forced his mouth open and fed him more poison."

"They what?"

Pietro shook his head. "I don't pretend to understand, but they say that some poisons are actually cures for other poisons. Belladonna cures foxglove, and foxglove cures monkshood. They decided that since the poison was slowing his blood through him, they would give him a dose of something to stimulate it and balance his humours."

"Is it working?"

"I have no idea. He seems to be breathing easier now, but that could just be hopeful thinking on my part. Morsicato says it's too soon to know. Maybe by morning."

"He'll pull through, he's got to," said Bailardino, adding a wry laugh. "How can he not? He's protected by a curse."

Pietro had often wondered if Bailardino knew of the prophecy of *Il Veltro* and its connection to Cesco. He settled himself on a stool by the wall, massaging the muscles of his right leg. "I don't put too much stock in prophecies. I've seen what happens to those that do."

"Cangrande, you mean," said Bailardino. Pietro had actually meant Bailardino's wife, but he chose not to clarify. Bailardino kicked off his boots. "Yes, he was always intent on proving that damned astrologer wrong, proving once and for all that he was some mythic figure who was going to pull Italy out of darkness by the hair. You weren't here these last few years. He grew really touchy about it."

Pietro had heard the stories. "Since everyone but us already thought he was *Il Veltro*, I'm sure it was a constant sore point."

"That damned astrologer," muttered Bailardino.

"You blame al-Dhaamin?"

"I do. He was the one made those hellfire charts for the whole family, Kat included. If he hadn't meddled..." Bailardino's voice trailed off as he closed his eyes, fatigue more immediate than a very old grudge.

To Pietro's way of thinking, it was not the astrologer who was at fault for Cangrande's lifelong disappointment. It was Katerina, the woman who had raised the Scaliger from the time he was six, all the while filling his head with the thought that he truly was destined for greatness – that *he* was the heroic figure of legend, the hound that would bring about another golden age. It was written in her stars that she was to have a dramatic role in the shaping of that mythic man. Cangrande had been her trial run, her testing of theories and methods.

When Cangrande turned fifteen, the official age of manhood, Tharwat had stepped in and revealed the truth at last – Cangrande was going to be a great man, a famous warrior and statesman, a patron of the arts. But he was not *Il Veltro*. That destiny belonged to another.

Bailardino opened his eyes and yawned. "Don't – ah, don't let me sleep, boy. There's far too much to do. God's bread, it was easier twenty years ago."

Pietro loosed a wearily malicious smile. "I was eight years old, then."

"Shut your face," groaned Bailardino.

"Make me, old man."

"By God, if I could get out of this chair I'd crush your skull."

He smiled wanly before gravity returned. "I'll tell you, though – just this once, I hope that heathen devil is right. Because God help us all if Mastino comes to council tomorrow afternoon and we show up without Cangrande's heir. That evil little bastard will string us up by our guts."

"We have the army," countered Pietro.

Bailardino waved that away. "Mastino'll have something better – public outrage. He'll accuse us of trying to kill the boy. Don't ask me why, he'll have some reason. It doesn't have to make sense. Mastino will appeal to the people that traitors, led by foreigners, have killed Cangrande's heir. He's clearly innocent – he was nowhere near the boy and everybody knows it. No, if your little Cesco snuffs it, we'll all have to run for the hills. Otherwise the crows will be pecking out our eyes by supper."

"Thanks," said Pietro. "I needed a good cheering up."

"Well, you'll like this at least – both your friends Montecchio and Capulletto came, trying to outdo each other in oaths to follow Cesco to the grave."

"They may get their wish. What did you do with our two Scaligeri guests?"

"Both Federigo and Alblivious are at the city council, under a heavy yet inconspicuous guard and told to keep their mouths shut for the duration. They make it look like Mastino's the only one not bowing to Cangrande's wishes." Bailardino chuckled. "Little Alblivious actually offered to be the one to treat with his brother."

"You didn't let him!"

"God, no. Not that I suspect him of any duplicity, but rather because I think Mastino would dig out his eyes with a splintered spoon. We sent Nico instead."

"And?"

"Mastino has agreed to come across to the Domus Nuova under truce at two tomorrow afternoon." Bail took a breath. "But an hour ago there was a new wrinkle added."

"Let me guess – a message from Giovanna."

"Right in one! That's why I'm here – I'm supposed to be consulting with Cesco and you. The bitch says that, as Cangrande's widow, she knows where all the bodies are buried. If we do not disqualify both Cesco and Mastino and elevate Paride to the Captainship, she'll reveal every trade secret and under-handed deal done in Verona's name in the last twenty years."

"Meaning if she can't rule the city, she'll ruin it."

"Yes. I have to say, after all this plotting, it was a refreshingly blunt message."

The lawyer in Pietro leapt up. "Not written down, was it?"

Bail shook his head. "Spoken by a page. Nothing we can use in a court."

"What do the Anziani say?"

"They're wondering what damage she can really do. You're the spymaster. What possible secrets could she know? How awful would it be?"

Pietro didn't have to consider at all. "However bad you can imagine, multiply it by a factor of ten. No, Bail, I mean it. Cangrande's reputation will be utterly ruined, and no Scaliger will ever be able to rule in his place."

Bail frowned. "What could he possibly have done?"

There was a large piece of Pietro that didn't want to speak. Bail had been part-father, part-brother to Cangrande. But Pietro's sense of outrage and injustice was even greater than Morsicato's. Now he could voice a fraction of his ire without feeling self-serving.

He started with an old example, the massacre at Calvatone. Bail had been there when Cangrande's word had been broken to the surrendering city and every last man, woman, and child had been slaughtered. "At the time, it seemed someone had betrayed Cangrande. But the orders were his."

"He had the offenders executed!"

"I heard it from his own lips."

"I refuse to believe it!"

"So will the people," answered Pietro honestly. "And they'll close their ears to one story, or three, or ten. But, Bail, there are dozens. *Dozens.*" He began to describe with precise detail a few of Cangrande's dealings in the last ten years – broken pledges, extortion, double-dealing, even murder. All of it to Verona's good, and any one of which was the action of a cynically practical man. But combined...

"I have proof. Or rather," said Pietro, correcting himself, "I had it. My strongbox in Ravenna was filled with evidence against him, just in case..." He paused to wonder where Giovanna had gotten her proof. His strongbox was built to survive even a fire, but they hadn't found it among the ashes of his house.

Bail was still struggling. "If you knew all this – you've been helping him all this time—"

"Helping *Verona,*" corrected Pietro. "For Cesco. Not for Cangrande."

"No," declared Bailardino, covering his ears. "I helped raise him, Pietro. He was my friend, and a good man. I mean, he was a little wild, and certainly he was cunning, but what you're hinting at – no, Pietro! I won't listen to him being spoken of like this—"

"Then don't!" snapped Pietro. "Just know that the threat is real, and treat Giovanna accordingly."

Bailardino eyed Pietro suspiciously. "True enough. Even if it's a pack of lies, she can make people listen. So what do we do? The people are all in a lather about your little ward. Even if we were to accede to her demands, they wouldn't follow Paride, not now."

"Bail, even if Cesco lives, there's no guarantee he'll ever leave that room under his own power."

"Truly?" Pietro's face carried all the answer required. "What are you saying?"

"I'm saying that there's nothing useful to do at the moment. Let Mastino worry about Giovanna – he has as much to lose as we do. Meantime, we just have to wait."

"That's something I'm no good at. I'm a soldier, I need to be doing!"

"I understand. But this isn't a battle fought with swords. I wish it were."

They sat together a long while. They had never been close, but always friendly. Pietro wondered if that was about to change. Bail had idolized his late brother-in-law. Pietro had sown a seed of doubt. He was already regretting speaking of it. *I could have given him a less pointed answer, let him keep his illusions, even if I've lost mine...*

Slapping his own face roughly a few times to rouse himself, Bailardino stood. "I'm going to check in, see how the boy's doing."

As he passed, Pietro touched his arm. "Bail – I'm sorry." Bailardino had nothing to say. His face was closed. "You're going upstairs?"

Bailardino nodded. The last time Pietro had been up there, the room had been a foul-smelling shambles. The doctors were now trying to sweat the poisons out through Cesco's pores, so the room was closed and stuffy with two braziers burning on either side of the daybed. Bailardino's sons were looking like ghosts, and Antonia had started reading to Cesco to keep his mind engaged. Pietro had needed to escape, however briefly, unable to watch his boy lying there, whimpering and struggling against the pain. "Be prepared."

With another curt nod Bailardino left the study. As Pietro sat back down, Tharwat appeared. "He needed to know."

"Listening at keyholes? Or after all these years can you hear my thoughts?"

"It is right he should be told."

"Not by me. Not now."

"Ser Alaghieri, you are a man who loves the intangible things that most men say they honour, but few do. Of these, the greatest is truth. Do not be ashamed of it."

Pietro shook his head. "I was hurting, and wanted to spread the hurt. I still do." He noticed Tharwat wrapping a scarf around his scarred throat and pulling a hood into place. "Where are you going?"

"To uncover another truth, one that has been too long in the shadows. If I do not return, it has been an honour knowing you."

Before Pietro could even rise, he was gone.

♦     ◊     ♦

The streets of Verona were a strange place that night. Part festival, part armed camp. The threat of civil war, though real, was overshadowed by the exciting arrival of the bastard heir of their beloved Cangrande. Tension was palpable. No one walked alone.

Traveling in groups from house to house, avoiding the public squares, the men of Verona's middle and upper-classes congregated and discussed the future of their city. The poor stayed home, sure that whatever fate brought they would endure it – even if it was a bloodbath in the streets.

The bloodbath would be short. Cangrande's soldiers had all defected from Mastino's cause. The only men still loyal to him were the German mercenaries barricaded in their barracks, or else in the palace with their master.

Most of the city's soldiers were on patrol, while the rest sought out taverns. Just before nightfall they had received a welcome if unusual order: each man was to raise his cup three times to the health of Cangrande's heir, paid for by Bailardino Nogarola. At the same time an order went out to all the churches: pray for the spiritual and mortal health of young Francesco della Scala.

In the streets, the Moor went almost unnoticed as he journeyed on his self-appointed mission. For the first time in his life he was defying the stars, taking preemptive action.

For Cesco he could do no less.

# SIXTEEN

ANTONIA WAS in the upstairs hallway, getting a breath of fresh air, when she heard a knocking below. There was a voice she knew, some small discussion, then a cry.

Quickly she descended the stairs. Entering the study, she saw her brother Jacopo laying flat on his back, hands over his head, face bleeding. Pietro had him by the arm, dragging their little brother up to his feet to hit him again.

Antonia ran forward and prised her way between them. "Stop it! Stop!"

Poco kept shouting, "What? What?" Seeing her, he cried, "Imperia, he's trying to kill me!"

"Pietro!" yelled Antonia. "What are you doing!? Cesco needs quiet!"

Knuckles bloody, Pietro reluctantly backed away. "Couldn't keep your mouth shut, could you! Had to let it drop! What was it – trying to get in good with Alblivious? Or did you just go straight to Mastino!"

"Wha – I don't—" stammered Jacopo.

"Pietro, he wouldn't –"

"Antonia, Cesco is laying upstairs because our little brother can't keep his mouth shut!"

"It wasn't that – I mean, I never —" protested Jacopo feebly around his bleeding lip.

"Pietro, he wouldn't —"

"Who else would have told them, little sister? You? Me? Katerina?

Castelbarco? We were all part of the plan. Only this little shitheel – dammit, Poco, we trusted you! *I* trusted you!"

Defiantly stepping out from behind Antonia, Poco kept the desk between himself and his brother. "Pietro, as God is my witness, I don't know what you're…" Pietro started forward again, fists raised. Poco scuttled back behind Antonia, who caught him by the sleeve and waved Pietro off.

"Listen to me, little brother," she said softly. "No one is going to hurt you for what you did, but you cannot lie to us. Two nights ago Pietro's house in Ravenna was burned to the ground. That means someone knew that Cesco was alive and in Ravenna. Did you tell anyone?"

"No!" cried Jacopo indignantly. Antonia slapped him across the face, and he yelped. "You said you weren't going to hurt me anymore!"

"I also said you cannot lie to us. We have to know. What did you tell Mastino, and when?"

"I didn't tell him anything!"

Antonia glanced over at Pietro, hovering at the near side of the desk, shaking with anger. Shrugging, she let go of Poco. Pietro started forward.

"No! I swear! Alberto and I are friends, and we joked once. Only once! I never told him anything!"

Pietro's voice was deadly calm. "Tell me this joke."

"I only said that – that maybe he shouldn't be so sure that he and his brother would inherit everything. That – that there was a chance Cangrande had a kid somewhere." Quickly he added, "I mean, everyone knows about how he got around! He was a real dog. There was that thing with that countess, that time! But that's all I said! How could I know they were going to find out about Cesco?"

Pietro closed his eyes, steeling himself while Antonia answered. "You gave them the hint. Didn't it occur to you that they might check into your family and friends to see what you knew?"

"You don't know it was them! Alberto laughed it off!"

"Antonia, I'm going up to check on Cesco." Pietro started to exit, but paused by the door. "Jacopo, you're my brother, and I'll always love you. But however long it takes for Cesco to mend, don't come back to this house for twice as long. If he dies, God help you."

Jacopo tilted his head. "What's this all about? Mend from what?"

"Listen to the important part, Poco. Leave. Now."

"This isn't your house!" retorted Jacopo.

"You think Nogarola will want you here? You're lucky I'm not off to tell Tharwat – he'd have that head off your shoulders. Or maybe Morsicato'll mix you up a matching poison."

"What poison? What are you talking about? I'm your brother!"

"And that's why I'm telling you to get out. Your life won't be safe here as long as Cesco's ill. In time, they might forget. I won't."

"Antonia, what's he talking about?"

"Someone poisoned Cesco today, in the street," said Antonia dully. "He's barely surviving."

"That's a secret, by the way," said Pietro. "Try to keep it inside your teeth. And don't look so surprised. By now you have to know what they're like."

Jacopo stuck out two open palms. "I didn't know – I didn't think…"

"You never do." Pietro shared a look with Antonia. She was glad he'd hit their little brother when he had, because she knew he was melting now. By tomorrow his fury would be replaced with a weary sadness. Poco was their little brother. They always forgave him in the end.

As Pietro left the room, Jacopo said, "I swear, they had no idea! I mean, I never told them anything real, I was just joking around…" Antonia made to leave as well. "Well, can I at least see Cesco? I'm his uncle, too – I mean, I was his—"

Antonia looked back. "Poco, if you're still here in ten minutes, I'll tell the Moor myself."

✦    ◊    ✦

At that moment the Moor was sitting in a large domicile several streets to the north-west, staring at an amazingly frescoed wall. It was done in the new fashion of geometric shapes, diamonds within squares of alternating colour. This was an unusual choice for decoration, eschewing family, religious, or mythological themes for anonymous designs that took an expensive skill to replicate frame after frame. Anonymity was prudent for the resident of this house, who was not the owner.

Odd, the effect art could have. Tharwat felt an unusual nostalgia for his youth. He'd seen walls like this, long ago. As always, the West was decades behind the East in terms of culture. But then, that particular culture had been eradicated, which led him to the obvious question – how advanced could a people have been if they no longer existed?

He had a long time to ponder the question. The wait was not unexpected. He made no sign of anxiousness. When the Giovanna da Svevia finally entered, she found him entirely composed. He rose and bowed. "My lady."

"We have never been introduced," Cangrande's widow said in flawless Greek.

"An error I am here to correct."

"I am gratified." She waved him to a seat. Dressed in the purest white, the colour of mourning, her face was hidden behind a lace veil. Sitting opposite him, she waved a servant to pour them refreshment. "It is a fruit-wine. I hope it will not compromise your standing with your god to share it with me."

"My god is your god. There is only one Lord in heaven."

"And his name is Allah," she finished the prayer, amused. "Praise be unto him. Tell me, were you able to practice your faith in Ravenna."

"In my own fashion," he said, receiving the cup and sipping it.

Watching him, she smiled. "You are a trusting man. Or have you divined that it is free of poison?"

"I do not fear death. I have lived long enough. I am here for the life of another."

Holding his eyes, she lifted her veil and drank. Gesturing to the fresco, she said, "Do you like it? In Antioch, in my youth, this was the style."

"I have never been to Antioch. But it makes me reflect on my childhood as well – much further removed than yours, I am sure." Giovanna accepted the social nicety, though both knew she was hardly younger than he. Her marriage to Cangrande had come late in her life, a political match to a prodigy barely in his majority.

So far he'd found the interview interesting. Her choice of language tested him, while at the same time excluding her Italian servants from their conversation. Her mention of Ravenna was deliberate, but had many possible meanings. Similarly, the mention of poison. So far she had hinted, but admitted nothing.

"Forgive me for prying," she said now, "but whatever is the matter with your voice?"

Tharwat removed the scarf from his throat. "An injury almost as ancient as I am."

She examined the bubbled scars that ringed his neck. "Tut. How terrible. I hope the man who caused it is dead."

"It was many men, and yes, they are no longer living."

"Did they die by your hand?"

"Yes."

"So you believe in revenge."

"I believe in the stars," said Tharwat al-Dhaamin. "And I grieve for your recent loss."

"Do you? How kind. Perhaps if he had been less conscious of your art, he might have lived longer."

"A man cannot deny his stars."

"A point he would have debated. In fact, that debate surely was the ultimate cause of his death, whatever the mortal event was."

"If you blame me, I am here to atone. With my life, if necessary. But before I die, I have a message for you."

"From my husband, perhaps? Can you commune with the dead?"

"After a fashion. The message is this – I have, at the late Scaliger's behest, made many charts over the years. One concerns you."

"I have seen my own star map," said the lady with amusement. "Nothing you have to say can impress me."

"I have seen it as well," said the Moor in his painful voice. "But it is not your chart I am here to discuss. It belongs to your charge. Young Paride."

Giovanna's face retained its tranquilly amused expression. The only gauge to her reaction was the length of the pause. "Paride?"

"The moment he was born, Cangrande had the local experts each create charts. The great Benentendi was one. I have compiled them into a master and studied it carefully."

"You are here to say he has a great future before him. I am gratified, but I knew it already."

"He has a distinguished life in store for him," agreed Tharwat. "But sadly short. He will not wed, he will have no heirs. He will not be Capitano. He will not be emperor. He will not be another Frederick. You must set those hopes aside. Your line is finished."

Now her anger was visible. "Am I to believe you? You, who stand to gain if he steps aside."

"I gain nothing in any event. My stars are set."

"Your charge, then. You dash my nephew's hopes to gain advancement for your boy?"

"Perhaps. But I do not lie. If there was a fault in my dealings with your late husband, it was an unwillingness to dissemble."

"If you are so bound to the truth, tell me what is so very special about this bastard you wish to elevate above the descendant of Frederick II. Will he be Capitano, and emperor in turn? Will he change tacks and become pope? What great destiny lies before him?"

"Would that I could say," replied the Moor. "Unlike young master Paride, Francesco's stars are in dispute. There were many portents, and too little observance of them that night. Two stars fell, and no one can say with accuracy which was the dominant."

"Cunning," said Giovanna. "And false."

"It is the truth, but also irrelevant." The Moor set his cup aside. "One point of interest, though. Paride's chart has made a portion of Cesco's history clear. Their fates are intertwined. Not their lives, but their deaths. The demise of one will lead to the death of the other."

The lady stared, then stood and crossed to the far side of the room. "A very convenient prophecy!"

"Madam." He stood and reached into his shirt. At once her steward drew a long dagger, but Tharwat merely produced a scroll. "This is a chart with the certainties of Cesco's life mapped out. I have removed all that is in dispute. I bring this as a gift. I am sure, despite your words, that you have a chart for Paride in your possession. You know what I have said of him to be true. Have your astrologer compare his data with mine. If he has any skill, he will tell you the same. I cannot say when, nor where. Nor can I say which will die first. It may be that Paride's death will lead to Cesco's. I tell you frankly, it is the only reason he is still breathing this night – to keep my charge alive." She turned a startled face to him. "Do you think the poisoning of my charge would have no consequences? I tell you, if Cesco dies from this, Paride will follow within the change of the moon. It does not matter where you hide him. He will die. If not by my hand, by another's. It is in his stars."

"I do not take threats kindly."

"Nor do I. Years ago you tried with all your might to murder this boy, yet he still lives. Now you risk your own chosen heir, and for what? You know his future to be less than—"

"Stellar?" she asked mockingly.

"Best, I think, to let him live his life. The alternative is to force him to a premature death in the name of your family. It will do you no honour. It will bring only disgrace."

The lady no longer watched him, but rather averted her gaze as he watched her. "You realize that, if it is as you say, by saying Paride's life will be short, you are dooming Cesco to the same."

"Yes." It was a humbling point, the worse because it was not as clear as he had made it seem. Always with Cesco there were inconsistencies. But he had not lied to her, strictly speaking.

"I will think about what you say. But if I relent and leave your Cesco unmolested, he will have to make an oath."

"I cannot speak for him."

"Nevertheless, this is the price of my forbearance. Whatever fate brings him in terms of fame, he must share it with my great-nephew. If this bastard's star is ascendant, I will affix Paride to it as to the tail of a comet."

"If he survives, I will speak to him."

"I will wish an interview as well."

"That I can promise."

"If he survives," she added.

"If that."

"You may go."

"Thank you for your hospitality." Leaving the star-chart on the low table, Tharwat bowed and turned to go.

At the door, her voice stopped him. "You have made it a point to be full of truth this evening. Allow me to return the compliment. You say your young ward is poisoned. I swear to you, in the name of your god and my own, in the name of my bloodline, that I had nothing to do with it. Poison may be a woman's weapon, but not one that I have ever employed. Look for the culprit elsewhere."

Bowing again, Tharwat departed the villa, considering.

◆     ◇     ◆

Near dawn, Pietro entered the sickroom. He was struck by an irony – ten years before in this very room, he'd first learned of the prophecy regarding Cesco. That Cesco was the Greyhound. Right here he'd pledged himself to protecting the boy. A task at which he had spectacularly failed.

The night had been trial for everyone. Each had taken turns ministering to Cesco for as long as they could endure. Since returning from his mysterious errand, the Moor hadn't stirred from beside the boy's legs, where his hands worked to keep the circulation flowing. Valentino was curled in a ball in a far corner, asleep. Detto lay on a pile of rushes after finally nodding off. The doctors spoke in tired whispers to a few of Fracastoro's more promising students, summoned to aid them.

The boy in the bed had lost weight overnight. Under the mop of damp curls his face was bloodless. Dark circles hung from his eyes, and his cheeks were sunken and pinched above the swollen jaw. He had been strapped down to restrain him from flailing as the waves of pain consumed him.

Antonia sat on the stool that had been her perch throughout, a book in her lap. Reading aloud in a determined voice, she tried to reach the mind of the invalid whose limp form was tied down to the daybed. Pietro listened to the words. They belonged to her father's epic:

| | |
|---|---|
| *...Al fine de le sue parole il ladro le mani alzo con amendue le fiche, gridando: "Togli, Dio, ch'a te le squadro!"...* | *...Then, making the figs with both his thumbs, the thief raised up his fists and cried: 'Take that, God! It's aimed at you!'...* |

Raised in Pietro's household with the old poet puttering about, little Cesco was well-aquatinted with the verses, which might be comforting. But Pietro wondered in what dreamland the boy wandered, and if the images of demons, fiery rivers, and unspeakable torments were really helping.

Antonia said nothing in greeting as Pietro sat down on Cesco's other side. As she read, he laid a hand on the boy's upper arm, following the Moor's example of rubbing gently on the exposed skin above the bandages and restraints. The doctors continued to whisper on the far side of the room. Otherwise all was silent except for Antonia's voice:

*...Io non li conoscea; ma ei seguette,
come suol seguitar per alcun caso,
che l'un nomar un altro convenette,
dicendo: "Cianfa dove fia rimaso?"...*

*...I knew none of them, yet it happened
as often happens by some chance,
one had cause to speak another's name,
asking: 'What's become of Cianfa?'...*

It was so slight that at first no one noticed. Then Pietro held up a hand, stopping Antonia mid-sentence. The doctors moved closer.

In the bed, the painfully swollen jaw was moving. Then the throat moved, swallowing involuntarily. The mouth moved again.

"*Cianfa...*" came the strangled voice. "*...dove fia...*" Then he sighed, not as one in pain, but as one relaxing from pain.

Pietro made way for Morsicato, who checked the patient's mouth, pulse and breathing. The excited stillness woke Detto and brought him tentatively towards the bed. He looked fearfully from face to face, trying to discern an answer without breaking this magical silence.

Morsicato stood back, letting his compeer in to second his judgments. They whispered briefly back and forth, nodding. It had been Morsicato's plan to use a second dose of deadly poison to cure the boy, so his was the honour of making the final pronouncement:

"He will live."

# SEVENTEEN

*Verona*
*Tuesday, 16 July*
*1325*

"YOU CANNOT GO," the voice said again and again. Perhaps it was more than one voice. It seemed to change in tone and intensity. "You can hardly walk," said the voice, low and gruff. "You have to rest," said the voice, soft and tremulous.

But being voices, they had no hands and so couldn't keep him from rising. How his fingers moved, his arms, his legs, he didn't care to know, so long as they did. He fumbled at the basin but didn't fall over as he washed his neck. He pulled at the loose gown he wore and dropped it to the floor. No, to the rushes. *Be specific.* Modesty was beyond him – nothing was real anyway, least of all his boyish body. Disjointed images with a single voice coming from many throats, saying over and over, "You can't go."

Those words were drowned out by a single, insistent voice inside his pounding head that said he must.

"It's the second dose of poison – it's a stimulant. He wants to be up, awake—"

"I'll stop this."

"No, don't fight him. He could hurt himself struggling—"

"He can't do this, can he?"

He didn't remember dressing, but when he looked down his feet were shod. "Nice shoes," he muttered. *Be specific, earn the right.* "Boots." His arms were encased in a marigold doublet. Beneath it, rough silk touched his chest and shoulders. He took one wobbling step, then another. Still the voice protested, only now it was becoming more distinct. He could swear he knew it. It sounded like his mother's voice. *I've never met my mother.* "I have no mother," he said angrily. *Everybody has a mother. Why are you so angry?* These voices in his head were going to hold him back. *I won't let them.*

He reached the top of the stairs and, without waiting to find his balance, started down.

"Oh Christ! Catch him!" The next thing he knew he was floating, his face up towards the ceiling. "Light as a feather," he laughed. In moments he was on his feet again and the voice was arguing with itself. He giggled.

"What the devil are you doing?" the voice demanded of itself. "He can't be allowed—"

"Tell him that!" the voice growled back.

"He's got to go, if only to be seen. Otherwise we're all dead."

"Bail's right. There are already rumours about poisoning—"

"The servants must have talked—"

"Then tell them the truth, he can't be moved—"

It was amusing to hear the voice yelling at itself. But the voice was boring, the same old tune. Don't let him, he can't, don't tell him, he shouldn't, don't touch him, he'll die. *If I die, don't deny, you'll cry that I never try.*

"Pietro, what do you say?"

*Pietro? I know a Pietro. He's a good man. He lied to me. He doesn't own me. I owe him. But he doesn't get to choose. The future will be. Amen.*

Before him was the door. He lurched for the handle and pulled. The sun was bright and the voice grew in volume as he blinked and saw a hundred faces grinning at him. Oddly, they were all black like the Moor. But the Moor had never cheered him this way. He liked it. He grinned back at the sight of so many funny faces. They cheered more.

"That's done it. Someone, take his arm. Bail, Nico, carve us a path. No, Antonia, you can't come, they won't let you in. Wait here. We won't be long, I promise."

"This will kill him," said his mother's voice in a fading whisper.

"You should be a ventriloquist." This was very funny because he heard laughter, which might only be inside his head. The Moors in the street laughed with him, reaching for him, clutched at him, begging for a scrap of him to take and eat to give them strength. "Plenty to go around!" It didn't sound right so he said it again in a funny tongue. "There will be plenty for all. Raisins for virgins, please."

"What's he saying?" demanded his father's voice. *I've never met my father.*

"He's delirious."

"This is madness," said his father's voice again.

"Papa Pietro," said Cesco.

"What? Did he just say my name?"

"Keep him moving."

Time was blurry, and Cesco felt like vomiting. The laughing and the waving went on and on and on. Then it was over and he was sitting in a cool chamber, a chill creeping up over his skin as someone mopped his brow. *I feel funny. Grandpa Dante, where's my head?* He reached up and felt for it. "Somebody, help me find my head."

There was a sharp pinch. The world snapped into sharp focus before receding into fog once more. But the pain had showed him the way, giving him a solid foundation for his sensations. He dug his fingernails into his palms. He ground his teeth, then bit his tongue. The sickening feeling of being tossed in a flowing river didn't go away, but he was able to think. *I'm Cesco, and this is — this is true. Time to wake up.*

The fog was still before his eyes, but it was entertaining, in its way. Shapes rose and fell in languid succession, some foreign, some familiar. Sound was easier to maintain than sight, so he let his eyelids fall shut as he listened to his own breath, his pulse. Had his heart always hammered this way?

Closing his eyes seemed to open his ears, as voices became distinct and clear.

"Ho, Pietro," said a polished voice Cesco didn't know.

"Mari." Uncle Pietro, warm with affection. An embrace, then the smooth voice said, "You know we're with you."

"I'm grateful."

"Gianozza sends her love."

There was a hesitation in Pietro's voice. "My sister is here. I'm sure she'd like to see your wife."

"Excellent! And you must come see my son! He's four and brilliant!"

*Brilliant?* wondered Cesco. *Does he glow?*

"I'd be honoured. When all this is settled."

"Of course! You can come see him after Cesco is elected Capitano."

"If we're all still alive," said a third voice, gruff and vaguely menacing.

Cesco opened his eyes and discovered his vision had improved a little. First he noticed he was sitting up on a dais, resting on a Roman-style chair. No back. *How am I sitting upright? Oh.* The Moor was at one elbow, the doctor at the other. It was the doctor who had pinched him. "Thank you." The doctor didn't seem to hear. *Did I even say it out loud? Can they hear me? Am I spirit or flesh?*

At the foot of the dais stood three men. Pietro was at the center. On his right hand stood a man of middle height who was very pretty. *Be specific, and you will be poetic.* Dante's advice. So, specifics – the man had shiny black hair and eyes as blue as snow at midnight. His features might have been delicately carved by an ancient sculptor for use in a temple to Apollo. His clothes were rich – *no, sumptuous, better word* – perfectly tailored, all in expensively dark colours.

He and Uncle Pietro were facing the newcomer, a man with shoulders so broad they made him look shorter than he really was. Almost a full head taller than Pietro, he had sandy-blonde hair and a beard with faint touches of red. His clothes were just as fine as the pretty one's, but had crossed the river of ostentation. *That isn't bad. I need to write that down. May I have some paper?*

"Antony." Uncle Pietro sounded vexed as he embraced the big man. Pretty man and big guy weren't hiding their antipathy. *Anti pathee. Auntie Pathino. Hmm.* Cesco's slowed brain finally realized who they had to be. *Mariotto Montecchio and Antonio Capulletto.* Former best friends, before Montecchio had run off with Capulletto's betrothed. Cesco had heard the story many times at the knee of Pietro's father. *How dark is it in Santafiora?*

Cesco faded away for a moment, and was surprised to return in the midst of a conversation. "...Magagnato,Villafranca, and Cristofoletto – all of them with us, with all their clients' wealth behind them. Thanks to my assurances that you were in the right."

"Thank you, Antony," said Pietro.

Montecchio scoffed. "Not that it was such a feat, convincing them. Pietro's got the army, both Nogarola brothers, Castelbarco, Bonaventura, and me behind him. And, out of the blue, Giovanna sent a letter of support this morning. It doesn't take much to see where the die has fallen."

"And what have you done, pipsqueak? Sat in your tower and waited to see who would win, same as always. Never willing to risk your own neck—"

Uncle Pietro was grinding teeth. "All of us are here to swear our allegiance to Cangrande's heir.That is proof enough of our commitment." Had Uncle Pietro learned to throw is voice? *No. I see. It was Castelbarco who spoke. And now they're looking at me. Smile! Wave!*

His head was fogging again but there was enough of his usual poise present to realize this was his moment. Cesco took a breath, hoping his voice would appear this time. "I was enjoying learning the ways of a courtier inVerona. Ravenna lacks this —" *be specific!* "— sophistication."

Uncle Pietro winced but it got laughs from the crowd. Montecchio looked rueful. Capulletto swallowed a scowl. *Picking on these two to win the others. Poor leadership. Bad orphan! Bad orphan!* But it was about as subtle as he could manage at the moment. His stomach was twisting and it took all his will not to clutch at it and retch. He dug his nails harder into his palms.

"That's the boy?" asked Capulletto. "I'd've thought Cangrande's son would be better fleshed."

"Not all of us can be built like aged oxen," retorted Montecchio.

"Aged!" sputtered Capulletto, but Montecchio pressed on. "He's probably just sick from laughing at your poor beard."

"At least I'm man enough to grow one…"

"The Triumvirs," muttered Uncle Pietro. "Together again."

Castelbarco said something and in moments the whole of the Anziani were seated on benches on either side of the dais. Before they vanished in another wave of dizzying fog, Cesco noticed that each the feuders were trying to draw Pietro to sit by them. Instead he remained standing close at hand with the Moor and the doctor.

*Thank you for not leaving me. But I can do this without you. I have to. So go away. Just don't leave me.*

Castelbarco's soothing voice droned on and on. Cesco forced his eyes to remain open, if half-lidded. He heard little of the oration, saw less. In his eyes were dragons and centaurs and vipers, all doing battle in a brown and orange haze. *What about unicorns? I want unicorns!* Then he realized he was staring at a tapestry. There were stitched rabbits doing battle with embroidered knights, with tiny demons hidden in the woven wood, egging the battle on. *I preferred the visions.*

Castelbarco was talking about an oath, and the mutters around the hall sounded favourable. Cesco reflected amusedly that the only thing keeping these noble men from swearing their undying oath to Cangrande's heir was the heir himself, sitting like a lump, half-dead, sweating and unmoving. *I should leap up and do some cartwheels for them. That is, if I could feel my feet. Can I even move my shoulders?* Only the sure grip of the Moor held him upright. *This chair is uncomfortable. Would they mind if I slip down and curl into a ball on the cool mosaic floor and die? Yes, they probably would mind that.*

One face briefly roused him from his reverie. A thin patrician nose cleaved a pair of eyes that were boring into him. The man wore a black robe, and it took Cesco several seconds to recognize the badge of Venice on it. Seeing himself scrutinized in return, the man gave Cesco a slight bow. Cesco winked at him, and grinned at the three-headed pixie next to him. The pixie waved back.

Cesco heard the doors open, and blinked at the influx of thick light. Out of the murky fantastic shapes of his fancy came a single visage, a solid dark face filled with malice.

Cesco was on his feet before he knew it, his voice ringing around the marble pillars and mosaic tiles. "Cousin! Here I am! Devilish forces do what they dare, I keep my word."

A fainting spell almost took him as he finished speaking, yet it didn't cheat him of the sight of Mastino's face. The Mastiff was framed by the open doors, gazing at the living Cesco, Nemesis personified.

The whole room came into focus. He felt sharp as a dagger. *It can't last! Make the most of it.*

The hall was silent with anticipation. The Mastiff slipped the gauntlets from his fingers and handed them to a servant, then strode to the center of the hall. "I never doubted you, cousin. It is those you serve whom I mistrust. Come, let us embrace and show these men that the blood of Cangrande cannot be turned against itself."

Pietro reached out a hand, but Cesco ignored him and took the three steps down from the dais. "Apt! The Greyhound's blood is stronger than even I knew." He felt his knees buckling, so he turned his stride into a low bow and knelt at Mastino's feet, arms outstretched. "Come, cousin!"

Mastino had no choice but to kneel as well. On the floor he did not have the pronounced advantage of height, and they were easily able to kiss each other's cheeks. Mastino started to rise, but Cesco put a hand on his cousin's shoulder and lifted himself back to his feet first, praising a merciful God above that his balance had returned.

Cesco made to return to the dais, only to find Mastino's hand restraining him. "That seat belongs to the Capitano of Verona, boy. Cangrande's heir you may be, but the people have not voted in their assemblies. Until they do, that seat is rightfully mine."

"If wishing made it so," said Cesco lightly. The vicious strength of Mastino's grip was a blessing, a new focus that distracted Cesco from the wicked nausea and the pain in his lungs, his guts, his head.

Without releasing his hold on Cesco, Mastino addressed the assembled nobility. "I have agreed to debate the future of this city, but I insist on taking my rightful place."

Castelbarco and Pietro opened their mouths to reply, but Cesco got in first. "I may be wrong – I *am* very young – but I think 'rightful' is the debated point." *If the seat is what you want, you can't have it.*

"Child, you have so many friends, allow me this one victory. A salve on my conscience," insisted Mastino in a commendably cheerful voice. Only Cesco was close enough to see the vein at Mastino's temple throbbing. *Can I make it burst?*

"I would, my ancient cousin, but where else can I sit? It's the only place in the whole hall where I can be seen." This was greeted with laughter.

"You have such a tongue, they would heed you wherever you sit, little master."

"And you have an ass' bray, cousin. They couldn't miss your 'nay nay nay!'"

It just slipped out. *Stupid!* He'd given Mastino the first victory by resorting to overt insolence. The red flush on his foe's face was pleasure, not anger. "A pity your teachers couldn't school you in manners."

"I learn from each new host in turn. Your hospitality hides poisoned strokes in honeyed words." *Did you do this to me? Come on, you can tell me, you want to!*

Mastino frowned. "You see poison where there is none, cousin. Nor honey. I am neither sour nor sweet. I simply am."

*That's not a denial! But, no, you would tell me. You couldn't resist. You didn't do this. But you see it, don't you? You can see there's something wrong in here. Well, go on! Say something! Taunt me again, so I can tear you to —*

Mastino suddenly redoubled the strength of his grip on Cesco's arm, then stepped back. Released, pain shot through Cesco and he nearly collapsed. Somehow he turned his gasp into a laugh. "Do you recoil at my touch, cousin? Am I so fearful?"

"I only fear the devil, boy."

"Then I shall call myself Devil-boy." The crowd laughed. *Mastino is losing an argument with a child. And thus I've found my theme!* Cesco started to sing. "Devil-boy, where are you – roaming?"

"Very droll."

"Don't you see your dog's mouth – foaming?" *Louder!*

"Do you want to be Capitano or Master of Revels?"

"Don't you fear the pain of – stoning?" *Play to the back!*

"Enough!" shouted Mastino over the clapping and laughing nobility. His calm was disappearing as the mirth grew. *Oh, you don't like being laughed at? A shame! Because a prince will always lose to a clown.*

Guglielmo da Castelbarco tried to take control of the situation. "If you please, masters, we have grave matters to discuss."

"Grave is the word," echoed Cesco.

Mastino turned on his new target. "I will not discuss them with a traitor."

Castelbarco was prepared to be called names. "I am a loyal son of Verona, my lord."

"You're a traitor, and these good men of the Anziani should know it. I don't care how many witnesses you drag forward, that will was forged. You've pulled the wool over the council's eyes – except maybe da Lozzo the turncoat and Bonaventura the lecher. I wonder what you promised them. Land? Gold? Whores?" Nico and Petruchio reddened in anger, but Mastino kept talking. "And for Montecchio and Capulletto to work together – well, perhaps they've finally reached an agreement on how to share the lovely Lady Montecchio. Does Capulletto get her on feast days?"

Montecchio gripped his stool hard to keep him from leaping up and throwing blows. Across the aisle, Capulletto managed to rise a few inches despite the hands of four men holding him back.

Castelbarco said, "Ser Mastino, a few days ago you were filled with sweet words, abasing yourself before this council. Now you seem to be alienating the great men of Verona just when you need them most. That isn't wise from a man who has usurped the rights of another."

"One man's usurper is another man's rightful heir. Why should I care what the council thinks? It wasn't me who abandoned the Anziani – the Anziani abandoned me. Some purported bastard shows up filled with pretty speeches learned by rote at the knee of a poet, and the great men leave their patriotic duty to embrace a myth, a puppet, a tool. Whose creature is he, Lord Castelbarco? Yours? Ser Alaghieri's? My Lord Nogarola's?"

"I am the Greyhound's heir, cousin." Close to falling down, Cesco had only moments more to give. *I have to strike, make my mark, then get out before I damage my cause. But how?*

"Cousin or no, you are a child, a creature of other men." Dismissing Cesco, Mastino addressed the council. "Masters, I say the Capitano's seat is mine."

Cesco turned to the crowd, managing a smile. "Masters, the will says it is mine."

A third voice boomed all around the hall. "And I, masters, say it's mine!"

Heads turned. The German mercenaries had retreated from the open doors, leaving a tall figure framed against the sunlight streaming in. A single sweep and the muffling cloak and floppy hat were cast aside. Taller than any in the chamber, Taller than any in the chamber, the intruder grinned at them, his chestnut hair cut close to his skull, his cornflower blue eyes twinkling maliciously.

Benches and stools scraped the tiles as men all around the chamber stood starting, gasping, laughing in relief. Many said his name, but Cesco didn't need to be told. He knew at once. *Father!* He started to say it aloud, but the title stuck in his throat.

Cangrande della Scala had returned.

# EIGHTEEN

"THAT BASTARD! I'm such a fool! I should have checked. I should have gone myself, seen his body, held up a mirror to his lips, sewed his nose shut, and buried him twenty feet under the earth before I even *thought* of bringing Cesco here! *Bastard!*"

"Well, Pietro, you've always said he's more fox than hound."

"Joke all you like, Antonia, this is a disaster!"

The two siblings were in the stony kitchens of the Nogarola house at the end of that very long day. Cesco was in bed upstairs, forced into restful slumber by Morsicato's poppy draught. Detto and Valentino, exhausted, had fallen asleep where they sat at dinner. The Moor was asleep too, unknowingly given a touch of Cesco's sleeping potion in his wine. Bail was off feasting with Cangrande and the rest of the jubilant nobility – all except Federigo della Scala, who was probably on his way out of Verona as fast as his horse could carry him.

Pietro had declined the invitation to dinner, pleading his charge's exhaustion as his excuse to escape the nightmare he found himself living. But after a whole day and night without food, he was famished. So he now carved hunks of roast lamb off a spit that rested over a cookfire in the warm, dimly-lit kitchen.

Sitting upright on a stool, Antonia said, "Tell me what happened."

Chewing, Pietro paced the kitchen floor, his words seasoned with bitterness. "He just strode in with a smile – that smile! – and pretended to be shocked at the goings-on."

"Don't let it upset you." Antonia calmly poured him out more thin wine from a clay pot.

"Don't let it..?! He was playing with us all! Because of him, Cesco almost died!"

"But he didn't. Cangrande won't do anything to hurt Cesco."

Pietro stopped and pointed a finger at her. "There you're wrong. He won't kill Cesco, true. But there are other ways to wound."

Antonia saw his eyes drift off again into darkness. Determined not to let him brood, she pressed the stone cup into his hand. "So tell me, what happened then?"

"The Anziani all stood and cheered, of course. Lasted an hour, it felt like. Then he walked over and sat in the chair that all the fuss had been over. He moved so calmly, so gracefully. Asked if anything interesting had happened while he'd been away. Everyone laughed."

"What did Cesco do?"

"Just stood and stared at Cangrande. I can't imagine what he was thinking. But Cangrande ignored him, so Cesco bowed his head and came to stand with me. I'm not sure how he was even conscious. Tharwat got a stool for him to sit on and we hid him between us while he closed his eyes."

"And Cangrande didn't say anything about him?"

"Not directly. He listened while Castelbarco outlined everything that had happened. Passerino Bonaccolsi, who arrived with him – he had to be a part of the deception. Another bastard. Anyway, Passerino stood by the doors and laughed the whole time. Then Cangrande called for his cousin Federigo. Bonaventura and Nogarola dragged Federigo up in front of the dais, and Cangrande publicly accused him of instigating the rumour of his death and starting what he called 'a war between children.' Then, before anyone could suggest Federigo be hanged, Cangrande said he was hungry and invited everyone to join him for a homecoming feast at the palace. Word had spread all over the city by then. The people were all coming to see Cangrande for themselves. The usual forum frequenters were outnumbered two to one in the crush. We smuggled Cesco past them and back here."

"And the Anziani accepted Federigo's guilt, just because Cangrande said so?"

Pietro snorted. "Of course they did. Even Mari and Antony bought it. The great man sacrificed his cousin to give the city just what it wanted – someone to blame for all the trouble. You and I know it's nonsense. Cangrande orchestrated it all. Damn his eyes!"

"Wait." Antonia held up a hand. "What do you mean, he was behind it all. Cangrande?"

Pietro's laugh was almost a spasm. "You had it right back on the road. Someone was flushing us out, you said. That's what he did."

"But he already knew where we were."

"Don't be dense!"

"Don't shout at me!"

Pietro scrubbed his hands over his face. "Sorry. *Sorry.* It's like this. Cangrande made a bargain with his sister and with me that he wouldn't send for Cesco until the boy reached his majority. By faking his death, he didn't break the agreement – he let us break it for him. Brilliant, isn't it? Cesco was supposed to live in Ravenna until he was fifteen. But now the world knows he's alive, he can't go back. His life would be in constant danger. As the fire was supposed to demonstrate."

"Cangrande—?"

"—set the fire, I'm sure of it." Pietro made a face. "I thought it was Giovanna or Mastino. Of course it was Cangrande."

"What about the poison? Who did that?"

That brought Pietro up short. "Honestly? I don't think that was him – too unsubtle. But it could have been any of them. The Moor says he's ruled out Giovanna. If I had to guess, my money would be on Mastino."

"But the curse – you said no one in the family would raise a hand against his own blood."

"They can't take Cesco's life, no. But they can hurt him. The curse is specific. Ten years ago Pathino refused to kill the boy, but he was perfectly willing to cut Cesco's eyes out." Antonia shivered, and Pietro pressed on. "I wonder if Cangrande isn't thinking along the same lines. Cesco is protected by a prophecy – he can't die until he faces the leopard, the lion, and the she-wolf, whatever they are. So if his life is in no danger, why not poison him? Cangrande knows that Cesco won't die yet, so there's no risk of incurring the curse."

Antonia considered this for a time. "You owe Poco an apology. We both do."

Pietro sagged. "If he'll even speak to us. If I'd thought about it for even a moment, I'd have realized that if Mastino knew, he would have been better prepared to face us. Damn me for a fool! I should have seen it. This was Cangrande's plan all along. There's no way to hide Cesco now. That curtain's been torn away. Damn him!"

"Aren't you giving him a little too much credit?"

Pietro laughed sourly. "You've never dealt with him, you don't know how his mind works. I thought I was a cynic. Turns out I'm not cynical enough. I just can't keep up."

"Pietro, it was Cangrande who insisted that Cesco be taken away. He's never tried to have anything to do with raising the boy, even before Ravenna."

"He plays a long game. Silver-tongued bastard! Why did I believe him? After everything I heard that night, all the precautions I took to keep him safe…" Pietro stilled for a moment, his expression searching. "Did she believe him, too? No, she had to – but then he was so damn triumphant, maybe she never saw that it was another game. And I never dreamed – I had eight years and I still didn't see it. He just wanted Cesco out of Katerina's hands until he was old enough – eleven is the right age to become a page or a squire. His father's squire," he added bitterly.

Antonia didn't understand all of her brother's rant, but his self-beratement made her reach out a hand to comfort him. "Pietro, he couldn't have planned this all out. Not back then."

"You spent, what, two years here at court? Was he ever anything but charming and in control? Did anything ever not go his way?"

"Well, no, but you've told me—"

"Yes, somehow, I'm not sure how it happened, but I got to glimpse something close to the real creature that lies under that golden skin. And for that knowledge, I get to be a puppet that can see his strings. But only after he's made me dance!" He slammed his fists onto the chopping block, sloshing some liquid out of the stone cup. His shoulders slumped and he rested his head on the gashed wood. "Everything's gone just as he planned it. As always."

Antonia hugged him, laying her head on his back. "No matter why he did it, Cesco still got to live with us and father for eight years. He has that solid core, a family that loves him."

Pietro was unmoving, unmoved. "He has the Scaliger's wildness."

"Yes, he does – but look how he uses it. He teased you into not tithing the poor, even though you both knew what it would cost you." Pietro's head came up and he turned to face her. "Father told me. I know it bothers you, but you made the right choice. Cesco was a part of that. However sharp he is, however cruel his tongue, he has a good heart. That, he got from you. He's Cangrande's blood, but he is your son."

That broke him. Pietro began to weep. Waiting for just this, Antonia took her brother's face in her hands. "Shhh."

"Not mine, not now. He's *theirs*." Tears ran down his cheeks. He ceased being able to speak for some time. Holding him, Antonia pondered everything Pietro had told her about the relationship between Cangrande and his sister, and wondered how it could have gone so wrong, and why.

When the tears were done and he had drunk some wine, they faced each other. Hiccoughing, Pietro smiled wanly. "What would I do without you?"

"You'll never need to know. Suor Beatrice will always have time for her big brother."

He took her hand. "And we have to make sure we'll always be

there for him."

"We will."

There was a pause while both of them followed different paths of thought. Suddenly Pietro said, "There was one fly in Cangrande's ointment today."

"What?"

"Dandolo. He didn't like the Venetian's presence. They've never gotten along. Cangrande and I once had a long talk about him. And he was right, Dandolo is definitely the coming man in Venice. I don't think Cangrande liked the way Dandolo was staring at Cesco."

"You mean…?"

"Oh no, not in a lecherous way. I suppose Cangrande would approve of that, if only to belittle Cesco. No, Dandolo's look was more… pensive." Antonia was about to voice her opinion of Dandolo, but Pietro got in first. "Listen. I'm probably going to be sent away."

Antonia's spine straightened. "What?"

"Cangrande will find a reason. He certainly won't want me here to interfere with whatever he has in mind for Cesco. Tharwat, too. And Morsicato will be sent back to Vicenza. But there's a slim chance he'll let you stay. He doesn't know you, might not see you as a threat. If he does try to send you away, make up some religious reason – an oath to God, something about Cesco's spiritual salvation. Tell him in front of witnesses. He won't be able to deny you, not if he wants to keep face with the church. Just don't cross him directly and you should be all right." Pietro stopped talking with words still hanging between them.

"What is it?"

"If – if he thinks you are too much in the way, too troublesome, he may have you killed. It would look like an accident, of course. You won't see it coming and we'll never be able to trace it back to him. There's no way to prepare for it except to be cautious." Pietro's mind was racing now. "We need to find you some kind of guard or companion. Someone local and inviolable who doesn't owe him anything."

"I don't want a guard," said Antonia with a touch of her usual stubbornness.

"I don't care what you want. I care what keeps you alive." He was back to being her big brother. "Cangrande isn't the only threat. I wouldn't trust Giovanna, no matter what Tharwat says. And Mastino might hurt you just to get to Cesco. From now on, they're blood enemies."

"You're a bundle of sunshine, you are."

"What are big brothers for?"

There was a respectful cough from the door as a servant entered. "Ser Alaghieri? The Venetian Ambassador requests an audience."

"With me?" Not being the master of this house, it seemed odd. "Tell him I'll wait on him in just a moment." When the servant exited, Pietro said, "Speak of the devil and he appears."

Antonia's face was grim. "Dandolo? Why is he asking for you?"

"He must know Bail's out celebrating. He met me in Vicenza years ago, and again when I was in Venice looking for Pathino." He sighed and started for the door. "Best go see what he – where are you going?"

"To meet the ambassador," said Antonia.

The dark glint in her eye allowed Pietro to divine her intent. "Antonia, no!" he hissed, reaching out to stop her.

Too late. She was already striding towards the receiving room. Damning his limp, Pietro raced after her. From the far room he heard her address Dandolo, first by his title, then with an additional name. "Murderer."

Pietro reached the door just in time to see Dandolo's reaction. Not shocked surprise. The regal figure simply arched an eyebrow at Antonia, then bowed. "Forgive the intrusion, Ser Alaghieri. I called to pay my respects to you and your charge."

"A little late for respect to our family," replied Antonia coldly.

"It is true, the hour is late. But keeping you from your rest, does that qualify me as a murderer?"

Before Antonia could clarify, Pietro said in his sharpest voice, "Antonia, be silent. Ambassador, forgive my sister. You are most welcome here. I regret to say that the events of the last few days have worn Francesco to exhaustion. I'm sure he'd wish to meet you, but he cannot receive visitors just now."

"Entirely understandable. Young constitutions are unpredictable, but resilient. I'm sure he will be in robust health tomorrow. I will entrust my goodwill to you, and you may pass it on as you please. Also, this gift." He removed a silver globe from a satchel and rested it on a table. After so many years with Tharwat, Pietro instantly recognized the etched constellations. "Great men need to be aware of their stars."

"You are too kind." As Dandolo made no motion to exit, Pietro sat and gestured the ambassador to join him. Antonia remained on her feet, glowering.

Crossing his legs, Dandolo straightened his gonella over his knees. "So tell me, Ser Alaghieri – what did you think of today's miraculous events?"

"I could hardly believe my eyes," said Pietro neutrally.

"Yes. In terms of the strife that was brewing, it was the most fortuitous of outcomes. And now the Scaliger has an heir."

"Pardon me, but he always had an heir."

"Ah, of course. But an acknowledged scion to carry on for him, that will be a great comfort to the people of Verona and Ghibellines everywhere. You have done him a great service. I am just glad it was my humble person who was deputed to Verona, so that I might witness the joyful reunion of father and son."

Antonia snorted. "Was it decided in committee who would come?"

"Actually, yes. It is the Venetian way." Dandolo turned his smooth, smiling features back to Pietro. "Ser Alaghieri, please tell me how I have offended the charming and pious Suor Beatrice, so that I may make amends."

"You can't—" began Antonia, but Pietro held up a hand and she clamped her mouth shut. Pietro looked Dandolo in the eye. "Antonia blames you for the death of our father."

Now came the shock, however feigned. "I? Responsible for the death of the great Dante? I am horrified!"

Fuming, Antonia had herself mostly under control. "Four years ago you were on the council he negotiated with. You remember – he was there to plead navigation rights on the Po for Ravenna."

"Yes, I met the man that once, for an hour. Most of that time, I spent in admiration of his talents. Why on earth would that connect me with his death?"

"Not only did you ignore his petition, you refused him safe passage on the way home."

"As I recall," said Dandolo, "he arrived safely in Ravenna."

"After having been forced to travel through a swamp! The *mala aria* took him, the marsh fever, the ague. He died of it!"

"Oh dear. I had not heard how he died. That is dreadful. I know it is belated, but please allow me to give my condolences for such a loss, which clearly still grieves you."

"Thank you." Pietro matched the man's diplomatic tones. "We are fortunate that he finished his epic poem. He died knowing his life's work was safe in the hands of posterity."

Antonia rounded on her brother. "Pietro, how can you stand here and be civil to the man who murdered our father!"

"Murder is a harsh term, *Suora*," said Dandolo.

"What else is it when you cause a man's death?"

"Politics," replied Dandolo simply. "For all that we respected him, nay, honoured his genius, he was in Venice as the representative of Ravenna. We must be firm in our dealings with our neighbours. They have armies. We have none. So we Venetians must use our trade routes as—"

"Weapons," finished Antonia.

"Levers," corrected Dandolo gently. "Ravenna was illegally using our routes. We couldn't allow the Ravennese ambassador return by those same routes they were trespassing upon. In this case, we treated the man according to the office he held, not according to his desserts. I am stricken to think it caused him any ill, much less led to his death. It is a loss for all posterity."

Dandolo's speech was a deliberate misstatement of the facts. Venice owned a powerful army, but on ships, policing the waterways of its territories and exacting an extortionate fee from any non-Venetian vessel. Moved by the plight of the Ravennese, urged by Guido Novello, Dante had agreed to use his way with words to bring relief to the port town. Pietro had joined in, throwing his weight behind Novello, speaking of justice and the law. Dante had died from the journey home.

Pietro wished he could blame Dandolo the way Antonia did. But things were never that simple. It wasn't as if he'd been poisoned. Unlike the plight of the boy upstairs, illness was illness.

Dandolo rose. "Ser Alaghieri, pardon me. I did not realize that my presence was unwelcome. I came only to inquire after the health of the boy. Forgive me for saying it, but he did not look at all well this morning. I thought perhaps he himself had a touch of the ague, and came prepared to offer my own physician. I am glad to hear such offers are unnecessary. I will leave this house in peace." He faced Antonia. "Lady, I had no idea you held me personally responsible for your father's death. Had I known, I would never have intruded upon your peace. I assure you, my grief at the death of Dante is second only to his children's. I hope some day I will be able to prove my sincerity on that score." He didn't try to take her hand. Instead he bowed to them both and departed.

Pietro saw the Venetian out, then returned. "Oh, well done. Are we going to plan a war with all of Venice, or just Dandolo?"

"Pietro, the members of that council caused father's death."

"True or not, telling him so doesn't help. We gain nothing. You've been worried about Cesco, and you vented your spleen on Dandolo."

"I don't trust him."

"A bit unforgiving for a nun in training, don't you think? No, please! I'm not looking for a fight. After what I said to Poco, you're all the family I have left. I'm going to look in on Cesco."

Antonia let out a long breath. "You need to get some sleep. You look worse than he does."

"Well, I deserve to, don't I?"

◆     ◊     ◆

Lighting a taper, Pietro climbed the stairs heavily. His sister was right, he was exhausted. He hadn't really slept in three days. Too much happening too fast, no time to think, only to react. Just as it had been planned.

*But now all the pieces are on the board. If it's an uneven game, at least we know the players. And Cesco is a prize worth playing for.*

Reaching the sickroom, Pietro swung the door wide and entered. The windows were covered, blocking out even the light of the night sky, and his eyes strained to find the boy in the bed. He heard a low voice from within. Drugged into sleep, Cesco was mumbling, "He's – no, my father – he's not…"

Carrying his lit taper, Pietro sat down beside the bed and brushed the hair from Cesco's face. "Shh, Cesco. It's all right. It's all right."

"He can't hear you."

Jumping out of his seat, Pietro turned so fast the taper guttered and almost went out. In the dim light he could see a figure lounging on the far side of the room. But he didn't need to see the face. Pietro remembered the voice all too well. "I didn't have a chance earlier. Welcome back."

Cangrande della Scala stepped into the light, his famous smile bright and open. "It should be raining, don't you think? Portentous, with thunder and lightning and eavesdroppers galore."

"It seems you took that role for yourself, my lord. What has he been saying?"

"He's been singing alleluias for your triumphant return to Verona." As Pietro made no reply, Cangrande's smile grew. "What, nothing? You've waited all these years to speak your mind, now nary a word. I'm disappointed."

"I don't have my father's way with words. My voice is lying here in the bed. The Greyhound will speak for me." In the dim light it was hard to tell, but Pietro was gratified to think Cangrande stiffened at that. "Aren't you supposed to be enjoying a homecoming feast?"

"I slipped away to fornicate. But the girl was drunk, and a whore to boot, so I came here to find fresher meat. How old is your sister now?"

It was a colossal insult, begging for a duel or an angry blow. Pietro controlled himself, barely. Years of living with Cesco had taught him the best counter to a verbal assault was to laugh. "You were subtler once. What exactly happened at Ponte Corbo?"

Pietro managed not to step back as the thirty-four year old master of Verona shot forward, barely restraining himself from the blow he had been goading Pietro into. Certain this, too, was a ruse, Pietro stared back, noting in the light of the taper how the great man had changed.

In size, Cangrande had both grown and diminished. His six foot two frame was more heavily muscled now, arms and chest thicker. Yet the swelling of the body had lessened the effect of the man. The old Cangrande had been stylishly lean, a true greyhound in form. Now he was more a bulky mastiff. Most tellingly, the face was heavier, burying those cornflower eyes in creased skin. Even the chestnut hair had been cropped short. Perhaps to hide some creeping silver?

Rage dissipating as swiftly as it had come, Cangrande nodded. "*Quel changement... quantum mutatus ab illo Hectore!* Everyone alters, and few for the better. What happened at Ponte Corbo, you ask? You must have heard the tales. I imitated you, my boy. I took an arrow to the leg and fainted dead away."

Pietro looked up into those clear blue eyes. "I don't recall ever running from a battle, my lord. Or leaving my army behind. What happened to those fourteen standards?"

"These stories do get around. But then, you hear everything, don't you? I appreciated your information about the mines, by the way. I was able to come into a great deal of copper cheaply."

"I do my duty, my lord."

"As true as my horse, more rabid than my hounds." Cangrande sat on a stool beside Cesco's bed. Pietro shifted uncomfortably. "O don't be an old woman! *Sanguis meus.* You of all people know how I honour an oath."

"To the letter."

Hearing Pietro's bitterness, Cangrande laughed. The old wonderful laugh. Like a tidal pool, everything was sucking Pietro back to memories he feared.

"So you figured it out? Well done! Better late than never. Perhaps lack of sleep dulls your wits. You look even more tired than you did on the road." The Scaliger grinned. "What, you don't remember? The woman in the coach?" Pushing his chest out, folding his hands in his lap, he was suddenly the exact posture of the busty woman they had passed leaving Ravenna. "How did I look as a red-head? The bosoms, alas, were false, yet I could not refrain from fondling them. Awkward. Thank Heaven Passerino wasn't there! But I had to keep an eye on you, Pietro. Your efforts are always so inept!" He waved a hand at the limp form in the bed. "I look at your handiwork and weep. But of course, it doesn't matter. He cannot die. The stars say so."

"He can feel pain. And fear. And hate."

The brows lifted. "What is that, to me? Our mythic beast can join the human race for a while. The least he can do, don't you think?"

Cesco muttered something unintelligible. Pietro knew what it was to hear conversations while in a fever, so he chose his words carefully. "The whole world, including him, knows that you are *Il Veltro*, and a great man. Perhaps someday you will try to live up to their expectations."

"Watch your tongue, boy. I've given you a fair lead, but be warned, insolence doesn't amuse me anymore."

"Did it ever?" Trembling inwardly, Pietro stepped around the bed to sit on the far side. "If that's true, I guess I have nothing more to say to you, my lord."

"Perhaps I ought to keep you around here with him. Teach you both how to be men."

"You won't," said Pietro simply.

"And why not?"

"Because you want him all to yourself."

Cangrande nodded happily. "That I do. Well, not all to myself. My little Mastiff can have a nip at him now and then."

"Is that why you threw Federigo to the wolves? To create a war between your heirs?"

"What good is a war if one side can't be here to fight it. It took a decade, but you're learning."

"What have I learned?"

"To think like one of the family." Reaching across the bed, Cangrande chucked Pietro under the chin.

"Does that mean I'll start poisoning children?"

"If you have any of your own, feel free. But let ours be." Cangrande stretched. "Ah, a very enjoyable day. I do love a crowd. I should have been in the theatre."

"Might have been better for us all," agreed Pietro.

"Now now, don't pout. You'll see him from time to time. Oh, and it may edify you to learn that I had nothing at all to do with the poison. Nor is Mastino so subtle. I understand you have ruled out my darling wife. So look elsewhere."

"I should just believe you?"

"Truly, I don't much care what you believe. But ask yourself – would I have gone to all this trouble to get my hands on a weak and sickly child? What would be the point of that? When you find you have no answer to that question, answer this – what if it wasn't any of us? What if someone was attempting to do to me what I was doing – bring the hidden to light? What, I wonder, did Dandolo *really* want here tonight?" With that Cangrande gave a little bow and, humming a jaunty tune, exited.

Pietro sank back limply. *He's changed! He knows it, too. Good lord, could a single humiliation in the field do all that?*

*No,* said the voice that spoke with Dante's voice. *It was the war of his youth that made him the thing he is now.*

Absently stroking Cesco's mop of curls, Pietro prayed he'd given the boy a solid enough foundation. Because from today forward, nothing would be easy ever again.

# NINETEEN

THE WHOLE OF VERONA clamored for a celebration of this newfound Scaliger, Cangrande's heir. They heard with sympathy that the young man had taken a slight illness from so much exertion, and the doctors insisted that any public event should be postponed until the boy was truly well again. All the more time to prepare!

Meanwhile, a carefree Cangrande went about the affairs of state – addressing crowds, paying his army, hearing major court cases. Together with his best friend Passerino Bonaccolsi, the lord of Mantua, he told a harrowing tale of Paduan murder-plots, midnight escapes, disguises, all leading to his triumphant return. The fact that none of it was true made Passerino even more joyous. Cangrande went so far as to tell his fool, old Manuel the Jew, to compose an epic ballad commemorating his 'resurrection.'

On a darker note, Cangrande was forced to imprison his cousin Federigo, who had foolishly not chosen flight. Into the cells with Federigo went his sons and close friends, their lands stripped and sold off to fill the public coffers. When asked for the whereabouts of Mastino and Alberto, Cangrande laughed and said he'd sent them to be grave-diggers for a fortnight, that they might recognize a dead man when they saw one. Whenever someone brought up the subject of his natural child, he smiled and asked, "Which one? There are so many…"

♦     ◊     ♦

Three days after Cangrande's return, Cesco awoke completely lucid for the first time. He gulped down the water Antonia held out. "I suppose I must be alive," he croaked. "Death couldn't smell this bad."

Antonia smiled. "As soon as the doctors say you can get out of bed, we'll burn the bedding – it's the only way, I think, to revive the room."

"Only if you burn me with it," he muttered weakly, setting the water aside and wrinkling up his nose.

"You've been burning up enough the last few days," said Morsicato, rising from a chair where he'd been napping. He was disheveled, the twin forks of his beard jutting out at odd angles.

"You look worse than I feel."

"You smell worse than I look." The doctor leaned down to take the boy's pulse. "Do you want food?"

"A bath," said Cesco distinctly.

"You *want* a bath, you *need* food. Let's see what you can keep down."

"I'll eat in the bath," said the boy stubbornly. Sitting up, he didn't fall over or look faint, though both the adults knew that even if he felt weak, his pride would never let him show it.

"It will take time to heat the water," said Antonia reasonably. "Until then, sit still and eat."

"I'll sit by the window, then. Fresh air." He swung his legs off the bed and set them gingerly on the floor. Both Antonia and Morsicato tried to help him, but he waved them off. "I don't remember having this much trouble walking when I was delirious," he said, rising and taking a few shuffling steps.

"Don't push yourself," advised Morsicato. "Youth may have saved your life, but you're not invincible." Cesco snorted and kept shuffling. "How much do you remember?"

"My name is Francesco, my favourite colour is sky blue, and when I sing little birds come to copulate in my hand."

Morsicato groaned. "You were easier to talk to when you were raving."

"Probably made more sense." Cesco lit on a bench near a shuttered window. His clumsy fingers found the latch, letting in a wall of sunlight. He held his face up and sighed in pure joy. "Didn't someone mention food?"

He ate, bathed, threw up, ate again, then lay in the shifting sunbeam for the rest of the day. When talked to, he spoke cheerfully from behind closed eyelids, replying to questions in anything but a helpful manner. Pietro, Antonia, Bailardino, and the two doctors all spent time quizzing him, all ending with the same expression of impotent frustration. Detto and Valentino were allowed to come in for a few minutes, but were packed off because Cesco was expending a great deal of energy entertaining them with stories invented from his fever dreams.

The setting sun made the room no less warm – the summer air around Verona was rife with humidity. But the threat of another attempt on Cesco's life was very real in everyone's mind – save Cesco's, it seemed – so the shutters were closed again and the room lit with candles. In the morning Cesco had asked for books to do with Verona, and by the end of the day a crate had arrived from the fabled Franciscan monastery of San Bernardino.

Cracking the first volume, he was instantly engrossed. So deep was he in study that when the door opened an hour later, it took the boy several moments to look up. "I'm still breathing," said the boy testily. "And enjoying being alone for the first time today."

"All things end, little dancer," said the Moor, seating himself on the floor, his back to the wall.

Marking his place with a rush-straw, Cesco said, "Did you know that the Roman general Gaius Marius defeated the Cimbric hordes not far from here?"

"Yes."

"Well *nyah*." Cesco extended his tongue.

"You were in the sun all day?" asked Tharwat.

Cesco stretched like a happy animal. "The reviving sun. Like a plant, I soak up the rays and it gives me growth."

"You don't want to appear pale when you go out."

Cesco shrugged. "I'm suddenly lacking both blood and weight. Can't let people think the Greyhound's heir is a daisy."

"And you plan to go out…?"

"Tomorrow," said Cesco.

"No."

"Yes."

"Not tomorrow. Sunday a week."

Cesco paused. "Because…"

"Ser Alaghieri's friend, the noble Ser Antonio Capulletto, throws an annual feast for all the great families of Verona and the Feltro—"

"Save the Montecchi," Cesco interjected.

"Save the Montecchi," amended the Moor. "It is the feast for the Christian Saint Bonaventura."

"Bonaventura isn't officially sainted, and his day was last Monday. Same as the sainted Holy Roman Emperor Henri II."

"Bonaventura was called a saint in his own time, and is celebrated as a saint in these parts, however uncanonical. As for his day, what you say is true. But due to a minor civil war, his festivities were postponed."

Cesco's face blossomed in pleasure. "Did Ser Capulletto, perhaps, wish to reschedule?"

Tharwat nodded. "In honour of Cangrande's return and your arrival, he has, at great personal expense, set a new date for his feast. The Sunday after next."

A short silence fell. Tharwat knew that Cesco would insist on venturing out sooner than he should, and Cesco knew he was being manipulated into at least a little rest. But he also saw what the Moor knew he would see – the possibilities inherent in making a grand entrance at the Capulletti gala. "Ten days. Will Mastino be there?"

"After a humiliating two weeks with the grave-diggers, yes."

Having not heard that news, Cesco's smile broadened. "A lovely *contrapasso*. And Donna Giovanna?"

"With her great-nephew in tow."

"Then I must be fresh, mustn't I?"

The Moor made no reply and they sat for a time, Cesco gazing at the open book without turning the pages.

Suddenly Tharwat spoke. "You have an appointment with the Scaliger's wife."

"The woman who tried to have me killed so often in my youth."

"The same. It was her price for promising to leave you alone in the future. That, and an oath that you will, in the course of your career, advance Paride above all else."

"Hmm. We'll see. As for the meeting, she could have had it without the promise. I want to know all my nemisises. Nemises? Nemisi?"

"Child, this is not a game."

"No, it certainly isn't," agreed Cesco. "This is better. The stakes are mortal."

"They are that." Standing, the Moor crossed to the center of the room. "Sit up."

Cesco recoiled. "I've been poked and prodded enough, old man!"

"This is a teaching hour. First, eat this." He passed across a small wafer of something sticky.

Cesco smelled it. "Sweet." He broke off a corner and dabbed it on his tongue. "Euh! What is it?"

Tharwat al-Dhaamin sat on the floor across from Cesco and folded his legs. "Eat it and then do as I do."

"Why?"

The Moor took up an erect posture and began to breathe rhythmically in and out. Overwhelmed by curiosity, Cesco swallowed the wafer and imitated the Moor's stance. They sat like distorted mirrors, old and young, dark and light. Every few minutes Tharwat would add an instruction. "Breathe into your back. Ease your shoulders down. Breathe. Straighten your spine. Breathe."

Slowly Cesco felt a swelling wellness within him, a sense of energetic ease and euphoria. Then, abruptly, the instruction was over. The Moor relaxed his stance, stood, and returned to sit by the door.

"What was that, if you don't you mind my asking?" said Cesco.

"I have begun your instruction in a new field."

"May I know what I'm learning, O my Chiron?"

"No."

"Oh. All right. Then tell me why I'm learning it."

"It might have helped you in this recent ordeal. If so, I was remiss in not instructing you before now."

"You don't think I'm too young?"

"I was a child much younger than you when I began."

Cesco blinked. "You were a child?"

"This will give you tools to—"

"Wait wait, I'm busy being shocked. You were young once?" When the Moor did not reply, Cesco rolled onto his back to stare up at the ceiling's beams. "You owe me a question."

"So I do."

"The trouble is, I don't know what I should ask you. Nuncle Pietro was easy, but you're an onion."

The Moor said nothing.

"Should I ask about your past? I know nothing beyond the languages you speak and the things you've taught me – and those magnificent scars. I must have some of my own. Though perhaps not on my throat, I enjoy talking too much. I know you are called the Arūs, meaning the Bridegroom, which I can only hope is ironic. This is the first time I've ever heard you mention your youth."

The Moor was silent.

"Or should I ask about me? There are things that I should know – my mother, for one. No one will tell me anything about her, and she's half of who I am. Then there's astrology – you're an astrologer, yet I've never seen my chart. Why is that?"

"Is that your question?"

"Oh no! At least, not yet. There's another whole realm of queries I could ask. I could have you tell me about my father – Cangrande. I listen to the stories and learn nothing. What wheels move him? How does he work? How should I approach him? What kind of man is he?"

The Moor said nothing.

"I suppose I'll learn soon enough. No teacher like experience, eh?" He smiled at the ceiling. "You see, this is my problem. I don't even know what questions to ask. So I suppose my question is this —" The boy rolled onto his side. "If you were to offer me a question after this one, what question should I ask?"

After a long considering pause, the Moor nodded. "It depends. Would you rather live a happy life in ignorance, or a troubled existence of knowing?"

"It's poor manners to answer a question with a question," replied Cesco scornfully. "Yet I will answer your absurd query with yet another question. If I chose ignorance, could you guarantee me a happy life? Is that within your power?"

Breaking eye contact with Cesco, Tharwat stood and crossed to the trestle table that yesterday had held doctor's tools. He poured himself some water from a flagon and drank it down.

"If you must break your promise and not answer, I won't hold it against you." When the Moor didn't reply, he added, "I'll only kill you in your sleep."

Tharwat nodded as if the boy were serious. He set his cup down. This was the room where, ten years before, he had showed the charts to Pietro Alaghieri at the behest of Cangrande's sister, Detto's mother. Thinking of her, the Moor turned. "When I have an answer, I shall tell you."

"I'm all aflutter with anticipation," said Cesco, closing his eyes. "Now I have that to look forward to. And the feast, as well. Ten days, you say?"

"Yes. There is much to be done between then and now. Try to be patient. And mend."

♦    ◊    ♦

Ironically, Cesco's private meeting with Giovanna preceded his public meeting with Cangrande. The Monday after Cesco's arrival in the city, a week to the day since his poisoning, Giovanna made her call on the Nogarola house. She arrived in broad daylight for all to see, and the crowd that daily gathered to see Cesco remarked how cheerful Cangrande's wife looked, visiting her husband's bastard.

Inside she was greeted by servants and shown into a freshly-cleaned sitting room – Cesco had been moved to a real bedroom, returning this room to its usual function. When Giovanna entered, she was greeted with a splendid vision of tranquility – Cesco in the window seat, fingers dancing over the holes of a fife; Antonia in her novice's uniform, working a hand loom; Tharwat standing placidly near the window; and Pietro, looking ready to pounce at the first sign of trouble.

Of the adults, Giovanna knew Antonia best. "Antonia, my dear girl." She held out her hands and Antonia laid her small loom aside to rise and curtsey. Gesturing to the loom, Giovanna said, "I trust that isn't the same piece you were working on in my service so long ago."

"It might as well be, lady," said Antonia awkwardly. "I've never been good with yarn."

"That's right, inks were always your specialty. Ser Alaghieri, you look well."

"And you, lady." Pietro bowed stiffly, recalling how often he had almost died because of her.

Making eye-contact with the Moor, Giovanna turned to the boy in the window. "And you must be Francesco."

"Must I? I'd rather be someone else."

"Quick," said Giovanna. "Or do you rehearse answers with your tutors?"

"I am nothing but what I am," said Cesco unhelpfully. Still, he made a good leg to her before returning to his pipe.

"You play well."

Cesco shook his head. "It's not my instrument. I like to sing as I play."

"Yet you try to master it, regardless."

Cesco shrugged, playing on. Tharwat cleared his throat, his usual prelude to speech. "You didn't bring Paride."

"They will meet soon enough." Giovanna's eyes were on Cesco. "I hope you will be friends."

Cesco lowered the pipe. "I hope so, too. Is he a friendly fellow?"

"He is. Are you?"

Cesco's teeth flashed. "Nothing but. I am, after all, here, making music for an ancient murderess." He returned to playing.

Giovanna's laugh carried a note of displeasure. "My boy, I don't know what these people have told you—"

"*In primis*, I am not your boy. Which is, I gather, the problem."

"It is rude to interrupt," she said sharply.

"Then you shouldn't do it. Secondly, *these people* are all the family I have ever known. You shouldn't scorn them, since it's because of you that I grew up with them. Thirdly, you are here on sufferance. You are a spent force. You've lost and are now trying to woo the winning side. That makes you at best a supplicant, at worst a whore."

Like lightning Giovanna moved forward, her arms raised before she knew what she was about. With Cesco reclining in the window, she could easily topple him over into the street below. It might even kill him, depending on how he landed.

Pietro bounded across the middle of the room. Tharwat came away from the wall. Antonia remained frozen in place, her hands over her mouth. Only Cesco remained unmoved, a slight curl at the corners of his mouth around the pipe. He played harder, a driving tune with a quick tempo. His eyes were wide in anticipation.

Giovanna did not make the final effort. Visibly stilling herself, she instead walked to stand beside him and wave at the crowd below. Then she turned away and started towards the door.

Cesco stopped playing. "Thank you."

She turned. "For?"

"For not murdering me. It answers my question."

"And what question is that? My belief in your heathen's prophecy?"

"Not at all," said Cesco, winking at her. "I was just wondering how diluted the temper of the terrible Frederick has become. Apparently his hot blood has been tamed. Three generations ago, you wouldn't have hesitated, and damn the consequences. But you took time to consider, to reason. Even made a good save of face at the end. And cousin Paride is two more generations removed from the great Hohenstaufen. He must be even more bloodless than you."

No one ever dared to speak to Giovanna in this way. As her mouth worked silently, trying to form her outrage, Cesco tossed his fife aside and leaned forward, his elbows on his knees, his hands clasped together to point at her. "Let me be plain. I bear you no ill will for past wrongs. But now it is more widely known that you tried to kill not only me, but Pietro here, his father, and Lord Nogarola's wife. That leaves you in a bit of a spot. Try to interfere with me and mine, and all fingers," he wiggled his, "will point at you. Even the great Scaliger, your husband, will not be able to stop them from seeing you hang. Though I think burning at the stake would be more appropriate, don't you, Guinevere?"

Glaring at him for a moment more, Giovanna turned to Tharwat. "This is how you make peace?"

The Moor shrugged. "You insisted on an interview. There was no promise of pleasantries."

The lady looked back to the boy. "Who are you to dare—?"

"Why wouldn't I dare? As I said already, you are a spent force. But if it pleases you, I will accept the bloodless Paride as my page. That way he can polish my boots as I claim my birthright."

Giovanna summoned all her dignity. "Your birthright? You are a bastard, a half-blooded little pinprick!"

"Better a half-blood bastard than a bloodless bitch of no birth whatsoever."

Giovanna's face flushed for a third time. The insult had many barbs, for she was in fact an illegitimate grand-daughter of an emperor. "I may not be able to murder you, but I swear I will see you destroyed!" With that, the lady swept from the room.

The moment the door was shut Pietro rounded on him. "You idiot. What were you thinking?"

Cesco retrieved his fife from the floor. "Actually, I thought it was quite gallant to allow her the final word. I had three excellent insults to hurl at her back, but I refrained. Gentlemanly."

"Why? *Why!?*" Pietro slapped a timber support in frustration. "We had her contained! We had her willing to help us!"

Cesco shrugged. "I don't want her help." And with that, he resumed playing.

Pietro walked up to the boy and ripped the pipe away from him. "That was the most asinine—"

Cesco glared up at him. "What do you expect, keeping me cooped up in here for a week. I'm going mad!"

"That's certain!"

"You can't blame me for having a little fun!"

"Fun!" Pietro pressed his eyes shut. "You just whacked a hornet's nest."

"And hit the queen," said the Moor.

Cesco looked at Tharwat. "She mentioned a prophecy. What's that about?"

"Nothing you need to know," said Tharwat.

"Or deserve to," added Pietro acidly. "You clearly only use what we give you to place yourself in more danger."

Cesco made a face. "What danger? The crowd below would have caught me."

Antonia cut off her brother's retort. "Pietro, wait. He's not stupid."

Cesco sent her a bow of his head. "Thank you."

She frowned back. "Rash, impulsive, bordering self-destructive, but not stupid. He must have had a reason for—"

"I did. A very good one. I *felt* like it."

Pietro threw the fife at the wall. "That's not a good reason to—"

Cesco suddenly flared to life. "Well, I also thought that Detto wouldn't like it if I was to make friends with the woman who tried to kill his mother. And maybe I don't like the idea of befriending the woman who tried to kill *you!*"

There were times when they were forcibly reminded that Cesco was only eleven years old. With his command of language, with his wit and agility, it was so easy to forget. Added to that was the fact he was still not recovered from his illness.

Pietro melted. Wrapping the boy in a tight hug, he murmured, "You idiot. You little numbskull."

Cesco did not hug Pietro back, but neither did he struggle to be free. They stood that way for some time. Finally Cesco lifted his wan face. "I saw you start when she came towards me. Do you think you could have caught me?"

"Well, we've had practice, Tharwat and I," said Pietro, wiping an eye. "You almost dropped off this very balcony ten years ago."

"Truly? O, I love my new life! I get to hear all these old stories. But let me see, I would have been about a year old…"

"Less."

"Carelessness?"

"No, a deliberate move on your part."

"Really? Was I being thwarted?"

Pietro considered. "Your cleverness wasn't being recognized."

Cesco gave a mock shiver. "Nothing worse in creation. I shall have to bend my mind to it and make sure it never happens again."

Pietro sighed. "You're off to a good beginning."

◆     ◊     ◆

They sent Cesco to bed, and to everyone's surprise he did not demur. Once they saw him settled with Antonia beside him to make sure he actually did rest, the Moor plucked Pietro's sleeve. In the hall, out of earshot of both the boy and the novice, Tharwat whispered, "Be ready to ride tonight. We must not be followed."

Momentarily perplexed, Pietro realized what the errand had to be. The only thing it could be. Against all his better angels, he was looking forward to it.

# III

## HEIR APPARENT

# TWENTY

THEY RODE SIDE BY SIDE through the moonlight, using every trick to lose the Scaligeri soldiers who were almost certainly following them. It was well past midnight when Tharwat and Pietro reined in before an old timber cabin to Verona's south, beyond Paquara, close to Tomba. An appropriate title for the place. It was certain to become one man's tomb tonight.

As they dismounted, a shape in front of the cabin shifted. Pietro reached for his sword, but Tharwat said, "It is I."

With a voice like Tharwat's there was no need for a password. The shape came shuffling out of the shadows. By the light of the moon Pietro could see he was a back-bent Moor. Missing fingers from both hands, clearly much abused by life, yet this crookback had muscles upon muscles, bulk that not even his rags could hide.

The man did not look once at Pietro, though if from fear or contempt, Pietro couldn't tell. "He stopped begging to be freed yesterday," the man told Tharwat. "Today he started pleading for me to kill him. He still drinks the water I bring, though, so he hasn't given up hope."

A wheedling voice came from within the cabin. "Who's there! I can hear you talking! Please, help! Help!"

Crookback grunted. "See?"

Ignoring the yells from inside, Tharwat handed over a satchel containing fresh bread, fruit, and clear water. "I thank you. Can you remain? We may not be done here tonight."

"I will stay as long as necessary. Tell me, does the child live?"

"He does."

"*Allahu akbar.*"

"*Allahu akbar,*" echoed Tharwat, heading for the cabin door. As Pietro followed, the crookback returned to his post, breaking the bread off between his teeth.

When they opened the door the shouting stopped. There was no light within, and they were silhouetted by the moon over their shoulders. There was a soft groan from the darkness, and a curse. "No no no – stay back, you heathen fiend!"

Tharwat struck a flint. Sparks danced in the air like little stars, but not far enough to illuminate the room. Again the rasp of the flint. This time the taper caught and light stretched out towards the corners of the cabin, not quite reaching the back wall.

In the middle of the room a burly man was bound to a central support beam. Thickly built, the poisoner was trussed like a holiday pig. Days of struggle against his bonds had torn his clothes, and there was blood on the ropes. Obviously the Moor and his friend outside were too expert in their knots. There were signs of abuse from the Moor's previous interrogation, but no permanent damage.

*Yet.*

Taking in the new face, the poisoner's eyes lit with hope. "Who're you?" The beard looked like a sickly ferret stretched across his jaw. Talking gave the illusion that the ferret was writhing. "Please, I beg you, get me out of this and anything you want, it's yours! I swear!"

Laying his sword close to hand, Pietro squatted down before their prisoner. "No need for oaths you don't intend to keep. You'll give me everything I want, now. Then we'll see about freeing you."

The man threw a nervous glance at Tharwat as the Moor unbuckled his massive falchion and laid it on the floor. The villain was now bracketed by swords. "Please – I have a family, they can ransom me."

"That's good. Start there. What's your name? Where are you from?"

"My name is Danno, my family's from Napoli. But no one calls me Danno."

"What do they call you?"

"Borachio." The man lifted his chin as he said it, proud of being a drunkard. Or, more likely, his ability to imbibe.

"Well, Borachio, my friend and I have questions. You'd best answer them truthfully."

"I already told him what the poison was," protested Borachio weakly.

"And we thank you. Now, who hired you?"

Borachio shook his head. "I don't know."

Tharwat removed a sickle-shaped knife from inside his doublet and held it gently against the drunkard's cheek. "Don't lie. For every lie, you lose a finger."

Like a pig smelling bacon, Borachio began to sweat. "I swear, I don't—" Sighing, Tharwat moved around to where Borachio's hands were tied. "No! Wait! It was in Venice – two men in masques dragged me to a casa."

"What kind of masques?"

"Those ones that cover the whole face."

"Bauta masques."

"Yes! They put me in a chair and bound me to it. They left, and I heard a voice. There was a screen – you know, one of those metal screens that courtesans use."

As Tharwat stepped back into view, Pietro said, "Was it a courtesan who spoke?"

"No, a man. Please, may I have a drink?" Pietro nodded to Tharwat, who brought a stoup of water from a bucket. Borachio grimaced. "I said something to drink, not something to wash in."

Cheeky, for a prisoner. Pietro decided it couldn't hurt to let the fellow slake his thirst. In fact, it might help. But not yet. "I have some wine in my saddlebags. First you have to earn it. Tell me about the man."

Borachio shot the Moor a nervous glance. "I don't know anything about him. Really! I told you, I couldn't see him, he was sitting behind the screen!"

"If the screen had holes, you must have been able to see something."

"Only that he was in a masque, too. There was very little light, one candle near me."

"How was he dressed?"

"I tell you, I couldn't see!"

"What about his voice? You could hear him well enough."

"I don't know, he was a posh. He spoke too well, you know?"

"Like me?"

"Better."

"So he was definitely noble?"

The drunkard clung to that word. "Oh yes. Yes, noble."

"Was the accent Venetian? Veronese? Paduan? Was he even Italian?"

"Venetian, I think. Yeah, I'm sure he was Venetian. Please, may I have that drink?" Pietro stood, and Borachio cried out, "No, please! Don't leave me alone with that monster!" Another wordless communication between Pietro and the Moor, and Tharwat exited the cabin.

Borachio stared earnestly into Pietro's face, his breathing laboured, his face lathered with sweat. Quickly he said, "Ser, you're a gentleman,

I can see it. You won't let him hurt me?" Pietro said nothing. "Come on, friend. At least loosen the ropes on my arms. I can't feel my fingers, they're so tight. I'm unarmed, I'm starving, I'm no threat to anybody!"

Pietro stared, studying Borachio's face. He'd expected to find someone evil, a man with a visibly twisted soul. Someone like Pathino. This big lout appeared completely normal, a fine drinking companion, maybe even a stout soldier once upon a time. Callow, to be sure. He wasn't even devious in his attempt to escape.

Yet he had poisoned a child. That simple fact identified him as lacking a soul. That fact also made it easy for Pietro to ignore his pleas. There was no mercy here.

Pietro thought of a new question. "What day did this happen?"

Borachio had to think. "What day is it now?"

"Monday."

"Well, this was either a Tuesday or a Wednesday. I never go to the Paradiso Trovato on a weekend – they're an unsavory lot, despite the name, y'see?" Pietro waited, and Borachio quickly went back to his calculations. "I think I remember drinking an honourific. Some priest. He said it was a feast day, and we had to drink seven healths."

"The Feast of the Seven Martyrs. That was Wednesday the Tenth. Are you absolutely sure?"

"Dead certain. I mean – yes. Always remember an honourific."

That date was twelve days past. Two whole days before anyone heard that Cangrande was dead. Meaning that it had to be Cangrande behind the poisoning – no one else knew. *And I believed him! Again!*

Tharwat returned. Taking the stone bottle, Pietro removed the stopper and held it to Borachio's lips. "Drink up. And then, like a true drunkard, spill your guts. Or he will." Tharwat again fingered his sickle-shaped knife.

Borachio gulped at the wine, slobbering some down his front, drinking without pause until Pietro pulled the stone bottle away. He sighed with relief. "Thank you. You are a good Christian."

Pietro set the bottle aside. "Now tell me, why did this masqued man choose you?"

Borachio got the crafty look drunks get when they're embarrassed. "I honestly don't know."

Pietro backhanded him, putting his shoulder into the blow. Lip bleeding, Borachio simply looked up at Pietro as if to say, *Is that all you've got?* Clearly the man had taken more than a few beatings in his life.

"Tharwat, our friend here was complaining that he couldn't feel his fingers. Test that statement."

Now Borachio squirmed. "No!"

"Why did he choose you?"

"He – he knew about a crime I had been a part of, dammit! He had evidence. He said that if I refused to do what he asked, the two men would take me to gaol and have me executed that very night. But if I did what he said, the evidence would disappear."

"So you agreed."

"Yes."

"To kill a child."

"What else could I do! Ever try to negotiate while you're tied to a chair? He wouldn't listen a whit. Said I would be doing my country a great service, and saving my skin besides."

"Your country? What does Napoli gain if—"

"I think he meant Venice," said Borachio simply. "Please, can you let me go now? That's all I know."

"Hardly," said Pietro. "What were his instructions. Exactly."

Borachio's brow furrowed in concentration. "He told me to go to Mantua, find an apothecary there named Spolentino. I was to buy a poison. The worst possible, the most deadly. Then I was to come to Verona and wait."

"For what?"

"For anyone claiming to be Cangrande's son."

Pietro exchanged a quick glance with Tharwat. "Go on."

Borachio shrugged. "I did it, just like he said. I went to Spolentino's shop, bought the poison, then came to Verona. I got a room and I waited. Every day I loitered in the square, listening for news."

"Then your target arrived."

"Yes." Borachio's sweat reached new proportions as he came to the most dangerous part of his tale – dangerous for him. "So I did what I was told. Worked my way through the crowd and pricked him. You understand, yes? I had no choice!"

Pietro was staring a hole through the man's head. It was Tharwat who acted. Standing, he reached into the satchel on his shoulder, removing a leather roll of tools. Borachio didn't need the Moor to unfurl it to know what it was. "Noo, nooooo!"

Tharwat rummaged carefully through the poisoner's tools and withdrew a long hollow metal tube. "You had this. Why didn't you use it? Answer!"

Borachio was shaking with dread. "Boy was too short. Couldn't get a shot through the crowd. Had to get closer. I'm sorry!"

"So you used this." Tharwat lifted a needle. It looked like it had a dirty end.

Borachio quailed, looked away, refused to answer.

Pietro's voice sounded like it belonged to a complete stranger. "You've only heard what it can do. We've seen it. Worse than you can imagine. Worse than losing a finger or two. And you did it to a child. A *child*."

"What do you want from me? I've told you everything!"

"Not quite. Describe the house."

"What? Oh. Ah, well, I couldn't see too good. The men jumped me as I left the alehouse. They pinioned my arms and threw me into a gondola. One shoved a masque over my face, but he pulled it low so I couldn't see out of it – the eyeholes were at my nose. Then one held a knife in my back and the other rowed."

Tharwat spoke. "Name the alehouse."

"I told him already, the Paradiso Trovato."

"The quarter?"

"Dorsoduro, west side."

"Say which way they rowed, and for how long."

"East, maybe? Yes, east. For about ten minutes."

"Rowed, not punted."

"No, you're right, he punted."

Pietro scowled. "That kind of mistake invites a pinprick."

"No! I didn't think – I didn't remember – I was drunk at the time!" As if that explained away everything, including the attempt on Cesco.

Pietro said, "Go on about the house."

"We stopped, they pulled me out. But they jostled me enough that they didn't notice when I shrugged the masque into place so I could see. There was a wall of pink flowers in bloom outside it. Not a few, a full wall. I could smell them over the river stink."

"What else about the casa?"

"It was three stories, well kept. The shutters were fancy, kind of oriental. And there was a carving of a three-headed man over the door."

"Describe it," rasped Tharwat.

"Like one of those Commedia-Tragedia masques – laughing on one side, crying on the other. But the middle face was the strange one. It was screaming, like it was crazy angry. Laughing and crying at the same time, you know?" Borachio surveyed the faces of his captors and decided he might have earned another slug of wine. Anticipating the request, Pietro lifted the stone bottle to his lips and held it there while the drunkard lapped. He had to pull it away before it was entirely drained. To be without wine was to lose their best enticement.

"Thank you," gasped Borachio.

"You're welcome. Now what was the crime?"

"What?"

"The crime you committed, the one the Venetian was blackmailing you with. What was it?"

Borachio's face squinched into a ball. "You want me to tell you?

How does that help me?"

"It keeps you alive a little while longer."

Drink made Borachio argumentative. "You're going to kill me anyway. I know that. So do it. Do it and have done!"

All this kneeling was straining Pietro's bad leg. He stood. "Borachio, use whatever passes for your brains. The only reason we have to keep you alive is to use you to hunt down this mysterious Venetian. You can lead me to the house, you can recognize his voice. As long as you're useful, you can live. But I have to know you won't run or betray me. I can already have you hanged for attempted murder and possession of illegal poisons. But to control you, I have to know what the other man has on you. It might help identify him. And," added Pietro, "if we know the crime, we can learn who betrayed you. One of your fellow criminals must have sold you out. If we can learn who did that, we can follow the chain to the man who threatened you, and eliminate him. It's the only way you'll be safe."

That speech had the drunkard furrowing his brow for a long time. Finally deciding he had nothing to lose, Borachio told his tale:

"I used to work under a *condotta* commanded by Lord Castracane of Pisa. You've heard of him, yes? We helped him oust that fool Uguccione della Faggiuola."

"The late Lord Faggiuola was a friend of mine," said Pietro coolly.

"Oh. Uh, sorry. Brave soldier. Well, things settled down in Pisa and us boys decided to go into business for ourselves. I was chosen as the *condottiero*, and we came to Venice to see what wars were in the offing. I was a fool, though, and quarreled with one of my officers."

"Over what?"

Borachio's face became a masque, half amused, half sad. "There was this girl…"

Pietro could hear Cesco's sarcastic voice saying, *There always is.*

"Anna. Little, dark hair, perfect nipples. She was engaged to this officer, Andreasio he was called, but fell for me. So she threw him over. Andreasio was furious. I paid him a bonus to recompense him, but that just made him angrier."

"He didn't like to be thought of as another Pander, I guess."

Borachio shrugged. "Whatever. So the wicked bastard puts a plan into motion to ruin me. He hires some local bint to dress like my Anna, then he gets a couple other officers drunk. This whore meets them dressed as my love, and this officer and she, they make a scene. Like a little play. All over each other. Damned bitch earned her fee right there in the back of the alehouse! Rot her!"

Borachio was beginning not to relate the tale so much as relive it, the anger in his voice doing battle with the tears in his eyes. "Word got back to me that same night. The officers told me what they had seen with their own eyes. Of course, they'd been drunk. But I believed them. I believed my Anna was untrue. Can you believe it? What a fool!"

"Your crime," said Pietro softly.

"My crime? My crime was that I killed her! I went to her rooms, had my way with her as she sobbed and wept and cried, said it was a pack of lies. That just made me angrier. I didn't mean to do it, but I broke her neck." Borachio's voice was level now, relating facts, despite the tears rolling down his cheeks. "I did that. To her. Me."

"What happened next?"

"Andreasio was waiting outside the room. He'd watched me go in, listened to the whole thing. When he was sure she was dead, he called to me. He'd blocked the door first – he knew I wanted to kill him, too. Through the door he told me what he'd done. That she'd been true. That I'd killed her over a lie. And that the law would have my head if they found out!" Borachio sagged. "He offered me an escape. Said that he wouldn't turn me in. All I had to do was sign the leadership of the *condotta* over to him, then disappear, and my name would never be linked with Anna's death."

A heavy silence. Borachio seemed unable to finish the tale, so Pietro did it for him. "You took his offer."

"Aye, I did. Gave up position, percentage, and pension. And I've been in that hellhole ever since."

"Is that why you turned to drink?" The question earned him a reproving look from Tharwat. Pietro knew why, but he couldn't help asking it.

Borachio looked up in surprise, then laughed. "That would be a good story. But no, I've always been Borachio. Probably the reason I ended up in this pig-sty of a fix in the first place."

Pietro asked a more pertinent question. "How did you make a living?"

"A little bodyguard work, a little crowd management here and there. Muscle, a quick club, and the stink eye."

"Any of your employers know your history?"

"Only my war record and employment history. All they needed."

"Could they have checked with Andreasio for your references?"

"Could have, but I doubt it. Not the kind of job you need references for. Either you look like a man who can crack skulls or you don't, you know?"

"Is this Andreasio still in Venice?"

"I don't know. I hope he shipped off to war and was drowned."

"You and Anna weren't married, were you?"

Borachio shook his head sadly. "Not yet."

Pietro and Tharwat asked a few more questions, probing certain areas further. But if Borachio responded, the answers were clearly inventions, attempts at pleasing his captors. When Tharwat threatened the needle the false answers dried up, leaving nothing at all. Borachio had spilled all he knew. His kind of evil was craven, easily turned. There was no loyalty in him. He switched masters as easily as he drew breath. Or downed a drink.

Pietro was glad they hadn't needed the implements in Tharwat's satchel. The thought of torturing a man, even a man as deserving as this one, turned Pietro sick at heart. *I'm too soft for this life.*

After giving the poisoner the last of the wine, Pietro and Tharwat lifted up their swords and started for the exit. Borachio called after them. "Wait! You're not just going to leave me here, are you?"

"We'll be back," assured Pietro.

Outside, Tharwat nodded to the crookbacked Moor, then continued walking until they were well out of earshot of the cabin. Stopping under leaves of a young oak, Pietro said dryly, "We should tell Cesco that his lack of stature saved him from the blowpipe. He might stop grousing about his height."

Tharwat was not in the mood for jests. "We have learned all he knows. What shall we do with him?"

"He's guilty of attempted murder."

"Yes."

"But do we want that to get out, is the question."

"Yes."

They didn't want it to get out. A rumour about an illness that looked like poison was quite different from a case at law, charging the poisoner and demanding his confession and execution. It was a matter of unforeseeable consequences. Best not left to chance.

But Pietro didn't want to let go of the law just yet. There had to be a legal solution to Borachio. "We caught him in possession of poison. That alone is enough to see him hanged."

"True."

*Damn you, Tharwat, argue with me!* "But even if we bring him up on charges, he'll have a chance to defend himself, speak, and he could say everything he knows."

"That is so."

The Moor was being too passive, and Pietro's frustration got the better of him. "Just say it. You think we should kill him."

"Are you saying you do not?"

"No, that's not it. But—"

"You wanted him dead when he was a thing, a poisoner, a murderer of children. But now that you've met him, seen him with your own eyes, you think he is a man, worthy of man's laws."

"He is!"

"He is not. He is still a thing, a poisoner, a murderer of children. That he did not succeed does not negate his intent, or his deed. You do not need to know what moves a man's soul to judge his actions."

"You mean I shouldn't have asked the cause of his drinking? I wanted to know him better."

"Immaterial to the matter at hand. It was sympathetic of you."

"You mean pathetic."

"I am not Cesco, nor am I Cangrande. I say what I mean. But you have fallen into a trap. He is no longer worthy of death. It is no longer justice. You see it as murder. You have stepped into his boots. Only, had you been in his boots from the start, you would not have committed this deed. A man's deeds are what there is to judge him by."

"You just said his intent was as important."

"You are a good lawyer, you have caught me in a contradiction. I confess it. Now, admit this – if Cesco were dead, you'd have chopped off his head before we left that room. No?"

Pietro considered a moment before giving a grudging answer. "Probably."

"But what if Cesco is permanently damaged by this? It is possible – such a shock to a young body, I know what it can do. It never leaves."

Pietro couldn't see them now, but could easily conjure the image of the scars around Tharwat's throat. Bubbly, like burn scars, but stretched so the discolouration became a great swath of pain around the whole neck. He had never thought about the stretching before, but now he realized that if a child had been tortured, the surviving adult would bear scars just like al-Dhaamin's. *A child…*

The Moor continued. "He is a criminal several times over. We'd be doing justice."

"We can't take the law into our own hands! Dammit, I'm a knight and a lawyer. I cannot betray those ideals."

"Not even for Cesco?"

Pietro sucked in a breath. "I would murder to save Cesco's life. But that's not the circumstance we're in. This is revenge, pure and simple. Vengeance isn't for me to mete out."

"Ser Alaghieri, nothing good comes from letting him live. The deed need not be done by you. Or even witnessed. Step down the road a ways. I will join you soon."

Pietro shook his head. "That's worse than doing it myself. I would still be complicit."

"I do not subscribe to the ancient Greek idea of transference. The blood is only on the hands of the man who does the deed."

"There have been cases at law that disagree."

"That law is to prevent future crimes as much as—"

"—as get justice for the dead, yes," finished Pietro. "Two men stop a traveler, meaning to kill him for his purse. The nearer strikes the blow. The other man isn't guilty?"

"Philosophy," rasped Tharwat. "Impractical. He must die. The rest is noise."

"Law is not noise!" said Pietro, a little too loudly. He moderated his tone. "Without the law, it is murder."

Tharwat remained unmoving, unspeaking. The argument, as far as he was concerned, had ended. Wanting to continue, Pietro saw the futility of it. Tharwat was correct. Nothing good came from letting Borachio live.

Tharwat must have sensed Pietro's defeat, even in the darkness, for he stepped past his friend and started back for the cabin.

"Tharwat, no."

The Moor did not stop.

"Al-Dhaamin."

The steel in Pietro's voice caused the Moor to turn. There was a tension in the air, as if the astrologer half-expected Pietro to fight him here, in the dark, in this cause.

Reaching out, Pietro laid a hand on Tharwat's sword arm. "I'll do it. I'm already damned. There must be some benefit to not being in God's view. I may sin with impunity."

"I am willing."

"If the deed is to be done," said Pietro, "I should do it. Anything else is cowardice."

Tharwat signaled his silent assent by stepping aside. Pietro led the way back to the cabin, where the light of the taper still flickered inside. At the door, Pietro drew his sword.

Borachio must have heard some of the argument, divined by tone if not words the debate being had. The sight of Pietro with naked steel in hand did not set him pleading again. Instead he simply muttered, "Oh Christ." He struggled against his bonds, but had no more strength in his final hour than he'd had before.

Pietro walked forward, the point of his longsword held low. *So this is it. I've killed men in battle. I've tried to kill a couple in single combat. But today I kill an unarmed man, bound hand and foot, helpless before me. Today I become a murderer.*

Reaching Borachio's side, Pietro raised his sword. The light from the taper reflected off it, sending a beam across the room. *Man's law is but reflected light from God's law. 'Vengeance is mine,' sayeth the Lord. 'Though shalt not commit murder.'*

But Tharwat was correct. Nothing good came from letting this man live.

*Nothing? Is that my decision to make, what a man has to offer?*

But for Pietro to let him live, there had to be a benefit to Cesco. And there was none.

Through a clenched jaw Borachio said, "Send my body to Naples."

Pietro swung the sword, hard. It bit into the wood beside Borachio's neck, sending a shower of splinters into the air. Borachio cried out.

And stopped. He looked up and up the length of sword that rested not an inch from his shoulder. At the final moment, Pietro had taken a slight step, causing the blade to bury itself in the wooden post at Borachio's back, just at neck level. Borachio shivered, then began shaking. An acidic smell filled the room as a dark stain filled his hose. Relief and rage fought to overwhelm the man. "Bastard. Bastard."

Pietro turned the blade, putting pressure on Borachio's neck. "Listen to me. You are no longer your own man. Your life belongs to me. If you even set a foot out of line, I'll give you to the Moor here."

Pietro exited. Tharwat did not follow. But neither did he draw his sword. Instead the Moor said, "My friend has offered you life. I offer you something else." Carefully he extracted the poisoned needle from the leather roll of deadly tools. Stepping around to Borachio's back, he laid it gently in the palm of the uppermost bound hand. "You may choose. Life, as he offers it. Or death. There is nothing else."

Tharwat witnessed the drunkard grasping the implied bargain. *We will return. If you mean to aid us, stay alive. If not, better to die now than die in the manner I will choose for you.*

Tharwat took the remaining tools and departed, pausing only to blow out the taper. He didn't look back at the angry, shamed figure in the center of the room, still affixed to the post.

Outside, Pietro had called the crookback over and was giving him instructions to feed the prisoner. When the man looked to Tharwat, the astrologer merely nodded.

They were mounted and already a mile on their way when Tharwat finally voiced the question. "Why?"

"Simple cowardice on my part."

"You are no coward. You thought of a reason to let him live."

"Maybe. I realized it could be useful having a *maladrino* in our pocket. In fact," added Pietro, "I have an idea how we can expose Cesco's enemy for all the world to see."

# TWENTY-ONE

*Verona*
*Tuesday, 23 July*
*1325*

## "I'M DAMNED. CESCO IS THE GREYHOUND?"

Morsicato was seated on a stone bench beside Pietro, across from Antonia and the Moor, both resting on the earth in the center of a walled yard belonging to the church of San Zeno. The burning summer sun beat relentlessly down upon them, and Pietro at least longed for the shade of the nearby arcade. But in the middle of the grassy square, they could see any approaching parishioners or clergy. As long as they kept their voices low, their words would remain private.

Pietro had learned long ago that houses have ears. Servants were unwitting spies, and in Verona's close confines there was no telling who else could be listening. Needing the council of Cesco's inner circle, Pietro found a modicum of privacy in San Zeno. He would have preferred the interior of the church, but that far the Prior was not willing to go. In spite of his knighthood Pietro was still anathema, and courtesy to the Scaliger only extended so far. Indeed, the Scaliger himself was excommunicated as well, barred from entering any but his own private chapel of Santa Maria Antica – though that edict had yet to be tested. Pietro supposed he was fortunate in owning a master who also laboured under Papal disapproval. Pietro's knighthood should have been revoked the moment he lost God's favour. His retention of the name Knight of the Mastiff meant he could demand certain concessions, such as the use of San Zeno's yard, and the entrance of al-Dhaamin within these holy confines.

Whom to invite to the meeting was almost as hard as determining a location. Antonia and Tharwat were a given. They knew every detail of Cesco's history. But Pietro balked at Castelbarco or Bailardino. Conspirators against Mastino, yes. But they were only in Cesco's camp out of loyalty to the Capitano. Already Bail showed unwillingness to believe ill of Cangrande, even when the tapestry was torn aside. So Pietro crossed them from the list.

The same went for Nico and Petruchio. Then there were Montecchio and Capulletto. There had been a time when he would have trusted them both implicitly. But that was before a woman had torn their friendship asunder. The worst part was that together they were a wonderful pair, a force to be reckoned with. Separate they were lessened, diminished, their potential reduced to mundane levels. And Pietro knew that if he reached out to one, the other would take umbrage. So they were both out.

That left the doctor. Certainly Morsicato had earned the right to be there. Privy to so much already, the doctor was ignorant of only one crucial fact – that Cesco was the fabled Greyhound of prophecy.

*Probably*, amended Pietro. With Cesco, nothing was certain.

For years Pietro had kept back this bit of information for the doctor's safety. But Cesco's destiny was the vital factor in divining Cangrande's motives. Therefore the doctor had to be told.

Pietro began by reciting the prophecy of *Il Veltro* – not his father's version of it, but the one that Cangrande himself had told him so long ago:

> To Italy there will come The Greyhound.
> The Leopard and the Lion, who feast on our Fear,
> He will vanquish with cunning and strength.
> The She-Wolf, who triumphs in our Fragility,
> He will chase through all the great Cities
> And slay Her in Her Lair, and thus to Hell.
> He will unite the land with Wit, Wisdom, and Courage,
> And bring to Italy, the home of men,
> A Power unknown since before the Fall of Man.
> He will evanesce at the zenith of his glory.
> By the setting of three suns after his Greatest Deed,
> Death shall claim him.
> Fame eternal shall be his, not for his Life, but his Death.

The next hushed words out of Pietro's mouth were to the point. "First, doctor, you must know this – Cangrande is not *Il Veltro*. The prophecy actually refers to Cesco. We didn't tell you to keep you safe. Cangrande's jealousy borders all rationality, and he'll hate anyone who even hints that he is not the Greyhound."

Morsicato asked Pietro to repeat his statement, and in a close whisper Pietro recited the words directly into the doctor's ear. "Cesco is the Greyhound."

To his credit, Morsicato did not reproach them with his exclusion from this information, though he did look a little gruff. But his answer was also to the point. "No wonder he hates the boy so."

Pietro shook his head. "Hate is too easy. He pities Cesco, maybe even loves him. But his goal is control. Hence faking his own death to lure Cesco back to Verona. But there is more to that story, which we only learned last night." Briefly, Pietro outlined everything they'd learned from Borachio.

At the end Antonia patted Pietro's knee. "I'm glad you let him live."

The doctor scowled at her. "I'm not. Damned poisoner!"

"Shh! Keep your voice down." Pietro glanced at the monks, obtrusively watching from the arcade – the Moor's presence unsettled them. *Or is it me?* "We need to decide what to do next."

Morsicato seemed surprised. "Obvious. We go to Venice, find the house."

"And do what? Storm in, demand to know who the man in the masque was? Even if it's not *carnevale*, masques are common in Venice. Everyone who wants to go unrecognized wears one and no one thinks twice about it."

"We could watch the house…" Even as the doctor spoke he saw the hopelessness of it. They didn't even know for whom they'd be watching.

Pietro nodded. "The house is irrelevant, because we already know who the man in the masque was." The others looked at him expectantly. He made a gesture with his hands, as if to say, *Isn't it obvious?* "The Scaliger."

"Cangrande?" asked Antonia, bewildered. "That doesn't make sense."

"Who else could have known he was going to fake his own death two days before it happened?"

"If it was he," said Tharwat, more careful than the others not to use names, "that means he hired the drunkard."

"Yes!" hissed Pietro, glad that at least the Moor saw the obvious.

"Which means it was he who wanted the boy poisoned."

"Yes."

The Moor shook his head. "I doubt that."

Pietro's mouth hung open. "Of all people, you know what he's—"

"What does he gain if Cesco dies? His father's curse on his head."

"Not if he believes in the Greyhound prophecy. He knows the boy won't die."

The doctor chimed in. "Even if that's true, Tharwat's right. It doesn't make sense. You say the Capitano staged his death to lure the boy back to Verona. Fine. What does he gain from poisoning Cesco? Why lure him out, only to make him helpless?"

Pietro recalled Cangrande saying almost those exact words. "It might amuse him to bring the fabled Greyhound low. Show us all he's mortal."

Antonia shook her head. "He would have admitted it. To you, at least. O, maybe not right out. But he would have let you know it was he. From what you've told me, he wouldn't be able to resist. Did he?"

Pietro's silence answered that question.

"*Is fecit, cui prodest*," said Tharwat softly. *The man who profits does the deed.* "The Capitano does not profit from this. And the drunkard said the masqued man had a Venetian dialect."

"The Scaliger once pretended to be a Spaniard and fooled me for days. He even pretended to be a woman on the road to Ravenna! He could easily mimic a Venetian accent."

"I don't see the gain," said Tharwat.

"Nor I," said Morsicato.

Pietro was adamant. "No one else knew!"

"Surmise, not fact," said Tharwat.

Pietro fumed. Yes, the Moor was technically correct. But the truth was so obvious! *Cangrande! It has to be Cangrande!*

The doctor cleared his throat. "I'm sorry, but aren't we missing the obvious name?" Everyone looked at him. "Mastino. Who stood to profit more from Cesco's death?"

"It a point," admitted Antonia.

Pietro shook his head. "This family – the curse of not spilling family blood weighs heavily on them. They're indoctrinated with it from birth. You should have heard Pathino back in that cave. He was a bastard, never knew his father, yet he believed in the curse with every fibre of his being."

Tharwat arched his brows. "That is as true for Cangrande as Mastino and Pathino. Moreso, perhaps."

Having depended on Tharwat's support, Pietro felt angry at being checked at each turn. When Antonia said, "We need to know more," frustration got the better of him, and he snapped, "That goes without saying!"

"Calm down. I mean specifically about the rumour that Cangrande was dead. How did he start that rumour? And how did this masqued

Venetian know about it ahead of time?"

Pietro could see the others needed logical proof. "Fine. Let's run down the list of suspects. Mastino."

Infuriatingly, Morsicato now reversed his position. "He couldn't have known, or he'd've been better prepared to challenge the will. Cesco would never have made it to Verona."

Pietro looked at the others. "Agreed?" They nodded. "Who else?"

"Cangrande's wife," said Morsicato, his voice overlapping with Antonia's as she said, "Giovanna."

Pietro pointed, as if dotting a name on a list. "Madonna della Scala. Certainly, she's tried it before. Tharwat?"

"No." The Moor was firm. When both Antonia and Morsicato began to argue, he said, "I believe her. Though, after his last performance, she might be thinking of it now."

"But she's the obvious person to benefit," protested Antonia. "If Cesco died, Paride would be next in line—"

"After Mastino, Alberto, and Federigo," completed Pietro. "That's too many bodies to climb over. She had better chances at law, and in court there were greater threats than a bastard son. Who does that leave?"

"Pathino?" suggested Antonia.

Pietro resisted a shiver. Gregorio Pathino had played a part in many nightmares these last ten years. Thankfully Tharwat answered that. "Even if he knew that Cesco was alive, how would he know about the fake death?"

"That goes for everyone," said Pietro. "Which brings us back to Cangrande—"

"Wait," said Antonia. "Wait. Clearly the Venetian didn't know where Cesco was, or else he would have attacked him in Ravenna. No?"

"That's right," said Pietro, the first real doubt coming home.

"Unless," said Morsicato, snapping his fingers, "the villain wanted Cesco killed just as he came to light."

"Who benefits from that?" asked Tharwat.

"Cangrande's enemies. Kill the heir just as he rears his head. Someone knew this was about bringing Cesco to Verona, and wanted to stop it. What if – what if this was less about the boy and more about hurting the Scaliger?"

"Scaligeri, you mean," said the Moor. "All of them."

It was a new thought, and Morsicato chased it as he would an unknown disease. "We naturally focus on the boy. But what if he's only a part of it? This could have been aimed at Cangrande – the whole family, maybe."

Antonia frowned. "Which means they're all in danger. Do we warn them?"

"Do we warn *him*, you mean," said Pietro.

"Yes."

Stubbornly Pietro shook his head. "I'm still not convinced he wasn't behind it. It could have easily been him behind the screen. The man was seated, so as not to give away his height…"

Antonia was his equal in stubbornness. "I simply can't accept it. It doesn't make sense."

Pietro threw a glance at Tharwat, hoping for eleventh hour support. The Moor inclined his head. "Anything is possible. But knowing the workings of his mind, I do not think it likely."

"Fine. How about this – we investigate the events around his fake death without talking to him directly. We can do that, surely!"

"It would be easier to ask him."

"And if it *was* him behind the screen? He'll know that we can link him to Borachio, and who knows what he'll do then."

"Have us killed," said Morsicato at once.

"Or removed some other way, yes."

"What's your solution, then?" demanded Antonia. "Kill him?"

"Before he kills us," said Pietro. "Yes."

The others stared at him. Antonia and Morsicato clearly thought he was mad. Tharwat was unreadable.

"Kill Cang– kill *him*?" gasped Antonia.

"Yes."

"Last night you refused to commit murder," said Tharwat.

"I also said I would murder to protect the boy. The drunkard is no longer a threat. *He* is." Pietro wanted to press his point further, but refrained. They had all the same pieces he did, they could reach their conclusions.

The Moor spoke first. "If it was he, then I agree."

The doctor was chewing his beard. "Me too. *If.*"

Antonia was staring at her brother as if she had never seen him. "I didn't know you would ever break the law."

"I would risk everything, even my immortal soul, for my family."

That was it, of course. Cesco was their child. No matter who his birth father was, they had raised him. They were the ones who loved him.

Antonia was a long time in giving her assent, but at last she nodded. Then, just as Pietro was about to ask how they go about it, she said, "*If* we can prove it."

"You want proof? Fine. I have an idea."

Quickly he outlined the plan he had conceived the night before. Antonia looked dubious, but Tharwat was brisk. "It is a good plan. One way or another we will be certain, and may proceed from there. But we will have to do it in public, someplace away from the court."

"Capulletto's ball," said Morsicato at once. "Cangrande will be there, and we can confront him away from his guards."

"Risky timing," said Pietro. "But better than trying at the palace or on the street."

"And in the meantime," said Tharwat, "the doctor and I will travel to Mantua and track down this apothecary. It bothers me, the instruction to purchase the poison in Mantua. There are enough disreputable apothecaries in Venice. Why add forty miles to the trip to procure the foul means of murder? I can only think that the apothecary is important. He may know something."

Pietro suddenly snapped his fingers. "Mantua! We can find out the events of those missing days without asking Cangrande! I know who we can ask!"

"Who?"

"Passerino! Lord Bonaccolsi was with him the whole time!"

"Excellent," said the Moor, nodding.

Visibly relaxing, Antonia said, "Somehow I always forget he exists – he's so eclipsed by the Scaliger. But Passerino is a good man, and he thinks this was an excellent joke. He'll want to tell the tale."

"Yes. But not until the party. We can't let the Scaliger know we're nosing around until we can confront him."

Morsicato held up a hand like a student. "Pietro, you may have thought of this, but how do we get the drunkard into the party without the Scaliger knowing?"

Pietro smiled. "I have an answer for that, too."

◆　◇　◆

Soon Pietro was crossing to the opposite end of the city, from north-west to south-east. His destination was an entirely different house of God, San Francesco al Corso. A modest establishment, as befit an Order that embraced poverty and humility. It was impressive only for its sheen, as the sun reflected off unadorned white walls and white paving stones leading to the open front door. This was not a church of massive grey stone. Nor was it made of the ubiquitous rose-marble and yellow brick that so defined the city. It seemed to glow, and in daylight it hurt the eyes. Perhaps that was why so many of the brothers had squints.

Pietro came at it from the side, following the path to the garden. Even the gravel was white, and Pietro's feet kicked up chalky clouds with each step. *I mar God's path*, he thought, wondering if it were true.

But it was too fine a day for such thoughts to linger. Light filtered down through trellised arbors wound round with bright green leaves. The white marble pillars holding up the trellises were thin, almost apologetic for being there at all.

The man Pietro sought was in San Francesco's garden. Once handsome, he clearly spent a great deal of time outside. His skin was dark with sun and his eyes had the smiling crows-feet of long days spent squinting. His hands were hard, his fingernails encrusted with soil. The knees of his brown robes were deep in the dirt as he instructed a teenaged acolyte in the nature of Nature. The sun reflected off the tonsured skin on their heads, but the elder man's hadn't been shaved in several days. Clearly he wasn't as careful about his appearance as once he'd been. No longer in the spring of his Orders, the thirty year-old still had a spry step and a genial smile.

Seeing someone approach, the friar paused until the hazy figure resolved itself. "Ser Alaghieri?"

"Good morning, Fra Lorenzo."

"*Benedicite*," said Lorenzo in cheerful welcome. "Is your young charge with you?"

"He's at home, mending well. Reading, probably."

"Delighted to hear it." Fra Lorenzo turned to the young man beside him. "See? Learning is a meal to be devoured, not a torture only inflicted on prisoners of youth. Ser Alaghieri, are you out for a stroll or do you have a specific destination?"

"I'm where I want to be." Pietro stepped into the shade of the garden wall. "I was hoping for a word, but there's no hurry. Please finish your lesson."

Lorenzo nodded. "Thank you. Brother Giovanni, stop staring at Ser Alaghieri. You'll make him self-conscious. Now, as I've said before, all creation is made for the express good of Man. No, that does not mean that everything is universally good. But there is nothing that exists on God's earth that doesn't have the *capacity* for good." His fingers brushed the rough twinned leaves of a tiny blue-stemmed plant. "Take this, for example. What's it called, do you know?"

"It looks like spinach," said the young brother.

"Do you want to eat it?" Lorenzo plucked one of the leaves free. "Smell this."

Brother Giovanni quickly turned up his nose. "Ew!"

"It tastes worse than it smells. Don't worry, son, I'm not going to make you eat it. Now, use your head. Name a plant that I might be interested in that looks like spinach."

"Umm." The novice gave a quick glance to Pietro, who shrugged.

"I'll give you one more hint. While it's poisonous to small animals when it's fresh, heat removes the harmfulness."

John took a guess. "*Mercorella?*"

"Good, good."

"I was right?"

"No. Well, a little. Part right in name, wholly wrong in fact." Lorenzo held up the sprig. "This is Dog's Mercury."

"Dog's Mercury? Like a Dog Violet or a Dog Rose?"

"Yes. Why do we call some plants Dog?"

"Because they don't – they lack the attributes of the regular species."

"Correct!" Fra Lorenzo twirled the stem to bring a leaf to the front. "You can tell that this is the commoner male by the leaves – more pointed, less serrated than those on the female, which have longer stalks." As the novice started looking for the female, Lorenzo clucked his tongue. "Sadly, male and female are rarely found together. They don't get on well."

"Then how do they thrive?"

"A surprisingly excellent question! They rely on the wind and, though I have yet to observe it, I think insects. Meanwhile they increase their numbers by spreading their rootstocks and stems. Rather like a man of considerable influence who lacks in potency of the loins." The novice reddened, causing Lorenzo to chuckle. "It flowers from March to May and seeds in summer. The Greeks called it Mercury's Grass, and the French call it *La Mercuriale*. Its name comes from an ancient legend that the pagan god Mercury came down and revealed its medicinal properties to man. Do you have any idea what those properties might be?"

"Ah. Poisonous. Um, good as a, a dye…"

Lorenzo gave Brother Giovanni's tonsure a light slap. "Don't guess."

"Was I wrong?"

"No. But I can still tell. To an adult, Dog's Mercury isn't necessarily deadly. Rather, it is an irritant. It will make you vomit, feel drowsy, or maybe twitch a bit in your face and extremities. As far as dyes go, the leaves and stem produce a muddy kind of indigo when steeped in water. It's permanent, but expensive, as a fair amount of alum is needed to bind it together. However, that's not what I asked you. I asked for the medicinal properties." Lorenzo sighed. "By the panic on your face, I see you haven't a clue. Fine. Listen. Learn. Hippocrates commends it for women's diseases – used externally, of course. If swallowed in a very watery concoction, it's a fine purgative. A solution of powdered leaves is good for sore eyes and pains in the ears. And if you're smart enough to pluck it while it's in flower, you can mix it with sugar or vinegar and create an excellent poultice for warts and ugly sores." Lorenzo stood and brushed himself off. "Now, here's the trick I use to keep my plants straight in my mind. I think of them as people. In time they become old friends, or at least passing acquaintances. So, Dog's Mercury or, as we shall call him, the Mercurial Dog. First, picture him physically. Blue eyes, feathery hair. He's smaller than his fellows and has extra arrogance because of it. He's not murderous, but neither is he friendly. A little prickly, he makes you uneasy when you're around him. But as he ages, he has hidden depths, and grows to a man of great, if unseen, influence." Hearing Pietro chuckle, Lorenzo said, "Ser Alaghieri, do you have anything to add?"

"I am only astonished at how well your little device works. I feel like I know him. I can see him before my mind's eye. But I imagine him with curling hair and a wicked smile. And his eyes are green."

"Indeed?" Lorenzo was bemused. "You are fortunate in your imagination. I always end up seeing faces of people I have known. Giovanni, can you picture him, too? Good. Keep him in your mind and make sure you never eat him. Now go back to the abbot and tell him what you've learned today. Ser Alaghieri has been very patient, but I don't think he's here to speak with you."

"Alas, no," said Pietro, patting the young novice on the shoulder as he passed. He waited while Lorenzo shook out his brown Franciscan robes from waist to ankle. He was barefoot according the rules of his Order. As he came near, Pietro breathed in the scent of freshly turned earth that by now had become the friar's own. Gesturing at the wide enclosure filled with plants, Pietro said, "A long way from tending Bishop Francis' little herb garden."

Lorenzo scrubbed his hands on the chest of his robes. "God's gift to me. I am blessed that I may put it to use."

"Doubly blessed," observed Pietro. "I hear even the Benedictines have swallowed their pride and asked you to instruct their young men."

"Only in matters of plants. I am under orders – from both Orders – not to discuss wider theological concerns."

Pietro cocked his head at the word *theology*. "I thought that both Franciscans and Benedictines frowned upon applying logic to God."

Lorenzo returned him a genially helpless smile. "Officially, yes. But in practice, it's what we've always done. And I like the word. *Theo Logy.* God Logic."

In the smile was the young man Pietro had met ten years before. Time had broadened his shoulders and added weight to his frame, as tended to happen with Franciscans. But his eyes were still the colour of a cloudy sky, his hair still raw black. His long, solid chin was now hidden by a bristly beard, which had the effect of making him less pretty than he had been. No longer could the women of Verona refer to him as another Brother What-A-Waste.

Indeed, if the rumours were true, Fra Lorenzo was one of the few members of any order who did not have a woman stashed away somewhere. It was noted that he always had time for the young men in need of work, or a kind word. Which gave rise to other whispers. Monastic life was the target of much speculation, and all too often the rumours of indecency between the brothers were true.

But Lorenzo didn't seem to be that kind of friar. His vow of chastity seemed as sincere as his other vows. His devotion to rules ensured that he would never rise to become a Bishop. But that, too, seemed to be fine with the man, who was happiest in his herb garden tending to God's creation.

Finished with his rough grooming, Lorenzo said, "How is Cangrande's son enjoying Verona?"

"He is as eager to soak the city in as a sponge for water."

"You say he's reading – books from the Chapter Library?"

"He's interested in learning as much as he can about the city."

"That library is indeed magnificent. Even I have found a few treasures in the collection. Several translations of Hippocrates' notes on herbs. Despite the common joke around the monastery that if you handed me a book, I'd try to plant it. Ha! Tell me, what kind of poison was it?" Pietro blinked, and Lorenzo gave him a shrewd smile. "I am not a fool. Fracastoro employs me as his personal apothecary. The brotherhood approves because he's the Scaliger's personal physician. When he sends to me for information about three separate poisons on the very night that the boy arrives in the city, it does not take a monumental intelligence to divine the cause." Lorenzo patted Pietro's shoulder. "Don't concern yourself. I know how to keep a secret."

"I'm well aware of it," said Pietro pointedly. "You see, I know a few secrets myself."

"Obviously! You raised the Capitano's son for nearly a decade and not a soul got wind of it. No small feat."

Hating himself a little, Pietro edged closer to his real reason for seeking out this holy man. "You know, it's funny, what sticks in the memory. As I remember it, you had only just arrived in Verona when we first met."

"True," said Lorenzo easily. "Ages ago."

"But now you pass for a native. Your accent is entirely gone."

And there it was. Just a flicker, but finally Pietro had prodded the man in a sensitive place. For the space of a single breath, Fra Lorenzo's face transformed from genial openness to wary suspicion. Then it was gone, vanishing as soon as it had appeared. Fra Lorenzo tried to laugh. "I wasn't aware I'd assimilated so thoroughly."

"Of course, they speak Occitan in Sebartés as well," continued Pietro. "The transition could not have been too hard."

"Sebartés? I'm sorry, I'm not sure what you mean."

"Really? If I were to mention that a Frenchman called Arnaud Sicre was in the area, what would that mean to you?"

Another breath of hesitation. "Nothing. Who is he?"

"A religious bounty hunter. You must have heard of him. He's the tool of a Dominican called Bernardo Gui."

Fra Lorenzo doggedly shook his head. "Another name that means nothing—"

Pietro sighed. "Fra Lorenzo, that's a ridiculous lie. Who doesn't know Gui? But we'll let that pass in favour of another name – Batto Tricastre. Does that—?"

With the suddenness of lightning from a clear sky, Lorenzo swung all his weight into a blow aimed at Pietro's chin.

Pietro Alaghieri was no longer the untutored teen who had arrived in Verona eleven years earlier. Any moment not spent learning law was spent in practice with Tharwat, and his swordsmanship now rivaled even the proudest soldier's. Training had honed Pietro's reflexes. Instinctively, he caught the blow on his own forearm. Stepping forward, he placed his weak leg behind Lorenzo's knee and unbalanced the friar by forcing that knee to bend. At the same time Pietro twisted his hips and shoved.

"Aaah!" Fra Lorenzo tumbled to the ground heavily enough to lose his wind, crushing the nearby crop of Dog's Mercury.

Pietro stepped out of arm's reach. "That's some temper."

"Wha – wha – wasn't it deserved?" demanded Lorenzo, red-faced.

"Probably," admitted Pietro. "I apologize."

"Is Sicre – in the area?"

"In Spain, last I heard. And as far as I know, he has no reason to come here."

Lorenzo hauled himself to a sitting position. Though flushed with rage, his grey eyes were filled with panic. "What do you want?"

"I wanted to warn you," lied Pietro. "If I know, you can wager that others do as well."

Tears forming in the friar's wide eyes. "It's been so long…"

A couple of Franciscans came around the corner of the wall, both running. "Brother, we heard a shout—"

Lorenzo clambered up to his feet. "I'm fine. Slipped. Stupid of me," he added, with a quick grin. It was convincing. The man was an accomplished liar. In moments Lorenzo had sent them off mollified, thanking them for their concern.

The instant they were gone, Fra Lorenzo turned back to Pietro. They held gazes for a moment, and there was something like hate in the holy man's eyes. Then the friar made a helpless gesture. "Will you walk with me?"

They left the grounds of San Francesco, turning to walk along the riverside where there was less chance of being overheard.

"I'm curious," said Pietro. "What would you have done if your blow had landed?"

"Tied you up, I suppose. Hidden you in the shade of the wall. Then I would have run." The friar uttered a sour chuckle of self-disdain. "It's something I'm good at. Running. How much do you know?"

"Enough. I wasn't lying when I said my father remembered you. When the trials started five years ago, he recalled you came from Sebartés, and how panicked you were when he discovered it. It was not a difficult leap."

Lorenzo sighed. "He was the only one who ever remarked it. It was because of him that I worked so hard to erase every trace of French from my accent. But you say others know?"

Pietro shook his head. "I've never told anyone. But the Scaliger must know. I have no idea who else."

Lorenzo was pensive. "If he's known, he could have done something else long before now."

Pietro didn't reveal what he thought of the Capitano. "He's a politician. He could be waiting until it's of use."

"True." Lorenzo's face was hangdog. "His father burned the Paterenes alive in the Arena."

"From what I understand, Alberto della Scala was a fanatically religious man. His son is devoted, but not cut from that cloth. He bears his excommunication with equanimity."

"Whereas yours bothers you?"

"Every day." It was a small enough secret to share, but Lorenzo could tell that it was something Pietro didn't like to speak of. An attempt to build trust.

They walked in silence for a time. At one point Lorenzo bent down once to pluck a plant growing along the water's edge. He studied it hard, as if hoping it contained the answer to all his problems. Finally he said, "How can I help you?"

"What do you mean?"

"Your motives are not altruistic. You're not here to warn me of impending danger. If you wanted to betray me, you would have done. You need me. There's no other reason to reveal your knowledge. So get on with it. But I warn you, I have very little influence with the Pope."

"I'm not here to extort your help," said Pietro, working hard to be persuasive. "The opposite, really. I'm going to trust you with a secret of mine. I wanted you to know that I can keep secrets. Besides, as you point out, I'm an excommunicant. What do I care about heresy?"

It was a lame attempt at humour, and Lorenzo's stare thoroughly chilled Pietro. But then the Friar shook himself. "A secret of yours?"

Pietro nodded. "You already guessed that Cesco was poisoned. We caught the man who did it. He was hired by someone in Venice, but I think that someone was really from Verona. The poisoner can't identify the man's face, but he can recognize a voice. It's my suspicion that the man will be at Capulletto's feast next week. What we need to do is sneak the poisoner into Capulletto's house in some disguise so that he won't be recognized by the man who hired him. Then, if he hears the right voice, he'll tell us and we can bring the real villain to justice."

"How do you know you can trust the poisoner?"

"We don't. We need someone with him at all times."

"And that's why you're—"

"—asking if you'll help."

Lorenzo considered for a time. "Why do you think it will be someone at the feast?"

"He said the man was noble, well-spoken. All the nobility of Verona will be at the feast."

"Except Montecchio," protested Lorenzo pointlessly.

"I seriously doubt Mari ordered the death of Cangrande's heir."

Lorenzo sighed. "What do you have in mind?"

"Disguise him as a vagabond friar visiting Verona, and have him accompany you to the feast."

"That might be a problem. I don't usually attend such things. Especially not at Capulletto's house."

"They've been throwing these celebrations for ten years. You've never been to one?"

"I have avoided Ser Capulletto's company ever since I caused the rift between him and Ser Montecchio."

Pietro understood at once. "*You* didn't cause the rift. You married Gianozza to Mari in good faith. No one blames you."

"That's not to say I don't deserve some blame."

"Then leave it to God. If Antony doesn't hold you responsible, I don't see why you need to hold him at arm's length."

"What if I say no?"

"To what?"

"To all of it."

"Fra Lorenzo," said Pietro haltingly, "I have a sister in the Order. I was raised to join it myself. I may be an excommunicant, but I have nothing but respect for the Church. You have nothing to fear from me." "There are many who would see it as their duty to the Church to betray me." "I am not one of them. I try not to judge a man without evidence." They reached a street that led back to the Franciscan monastery. Lorenzo stopped. "You have me over a barrel. I'll aid you in your deception, but only because it will aid the child and the Capitano." The friar studied Pietro from head to toe. "You know, I always understood you to be an honourable man. I watched you fight a duel once. I even cheered for you because you were in the right. I mourned your excommunication when I heard of it because I thought you were the wronged party. But now I see the Pope was guided by the Lord in making his decision. You are in league with the Devil."

Barbed words. Pietro answered in kind. "Of the pair of us, I'm not the one the Pope would like to see burned at the stake."

It was past the hedge of Pietro's teeth before he could stop it, and at once he tried to mend his gaffe. "When he was five, Cesco asked me a question. 'Uncle Pietro,' he said, 'how do you put your talk back in your mouth?' I wish I had an answer now. That was unworthy. I apologize."

The friar just stared, mouth set in a deep grimace.

After an uncomfortable silence, Pietro said, "I'll send my sister to you. She knows nothing of your secret. Nor does anyone else. I mean it. I will not betray you."

Lorenzo said nothing. There was nothing to say. But Pietro made a last stab at amends. "You told Brother Giovanni that everything on earth has the potential for both good and evil. Consider this me doing evil for a good cause."

Fra Lorenzo studied Pietro as he would a weed in his garden. "Matthew 7:17. *Every good tree bringeth forth good fruit; but a corrupt tree bringeth forth evil fruit.* It says nothing about good fruit from an evil tree." Turning, he left Pietro standing at the water's edge with the thought.

# TWENTY-TWO

*Verona*
*Thursday, 25 July*
*1325*

IT WAS THREE DAYS before the Capulletto feast when Cesco was well enough to join the household for both the noontime dinner and evening supper. The sun was in the middle of the sky when he met Pietro, Bailardino, Antonia, Detto, Valentino, and the visiting Castelbarco at the boards.

"Where's the doctor?" asked Bailardino.

"And Tharwat," added Cesco, amused by Bail's persistent dislike of the astrologer.

Tucking in, Pietro said, "On their way to Mantua to discover who made the poison."

That rocked everyone back on their heels. Even Antonia looked surprised. But Pietro knew the best way to make Cesco curious was to evade the truth. Lay it bare and he might just let it alone.

*You really are starting to think like them.* It was an ugly thought, one that had haunted him since his interview with Fra Lorenzo. Focusing on the dish before him, Pietro said, "This looks excellent." It did – horseflesh in an apple sauce.

Bail laughed. "The cooks choose my meals for me. I have no say in it. And I have to admit, it's always better than what I could have come up with – warm bread, a bowl of porridge, and a salted hunk of game, probably. Kat picked our servants years ago. Even unable to enjoy it, her meals always consist of the best dishes."

Castelbarco said, "You don't strike me as an Epicurean, Bail."

"O, I'm no Morsicato when it comes to these things. The cooks know their master is no effete. But they make sure that sitting down to table is a pleasure."

Detto was focused on Pietro's statement. "Do they have a lead on the poison maker?"

"Yes," said Pietro.

"Will they kill him?" asked Valentino.

"That depends on what he tells them."

"But it's illegal to even own poison," argued Detto.

Pietro had filled his mouth, so Antonia answered. "A law is only as good as the men who enforce it."

Castelbarco applauded. "How well put! Mind if I quote you next time I'm wrangling with the Anziani?"

"Feel free," replied Antonia. "It's hardly original – father used to say it."

"Speaking of fathers," said Pietro, blatantly opening up a new topic. "Cesco must be dying to know what Cangrande was like as a boy. Bail, you knew him then. Any good stories come to mind?"

Cesco gave Pietro a curious look, but Bailardino was already laughing with pleasure. "O dear Lord! A million! Which do you want to hear?"

Castelbarco groaned, a rueful smile on his face. "What about the time he stole the clappers to all the city bells? Or the time we thought he'd drowned in the Adige, teaching himself to fish with a spear? We spent hours in the freezing water, only to find him safe at home, eating salmon."

"Which he'd bought," added Bailardino, leaning his chair back against the wall.

Pietro had a particular story in mind. "I recall hearing something about him showing up uninvited to a knighting ceremony wearing a masque."

"Ah!" cried Bailardino as Castelbarco sighed with mock wistfulness. "I remember all too well! Many worthy men were invested that day. The very soul of chivalry, those men were— "

"Could you possibly have been among them?" asked Cesco, laughing already.

"Come to think of it, I was! And lesser men, too, like Castelbarco here." Castelbarco responded by tapping the bottom of Bailardino cup in mid-sip, spilling just enough to make the speaker appear to be dribbling. Guffawing, Bailardino mopped his chin. "Must be getting old. Anyway, it wasn't our knighting that made that day memorable. No, it was himself the elf. Not so small as you, boy, but close."

"Thank God," said Cesco. "There's hope for me yet."

"I remember that day as well," said Castelbarco, explaining to

Bailardino's sons, "It was at the *Corte Bandita*, almost thirty years back—"

"Dear God, I'm getting old," moaned Bail.

"—it was your father's big day. Married in the morning, knighted in the afternoon!"

"But the little puppy pissed all over my big day!" Bail pointed to all three boys. "Your grandfather was celebrating a victory over the Paduans – they never learn."

"The city was thronged—" said Castelbarco.

"Noble guests, actors, jugglers, and minstrels—" Bail interjected.

"Alberto della Scala showered us new knights with gifts—"

Bail grinned at the memory. "Flemish cloaks, scarlet, purple, green, white, and all lined with lamb's wool or fur—"

"I still have mine."

"Thrifty, my friend, thrifty."

"Now, boys, your grandfather was a favourite of the last pope's—"

"Unlike Cangrande and our friend here." Bail jerked a thumb at Pietro.

"—so he invited lots of cardinals and priests close to Boniface."

"In front of them all I knelt for blessing and he knighted me."

"Only you?" asked Antonia airily.

Bailardino harrumphed as Castelbarco grinned. "Well no – but no one of any importance." Ducking a swipe from the aging noble beside him, Bail fended off continued attacks while he told the story. "Like I said, Castelbarco was knighted. My brother was there, too, but he's so small I'm surprised anyone noticed. Oh, and Cangrande's brother Bartolomeo was knighted, but everybody already loved him. Cangrande's cousin Nicolo was knighted that day, wasn't he?"

"That's right, he was!" nodded Castelbarco, still making mock sword strokes. "I'd forgotten him completely!"

"Who was he?" asked Cesco between laughs. The boys were thoroughly enjoying seeing their elders be foolish.

"The first Mastino's only son," explained Bailardino. "Dead, what, twenty years? But he was made a knight that day. Not that it mattered, really, because all eyes were on me. Y'see, I'd just come from my wedding, and there was my Katerina, as refined as a Giotto, lovelier than Venus at her bath. So all the crowd was looking at me and whispering—"

Pietro broke in. " '*Who's that big ox with the beautiful wife? He must be somebody's brother, or rich, because he's so ugly. Poor lady!*'"

Detto came to his father's defence, flinging an apple slice at Pietro. Cesco rallied for Pietro, hitting Val with some hard cheese. Amid the flying food Bail shook a fist. "Were you even alive then, Alaghieri?"

"Wait wait wait!" cried Cesco. "You said Venus at her bath! So *La*

*Donna* came to the festival naked?" Detto and Val turned their full attention to attacking Cesco, who gleefully defended himself as everyone at the table laughed harder.

The only woman present, a sighing Antonia gently put a stop to their antics. "What happened then?"

Bailardino was busily mopping apple sauce from his forehead, so Castelbarco picked up the narrative. "Alberto della Scala was on the dais doling out knighthoods, surrounded by a few thousand well-wishers. Suddenly this horse starts pushing through carrying a little fellow in a masque and cape."

Bail's face came up out of his shirt. "I remember thinking, 'Oh, a midget! This'll be good!'"

"We all thought he was there to perform tricks because he was riding bare-back, with only a rope halter for steering. And we were right. He begins this course of acrobatic moves, handstands and flips, all while he's racing a stallion around and around the dais —"

"The crowd went mad applauding and laughing."

"Nogarola, who's telling this story?"

"I am," replied Bail. "The little twerp plucks a spear from one of the guards and hoists it up over his head, twirling it like a girl with a needle. Well, suddenly what's been amusing antics become threatening. Some men step out to grab him, but the spear lashes out, cracking a skull, trapping a knee. The imp doesn't stop until he reached the podium where we're all standing with our thumbs up our – noses. Up our noses. He leaps at us, spear in hand. He lands all set to attack, then, just before I chop him in half —" He paused, considering. "There's a joke there. Cutting a midget in half. Would that make him a quarter-man —?"

"Half a half-pint?" suggested Pietro.

"A demi-dwarf," said Cesco.

"This is why you can't tell stories," said Castelbarco sourly.

Bail made him a face. "So the insect is about to sting our beloved leader in the gut when he drops down on his knees, holding the spear out like a gift, calm as you please. Now old Alberto was a cool one. He booms out, 'What do you mean, stranger, invading our lands and disrupting our festival?' And the midget, sounding just like our Cesco here, whimpered and sniveled —" Cesco launched a piece of food at Bailardino's head. "I mean, in a manly voice, nothing at all like a little girl-child, he says, 'I come to claim knighthood. Try me as you might.'

"Well, after a moment of thought, Alberto calls forth his new knights – eleven in all, I think – and tells us to devise tests for the little puke. Some of them didn't quite take it seriously, making him recite poetry or swish his sword through the air!" He made a couple of weak slashes at Castelbarco, informing his audience who had come up with that particular lame task. "Whereas I understood how important, how truly fraught with meaning, the charge of knighthood is. I made him parade around the dais ten times, holding a banner over his head."

"A banner covered in nightsoil," supplied Castelbarco.

"A mark of his courage and dedication!"

"Defecation!" cried Cesco, wincing.

"If he let it fall, he wasn't fit to become a knight!"

"If he'd let it fall," said Castelbarco to Cesco, "it would have landed on his head and he'd've been covered in – well, in —"

"Shit," finished Antonia with a disgusted look for all these idiots.

"Er, yes, exactly." Castelbarco quickly moved on. "At the end of eleven trials, the boy climbs up the dais to claim his reward. Alberto then delivers the charge of knighthood and helps the little imp to stand. 'What shall we call you, my boy?'"

"He almost said son." Bail was determined to finish the story himself. "And though we all know who he is, the little guy's earned the right to unmasque himself. Well, he grins at us, for the first time looking his age. He tears the masque off his head, turns round and asks the crowd, 'What's my name?'"

"Cangrande!" cried the table in unison.

Bailardino nodded, his smile fading a little. "Then he collapsed. It was Kat who picked him up. She had a good joke about it – something about him carrying a sword and a rattle. She had to play his nurse for eight days. I could have killed him! Some honeymoon!"

Pietro was smiling and laughing with the rest until Antonia caught his eye. She had no trouble communicating her thoughts: *Why did you want Cesco to hear this story?*

Pietro had good reason. Armed with an example, Cesco's official entrance to Veronese life would have a sense of tradition, bolstering his claim. Already he could see the boy's mind considering how to make the biggest splash.

Of course, it had always been likely that Cesco would outdo himself to create a spectacle. That didn't worry Pietro. What frightened him was what Cangrande might do if he felt himself being eclipsed.

◆     ◊     ◆

## Mantua

A mass of bricks surrounded entirely by water, that was the impression Mantua gave the eye. No plaster on the walls, and therefore no frescos upon the plaster. Just brick upon brick, topped by clay tile. A functional city, a serious city, a city without a sense of play.

Perhaps the reason lay in its history. Founded three thousand years earlier on the banks of the Mincio River, Mantua was built upon a quasi-island. Sadly, this defensive position did not prevent it from being conquered time and time again, first by the Gauls, then the Romans. Augustus settled his veterans around Mantua in the hope of bolstering its backbone. But the moment Rome collapsed, so did Mantua. Goths, Byzantines, Longobards, Franks, and Tuscans all took Mantua for their own. Though not valuable in itself, the city was a perfect staging area for northern Italy. Which led to its being named the capital of Lombardy.

For two hundred years Mantua had been a free commune. Determined never to be ruled by outside forces again, the citizens fought strenuously to defend themselves from the growing Holy Roman Empire. One ingenious Mantuan had altered the flow of the Mincio, creating four 'lakes' to reinforce the city's natural defenses.

Then, just fifty years past, the Bonaccolsi family had seized control of the city and switched allegiance from Guelph to Ghibelline. Which made Mantua an ally to Verona. Not as populous, Mantua had benefited from the alliance with its northern neighbour. Trade flourished, and a new militaristic fervor rose. For the first time in its history the city could look forward to being the conqueror, not the conquered.

Unlike Verona, Mantua had not invested in towers. There were a handful, yes, but as a whole the city felt squat, crouched, wary, waiting for the next blow to fall. The people of Mantua bore a similar look. Stern, guarded, reserved.

Amidst this serious community walked two unusual figures. One was a stout, long-armed, fork-bearded fellow wearing a urine-glass about his throat, declaring his medical profession. The other was a Moor in fine clothes with a big falchion on his back, carving a path through a sea of Mantuans.

As citizens made way, the doctor grunted. "What I don't understand is why you don't wear that all the time."

Tharwat glanced down at his finely tailored garments. Worked into every piece was the Scaligeri crest. He shrugged. "Itches."

"It damn well doesn't itch and you know it," groused Morsicato. "It looks magnificent. And no one will bother you with that crest on your sleeve."

"Which is why I wear it this day. Mantua is hardly less hostile to men of my colour than Venice. We have enough difficulties." He paused at the intersection of three streets. "Do you see a sign? Or is this another Venice, where the streets have no names." They had been forced to leave their mounts at a stable outside the walls and cross a bridge spanning the man-made lakes. But on foot, the city design made no sense.

Morsicato was not inclined to let his companion escape the topic. "I just don't see why you make it hard on yourself when you could wear that every day."

"It would ruin me," said the Moor. "Let's try this way." He set off, and Morsicato trotted to keep up.

"Did you see a sign?"

"No."

"If you didn't see a sign, how do you know where we're going?"

"I don't."

"We should just ask," suggested Morsicato.

"And let everyone know our destination? No."

"But just wandering the streets, it could take days!"

"Then days it takes."

"It better not take days. We have to be back by Sunday. I'm not missing Capulletto's feast. I'm sure it will be memorable."

"We will be back in time."

"I've only been to one – the first one, in fact. Oh damn, what food he serves!"

The Moor eyed the doctor. "I always wonder you are not fatter."

"A discerning palate does not lead to gluttony," replied the doctor haughtily. "In fact, if you have a taste for good food, you tend to starve among the common fare." Hearing an odd sound, Morsicato rounded on his companion. "What was that?"

"Nothing."

"I heard it, what was it?" The doctor saw the flicker of a smile curling Tharwat's lower lip. "Damn me. Was that a laugh?"

"No."

"You're right – that was no laugh. That was a titter."

Tharwat was solemn. "I do not titter."

"Admit it! You giggled like a girl!"

"I had something in my throat. My scars make strange noises sometimes."

For years Morsicato had longed to examine al-Dhaamin's throat. By now it was far more than professional curiosity. He wanted to know who had inflicted such a disastrous injury upon his friend. But now was not the time to ask. "Deny it how you like, I'm telling Pietro what I heard. And Cesco."

Tharwat gave the doctor an evil glance, then continued walking.

"They certainly like identifying themselves with Virgil," observed the doctor. "That's the third house I've seen claiming to be his birthplace."

"Blame Pietro's father. He made Virgil popular again."

"Popular is the right word," replied Morsicato. "Did you know there's a movement to translate *The Aeneid* into the *vulgare*. I wonder who will attempt it?"

"Cesco should do it," said Tharwat.

"He'd try to improve it. Is that the church?" Morsicato pointed at a round brick building two stories tall, with another ring at the top.

"It is a rotunda," said Tharwat. "I see nothing to mark it as a church."

"There," said Morsicato, squinting at the wooden doors. "Inscribed, the sign of San Lorenzo."

The Moor squinted at the image of a man beside a flaming grid-iron. "I have never understood why Christian saints are depicted with the means of their deaths."

"Christ died on the cross," said Morsicato simply.

"Then why worship the cross? Shouldn't you worship the man?" The doctor shot the Moor a scandalized look. At once Tharwat bowed his head. "Forgive me. Arguing with Cesco is enough to corrupt the purest heart. Please, go in so you may keep your promise to Ser Alaghieri. I will find the apothecary and return in fifteen minutes."

The doctor didn't want to waste time in church, but Pietro had made him promise. So he stepped through the door, bent a knee, crossed himself, and prayed in a pew. Finished, he made a donation with money Pietro had given him. Morsicato didn't know why Alaghieri wanted forgiveness from San Lorenzo, but he was more than happy to pray on behalf of Pietro, who was unable to pray anywhere.

Emerging, Morsicato found al-Dhaamin waiting for him, drawing curious glances. "It's the clothes," explained Morsicato. "You'd draw less attention naked."

"I doubt that. Come. It's not far." Tharwat led him around two corners to a short flight of steps leading down to a cellar door. Over the door was a wooden plank with two words scrawled across it: *Lorenzo's Apothecary*. "It matches Borachio's description, and the name is correct."

Morsicato's lip curled. "A little presumptuous, naming your shop after a saint. Especially a saint not interested in nature."

"Geographic reference," replied the Moor. "It notes his nearness to the Rotunda."

"Do we just go in?"

"I'd rather we weren't seen entering," said the Moor. "We are somewhat conspicuous."

"What then, start a fire and smoke him out?"

"There is a rear entrance."

"You'd rather we broke in the rear?"

The doctor's deliberate unhelpfulness never seemed to discommode the Moor. "I will go to the rear and wait. Count to twenty, then go in and sound him out as a man of medicine. If he is unhelpful, call for me." Without awaiting a reply, the Moor strode away.

Morsicato counted twenty, then descended and knocked on the apothecary's door. No response. Knocking a little louder, Morsicato could hear a shuffling within. Then nothing. Morsicato began to hammer on the door's wooden frame. This elicited an unintelligible cry the door's other side. Morsicato banged the palm of his hand so hard he feared he might split it open.

This time the voice within was quite clear. "Go away!"

"I have business!" called Morsicato.

"Take your business somewhere else!"

"I am a doctor, I require herbs!"

A suspicious pause. "What do you want?"

"What I don't want is to be standing in the street, shouting my fool head off for all to hear. Open this damned door!"

There was muttering and a scraping of a barricade, then the door swung wide and a lean man of forty or more peeked out. His face might have been unremarkable but for the brow – the apothecary had the most prominent forehead that the doctor had ever seen. Adorning it was a single eyebrow that twitched and danced as if it lived independently of its owner. Morsicato couldn't decide if it was the massive brow that dwarfed the rest of the features, or if God had played a cruel joke on this man, giving him small eyes, nose, and lips against the monstrous fuzzy Alp above them.

The chin bore whiskers. It wasn't a beard, but neither was it clean-shaven. It was the growth of a week or more. Bizarrely, the man wore the robes of a Franciscan friar, but the homespun brown was tattered and worn. A cast-off from an order that embraced poverty. This was a poor man.

Belatedly, Morsicato noticed the apothecary held a club with nails crudely hammered into it at all angles. Seeing Morsicato's *jourdan*, the man relaxed his grip on the home-made mace. "You really are a doctor."

"I said I was," retorted Morsicato.

"My mistake," shrugged the apothecary. "I thought you were a bill-collector." He glanced nervously into the street above them. "Hurry, come in."

Morsicato did not wish to hurry into the dark, dank space on the other side of the open door, but did as he was bid. Instantly he started to sneeze, though what was assaulting his senses he couldn't tell. A single taper burned on a scarred table. Through watering eyes, Morsicato peered around at the chamber that was both shop and home to the apothecary. The floor was littered in packthread and the remains of dead roses. In the corner was a truckle-bed, barely off the floor. Skin crawling, Morsicato imagined he could actually see the lice in the straw.

The wall-shelves were bedecked with cracked and crumbling earthen pots, bladders, and boxes filled with the instruments of the man's trade. Yet despite the apparent poverty, Morsicato perceived the care taken to separate items. Instead of jamming the shelves to overflowing, many of the larger items hung from hooks in the ceiling. Snake skins, tortoise shells, cured fish turned inside out. On one wall hung a ragged old tapestry, probably thrown out by some local lord.

The apothecary shut the door, bolted it, and dragged a trunk against it for good measure. In the dim light he studied Morsicato. "You're not a Mantuan doctor."

"I'm traveling. My name is Pathino," lied Morsicato, using the name of a man they all owed a bad turn.

"Never heard of you."

Morsicato waited, but the man didn't say anything more. "I like to know the name of the men I do business with."

The apothecary's beady eyes became hooded with suspicion. "You need herbs, I have them. If you can pay, why do we need to know names?"

"What if I want to recommend you to someone?"

"You know where to find me. I've been in this shop for fifteen years. Three fires, a hundred break-ins, and one flood haven't changed that."

"Very well. I'll just ask you neighbours your name when I leave. They're bound to know it."

The doctor could see the other man's mind working. If Morsicato paid for herbs, then went asking the neighbours his name, they would know that he possessed some money. He was the kind of man who owed everyone money.

"Spolentino. That's my name. Now what herbs does the fine traveling doctor need?"

Instead of answering, Morsicato looked around. "You have an extensive inventory. Do you have steady business?"

"Does it look like I have a steady business?" demanded Spolentino angrily. "What do you need?"

Morsicato felt something brush his shoulder. "Is that an alligator skin?"

"It is. Brought all the way from Egypt, where it was caught at great personal risk and expense."

"I'm sure. But I have no need of alligator scales. I was just curious—" Morsicato examined some musty seeds that lay on the old table. But the apothecary swept them onto the floor in an angry gesture. He still held the club in his other hand.

"Look, I'm not here to satisfy your curiosity. Tell me what you want, I'll tell you how much. Else you can get out."

Time to broach the subject. "I'm looking for scorpion venom."

Spolentino recoiled, his massive brow bristling with suspicion. "And you came to me specifically?"

"You *are* an apothecary," said Morsicato lamely.

"I assume you know, doctor, that scorpion juice can be deadly."

"Yes," said Morsicato. "But it can be —"

"As a traveling doctor you might not know it, but Mantua's law says it's death to even own the means of making poison. Which, as a doctor, you must admit is ridiculous. The same things that kill can cure. It just takes a skilled hand to know the difference."

"True, true," agreed Morsicato. "Now, for the venom —"

"I don't have any," said Spolentino bluntly.

"Oh? But I heard —"

"What? What did you hear? From whom?" Spolentino was working himself in an apoplexy. His panic was clear. "I don't deal in poisons, never have! Who sent you? Who?"

The agitated apothecary was between Morsicato and the door, the ugly club raised high. Tharwat had mentioned a rear exit – it had to be behind the moth-eaten tapestry. Backing towards it, Morsicato held out his empty hands. "Wait, I just —"

The spiked club started making arcs in the air. "*Who sent you?!*"

Morsicato was on the verge of doing something desperate when there was a cracking sound at his back. The tapestry fluttered behind him and Tharwat appeared, falchion in hand.

Horrified, Spolentino instantly dropped his club and fell to his knees. "I don't have the money!"

Eyes on the apothecary, Tharwat said, "Are you well, doctor?"

"Fine." Morsicato cleared his throat. "I'm fine. Thank you."

"I don't have the money!" cried Spolentino again.

"Stop talking," said Morsicato testily. "We're not here for money."

That brought the apothecary up short. In his mind, all anyone wanted from him was money. His eyes narrowed. "What is this? Who are you?"

"We need to ask you some questions." Morsicato reached into his robe and produced a bag of coins. "If you like, we could torture you, maybe maim you for life. But we'd much rather bribe you."

Spolentino's eyes fixed on the purse. "How much?"

"Depends on what you know. We'll start by talking about the poisons you don't sell."

♦     ◊     ♦

## Verona

Undressing for bed, Pietro was struggling with tangled points when Cesco knocked on his door. "Nuncle?"

"What can I do for you?"

Entering, Cesco nudged the door shut with his toe. "That wasn't an accident, me hearing Bail's story."

"No, it wasn't."

"You *want* me to make a scene?"

Pietro freed his shirt from the tangle of cords that held his small-clothes. Even though he had started wearing trousers years ago, he had never quite given up on the trappings of hose. "You object?"

"I'm suspicious. You've never wanted me to make a scene before."

Pietro sat on the bed. The starlight from the single window gave plenty of light to see by. "We were in hiding then. It was unwanted attention. This is different. You won't be happy unless you live up to expectations."

"Or flout them," said Cesco. "I could be the model of filial piety."

"Is that what you want to do?"

"No," admitted Cesco. "But by telling me that story, you seem to be insisting I out-shoot the target."

"I suppose I am." Pietro waited a moment. "So do it."

Cesco grinned. "I like the Verona you. You're a little meaner, more determined. It suits you."

Pietro didn't know how to respond to that, so he stood and crossed to a bundle lying beside a bowl of water, on top of his shaving tools. He picked up the package and tossed it to Cesco. "I got this for you."

Unwrapping the cloth, Cesco held the object to the starlight. It was a masque, a grotesque *carnevale* affair with three faces connected at the cheekbones. One face laughed, one screamed, one cried. Cesco fitted the hard leather into place. The screaming face was at the center, the others curved to cover the sides of his head. "How do I look?"

"Horrific," echoed Pietro.

"Is this like the one he wore?"

"I doubt it. It isn't meant to be."

Cesco slipped it off and looked at it again. "I like it. But isn't it a little predictable?"

"Yes. But that's me. I thought it was a nice homage. It's up to you to flout expectations. Just let us in on what you plan."

"So you can censure me?"

"So we can help." Pietro smiled. "You have an idea, don't you?"

"I do. But what I have in mind may not be possible."

"*Do what is possible,*" said Pietro, quoting the saint that shared Cesco's name. "*And soon you will find yourself doing the impossible.* What did you have in mind?"

# TWENTY-THREE

*Verona*

*Sunday, 28 July*

*1325*

THE SKY WAS MAGNIFICENT, a blue of purest summer. The sun had barely begun its descent when the gates to the Capulletti house were thrown wide to welcome revelers. Servants in tricked-out particoloured tunics and expensive hose began to usher the guests through the arched brick tunnel into the courtyard.

Pietro Alaghieri approached the gates, dressed to the hilt. It was not his habit to wear expensive clothes. Until today he'd believed his days of fancy hats was behind him. But for this occasion he had gone out of his way to dress sumptuously. From the tip of his high feathered cap to the soles of his tall leather boots, he was a vision of sartorial splendor.

His shirt, which showed only at the cuffs and collar, was of a pristine white batiste. His farsetto was of the old style, hanging down almost to his knees. So blue it was nearly black, it had a pattern sewn into it using the same colour thread creating the Alaghieri family crest - *per pale or* and *sable a fess argent* - interwoven with a running mastiff, the symbol of his knighthood. Its sleeves billowed out at the elbow, short in front, long and pointed in back, reaching past his knees.

The one garment he'd refused outright to wear was hose. He'd not donned a pair of skin-tight leggings since receiving the ugly wound on his thigh. Thus he wore knee-length breeches that matched the doublet, tucked into his tall boots.

Belted and trimmed, the whole affair was topped with a short, brocaded cape of blue with real silver accenting the edges. "To be removed only when you sit to eat," he'd been instructed by his eleven year-old goad. Of course Cesco had chosen his clothes.

One matter he hadn't thought about was his complexion, the deep circles under his eyes. "We want you to look as young as you are," Cesco told him. "If your clothes attract a potential wife, we don't want her to look at your face and run." So two weeks of lying awake fretting was masqued with the aid of tinted beeswax, lightly applied. *Like a whore trying to hide her age.* Pietro felt ridiculous, and was uncomfortably aware of the admiring glances he was now receiving.

Standing at his elbow was Antonia, dressed far more demurely in a simple Germanic gown, embroidered with ribbon trims on the neckline. The sleeves ended in a point over the hand with a loop to go over the second finger to keep them in place. Her head was covered and there was no plunging neckline on her gown ("Not that I have so much to display," she'd muttered as she'd dressed). She was thankful that she hadn't yet cut off her hair for the Order. It wasn't entirely vanity. A shorn woman was noticeable.

Her simple appearance was by design as well as inclination. The idea was for Pietro to draw attention to himself while Antonia faded into the background. "You can be the sun," she'd said, "and I shall be a cavern."

"If you go unnoticed next to me, when Cangrande arrives you'll be positively invisible."

"Isn't that the whole idea?"

Standing just behind them in the teeming mass of party-goers was Fra Lorenzo. He didn't look happy to be there, though he was pleasant enough to Antonia when she spoke to him.

Beside Lorenzo was another man in Franciscan robes. He didn't look happy, either. "Wish I had shoes," said Borachio, shifting his weight on the cobbled street.

"You get used to it," said Lorenzo.

"And my head itches," complained Borachio, feeling the bare patch on his head for the umpteenth time.

"You get used to that, too."

"I'm surprised you haven't already," said Pietro pointedly. "After all, Brother Lucius, you've been in orders how long?"

In response to Pietro's warning look, Borachio answered dutifully. "Three years. But it was a very lax house of God. The abbot had three sons in the order with him." He grinned, and once again Pietro fretted. In the abstract, it had been such a marvelous idea. But the reality could light a fire to engulf them all.

Spolentino had been a disappointment. He had indeed sold the poison to Borachio, but had no idea why his shop had been chosen. He listed many of the people who had bought from him over the years, but since that list had included nobles as high as Passerino Bonaccolsi's late brother, there was no help from that quarter. So Pietro's best hope for exposing the man behind Cesco's poisoning lay with this poisonous drunkard dressed in friar's robes.

As the quartet entered the passage, other guests greeted Pietro warmly. Antonia whiled away their slow progress in the tunnel by talking to Lorenzo about his Order, and thus covertly instructing Borachio on his role.

After three minutes of inching forward in relative darkness, they emerged from the tunnel and gazed up at the three-story building on their right. "This is a beautiful house," said Antonia.

"Your brother said he's never been here," said Lorenzo politely, pushing back his hood and patting the sweat off his forehead. "But you left Verona after he did. Did you never attend a Capulletto ball?"

"I did, but they were still living on their country estates. Before Old Ludovico died."

Hand sore from successive shaking, Pietro pointed. "The fresco work is beautiful." The walls were probably brick like most of the city's buildings, but it was impossible to tell because they were entirely covered with plaster and a painted story. "Can you tell the subject?"

"Ask Brother Lucius," said Lorenzo unhelpfully.

"I, ah, I don't —" stammered Borachio.

"David and Uriah the Hittite," supplied Antonia. "From the second book of Samuel."

Pietro suppressed a groan. "Of course it is." He saw now how the story began on their left, where a lower building, two stories tall, depicted King David on a rooftop spying on the happy couple of Uriah and his wife Bathsheba. Husband and wife were embracing by a pitcher of water, washing each other and laughing, while the jealous king looked down on them.

The cycle continued on the wall opposite the tunnel, also only two-stories high. Here Uriah was in the forefront of the battle against the Ammonites, cut off from aid. A magnificent warrior, he fought valiantly, but there was little doubt he was finished – a figure loomed behind him, ready to stab the Hittite captain in the back.

High in the corner of the same fresco stood David and Joab, David's warlord. David was pointing to the field and handing Joab a note. Despite the ban on church-going, Pietro had kept up his bible readings, and easily recalled that message: *'Set ye Uriah in the front of the battle, where the fight is the strongest: and leave ye him, that he may be wounded and die.'* The jealous king wanted the valiant soldier dead so he might marry Bathsheba himself.

The third panel was striking, covering the wall of the house proper, a full story higher than the other two. Around windows and doors, the background was a deep and impenetrable blue. The foreground was covered with snow. Just to the left of the tall arched door in the wall, David was dragging a weeping, widowed Bathsheba towards an altar, only to find his path blocked by a haloed man on the door's other side. This was Nathan, sent by God to rebuke David's act. Cleverly, the torch sconce beside the door was placed to rise out of Nathan's hand.

In the distant hills behind the three main figures were several smaller scenes, which Pietro knew to be the events of the parable Nathan tells David:

> *There were two men in a certain city, the one rich and the other poor.*
>
> *The rich man had very many flocks and herds.*
>
> *But the poor man had nothing but one little ewe lamb, which he had bought. And he brought it up, and it grew up with him and with his children; it used to eat of his morsel, and drink from his cup, and lie in his bosom, and it was like a daughter to him.*
>
> *Now there came a traveler to the rich man, and he was unwilling to take one of his own flock or herd to prepare for the wayfarer who had come to him, but he took the poor man's lamb, and prepared it for the man who had come to him.*

Pietro saw both men, one surrounded by sheep, the other cradling his single ewe. Further on, the rich man stealing and killing the lamb. David was angry at the thief in Nathan's tale, until he was told he himself was the thief – he had plenty, and yet had stolen from a man with only one precious thing. Nathan then said that justice demanded the king's most precious thing be sacrificed in return.

Turning, Pietro looked up at the archway over the tunnel from which he'd just emerged. Sure enough, there was the end of the tale, with David weeping as his newborn son was taken to Heaven. Bathsheba was mourning nearby, but the artist had performed a neat trick by having her face turned towards the first frame of the cycle, thus making her seem to mourn the idyllic days with her former husband. Nathan watched the scene, crowned with God's righteous light. Over his shoulder hovered the dead Uriah, an angelic forgiveness on his face.

Astonished, Pietro stared at the painted faces with a sick feeling in his stomach. Uriah wore the unmistakable visage of the master of the house, Antony Capulletto himself. The wicked David bore the face of Mariotto Montecchio. And Bathsheba was a perfect rendering of Gianozza della Bella. Or rather, Gianozza Montecchio, once Antony's betrothed, now Mari's wife of ten years.

Most disturbingly, the saintly Nathan wore Pietro's own face – the straight brown hair, the sharp cheekbones and the slightly flat chin below the crooked smile. There was even the slightest hint of lameness on Nathan's right side.

"Oh dear Lord!" Pietro exclaimed as the idealized likeness of himself gazed sternly down at him.

Antonia snickered, and even Lorenzo had to smile. "It seems Capulletto has declared you his champion for all eternity."

Pietro closed his eyes, thinking back. When Mariotto had secretly married Antony's bride-to-be, Antony had been suffering a broken leg and was unable to properly challenge his former friend to a duel. It was Pietro who'd thrown down the gauntlet in his place, though not to fight Mariotto. Pietro had wanted to draw out the bride's cousin, Marsilio de Carrara. It had worked the way he wanted, and he'd fought in Verona's famous Arena, surviving only by intercession.

Lorenzo was speaking again. "...had a minor hand in it. I was asked by the Prior, as a favour to Ser Capulletto, to mix some red ochre for the – what's it called, the *sinopia*?"

"Yes," said Antonia absently, eyeing the majestic expanse of fresco. "It's a part of the process, named after Sinope, a town on the Black Sea that's known for its red pigments." Pietro shot his sister a quizzing glance. "I've had a fair amount of truck with artists and painters." Lorenzo turned to stare at her. "For illustrating manuscripts!"

"Ah." Chastened, Lorenzo grinned ruefully. "Forgive me. Though ordained, I am still of a sinful mind."

"Me, too." Borachio did not look at all abashed.

Antonia said something low in Latin that Pietro missed. He turned back to the tallest wall. "The snowy night at least is apt." It had been snowing during his duel in the Arena.

"God's light is even moreso," said Antonia. "Look at it closely."

Hidden in the rays of light from heaven were thin golden rungs, just like the rungs of the ladder in the Scaligeri crest. As Pietro had been fighting for justice in Cangrande's court, so Nathan was issuing divine retribution in the name of God.

"What poor sap did he get to paint this?" asked Pietro with a snort.

"Maestro Giotto himself, of course!" The answer came from Antony Capulletto, merrily elbowing other guests from his path. Their host was decked out in a gorgeous robe full of geometric shapes trimmed in gold on black. On a smaller man it would have looked ridiculous, but Antony had both the height and the breadth to pull it off. As ever, his sandy hair was tousled, as if he'd just woken from sleep and slapped it into place.

"How now, how now!" Antony's greeting was loud enough for the world to hear. "Pietro Alaghieri, my dear friend, guardian to the Scaliger's heir, welcome to my house! I've had to wait so long for you to visit. And Antonia! More beautiful than ever – please tell me that you're not still planning on joining the Order?"

"I am, yes." Antonia received his welcoming kiss with grace. "It will soon be Suor Beatrice."

Antony shook his head. "God's gain is a loss to all lusty men, I guess." He frowned at Lorenzo and Borachio. "Forgive me, Brothers. I don't recall your name on the invitation list."

"They are my chaperones," explained Antonia quickly. "Brothers and sister in Christ, you know."

"Ah." Antony eyed Lorenzo in distaste. It had been Lorenzo who had married Mariotto to Gianozza. Though an unwitting sin on Lorenzo's part, clearly Capulletto had not forgotten. But to his credit, Antony welcomed the holy man, then turned to Borachio. "And this brother? I don't recall —"

"He's newly arrived in Verona," said Lorenzo. Pietro was glad to see the friar pick up his cue without prompting. "May I introduce Brother Lucius, late of Naples."

"An honour," said Borachio, bowing from the waist and steepling his hands.

Antony spared the disguised drunkard barely a glance. "What a terrific fortnight! Cangrande alive, his son and heir here and safe, and my dear friend Pietro returned to Verona at last. Any one of them deserves a feast, let alone all! Now tell me truly, what do you think of my fresco?"

"It's – breathtaking, Antony." Before Antony could press further, Pietro added, "You say Giotto painted it? I thought he was too busy in Florence these days to take outside commissions."

"Well... I might have overshot myself. I mean to say, Giotto *designed* it. I met him some years ago, and he agreed to a commission. He did the walls of Verona's palace, remember? But it was his godson and his best student who actually came to oversee the painting. Still, the designs and colours are pure Giotto!"

"His godson?" asked Pietro.

"Boy called Taddeo Gaddi. But, I assure you, this is Giotto's work. You recognize the story?"

Antonia came to her brother's rescue. "I'm surprised you chose a

Biblical story. The new style is market scenes and city life. I hear it's all the rage in Avignon."

"That's no surprise," said Lorenzo with feeling. "The French have no sense of true piety, God rot their hides."

Pietro said nothing. If Lorenzo's own disguise included a vocal hatred of all things French, it was no business of his.

Antony was nodding vigourously. "I completely agree. Your holy fervor serves you well! The next time Cangrande dies, we'll call you to perform the last rites!" Antony burst out laughing. Pietro and Antonia chuckled dutifully, while Lorenzo crossed himself and said, "God forbid. Now, if you will pardon me, my lord, I'd like to look at your garden – your olive trees are doing better than mine. Come, Brother Lucius."

Clearly Lorenzo wanted out of this engagement, which suited Pietro to the ground. The plan was for him to keep Borachio out of the way until the moment of truth.

As the bemused Friar and his captive wandered off to look at the shrub-like trees, their host rubbed his palms together. "So, Pietro, where is your protégé? Tell me he's not still ill!"

"He'll be here shortly," Pietro assured him. "He likes to make an entrance."

"Like his father! Well, while we wait there are introductions to make. Let's see. Pietro, you've never met my father's brother. He came from Capua just after us. Then there's my brother-in-law and his wife – they're over there near the wine. Yes, what is it?" Antony snapped at a young girl plucking his sleeve. Pietro assumed that this was someone's daughter until he noticed her swollen belly.

"My lord husband, the musicians have arrived."

"Very good." Antony hesitated, then said gruffly, "Pietro, Antonia, this is my wife, Tessa."

Trying not to be shocked, Pietro bent into a full bow. "Pietro Alaghieri, at your service. Allow me to name my sister, who is studying Orders in Ravenna. She was born Antonia di Dante, but now she is Suor Beatrice."

Eyes bulging at the incongruous husband and wife, Antonia hid her wonder by dropping into a curtsy. "My lady Capulletto."

"You are most welcome, both of you." The girl's status as lady of the house was displayed by the ring of keys that hung awkwardly over her giant belly. "I've heard my husband speak of you often, with great fondness."

Pietro had heard of the marriage, of course, and clucked his tongue and tut-tutted like everyone else. Facing the living girl, pregnancy overwhelming her delicate body, it was far less amusing. Not that this was the youngest marriage ever consummated. But that didn't keep Pietro's skin from crawling as he imagined the wedding night.

Forcing himself to speak, Pietro congratulated the couple on their impending happiness. Capulletto nodded. "A girl, the old women tell me. Not that I'm disappointed. Not at all. Plenty of time for a boy, isn't there?"

*An abundance of time,* thought Pietro, *if she survives the birth.*

"She's of the best family," Antony continued, patting his wife on the head. "I mentioned my in-laws, Tessa's brother. He's been plagued with girls as well. What were their names?"

"Lucia, Olivia, and Rosaline," said Tessa without inflection.

"Girls! Fortunate for me that the Guarini throw so many females. They practically begged me to take this one off their hands. And she'll grow to be a beauty, I know it."

"Wasn't she engaged to your nephew?" asked Pietro.

"Why be a princess when you can be a queen? Isn't that right, girl?"

Tessa smiled dutifully, a smile that changed to something more vibrant as her eyes fixed on something across the yard. Following her gaze, Pietro spied a blond boy about Cesco's age, strutting about with a wooden practice sword on his hip.

Antony saw him, too, and scowled. "Tessa, go tell my nephew that he's to get to the kitchen, or else. He knows he's not allowed to mingle with the guests tonight."

Tessa was off at once, rushing through the crowd to guide the young man out of sight.

"Sorry about that," said Antony. "Little monster has been up to all kinds of mischief today. He's on probation."

"A shame he won't be here," said Pietro. "Cesco doesn't know anyone his own age from Verona. They could be friends."

Ignoring that suggestion, Antony stepped close. "Speaking of Cangrande's boy – Cesco, do you call him? Good name. I was wondering, do you have any plans for him to marry? Because, let me tell you, there's one thing that would earn him the love and respect of the city, and that's to be betrothed to a true daughter of Verona —"

Seeing where this was headed, Pietro broke in. "Antony, nothing would please me more, but I think it's up to the Capitano now, don't you?"

"But you can still put in a good word. I mean, you've been his guardian, haven't you? And let me tell you, there are a lot of men shitting themselves in envy. We all thought the old boy hated you. Turns out you're his favourite! You're going to have lots of marriage offers yourself.

In fact, if I weren't certain that Cangrande will accept my little girl for his son, I'd say wait ten years and I'd marry her to you. You could be my son!" Antony laughed, grasping a goblet off a passing tray.

There was nothing Pietro could conceivably say to that. Antonia pretended a cough, then said, "I'm going to find Lorenzo and Lucius. They're my chaperones, after all."

When she was out of earshot, Antony frowned. "Since when did she need chaperones? I remember when she was the terror of copyists and booksellers, stalking around the city as if she owned it!"

"She's a novice in orders. As such she has to be with a member of the church whenever possible. It's a matter of form." It rang rather hollow, but since Capulletto was at least one sheet to the wind already, it held up. In truth, Antonia was keeping an eye on Borachio. "Are you too busy playing host to give me a tour?"

"Not at all, not at all. Delighted!" Antony pointed off to the left side of the yard. "There are my offices — not that you should believe those vicious rumours about simony," he added darkly. "I just advise people what to do with their money, I never lend. Well, I do, but never with interest."

Well, never with more than twenty percent interest, thought an amused Pietro, who knew far more about Antony's business dealings than the other would find comfortable.

Antony indicated the guest house along the East, then led the way through the door along the South wall of the yard into the house proper. "This house belonged to the old Capelletto clan, which is why we bought it when we inherited the name."

*Inherited?* The way it was said, Pietro knew it had been repeated so often Antony now believed it himself.

"But it wasn't large enough for my father," continued Antony, "so he bought the building next door and knocked out all the walls. We now own one of Verona's forty-eight towers!"

They passed through the ground floor, which was set up for the feast. Benches lined the walls while tables destined to be laden with food surrounded a central pillar. Off to the right was a door from which emanated the smells of a sumptuous feast. This was a little unusual — kitchens were often higher up so the smoke and smells wouldn't filter through the whole house. *They must have excellent ventilation.*

He followed Antony up a trio of stairs to a short landing, then an L-shaped staircase to the first floor. Reaching the top, they emerged into a bright room with rose-marble pillars holding up a wood and plaster ceiling. It was empty of people at the moment, so Pietro could see the dazzling tapestries hanging over the ochre-coloured walls. Elegant three-lobed windows spilled light from both sides, meaning this floor was higher than the house next door.

There were more benches and stools, with trestles along the walls to hold the food. There was a little sitting area on the far side of the room to the right of the stairs. Through an archway bracketed by twin rose pillars, the wooden floor changed to a marble checkerboard pattern of white-rose and pink-rose.

"This is the receiving room, with a parlor for ladies to enjoy over there."

"There's a lot of light," said Pietro admiringly. He gestured to a nearby tapestry. "I can make out every detail."

Antony beamed. "Fresh from Florence – oh, that's right! I meant to ask. Are they still after your head?"

Pietro laughed. "I suppose, but they're not trying very hard. Though they recently made an attempt to steal my father's bones."

"Silly buggers. If you ever need any help dealing with them, I have a lot of connections there."

"I'm sure," said Pietro dryly. "You're quite the man of the world these days."

"I'm sure I'm the same man you knew back when. Just because I've done well for myself —"

"Don't get your back up, Antony. It's just, well, look at you! Not even thirty and a wealthy man, one of the Anziani, and married to boot!"

The compliment didn't have the intended effect. Instead of swelling with pride, Antony leaned up against a wall and looked deflated. "Ridiculous, isn't it? Me, married to that child."

Pietro blinked. "Antony, I – didn't you want to marry her?"

"She's not bad, I guess," grumbled Antony. "But I – well, I know I can trust you, Pietro. Her family got wind of some of my, well, a questionable business dealing. When I started looking for a bride, they threatened me with exposure."

That was news to Pietro. "Was it that bad?"

"They had documents. It would have hurt my public standing, maybe even a censure from the Church."

"That can sting," admitted Pietro.

"I know. Look at you." Antony sat down heavily on a bench, careless of his fine robe. "They told me to break Theobaldo's engagement and marry Tessa myself. Not a bad deal, business-wise. And I'm sure she'll give me lots of children. But it was hard to – I mean, I only... The moment I was sure she was pregnant, I moved down to the bedroom at the back of my office."

When you were away from Antony, it was easy to remember only the brash and churlish side to his personality. Being with him, you could always see the enormous heart. *If only his pride wasn't so great, his insecurity so deep.* "Does the girl know why you married her?"

Antony looked up, surprised. "What? No, I don't think so. I hope she believes I asked for her hand. She wasn't pleased at the time, but as she grows up she'll come to like being the lady of the house. Much better than being married to my brother's brat, anyway."

Pietro sat down beside him. "Why get married at all? I mean, what made it so important that you had to marry now?"

"You know why."

Pietro saw the old hurt in his friend's face. Yes, he knew. Five years ago Montecchio and his wife had gone to Rome, and returned to Verona last year with a child, their pride and joy. "Mariotto's son."

"Her son," corrected Antony. "Giulia's son."

*Oh for pity's sake!* Antony had always called Mariotto's wife by that name, an affectionate reference to Julius Caesar's daughter Julia, the perfect woman. It was always said that a Julia had the ability to make her man happy. A foolish pet name, as Mari's wife had caused no happiness in Antony's life, only misery.

But Pietro kept his thoughts to himself. Aloud he said only, "I'm so sorry, Antony."

"I had thought—" Antony cuffed roughly at his face. "Life was passing me by, you see? She and Montecchio were moving forward. Even his little sister has a son. And there was me, standing with my thumb up my ass. I need an heir. I'm a man without a son..."

Servants appeared at the far end of the room bearing trays, and Antony leapt to his feet with a forced smile. "Good. Good! The Scaliger will be here soon. Come, Ser Alaghieri – up to the Grand Salon."

Ascending another flight of stairs, they came to a long room where fine oak tables were ready for the guests of honour. No rushes here. The wood floors were polished so bright they shone. Frescos decorated the walls in tight geometric patterns, every so often making room for a fine rendering of a saint.

At the far end was a large fireplace displaying the ancient Capelletti crest, a two-tiered hat in stone. Overhead, the wood cross-bracings steepled up to a point. This, then, was as high as the original Capelletto house went.

Tall windows on both sides let in the light of day, but near the staircase a door led out onto the long balcony Pietro had seen from below, connecting the old house with the new one. "That's where your household actually lives?"

"Oh yes. The tower goes up two more flights, with room enough for nearly everyone. A fireplace in every room. Some even overlook the *via Cappello*."

Antony was about to take Pietro through when they heard the sound of hoofbeats, barking dogs, and a great cheer from below. Stepping quickly onto the balcony, they watched a rider on a snow white horse come galloping through the tunnel followed by six great mastiffs and twin spry greyhounds. The mingled nobles and their wives retreated to the walls. Cangrande had arrived.

Pietro spied Lorenzo, Antonia, and Borachio off in a corner of the yard. His sister caught his eye in a moment of anticipation. This was it, the moment of truth.

Antony's eyes were on the Capitano. "The boy's not with him?"

"They haven't actually met yet. Not formally. We'll present him after the feast."

Antony beamed at this unexpected honour. Uttering a perfunctory excuse, he vanished back down the stairs to greet his most important guest. Pietro remained on the balcony, watching carefully. The Scaliger was a master of these situations. Motioning his dogs to stay, he greeted Antony with grace and humour, then made the rounds of important men, each one treated to the famous *allegria*. Poise perfected. Antonia and Lorenzo were passed by, unremarked.

Pietro's eyes were on Borachio. The disguised poisoner was looking right at Cangrande, listening to the words the great lord passed with his fellow nobles.

Nothing. No reaction, not even a flicker of recognition.

Antonia looked up to Pietro, wondering if he had seen something she had not. But Pietro just shook his head.

*Damn.* The others were right. Cangrande was not the man who had ordered Cesco's poisoning.

*Now what do we do?*

# TWENTY-FOUR

THE BLUE SKY was giving way to red and exterior torches were being lit when everyone was finally seated for the first course. Merchant families, the 'new nobility', were placed on the ground floor with the least influential nobles, while the first floor housed the middle tier of the city's best and brightest. The top thirty nobles found themselves guided to the best table on the second floor.

The division made it impossible for Antony's servants to create the formal *entrée*, the traditional bringing in of dishes on horseback. Instead they cannily made the household dogs the bearers of each dish, low trays strapped between paired hounds matched for height.

The bread was still blackened from the ovens, and Pietro broke his with the rest of the honoured guests on the highest floor. The faces here were all familiar: Nico da Lozzo and his wife Imogen; Lord and Lady Castelbarco with their mature son (who shared a name with his father); sallow-faced Bernardo Ervari, one of the Anziani and a widower; Petruchio and Katerina Bonaventura. Bailardino was there with his brother and sister-in-law, who was from Cremona. The Mantuan lord Passerino Bonaccolsi was all smiles. A few other famous couples were present, chosen for their influence and wealth more than their ancestry. The only noble exceptions were Montecchio and his wife, who had never been invited to the Capulletto feast.

Not every face was friendly. Mastino and Alberto were both there, seated far from the Capitano, a demotion that clearly didn't sit well. With Alblivious came Jacopo, who avoided Pietro's eye. Twice last week Pietro had tried to apologize, but Poco had ducked his visits.

Even Verde della Scala, present with her husband Rizardo, sent Pietro chilling looks. She had likely fancied her little brother ruling Verona, with Rizardo in charge of Serravalle. Fortunately she took more after Alberto than her uncle, owning neither great ambition or deviousness, just loyalty.

One particularly unfriendly face was the Bishop of Verona. At the end of his life, Pietro's father had eviscerated the incompetent Benedictine friar in several letters to the Capitano. But Bishop Giuseppe was a distant Scaligeri cousin, though from the wrong side of the sheets. *The same side as Pathino, come to think of it.* Most of the duties of the Bishop had been transferred to Lorenzo's master, the Franciscan Prior, who was absent. Probably to avoid the Bishop.

*Lucky for me. Otherwise he might ask who this drunken brother with Lorenzo is.* Antonia and Lorenzo were at the far end of the table, as a favour to Pietro. Taking the place of a servant behind them was Borachio, who eyed the wine longingly.

Cangrande sat at the center of the table rather than its head, the better to hold court, his hounds ranged about him. Arriving in her husband's wake, Giovanna sat on his left beside the feast's host and hostess, with a large-boned nurse fussily hovering over the pregnant mistress of the house.

Awkwardly, Pietro found himself placed on the Capitano's right hand. He stood through the Bishop's blessing, but when he began to sit, Giovanna forestalled him. "Ser Alaghieri, should you even be at this holy feast?"

"Where else should he be?" called Cangrande.

"I mean no disrespect, of course. But he has been declared *nefas* by mother church."

"As have I." Nudging a hound aside, Cangrande settled himself in the backless chair. "We'll just have to beg you all to overlook us heretics in your midst."

Giovanna bowed her head graciously. "When have I ever been unwilling to overlook your sins?"

A fine opening sally. In just a few words she had reminded everyone of Pietro's excommunication and her husband's philandering. *It's going to be a long evening.*

The salutary drinks came next. They first raised their cups to the newly resurrected Capitano. "Long may he keep returning from his grave." The next salute went to the host and hostess. "Long may they prosper and flourish."

Distaste was etched on the face of Petruchio's wife. Pietro had only seen Katerina Bonaventura once before, on a snowy day several years earlier. However, he'd seen a great deal of her, and in the years between he'd heard many a tale of this remarkable couple.

Her husband was the next to receive a salute, sharing the name of the holy man whose day they were belatedly celebrating. This made them the ostensible guests of honour, seated across from the Scaliger.

Cangrande quaffed his cup and held it out for more. "I trust the brood are well?"

"Very well, my lord!" replied Petruchio, waving away almonds in coloured garlic sauce in favour of a tray of Golden Morsels. These were a new favourite in Verona – toasted bread crumbs soaked in rosewater with beaten eggs and ground sugar, then fried with chicken fat and dusted with more sugar.

The tray of Morsels was taken from Petruchio by his wife and passed along before he got one. Petruchio kissed her fingers, laughing. "My eldest son is so taken with horses, he might as well be a centaur."

Castelbarco took the denied Morsels happily. "How do you count him eldest? They're twins."

"My Kate tells me he came out a full two minutes ahead of his brother, so he bears my name. The other is named for my friend Hortensio."

"I knew a Paduan of that name," said Nico.

"The very man," agreed Petruchio.

"My first was named for me, too," said Bailardino. "But I have no idea where my wife came up with Valentino. I had planned on Nicolo, but was over-ruled in the strongest terms."

"You must have a happy marriage," said Kate. "How does your wife fare?"

Bail was in high spirits. "Coming along, coming along. Sadly she cannot join us, though I pleaded. But she's delighted that Cangrande's brat is back where she can keep track of him."

All eyes shifted to Giovanna, but the Scaliger's wife disappointed everyone by ignoring the bait. "Speaking of your family, Donna Bonaventura, how is your father? He hasn't visited us in months."

Petruchio cut across his wife's answer. "Baptista? The codger's surviving, lady. Though he's spending less time in the city. Padua's not a safe place to be at the moment. Even for Paduans!" There were more cheers at this, and another round of salutes for the foolish Paduans.

"Your girls are well?" pressed Giovanna.

"Thriving!" Petruchio waved a hand at his wife, nearly overturning a goblet of wine in her lap, if not for her deft removal of the vessel a moment before. "The younger one takes after me – peaceful, mild, kind-hearted. A real joy."

"A joy to her father," corrected Kate. "She reminds me of my sister."

"For shame, Kate! Vittoria is an angel! But Evelina takes after Kate. The harridan never lets me sleep."

"Turnabout is fair play," Kate replied with a wicked smile.

"A willful and spiteful girl! Hisses like a cat if I don't spoil her rotten."

"The apple of her father's eye."

"As I said, just like her mother." With one arm he pressed her close to him and bussed her cheek. The other guests shifted. Such public displays were against custom, but Petruchio didn't appear to care.

Kate held up a table knife. "Husband, watch ravaging me when I'm armed. This could end up in a dangerous place." She let the knife fall between his legs.

Petruchio caught it and flourished it in the air. "I'm married to a madwoman! You're all witnesses! She tried to caponize me! Kate, I demand satisfaction!"

"Here? As you wish. I am nothing if not a dutiful wife." She began unbinding the laces of her dress.

Petruchio quickly laid the knife aside and stopped her. "Not that kind! Christ, save me from an obedient spouse!"

Laughter led to more drinking and the next round of appetizers — armoured turnips, fried cheese discs, and a selection of plums and late cherries. Conversation gave way to good food until the plates were cleared for the first course of meat.

Nico da Lozzo turned in his seat to waggle his fingers in a passing bowl of sage, rosemary, and orange-peel water. "So Pietro, tell us. We're all in a frenzy to hear tales of this boy Cangrande has kept hidden all these years."

Pietro sipped his wine. "What do you want to know?"

"Well, we know he's daring. Can he ride?"

"He can." *Better than anyone I've ever seen.*

"Does he know one end of a sword from another?" asked old Arnaldo Capulletto.

"Better than I did at that age."

"That doesn't mean much!" laughed Antony.

"It wasn't supposed to," observed Cangrande. "Ser Alaghieri here is doing an excellent job of deflating our expectations."

Petruchio pointed his knife at Cangrande. "Is he anything like himself here?"

"Yes," said Cangrande. "Is he?"

Pietro pursed his lips. Best, he decided, to give an example. "I'll tell you a story. This happened fifteen days ago." Once more he related Cesco's thwarting of the theft of Dante's bones, assuring them all that his father's remains remained safe.

"Sounds foolhardy," said Castelbarco's wife.

"What boy of his age isn't?" asked Bailardino.

"Of any age," amended Kate Bonaventura. Cangrande raised his goblet to her.

The meat arrived, suckling pig with sky-blue summer sauce smelling of ginger and blackberries. Petruchio asked if Cesco hawked. Upon learning the boy had never had a lesson, he offered to take young Cesco out and teach him. "If the Capitano can spare him, of course."

"Who better?" said Cangrande.

Kate elbowed her husband in the ribs. "Who indeed?"

"You'll have to take my boy Detto with you," said Bail. "They're inseparable – a third generation of Nogarola and Escalus."

"Let's hope they don't end up like the first," said Cangrande.

The unlucky reference was missed by most of the table, though not by Pietro. He chose to ignore it, instead asking, "Escalus? Who is that?"

Cangrande laughed. "An Imperial title. Ludwig apparently has trouble pronouncing 'della Scala,' so some ingenious courtier gave him a Latinized variation to cover his inability. I am now called Prince Escalus by the Holy Roman Emperor."

"A well-deserved honour," said Antony, slamming his hand repeatedly on the wooden tabletop. He was joined by all the men and the thumping on the table brought echoing noises from the floors below.

While Antony was busy speaking to Giovanna, Pietro murmured to Cangrande, "Has he been trying to get you to betrothe Cesco to his unborn daughter?"

The Capitano chuckled. "Yes, the latest in a string of Capulletti offers. Only last month he was trying to marry his still-wombed brat to Cecchino's son." The great man's face grew solemn and he stood. The table stilled as he raised his goblet. "To Cecchino."

"To Cecchino," Pietro echoed among the chorus. His very first day in Verona had been Cecchino's wedding day. He'd liked the late knight, and it was Pietro's instinct to suspect Cangrande. If Cecchino had lived, there would have been no question of succession, and Cesco would have been safe for years to come.

"Paride!" Cangrande called out for his great-nephew. When he didn't appear, Cangrande beckoned a servant nearer. "Have someone find where he's dining and tell him we're honouring his father."

"Why Paride?" asked Kate. "The name, I mean. It's unusual."

Giovanna explained. "My niece has always been a romantic. She fought for Tristano, but was willing to settle on Paride."

"For Paris? Helen's lover?"

"Exactly. It seems Costanza fancies herself as Hecuba."

"If I remember my poetry," said Kate, "that's an unfortunate likeness for a mother to her son."

"Nico and Antony look confused, poor fellows," said Cangrande. "We are fortunate in having a poet's son with us. Pietro?"

Having been put on the spot often by his father, Pietro hardly blinked. "Hecuba, wife of King Priam. She witnessed the fall of their city, the suicide of her daughter on the tomb of Achilles, and the deaths of her sons."

Castelbarco joined in. "After being enslaved by Odysseus, she went mad, killed – someone, and was transformed into a dog for her troubles." He noticed the looks he was receiving. "I don't just read law, you know."

"A man of hidden talents," said Petruchio.

"An unfortunate name," observed Bail. "If one gives a fig for such things."

"Which you don't," said Passerino Bonaccolsi.

"True," replied Bail happily.

Castelbarco was determined to share his learning. "It's worse than that. If I've learned my Greek right, Paris actually means 'married to death,' doesn't it?"

Cangrande laughed. "It does indeed! Well, if it must come true, let's hope that young Paride is married to several women, all of great appetite, who eventually wear him to death."

"Hear him," said Petruchio, slapping his wife's backside. A moment later he grimaced, a look of extreme discomfort on his face. Pietro didn't want to know how she'd retaliated. Both her hands were in plain view.

Young Paride arrived to make a leg, allowing Pietro his first view of the boy. Not pretty, not ugly, not happy, not sad. He was a perfect neutral. Well-spoken for a ten year-old, his manners were impeccable. Pietro found himself liking Paride, mostly because this boy was Cesco's complete opposite. Nice enough, but entirely dull.

The feast continued, course after course. Eventually Cangrande and Antony left the table to make politic visits to the revelers on lower floors, and soon the noise was increased by music. Pietro smiled at Castelbarco. "Manuel?"

"He had to arrive sometime." They referred to Emmanuele di Salamone dei Sifoni, also called Manuel the Jew, the Master of Revels at Cangrande's court. He and Pietro were old friends. Now he was somewhere below, his arrival heralding the end of the feasting portion of the evening and a start to the dancing.

"I hear he's not well."

"Well or no," replied Castelbarco, "there's nothing in God's Creation that can keep Manuel from a feast. When does the boy arrive?"

Pietro put a finger to the side of his nose. "Soon, I hope."

◆    ◊    ◆

It had been decided that Cesco would arrive mounted. "You're too small for men to see, little dancer," the Moor had said. "It will give you dignity, and keep you from exerting yourself." Thus he rode the short distance to the feast while Morsicato, Tharwat, and the boys flanked him on foot.

Cesco fidgeted in the saddle. "This is ridiculous. He won't respect this."

"He knows about your health," said Morsicato. "There is no shame in this."

"You can put on the masque," said Tharwat.

Cesco took out the masque Pietro had given him and stared at it. "He'll be expecting something more."

"Then flout his expectations," said Morsicato tartly. "You excel at that."

By now they could hear the echoing music and laughter. Looking up, Cesco said casually, "That building must back onto the Capulletto yard."

"Why, so it must!" said Detto, grinning. He knew the real plan.

Suddenly Cesco started to cough. Tharwat stopped the horse as the boy doubled up, knees to his chest. The three-faced masque fell to the cobbled street.

"He's having a relapse!" Morsicato fumbled for a wineskin at his hip. He got it unstoppered and turned to pour some down Cesco's gullet.

But Cesco wasn't there.

Looking up, Morsicato saw the boy dangling from a shop-owner's massive sign. "Cesco!" His reaching hands were instantly pinned to his sides by Detto, the wineskin falling to their feet where it burst, creating a crimson pool about the masque.

"All better now, thank you, doctor!" A kick out with his legs, a twist, and Cesco was standing atop the sign. "Detto, my visage!"

Releasing the doctor, Detto picked up the wine-covered masque and flung it upwards. Val was hopping with sudden excitement.

"Tharwat! Get him!" roared Morsicato. But the Moor stood placidly holding the reins.

"The sign wouldn't hold him. Shall he shoot me?" Deftly slipping the masque into place, Cesco probed the wall. The building was frescoed with the image of a slaughtered pig, but there were patches where the plaster had broken away. Finding a fingerhold, he began to climb.

"This wasn't the plan," rumbled Tharwat.

"Correction – this wasn't *your* plan."

"What should we do?" Valentino hadn't been told the plan either, for fear he'd tattle.

Cesco reached the rooftop. "I think more horses are advisable." With that he vanished.

Morsicato turned to berate the Moor. But the horse's reins dangled idly – Tharwat had vanished as well. The doctor turned to yell at Detto, but the two brothers were bolting away to procure more horses. Morsicato was left all alone, sputtering in the middle of the street, wondering what to do.

# TWENTY-FIVE

MASQUED, CESCO slithered on his belly like a serpent across the tiled roof. Through the eye-slits he was able to see the lights on the top floor of the Capulletto house. The feast seemed to be a smashing success, with music and laughter and the barking of happy hounds. The festivities had spilled into the courtyard, where men and women danced and talked and flirted and drank.

Watching them, Cesco sighed. "If you must trail me, do it in the open."

The Moor stepped into view, arms folded. Behind the masque, Cesco grimaced. "You could respond once in awhile. It won't kill you."

"It might," said the Moor.

"Ah-ha! It has a tongue! Excellent. Now get down before they see you and declare a Crusade."

Reluctantly, Tharwat knelt. "This was not part of the plan you told Ser Alaghieri."

"Oh please! As if he expected me to tell him what I really had in mind!"

"What *do* you have in mind?"

Cesco slithered further. "I want to see what we're walking into, that's all."

"No foolishness. You're still —"

"You drip drip drip, old man, but you won't wear me down."

"You have to learn your limitations."

"For a man who doesn't like speaking, you spend an insane amount of time repeating yourself. Now hush. And keep lower!"

This rooftop sloped steeply down, and two tiles slid past Cesco as the Moor navigated the descent. "Don't move. The roof might collapse under us." Cesco was much lighter, especially since the illness. The roof barely acknowledged his presence as he crept to its edge, overlooking a flat rooftop that extended right up to the Capulletto yard. The L-shaped rooftop was over Capulletto's office and guest house, across the yard from the main house. It held a dovecote, and the gentle cooing was a happy, soothing sound.

Resting on his haunches, Tharwat rasped, "Seen enough?"

"Back in a moment." Before the Moor could stop him, Cesco rolled lightly over the edge to the roof below.

He was now only one floor up from the ground. At his back, two short sets of stairs led up to well-barred doorways. Capulletto shared this roof with his neighbours. Having landed just in front of one of the doors, Cesco crept slowly past the dovecote, meaning to scout the layout of the courtyard and perhaps eavesdrop a bit on the party.

Hearing the crunch of a step behind him, he knew at once it wasn't the Moor – never in his life had he heard Tharwat's step. Someone had been hiding in the shadow of the dovecote wall and was coming up fast, too fast for anything but an attack. Cesco rolled, feeling something glance off his ribs. Not a weapon. A fist or a foot. The first blow was closely followed by another, and Cesco realized he was being kicked. Someone was trying to crush his ribs.

He continued to roll until he reached the very edge of the flat rooftop. He nearly rolled too far, and flung himself over onto his back. Masque knocked askew, he could only half-see out the eyeholes. Looking up, the stars outlined his attacker. Who was almost the same size as Cesco. Another boy!

Cesco threw a wild kick. It was easily dodged, and a foot descended to stomp at Cesco's face. He grasped the heel and twisted, throwing his assailant stumbling backwards.

Cesco took a moment to fix his masque. Eyeholes in place, Cesco now saw that his dancing partner had ice-blond hair and a thin, angry face. That was all he could make out before he was attacked again.

A floor above the oblivious revelers, the two boys traded blows. Cesco laughed as he ducked and dodged, every few seconds hitting the other boy with his open palm. This only enraged the blond boy further. Though strong for his age, it was painfully obvious he hadn't had any real training.

"Come on," hissed the lean blonde boy. "Fight!"

"If you insist," replied Cesco.

♦   ◊   ♦

Bailardino's ears pricked up. "Does that sound like a fight?"

"Where?" demanded Bail.

Passerino rubbed his hands together. "That's more like it!"

"Is anyone taking bets?" asked Petruchio.

"Darling, no more betting, you promised," said Kate.

"Some of the revelers must be wrestling," said Castelbarco.

"Sounds like birds flapping to me," said Antony dismissively. "Maybe a cat near the dovecote."

♦   ◊   ♦

Cesco was growing annoyed by the other boy's insistence on continuing a losing fight. When a fist came winging at his head, Cesco caught it at the wrist. Stepping his right leg around his attacker's, he struck the boy on the left shoulder while hitting the right knee from behind. They went down, and Cesco quickly pinned the boy. "Another gate-crasher? Or a young watchdog?"

The boy stared at Cesco's masque. "What are you?"

"I am the night, the bringer of evils. I am − Beelzebub!"

The mockery made the blond boy hiss. "Get off me!"

"Since you asked so nicely." Cesco rolled away, easily ducking the wild swing that followed him. The other boy retreated into one of the low arches under the nearest stair, disappearing into the shadows. There was a pause. "Oh. It's a masque."

"Of course it's a masque. What, did you think it was my face?"

"I thought you were a demon. My uncle says I'm going to Hell."

"We're all going to Hell," replied Cesco lightly.

"Why are you wearing a masque?"

"It's comfortable, and oh so fashionable. Everyone will be wearing them next year." He began to stroll towards the yard.

The other boy reached out urgently. "Don't let them see you!" Amused, Cesco crouched down in the shadow of the dovecote as his attacker continued. "My uncle doesn't take well to intruders. He'll have half the hide off your backside if he finds you."

"Is that why you tried to do his job for him?"

"I'll never help him!" hissed the boy fiercely.

"So-ho! Such passion! Not admirers of our uncle, I take it. Are you exiled from the party? Are you trying to get in?"

"If I wanted in, I could go through there," he said, pointing to the nearby wall where crumbling bricks made the perfect handholds to climb level with the long balcony a floor higher.

"I see. Then what are you about, that you don't want to be discovered?"

The blonde boy puffed out his chest. "If you've come to ruin the feast, don't worry. That's *my* job."

"Your dislike of your uncle must reach Mount Olympus. How did you plan to topple Chronos, O mighty Zeus?"

The boy frowned. "What?"

"How were you going to ruin the party?"

The blonde boy nearly jumped out of his skin as a rasping voice provided the answer. "Fire. There are two buckets of pitch here."

Not acknowledging Tharwat's sudden appearance, Cesco whistled in admiration. "Fire?"

The icy boy recovered quickly from his fright. "My uncle has all sorts of important papers in his office over there. I'm going to burn it down in front of everyone. He's a law-breaker. He'll lose all kinds of money, and never be able to admit it!"

"You mean to both expose and ruin him at the same time. Daring. They'll hang you, but it's daring."

"Hang me? No, he'll only beat me. I'm used to it."

"No, I mean the city will hang you. Arson and horse-theft are the greatest crimes a body can commit this side of sacrilege. Even treason comes in third. Murder is usually next, then dueling, then spitting in public—"

Flustered, the boy demanded, "Who are you? And who is he?"

"Just a monkey and his master." Cesco jerked a thumb at the Moor. "He plays the fife and I dance for him."

Tharwat said, "Your friends are waiting."

"The doctor won't go into a real snit for another minute or so." Cesco turned to his assailant. "My name is Francesco, and this little festival is for me, so I'd rather you didn't ruin it completely. Still, it *is* a little boring. How about helping me liven it up?"

"Cesco…" said Tharwat warningly.

He ignored the Moor, asking instead, "What's your name?"

"I – I'm called Thibault."

Cesco winced. "Thibault the Cat. Of course. Only a cat could take a piece from my poor hide. Well, my fine feline friend, tell me – is that the Capitano's horse down there?"

"Yes."

"Are there any other horses around here?"

"They're kept down the street."

"Perfection, divinity, serenity. Come along. Bring those buckets of pitch."

Thibault hesitated. Cesco clapped his hands once, sharply, and the blond boy scampered off to obey.

Tharwat was stern. "Francesco, when I said no foolishness—"

"See you soon!" Saluting, Cesco rolled off the roof's edge, landing in the corner of the yard behind a tall screen. From the continued sounds in the yard, no one had noticed.

Returning with the buckets, Thibault saw Cesco down below unhooking a torch from its bracket.

"Don't get mixed up with him, boy," rasped the Moor.

Though frightened of the huge dark man with the broken voice, Thibault couldn't abide being told what to do. Recklessly, he dropped down with the buckets of pitch to where Cesco waited, torch in hand.

For an instant, Al-Dhaamin considered warning the crowd. But if he spoiled Cesco's design, the boy would only do something wilder.

And in just a few moments, it was too late.

◆    ◊    ◆

*"Fire! Fire!"*

The shouts from below brought Pietro and the others out to the balcony. Guests were spilling out into the yard below to battle a smoking thing on the far side of the yard.

Suddenly there was a commotion from the center of the yard. Cangrande's unsaddled snow charger was free of its tethers. On its back was a boy in a grotesque leather masque with three mad faces. "Cangrande della Scala," called the little lunatic. "Won't you come out and play?"

More shouts and confusion as a second boy came running to leap up behind the masqued Cesco, who kicked the mount. Men leaped back as the lovely horse raced past them and into the tunnel leading towards the street.

"The Capitano's horse! He's stolen Cangrande's horse."

"Of course he has," muttered Pietro angrily. *A fire? That wasn't the plan!*

Emerging into the yard, Antony shouted, "Andriolo! Andriolo! My horse!" A burly groom dashed down the tunnel towards the stables.

In moments the whole household was rushing out of doors. Half drunk, Nico, Petruchio, Bailardino, Passerino, and many more went gleefully pounding down the stairs in pursuit. Cangrande was in the lead.

In Pietro's ear, Antonia said, "I think I'll have the friars escort me back to the house."

"You're leaving?" asked Pietro incredulously.

"Borachio hasn't recognized anyone. Best get him out of here before he's discovered." She bussed his cheek. "Go, join the chase. Make sure he isn't harmed. And tell Ser Capulletto it was a lovely meal."

Nodding grimly, Pietro started for the stairs.

◆　◇　◆

Two streets away the young horsethieves met Cesco's confederates, now also mounted. The doctor was there, scowling. "What have you done this time, you little maniac! What are those shouts?"

"We got horses," said Valentino proudly.

Detto pointed at Thibault. "Who's he?"

" *'The fox and the cat, two saints indeed, to make a pilgrimage agreed.'*" Cesco jerked his thumb. "Another exile from the party."

Morsicato saw the sigil on the blanket under Cesco's rump. "Is that Cangrande's horse?"

"Yes. Arson and horse-theft. It's a hanging matter now."

Thibault was grinning, and Detto let out a whoop of laughter. "Are they chasing?"

"I'll be very disappointed if they aren't. Hold on, kitty!" Kicking at the fine white mount, Cesco led the way, Detto and Valentino right behind.

Watching them go, the doctor let out a yelp as the Moor landed on the road beside him. Without a word, Tharwat leapt into the saddle of the remaining horse and turned its head to follow his charges. "Get on."

Morsicato clambered up and locked his knees in place as Al-Dhaamin whipped the reins. "What in the name of a merciful God are we doing?" moaned Morsicato through his bouncing teeth.

"Seeing he lives."

"Give me one good reason why."

"A shame to waste all your hard work, doctor"

Morsicato buried his face in the Moor's back. "It's not good. But it's a reason."

◆　◇　◆

Somehow in the press of men and horses in the street outside Capulletto's house, Cangrande found Pietro. "He was wearing a masque."

"I wonder where he got the idea."

Cangrande laughed. "Any notion where he's headed?"

"None at all," lied Pietro. "He's trying to make an impression."

"He's succeeded. Now he just has to live through the night. Capulletto is livid."

"They got the fire out," said Pietro defensively.

"But his precious Giotto fresco is ruined."

"Good," snapped Pietro. "Besides, everyone else sees it as a romp."

"Not everyone." Cangrande jerked his head towards a pair of horses already racing away. Mastino, in the company of his German friend, Fuchs.

Pietro swore and grabbed at the saddle of the nearest horse, tearing it away from another knight. Cangrande quelled the offended man with a firm grip. "Leave him be, Ser Bellinzona. He's a man worried about his son. Myself, I have plenty of heirs."

Pietro was galloping away. With a joyful laugh, Cangrande mounted and spurred with a shout of "Scala!"

◆       ◊       ◆

"Where are we going?" asked Detto as they turned down a side street.

"No idea," snapped Cesco. "I'm new here, remember?"

"Turn left ahead," said Thibault, clinging to the horse behind him.

"No," said Cesco.

"We're heading for the river," Detto called.

"Are we going to Vicenza?" asked Valentino.

"No," said Cesco.

"I said turn left," Thibault insisted.

"I said no." There was a sharpness to Cesco's tone.

"That's not fair!"

"Life is flawed and unrelenting."

Thibault reached around Cesco, grasping for the reins. "Don't be a pain, *mon petit chat*," chided Cesco. "You're only here, my artful hypocrite, because the fox invited you!"

"You're not my master! Turn left!" shouted Thibault, again grabbing at the reins.

Cesco locked his knees and jerked the back on the leather reins. The horse reared, and Thibault found himself first slipping, then toppling backwards off the horse's rump and onto the cobblestones.

Galloping away, Cesco waved back at him. "Climb a tree, friend cat, while I search my bag of tricks!"

"What was that?" asked Detto as they turned the next corner.

"This time the fox warned the cat."

"So, where *are* we going?" demanded Val.

Cesco smiled. "Detto?"

Detto grinned and pointed. "Montecchio's house is that way."

# TWENTY-SIX

KEEPING MASTINO IN VIEW, Pietro found himself riding alongside Antony. "Just like old times."

"I'll murder him. I'll *murder* him!" Antony turned his head. "What?"

"I said, just like old times! Who are you going to kill? Not Cesco!"

Capulletto snorted. "Hardly! He's just being Scaligeri. His father will make good the damages. But I saw that nephew of mine tagging along on the back of the horse. Little shit. Destined for a cloister before tonight. Now. He's. As. Good. As. *Dead!*"

Shaking his head, Pietro kept his gaze on Mastino, who was whipping his horse in mad pursuit. Mastino's friend Fuchs was a better horseman, and knew that beating the horse wouldn't serve.

Urging his own borrowed horse on, Pietro heard laughs and shouts all around him. Nico, Petruchio, and Bailardino were among the two dozen knights and lords chasing after Cesco. Cangrande was in the center of the high spirited pack, trailing Mastino and Fuchs by about a city block.

*He's letting them get ahead. He wants to see what happens when Cesco and Mastino come face to face.*

Pietro knew where Cesco was heading. He had to do what he could to make sure the pack didn't catch up too soon.

♦   ◊   ♦

Tharwat and Morsicato were catching up. Cesco's first order of business was to lose them. Seeing a shadowy lane ahead, he called low instructions to his companions.

When the horse bearing the combined weight of doctor and Moor entered the same lane, it kept on through, chasing the telltale sounds of horses ahead of them. Neither man saw the lone white horse down an alley with the two figures on its back, because Cesco was holding the dark saddle blanket up to hide them, the crest facing inwards.

Cesco and Valentino listened to their minders pass, followed moments later by another set of pursuers, with Mastino in the lead. "I hope Detto leads them on a good chase," whispered Cesco.

Val giggled. "What now?"

"Now you can direct me to Montecchio's house. Quickly, before they lynch us as horse thieves."

They clopped slowly out the other end of the alley, and in just a few minutes they reached their destination. The Casa Montecchio was close to the river, and a massive bridge was visible between the buildings.

Looking up at the house behind the high wall, Cesco saw light coming from an upper floor, casting shadows within. "They have stables, don't they? I don't see them."

Valentino pointed. "Around that way, next to the main gate. But there's a side door around the other way."

"Show me."

They entered a lane beside Montecchio's house, passing out of sight of the river. Reaching the spot Val indicated, Cesco saw there were in fact two doors set into the wall. One was tall and wide enough to allow horse and rider through. The other was a short arched door that didn't even reach the ground. Death's Door.

By church law, the living and the dead could not use the same entrance. To that purpose, every house had a death door, and the ceremony of removing a corpse from a house required a priest and a city official. The rest of the time the door was kept firmly shut.

Cesco looked around in frustration. "What's the matter?" asked Valentino.

"No way in. We'll have to ride around—"

He and Valentine froze. There were voices nearby. Listening, they came from the far side of the wall, inside the house. The voices were calling out a single word. Val whispered in Cesco's ear. "What are they saying?"

Cesco cupped a hand to his ear. "It sounds like – *Roma*?"

A small laugh quite close made them start. Dropping to the ground, Cesco crossed to the death door and pressed an ear to it. He smiled, then knocked.

A startled intake of breath from the other side. "Who's it?"

"Death," answered Cesco conversationally. "I want to come in my door."

A pause. "I don't believe you."

"I'm a baby horse-thief, looking for tips."

"You steal baby horses?"

"No, I'm just being funny. Really, I'm a boy hiding from grown-ups, just like you. Why don't you let me in?"

Val's eyes were wide. "You can't go through a death door! It's bad luck!"

"Luck is what you make it." Cesco knocked again. "Who is this?"

"Not telling. Go away."

"Look, I'm going to keep knocking until they hear me and find your hiding place." Cesco rapped harder.

The reply was immediate. "No!"

"Then open the door."

There was the sliding of wood and the death door swung wide, leading into darkness.

"A shame the cat isn't here. Horse-theft, arson, and sacrilege all. A trinity of criminality." Cesco started forward.

"I can't believe you're doing this," gasped Val.

"Yet here I go. Coming?" Cesco reached out a hand and Val recoiled in horror. "No? Suit yourself." Cesco slithered through Death's Door. As soon as he was through, it was shut behind him. Val whimpered.

Inside, Cesco brushed off his hands and knees and squinted at the boy in the shadows. He couldn't be much more than four years old. "Thank you, Master Montecchio."

The child studied him. "You've got a masque."

"I'm very ugly."

The boy frowned suspiciously until there was another shout from the house. Shushing Cesco, the boy pulled him into the deeper shadows of the walled yard. Unlike the Capulletto courtyard, this one was bricked and unadorned by paint. Cesco could smell stables close by.

"Baby horses are foals," said the boy.

"Oh?"

"Quick!" The boy pulled Cesco by the arm across the yard to a fresh hiding place. Passing through a patch of light, Cesco's breath caught in his throat.

The boy was beautiful! Even so small, everything about him was perfect. Hair so brown it was almost black, eyes as blue as the sky, a strong nose, and a proud chin just barely turned up at the end. Carrying no extra child-heaviness, his limbs were strong and proportioned.

Hearing Cesco's gasp, the boy's eyes darted furtively around. "What's the matter?"

"Nothing. Nothing at all. Tell me more about horses."

The original Montecchi clan had been horse-thieves hiding in the hills that gave the family their name. Though now respectable, their connection with equestrian endeavors hadn't lessened. Montecchi horses were among the best in Lombardy, always fetching a good price.

The boy knew little or none of this history, of course, but horse-breeding was in his blood. He told Cesco all sorts of things he'd learned here and at their castle in the country, relating the details of a fine pony he was allowed to ride and feed and even name.

"What did you name him?"

"Nardo."

"Is that your name?"

"No," said the boy. "My name's—"

"Romeo!" Two women burst from the house with candles in their hands. "Where the devil can this Romeo be?"

"Romeo! Romeo, you naughty boy, come in here this instant!"

"Romeo Romeo Romeo!" called another little boy, toddling out to follow the two women.

Young Romeo pulled Cesco into the shelter of the stable wall and pointed to a beautiful woman with just his colouring and hair. "That's Mama."

The famous Gianozza, cause of the feud. "She's very beautiful. Who's the other woman?"

"Auntie Aurelia."

Cesco pointed to the toddler. "And that?"

"Benvolio," said Romeo, with an *of-course-it-is* sort of voice.

"Your brother?"

"My *cousin*."

"Ah. What happens if they catch you?"

Romeo covered his bottom with both hands. "Nothing."

Cesco tried not to laugh. "I don't see your father. Is he home?" Romeo nodded. "Good. Now listen. I'm playing a kind of game of hide and seek myself. Do you know about the big party tonight?"

Romeo face turned down. "Papa doesn't get to go. It's not fair!"

"I agree, it isn't fair. I want your papa to go. But I don't think he'd go to a party uninvited – he's too good of a man, isn't he?" Romeo nodded. "But what would happen if he thought his horse had been stolen? He'd have to chase it, wouldn't he? And if it ended up at the party, he'd have to go too, wouldn't he?"

"You're taking a horse to a party?" Romeo sounded awed.

"It's only fair. The one I was riding came from the party. I need to take one back. What do you say? Do you think you could help me take a horse?"

Romeo frowned. "You could be trying to take a horse for keeps. I showed Benvolio a bird's nest and he kept it."

"That dirty Benvolio," said Cesco, shaking a fist.

"Will you bring it back?"

"Yes."

"How do I know?"

"By taking a leap of faith, little Romeo. I promise, I won't do anything to hurt your father, or you."

"Ever?"

"Ever."

Romeo's voice pressed him urgently. "Swear."

"I swear." Cesco made the sign of the cross. "In the name of my father."

Stealing his hand into Cesco's, the little boy pulled him into the stable. A minute later they were guiding a fine stallion out of a stall, a halter in its mouth. "Don't you want a saddle?"

"Saddles are for sissies," said Cesco, making Romeo laugh. "I will take this rope, though. And this too." He lifted an object from its slot on the wall and tucked it into his belt. "Now, when I go, you have to raise a ruckus and say you were hiding from a horse-thief. Just give me a head-start, then make lots of noise and get your father to come after me."

"And you'll get my Papa into the party?"

"I'll try my hardest."

Romeo's eyes were endlessly deep. "Can I come too?"

A wicked grin crossed Cesco's face as he considered. Then he shook his head. "Not this time. When you're older, I'll take you to a party too, I promise."

Mollified, Romeo helped open the tall door as quietly as possible. Valentino was waiting on the other side. Cesco grinned at him. "See? Death in, birth out. We've given birth to a horse."

"I think Detto's coming this way," said Val urgently. "I heard the chase."

"Good." Stepping on a barrel, Cesco leapt to the horse's back. The horse whinnied, and a sudden shout from across the yard told them they'd been seen. "Now, Romeo, holler for all you're worth. I'll see you later."

"Remember, you promised!"

Cesco winked. "Someday an adventure all our own. Now get going!"

Romeo leapt into the light, pointing. "Thieves! Thieves!"

"Romeo? *Romeo!* Get away from them!"

Cesco and Val rode off, Romeo shouting after him. "There they go! They're getting away! Thieves! Papa, they've got your best horse! Go after them, go after!"

Bolting back towards the river, Cesco and Val almost collided with Detto, still leading the spare horse behind him. "Perfect timing! Jump!" Without hesitation Detto leapt from the back of his tired horse and landed across the rump of Cesco's. The three boys raced off. "We're not very good at this business."

"What business?" asked Detto, trying to find his balance to sit.

"Horse thieving! We had four, now we have two, though this one is probably worth those two put together. How are you?"

"I saw Mastino pass Tharwat and the doctor."

"With blood in his eye, I'm sure. Let's turn that blood into mud." Leaning close to the horse's bare neck, Cesco veered down a path to the damp banks of the Adige. It was a steep incline, but both horses performed admirably. Cesco patted his mount's neck. "Good boy!"

The river's bank had a brick wall that separated it from the road above. They raced between the wall and the water, across the narrow strip of gravelly earth. The river was low, creating a shoulder on either side just wide enough for four horses abreast.

There was a cry from behind as the hunters spied them. Some angled down the path to the bank, hot in pursuit. But higher up, Mastino and Fuchs were flanking them on the road, making good progress. In another minute he would pull ahead, then find a place to descend and cut them off.

"Come and get it, little doggie. Detto, take the reins. Take this too. Don't drop it. Val – watch it, I'm coming over!" Hitching his legs up under him, he leapt from the back of his horse, racing full tilt over the mud, and landed neatly just behind Valentino.

Valentino was growing tired – the strain of managing a full-sized courser was too much for an eight year-old. But the saddle was big enough for them both, so he could lean back and rest for a moment as Cesco took the reins.

He was surprised when Cesco thrust something into his hand. "Loop this around the saddlehorn and hold it tight!"

It was the end of a rope, stolen from Montecchio's stable. The other end was in Detto's hand.

Fatigue forgotten, Val tittered in excitement as he obeyed.

♦   ◊   ♦

Taking a cue from Mastino, Pietro kept to the road. His eyes remained fixed on the horses sending up sprays of mud on the riverbank. It took someone shouting in his ear to gain his attention.

"Pietro! Pietro! What the devil is going on?" Mariotto Montecchio was coming up easily next to him on a magnificent horse that put Pietro's borrowed one to shame.

"Cangrande's son! He's out to prove how daring he is!"

"By stealing my best horse?"

"Not just yours! That's Cangrande's horse he's on now!"

Anger subsiding, Montecchio let out a rueful laugh. "He must have half the city after him!"

Cangrande and Capulletto hadn't taken the river route either. Seeing Mariotto, Antony snarled. "What's *he* doing here?"

"Cesco stole his horse," explained Pietro.

"Good for Cesco!" cried Antony with real pleasure.

Mariotto ignored his former friend. "Look! Mastino's got him!"

Below, Mastino and Fuchs were descending to the muddy bank in front of the fugitives, cutting off their escape. Mastino and Fuchs charged, and the four horses drove together like matched pairs of *giustani* on a tilting yard. Unlike jousters, no one bore lances. But Pietro saw a shimmer of metal in Fuchs' hand. Cold dread gripped him. "Cesco, look out!"

◆     ◊     ◆

As they drew nearer, Cesco called out, "Good morrow, cos!"

Mastino shouted back an unmistakable insult, raised fist ready to smash down as they passed. Detto was riding south along the wall, while Cesco and Val's horse would thread the needle between Mastino and Fuchs, nearest the water.

Like the teeth of a water-wheel, the horses came together. In the instant, several things happened:

Fuchs swung his blade, and Cesco forced Valentino's head down.

The rope between Val and Detto went taut.

Fist raised, Mastino cried out in surprise as he was lifted out of his seat as if by an invisible lance, dropping to the muck and dragged between Detto and Val's horses.

"Detto!" cried Val.

Detto was laughing until he heard his brother's frantic shout. "What is it?"

Dropping his end of the rope off his saddle horn, Val turned to stare behind him. "Cesco's gone!"

♦        ◊        ♦

To Pietro's relief, the boys let Mastino go after a few yards. But his relief was shattered when he saw there was one less boy on Cangrande's horse. *Did Cesco fall off? Is he hurt?* Pietro scanned the riverbank for a body. Cangrande, Mariotto, and Antony did the same.

Tharwat and Morsicato arrived. The doctor was panting. "What's happening?"

Pietro shook his head fractionally. "I can't see—"

Antony pointed. "What – there, is that..?"

"Yes! Look!" Mariotto was pointing at Fuch's horse, still galloping full tilt. A small figure was hanging from the saddle on the underbelly of the beast.

"Oh dear God," murmured Pietro.

"He'll be trampled!" cried Morsicato. "We have to stop—"

"Too late!" Cangrande leaned eagerly forward to watch.

♦        ◊        ♦

Hanging upside-down from Fuchs' stirrup, Cesco braced his feet against the horse's belly. The mud that spattered up into his face was nearly blinding. The kicking foot in the stirrup was especially unhelpful.

"Whoreson brat," Fuchs hissed in German, his long dagger flashing down.

Cesco's face swayed inches from the horse's testicles – this was no gelding. *Impressive. But it will make this more difficult.* Groping out with a desperate hand, Cesco swung to the horse's left side, snatching at the opposite foot. *Thank heavens Fuchs isn't wearing spurs.* Cesco longed to taunt, but he'd only swallow mud. His fingers were already slipping. The masque had shifted down to half-blind him. *It's possible this was a bad idea.* Taking a shallow breath, Cesco let go with his right hand and cast back with his left, pushing his legs off the underside of the saddle. *Here goes!*

Above, Fuchs glimpsed the disappearing hand and laughed, waiting to feel the brat's body under the hooves.

Below, Cesco hung in the air for a terrifying moment, floating face-up between the thundering legs of the horse, brushing its massive penis and grazing the inside of its thighs. Then Cesco found the lifeline he was grasping for – the braided tail. Gripping it tight, he put all of his weight on it. Hanging upside-down by the tail, he braced his feet against the horse's backside and pulled with all his might.

The steed reacted to the yanking on its tail in the only sensible manner. It reared.

Fuchs was an excellent horseman. Though unexpected, the sudden rearing failed to unseat him. But for that moment the horse was no longer running.

Cesco's head brushed the ground as the horse stood tall on its hind legs. Having survived this insane stunt, it would have been simple for Cesco to touch his feet down and leap up behind the rider. But Cesco was determined not to touch the earth at all. So as the horse descended, he stepped on the horse's rear legs, turned his right shoulder, and rolled up over the horse's rump. An inelegant move, it left Cesco lying sideways behind saddle.

Fuchs felt the bump at his back and, even as he sawed the reins with one hand, he flipped his long dagger into a stabbing position and swung backwards blindly. Cesco's knee blocked the blow at Fuchs' elbow. Right hand darting to his belt, Cesco retrieved the object he'd borrowed from Montecchio's stable. Like the dagger, it glinted in the moonlight.

Ducking another backwards stab of the dagger, Cesco brushed the object against the strap to Fuchs' saddle. Then he flopped onto his back and aimed a sideways kick at the German's head.

Half-turned in his saddle, Fuchs easily caught the childish kick on his forearm. As he brought the knife up again, he suddenly he felt himself slipping, falling sideways. The saddle rolled off the horse's back, taking him with it, and Fuchs landed hard in the muddy grass and pebbles.

More horsemen were thundering down the riverbank towards them. Cesco took the reins and turned the horse about, careful to keep the horse from stepping on the sputtering German. "Sorry, no time to stay!" Galloping off, he tossed aside the instrument he'd used to cut the saddle strap, a sickle-shaped blade used for trimming manes, curved like the waxing moon above.

♦   ◊   ♦

The crowd on the road above watched all this over the course of thirty seconds. Seeing Cesco ride away unhurt, Pietro told his heart to start beating again. The masqued boy waved up at them as he passed them by.

"He rides well enough," mused Cangrande. "But what does he have against saddles?"

"Amazing," said Petruchio, having just arrived.

"Never seen anything like it," said Mariotto.

Unable to disagree, Antony grunted. "Where's he going now?"

"Back to the feast, I hope." Cangrande sounded bored. "I've not had my dessert yet."

"No!" cried Mariotto. "Look!"

Cesco had disappeared about a quarter of a mile south, hidden by the curving wall. The pursuing horsemen on the bank pulled up sharply at the same spot, gazing upwards. A moment later Pietro saw why.

Clambering over the top of the wall, Cesco dusted himself off, wiped the mud from his masque, then turned to face them. It was a clear night, brightly lit by stars and moon, and the hand gesture the masqued filthy child gave them was startlingly clear. "Khan Grande, Don Worm, you fashion-mongering poor inch of nature, you cowardly, bowelless, wrathful mouse! Do you always let your men fight in your place? I had thought better of the Greyhound! Grey*hind* is more like it!"

With a roar of either rage or laughter, Cangrande lurched forward, spurring his horse into a run. Pietro swallowed and joined the others as the chase began anew.

Only this chase was to be vertical. Cesco had already leapt from a barrel onto a balcony, and was proceeding to scale the side of a three-story building.

Reaching the edge of the same building, Cangrande didn't hesitate. From his horse's back, he leapt to grasp the edge of the balcony. Hauling himself upwards, he glanced down. "Surround the building. Pietro, bring my horse." He grabbed at a window frame just as Cesco disappeared over the roof's edge. A few dislodged clay tiles came slipping down.

Pietro called after the Scaliger. "Remember, he's just a boy!"

"Not tonight," replied Cangrande, stepping up onto a windowsill and grasping the roof's edge. "He chose to play a devil. Now he'll collect the Devil's due!"

# TWENTY-SEVEN

HEAVING HIS SIX FOOT and more frame over the lip of the roof, Cangrande studied his surroundings. His weight was far more than a child's. Yet the incline of the foot-long clay tiles wasn't impossible, especially if taken quickly. He pushed off and dashed to the peak of the roof where he halted, looking about.

The boy was perched on a stone gargoyle the next roof over, his masque's three faces all mockery.

"You'd be wiser to run," said Cangrande.

"Oh? Is that how we justify cowardice? As wisdom?"

Cangrande took a step but the tiles slipped underfoot, cascading down to shatter on the street below. He sprang back and Cesco laughed. "I must have taken out a few too many on my leap. Sorry."

Cangrande examined the boy through narrowed eyes. "I'd have thought you'd be taller."

"I hope I manage more surprises than that."

"So far, just a poor copy. The masque – it's been done."

"An homage, my lord. Flattery. Are you susceptible?"

"As much as any man. But perhaps less, by you."

Cesco cocked his head theatrically. "However shall I gain your admiration?"

"You've begun with theft, assault, and insult," said the Scaliger.

"Don't forget arson. And there's a minor sacrilege you don't yet know about."

"When you arrive at murder, you will garner my full attention."

Cesco clicked his tongue. "I don't have it yet? I suppose this roof-top is just a favoured locale."

"I came to see if you were at all interesting. So far you may colour me unimpressed."

Cesco switched to Arabic. "*God shall not charge any soul save to its ability.*"

Cangrande answered in kind. "*No soul shall be wronged at all, nor shall ye be rewarded for aught but that which ye have done.* Thou dost disappoint. Before he was thy tutor, the noble bridegroom was mine."

"I can tell by the accent." Cesco's voice was lazy but his eyes were bright in the central, screaming face. "Well, if words will not suffice, shall we dance?"

"Let's." Cangrande lunged. Tiles fell away under his feet, but he was already airborne, spanning the gap to the next building.

Cesco rolled backwards off the gargoyle and fell out of view. By the time the Scaliger had his feet under him, Cesco was already leaping to another roof. Shouldering through a balcony door, the boy vanished inside. There was a moment of surprised silence, then a woman's screams.

Cangrande reached the balcony scant seconds later to find pandemonium within. In the dim light two naked figures could be seen. The woman was trying to cover herself while her lover grasped a chamber pot to strike at this second intruder.

"*Coitus interruptus,*" said a voice in Cangrande's ear – the boy had hidden in the shadows by the open balcony door. "Apologize for me."

Shoved forward into the room, Cangrande was forced to duck the pot, smelling its contents as they sprayed the wall to his right. He lashed out with his fist, knocking the naked man to the floor. "Dreadfully sorry. The boy will have a lesson in manners, you have my word." Giving the woman an appreciative glance, the Scaliger bowed and exited the way he'd come.

Outside, Cesco was nowhere in sight. Smiling to himself, Cangrande began to climb.

♦   ◊   ♦

Below, Morsicato was riding beside Pietro, having taken the saddle of Cangrande's horse. "Well, he threw the plan out the window. Unless this something else you decided not to tell me?"

"This was his alone." The plan had been for Cesco to arrive at Capulletto's house and start singing, showing his talent for invention. He would then lead his Capulletto host to Montecchio's house, hoping to effect some sort of public reconciliation. "I should have known. He was far too obliging."

"In his defense, he *did* go to Montecchio's house," noted Tharwat from Pietro's other side.

"Was he supposed to?" demanded Capulletto. "Why?"

"Maybe he was hoping for a decent meal that wouldn't turn his stomach," said Mari.

"I have the best cooks in the Feltro!"

"I know. You hired them away from me!"

Pietro sighed. It had been Cesco's idea to bring Mari and Antony together, make them put aside old wounds. But already they were sniping. Pietro told Mari to go with the Moor and the doctor to the north side of the building. "Antony and I will circle around to the south."

"Yes, do go on," said Antony in a scathing tone. "Pietro and I have more important—"

"Antony!" Pietro cut across him in exasperation. "Stuff it, or I'll go with Mari instead."

There were nasty stares between the rivals, then they separated. Pietro and Antony turned the corner in time to witness a cursing man wrapped in a blanket, standing on a balcony and shaking a fist at the rooftop. "Which way did they go?"

"To the Devil for all I care!" shouted the naked fellow as he slammed the broken balcony door shut.

Antony chortled. "So much for the boy getting hurt! He's remarkable."

"Yes, he is." Pietro was torn between laughter and tears. Where Cesco was concerned, it was a familiar sensation. "The problem is that he knows it."

"Just like his father. Where did he learn to ride like that?"

Pietro shook his head. "I have no idea. From Tharwat, maybe?"

"Who?" Antony had never known Tharwat's true name.

"Theodoro. The Moor." *So many secrets.*

"Remarkable," repeated Antony.

Pietro's eyes were trained upwards. Suddenly a moving shape overhead caught his eye as it soared over the narrow street and onto the building opposite. Cupping his hands to his mouth, Pietro shouted, "Cesco!" But the boy was already flying across the next roof. "*Dammit!*"

"He'll be fine," consoled Antony. "He moves like a cat."

"Don't tell him that."

A second figure hurtled overhead. "Look out below!" cried Cangrande as more tiles came slipping down. Pietro and Antony shielded themselves from the shower of shattering clay. They calmed their horses, dusted themselves off, and were about to follow when they heard a patter of footfalls behind them. "Ser Capulletto! Ser Capulletto!"

"Andriolo, what's the matter?"

Capulletto's groom was a hulking fellow with a bright genial face. He wore an unaccustomed look of worry as he breathlessly related the news. Capulletto turned his horse about and raced back to his home, leaving Pietro all alone.

♦    ◊    ♦

Three roofs away, Cesco hid in the shadow of an overhang. The drying mud made him nigh invisible. His sat with eyes closed, posture erect, the perfect mirror of Tharwat's posture ten days earlier.

A single footstep. Cesco could almost feel the nearness of the hunter. "Atropos, is that you?"

"With my shears." Cangrande leapt off the overhang. Cesco twisted away, but his ankle was caught. He kicked uselessly as Cangrande lifted him bodily, dangling him inverted in the air.

"A quick lesson in keeping a civil tongue." With his free hand, the Scaliger struck five times across the masque. "One for each accusation of cowardice."

Cesco curled, hands deflecting the worst of the light, open-handed blows. When they were done he went slack, unfurling upside-down. His lip was split and he hawked bloody bile to the tiles. "I'm sorry..."

"That's a start."

"...sorry you ever learned to count. My, you're big."

Cangrande shook the boy. "And you're lighter than you should be. Have you lost weight?"

"I've been starving myself out of fear. I didn't want to vomit on sight of you."

"Am I so hideous? You're the one under the masque."

"For fear of every soul in the city falling to my charms. I'm such a beautiful boy, you see. That's why your soldiers like me."

"Hah! Competition I don't need. Perhaps I should throw you back, little fish."

Cangrande drew his outstretched arm a trifle closer to shake the dangling boy again. Serpent-quick, Cesco's hand shot out and twisted the nipple under the Scaliger's loose shirt, hard.

Surprise caused Cangrande to drop him. Cesco landed on his shoulder, rolled over backward, and stood with his back to the wall of the next building over. "Why, Atty, you've lost your bubbies!"

Rubbing at his sore chest, Cangrande's smile was thin. "I feel no need to suckle you at my teat." A swipe, a duck, a roll. Cesco came up a few feet away. "Is this the milk of your kindness? I'll take wine."

"All you do is whine," said Cangrande, advancing.

Cesco winced. "He who puns would purloin a purse. Grandfather would be appalled."

"You never met your grandfather." Cangrande dove forward, hands outstretched.

Cesco darted right, kicking off a carved saint for redirection. Using Cangrande's shoulder as a step, he hopped neatly onto the lowest edge of a close by roof. "Join me, dear lout! *Qui m'aime me suive.*" Cesco turned and ran, Cangrande hot on his heels.

♦          ◊          ♦

"He's going to kill himself," moaned Morsicato, riding along with Montecchio and the Moor. "He wants to die, that has to be it. He's got a death-wish."

"He'll be fine," said Mariotto. "I'm sure the Capitano will look after him."

"Hmm. Well, if he doesn't die himself, he'll be the death of me."

"He *is* a wild one," laughed Mariotto.

"And reckless! Only a dozen days after—" The doctor found his horse bumped by al-Dhaamin's. "—ah, after coming to the city, and he's running around the rooftops, scaring the citizens?"

"Worse, he frightened my son," said Mariotto. "I can't say he doesn't deserve a fright himself."

The Moor grunted. "He'll get one."

♦          ◊          ♦

Slipping through a window, Cesco dropped into a storehouse. He landed on pipes of tallow, then a crate, finally coming to rest atop a barrel. He laughed softly. He would give his hunter another ten minutes of fruitless searching, then sneak back to the party and wait. In the meantime, he opened a pouch and removed a small metal tin with blueberries inside.

"Hungry?"

Cesco whirled about to face the figure on the far side of the room. The voice alone told him who it was. "I'm impressed. Not even the Arūs could have slipped in that fast and that quietly."

"I have a secret to tell." Striking a taper, the Scaliger lit a candle that cast a dim flickering light over stacks of goods. "I've been waiting for you."

Much as he tried, Cesco couldn't hide his surprise. "You knew I'd come. How?"

Cangrande made a shrugging motion. "I don't often sleep, you see. I find myself awake in the small hours with nothing to do but deflower virgins."

Cesco sighed. "Or trail young hounds."

"I can't tell you how much I've enjoyed your nocturnal wanderings this last week."

"I came here thrice. That's how you knew."

"You wanted to be sure you could find it, even turned around. Perfectly sensible."

"Perfectly asinine." Scowling, Cesco slapped each of the masque's varnished foreheads for effect. "Detto's the one with the perfect sense of direction, you see."

"I thought you'd spotted me two nights ago."

"I took you for the Moor," explained Cesco. "I've given up losing him for any length of time."

"I made certain the Moor was detained." Sitting atop a wooden box with chalk scrawlings across it, Cangrande made no move to approach. "He used to dog me the same way."

Cesco held out his clasped hands. "I beg, no more puns."

"Unintentional," waved Cangrande.

"You couldn't be unintentional if you tried."

"Interesting. Only an hour of acquaintance and already I'm a liar and coward."

"While I'm a tiny upstart thief of no family."

"We have yet to determine your parentage."

"*Ap neb,* as the barbarians say. A mere mule. The wrong side of the sheets. *Il veltro.*"

Cangrande was silent.

"I notice you haven't tried to corral me," said Cesco. "I could dance up these crates and out the way I came before you reached me."

"I thought we might pass a few words before you traipsed off into the aether."

Cesco squatted on the barrel, tucking his knees under him. "So?"

"So." Cangrande leaned back in his improvised seat. "Do you wish to shoulder the burden of being my heir?"

"*Post equitum sedet atra cura!*" Cesco's words dripped with feigned surprise. "You mean there's a choice?"

"There is," replied the Scaliger levelly. "You can't return to Ravenna, but I have friends in many places. My enemies would never smoke you out. If you wish, you may lead a fruitful, uneventful life."

"You have enemies? I find that hard to believe. Such a very gracious host."

Seated, Cangrande made a quarter bow. "I live to serve. Yet, alas, there are some who do not appreciate my need to serve them. Hence, enemies."

"They'll learn the errors of their ways, I'm sure."

Cangrande's smile was grim. "Yes, they will. But that's not to say there won't be more in their wake. You should be aware that if you take up the name of Escalus, you will never be rid of it. Already you are tainted. We're not a wholesome bunch. I believe God likes to test us often to keep our mettle pure."

"God as blacksmith, always forging ahead." Cangrande winced and the boy opened his palms in apology. "You set the tone. However it pains me, I must prove my mettle the equal to yours."

"Life as a Scaligeri would not be life as an Alaghieri."

"Confidentially, if you asked Ser Pietro, he might say my deeds stretched what it was to be an Alaghieri."

Cangrande stood. "You are determined, then, to take up the title?"

"I am, lord, if you wish to bestow it upon me."

"And if I don't wish to?"

"I cannot dream of a time when you could be compelled to do something you didn't wish to do."

"Expand your dreams, then. It happens all too frequently. Take tonight. I had planned on a lovely meal and a few words, then seduce a few maids before stumbling off to my bed. I haven't been getting much sleep of late."

"That's the second time you've alluded to lovemaking," said Cesco. "Are you flirting with me?"

Cangrande allowed himself a laugh. "Perhaps I am! But not in the way you mean. You're baptized for me, you know."

"I rather thought so. You won't mind if I don't take your cognomen."

"Don't like dogs?"

Cesco's fingers brushed the coin hanging at his throat. "Adore them. But I wish to be my own man."

"I hear the ring of Ser Alaghieri's voice in that sentiment. I said something quite like that to him once. And yet, *Omne quod est, aut habet esse a se, aut ab alio.*"

"I see," said Cesco. "I am the latter to your former, then? I think I am resentful." Popping another blueberry into his mouth, he chewed while tapping his fingers absently on the tin lid.

Cangrande said, "Aren't you ever still?"

Cesco shook his head. "Enough time to be still when I'm dead."

"When you evanesce, you mean."

"Evanesce?" asked Cesco, puzzled. "Am I made of vapor, that I'll evaporate with the morning dew?"

"No," said the Scaliger, approaching. "Light as you are, I believe you're made of more solid stuff."

Cesco didn't flee. "Almost a compliment. What do I need solidity for?"

"For what comes next. Creative you may be, but you will have responsibilities beyond your imagination. There are twin offices, military on the one hand, judicial and financial on the other. You have to be prepared to overrule men four times your age. Not just Castelbarco, Bonaventura, and the rest, but wizened fools who resent any form of change or innovation. To them the old ways are always the best, no matter how ineffectual they may be. You must be willing to judge your friends, even sacrifice them for the sake of the city. All concerns are second to the welfare of the city."

"This offer grows more seductive every moment. I'm awed you haven't slit your wrists by now."

"Expect no help from anyone, even your friends. Especially your friends. Everyone wants something. It's what you're willing to sacrifice that matters, and as Capitano you have to be willing to sacrifice anything and anyone."

"Even your heir?"

"*Especially* your heir."

"Poor me. Though from what I hear, there are more where I came from. Are the nobility at all useful, or are they the children you paint them?"

"Not all are bad. Castelbarco is capable, if unimaginative. His son looks to be cut of the same cloth. Nogarola is steadfast and a true leader of men, but not much as a general. Lozzo is genial, but under his cheerful façade he's ruled by self-interest alone. Bonaventura is somewhere between those last two, but has a fascinating wife to guide him."

"You left out Montecchio and Capulletto."

"Ah, our own Eteocles and Polynices," said Cangrande. He raised a probing eyebrow.

Cesco groaned sourly. "Another test? I *was* raised in Dante's house, you know. Tests were the alpha and omega of my existence." He uncurved his spine to sit upright and recite. "Sons to Oedipus and Jocasta. Forced their father to abdicate, and thus were cursed to be enemies forever. I made some small attempt tonight to bring them together."

"By provoking them both into chasing you? An interesting tactic, if futile. I've tried everything. I think Montecchio might be willing – he's long gotten past the belief that Capulletto murdered his father. But our Antony is still stung by the thought of his lost love. Myself, I cannot understand it. The girl is pretty enough, but insipid to the point of absurdity."

"Those do seem to be the women who cause the most trouble."

Cangrande barked out a single laugh. "Too true! What about you? I had my first real woman when I was your age. Have your balls dropped yet? Have you been bedded?"

Cesco shook his head. "I am sadly ignorant of the skills, if not the act. Though I was recently witness to the most fascinating wooing scene…"

"You must tell me all about it, tomorrow. Tonight, we must find you a willing girl. There's one back at the palace —"

"O please, no," said Cesco. "Not one of your courtesans. I'm going to be doing enough treading in your footsteps. To complete your list, what about my erstwhile rivals, Mastino and Alberto?"

Cangrande now stood before Cesco. "What, am I supposed to give away everything at once? Probe their stuffing yourself."

Cesco rose to his feet, looking up. "As you wish, *pater mi*, oh great Greyhound!"

Cangrande slapped Cesco across the face so hard it cracked the masque. Broken, the three varnished faces slipped to the floor, Comedy to one side, Madness and Tragedy to the other. "*Never* call me that again."

Cangrande watched Cesco's head come slowly up, furious tears in the boy's eyes – tears of outrage, shame, and surprise. They fell freely, carving their passage down his flushed cheeks. For the first time in his life the Scaliger saw a naked rage that dwarfed his own temper. He readied himself for the blow that had to be coming. He wondered if it would be to maim, or to kill.

But Cesco simply turned his face, offering up his other cheek. "Please. I value balance in all things."

Cangrande felt an unwelcome shiver run through him. "Christ-like. But heed my words. In public, in private, in my company or out of it – never call me that."

"Which? Greyhound? Or father?"

"Either."

Cesco's tongue worked at the blood filling his mouth. "I suppose I should have accepted the whore."

"I suppose so." Cangrande stooped and took up the broken halves of the masque. "A visor, for a visor?"

"We all wear masques, my lord. Some are just more grotesque than others."

With galling defensiveness, Cangrande offered a kind of apology. "Only blood of my blood could fray my temper so much. Yes – you are a true della Scala."

Cesco managed a bloody smile. "Was there doubt?"

Cangrande stared down into that face a long time before answering. "Once, perhaps. But now? No. No doubt at all."

♦       ◊       ♦

Pietro was among two dozen horsemen gathered in torchlight just outside Cangrande's palace in the Piazza della Signoria. With the aid of many other hunters Bailardino had managed to trap his sons, letting Montecchio repossess his stolen horse. Of Mastino and Fuchs there was no sign. No one expected them to show their muddy faces for days.

By now they had given up all hope of tracing Cangrande and Cesco from the ground. Instead they speculated, giving odds on how long it would take for the Scaliger to return with his wayward heir in tow. Some of the younger lords stared at the Moor, sitting calmly atop his horse, having never known him in their time at court.

"Ho! Look out below there!"

Faces turned up to behold two descending figures. Pietro released a long breath, and Petruchio cheered. "See, see! They're back together, and before midnight. That means I won!"

"Only if the race is over," said Nico da Lozzo. "My lord, have you driven the prey to us? Should we bring him down for you?"

"Lay a finger on him and you'll regret it," replied Cangrande loudly, hanging from a grating on a palace window. "Oh, I won't stop you, but your nipples may be sore on the morrow." He rubbed his own for emphasis.

Every man laughed while openly they studied the pair, so unlike in size yet so very similar in gait and bearing. As the Scaliger and his heir dropped to the earth, the assembly felt the weight of the moment, and as one they dismounted and wordlessly knelt.

"My friends," said Cangrande in his expansive public voice. "It is my duty to present to you Francesco della Scala. My heir."

"Sca-*la!*" In seconds the cry was taken up by the assembly as they rose and pumped their fists into the air. "Sca-*la!* Sca-*la!*"

As Cangrande smiled and waved, his heir stood looking from face to face, his expression sardonic. Then the crowd surged forward to lift Cesco up onto their shoulders, bearing him back towards the Piazza delle Erbe.

Watching the boy go, Pietro felt an enormous rock lodge between his ribs. *He will never be free now. They will both strive for mastery. Who can say which will win? Prophecy says only so much.*

Cangrande mounted his white horse, and grinned at Pietro. "See? Entirely unharmed."

Pietro was too tired to spar. "It doesn't matter. He's yours now."

"I suspect he will never be entirely mine. For that, I congratulate you." The Scaliger clicked his tongue, urging his horse to follow the impromptu parade.

Pietro, Tharwat, and Morsicato followed. "At least he's still alive," said the doctor.

"He will need us more than ever now," said the Moor.

*And I won't be here. Cangrande's already made that clear.* Pietro suddenly noticed that the revelers were returning to the Capulletti house. "Oh, no." Kicking his mount, he called out Cangrande. "We shouldn't return to the feast."

"Whyever not, Ser Alaghieri, Knight of the Mastiff? Did my hounds get into the pudding?"

"Word came while we were chasing about. His wife is giving birth."

"Excellent!" said Cangrande, unperturbed. "Another reason to celebrate. And if it is indeed a girl, perhaps we can delight him with an alliance, my heir with his. What do you think?"

"I think now is not the time to disturb their household."

"Nonsense! He'll welcome the distraction. No, Montecchio, don't slink off! Young Cesco made an effort to draw you out tonight, and I won't let his first act of diplomacy go to waste. Truly, you're coming, I insist! Won't that be a surprise for our host!"

But Antony was not the only man surprised. When the group dismounted at the tunnel to the Capulletti household, there was an odd tension in the air. Antony rushed forward. Unbelievably, he didn't even bat an eye at Montecchio's presence. "My lord —"

Cangrande took Antony in his arms and kissed his cheeks. "I understand you are about to be a father! A night for heirs!"

"Yes, lord, but —" Antony paused, trying to frame his words. "Another guest has, I mean, she's here, she —"

"What is it, man? Did one of my mistresses show up?"

"Given their number," said a cool voice from the door of Antony's house, "that would be far less surprising."

Audible gasps. For several seconds Pietro couldn't believe his eyes. Even Cangrande seemed taken aback. Only Cesco was unmoved, looking curiously at the newcomer.

"I'm sorry I'm late," said Katerina della Scala, striding gracefully forward. "I seemed to have missed some excitement. Won't you tell me all about it?"

Not a word was slurred.

# TWENTY-EIGHT

"I FEAR I AM one of Horace's slavish herd. I decided if you could come back from the dead, the least I could do was overcome a simple stroke."

Ensconced in one of Capulletto's chairs near her sons and husband, Katerina gazed levelly at her brother, leaning casually between tapestries on a nearby wall. His answer was smooth, his famous *allegria* firmly in place. "All artifice is but imitation of nature. I'm flattered."

"To misquote a poet is a sin."

"Not a mortal one, though, I'm sure. What do you say, Ser Alaghieri?"

"Are you really better, mother?" asked Valentino, her gloved hand stroking his hair as he sat at her knee. Detto was seated on her right, holding her other hand and happier than Pietro could remember him being.

The lady spoke crisply. "I'll never be all better, my boy. But I decided enough was too much."

Cangrande was darkly amused. "I'm sure you did."

Pietro watched the family reunion with interest. Cangrande's manner was predictably careless and sardonic. The two boys were overjoyed. But Bailardino's brows were drawn together in a frown. *Wonder what he's thinking right now.*

Bail wasn't the only one fretting. In Antony's house for the first time, Mariotto was stiff and wary. He'd viewed the fire-scorched fresco in the torchlit yard with a sour face. Pietro tried to ease his friend's discomfort by observing, "Petrarch says hello."

Mari's face brightened. "How is he? Still lusting to be like you."

"Like my father," corrected Pietro. "All he cares about is poetry."

"He should meet my Gianozza," laughed Mariotto, then frowned. "Or maybe he shouldn't. I've already had one friend turn on me over her."

*Over her idiocy. Well, so much for distracting him.*

Adding to the general awkwardness, every few minutes an agonized cry would issue from somewhere in the attached building. Antony pretended not to hear his wife's shrieks until it became too much and he whispered to his servants to have the girl gagged if need be. "She's disturbing our guests."

The center of all attention, Katerina looked around. "I understand there was a fuss over my former ward. May I be introduced?"

Heads turned in the crowded feasting hall, but Cesco was absent.

"Dammit," said Morsicato through a full mouth – quite the gourmand, he was trying to catch up on the courses he had missed. "Not again."

"Never you mind, doctor," said the lady. "I'm sure he'll turn up."

But Pietro was concerned. "Excuse me, Mari. I have to look for him."

"I'll go with you." Pietro tried to wave Mari off, but he persisted, so together they stepped out onto the long balcony and followed it left towards the living quarters. Cesco couldn't have gone to a lower floor without slipping past them, which meant he was somewhere in the Capulletto's private rooms.

Both Pietro and Mariotto winced at a smothered moan from above. "With Romeo, Gianozza had an easy birth. At least that's what they told me. She sent me away."

"Probably for the best," said Pietro absently. He'd just spied Tharwat at the far end of the hallway, at the foot of a staircase. Pietro made to call out, but a gesture from Tharwat cut him short. Approaching, he saw why.

Cesco was huddled in a corner, curled into a ball and shivering. His eyes were closed and sweat poured down his face.

"The reaction," whispered the Moor.

"*Jesu Christo*," murmured Mariotto. "What's the matter with him?"

Pietro knelt. "Can he hear us?"

"If he can, he should not try to answer."

"Shall I fetch Morsicato?" asked Mariotto in genuine concern.

"N-n-no," said Cesco through chattering teeth. "F-f-fine in a m-minute."

"Don't talk." Tharwat forced the boy to swallow some wafer, then produced a flask and pressed it to Cesco's lips. Drinking, the boy breathed in through his nose several times.

"What's that you're giving him?" asked Pietro.

"Something to give him strength."

"What's wrong with him?" intruded a younger voice. Thibault was watching through the slats of the banister above.

"Should you be spying on people?" asked Mariotto.

"I know who *you* are," sneered Thibault. "You shouldn't even be here." He jutted his chin towards Cesco. "Is he going to die?"

"No," said the Moor.

"I hope he does die," said Thibault. "He deserves to die!"

Pietro took a step towards the stair and the boy covered his mouth with his hand and ran from sight. "What was that about?"

The Moor shrugged. "On the road to friendship, they veered."

Cesco spoke through chattering teeth. "C-could n-never be f-f-friends with the K-king of Cats."

Capulletto appeared. Seeing Cesco, he blanched. "What's the matter? He's not ill? Not here, not tonight!"

Shoulder to shoulder with his former friend, Montecchio asked, "What *is* the matter with him?"

*The truth is better than the rumours they'll start spreading.* "Antony, Mari, not a word of this to anyone. He was poisoned when we first arrived in the city. He's recovering, but he pushed himself too hard tonight. Idiot boy," he added.

Cesco's deep breaths seemed to be helping. He flexed his trembling fingers, staring at them with concentration, as if willing them to stillness. "If I'm weak, h-he'll send me a-away."

"Cangrande collapsed when he was knighted."

"He was six," said Cesco dismissively.

"And he hadn't been poisoned," said Tharwat.

"Poisoned," murmured Antony in disbelief.

"Was it on the day he arrived?" asked Montecchio.

"Yes," said Pietro.

"I thought he seemed unwell in council."

"Anyone could see that," snapped Antony. "Pietro, do you know who did it?"

"No."

"It has to be Mastino!" cried Antony in disgust. "He's the only one who stood to gain."

"Maybe," said Pietro doubtfully.

"Why keep it a secret?" asked Mariotto. "Why not tell the world? We could string up Mastino once and for all. At least send him into exile."

Pietro said nothing. In truth, he'd considered blaming Mastino, if only to thwart Cangrande's plans to set the Mastiff at Cesco's neck. But they lacked proof. And whatever they did, Cangrande would be three steps ahead. Sometimes the best way to deal with this family was to wait and see. Katerina had just provided a strong reminder of that.

*Yet* – perhaps he could plant the seeds in his two oldest friends. "Cangrande knows and hasn't done anything. I don't see how things would change if it became public. But the council should know."

"They'll be eating out of this one's palm after tonight," said Mariotto. "I've never seen riding like that."

"Uncle Tharwat saw such tricks once," said Cesco. His shakes seemed to be behind him. "He told me. In Damascus. What were you doing there again?"

"Picking apricots," replied Tharwat.

Cesco was recovering. Whatever the Moor had fed him, it was giving him strength. Pietro ruffled his hair. "You little menace. How long?"

Cesco had the good grace to appear abashed. "Almost a year. In those few moments when I'd eluded my Shadow. My arms aren't long, but I'm small so I don't get hit by the horse's legs." His words came in short bursts, quite unlike his usual flow of speech. But the grin was entirely his own. "Never tried it without my harness. Glad it worked."

A cry from upstairs caused Mariotto to glance awkwardly at Antony. "I hope congratulations are in order."

Antony threw civility in Mari's face. "My line will bury yours."

"So your nephew learned his manners from you. Your line isn't much to brag on."

Cesco shakily climbed to his feet. "Dear lord, do they never stop?"

"I wish." Pietro reached out a hand. "Let me help you."

"I can manage."

The Moor stared down at his charge. "Are you recovered?"

"Enough to slip away from this venomous cant." Cesco looked sideways at both Montecchio and Capulletto. "*Vieni a veder Montecchi e Cappelletti, uom sanza cura: color gia tristi, e questi con sospetti.* I came, I saw, but I could not conquer. So I leave."

Recovered, Cesco headed back towards the festivities, Tharwat right behind. Pietro started to follow, but was forestalled by Antony. "What was that, a quote?"

Mariotto snorted. "Feh! If you read, you'd know."

Pietro sighed. "A line my father wrote, a very long time ago." He stalked away, leaving the two enemies standing nose to nose in the dim hallway. Above them little Tessa was again ripped through with screaming as she brought her daughter forth into the world.

♦ ◊ ♦

"Here's our chief guest," called Cangrande as Cesco appeared from the balcony doors. Men made room for him, clapping and whistling. "I doubt he could have been forgotten," said Petruchio. At his side, Kate added, "Not for long, in any case."

Guessing her identity, Cesco bowed to her. "Donna Bonaventura, this is your namesake's day. Thank you for sharing it."

Kate brushed back her russet hair. "I am only a Bonaventura by marriage."

"And I a della Scala by default. We are kindred souls, known for our masters, not our selves."

"Don't go calling me her master," said Petruchio. "I had her do it once, and she's never stopped since!"

"I obey your every command, my lord," said Kate, a twinkle in her eye. "Master Francesco, I believe there is another Katerina here you should be addressing. She waits for you."

Cesco turned dutifully towards Detto's mother, who rose. Cesco bowed deeply. "Madonna, it has been far too long."

"Nearly three years." Brushing her fingers through his hair, Katerina addressed the crowd. "Before my illness, I went with my son to visit him, in secret."

"Of course, her true identity was kept from me," said Cesco, continuing the tale. "For a long time I thought she must be my mother. Now I know I am not so fortunate. Lady, please do not stand on my account." Taking her arm, he guided her back to her seat and sat on the floor beside her.

Pietro watched from the balcony door. *He's good.* First the boy had showed off his physical prowess and daring. Now he was charming them, just moments after shaking and feeling wretched. *He never ceases to amaze me. Yet my heart breaks for him, over and over. Why is that?*

Katerina was examining his face. "Handsome. In a rather feral way."

"He needs a haircut," observed Cangrande. "He looks like a dancing girl."

"Only because I am one." Cesco leapt up and launched into an elaborate series of steps without faltering. Feeling a tear welling in his eye, Pietro blinked it away.

*Over and over.*

♦ ◊ ♦

The rest of the night was a hot blizzard of conversations and asides, cheers and proclamations. During the course of it, Pietro kept himself at a little remove, mostly to keep an eye on Cesco, but also because he was still bitterly disappointed about Borachio's failure to recognize Cangrande's voice.

Yet the night still afforded him one hope of tracking down the man behind the poison. That hope lay with Passerino Bonaccolsi. Pietro just had to wait for an opportune moment.

It came when Passerino stood up and said, "I have an announcement! It will seem a little anti-climactic after all this excitement – but I'm to be married!" There were wry cheers and well-meant jeers as everyone asked to whom. "To Ailisa d'Este, sister to Rainaldo and Obizzo. Sews up a nice little backyard alliance with the city of Ferrara. And she's not hard to look at, thank God!"

There were salutes and oaths and much more wine, though Cangrande himself seemed much bemused by the match.

Having made his announcement, Passerino slipped down the servants' stair to make water outside. Recognizing this as his moment, Pietro fell in step behind the Mantuan. "I need to clear the pipes. Have the same idea?"

"More like the need made itself known." Passerino was weaving a little. "Capulletto's wine goes down too easily. Even if it is horribly watered-down." Once in the yard, they took places side by side and fumbled with their points before relieving themselves.

"Congratulations, by the way."

"What? Oh, yes. Thank you."

Pietro stared at the wall in front of him, as protocol dictated. "You've had an interesting couple of weeks."

"Not as interesting as yours. Raising Cangrande's brat – that's something!"

"Something," agreed Pietro. "The news of his death turned our world upside-down."

"I can imagine."

"How did that rumour even get started?"

"What? Oh, I can't talk about that." Passerino gave Pietro a conspiratorial wink.

"Ooo!" said Pietro, as if he gleaned Bonaccolsi's meaning. "He started it himself!"

"Shhh! That's a secret!" Passerino sighed, placing one hand against the wall. "I thought it was a good prank."

"A dangerous prank. It kicked up a lot of chaos."

"You know, I did point that out. But he was determined. Damn. Need more light out here. Think I'm hitting my shoes."

"And you didn't know anything about Cesco?" pressed Pietro.

"What? No. Not until we came back to Verona and stumbled into the whole hornet's nest." Finished, Passerino was retying his laces.

Pietro started doing the same. "Were you with him the whole time?"

"Oh yes. We laughed for days, watching everyone scramble. A great joke." He patted Pietro on the shoulder. "Good to have you back, lad."

Passerino stumbled off, leaving Pietro wondering if he had learned anything, and which hand the Mantuan had patted him with.

♦     ◊     ♦

The revelry continued unabated into the small hours. Cesco was witty and lively, displaying no further sign of weakness. Twice he was persuaded to sing in concert with Manuel, the Master of Revels. They took turns at instruments, throwing them back and forth as challenges until each was playing three at once. An impromptu dance found men capering with men to off-set the lack of women. At the end of it all the dwarf bowed to the boy, sleeve-bells jangling. "I would sell my soul for such a voice."

"For such a price, you may have it and welcome." Cesco kissed the old fool on both cheeks. They were much of a height.

Pietro informed Morsicato of Cesco's episode, which kept the doctor hovering with hawk eyes for any sign of fatigue. The Moor, too, was never far away. Twice more he gave the boy some little brown wafer to eat, followed by a pull from the flask.

"What's he giving him?" whispered Pietro to Morsicato.

"I have no idea," grumbled the doctor. "But I don't like it."

"Whatever it is, it's helping him to get through."

"Hmph. You'd think he was the doctor, not me."

With the cessation of the cries from above, the only dampening on the evening were the dour faces of Capulletto and Montecchio. That, and the grim mood of Bailardino Nogarola. He put up a decent front, smiling when spoken to. But when not engaged his face returned to an unusually austere countenance.

Cangrande himself broke up the evening. "It is so late it will be early, by and by. We should impose no more on our host, whose happiness has caused his wife so much distress."

"No no, my lord!" cried Antony. "She's a hearty girl! Stay!"

"If I do, I'll have to be carried home in a cart! So much to cele-brate – an heir to each of us, my sister returned to me, Ser Alaghieri as well, a wonderful romp through the streets, and the best food I've tasted since I died! Truly a night to be fabled in song. You hear, Manuel! I want a song!" Manuel was under a table. "Yes, a song! And paintings! We'll have Taddeo back to repaint your walls, Antony, and this time it'll be naked girls and flowing wine, a Dionysian Bacchanal!"

"A fitting way to honour a holy man," said Cangrande's sister, quite sober.

"As fitting as honouring Christ with a cross," said the Moor. He meant it only for Cesco's ears, but Cangrande repeated it, adding, "How would it be if we only honoured every man for the way he died?"

Cesco said brightly, "Then every man would get what he deserves."

It was generally agreed to be the wittiest remark of the evening.

# IV

## Towering in Pride of Place

# TWENTY-NINE

EMERGING FROM CAPULLETTO'S tunnel, Pietro and company were waylaid by one of Cangrande's servants. "Ser Alaghieri, your presence is requested at the palace."

Yawning, Pietro blinked. "Mine alone?"

"Yours specifically."

Nodding tiredly, Pietro continued to walk along with Tharwat, Morsicato, and Cesco. Detto and Valentino trailed along behind them after saying goodnight to their mother, who said she would see them in the morning. A morning not so very far away. Bailardino had already left, asking Pietro to take all three boys back to their over-crowded house.

Once on the street, Cesco became a limp doll, muscles suddenly replaced by straw. Tharwat lifted him in his arms and the boy closed his eyes. Suddenly he was a babe in arms again.

"What do you think he wants?" asked Morsicato softly.

Pietro didn't want to speculate in front of the boys. "I'll find out soon enough."

They passed through the Piazza delle Erbe, under the monstrous bone of *la Costa*, and into the Piazza della Signoria. On the far side of it, Pietro broke away. "I'll see you. Cesco, you're not fooling me. Be sure to sleep."

From behind shut eyelids, Cesco said in a sing-song voice, "Nor riddles, nor mysterious parents, nor even the chance of flinging more mud in Mastino's face, could keep me from my bed."

Pietro glanced at Tharwat. "You have a package to retrieve from the friar." As the Moor nodded, Cesco raised a curious eyebrow over one closed lid. *Let him wonder.*

Pietro entered the palace, passing between guards bearing halberds and axes. He climbed the stairs to the first floor. So tired was he that at first the voices didn't penetrate his consciousness. When they did, he stopped in his tracks.

"Dammit, Kat! I've tolerated a lot of nonsense between you and him, but this is the limit! Two years! Two years denying your children! Denying me, your husband!"

Katerina's tone was her most infuriating, completely calm yet sharp. Pietro had heard her use it before, but never with her husband. "You accuse me of feigning the stroke?"

"You damn well didn't just recover in the last two weeks! How long have you been able to—"

"A short while," said Katerina soothingly. "It's been slow progress, and it tires me. I wanted to surprise you."

Frozen on the stair outside, Pietro was considering turning right around when a voice in his ear said, "Quite a row."

Startled, Pietro lost his footing on the stair. Cangrande caught his arm. "I'll have to create a new order of knight just for you. The Keeper of the Keyhole."

Flushing, Pietro removed his arm from Cangrande's grip. "You asked me here."

"I did no such thing." Cangrande glanced at the door. "It must have been some other in my name. My apologies. And in fairness, they can be heard in the Antipodes. Well, come along. She's summoned us. I'm dying to know what she wants, aren't you?"

The Scaliger happened to be standing beside a likeness of himself painted on the wall by Maestro Giotto. The look of fierce joy on the frescoed Cangrande's face as he rode to battle was a stark contrast to the grim expression he wore as he turned to wage an entirely different kind of war.

Cangrande pushed wide the double doors. Following, Pietro saw a red-faced Bailardino opposite his wife, who was bolstered by a cane. "Ah," said Katerina, "the rest of the hanging party. If Ser Alaghieri will be so good as to close the door, you may both join my husband in venting your spleen."

"I have none to vent," said her brother, languidly seating himself on a box-bench. "But I will gladly watch."

Throwing up his hands, Bailardino fell into a chair. "I'm sick with it! All of it. Kat, Francesco – I'm tired. Of you both. I love you, but – Kat, the children! Is it worth depriving them of a mother just to win this endless—"

"I know, dear." Katerina crossed to scratch the nape of his neck with the fingers of her good hand. "I admit, it looks like I've been playing you for a fool."

Bail shrugged her off. "Because you have."

Pietro had always liked Bailardino, sometimes envying him, sometimes admiring him. Never before had Pietro pitied him.

"Not intentionally," protested Katerina. "You know how I hate solicitude. I wanted to be fully well before I returned to the public sphere."

Cangrande pointedly studied her cane. "I take it you were thwarted. Or was the opportunity of stealing my thunder too much?"

"Not at all. As pleasing as it might have been, I have never been one for creating a scene. That was always your way. Or has resurrection changed your nature?"

Bailardino waved an angry hand. "There you go again!"

Cangrande clucked his tongue. "Yes, Kat, please. You're upsetting Ser Alaghieri. For God's sake, boy, sit down. This isn't formal court. This is family."

Pietro remained on his feet. "I'm fine."

"Well I'm not," said Bailardino. "Thank God for you, Pietro. You took the boy away – dammit! Tomorrow I'm sending both my boys back to Ravenna with you."

"No you're not." The smoothness vanished from Katerina's tone. "Cesco will need all his friends around him."

"Besides, Pietro's not going back to Ravenna." Cangrande was sympathetic. "There's nothing for him there, anyway."

"Bail darling, I truly did want to surprise you first. But my plans were upset by a new element. While I sat in my room, listening to the reports of my brother's miraculous resurrection, I had a visitor."

Cangrande did not speak, yet from across the room Pietro could feel him tense.

Bailardino frowned. "A visitor? You won't let anyone —"

"She is unique," said Katerina. "I had to hear her out."

"She? She who?"

Katerina's eyes may have been on her husband, but her answer was for her brother. "Francesco's mother."

"His mother?" asked Bail in confusion. First he looked at Cangrande. Then realization hit. "You mean little Cesco? His mother is alive? She's here?"

Cangrande shook his head. "Don't look at me, Bail. I didn't send for her."

"No," said Pietro. "Donna Katerina did."

"She would have come regardless." Taking a seat beside her husband, Katerina laid her cane across her lap. "Thinking you dead,

Francesco, she wanted to be certain her son received his due. That was the bargain, after all. She was concerned there would be trouble with the will. As you must admit, there was. Her intent was to testify in court as to who Cesco's father was. But by the time she arrived, you were alive again and Cesco nowhere in sight. She was naturally worried, but didn't wish to create a scene. So she came to me."

"Ironic, that." The Scaliger sent a meaningful glance at Pietro, who knew Katerina had arranged an attack on baby Cesco while he was still in his mother's arms. "And where is the good lady now?"

"Here, in the palace. I took the liberty of setting her up in the guest-suite disguised as one of my servants." Sensing her husband was somewhat mollified, Katerina gestured to Pietro. "Ser Alaghieri can tell you if it's her. He has met her before."

Under Bailardino's stare, Pietro had to nod. "We weren't introduced, but I've seen her." It was true. He'd met Cesco's mother on a stormy night long ago. His recollection of her was as a beauty, but he might have romanticized her in his memory. *Lord knows I've been guilty of that before.*

Feeling his gaze, Katerina smiled at him – a lop-sided expression, proving that she was indeed not fully recovered from the stroke. "It is important, I think, to have a witness who knows the principals involved. Also, you have been Cesco's primary guardian and know him best. She wants to meet him."

"What's wrong with that?" asked Bailardino. "It's natural for a mother."

"In a natural mother, you mean," remarked Cangrande dryly. "The lady in question, like your own wife, is anything but."

Katerina ignored them both, focusing on Pietro. "I want to know if Ser Alaghieri thinks it wise."

Pietro's first instinct was an unconditional 'no.' After all the plots and schemes of this family, who knew what machinations were behind this? Yet he made himself withhold judgment. "I'll need to see her first."

Katerina placed her cane on the floor, meaning to rise. "I'll send for her."

"No. I'll go myself." Before she could argue, Cangrande had vanished through the double doors.

Bailardino was baffled. "Why not send a servant?"

"Because this is a family affair." Katerina sat with her eyes closed, reminding Pietro of Cesco an hour before. Clearly she was not as well as she let show, nor had she been as ill as she'd let on two weeks before. *A family of onions, layers and layers. And all so similar.*

A memory came bubbling up, something a very young Cesco had said. Returned from University and introduced to the toddler, Pietro's limp was evident. Noting it, Cesco had said, "You're hurt. Don't show it. No one will help."

They waited for ten minutes in silence. There was nothing to say. Katerina reached out her good hand to rest upon her husband's. Bailardino looked at it, but did not remove it. Pietro felt like pacing, but his leg was throbbing. He sat by the open windows, smelling the freshness of the night air. An electricity in the wind foretold rain.

Hearing footsteps in the corridor, they all watched the door keenly as Cangrande ushered a woman into the room.

She was shorter than Pietro remembered, and the pearls were gone from her dark hair, now daubed with silver. But pale her face was the soft-skinned oval he remembered. Her eyes were entirely unlike her son's in shape, yet they retained his liveliness.

Her expression now was guarded as Cangrande closed the doors firmly behind them. "Donna Maria, allow me to name my brother-in-law, Lord Bailardino Nogarola, Podestà of Vicenza. His wife, my sister, needs no introduction. And perhaps you will remember Ser Pietro Alaghieri, Knight of the Mastiff, son of the poet Dante and until recently Cesco's guardian."

Pietro felt a mixture of warmth and envy coming from her. "I remember him." Her words carried a lilt that Pietro had forgotten, an accent he had heard nowhere before or since.

Pietro and Bailardino both bowed to her, and Bailardino baldly asked, "Donna Maria what?"

Pietro could have kissed him. There were times Bailardino's lack of social grace was an asset.

"Donna Maria will do for the moment," answered the Scaliger. "Now my lady, you have questions for us all. I imagine Ser Alaghieri will bear the brunt of your inquiry, but first you must be wondering about our blunders of the past few weeks."

"Yes. How did things take such a turn?"

"I admit, mistakes were made. A rumour of my death set in motion the wheels we'd hoped we'd never need. You know the old plan – when the boy turned fifteen he would have been brought forth and declared my heir. Events forced our hands, but the end result is the same."

"But another heir tried to take your city," protested Donna Maria.

Cangrande guided her to a seat not far from his sister. "Having seen what occurred, we can take steps to ensure it never happens again."

Katerina smoothed the folds of her skirts. "As I said before, my dear, consider the past two weeks a practice run in the tiltyards."

"Just so," concurred Cangrande. "All the plans were executed neatly. In the end, your son would have taken power. Fortuitously, it was not required of him just yet. But tonight I tasted his mettle and there is no doubt in my mind he will make a fine ruler for our fair city."

Donna Maria's silence lasted an uncomfortable interval. Neither Cangrande nor Katerina made any attempt to further allay her fears. Pietro himself had no idea what to say. He couldn't bring himself to tell her how close the boy had come to death. What he wanted to do was lay all Cangrande's crimes at her feet. But he couldn't be sure that, spoken, they would alter anything. So he kept his mouth closed.

Bailardino finally broke the tension. "That's all fine and good. But I imagine that, now she's come, she'll want to see him."

"I should like that," said Donna Maria cautiously.

"And we should like nothing more than to fulfill your desire," replied Cangrande. "But I confess, I think it might be unwise. Katerina?"

Katerina frowned kindly, her brow furrowed. "I am conflicted. As a mother, I cannot imagine not knowing my child. The temptation to meet would be too strong for words. Yet I don't know what it would do to the boy."

Bailardino was incredulous. "You think he doesn't want to meet his mother?"

"I'm sure he does. But I'm not certain that, meeting her, he would behave himself."

Cangrande folded his arms and leaned against a pillar. "Explain."

"He knows now the history of his first few years – that his mother gave him into our care, and that we, after failing spectacularly to protect him, passed him off to Ser Alaghieri and pretended he was dead. What he may wonder is why his mother did not join him there." Katerina's eyes were soft, considering. "Of course Cangrande couldn't visit, or else word might have reached the very people who wanted the boy dead. But Donna Maria – no one was watching you. He might be tempted to blame you for any feeling of abandonment he harbours."

Donna Maria looked furious. "I was told not to go to him. By you."

Katerina didn't bother with excuses. "Will that matter? All he will know is that his mother abandoned him to the care of strangers."

The lilt of Donna Maria's accent belied the steel in her tone. "I desire a meeting with my son."

"And you shall have it," said Cangrande suddenly. "It would be inhuman of us to deny you. Yet misgivings still gnaw at me. I'm not sure my sister is correct, but it sounds plausible. My own mother had nothing to do with me as a boy. I was raised by my sister, and I admit that somewhere in my soul there is an irritating grain of resentment." He smiled winningly at Katerina, who ignored him. "On the other hand, even if he bears you no ill will, there are questions he will inevitably ask. Awkward questions about your self, your line, and your husband. Questions none of us want answered. It would undo the arrangement we made so many years ago."

Donna Maria sat with the expression of a basilisk, her gaze divided between brother and sister. It was almost a look of hatred. Bailardino wore the same puzzled expression Pietro could feel on his own face. Both heard the thinly veiled threat beneath the fair words, but neither had an inkling as to the nature of that threat.

"Perhaps, brother, we may compromise. They may meet, but under some pretense."

"Pretense?" asked Cesco's mother.

"For your sake and his, we will not let on your true identity. You've arrived here as one of my ladies. Tomorrow you will be introduced to him as such. Ser Alaghieri will bring the boy to visit me in my suite here in the palace. I shall contrive to be away for some little time. He shall meet you instead."

Donna Maria considered. "We'll be alone, will we?"

"I think Ser Alaghieri might remain, or perhaps another of the boy's guardian angels. But neither my brother nor I will be there. Is that satisfactory?"

"It will have to be, won't it?"

"Done and done." Cangrande yawned and stretched. "It's late, and after all the excitement I'm done in. Pietro, stay as long as you wish. I'm sure Donna Maria would like to hear tales of her son." On the verge of exiting, he called over his shoulder, "Oh, Pietro? Please don't pester Donna Maria. She's already had a more wearing few weeks than either of us." With that, he was gone.

Noting Pietro's expression, Katerina smiled. "I'm afraid his enigmatic nature sometimes makes him difficult to obey. He means you are not to question our guest. They have an arrangement, with various mutual conditions. Bail? I am ready for bed. Pietro, you'll see Donna Maria back to our suite here in the palace?"

"I will, Donna."

"Then goodnight. Or shall I say good morning?" She allowed her husband to guide her out and close the doors behind them.

Pietro saw that Donna Maria was trembling. There was a moistness in her eyes. He averted his gaze, examining the sky outside until the lady had composed herself. At last she said, "You've been raising my son."

Pietro rose and crossed to her. "Ask me what you want to know."

She looked up into his face imploringly. "Anything. Anything at all."

Pietro discovered that his natural reticence regarding Cesco's secrets did not apply to this woman. He sat close to her and related everything he could think of. Early adventures, the loneliness, the keen appreciation of music and mechanics. Some tales were funny, like Cesco's first curse word. Others were poignant, like the first time Cesco had questioned the nature of God. He told her of Cesco's vulnerable side, his frailties, his strengths, his dreams, and his passions. A catalogue of the funny, the mundane, and the heart-breaking. A parent's stories.

At one point he described Cesco's tendency to shiver uncontrollably whenever he thought about his own failings, his blunders. "Cesco never does it anymore, but I'm certain he still has those moments in private. He relives each failure."

"His father was the same, once," said Maria.

"Really?" Somehow that did not fit his image of Cangrande. "It worried us when he was young, and doctor Morsicato kept alert for signs of disease or nerve damage. My father guessed the cause of Cesco's shaking was emotional. He used to call Cesco a lute with the strings wound too tight." Thinking of his father, Pietro paused.

"What is it?" she asked.

*If there is anyone who should know, it's this lady. A mother should be able to take pride in her son.* "There's one thing, a story no one's heard. I don't have any proof, but – you know who my father was?"

"Of course. I've read his Commedia."

"The whole of it?"

She took that as an insult. "Yes."

Pietro gave her a wan smile. "Then you've also read your son's work."

When he finished explaining, Donna Maria gazed at him skeptically. "When was this?"

"My father died four years ago."

"Cesco was seven."

Pietro opened his hands. "I know, the thing's impossible. Only it's not. My father was grooming him. In Cesco, I think he finally had the son he'd always needed."

Maria placed a hand on Pietro's knee. "Surely not."

"No, I only mean that everyone seems hell-bent on having Cesco as an heir. Father wanted the boy to take up poetry. Cesco listened politely and, as always, went his own way. It made my father furious. He'd kick Cesco out of his study. A week or two would pass, then they'd be in there, starting over again."

"That must have been hard for you."

"I have none of my father's skill with words. I tried keeping a journal once. It just didn't take. Besides, when the two of them were closeted together, I never had to worry about what the little monster was up to."

Maria raised an eyebrow. "Monster?"

"Forgive me, that's extreme. It's just that he's so capable! You should have heard him sing tonight. He can tear your soul from out your breast one minute, make you cry with laughter the next."

Maria's expression held any number of conflicting emotions. "He sounds remarkable. Like his father."

His hand in hers, Pietro felt the wedding ring on her finger. He saw it was a mixture of gold and silver, with a curious knot repeated over and over across the tiny band. It was ludicrous not to ask. It even seemed that she was waiting for him to do so. "Lady—"

"Yes, Ser Alaghieri?"

"I don't mean to pry, or to interfere, but I've always… I mean, I – I disagree with Donna Katerina. I think Cesco should know who his mother is. There are too many secrets."

"I understand. But this is one more that *must* be kept from him. For his sake, the sake of his future."

"Lady – the arrangement you have with Cangrande… does it affect Cesco's well-being?"

"It does."

Pietro paused to compose his words. "The Scaliger hinted at a threat. Is that why he went to get you himself, to threaten you?"

It was Donna Maria's turn to weigh her words. "To remind me of our agreement."

Pietro had to tell her. He couldn't not. "Lady, that agreement was based upon a falsehood. The Scaliger's sister was the one who sent the murderer to your house all those years ago, to make you fear for Cesco's life."

Maria's breath grew still. "You know this?"

"I was told by the lady herself. It was part of how they convinced me to take him into my care. If I'd known how to reach you then, I would have."

Expecting rage, Pietro was astonished when she nodded. "I suspected as much. It didn't make the threat less real. I suppose it's occurred to you that she was lying?"

"She wasn't. But lady, if you knew…?"

"Ser Alaghieri – Pietro – I was not coerced into giving up my son. It was a choice I made to ensure he gained his birthright. It remains the most painful decision of my life. I have missed him more than I can say. No matter the circumstance, I will be happy even to see him tomorrow, and to know him a little through your stories."

"I can't imagine a reason to deny him the pleasure knowing he has a mother who loves him."

"There is a reason for everything." The way she said it, the matter was closed. "He's had a better life than I could ever have hoped for him. For that, I thank you." She kissed his cheek.

Though Pietro had a thousand more questions, there was clearly nothing left to say. He rose and escorted her from the loggia.

The moment Ser Alaghieri escorted the woman out of the room, Mastino stirred from his place of concealment at the far end of the loggia. Massaging life back into his limbs, he reflected that the pain was a price gladly paid for what he now owned – a lever to topple the beloved Cesco from favour.

An hour before, red faced and raw from scrubbing the mud off his body, he'd been pacing the loggia end to end. Imagine! Two weeks ago he'd been the hero, cheered by the whole city. And tonight he had been literally dragged through the mud! By children, no less! The ignominy had only added to his already towering hatred for the Capitano's anointed heir.

His pacing ended when he heard an animated exchange on the stair between his aunt and uncle. Thinking quickly, he'd concealed himself in a nook behind a tapestry, an old hiding place he hadn't used since he was younger than Cesco. It was cramped, too small for an adult. Yet he'd forced himself to be still and listen.

Emerging now, he considered what he had learned. Then he went to wake Fuchs.

◆　　◊　　◆

Arriving back at the Nogarola house, Pietro found a stony-faced Tharwat waiting for him. "The drunkard is gone."

Pietro was too tired to be angry. "Escaped, or released?"

"The latter. Lorenzo decided that the man's work was done."

"That wasn't his decision to make."

"He wasn't able to identify his employer in any case. Should I pursue him?"

There were far too many threads unraveling in Pietro's mind to keep track of them all. "No. He's a coward, he won't try again. He'll just vanish." He paused. "I'm sorry. You were right. We should have just killed him."

"No, your decision was sound. It is worth his continued existence to be certain the Scaliger was not behind the poisoning."

"Terrific. Now we only have to rule out the rest of the world." Releasing a magnificent yawn, Pietro shook his head. "I'm going to bed. Have someone rouse me an hour after dawn. We have a big day ahead of us. Cesco has a meeting with his real mother in the morning."

Tharwat might have desired an explanation, but Pietro was too exhausted to give it. Instead, he climbed the stairs and fell fully-dressed into bed and closed his eyes.

But try as he might, he couldn't staunch the flow of worries assaulting him.

# THIRTY

AFTER A PITIFUL handful of hours lying awake in darkness, Pietro stared listlessly out the window as the sky broke and rain began to fall. Not a sweet summer shower. A deluge. Pietro resisted the urge to see portents in the weather.

The door opened and Cesco stuck his head in, looking maddeningly fresh-faced and bushy-tailed. "I hear we're invited to the palace. What does the Capitano want today, to take me bear-baiting?"

"The invitation's not from Cangrande," said Pietro, rolling out of bed and pulling on his tunic. "It's from Donna Nogarola."

"*La Donna*? Then why risk a drenching? This is her house, isn't it? Let her come to us."

He wasn't fooling anyone. Cesco was eager to get into the palace for the first time. "How are you feeling?"

"Ask me that again and I'll vomit. Otherwise, fine."

"Then make yourself presentable. And try combing your hair." They both dressed formally, covering their finery under heavy cloaks. At the main door they were met by Tharwat and Morsicato.

"The boy shouldn't be running around in this weather," said the doctor.

"I'll dash between drops. Are you coming, doctor? No? Pity. I always wanted to see how much water that beard could hold. What about you, Nuncle?" The boy paused. "You know, I've been meaning to ask you. Should I still call you Nuncle? Or would you prefer Ser Alaghieri?"

Antonia appeared at the top of the stairs. "If you start addressing him formally, you'll have to do the same for me, and I simply refuse to hear you call me Donna."

"But soon I'll be calling you Suora," replied Cesco brightly. "What if you become an abbess? Could I then call him uncle for real, as the brother to the Mother Superior?"

Pietro's head hurt enough already. "Uncle is fine. Antonia, where are you going?"

"With you," she said significantly. Al-Dhaamin must have told her of the meeting with Cesco's mother, just as he had obviously decided to leave the doctor in the dark. Pietro understood why. Cesco found it too easy to read the antics of that forked beard.

Pietro could wish Antonia well away from the palace and Cangrande. But she wouldn't willingly miss a chance to lay eyes on Cesco's mother. "Very well. Come along."

Hurrying through the rain, the four of them passed the graves beside Santa Maria Antica and entered the rear palace gate. Across the busy yard and the old familiar stables, they achieved the inner stair, shaking their cloaks free as they climbed.

At the top they were met by Tullio d'Isola. "I am afraid Donna Katerina is engaged with her own children at the moment, but she has asked her lady to entertain you until her return." The Grand Butler showed them into the front room of the guest suite and left.

Donna Maria was waiting beside the window, watching the rain. *So far, so good.* Cesco didn't know the Katerina's retinue, so he wouldn't suspect a switch.

Seeing them enter, the short woman didn't look twice at Tharwat or Antonia. She stood and curtsied to Pietro, then invited Cesco to sit with her. "Donna Katerina has asked that I pass the time of her absence with you."

Cesco rudely dropped his sodden cloak to the rushes. "Take my measure, you mean. My entire existence consists of one person or another trying to sound my depths. I shall save you the trouble. I am a pond so shallow even Narcissus would pass me by."

The lady was visibly startled. Pietro intervened. "Perhaps you can disguise your lack of personality – and decorum – by playing for us."

With a deliberate sigh, Cesco took up an idle lyre, wasted a few seconds tuning it, then launched into a section of a popular French ballad about the life of Charlemagne, regarding the redemption of Elegast the Thief.

The story was famous, if absurd. Young Charlemagne was commanded by an angel to go out at night and try his hand at thieving. With the aid of the disgraced noble turned thief, the disguised

Charlemagne roams the rooftops of his city learning how to steal in secret. Elegast, alone, discovers a traitorous Earl attempting to gain the help of Charlemagne's wife in an assassination plot. Elegast runs to his companion for help, unaware that this is the lady's husband. Charlemagne returns in time to hear his wife's refusal.

Cesco's voice was high and clear as he sang the tale's climax:

> *The Earl angered at the thwarting of his deed.*
> *He hit the countess a nosebleed.*
> *Outside stood Charles, Prince Royal, listening to it all.*
> *'Soon this will end and he will fall!'*
>
> *Charles prince royal jumped in to make a stand*
> *With drawn sword ready in his hand.*
> *'Now you won't ever again, sir,*
> *Hit the king's daughter!*
>
> *'Nor will you be troubled any more*
> *By Royal Princes at your door.'*
> *And as his golden locks turned red,*
> *The Earl lost his head over the side of the bed.*

The song ended with Elegast, for his loyalty, being reinstated as a knight and Charlemagne on his knees thanking the angel that sent him out thieving in the night. Cesco let the last note linger, then placed a hand over the strings and set the lyre aside. "What next, Nuncle? Shall I dance? You could play while I caper."

"You could show some manners." Pietro wanted Cesco at his best, but the boy wasn't cooperating. A violent drinking song and boorish behavior wasn't how Pietro wanted Maria to remember her son.

But the lady seemed to have grown accustomed. "I think he resists being ordered or controlled. Isn't that so, young one?"

Cesco sighed. "So instead of putting me up for display like him, you'd rather talk down to me as if I were a mewling brat on someone's knee. Honestly!" He threw up his hands in despair.

"How would you like to be treated, then?"

Predictably, the boy feigned shock. "You mean I can choose?"

"If you wish to be treated as an equal, then you'd best be doing the same for me. I'm not one for games."

At first Cesco looked angry, then chagrined. Finally a genuine smile played at the corners of his mouth. "An equal, then. If you'll forgive me, lady," he said, intrigued, "I can't place your accent. I'm sure I've never heard anything like it, but somehow it sounds familiar."

"I come from an island far from here, *mo chridh*," said the lady. "Home to a great and pious people. What's this?" Her fingers touched on the silver disc hanging under his Adam's apple.

"An old coin," said Cesco. "I've always had it. Ser Alaghieri says it belonged to my first dog. What was it you just called me?"

The woman ignored the question, studying the image on the coin instead. "Who is this?"

"Mercury. God of messengers, poets, and dying."

"A planet as well."

"Yes," said Cesco. "Smallest of the seven planets, where dwell *i buoni spiriti, che son stati attivi perche onore e fama li succeda*. Yet it is the reason the rays of true love flow less easily to Heaven. A troubled sphere, to be sure."

"But a noble one."

"I suppose," shrugged Cesco.

"You must have been born under it, to have such a strong attraction." Her tone was probing.

"Grandfather Dante was. He thought it was the source of his genius. As for myself?" He shrugged and jerked a thumb at al-Dhaamin. "No one has ever seen fit to tell me my birthdate."

"Friday the Thirteenth," said Pietro, referencing the unlucky day two decades before when all the Knights Templar were arrested by the French king's puppet pope.

"You see?" smiled Cesco. "They think it's dangerous knowledge."

"All knowledge is dangerous," answered Donna Maria. "It leads to more questions."

"Ha-hah! Too true. Lord knows they hate questions. Though the Arūs still owes me one."

Not understanding the reference, the lady continued in the former vein. "Mercurio. He suits you, my boy."

"True, I am light on my feet, even without the wings. But sadly all accounts have him tall, and I fear I shall never grow to great heights."

"The little Mercury, then. Mercutio."

Cesco cocked his head to one side, a slow smile spreading. "I like it. But I have too many names already, I'm afraid. Another one will just confuse the matter. You still haven't told me yours."

"Nor have you told me yours. I am a *siabrae*, you are an *uirisg*. They never share their names."

Cesco stared, then laughed. Turning to the Moor he said in Arabic, "It's not often I'm shown up in another tongue." Seeing the lady's blank gaze, Cesco returned to Italian. "Now we're even, having both proved our talent with words. Shall we—"

But what Cesco was about to propose was never discovered. At that moment, Katerina entered, Detto and Valentino by her side. They waved to him, and Cesco stood to bow to Maria. "Alas, I am called to perform once more. Lady, it has been a pleasure. We will continue our discourse another time, I'm sure."

The interview was over. *Too short by far*, thought Pietro resentfully. Donna Maria, however, rose with a smile and a curtsey that somehow had a regal air to it. For all Katerina's power upon entering a room, this woman matched it. A gentler presence, but no less impressive. "Fare well, *mo chridh*."

As Cesco was dragged into the inner room, he cast a final look back at the lady. She inclined her head to him, and he to her. Then he was gone to laugh and play with his friends.

Pietro crossed to take Maria's arm. "You didn't even tell him your name."

"Maria is only one of my names. Just as Francesco is only one of his. He knows the name of my soul." Her face brightened. "Thank you. Despite the restlessness he is – remarkably whole."

Pietro had nothing to say to that. Instead he made introductions. "Lady, this is my sister, the novice Beatrice."

"A pleasure," said Maria with another regal nod. Antonia was uncharacteristically quiet as she curtsied.

"And this is Tharwat al-Dhaamin, my friend and your son's protector."

Tharwat bowed in the Italian fashion. "It is an honour, lady."

"He called you the Arūs," said Maria.

"An ironic name, meaning bridegroom. He uses it to taunt, because he does not know why I bear it."

"I see. Am I to understand you are an astrologer?"

"I have some skill, my lady."

"You have made a chart for my son?"

"Several. There is conflicting information regarding the night of his birth."

"Conflicting?"

"There are reports of two separate shooting stars that night, crossing in the sky. Perhaps you can assist me…?"

Donna Maria's smile was apologetic. "I'm sorry, I cannot help you. I was somewhat occupied at the time."

A deferential knocking at the door produced Tullio d'Isola. "Madonna, your carriage is prepared, your effects on board."

Pietro said, "She'll be along in a moment." Tullio nodded and shut the door as respectfully as he'd come. "So soon?"

"I must go." Yet she sent a longing look to where Cesco had disappeared.

"Lady – if I ever need to find you…"

"You cannot. Today was a gift not to be repeated. It is the old arrangement. If my son is to be the Capitano's heir, I must relinquish all rights to him. He must never set eyes on me again."

"But the time may come – I mean, if there ever were need to reach you… I don't even know your family name, where to look for you."

"That is as it should be." Approaching him, Donna Maria kissed Pietro's cheek, then departed. The Moor excused himself as well, leaving Pietro and Antonia alone.

"A remarkable woman," said Antonia. "I can see why Cangrande was attracted to her."

Unbidden, an image of Cesco's two parents lovemaking flashed before Pietro's inner eye. It seemed incongruous, even indecent. Yes, Cangrande had treated her with deference, but without a hint of intimacy. For the first time, Pietro wondered how the liaison had come about. *One more question I'll never have an answer to.*

◆    ◊    ◆

Inside Katerina's chamber, Cesco was seated at her knee. The lady had dismissed her other attendants, then sent Detto and Valentino on an errand. The two sat near a smoking brazier in silence, listening to the rain, eyes on each other.

Cesco eyed her warily. "I remember you."

"Yes," said Katerina. "*La Donna*, Detto's mother."

"Before that."

"Oh?"

"Yes. When you visited us in Ravenna, before your illness, I was always uneasy. Now I know why. I was raised by you, in that palace in Vicenza."

"Did Ser Alaghieri tell you that?"

"I had already begun remembering. I don't think I liked you very much."

Katerina nodded, unconcerned. "That is probably true. But you can't take your eyes off me now. Is that hatred as well?"

"No," admitted Cesco. He felt naked before her gaze, and his words were equally bald. "I badly want to impress you. It's why I worked so hard to charm your maid just now. Your opinion matters to me on a level so deep I hardly recognize it. I don't like it."

"Then why worry about it?"

"Because…" He trailed off, not having an answer. She discomfited him in a way even the Scaliger did not. "You asked to see me, not the other way around. Do you want something?"

"Only to see you, have this conversation. You realize that my brother faked his death to gull you out of hiding."

"I guessed as much. Though since I wasn't aware I needed to hide, I don't feel any loss. But I've wondered why."

"To win a war with me. I had you in your earliest years. We fought, and since neither could win, we handed you to a neutral party. The arrangement was that when you turned fifteen, you would come here and be made his heir. Only he has accelerated that timeframe, thus inflicting a defeat upon me."

"So you came here to show him you are not defeated."

"Yes."

"Has it occurred to you that perhaps you deserve defeat?"

"Yes. But I am willing to wager my life against his that my brother has never thought he deserved defeat."

"You argue that self-doubt is a virtue. It makes sense, as I feel tremendous self-doubt just being in your presence. You must have instilled it in me very young."

"You hide it well," said Katerina. "Just like my brother hides his."

"You just told me that he doesn't own any."

"No, I said he believes he deserves to win, no matter what. He is plagued by doubts, even moreso than I. He simply has no scruples."

"Are you trying to turn me against him?"

"I wouldn't presume. You are to be with him from now on. I only wished to impart this piece of wisdom to you – there are more sides to this die than just his. When you are ready to be rid of him, come to me. I will be waiting."

"Then I can only hope you have the patience of Penelope. I'm still trying to figure out the rules, but I'm fairly determined to win by fair means, not foul. Coming to you would be cheating."

"You are young," said Katerina with an infuriating condescension.

Cesco felt an old panic roiling his gut. Hating himself, he tried to form a cutting exit line, but his wit was as empty as a pricked bladder. Lacking his usual *mot juste*, he rose into a neat little bow and tried not to run for the door.

# THIRTY-ONE

WHILE CESCO was ensconced with Katerina, Pietro received a summons to attend the Scaliger in the Domus Nuova. Expecting something of the sort, Pietro took his leave of Antonia and pulled his cloak up over his head, following Tullio across the wet stones of the Piazza della Signoria. Knocking, they were admitted at once.

Cangrande was seated in state upon the dais, papers spread on a table beside him. With him were two men. The first, predictably, was the Mantuan lord Passerino Bonaccolsi, the Scaliger's fast friend. It was the second man whose presence was surprising: Federigo della Scala, removed from his cell.

Federigo was not in good humour. "Cousin, you owe me more than—"

Cangrande cut across him sharply. "You should have fled, cousin. Your staying has placed me in an impossible position. By law, I should have you executed. But until now you have always been a loyal and able defender of Verona."

"I still am!" protested Federigo, thumping his chest angrily.

"You maneuvered children into my place without checking the facts of my supposed death. But your grab for power would not have been so transparent had you not tried to take control of my armies. Fortunately for us all, you bungled that so efficiently that I didn't even have to put up a fight to get them back. For Heaven's sake, they were willing to follow an eleven year-old rather than stay with you. Doesn't that tell you how badly you managed affairs?"

"I was following the instructions you left behind!" cried Federigo, suddenly commanding Pietro's full attention. "You said to stop the army's pay while a new system was laid out—"

"That was when all was well! In a crisis, the last thing you do is stop a soldier's pay! There's nothing that better ensures their quick defection!"

"But you were explicit, you said that nothing should stop me from—"

"I didn't foresee my premature demise!"

Federigo threw up his hands. "So you're just going to kill me?"

"No. You're going into voluntary exile. Passerino has generously volunteered to escort you to Mantua. Where you go from there is of no concern to me. I'll make sure you have a pension to live on – secretly, of course."

Federigo began to plead. "Cousin—"

"Do not mistake mercy for softness. I am repaying you a debt I owe you. If you return to Verona, I will have no choice but to have you killed. Passerino, he's all yours. There's an escort waiting outside. His belongings are waiting there, as are his sons. Go." Pretending to just notice Pietro, Cangrande smiled broadly. "Ah! Ser Alaghieri! Welcome, welcome. Tullio, you may leave us. And stop fretting! You did well, considering the circumstances. When I'm in the mood to read, I shall just have to hop over to the monastery, that's all. Or do you think I could borrow one of my books back from time to time?"

"I am sure the brothers would return the collection," said the Grand Butler, making way for Passerino and the sullen Federigo. "You have only to ask."

"And how much of a churl would that make me? No, resurrection should require sacrifice. And as you say, you saved them from the fire. For that you have posterity's undying thanks, and mine. You may go."

Despite the rough tone, Tullio was smiling as he bowed. Collecting Pietro's sodden cloak, he exited with a surprising spring in his step. Cangrande waved the guards to follow. Alone with Pietro in the high chamber, the Scaliger shook his head. "They gave away my books. Years of hunting up old manuscripts, collecting, though with little time to read them. But it seems young Mastino has no appreciation for the less physical delights of this world. So in one fell swoop they were donated to the Church, no friend of mine. Or yours!"

Pietro had no immediate reply. He was staring at the papers Cangrande had been sorting through – the contents of his strong-box, the one that had vanished in the fire in Ravenna. The box itself was visible behind the dais, its metal scored with burn marks. Woodenly, Pietro said, "That is a shame, lord."

"Still, they're in good hands. But to see them I will probably have to remove the odium of excommunication from my name. I'm thinking of erecting a church in honour of my miraculous recovery from death. *Santa Maria della Scala* – it has a ring, don't you think? It will certainly be finished before Anastasia is ever done. Thirty-five years and still no roof. Sad."

"Is that why you wanted to see me? To solicit a donation?"

"Not unless you've been shirking your law studies to delve into architecture. Otherwise I have better use for you elsewhere." Cangrande ruffled the papers on the low table. "I'm afraid your prognostications have come true, my noble knight. You're leaving Verona tomorrow. Wednesday at the latest."

"Am I?"

"Take off your hat, *cavaliere*," said the Scaliger, a little sternly. "You're having a private audience with the Capitano of Verona. A little respect is due. That's better. So, you're leaving. Why, you ask? Because, I reply, I need you to do me a favour."

"Why would I?"

Cangrande stared pointedly.

"Lord," Pietro added.

"There was a time I had to beg you not to call me lord. Ah, how the wheel does turn." Cangrande sprawled sideways in his backless chair. "Why do me a favour? The oldest reason in the world. I plan to bribe you."

"Nothing you can offer will tempt me, my lord."

"Now now, don't be hasty. Tell me truly, how are your studies coming? You're, what, a year away from your examinations? Will they let you finish after your recent abrupt departure?"

"They will." Pietro was not as sure as he sounded.

"What a relief! I'd hate to think you'd burned any bridges behind you. Like your house burned. Thankfully, these documents survived." The Scaliger tapped the papers with two fingers. "It's such an interesting choice, the law. Whatever made you choose it?"

"I couldn't say, lord."

Cangrande laughed. "I think I could! But that's neither here nor there. You'll make an excellent lawyer. You have the right combination of brains and moral outrage. But I sense a lack in your life. Since your dear father is no longer with us, you need your patron more than ever. What if I told you that I could accelerate your rise?"

"I'd say I can find my own way, lord Capitano."

"I thought that might be your answer. But it really is unavoidable. The papers have already been signed and witnessed. You are to be my special envoy, an acting judge for the Trevisian Mark. Quite a plum assignment. Isn't that nice?"

Pietro's pulse began to race. "Special envoy?"

"Yes. A minor thing, really. You can pop off and take care of it on your way back to Bologna. With my title behind you, I daresay they'll expedite your degree."

"Or hold it up forever." Verona was allied with Bologna's enemies.

Cangrande shook his head. "Even Guelphs are not so short-sighted. The University may need my help one day. Or at least my money. Why worry? You're the son of the greatest poet since Virgil, so of course they want to say you got your degree from them. I predict that within a year you'll be teaching their classes on telling right from wrong. It's so very clear for you," added the Scaliger with unmistakable irony.

"I wasn't planning on leaving Verona yet."

"Oh, you can stay if you want. But it will get about that you refused this commission – one that's been voted on by the Council. It doesn't just bear my signature. Bail, Nico, Petruchio, Antony, Mariotto – even Castelbarco signed it. Thought it a fitting reward for your hard work all these years. Won't it look churlish if you refuse? Worse than demanding my books back."

Pietro flushed. "I'm not done here yet."

"Of course not! Just as in your past exiles, extended though they were, you will return. It's only that you've had him all to yourself for so long, I thought you might be willing to share him with me for a few months. You can come and visit at Christmas." Cangrande sipped from a goblet. "You haven't asked me what the chore is."

"I don't want to know."

"Afraid of the Sirens' song, eh? Stout fellow. Too much temptation is bad for the soul. Still, it's quite plum!"

Pietro stood there hating himself for wanting to know what Cangrande needed a special judge for, forcing himself to keep his lips pressed tight lest the question pop out.

Clearly able to read Pietro's thoughts, Cangrande's smile was prodigious, a cat with a mouthful of canary. "I need a reliable man of discretion for a mission of diplomatic delicacy. Summarize the state of Padua for me, please."

Pietro could see no harm in this. "Technically the city is under the protection of the Emperor through his agent, Heinrich of Corinthia."

"Ironic, since I'm the local Ghibelline."

"A fact not lost on Heinrich. The Paduans went running to him for troops, letting the Emperor in just to keep you out."

"Rather like turning whore to avoid being raped," mused Cangrande. "The end result is the same. Pray continue."

"So now there's a titular Imperial Vicar and their usual foreign podestà – odd that Paduans refuse to be ruled by other Paduans. But the Germans don't care what happens to the people as long as the taxes flow into Heinrich's coffers. And the podestà is another straw man. Napoleone Beccadello. I met him in Bologna a few years ago, and he's just a puppet for the real power in the city – the Carrara family."

"Ah, the dear dear Carrarese, beloved of us both."

"They're in a shambles. The death of Giacomo Il Grande left his nephew in charge."

"Marsilio," said Cangrande. "Your friend and mine."

"Friend is not the word I'd use." It had been Carrara that Pietro had dueled that snowy day ten years earlier. He was related to Mari's wife. A family of trouble-makers. "Moreover, the death of Perenzano, Marsilio's father, left no one of the old generation to hold the family in check. This younger generation is nothing like the last one. Headstrong, arrogant, and violent. Marsilio's cousins Ubertino and Niccolo are accused of all sorts of crimes – violence, extortion, rape. They've organized street gangs to terrorize the Paduan people in the name of law and order."

"Irony always was lost on that family. I hear even Marsilio's sister Cunizza has gotten involved in some unsavory business." The Scaliger bowed his head. "I keep interrupting. Please, go on."

Pietro wet his lips. "As you say, it's an ironic situation. There's a truce between Verona and Padua, and with no war to fight, their city has fallen into a shambles. A few weeks ago opposition to the Carrara family came to a head. The Dente family started to put mobs of their own together to oppose the Carrara gangs. While the other city leaders, including your devoted admirer Albertino Mussato and Pietro da Campagnola, were sent to Innsbruck as ambassadors to Heinrich, Ubertino Carrara and a friend murdered Guglielmo Dente in the street. This was just a month ago."

"Awkward, as Ubertino's mother was a Dente. Still, trouble for Marsilio."

"He seems to have made the best of it," said Pietro, too fair not to give even an enemy his due. "He seized the chance to declare a truce with the Dente and at the same time get rid of a troublesome relative. He exiled the murdering pair to Chioggia. That leaves Niccolo, whom he despises for being too friendly with you, and the Papafava branch of the family, who are all dogs on his leash."

"Strong dogs, though. They're as warlike as himself."

Pietro was caught up in his narrative. "There's something I doubt you've heard. Before I came from Bologna, I got my hands on a copy of a letter. Padua's given up all government to Heinrich's men. When Mussato and Campagnola went to Treviso on their way to Innsbruck, they were asked about some contested deeds. They said they'd made the matter known to their lord the Duke of Corinthia, *'without whose consent we can do nothing.'* That's a quote. But even though Heinrich's men control the taxation, the law, the mint, both treasuries, and the guilds, they're either unwilling or unable to put an end to the violence in the streets."

Cangrande clucked his tongue. "Poor Padua. Always caught between Scylla and Charibdis. They haven't had a single year in the last twenty when there wasn't some sort of riot or revolt. You'd think they'd be tired of it all by now. Or perhaps they just don't think much of their leaders."

"They shouldn't. Those leaders have broken the bank. The people are being doubly taxed – once for the commune, once for Heinrich. That doesn't even take into account the extortion gangs. How many men did the Germans send to help Padua last year?"

"Fourteen or fifteen hundred horse," supplied Cangrande, "with three hundred crossbowmen for good measure."

"Well, between paying for them and the extra taxation for the Emperor, they've run out of money. The new mint Heinrich's men set up hasn't spurred the city economy the way they'd hoped."

"*Padva Regia Civitas,*" said Cangrande, quoting the latest motto for the city. It was on all the new coins. "I wonder if Marsilio misses his beloved *patavinitas.* What about the attack on Vicenza?"

"As far as I can tell, with Ubertino out of his hair, Marsilio saw the fire as the perfect chance to take it from you. It would save him – loot to fill Padua's coffers, a personal victory to prove he's a strong leader, and a stick in the eye to you. But the moment he marched, cousin Niccolo started stirring up trouble back home. Since the Germans are keeping their noses out of Padua's internal affairs, Marsilio had to beat a hasty retreat and put his cousin back in line. He must be hating the fact that he has any family at all."

"We all do," said Cangrande. "The price of being prince."

That brought Pietro up short. Beyond the implied jab at Cesco, suddenly Pietro's mind was running along another track. *The aborted attack on Vicenza – did Cangrande know that it would come to nothing? Was that why he risked faking his own death? But how could he know, unless—*

*Unless he has an agitator in Padua.* The corresponding leap was an obvious one. *Niccolo da Carrara. Cangrande is paying Niccolo to stir up trouble and undermine Marsilio.* His next thought was, *How can we use that to our advantage?*

Cangrande prompted him to continue, but Pietro wasn't much interested anymore. "That's about all. Except the poet Mussato has been exiled again for stirring up resentment, and he's ranting about Marsilio to anyone who'll listen."

"Then Carrara and I have an enemy in common," said the Scaliger with amusement. "It strikes me, Pietro, that we've had this conversation before." Cangrande studied him with an arched eyebrow, then gave him an approving nod. "You are the soul of patience. Any other man would have asked after their mission by now. But not Ser Alaghieri. I applaud you."

"I imagine you won't be able to resist telling me, lord."

"I resist few base impulses." Cangrande took on a thoughtful expression. "What motivates man, do you think? Is it an inner force that propels us forward, or circumstance? Are we moved by morality or venality? Or is it as the poet says, *Omne quod movetur, movetur propter aliquid quod non habet.*"

Pietro bristled. This last quote was lifted from an open letter his father had sent to Cangrande discussing what was necessary in a prince. Because Pietro had never revealed Cangrande's secrets to his father, Dante had died admiring Cangrande, dedicating the last part of his Commedia to the Scaliger.

There were moments Pietro regretted his restraint. "That's certainly true for you. Not by what you cannot have, but what you cannot be. *Est eius appetitus,*" he added, quoting the same passage.

Cangrande made a weary sigh. "Pietro, you must sheathe that weapon. It grows tarnished with use."

"I use what I have."

"Then I'll dispense with philosophy, since you cannot keep up. You mention the Dente family. You know of Paolo Dente?"

Pietro had to think for a moment. "The late Guglielmo's half-brother."

"Illegitimate. Now *he* is a man motivated by what he lacks – his sibling. He is ripe to be moved, and you are the man to move him, owning nearly as much reason to detest Marsilio da Carrara as he does. I want you to go to him and encourage him to follow his bliss – as long as that bliss is the overthrow of the Carrara clan. I will provide him connections and money, but no troops. Those he must find for himself."

"I haven't said I'm going," said Pietro.

"You will."

"Why?"

"Because you're not like me." Cangrande fingered a cross hanging at his neck. "It has never really bothered me, my excommunication. I believe that the Virgin watches over me, and can easily make the argument that a church based in Avignon is no church at all. But you — tell me, Ser Alaghieri, how does it sit with you, being out of God's view? What ring of Hell will claim you? The Sixth? Or would your father put you in Cocytus' Pit? Are Brutus and Judas good company, do you think?"

"I hope I do end up there," said Pietro. "Then I can visit you in Antenora."

"I'd rather a little lower, if you please," countered Cangrande. "I haven't betrayed my country, just my friends. Poor Federigo. I knew I'd need a sacrificial lamb once the dust had settled. Nevertheless, I plan on buying my way into Heaven — French coffers are never full enough, as you already know to your sorrow. Yet, in spite of my current state, I have a great deal of influence. I can have you reinstated."

Pietro's hands began to tingle, his head felt light. "What?"

"Your excommunication. I can have it expunged. Removed. Bring you back into the fold of holy mother Church."

Cangrande was offering nothing less than salvation. Pietro was stunned. Entirely without volition he said, "What do I have to do?"

"Go to Vicenza as my anointed judge. There you will set up a special tribunal and accept all accusations of murder. Paolo Dente will arrive with other members of his family. He will petition your court and you will hear him out. He will present evidence, and you will publicly condemn the whole Carrarese family for their complicity in the murder of Paolo's brother. Then in private you make my offer."

"Which is?"

"Funds, weapons, and a base of operations. No troops. As you know, I adhere strictly to the conditions of any truce. I will not let Verona's soldiers attack Padua. But an army of exiles is completely outside my control."

"What do you want in return? From Dente, I mean."

"My only condition is that Dente throws out Heinrich's minions and restore Nico da Lozzo to his proper place on the Paduan Anziani."

"Effectively giving you a voice in Paduan politics. Paolo takes on Marsilio, you reap the rewards if he wins. Why should he do this?"

"Because he has a mean spirit, and a weak, petty mind. He is almost womanish in his need for revenge. Not at all like you."

Pietro shook his head. "I already told you I won't go."

"Ah, so you did! But that was before you knew what the chore was. I thought that dispensing real justice at law combined with a chance to see Carrara's face rubbed in the dirt *and* your promised return to

God's sight would stir you to break your knightly word, just this once. Perhaps I am the Biblical serpent, but instead of offering forbidden fruit, I offer a return to the garden. You are truly a man of honour to refuse. I stand in awe."

What hurt Pietro was that his heart's desire was so painfully obvious. Cangrande had indeed plucked not one but three of Pietro's heart-strings, playing him like Cesco's lute.

But after all, wasn't it Pietro's plan to let himself be sent away so Antonia could stay without suspicion? Still, it couldn't look too easy. "Man of honour or no, I'm not going."

"Stubbornness is not a quality I admire. I offer you the world. Is this enough? It is not, says he, and spits in my eye. Fame, titles, restoration of your honour – what more can I give?"

"A promise," said Pietro quickly. "That I may return the moment the trial is concluded and the offer made. Whether Dente accepts or not."

"Your professors may not like that," said Cangrande, tactfully hiding his pleasure at Pietro's implicit acceptance. "But then, you'll already be a consul with a better income than they can dream, it being added to your knight's portion, also from me. So let them hang, I say. Yes, Ser Alaghieri, I will do nothing to prevent your return to Verona. But only after the attack on Padua is made."

"And if Dente refuses to attack?"

"He won't. Either way, the moment this expedition is done, I give you full permission to return to Verona."

"You should know, I will try Dente's case on its merits. If the evidence does not meet my satisfaction, I will throw out the case."

"Mmm. I suppose it was too much to hope that you would fix the case for me. Fine. But then it won't be you making the offer to Dente. I'll send Nico with you. He'll be the one who has to rule Padua if this works, he might as well have some hand in it."

"I need a few other assurances."

"Anything for my faithful servant, *Ser Giudice*."

"I want you to appoint my brother Jacopo to the Anziani."

"Nepotism!" Cangrande shouted in delight, pointing an accusing finger. "Wonderful! You're already starting down the path of corruption! Your wish is granted. What else?"

"I want your word that Tharwat will not be forced to leave Cesco's side."

Cangrande raised his right hand. "I swear by the Holy Virgin that I shall do nothing to divide Cesco from his keeper. What else?"

"You'll let Morsicato choose his post."

Cangrande considered. "As long as he doesn't displace Fracastoro. I loathe change. But I imagine that personal doctor to the Heir was more what you had in mind."

"Morsicato can make that decision. If he wants out, you'll let him go."

"Such a lawyer! You're proving my appointment so very sound. Very well, Morsicato can write his own pass. What else? Would you like to bed my wife? It might be a little frosty, but I'm sure I could bribe her with something – these papers, for example." He waved his hands at all Pietro's correspondence.

It was tempting to demand their return, but Pietro held firmly to his line. "I want you to declare Cesco your heir in writing and in person before I leave."

This brought a stiffness to the Scaliger's posture. "I thought I did well enough last night. But of course, if you wish it, I shall call a special council and perform a ceremony here in the Domus Nuova. Or should I parade him through the streets on my horse, with me shoveling the shit behind him?"

"No. You'll extract an oath from Mastino, Alberto, and the nobility that they'll see Cesco made Capitano upon your death."

Cangrande was no longer smiling. "Done. Anything else?"

"That will do," said Pietro.

"Nothing about your sister?"

The chill was back, but Pietro managed not to show it. "I don't imagine you'll be troubled by her. Or she by you. She is under the protection of her Order. When her oath to her abbess is performed, she'll go back to Ravenna."

Cangrande's brow furrowed. "Oath?"

"She swore before God that she wouldn't leave Cesco until she is certain of the state of his soul. Until then she will remain here, in the cloister. I'm not happy about it, but she's as stubborn as I am."

Cangrande was nobody's fool. "I see. An inviolable queen to put me in check. You're quite the monster, to use your family so. I thought that was the very reason you abhor me."

"I had nothing to do with it," said Pietro with the ring of absolute truth. "She made the pledge first to my father, then to her abbess. I'd rather she wasn't here at all."

Cangrande grinned. "So she's her own mistress. Excellent! The game needs more spice. Suor Beatrice. A funny name, that. Are you sure she's your sister, and not your father's whore? Or both, perhaps?"

Pietro was too shocked to even speak, much less issue the challenge that remark deserved.

Cangrande waved dismissively. "As amusing as you've been, Ser, you have packing to do. The council will be called tomorrow and I will invest your little Cesco before your eyes. The next morning you will be escorted east with an honour guard of my soldiers. Now get out. I have real work to do."

Fuming, Pietro made for the exit. He didn't know how many more interviews like this he could stand. He hoped he'd thrown enough dust in Cangrande's eyes to blind him towards Antonia. If Cangrande thought that Pietro didn't want her there, perhaps she was safe. Cangrande saw Pietro's truthfulness as a weakness. This once it might work in his favour.

His hand was on the door when Cangrande called out, "It was a girl, by the way."

Pietro turned. "What?"

"Capulletto's child. It was a girl. He's named her already." The Scaliger paused. "He calls her his Giulietta."

"O Jesus Christ!" exclaimed Pietro right from his heart. As he elbowed out the door, Cangrande's laughter rang after him.

# THIRTY-TWO

As PIETRO SUFFERED through his interview with the Capitano, Antonia conscientiously followed his instructions, insinuating herself back into Veronese life. Braving the elements, her first call was to San Francesco al Corso. Even in this tempest, the white walls were a shiny beacon.

Naturally, she found the man she sought in the garden, pinning down a tarp to protect his plants. "Devilish weather!" cried Fra Lorenzo before he even knew who it was beside him.

"I need to talk to you!" she shouted over the torrent.

He waved her into an arched arcade. Throwing back his cowl, he looked at her warily as she said, "I'm afraid I need my chaperone again."

"More heretics to expose?" There was some bite in his tone.

"More acquaintances to renew. But I also need an introduction to the sisterhood here in the city. Who better than a brother of the Order?"

"Did your brother send you?"

"No. Why?" The friar only grunted. "Brother Lorenzo, you've made your dislike of my brother plain. But I know no reason for it. He is a good man, honest and loyal to a fault."

"We have seen different sides to him."

"Perhaps," said Antonia tartly. "But does your dislike of him extend to me? Should I look for another companion?"

Fra Lorenzo heaved a sigh and looked out over his garden. "There's nothing much for me to do in weather like this, anyway. And no, I bear you no ill will. How could I? You are a sister in Christ. Allow me to mention my absence to my Prior, then we'll be on our way. Though I hope we aren't traveling far."

Minutes later, huddled beneath heavy cloaks, they set out. "Where first?"

"A return to the Capulletto household. I want to see if there's anything to be done for the new mother or her daughter."

Lorenzo looked pleased at the Christian nature of the call, but suspicion crept in. "No secret agenda? No one to interrogate?"

"No!" laughed Antonia. "Though I suppose we should keep an eye open for Borachio—"

"According to your brother, they had a bargain. Borachio would attend the ball. If he recognized a man's voice in the crowd, he would say so. He did not recognize anyone's voice, and so he had fulfilled the bargain. I took it upon myself to release him, in case your brother did not."

*Pietro, what did you say to this holy brother to make him detest you so?*

Due to the rain, their conversation progressed in fits and starts as they raced from shelter to shelter, a doorway here, an archway there. Each time they were joined by other Veronese unfortunate enough to be out in this weather, and Lorenzo would greet them, introducing Antonia as Suor Beatrice.

"I am glad of this visit to Lord Capulletto," admitted Lorenzo at one point. "Last night I realized I've been remiss. I've avoided him these many years for fear of the anger he bears me, when I should be mending fences with him. Who knows? Perhaps in time I can effect a reconciliation between he and Montecchio!"

"Good luck in that. They're intractable. If you succeed where so many have failed, then my brother will love you the rest of his days." Lorenzo considered that statement with interest.

Reaching the brick tunnel to Capulletto's house, they ran right into Antony, accompanied by several servants dressed for riding. "Sister! Father! To what do I owe the pleasure?"

Antonia answered. "We came to visit the new mother and child, to bestow on them what comfort we can. If I'd known, I wouldn't have left so early last night. But I thought the party would end with the impromptu race."

"That boy is a scalawag, isn't he? Hey – Scala-wag! Ha!" Antony chortled, enjoying his inadvertent pun. "But you've come at the perfect time! She's awake now, so go see her. She's a delight! I've been holding her all morning. Me, myself! Can you imagine? She doesn't look like much, of course, but her eyes are so bright. And she has my hair!" At the moment his hair was hidden by the hood of a heavy cloak. "As you can tell, I was on my way to my estates – a bridge has washed out, my tenants are in dire straits."

"Do you need my help?" asked Lorenzo instantly.

The offer both surprised and pleased Capulletto. "Thank you, Fra Lorenzo! But no, we can take care of it. Have to keep the tenants happy. But you *can* do me a kindness."

"Anything," said Lorenzo.

"Well, with this weather… I wonder, could you baptize my little girl? It's hardly the form, I know, and I'll have the whole ceremony again properly in a few months time. But so many infants die untimely. Not that I think she will, she's the hardiest little thing. But I dread the idea of my sweet treasure going to Limbo."

"I cannot think the Bishop would object."

"Cesco was baptized twice," said Antonia.

Antony blinked in pleasure. "Was he? Then my girl is in good company!"

"What's her name?" asked Lorenzo.

"Giulietta," said Capulletto with a happy sigh.

Upon hearing the name, Antonia had a reaction similar to her brother's, if not so blasphemous. Giulietta. The Little Giulia. *Oh Antony..!*

"And do you have god-parents chosen? Or shall that wait?"

Capulletto turned to Antonia. "Would you consider it? You, and your brother? I can think of no one more choice!"

Lorenzo spoke before Antonia could answer. "Ser Alaghieri is sadly ineligible. He is out of God's view."

Antony scowled. "What nonsense that is! There's no better man in the world. Well, Antonia is enough for the moment." Horses were arriving, brought by the huge groom Andriolo. "I must be off. Antonia, thank you. And Fra Lorenzo – I am in your debt for this." He said this last with some weight. Lorenzo bowed his tonsured head.

Antony was heaving himself into the saddle when someone pressed a message into his hand. He snorted and, breaking the seal, struggled to read it in the poor light of the tunnel. The blood had seemed to drain from Capulletto's face and he let out a peculiar sound, rather like a mew. "Who gave you this?"

His servant stepped back. "Someone on the street. I couldn't see his face."

"Ill news?" asked Antonia.

Capulletto crumpled up the paper and shoved it into the neck of his doublet. "Just a trifle. Money matters." He kicked his heels and, without a farewell, rode out into the storm.

"What do you think was in the note?" asked Antonia.

"Exactly what he said. Money matters. He's not a natural noble-man. He'll have his fingers in some sordid business affair until he dies. Which is no sin, so long as he avoids usury."

"No sin," agreed Antonia. "But hardly respectable."

"That is his affair. I'm content that he asked my help. A simple enough request, for so great a reward."

"Yes, a lovely olive branch for the new generation. Besides, Antony is not a man to—" She'd been about to say *hold a grudge*, but realized how untrue this statement was.

Led to the highest room in the tower, they were greeted by clucking and cooing women. Holding court over them all was the nurse Angelica, a woman of broad shoulders, broad hips, and broad breasts.

The young mother was abed, the bundle of joy in her arms. Announced, Lorenzo and Antonia were instantly brought to the bedside to view the little miracle.

While Lorenzo asked for a bowl of water for the baptism, Antonia took a seat on the edge of the bed. "May I hold her?"

Tessa handed the child over as if relieved to be rid of her. Antonia took the tiny, fragile thing in her arms, making sure to support the head – newborns were like wooden-headed puppets, giant heavy heads lolling about.

The nurse hovered at Antonia's elbow. "God love her, look at that face. She'll be pinched raw by the time she's five with cheeks like that! And look at me, fussing over her when I have my own baby girl to cuddle and coo. It's sinful, I know, but I think I like this one even better than my own – I mean, she's so fair! Susanna is a screamer, we have to bribe her with a touch of wine just to get her to sleep. It was my husband thought of that, God bless his heart. Just a little nip and she's out like a candle in the wind. Thank God she's thriving, so many babies die young. Our first two both died in their first weeks, which is how I became a nurse – all this milk and no one to drink it! Ah well, they're with God, aren't they, and living happier lives nestled into the Lord's bosom, isn't that right sister? Oh all right, Susanna, I'm coming!"

As Angelica the nurse moved across the room to suckle her own daughter, Antonia pulled back the swaddling hood and took a close look at Giulietta.

Capulletto was deceiving himself in thinking she had inherited his hair. Though as yet there wasn't very much, hers was a purer blonde. But he was certainly right about her eyes. Like most newborns' they were blue, but so light in hue they would likely retain that colour.

Her nose was small and thin, like her mother's. And her ears stuck out a little – not enough to make her look like an amphora, but it marred her perfection enough to be endearing. She didn't scowl the way new babies often did, didn't squint or frown or wail. Instead she looked up with excitement at each new thing, bright and alert, surprise in every glance. *Smart,* thought Antonia. *Of course, she is a girl. That gives her a head start.*

The nurse returned with Susanna, only two weeks old. Cribmates, the two infants would grow to adulthood together, mistress and servant. The women passed several comments back and forth, and Antonia had no trouble adding her compliments to theirs. Hearing Capulletto's request, Angelica was instantly panicked that her own little girl would also die and never get to Heaven. "She's only two weeks old, and weather like this carried off my little Sylvia when Mistress Tessa here was only a babe."

Lorenzo agreed to baptize both girls. After blessing the water, they stripped both children bare and lay them in the basin of holy water, side by side. Both began to cry, but Lorenzo had his prayer ready, and in just a few moments he had completed a perfunctory baptism.

Angelica clamped their mouths one to each breast to silence them. Red-faced, Lorenzo withdrew. The other ladies said their farewells. Antonia wished to stay and befriend the young mother, but Tessa complained of tiredness.

"Perfectly understandable." Rising, Antonia was intercepted at the door by the nurse, a sucking child on each teat. In an over-loud confidence, Angelica said, "She lost a lot of blood, but that's not it. She wants to keep the master away from her as long as possible. Never met a girl who thought sex was as dirty as she does – except you maybe. You're going to be a nun, aren't you? What's the matter? Don't like men?"

Antonia quickly joined Lorenzo in the stairwell, and they fled their individual embarrassments, heading back into the rain that was coming down in sheets. Cowl over his head, Lorenzo observed, "I notice Ser Capulletto is very fond of you."

"Antony and I have been friendly since my first day in Verona. Sadly, that was the same day he and Mariotto fell out."

"Over another friend of yours." In response to her curious look, Lorenzo added, "Lady Gianozza has long come to me for confession. She has nothing but praise for you."

"Ah. Yes, we were close, once. I haven't seen her in years."

"She mentioned her desire to call upon you, but she is much taken up with her son. Young Romeo."

"I haven't met him yet," said Antonia. "But I plan to rectify that now. She is our next call." Lorenzo was holding her arm, trying to shelter her from the dousing with his greater size. Ruefully, she said, "Perhaps I should leave it for another day."

"We are already drenched, and I am sure the lady would welcome the visit. Though—"

"Yes?"

"Forgive my saying this, but it seems an unlikely friendship. I remember you well enough from your previous stay to know how very practical you are."

"Whereas Gianozza is anything but practical," said Antonia with a laugh. Gianozza Montecchio lived in a near-fantasy world, a romantic existence with Guineveres and Lancelots, a world where *La Roman de la Rose* actually happened. It was this view that had cast her and her husband as the principal players in a great melodrama – not a passion play, but a play of passion.

"She may be less earthbound than I, but there are few women who have read as extensively. She knows literature, and her letters are always long and involved on some literary dissection. Her appreciation for meter and structure is above most poets'!"

"I know little of poetry. I must confess, I haven't even read your father's epic. But now that I have you as a guide, perhaps I'll give it a try. You are staying in Verona for some time?"

"I mean to," said Antonia. "That's our third errand, the one for which I most need your help."

"Yes, the abbey. Well, best get moving!"

Out in the storm, Antonia voiced one question about the lady they were to visit. "How is she coping with life as a wife?"

Lorenzo considered, weighing his words as the lady's confessor. "She seemed restless until God granted her a son. He is her true passion these days."

A statement proven true the instant they arrived at Montecchio's house. Barely were they out from under their sodden cloaks before Gianozza had her son brought before them.

Romeo had shining black hair, which he could have gotten from either parent. He had much of Mariotto's overt beauty, but his features seemed more delicate than his father's, as if Gianozza's blood had refined Mariotto's good looks even further.

Presenting him, Gianozza smoothed her son's hair. "Isn't he precious?"

*That's the very word,* thought Antonia. *Precious.*

"My little angel. Romeo, show Auntie Antonia how you make a leg." Romeo dutifully bowed, one leg forward and straight, the other bent behind him. "Isn't he brilliant?"

Knowing what true brilliance in a child looked like, Antonia nodded neutrally. "He's about the same age Cesco was when he came to Ravenna."

Romeo's little head popped up. "You know Cesco?"

"I am his aunt." As she said it she remembered it wasn't true. But it felt true.

"Momma called you *my* aunt!" cried Romeo excitedly.

"A different kind of aunt," said Gianozza, laughing.

"Oh. Can Cesco come and play?"

"Not today." Romeo's face fell and his eyes began to fill. "But I'll ask him to come see you sometime when he's free."

Tears vanishing as swift as they had come, little Romeo smiled from ear to ear. In a moment his face had transformed from his mother's mournful expression to something like Mariotto's bright humour. He clapped his hands excitedly and dashed from the room.

"He has high spirits," said Antonia, politely hinting that he was overly emotional.

"He has that," said Gianozza happily. "He really *feels!* I mean, he feels his life! It's how we've been raising him, to be deeper than other boys."

Antonia understood what Lorenzo had been hinting at. No longer at the crisis point in the novel of her life, Gianozza had been bored until her son had come. Typical Gianozza, she was attempting to mold the boy into Paris, or Tristan, or perhaps Pyramus. There was a part of Antonia that believed the boy would have been better off if his mother ignored him. *Deeper than other boys indeed!*

They exchanged kisses, and while Gianozza greeted Lorenzo, Antonia took in her friend. Gianozza was still a breathtaking beauty. Motherhood had added a little to her figure, which suited her, made her voluptuous. Those large sad eyes were untouched by lines or care, as if age were giving her free passage. But then she was only, what, twenty-five? Barely older than Antonia herself. Yet infinitely more immature.

They settled in upstairs, and Gianozza's first questions were naturally all about Cesco. "So you've been living with the Greyhound's heir all this time? Hiding him from the Capitano's enemies? How daring! And never even a hint in your letters!" she added reproachfully, as if it were Antonia's duty to pass along anything so utterly dramatic. Clearly the notions of consequence, of responsibility, and of restraint of continued to elude her.

Eventually talk turned to Antonia's joining the convent. "Don't tell me you actually enjoy a cloistered life!"

"I do," said Antonia simply.

"But it must be so *dull!* Wouldn't you rather find yourself a husband? You say you haven't taken your final vows yet, you could still meet the perfect man…" She trailed off, putting a hand over her mouth as if she had trespassed. "Or – oh, of course, I'm so sorry. That is why you're becoming a nun! I understand!"

Whatever Gianozza understood, it was lost on Antonia. "What do you mean?"

Gianozza laid a hand over Antonia's, clasped it tight. "You already found your one true love, and now he is gone. Tell me – do you ever think of your poor lost Ferdinando?"

It was as if Gianozza had her smacked in the face. Antonia had, in fact, thought of Ferdinando just the night before. How could she not see Petruchio without recalling his awkward, rude, garrulous cousin?

Antonia removed her hand from her friend's grip. "So Gianozza, tell me, have you read the *Sonetto per Selvaggia* yet?"

Gianozza gave Antonia a sad and understanding smile, then launched into a recitation of the new poem's flaws and genius.

◆　◊　◆

Their final call was at the convent of Santa Maria in Organo. Antonia tried to hurry, but it didn't stop Lorenzo from making the obvious inquiry. "You were to marry?"

"No," said Antonia discouragingly. Then, thinking that a short answer might only make matters worse, she elaborated. "Matters never progressed that far. We were – friends." Fra Lorenzo kindly let the matter slip.

Several minutes of dashing between raindrops and a quick crossing of the Adige over the Ponte Nuovo brought them to their destination. Outside the original city walls, the convent lay nestled against the river's east bank. Rebuilt after an earthquake two hundred years earlier, Antonia had always found it one of the most unassuming convents she'd ever seen – brick, covered with a thin layer of plaster that was already bare in places. But inside there were ancient pillars dating back to the convent's founding in 745.

After making her purpose known, Suor Beatrice was granted an interview with Abbess Verdiana, a kindly woman with a face so wizened it looked humourous. After Lorenzo made the introductions, Antonia told her history, concluding, "If it pleases Mother Abbess, I shall take up residence here tomorrow."

The Abbess granted her leave. "On condition that, for the time-being, you reside in the guest suite, away from the common dormitory. Until we know you better." Suor Beatrice might be welcome for her father's sake, and the Capitano's, but they were not going to be responsible for her.

Antonia was content. It was enough to be able to pray, work, and sing in company. Who cared where she slept?

She thanked Lorenzo, who departed at a run, impatient to see what the storm had done to his gardens. Alone, she walked around the church's interior, feeling calmness descend. Her shoulders lifted, relieved of a weight she hadn't know she was carrying. She felt the shift as Antonia Alaghieri slipped away. If she had ever doubted, she was now certain. Though she loved her brothers and her friends, this was where her true life was. Deprived of her beloved father, she could devote herself to the Father of all. She was meant to be Suor Beatrice.

But there were still ties to her old life. Until Cesco became a man, able to fend for himself, and until Pietro was wed and content, she would continue to straddle two worlds. She had to keep Antonia Alaghieri alive until Cesco and Pietro didn't need her anymore. Then she'd be free to be Beatrice forever.

# THIRTY-THREE

THAT NIGHT, as the rain poured down and Cesco's few belongings were moved into the Scaliger palace, Pietro called another meeting of Cesco's inner circle – himself, his sister, Tharwat, and Morsicato. They met, not in the Nogarola house, but in a rented room above a tavern, part of an inn called the *Albergo delle Quattro Spade*. The Inn of the Four Swords had been a haunt of his during those halcyon few months when he, Mari, and Antony had all been friends, free from care. Ten years past, he still associated this place with good times and good friends.

The door closed, Pietro succinctly laid out the details of the Scaliger's mission. "In essence, I'm being sent to give a legal pretext to an uprising against Padua."

"Isn't that dangerous," asked Antonia. "What if Carrara learns of it?"

"Well, he already dislikes me…"

"Don't be glib. Does this put you in peril?"

"In peril," repeated Pietro with his crooked half-smile. "You've been talking to Mari's wife."

Antonia blushed, stubbornly repeating, "What happens if —"

"If Carrara hears, he'll assume I'm acting on an old grudge. Trust me, he's got enough troubles at home. He won't come looking for me."

Morsicato held up his palms. "Wait, wait. I'm still choking on the fact that you accepted the Capitano's order."

"If I didn't, he'd have some other way to get rid of me. Just as he'll be looking to fob off you lot. That's why we're having this discussion. First and foremost, protecting Cesco from future attacks. I was wrong and you all were right. Cangrande was not the man in Venice. Which does not mean," he added quickly, "that he did not hire the man."

"Makes it less likely. What did Passerino have to say?"

"That he was with Cangrande the whole time. They stayed in hiding in a monastery while the rumour spread."

"They must have paid someone to start the rumour," mused the doctor. "We could find that person, learn who they told and when. That might tell us who knew—"

"Wait," interrupted Antonia. "He said they stayed there the whole time?"

"Yes. Until they returned to Verona, they were in hiding in—"

"But that's not true!" protested Antonia. "Didn't Cangrande tell you he was the woman in the carriage on the road? Why wouldn't Passerino mention that? If it was such a great joke, wouldn't that be the best part?"

Pietro could have kicked himself. "A sin of omission? It's something else to look into. On my way to meet the Paduan exiles, I'll stop in at the monastery and —" His voice trailed off at the obvious objection.

"I'll write them," suggested Antonia.

"No no. If they turn me away, I'll just bribe them with Cangrande's money. I can also look into Cangrande's movements prior to the rumour of his death. He was on his way to Vicenza because of a fire. Maybe I have Cangrande on the brain, but I have to think he ordered the fire set as an excuse to leave Verona quickly and disappear along the way."

"That I agree with," said Tharwat. "It suits the workings of his mind."

Morsicato raised an objection. "But he was risking all of Vicenza! He couldn't have known that the Paduans wouldn't attack."

"Couldn't he?" asked Tharwat. "He's sending Ser Alaghieri to stir up revolt inside of Padua. Who's to say he's the first? It is convenient that at the moment Vicenza is most vulnerable, civil strife keeps Carrara from pressing his advantage."

Pietro waved his hand. "We'll know more soon. We have to decide how we're going to protect Cesco from this unknown menace. I've started by extracting promises from Cangrande. What else?"

They spent an hour shuttling ideas back and forth. Some were rejected, some adopted. In the midst of discussing food tasters, Morsicato snapped his fingers. "I just remembered! Tharwat, tell me – what was it you were feeding Cesco?"

Pietro had entirely forgotten the little wafers the Moor had been slipping Cesco. For the first time in memory, the astrologer looked discomfited. At last he answered. "Hashish."

Pietro goggled. "What?!" Antonia echoed her brother while the doctor angrily exploded, "You damned fool!"

"Please lower your voice, doctor," said the Moor. "The walls have ears."

Morsicato didn't hear him. "You idiot! You monster! Why on earth…?"

Tharwat al-Dhaamin replied in a tone so soft it was almost inaudible over the rasp from his throat. "It eliminated his pain and gave him energy to get past the ordeal."

"You've made him an opium eater!"

"No. I appreciate your concern, but it was a small amount, mixed with other herbs. You use more opiate in your sleeping draughts."

"When did you become a doctor? Shall I begin fiddling about with charts and pendulums?"

"I have some experience with the substance. If the boy had been wholly well, he would not have needed it. In the aftermath of the poison—"

"You decided to poison him more!" The doctor pointed an accusing finger. "*Never* do that again."

"I will do what I deem necessary."

"I wasn't asking a question," said the doctor icily.

"Tharwat," said Pietro. "Promise me, no more."

"That is a promise I cannot keep. He has tasted it, knows its strengths. If I cease his training now, he will never learn of its dangers until it is too late. He will indeed fall into the pit you fear so much."

Morsicato's fury was replaced by incredulity. "Training? In opium eating?"

"It is a discipline like any other. So far he is managing it."

Pietro's feelings were in tune with the doctor's. "Dear God, Tharwat! He's a child!"

"I was even younger."

"What in the name of all that's holy does that mean?" demanded Morsicato, his beard bristling.

Antonia provided a calming voice. "Tharwat, what do you mean?"

The Moor's expression was a blank. "I was seven, at most. As you see, it has done me no harm."

"Why were you given hashish as a child?"

"As part of my training."

Pietro was perplexed. "As an astrologer?"

"No."

"What, then?"

It was clear Tharwat did not like the question. That he answered it was a triumph of his friendship, his trust for these three people with whom he had shared so much.

"As an Hashashin."

Antonia put a hand to her mouth.

"Dear Christ," swore the doctor.

"You were a – an Assassin?" said Pietro.

"No," said Tharwat.

"You just said—"

"I was trained to be one of the Order. But as I came to manhood, the Order was hounded out of formal existence." He touched his neck. "I barely escaped with my life." Never in all the years they had known him had the Moor made reference to the origin of the disfiguring scars that had damaged his voice.

"Beloved Christ." Pietro was shocked to his core. Tharwat's reluctance to share this piece of his history was understandable. He seemed suddenly so foreign, so frightening, the others had difficulty looking at him. Bad enough his dark skin marked him as a Moor, a born heathen. If it was known that he had been part of a sect of Muslim murderers, trained to mete out death in secret and stealth – if that got out, he would be dead in an instant.

Tharwat gazed at them with sad eyes. "I understand your unease. I always meant to spare you this. I promise, there is no one living outside this room who has this knowledge." The way he said it, they knew that he had personally made certain this was so. "But we are here to safeguard the boy. I suggest that you put aside your discomfort for a few moments more, that we may finish laying out our precautions." He turned to the doctor. "For the substance you object to. You will admit now that perhaps I understand it better than even you. It is a tool. Like any tool, it may be abused. But if I have at my disposal skills to help him through the ordeal to come, I am remiss in not teaching them to him. I suggest that you, doctor, do the same. Teach him medicine, science, anatomy, anything that may stave off the darkness until he has achieved his destiny. For he has one. Remember, Cesco is the Greyhound. He will unite this land and bring forth a new age of man. But the prophecy does not say what that age will be – will it be to mankind's benefit, or the Beast's? His stars are uncertain, confused. He needs every tool we possess if he is to rise above his darker portents and shine like the star we all know he can be."

It was the longest unbroken speech al-Dhaamin had ever made, and the most passionate. By the end of it, his voice was ragged, worse even than the rasp they were accustomed to. Indeed, he seemed to speak with two voices in disjointed harmony, one rasping, one pure. He sounded like a lute whose middle strings were cut, leaving only the top and bottom of the scale. It gave the merest hint at what his voice had been like before the injury.

More than his pleas, the use of his true voice silenced them. Pietro took a breath. "I think we've covered everything we need to tonight."

About to say something, Morsicato thought better of it and headed for the door. After a brief pause, Antonia went up on her toes to kiss the Moor on both cheeks, then left.

For some unfathomable reason, Pietro felt betrayed. Reason told him that Tharwat's silence was a wise precaution. But he had placed his life in the Moor's hands so often, he'd believed the trust between them was absolute. This secret felt like a knife through trust's heartstrings.

Struggling to find words, al-Dhaamin saved him the trouble. "One thing more. Cesco's mother has vanished."

Pietro's brow furrowed. "Wasn't she supposed to?"

"That was your arrangement, yes. But we needed to know more about this woman and the bargain she has made with Cangrande. So I followed her."

Another betrayal. But then, what did an Assassin know of honour? "I gave her my word."

"I do not deem myself bound by your promise to her. But it does not matter now. Her carriage was assaulted on the road away from Verona. Her driver is dead. There is no sign of the lady or her belongings."

"A robbery?"

"No reason for robbers to take the lady."

"Ransom?"

"If so, then the Scaliger will receive a demand."

"And we'll hear about it, or not, depending on his whim."

"That is not the possibility that frightens me. I fear that some person has divined the lady's relationship with Cesco, and is asking her for the answers we also wish to have, but with more – forthrightness."

Pietro realized what the Moor was saying. If someone laid hold of Donna Maria, tortured her, that person could learn all the secrets of Cesco's past. Whatever Cangrande and Maria were hiding, it was important. Not knowing what that secret was, Pietro had no way to protect Cesco from it. "I suppose you discarded the possibility that the kidnapping was staged just to stop you from following her."

"It's possible, but it gains us nothing. We must assume that she is in peril."

"And we don't even know where to start looking for her. Hell, we don't even know her name." Pietro threw up his hands in exasperation, then subsided. "I'm glad you went after her."

Tharwat said nothing.

"You're sure Cangrande doesn't know about your past? Because if he does, that would be the most expedient way to remove you from Cesco's company. He could burn you at the stake, based solely on the accusation."

"Then I hope you do not tell him."

That cut Pietro to the quick. "Of course I'm not going to – Tharwat, you just admitted to being an Assassin! You understand why I'm wary?"

The Moor's brown eyes were puffed and bagged from a fatigue greater than Pietro's. The two gazed at each other for the span of a beating pulse. Finally al-Dhaamin answered. "I have lived all my life among men who wish me dead for the place of my birth, the colour of my skin, the practice of my faith. I have been the Other, the alien, through all my adult years. I know that but for my skill with the stars, I would have been long dead, murdered by men who fear me."

Pietro tried to interrupt. "I'm not—"

"What these men did not understand, what they could not know, is how I fear their fear. I fear them, Ser Alaghieri. I have lived fifty years among men I fear. Every face I see is potentially the man who will undo me. It is why I go about in the guise of slave or servant. Before you, there was Ignazzio. There were others before him. There will be more before I die. As long as I seem servile, I am welcome everywhere. My skills are recognized as having value, which lends value to my life. But I cannot go home. I have no home. I was stolen from my parents, raised in captivity to be something terrible. But those evil men became my brothers. Then those brothers were slain and I was left for dead. It took years, but I repaid their killers in kind. It meant forever leaving the only place I ever knew as home. Even now, returning would mean death."

Tharwat al-Dhaamin spoke more softly now than in his earlier impassioned plea. This was again a rumble from his chest voice, rasping but whole. "You ask if I understand why you are wary. I do. I have lived with that same wariness for almost as long as I have been alive." He paused. "But I had hoped that you, the man who loves law and the concept of justice; you, son of your father, father to the boy we both love; you, who have been my friend – I hoped you would not find it in your heart to despise me for being what life has made me."

Before Pietro could think of an answer, Tharwat had opened the door and gone.

# THIRTY-FOUR

*Verona*
*Wednesday, 31 July*
*1325*

AMAZINGLY, THE SCALIGER kept his word. Two days after his interview with Pietro, at a special session of the city council, Cangrande formally adopted Cesco as his heir. The ceremony was remarkably brief. The bishop intoned prayers, Cangrande made the announcement, the assembled nobles applauded as Cesco took his place by Cangrande's side.

As the applause died away, Cangrande spoke. "It's time for this wayward youth to learn the duties of a knight. He is of the age to act as squire to one of Verona's many distinguished nobles. The question of which to choose has been weighing heavily on me these last few days. To show favour to one is a slight to another."

*Oh please God,* thought Pietro. *Don't choose Mari or Antony. The other would never let it go.*

"So rather than elevate one, I will elevate you all. Each one of Verona's knights and nobles will participate in young Francesco's training. In the meantime, he will act as my personal squire."

That raised several eyebrows. It was unheard of for a knight to mentor his own son. But Cangrande had an explanation waiting. "For the last eight years this lad has been raised by the brave and resourceful Ser Alaghieri. No one could have been a better foster-father." He bowed his head gracefully to Pietro. "However, I want to have a hand in the shaping of this young man. If he is to be my heir, he must come to know me. Fear not! Lest I prove too forgiving a mentor, Verona's best and brightest will help me overcome familial fondness."

To the assembly, this statement made perfect sense. Of course a man should know his heir! For his part, Cesco showed no reaction. Which did not mean he did not have one.

"Lord Nogarola," said Cangrande, formally addressing his brother-in-law. "You were my master when I was young Cesco's age, and I had planned to return the favour by mentoring your eldest son. Will you forgive me if I renege on that agreement. I think," he added with a sly smile, "that I shall have my hands full."

There were chuckles, and Cesco was smiling too. Pietro was not.

"Of course," rumbled Bailardino. "But then who will take my little brat?"

"Little?" asked Petruchio Bonaventura. "He's as big as my twins put together!"

"Then why don't you take him off my hands?" demanded Bailardino.

"Only if you'll do the same for me when mine are of age!"

"One! I'll take one."

Petruchio shook his head. "It's double or nothing! I bet my best horse you can't manage both at once."

"You're cruel to an old man!" cried Bailardino, amid a chorus of light-hearted jeers. "Fine. Both. I'm sure each will turn out to be twice the swordsman their father is."

"Care to bet on that, too?" challenged Petruchio with a grin.

Cangrande cut off their boisterous good cheer. "Now that Bailardetto's future is certain, let's go out and amuse the people rather than ourselves."

On the way out, Pietro touched Morsicato's shoulder. "Have you seen Tharwat?"

The doctor shook his head. "Not since he told us about – about his past."

"He hasn't been back to the Nogarola house. Cesco is worried."

"Cesco doesn't know what we do, now, does he?"

Tharwat's parting words repeating in his mind every hour, Pietro had been wracked by guilt for two days. Thus he was quick to come to Tharwat's defense. "He's the same man he's always been."

"That was true about the Scaliger. Before and after you found out about his real nature. His deeds were the same, only his motivations were blacker. Who's to say that isn't more true of the blackamoor?"

"*The blackamoor?*" echoed Pietro. "That's a friend you're talking about."

"A friend of circumstance," retorted Morsicato.

The crowd was almost done filing out of the Domus Nuova, and servants were busily clearing benches. Pietro guided the doctor outside where the noise of the mob covered their talk. "We owe him. And we need him."

"I know we do," said Morsicato grudgingly. "What I can't decide is, now that we have an Assassin on our side, do I feel better or worse?"

"Keep that word inside your teeth," warned Pietro.

Morsicato scowled. "Well, wherever he is, I hope he stays away a few more days. Between watching Cesco for signs of addiction and treating my wife for nausea, I'd have no idea what to say to him."

"Esta's unwell?"

"Stomach's bothering her. Change in venue, I think. Recent events have certainly upset my innards."

"Stop that," said Pietro.

"I don't just mean *him*," said the doctor hotly. "There's also the little matter of a poisoner. It's funny, though – isn't that the chosen weapon of an Assassin?"

Biting back his angry answer, Pietro shouldered his way through the crowd, leaving Morsicato behind. It felt like he was losing his grip already. He'd hoped to see Tharwat before he departed. He desperately wanted to make amends. But clearly that was not to be. *And now I'm quarreling with the doctor. Terrific.* It was not lost on Pietro that the close-knit group of protectors around Cesco was beginning to unravel. *Friends quarrelling, secrets, lies, ambitions. I must be in Verona.*

Not for long. Saddlebags packed, groom and bodyguard hired, Pietro had already taken leave of Antonia and given a few wise words to Cesco, which he was sure would be ignored. Slipping through the crowd, he mounted his horse and met the waiting Nico da Lozzo.

"Exciting stuff," said the former Paduan, rubbing his hands together. "Murder trials, secret offers, treachery, revolt – epic! And us as the heroes. It doesn't get better than this. A shame that your father isn't here to put it into verse."

Fortunately, Nico wasn't a man who needed a partner for conversation, just a vessel. He talked incessantly as their party exited Verona across the Ponte Pietro. The last time Pietro had passed under the massive stone arch and onto the bridge, it had taken him ten years to return. Now he hoped it would only be a matter of weeks – days, even, if Nico could persuade Dente to move in haste.

Against his will, a slice of him burned with excitement. Cangrande had known just the levers to pry Pietro's feet from the earth. The title of judge was something by itself. But to regain his place before God, and do so by unseating the man responsible for the rift between Mari and Antony – it was too much temptation.

A warning voice told him that things would not go as planned. No matter the assurances, the Scaliger had something up his sleeve. *I am being played upon like a pipe, or a pawn on a board. But I'm not a lost teen anymore. If I am a pawn, I'm a pawn able to conspire with the other pieces against the player.*

♦        ◊        ♦

Cangrande summoned Cesco to the loggia overlooking the rear of the palace. "Pack my bags, squire, and order the grooms to prepare the horses. We leave before dawn."

Cesco bowed. "Of course, lord. What will you require?"

"Tullio will show you how I like to travel. Pack your own bag accordingly. Bag, not bags. I do not like a parade of pack animals behind me. Light is the word."

"Will we have any train, lord, or is it just us two?"

"A small train, a dozen or so."

Cesco blinked in surprise, then bowed again. "Good night, lord."

"Sleep well." The tone of the order conveyed a private amusement.

Closing the door to the loggia, Cesco decided to speak to the groom first – better to order the horses before packing. Skipping down the stairs and through the private yard at the back of the palace, he'd just entered the stable when a fist slammed into his bicep.

"What the hell are you doing here?" demanded Detto with a smile. His language was already growing saltier now that he was a squire.

Cesco rubbed his arm. "Haven't you heard? I'm the new stable-boy."

"Demoted already? Too bad. But maybe you can help me. Petruchio wants some horses for tomorrow, break of dawn."

"That's funny," said Cesco. "So does Cangrande."

Detto beamed. "Does that mean—?"

"I think it does."

Detto gave a little whoop at the idea of having Cesco along for his first day as a squire. "Any idea where we're going?"

"None at all. Nor do I want to. Let's agree to be surprised."

"That's amusing," said a voice from the doorway. "I thought you liked giving surprises, not getting them." Framed by the darkening sky behind him, Mastino leaned against the stable door.

"Ho, cousin," said Cesco genially.

But Detto placed himself between Mastino and Cesco, fists raised to the ready. "Don't come near him!"

Mastino gave Detto a withering glance. "Step off, child, before you get hurt."

Cesco laid a restraining hand on Detto's arm. "Yes, Detto, do be careful of the muddy Mastiff." To Mastino, he bowed jauntily. "Another day, cos, another meeting. I haven't seen you since our little *giostra*. Are you here to chastise me? How very wise. Pardon one offence and you condone many, they say."

Mastino grimaced. "You definitely like to talk."

"I do. It passes the time. Where's your friend Fuchs, O he of the slippery saddle?"

"Looking after some chores for me," said Mastino airily. "You might not realize, boy, how lucky you were to slip away from us."

"I'm sure your riding shames ours," said Cesco. "In fair weather. If our horses were blown. And lame. And dead."

Detto snickered, but Mastino was unmoved. "So young to have so many enemies. Aunt Giovanna, my friend Fuchs. This Donati fellow can't be pleased that the story of his being bested by a child is beginning to spread back to Florence. And then there's me."

"You, cousin? Say it isn't so!"

"Funny little fellow. You have some wit, I grant you that."

"Generous of you."

"But that is just the personal list. Then there are Cangrande's enemies, who will all look at you as a way of hurting him."

"As edifying as this is," said Cesco, "you're not telling me anything I haven't already sussed out. Perhaps that's why you aren't the heir – mastery of the obvious is not enough to rule the Feltro."

Stepping around Detto, Mastino used his height to tower over Cesco. "You are insolence personified, aren't you?"

Looking up at him, Cesco sniffed the air. "How do you get your breath so fresh? Do you chew mint leaf? May I try some?"

Mastino smiled in one corner of his mouth. "You're not at all afraid of me, are you?"

"I should be, I know. But it's hard to hate the first family member you can ever remember meeting."

Detto piped up. "I'm more family than he'll ever be!"

Mastino stepped back to lean casually against a post. "Speaking of family, how was your chat with your mother?"

Cesco's eyes glazed for a hair's-breadth of time. Then with an excited smile he said, "It was wonderful. At first I wasn't sure it was her, but after she'd suckled me at her teat, I was sold. Then she bathed me and dressed me and sang me a lullaby. Enough mothering for a lifetime."

"It will have to be," said Mastino. "You know you'll not be allowed to see her again."

"Then I shall treasure our time to the end of my days. If you'll excuse me, Tullio is expecting me. You know how it is – one child disappears and everyone goes into a frenzy."

"That's not true of an adult," said Mastino.

"Then I am fortunate, am I not, that I'm not yet as fully grown as, say – you. Detto, let's find the groom. Cheers, cousin!" Cesco gave Mastino a light salute and walked away. Detto followed, staring daggers at Mastino.

When they were both gone, Mastino began to whistle cheerfully as he mounted his horse and rode off to meet Fuchs.

# THIRTY-FIVE

*Illasi*
*Thursday, 1 August*
*1325*

THE PARTY OF FOURTEEN departed before the break of day. The purpose of the outing was immediately clear – six servants bore great hunting birds on special perches built onto their saddles.

This was no normal hunt. Cangrande's usual expeditions numbered over a hundred knights, each with attendants to swell their ranks even further. Today the only lord in company was Petruchio Bonaventura, renowned for his skill with falcons and hawks. If not the best hunter in Verona, he was acknowledged the preeminent expert in hunting birds.

Cangrande and Petruchio rode together, as was fitting, with their two squires just behind. The rest of the riding party trailed back at a decent distance, within reach of a raised voice but not close enough to overhear private conversations.

"Weather couldn't be better for it," said Petruchio.

"Really?" said Cangrande, amused. "The weather?"

"Well, what should we talk about with those two in company?" Petruchio jerked a thumb at Cesco and Detto. "Never had a squire before."

"I don't think it's your squire you're fretting over," laughed Cangrande. "Cesco, would you be offended if we discussed gambling?"

"Yes, unless I'm permitted to make the odd wager. Then feel free."

"We have to do something about your manners," Cangrande told him. "You may have been brilliant against the lesser lights of Ravenna. But it's clear you were raised in the house of a poet. A touch too artistic for court."

"I shall mimic you in all things," said the boy, and for the next few minutes aped the great man's every move and word, to the great man's extreme consternation.

"A squire should be neither seen nor heard," said Cangrande at last. "Invisible. But if this is to be an egalitarian outing – Lord Bonaventura, where is that amusing groom of yours?"

Petruchio's beard twitched in a smile. "Grumio! Front!"

From the saddle of a dappled grey mare a middle-aged man in rough clothes groaned. "Now?"

"Not later!" snarled Petruchio.

Grumio clicked his tongue and the mare cantered forward until it was level with them. "Shall we set loose the birdies?"

"Not yet," said Cangrande. "We just wanted your company."

Grumio tugged his cap. If he was surprised at being summoned to join the nobility, he didn't show it. "Right kind of you, m'lord."

"We desired a touch of eloquence," explained Cangrande.

"Just a touch? Tcha, all right. I'll try to hold back." Grumio winked at Cesco. "Lords and hordes, little master. Always pays to leave 'em wanting more." The way he said *hordes*, it was quite clear he was referencing another word.

Cangrande laughed. "A lesson the boy has yet to learn."

"One of oh so many," said Cesco.

"So, bumpkin," said Petruchio to Grumio, "what had you so busy that you answered me roundly in front of the Capitano?"

"We had a wager going."

"And you didn't invite me, churl?"

"The wager wasn't genteel, lord."

"We're not genteel lords," said Cangrande. "What was the wager?"

"Well," said Grumio seriously, "we were wondering – since most women's privates smell of fish, and the fish is the sign for our Lord," he crossed himself, "I was willing to lay a bet that any theologian worth his salt would say that the best path to redemption lies in the conjunction between a lady's legs."

Cangrande bit his tongue to keep from laughing aloud. Cesco and Detto made disgusted faces, Detto mouthing the word, *Fish?*

"Heretical lecher!" Amid his roaring laugh, Petruchio slapped his groom upside the head. "Impious villain!"

Grumio bent under the open-handed assault. "Begging forgiveness! But it strikes me as I'm being the soul of piety!"

"That's me striking you, fool!" Petruchio used his reins to whip his groom's knee.

The older man recoiled. "Mercy, mercy! Lord Capitano, is it right that a man should be beaten for seeking salvation?"

"For that, perhaps not. But for wagering on it, absolutely."

"Ah," said Grumio, nodding at the Scaliger's wisdom. "Then while my master beats me, you can beat him."

"Beat me, fellow?" cried Petruchio.

"Beat you, master. For I have often heard you cry out, 'I'll bet on that, by God!' Now, if wagering on God is sinful, then placing a flutter in His name must be a hundred times worse. I've sinned this once, and it's earned me a half dozen blows. You've sinned a hundred times, and every sin a hundred times worse than mine. Let's see, in blows that comes to—" He screwed up his face, counting on his fingers.

"Grumio?"

Grumio's head came up. "Aye?"

"Mum."

Grumio's head went down. "Aye."

Delighted, Cangrande pointed at Grumio. "Master groom, if Lord Bonaventura ever releases you from his service, look to me for hiring. As a fool," he added.

"What's a fool?" asked Grumio.

"Asks the walking definition," muttered Petruchio.

"Beg pardon, master," corrected Grumio, "but I'm riding."

"Yet somehow you knew I meant you."

"A fool is a teller of amusing truths," said Cangrande.

"Or a teller of truths as amusement," added Cesco.

Grumio scratched his chin. "And what's a fool's pay?"

"Fool's gold, of course," said Cesco and Cangrande together.

Grumio nodded wisely. "Then if you please, I'll keep to my station. To be paid for foolishness is beyond me. I don't want to be putting on airs."

"Magnificent." Cesco grinned from ear to ear. "Capitano, can I become the groom's apprentice instead?"

"I can certainly arrange it. But you'll miss the hawking. Grooms don't hawk."

Grumio made a disgusting sound and spat into the grass.

"I stand corrected," said Cangrande, wrinkling his nose.

Casually slapping Grumio, Petruchio asked, "What do you boys know of falconry?"

At once Cesco began to recite:

*I nurtured a falcon for more than a year.*
*When I had him tamed exactly as I wished*
*And had gracefully decked his feathers with gold,*
*He raised himself so high and flew to other lands.*

*Since then I've seen that falcon flying superbly;*
*He was wearing silken fetters on his feet*
*And the whole of his plumage was all red gold.*
*May God bring those together who want each other's love.*

"Amen to that," said Petruchio. "Though I don't know about loving a male falcon."

"Kürenberc was a German," said Cangrande. "And enjoyed symbolism more than substance, like some others I can name." Cesco stuck out his tongue at Cangrande's back.

"Very true," said Petruchio. "But we're going to be handling females." Grumio opened his mouth and Petruchio opened his fist. "Mum. Most often they're the better hunters, and they're always the more dangerous. Can either of you name for me the different types of falcon?"

Detto was eager to impress his new lord. "The peregrine for the earl, the gyrfalcon for the king, the saker for the knight... ah, the, ah..."

"Lanner," prompted Cesco softly.

"Yes, lanner for the squire, the merlin for the lady, the hobby for the boy, the goshawk for the yoman, the sparrowhawk for the priest, the musket for the clerk, and the tercel for the poor man!" Detto concluded proudly.

"Don't forget the eagle," said Cangrande.

"Which belongs to the emperor," replied Cesco.

Petruchio appealed to the heavens. "God save us from poets. Look, I grant it's a pretty list, but in practical terms it's nonsense. Eagles, kites, vultures, muskets, and hobbys are for all intents useless. As for the rest, it depends what kind of game you're after. So do me a favour, forget literary symbolism and start your list again."

Crushed, Detto quickly complied. "The peregrine."

"Good for winged game, especially water fowl. Has two types of flight – it can wait on over a fixed ground, or chase through the air in these marvelous, unpredictable swoops. To kill, it can either strike with its pounces or bind its game and tackle it to earth. Next?"

"Gyrfalcons," said Cesco.

"Bigger, heavier than the peregrine, but basically the same. A little harder to train, but being so light-coloured, you'll see a lot of them at court. They're pretty, make nice ornaments. The more the court has, the less interesting in real hunting they are."

"Noted," said Cangrande, smiling.

"The saker," said Detto.

"I could use a good saker right now," muttered Grumio. "I'm

thirsty."

Petruchio ground his teeth. "Arab bird, looks like a dark gyrfalcon. Hardier than the peregrine, but not as good at catching water game. Next."

"Lanners," said Detto quickly. Cesco's mouth was open, and he made a face at Detto as he closed it again.

"Only really good in conjunction with another bird, but strong and reliable. Less temperamental than the peregrine. Decent at the river, good with hares."

"The merlin." This time Cesco beat Detto to the answer.

"A tiny peregrine. Good against small birds." Petruchio nodded at Cangrande. "The Capitano here used to fly the most magnificent merlin I ever beheld. Trained it for war, though, so it was no good as a hunter." Cesco raised a hand. "Yes?"

"I thought," said Cesco hesitantly, "excuse me, but I thought a merlin was a woman's hawk."

Cangrande said, "Do I look like a woman?"

Cesco considered. "Not in this light, no."

Petruchio shook his head. "Forget those idiotic appellations. Merlin's a small bird, about as big as my arm, that's all. So smaller arms can launch them. What's next?"

"The hobby," said Detto.

"He said hobbys were useless," snapped Cesco. "The goshawk."

"Ah, now, that's a fist bird—"

"Bird on the fist worth none in the bush," muttered Grumio.

With heroic effort, Petruchio pretended not to hear. "Again, good for smaller birds and hares. Maybe it won't kill, but it's strong enough to hold its prey until the dogs show up. But they're a bitch to train."

"The sparrowhawk," said Detto and Cesco in competition.

"A stubborn and unhelpful bird. This one really is a lady's bird. Also a fister – don't!" Grumio clamped his mouth shut and started humming innocently. Petruchio continued. "The sparrowhawk is a savage little bird, though, and would as soon peck out your eyes as look at you."

"The tercel!" cried Cesco and Detto together, now so intent on the game they forgot to listen.

"You want a male, if you wanted a tercel at all, which you don't. Anything else?"

Cesco and Detto looked blankly back at him.

"Your list forgets the alphanet," instructed Petruchio. "But since she always flies back to Africa whenever she feels the sun on her back, you're right to forget her. Don't ever waste your time with an alphanet. Trust me, I know."

Cangrande clucked his tongue. "Now you've done it. That's the only one our little princeling will want."

"His loss. Now boys, we have with us today a sparrowhawk I've managed to train, one peregrine, a lanner, a merlin, and pair of sakers. Up ahead is a clearing that's familiar to them all. It's where they were first aired, so it'll feel like home."

Detto looked at the trees. "Is this nesting land?"

"Indeed it is," said Cangrande. "One of my many fights with the clergy has been over a monastery not far from here. The friars were chopping down trees that had been used as nests by the local hawks. If not for their holy status, I could have confiscated their land and had them blinded. Instead I had to take the whole thing to court. I won, of course. You don't disturb a falcon's nest."

"What was their penalty?" asked Cesco.

"Money, land."

"But no eyes?"

"Of course not." Cangrande's perfect teeth shone in the summer sun. "I am generous to a fault."

"Whose fault?"

Grumio sat up straighter. "I'm sorry – do you smell a fault? I thought I was downwind."

Petruchio rolled his eyes. "Our own Aeolus."

Grumio shrugged. "I've been called worse."

"Lord Petruchio," said Detto, "what's your favourite bird?"

"O, don't force me to choose! They're like women – each with her own qualities. I actually like troublesome birds—"

"And troublesome wives," said Grumio in a loud *sotto voce*.

"Exactly!" said Petruchio, as if Grumio's comparison were actually helpful. "Peregrines are like red-heads, hot and fierce. Goshawks are blondes, but the kind of blonde that knows she's attractive, and so turns into an absolute bitch. Lanners are brunettes, good, reliable, a little uncertain."

"Listen close, boys," chuckled Cangrande. "Two lessons for the price of one."

"Girls!" said Detto, squinching up his face. "Bleah!"

Grumio instantly turned to Detto, feigning solicitousness. "Are you feeling well, young lord? It's been a goodly ride already. Perhaps, masters, we could rest for a bit – even nap under the shade of that oh-so-inviting tree. Master, the young squire looks a bit peaked, and he's making the oddest noises…"

Petruchio eyed his servant. "You, of course, could ride all through the day and into the night."

"Of course I could!" declared Grumio, thumping his chest. "I am the picture of rude health! As long as my lord wishes to ride, I shall ride! Not even a hundred blisters would keep me from my saddle! Let my legs lose all sense of feeling – as, being an honest man, I must say they have – it makes no difference! I will trace my lord's steps through the Gates of Hell or to the Court of England, whichever is farther! I only thought of the young men – you know how it is with the young, my lord. They need their rest. No, it is the old men who need no sleep! We are near enough the final sleep, and need no reminder that soon we shall sleep forever in the earth's cold embrace. My lord rides, so Grumio rides! It was only for their sake—"

"Shut up, rascal," said Petruchio. "You're in your prime!"

"So I am! Which makes you a youth, a mere stripling, though stripped from what I cannot say."

"I'll strip your back and have it striped with my lash, you crusty knob of insolence."

"If he's the knob," said Cesco, "where is the door?"

"Another insolent country heard from," said Cangrande.

Petruchio pointed. "There's the clearing, thank God. Let's dismount here and I'll show you how to air each kind of bird in turn."

"Only if you keep talking about girls," said Cesco. "I want my money's worth."

♦     ◊     ♦

The entire morning was taken up with the flight of birds. From tamest to wildest, Lord Petruchio set each into motion, pointing out the differing flight habits. Then he would call the bird home, feed it a treat, and prepare the next.

"When I'm hunting, I like to air them in pairs. They respond better to their calls, and keep each other from ranging. A lanner is the best to pair the others with. She'll learn the other's good habits, and she'll break them of their bad ones. She's reliable, but uninspired."

"You never fly a lanner alone?" asked Cesco.

"Rarely. And only if she's lived her life around peregrines and gyrfalcons. She has to learn to be wild, whereas they're wild by nature. Temperamental isn't always bad."

"I'll remember that," said Cesco seriously. He didn't return the look he knew Cangrande was giving him.

To the amazement of everyone save Cesco, Detto was a natural. Like all animals, the birds took to him at once, and even if his arm sagged under their weight, they trusted him. Whereas Cesco had to be careful not to be nipped. "A few more lessons and my squire will be better than me," groused Petruchio cheerfully. Detto preened, and Cesco scowled.

Cangrande laughed at the scowl. "Don't fret, boy. We'll find something you're good at, I promise. We'll start tonight with raking out the stables."

At morning's end they all sat down to eat. Two of the birds had brought back game, which joined the fare they'd brought with them. They ate around a firepit, some ways off from the airing ground.

From his place behind his master, Grumio pointed. "Master, what kind of tree is that?"

"It is a Damned-Be-Fools," replied Petruchio. "It's the place where we hang men of idiotic dispositions who always ask stupid questions."

"Then I'm glad I have this belly, sir," replied Grumio sagely, patting his stomach, "for those limbs wouldn't hold me."

"Keep eating like you have and your horse won't hold you."

"I've barely touched a morsel this whole day."

"You filched that rabbit's leg not five minutes ago."

Grumio's eyes grew wide. "God save me if I did such a thing!"

"Yes, pray to be saved, because your time is soon coming."

"I've not an enemy in this world."

"Perhaps, but you're not that young anymore."

"While my master stays the picture of youth. Even your grey hairs try to look blond."

"Wretch!" Petruchio scrambled to his feet and swung a fist.

Grumio ducked and backed away. "Master, pardon! I mean you're going grey by trying to look blond!"

Petruchio kicked the groom's legs out from under him, sitting Grumio down hard. "Ass!" declared Petruchio, dusting off his hands. "You're lucky if you have three hairs left to turn grey."

"Too true." Sighing, Grumio removed his cap and stroked his bald head. "My pate's as spare as my tool is long. Consequently, I have to make relations with my wife from the next room."

"That must be hard," mused Cangrande. "Never sure if you're coming or going."

"Hard it is. Hard as the day is long, and long as the day is hard."

"Are we back to women?" asked Cesco. Detto made puking noises.

Cangrande looked to Grumio. "He does need a lesson, doesn't he? Because it's the men are hard, not the women."

"But," said Cesco, "as I understand the mechanics, the men grow hard for women."

"Unless you're Grumio," said Petruchio, settling into his seat again. "Then you're hard for horses."

Grumio bobbed his head. "It's true. Makes for damn awkward riding, I can tell you. Pardon my language, lord," he added.

Cangrande replied, "If you'll pardon my squire's lack of sophistication. He's not very worldly yet."

"Takes time, sir, it takes time. Not everyone is as fortunate as we are, to be born with *savoir faire*. O!" he cried, shifting his weight. "Pardon, masters. That hare gave me the windigalls something fierce! Ooh! Allow me to remove myself." Bowing, he crept away to stand by the horses, making the other servants frown as he passed.

"You're quite lucky to have him," said Cangrande.

"Aye, but don't tell him I said so," replied Petruchio ruefully. "He's the best groom in the land, and his wits keep me sharp. Even if he has made my oldest girl a trifle coarse."

"Nonsense, she is an ideal young lady. Not demure or coy, but strong-willed like her mother. I tell you, Petruchio, if I were younger, you'd have a match."

"As high a compliment as there is," said Petruchio with a salute.

"Maybe I should meet her," said Cesco. "Isn't she about my age?"

"A year or so younger," said Petruchio. "And you're both too young to marry, no matter what Capulletto does. You must first thrive, young Cesco, before you wive."

"Were you forced to marry your Kate?"

Petruchio chuckled. "Rather, I forced my way into her heart. Though she tells a different story. Wooing is a game, and you two boys should play for lesser stakes before you try it. Which is why," said Petruchio slowly, anticipation in his eye, "starting tomorrow, you're going to learn how to woo a hawk."

"A skillful segue," admired Cangrande.

"Thank you. Boys, at the Capitano's suggestion, each of you is going to pick out a red hawk – that's the term for an inexperienced hatchling. And you're going to train it. You'll soon learn that every falcon is a lover. You have to know the best way to woo her. Some respond right away, fall for you and are eager to please. Some play coy, but all they want are treats and a little petting. And then there are those hellkites that fight you every step of the way. Those are the most dangerous, but also the most rewarding. Because once she's tamed, she's yours forever."

Cesco was practically bouncing up and down for the challenge. "How do you tame a bird like that?"

Petruchio stroked his beard. "Eager, eh? Well, like most birds, you keep her in a place removed from home, a place she's not used to. You keep her away from her food and never let her rest. Loud noises all through the day and night. Then you keep her busy – don't let her fly, or she'll escape."

"How do you keep her from flying?" asked Detto.

"A hood is the common way. Though with some birds you have to sew their eyelids shut. You keep all this up for as long as it takes, and every once in a while you offer her a little kindness – a mouse, a hunk of meat, a compliment. Soon she's doing anything you want for that mouse, that compliment. Pleasing you is the only thing that matters. That's when you take the risk and air her. If she comes back, she's yours for life."

"And if you judge it wrong?" asked Cesco. "If you air her too soon?"

"Then she flies off, but not before taking a nip at you. It's happened to me a couple of times. They're always the hardest, because you spend the rest of your life cursing them and worrying about them all at once." Petruchio stood and dusted himself off. "All right. Stand up. This afternoon we'll try you both on launching and recalling a bird. Then you can watch as the Capitano and I do a bit of real hunting."

"And our hawks?" asked Cesco.

Cangrande said, "When we get back to the palace, you may choose. Or, rather, let her choose you."

♦   ◊   ♦

Later, while Cangrande and Petruchio were off hunting, Detto drew his horse close to Cesco's. "That was exciting!"

"You did well," said Cesco sourly.

"The merlin was just in a bad mood. Not your fault."

"Mmm." Cesco was fussily stripping off the hard leather glove that stretched from knuckle to elbow, protection from razor-sharp talons.

"Not that I'm complaining, but any idea why this is our first lesson?" asked Detto. "I mean, why not swordplay or horsemanship? Why falconry?"

The furrow in Cesco's brow altered from angry to pensive. "I'm not sure. It's been much friendlier than I expected."

"Yeah, we weren't even made to clean or cook or scrape after them the way some squires are."

"Oh, I'm sure that's coming. But today was like a holiday, almost."

"Is that bad?" asked Detto.

"I don't know. I can't shake the feeling that it was a message of some kind."

"Message?"

"Maybe a threat. A gauntlet thrown down, some kind of challenge. But for the life of me I can't figure out what kind." Instead of being put out by his lack of understanding, Cesco looked delighted.

Detto made a face. "Oh, good. Another puzzle. Let me know when you've solved it."

Cesco nodded, brow still furrowed. "As soon as I see the pieces."

# THIRTY-SIX

*Vicenza*
*Wednesday, 7 August*
*1325*

"YOUR HONOUR, it was just after noon. My father and I had supped at home, and we were walking from our house, past San Matteo, towards the Porta Altinate when there was a commotion behind us. Some kids were pelting our servants with clods of earth. It was silly, but a nuisance, so my father sent me back to take care of it. But the brats had been paid to create a distraction—"

"Your honour!" objected the advocate. "How does the witness know the boys were paid?"

"Signor Dente, do you have any proof that they were paid?"

"They told me," said the witness. "Later, when I was beating them for their part in it."

"Your honour," said the advocate, "the confession of a beaten child is worthless! He'll say anything to stop the beating!"

"He also showed me the coin he had been given. It was fresh from the new mint, no wear at all."

"That's hardly proof, my lord judge! The child could have stolen it!"

"Your point is taken, advocate. The witness may continue."

It was just after dawn and already the heat was rising. In the witness box, Vitaliano Dente was fanning himself, and several of the lawyers had begun loosening their gowns.

At the head of the room, Special Consul Ser Pietro Alaghieri sat refusing to make any concession to the weather. His deep crimson gonella remained laced, the long cap remained straight on his head, its tail trailing down over his right shoulder.

This was the fourth case Pietro had heard in the last three days. He'd wanted to whet Justice's wheel a little to test his mettle before taking up a case he had a stake in.

The arrival of a consul – a judge – from Verona had been hailed as long overdue, and on his first day Pietro had created a sensation by ordering the drawing of lots to see which case would be heard first. Usually matters were heard in order of social status. At once he was popular with the people, less so with nobility.

Two of the first three had been local matters, the other a Trevisian exile looking to have justice for his dead son, killed while being evicted from their estates. Pietro dealt with each of these with quick, decisive judgments, pleasing both plaintiffs and defendants with his alacrity, if not the decision itself. Most men had to wait weeks while the judge weighed the various bribes in offer – what was worth more, that bag of gold, or that parcel of land? Did the plaintiff's cow still give milk? Was an interest in the defendant's wool business enough to warrant an acquittal?

But Pietro did not even entertain the offer of a bribe, causing him to be both admired and reviled. Admired by the poorer people who always lost such cases, reviled by the lawyers who were now forced to practice actual law. After only three days in the judge's throne, Pietro was feeling virtuous.

Until this morning. Dente had drawn the proper coloured stone from the water jug, so his case had to be heard. Pietro suspected Dente of bribing the clerk, but it didn't matter. The witnesses had been ready, and Pietro had begun the proceedings.

Owning qualms about condemning a man *in absentia* – even Marsilio da Carrara – Consul Pietro had done what he could as a sop to his conscience. He'd appointed one of the brightest lawyers in Vicenza to represent Carrara's interests (something he was not, by law, required to do), and the man was doing his work splendidly. This was no show trial – or, if it was, it didn't look like one. Pietro was giving the defender a great deal of leeway, more than he afforded the plaintiffs. Gaining a confession through torture was standard practice, and therefore one obtained through a common beating must be accepted as well. But Pietro had listened to the lawyer's objection, and promised to take it into consideration.

Vitaliano Dente continued the tale of his father's murder. "Well, I ran back up the street to stop the clods of earth from flying. Our servants were all hiding their heads or chasing the kids. I had just got ahold of one of them when I turned and saw my father. He was being held by three men, all the servants of Ubertino da Carrara—"

"How do you know this?" demanded the defending advocate.

"They were wearing Ubertino's livery—"

"Which they could have stolen!"

"— and Ubertino was with them," finished Vitaliano.

The defending advocate opened his mouth, thought better of what he had to say, and resumed his seat. Pietro said, "Go on."

"Ubertino and his right hand, Tartaro da Lendinara, faced my father. Tartaro handed Ubertino a knife and—" Vitaliano's jaw became tense as he forced out the words, "— and yerked him."

"Where?"

"Here, under the ribs," said Vitaliano, pointing to the left side of his own chest.

"You saw this with your own eyes?"

"I did," said Vitaliano.

"When did this happen?" asked Pietro.

"The seventeenth of June. Four days after the feast of Sant'Antonio."

"What has happened since then?"

"Ubertino and Tartaro were banished from Padua, and their heirs to the third degree."

"By whom?" asked Pietro.

"By the podestà, Napoleone Beccadello of Bologna."

"My lord consul," said the defending advocate, standing, "we are not here to dispute these events. Detestable as it was, the murder of Guglielmo Dente has already been addressed by a Paduan court of law. As the witness freely admits, the men responsible have been exiled from their homeland, their property forfeit to the state. I cannot understand why we are wasting your honour's time with this."

"My lord," said a voice from the other side of the aisle, "if you'll allow me to call another witness, I will show that this foul murder was planned by the whole Carrara family, not just Ubertino." The voice was smooth, and quite rehearsed. It emanated from Paolo Dente, natural half-brother to the deceased and the man with whom Cangrande wished to conspire. Built like a spindly chair, too thin by half, he had a cocky half-smile and a glint of righteous indignation in his eye.

"This is a matter for the Paduan courts!" declared the defense.

Pietro nodded. "The advocate for the defense makes a good argument. Why have you brought charges before this tribunal? Why not raise these charges in Padua?"

"We are appealing to the justice of the Imperial Vicar of the Trevisian Mark," said Paolo. "We tried to bring our case before the representatives of Heinrich of Corinthia, but they told us they couldn't be bothered."

*That's probably true.* The German garrison in Padua was there as a defense against Cangrande, nothing more. "Call your witness."

Nico da Lozzo sat in the gallery looking bored. Around him were several men that Pietro had come to know this last week. These were the Maltraversi of Castelnuovo and the Schinelli of Rovolon, Nico's kinsmen, former Paduans who had defected with him years ago.

There was another oddly familiar face in the crowd today, a man in Franciscan friar's robes. Pietro was sure he had never seen the old man before, yet this face was reminiscent of one he knew. Who was it that this man reminded him of?

Paolo Dente cleared the matter up when he said, "Abbot Gualpertino, will you come and give testimony?"

Gualpertino Mussato! Brother of the poet laureate of Padua. Pietro knew Mussato, having both fought against him in battle and dined with him after. His ecclesiastic brother was more renowned for his skill at swinging a mace than reciting holy writ. When the holy man took his place before Pietro, Dente asked, "Father, what light can you shed on the death of Guglielmo Dente? Were you present for it?"

"I was not." For a poet's brother, his speaking style was remarkably blunt. "I was at Innsbruck, as were all the other Paduan leaders. Except the Carrarese, who remained behind."

"Why were you at Innsbruck?" asked Dente.

"I was part of a Paduan delegation sent to beg aid of Heinrich of Corinthia. I was sent on that errand by the Podestà of Padua, Napoleone Beccadello. He has since told me that he sent us all on the orders of Marsilio da Carrara."

Dente feigned shock. "Why did the Podestà obey an order from a common citizen?"

"Marsilio da Carrara is no common citizen. At the death of his father, he inherited great riches and even greater power. He wields massive influence. There are many Paduans loyal to him, more than to our current German overlords. There are only a few men in Padua willing to oppose him. Most of them were sent on the delegation to Innsbruck. But Guglielmo Dente was not. His was the loudest voice raised against the Carrarese family, and he was deliberately kept in Padua in order that he might be murdered."

"How do you know this?" demanded the defense.

"Because Podestà Beccadello wept as he confessed. As a man as well as a penitent. I don't mean to imply he was a willing party to this murder. He was Carrara's tool. Beccedello told me in no uncertain terms that Marsilio da Carrara sent the rest of us away so that Guglielmo Dente might be murdered when his friends were absent."

The defense made an impassioned argument, pointing out yet again that the murderers had already received justice. But Dente argued that, by exiling Ubertino and Tartaro, Paduan law had missed the organizer of the plan: Marsilio. "For Lord Carrara is wily. He used his cousin to remove a rival, then used that deed to banish the cousin from Padua. It is my family's wish to have a judgment at law against everyone involved in this foul act!"

This time Pietro took extra time considering the evidence. He had to be certain his own prejudices were not swaying him for or against. But according to the law, Abbot Gualpertino's testimony was absolutely damning. He returned his decision before noon. Marsilio da Carrara was guilty of the murder of Guglielmo Dente.

♦     ◊     ♦

"We needed this," said Gualpertino candidly. "There has to be some justification at law, some pretext, no matter how slight, for us to overthrow Carrara."

"Even if it's Cangrande's law that gives it," added Nico da Lozzo with a grin. "Delivered by an excommunicant judge at that."

Nico, the abbot, the two Dente, and Pietro were all sharing a flagon of wine in Nico's Vicenzan house. Though it struck Pietro as vaguely improper for a judge to drink with the plaintiffs of a case he'd just decided, there were certainly no rules against it.

In response to Nico's wry smile, Gualpertino shrugged. "The irony isn't lost on me. But I would endure more than accusations of hypocrisy to see Padua whole again."

"Blame your fellow Paduans," said Nico. "It's not the foreign wars, it's the in-fighting!"

Having endured several days of it, Pietro was in no mood to hear yet another of Nico's dissections on Paduan politics. To the abbot he said, "And the fact that the judgment came from me won't taint it?"

Gualpertino patted Pietro on the shoulder in a fatherly way. "In some eyes, perhaps. But you have a reputation for being scrupulously honest – even your excommunication is spoken of well. You have no idea how much the Ravennese admire you for standing up to the pope for them. And in Bologna your name is uttered with high regard. My brother says what your father was to poetry, you will be to the law." Seeing Pietro's embarrassed flush, the abbot did him the favour of tempering his praise. "Your only flaw is that you share your father's love of the Greyhound!"

This was truer than the abbot knew. Unable to hint at that secret, Pietro said, "Who doesn't love Cangrande?"

"Anyone who has read my brother's play," replied Gualpertino enthusiastically. "If they have the wit to see the warning."

"Play?" asked Nico.

"*Ecerinis*," said Pietro.

The abbot was visibly pleased. "You know it?"

"I heard about it. But when I went to purchase a copy—"

"— it wasn't there. Yes, your beloved Cangrande suppressed it. Or rather, he bought all the copies he could find. We don't know it for a fact, but we suspect him of having them destroyed."

Pietro hadn't heard *that*. "But he promised to pay for it to be produced! I was there!"

"Oh, he did! A stickler for his word, your Capitano. But he hired a troupe of actors known for their skill in comedy, not drama. A crew of patches, clowns and fools all. And he had it performed in a closed court, for my brother and a few Veronese only. A gesture of spite, but it paid Albertino a greater compliment than he knew. The Scaliger fears this play. Such is the might of the playwright's pen! It can raise fools and bring low princes!"

"Where is your brother now?" asked Pietro.

"Still in Innsbruck. I hurried back after the murder, but he stayed to finish what is indeed a vital chore – the removal of these Germans from our midst. Or at least the cessation of the taxes. Why do you ask?"

"I'd like to thank him personally for his kind letter at the death of my father."

"I know Albertino viewed it as a great loss. It's a miracle that your father was allowed to finish his great epic."

Pietro gave a non-committal nod, then changed the subject. "Tell me, how does a fierce Paduan patriot come to conspire with Verona against his countrymen?"

"I'm not conspiring with Verona. I'm here with a Florentine judge, a wayward son, and two honest and true Paduans. I don't see the tyrant of Verona anywhere."

"Because you choose not to," said Nico wickedly, pricked by the wayward son comment.

"I am a true Paduan. We do not believe in rule by one man, be he emperor, king, or capitano. The fact that Il Grande da Carrara was ever elected to such a post is a disgrace. And he was a far better man than his nephew, who in turn is far superior to his cousins. This is the problem with heredity in a nutshell – there's no telling what the next generation will bring!" The abbot flexed his beefy hands, reaching for the sky. "And I mean to fight with every ounce of my strength until Padua is once again in charge of herself, ruled by a council, and free from the spectre of war!"

"Hear hear!" cried Dente.

Nico applauded. "Oh, Abbot, how I have missed your sermons. *Patavinitas* above all! But, sadly, this isn't to the point."

Dente nodded. "He's right. Abbot, we've got what we wanted. Carrara is condemned at law. Will you and your brother now join us?"

"It depends," said the abbot, "on the date you choose for your uprising. Albertino doesn't travel as quickly as once he did."

Pietro had been at the battle where Albertino Mussato had broken what seemed like every bone in his body, trampled by a horse. The fact that he had lived at all was a miracle, let alone his retention of all his limbs. Bailardino's brother had lost an arm that day.

"He doesn't have to be there," said Vitaliano Dente. "All we need is his support when it's over."

"That, you'll have," said the abbot with certainty.

Nico leaned forward eagerly. "Who else will be in this?"

"Marco Forzate and Traverso Dalesmanini. They've been in voluntary exile for six years, but they still have pull in the city. And the son of my late friend, Maccaruffo da Maccaruffi."

"An old friend of Cangrande's as well," observed Nico, smiling still.

The abbot shrugged. "I have friends my brother would not like. No man is just one thing."

"Here's the real question," said Paolo Dente. "Does Cangrande mean to help us? I don't mean to say this little tribunal hasn't given us an air of legitimacy, and we appreciate it. But it can't be all he sent you here for. There's an offer."

Nico looked cagy. "I believe there might be."

"Before we hear the carrot," said abbot Gualpertino, "I'd like to hear the stick. If he's asking to be our overlord, we don't need his aid. We already have one bleeding us dry."

"He wants what you want," answered Nico. "The removal of all Heinrich's men."

The abbot was unimpressed. "So that he might more easily overwhelm us. What else?"

"Nothing," said Nico airily, then amended, "Well, not nothing. It's a trifle, hardly worth mentioning."

"Please mention it."

"He would like me to be restored to the rolls of Paduan citizens, and given a place on the city council."

"Hmph!" snorted the abbot. "I can't say we've missed you all that much! And how clever! Cangrande is nominating his puppet to the Anziani!"

Nico's eternal smile became a shade darker. "Now Abbot. One

thing you must know about me by now – have I ever followed anyone's advice but my own? Cangrande knows it, and still thinks me smart enough to see that the war between our two cities must end. It can't last forever! Right now Padua is losing. Don't you think it would be helpful to have someone around who can treat with the Greyhound?"

"It's a small enough price," said Paolo Dente to the abbot. He gave Nico a sidelong glance. "Provided that he's offering us real help."

Gualpertino nodded. "Very well. What is your master willing to offer?"

"As much money as you need and as many arms as you can carry. But no men."

Paolo and Vitaliano looked angry, but Gualpertino nodded. "That is as it should be. This is a Paduan matter. There can't be a mass of Veronese pouring in. This needs to appear as it is – a civil revolt against the Carrarese. If foreigners and exiles begin to threaten the walls, the Germans will come to Carrara's defense. Whereas if this is an internal uprising, they'll stand on the walls and watch. That means, Ser Nicolo, you cannot be a part of this."

"Oh, you're not keeping us out of this fight!" laughed Nico with a dismissive wave.

"You can't—!"

"Don't waste your breath, abbot. You're not your brother, men don't flock to hear you express a fart. And don't look so bothered! We won't ruin your uprising. We'll wear, I don't know, fake beards or something. But nothing will stop us from wiping Carrara's eye. Aren't I right, Ser Alaghieri?"

Without warning Pietro was confronted with the unexpected. *Go into battle?* It had been years, but there was no denying that he was far better trained for it today than he had been then.

No, it wasn't the risk to his life that gave him pause. *If anyone learns that I was among the attackers, Cangrande will disavow me. He will swear that he gave no Veronese knight permission to attack Padua during the truce. And it's even true. Nico knows he's disobeying a direct order. He just doesn't care. And he doesn't have nearly as much at stake as I do.*

*But if we do go in disguise, no one will know I was there. And Carrara will already want me dead for the judgment I just passed on him. Most important of all, if we can conquer Padua, that's one more city that will come to Cesco when he inherits Verona.*

"Pietro?" Nico was demanding an answer.

Slowly Pietro nodded his assent.

# THIRTY-SEVEN

*Verona*
*Tuesday, 27 August*
*1325*

IN THE WEEKS after the Capulletto ball, Verona resembled an ongoing festival. At a moment's notice all work would cease and the populace would throng the streets to cheer some new wrinkle in the saga of the Greyhound's Heir.

Not that the heir was in the city much. Nor was he with the troops. Without a major war to fight, Cangrande's army remained active by hunting down roving highwaymen, building roads, and training. There were a few minor skirmishes with rebellious towns, but those were handled by Castelbarco or the Nogarola brothers. Cangrande's army saw very little of their commander, and the city saw him even less. When he did appear, it was with Cesco in tow, both looking tired, both in seemingly good spirits. And the people would flock to see them both.

Soon Cesco's novelty would wear off and life would return to its usual ebb and flow, but for the moment the people of Verona were enjoying having an assured future.

Certainty was lacking in Suor Beatrice's life. She was slowly acclimating herself to Verona's nunnery, where as another house's novice she was eyed with kindly suspicion, neither fish nor foul. She took comfort in the hours of observance. Up at Matins, three hours before dawn, then again two hours later for Lauds. Prime came with the dawn, starting the day of work. She returned three hours later for Terce, and at noon for Sext. After noon there were only three divisions, None and Vespers being three hours apart, with the final Compline two hours after the latter. And then to bed for personal prayers.

The ritual was soothing, much needed in her current state. Unsure of how to pass her time, she returned to the familiar. Between the hours, she taught the sisters the value of an income derived from copying. The scandalous nature of women writing was quickly forgotten as money started changing hands, and soon she was again in charge of a few women of good eyesight and steady hands. Many of the sisters were unable to read, so Antonia's time was greatly taken up overseeing their work as they produced a bible for their first client, Guglielmo da Castelbarco.

It was fortunate that Suor Beatrice had so much to occupy her daylight hours, because Antonia Alaghieri spent her nights in sleepless concern. She began each night in prayer, and slept only when fatigue overwhelmed her. Her days she kept filled to overflowing, so that no trace of her worries could interrupt her thoughts.

She hadn't seen Cesco since the day Pietro had left the city. Not once. And the stories made her fear for him. Not for his safety, exactly. In the field with Cangrande, Cesco at least was protected from overt danger. But if the tales filtering back to the city were true, Cesco was his own worst enemy, always attempting some stunt to out-do his teachers. *At this rate he'll burn out like an over-used lamp.*

She was also concerned for Cesco's other protectors, each for quite different reasons. Morsicato's wife hadn't recovered from whatever malady was afflicting her – though Antonia wondered if Esta wasn't faking some mysterious illness to get her husband's undivided attention. It wasn't beyond imagining.

But if she prayed to ease Morsicato's suffering, at least she knew enough to plead her case. If the Moor was suffering or not, she had no idea. No one had heard from him. He was not within the city walls, was not traveling with Cangrande and Cesco, nor was he with Pietro in Vicenza. Had he gone? Had their rejection of him been so devastating that he'd simply packed up his bags? Did he fear they would betray him to some papal inquisitor and have him put to death?

Antonia refused to believe he had abandoned them. Even if he feared those things, Tharwat al-Dhaamin would never leave Cesco. Which meant that he was about some specific task and no longer trusted them enough to share it. Antonia felt the proper amount of shame, tempered with the knowledge that what he had hidden from them was indeed monstrous.

*An Assassin! Thank God Gianozza doesn't know,* thought Antonia. *She'd be thrilled and shout it from the rooftops.*

Lastly, she prayed for her brother. The reward Cangrande had dangled was indeed what she had prayed for all this last year. But she felt certain the Scaliger's promise meant nothing. And though her brother had downplayed the danger, Antonia knew that even if Marsilio da Carrara did not discover his part in the Dente conspiracy, the judicial condemnation alone would be enough to make the Paduan demand Pietro's life. Had she known he planned to risk life and limb himself, her nerves would have been stretched past breaking.

These worries gnawed at her innards, made her stomach roil throughout each night. So she worked all the harder to stay occupied during the day, hoping to wear herself out.

On this particular day late in August, she was busy teaching letters to a few of her better pupils, all a great deal older than she, when the bells for Compline sounded. Quickly she set aside the book she was teaching from and joined the others as they gathered to intone psalms one hundred twenty-eight through one hundred thirty, sing the daily Compline hymn, and listen to a chapter from Ecclesiastics. Then a second hymn before the abbess recited the final prayer:

> *We beseech thee O Lord that the*
> *glorious intercession of the ever*
> *blessed and glorious virgin Mary,*
> *may protect us, and bring us to life*
> *everlasting. Through our Lord Jesus*
> *Christ thy son: who liveth and*
> *reigneth, God, with Thee, in the*
> *unity of the holy Ghost, world*
> *without end.*

Suor Beatrice mentally translated the Church Latin easily, unlike some around her who recited the words by rote. Her father had been certain the Italian he spoke in his life was the same as that uttered by Virgil, and that it was the church that had altered the true tongue of Italia.

Antonia recalled Cesco challenging this, as he'd challenged all of her father's assertions. Though it had infuriated Dante that the boy of six or seven had more languages than a middle-aged poet, they'd still enjoyed each other so much. If only he had known that the boy was the Greyhound he'd alluded to in the first canto…

Lost in thought, she almost missed her cue for the chorus of "Amen."

"*Domine exaudi orationem meam,*" said the Abbess.

"*Et clamor meus ad te veniat,*" replied the chorus.

"*Benedicamus Domino.*"

"*Deo gratias.*"

They made their obeisences and left the chapel for the open air of the yard. The structure of the nunnery was articulated around a square courtyard with a garden. Peaked roofs of orange clay tiles angled down from above. The common halls were located on the ground floor – rooms for eating, meeting, teaching, and healing. Beyond the north walls there was a large kitchen-garden extending up to a high and thick stone wall that was the boundary of the property.

The entrance to the upper complex was on the west side of the building, a single set of doors atop a stair. This led into a greeting room on the first floor, separate from all other rooms and leading back down to the yard on the ground floor.

The individual cells were one floor up on the south side. These rooms were accessible only by two means – the stair leading to the yard, which led right up to the Abbess' chamber, and through the church.

Antonia was housed on the opposite side. Scaling the flight of steps to the guest wing, she glanced out of the narrow slit window. It was already dark, the stars bright above. Below, girls her age and older were crossing the yard. They hadn't taken the stair from the church, but had chosen to enter the chilly dark outdoors one last time this day, chatting and checking this or that vegetation.

It was this time of day she was loneliest. She was used to sleeping in a long room with six beds, attached to another room with six more. There was a warmth to such company that no book could ever replace, something she had never understood as a child. She'd dreamed of a cloistered life as one long pursuit of knowledge. Now she knew there was more, and wished she could return to Ravenna to experience that sense of belonging again.

But the wish never became a prayer. It was a selfish desire. She had work to do here.

Quite used to the dark – candles were expensive, as her own Abbess let them know nightly – she entered her cell without striking a light. She moved about this way and that, removing her outer clothes, fiddling with her shift to open it at the neck – even at night the August heat showed no sign of relenting. There was a window even narrower than the one in the yard, but she kept it shuttered. Birds flew in by day and bats by night. Better to rest in darkness, undisturbed.

"You must have eyes like a cat."

Antonia gasped. Instinctively, she took a step for the door.

"Shhh! Don't call out. Now is the hour that turns back the longing of soldiers and melts their hearts. It would be a shame to disturb them."

Hearing the deliberate misquote of her father, she relaxed. "I should have known. How did you get in?"

"The windows are narrow," said Cesco, "but so am I. Moreso now than when you last saw me, I'm afraid. I don't suppose you have anything to eat?"

"I'm sorry, no," she whispered, closing her door. "When did you get back?"

"Tonight. There's something in the offing. Whatever it is, Cangrande had to come back to plan it. Maybe it's a war. I hope so. I'll have to actually be a squire for a couple of weeks."

"What are you now?"

Cesco's chuckle was as dark as the room. "His hawk. His hound. His horse. His ass."

"You said you're hungry. Isn't there enough food in the field?"

"For him, yes," said Cesco. "For me, no."

As she started to light the taper by her bed, he said, "Don't bother. You wouldn't like what you saw."

"Are you ill?"

"Perfectly well. Only tired." He stifled a yawn. "I slipped out of the palace. No doubt tomorrow I'll be punished past enduring. But I needed a reprieve."

"I can go to the kitchens," said Antonia.

"Don't trouble. I'll steal some bread before I return to the slave-driver. I just wanted a familiar voice. A familial voice," he said almost wistfully.

Antonia had never heard him sound so – lost. "What's he been doing to you?"

The boy managed a weak laugh. "Hawking me."

Drawing him to sit on the only furniture in the room, her bed, Antonia took his hand. "What do you mean?"

"I'm his new falcon. It's amusing, really. He wanted me to know it. I am a new toy, a knack, a beast to be broken. He's tamed hundreds of birds and hounds, I suppose it's what he knows best."

Antonia grew more anxious with each word. "What is he doing to you?"

She felt him shift his weight to lean against the wall. "He's wearing me down. I know the method because he cheekily had it demonstrated to me. Lord Petruchio has been showing me how to break in a new bird – you starve it and don't let it sleep."

"And that's what the Capitano is doing to you," said Antonia dully.

"A month with him, and I think I've slept and eaten enough for a week. I'm off for days at a time, first with this lord then with that, receiving instruction. Castelbarco for horsemanship, Passerino or Bailardino for swordplay. Bonaventura not only instructs me in hawking but also in axe-work and hunting – though sometimes dell'Angelo takes me out for bigger game. The moment one is done with me, I'm fobbed off to the next. At the end of each day, Cangrande has me hunt for our food, his and mine, long after all the other foragers have run the easy game to ground. I bring back whatever I can find, cook it, and he eats it, sharing just enough to keep me from starving."

"My God," whispered Antonia.

"No no. Knowing what he's doing only strengthens my resolve. My real nourishment, as it were."

Antonia felt tears in her eyes. "And the other lords – they don't feed you or let you sleep?"

Cesco patted her hand. "You think they know what he's up to? Not from me! No, if I told anyone they'd slip me food or order me to bed down for a night. That's why I can't. He'd win."

"What about Tharwat or Morsicato?"

"Haven't seen hide nor hair of them."

"Well, the doctor is busy tending his wife."

"And Tharwat?" He sounded casual, but she could hear eagerness in his question.

"We don't know. He's disappeared." *And that was our fault.*

"Just like that monstrous old man, to vanish when I actually need him."

She wondered if it was the Moor he needed, or the hashish. "What about Detto?"

"Oh, he's fine! Busy squiring for Petruchio. I see him sometimes at night, when we're taking our hawks out in their hoods to get them used to us."

"This is dreadful!"

"They don't mind the hoods, really."

She made a playful punch at his arm, as she had a hundred times before. But this time he flinched and recoiled. "Sorry. I'm all over bruises."

"Does he beat you?"

"Absolutely. Just not the way you mean it. He spars with me every night, late. Last night I had to fight him blindfolded, the better to learn how to fight in night battles. Needless to say, he was the victor. I always lose. He wants me to break. It's what he's waiting for."

"You make it sound like he's your enemy," said Antonia.

"Not an enemy. A Nemesis. But I've heard of squires treated much worse than this. He never lifts a hand to me except in training, and he's really quite polite. An interesting conversationalist, too. I don't mean to worry you, truly. I just wanted a night off, is all."

"You're more than welcome," said Antonia. "But you say he'll punish you?"

She felt him shrug. "One becomes accustomed. Besides, I'm here already, so I may as well enjoy my time with you."

She reached up to stroke his beautiful curly hair, only to find it gone. "Oh Cesco..!"

"Shamed, starved, and shorn. I can almost like it. It is certainly easier to keep, and the Scaliger is right, it's more practical. But it's the impracticality I miss. That, and getting it in my eyes." He curled into a ball, his head in her lap. "But enough of me. Tell me about your life here. Why don't they let you join the others? They don't think you've got a lover?"

As Cesco laughed at the thought, Antonia heard a step outside her door falter, then keep on. *Damn*, she said inwardly. There was nothing to do but ignore it. This was far more important. She was at last fulfilling her purpose here, providing a haven for her little boy. Who for once was behaving like a boy instead of a prodigy, in need of compliments and affection and comfort.

That brought to mind another little boy. "Oh, Cesco, before I forget, I have a message from Montecchio's son. He wants you to come and play."

"Romeo?" Cesco chuckled. "Tell him I will as soon as I'm done playing with the Capitano." He yawned and Antonia said, "Do you want to sleep?"

Cesco snuggled in against her. "Soon. It's just nice to sit and listen."

So she talked about trivialities, about daily life in the convent. She described Fra Lorenzo's gardens and told him about teaching the other sisters to copy. "Oh, and I've become a frequent guest of the friars at the Chapter Library. There are more books there than I have ever seen in my life. Scrolls dating back a thousand years, and translations from Arabic texts that must have come from the ancient Greeks. I've hardly scratched the surface of what's there, but I found some plays and poems I've never heard of before. I'm trying to figure out who wrote them. And letters, lots of letters."

"From whom?" asked Cesco sleepily.

"I've been focusing on the poems."

"Naturally. Your father would be proud that you haven't entirely given up his passion."

"He'd be more proud of you," said Antonia. "I know I am. And Pietro, more than he can say."

She was brushing his short hair with her fingers, the way she had when he was smaller. There was a slight tremble under her hand and she realized that he'd begun to cry. Silently, but she felt him shaking. Then he drew in a single raggedly audible sob. She clutched him tight, saying nothing for fear of shaming him. She made sure her own tears were silent. Eventually he fell asleep in her arms. She fell asleep as well, propped awkwardly upright against the corner of the wall, Cesco's head in her lap. It was, perhaps, the closest she had ever felt to him.

When the Matins bells rang she woke and found him gone. Reaching the chapel, she knelt in the aisle and moved into her row. She joined in the first prayer of the new day.

*Ave Maria, gratia Plena; Dominus tecum: benedicta tu in mulieribus, et benedictus fructus ventris tui Jesus. Sancta Maria, Mater Dei, ora pro nobis peccatoribus, nunc et in hora mortis nostrae. Amen.*

As her head came up and she rose to her feet she felt the disapproving gaze of the abbess on her. *She thinks I have a lover,* thought Suor Beatrice with an inward sigh. *Well, let her. If I sacrifice my reputation to give that boy one night of ease, it's a price I'll pay, and gladly.*

"*Domine labia mea aperies,*" said the Abbess.

"*Et os meum annunciabit laudem tuam,*" said Suor Beatrice in unison with the others.

"*Deus in adiutorium meum intende.*"

"*Domine ad adiuvandum me festina.*"

*And Lord,* added Suor Beatrice, *haste to help him as well.*

# V

## PRISONER IN TWISTED GYVES

# THIRTY-EIGHT

*Padua*
*Tuesday, 17 September*
*1325*

FOR TWO DAYS Pietro had been sitting in a Paduan inn not far from Vitaliano Dente's house. With him were Nico da Lozzo and his fellow expatriates. They had all ridden into the city separately using assumed names, and refrained from intermingling except in the common eating area, where they played at dice or chess as strangers. Avoiding each other would have been as obtrusive as hiding in their rooms.

Pietro was supposedly a Florentine alum speculator for a syndicate of Nice dyeworks. The choice of city was a whim. He'd passed through Nice thirteen years ago and had liked the city. An Italian working for foreign interests was no great novelty, so he attracted little attention and less respect.

Nico, however, was thriving in his disguise. Unlike Pietro, there were many in Padua who might recognize him, so he'd spent the last month growing his beard and taking care to be neither clean nor respectable. He played the part of a pilgrim traveling to Brindisi, the launching point for the Holy Land. He'd considered playing a leper, but the goal was to remain in the city, and inconspicuous, and a leper would achieve neither.

Remaining unrecognized was hardest for Nico's two friends, whose departure from Padua was far more recent. Maltraverso and Schinello were disguised as horse-traders fallen on hard times. Of the pair, Schinello embraced his part with more gusto, describing his fictitious decline so tediously that no one wanted to listen. It was, Pietro reflected, a perfect way to wear a disguise – tell everyone everything about yourself in the most pedantic way, and no one will think you have something to hide.

Of course, the easiest thing would have been for the four of them to pretend to be friars and stay with Abbot Gualpertino, but this way, even if one of them were found out, the others would have some modicum of safety.

Pietro had taken a page from Schinello's book and started asking if anyone had been looking for him. "I'm supposed to meet a man here for some business. I'm in the alum trade."

"You don't say," replied the innkeeper in complete disinterest.

This morning he'd come downstairs to the common room just before dawn. Spying the innkeeper, he opened his mouth, only to have the fellow answer without being asked. "No, no one looking for you."

"One more day," said Pietro in frustration. "If the fellow doesn't show, I'll go further south and try to find him."

The innkeeper said something under his breath and continued laying out new rushes. Pietro stepped on the fresh straw and made for an open space on the bench.

Nico was already there. "Beautiful day, isn't it?" His pilgrim was unrelentingly cheerful.

"The sun isn't even up yet." Pietro's alum merchant liked to goad the pilgrim.

Schinello and Maltraverso joined them, demanding, "Is breakfast ready?"

The innkeeper shook his head. "Not for another hour. Stove refused to take a light."

"But I'm hungry!" cried Schinello.

"You still haven't paid for last night's meal!"

"Well, I'll pay for it when I've had my egg!"

"And when will you pay for the egg?" demanded the innkeeper.

"Tonight, when I get my dinner!"

Pietro rose. "If it's going to be that long, I'll take a walk."

"A wonderful idea!" exclaimed Nico, also rising. "We can watch as light spreads over God's creation."

Pietro made a face. "If you're coming, I'm not going."

"We'll all go," said Schinello. "Maybe we can find an inn with a decent stove."

"Fine," snarled the innkeeper to their backs. "I wish them luck of getting you to pay!"

As the four conspirators emerged into the pre-dawn light, Pietro looked around. "Where to?" he said loudly.

"Let's go this way," said Schinello with indifference, setting them on the road to Dente's house.

Pietro had never been to Padua before, and before leaving Vicenza he'd asked Nico to draw him a detailed map. "It would be nice to know where I'm going."

"So go out! Explore!" Nico had said. "It's not as if you'd be recognized!"

"Really?" Turning his head to show his profile, Pietro had addressed Nico's two friends. "Who does this look like to you?"

"Dante," said Maltraverso.

"Yeah, Dante," agreed Schinello.

Nico had been dumbfounded. "Dante never looked like that! He wore a beard!"

"You know that because you met the man," Pietro had replied. "But he always shaved when someone was taking his likeness. More Roman. People who've only seen his portrait stamped into the pages of his books think he looks like me."

"You should grow a beard."

"But then I'd actually look like him!" A horrifying thought.

"Whereas now you look like what people think he looks like." Nico had laughed. "Scylla and Charibdis." But he'd drawn the map.

Pietro was now running over Nico's map in his mind. That church would be San Matteo, which made this the very road on which Guglielmo Dente was murdered. But they were heading away from the spot itself, angling north back towards the house Vitaliano had inherited from his late father.

A high wall surrounded it, almost butting up against the external city wall. Padua was a city surrounded by water, an island in the middle of rivers. This was the true reason the city had been able to resist Cangrande for so long, its natural defenses. The Paduans had built their walls just above the riverbanks, enclosing almost the whole island, except for a jutting spit to the north.

What surprised Pietro was how similar Padua's architecture was to Verona's. Brick, rose marble, columns, crenellations. He could lift any castle or home and drop it into Verona and it wouldn't look out of place. Was the reason for the war the similarity of the two cities? Was it envy? And who was envious of whom? Was one copying the other? It was impossible to say.

Dente's house was inside the wall, near the bridge that led to the small Roman arena on the river's far side. The password ushered them in, and Pietro had to admire the preparations. From outside it sounded as if a few men were working with an anvil. But through the thick door, the wide yard teemed with nearly a hundred men arming or praying, and doing so in commendable silence.

It was agreed beforehand that none of the Dente would speak to the four outsiders, so as not to single them out. Instead the quartet sought out Abbot Gualpertino, who greeted them roughly, saying, "My sons." At first Pietro thought it was a holy blessing, then noticed two burly men behind the abbot that bore him a striking resemblance. One of the ecclesiastical bastards shoved tunics into their arms.

The condition of their participation was that, while Schinello and Maltraverso could ride, he and Nico could not. They had to mingle with the common men-at-arms. Schinello and Maltraverso had never betrayed their country, they had only gone into voluntary exile to protest the rise of the Carrarese. So their return would be a beacon. Whereas Nico had most definitely changed sides, spending the last ten years fighting his brother Paduans. And Pietro was known to be the Greyhound's creature. So they would fight among the anonymous foot, or not at all.

Pietro had agreed despite his qualms. His right leg made running difficult. He'd always done his heavy fighting from the back of a horse, where he could adjust the saddle to compensate for his leg. But as long as he wasn't wearing heavy armour, he thought he could manage.

Pietro stripped to the waist and put on the Dente livery. *Why am I always fighting in disguise? Does that make me a coward?* Over the tunic he wore a gambeson, a short tunic sewn in vertical stripes, each one stuffed with tallow and cloth. It might not deflect a stab the way a chest plate would, but it could blunt any swinging attack.

The most important piece today was the helm. He couldn't wear a fancy affair that hid the face, it wasn't in keeping with his role. But he did have a fine round helm with a chain mail coif that buckled under his chin. There was a nose bar as well, so chin, nose, and forehead were all obscured. All that could be seen of Pietro's face were his eyes and mouth, hopefully enough to keep Marsilio from recognizing him. *Though if we succeed I won't have to worry if he recognizes me or not.*

He was handed sword, knife, and gauntlets. Someone offered him a large club, but he refused it. Though pretending not to be a knight, he couldn't bring himself to carry anything but a sword.

Not that this sword was particularly good. It looked rather chewed on one edge, as if someone had been hacking at a stone wall. And the wire binding the grip was coming apart. He turned to Gualpertino. "Is there another I could use?"

"Beggars, choosers." The abbot hefted his famous mace, flexing his arms and swinging it by his side.

The abbot didn't want him here, and this was only one more inducement to make him quit before things started. But Pietro wasn't leaving, and he refused to carry a weapon liable to break. Ramming the point of the toothy sword into the earth, he reached to the abbot's belt and drew the Gualpertino's own sword. Beautiful, thick but perfectly balanced, with enough nicks to show it was battle-worthy, not enough to make it look weak.

The abbot grasped furiously for it, and one of his sons made to pin Pietro's arms. But Pietro simply said, "Whose money?"

Angry, Gualpertino waved his son off. Cangrande had paid for the weapons, so it was only fair that Cangrande's agents carried the best of them. Amusingly, the abbot refused to take the chewed blade still sticking out of the earth, instead stealing someone else's.

Pietro turned to see that Nico had chosen a quarterstaff rather than a sword. "I like the balance," Nico explained. "Besides, I'm a little bastard, and on foot I'll need a longer reach. Speaking of little bastards, I saw your boy a few days back."

"You saw Cesco? How is he?"

"The Greyhound's running him ragged, to be sure. But he's whole, and still smart as a whip. Wants to know what we're up to together." Nico chuckled. "Nothing slips past him."

"Don't speak," growled Gualpertino as he passed by, the long mace cradled in his arms like a child.

Pietro was reassured to hear Cangrande and Cesco hadn't killed each other yet. Antonia had written about the 'hawking' and Pietro was sure the boy was pushing himself hard to prove his merit. Neither could maintain that pitch forever, and he wondered which would be worse – if Cesco broke first, or Cangrande.

Pietro heard a rustle and saw Paolo Dente mounted on a fine stallion. Despite his thin frame, in his armour he was almost passable as a leader of men. Flanking him were Vitaliano and Gualpertino.

Dente gave no speeches. Everyone had their instructions. Surprise was the key, and surprise was only achieved in silence.

The main gates opened and the mounted men started out into the street, to the surprise and horror of passersby. Taking his place beside Nico in the crowd of Dente foot soldiers, Pietro gripped his sword.

*Here we go.*

◆     ◊     ◆

## San Bonifacio

*Day forty-eight of my captivity*, thought Cesco. Early on, thinking of his squireship as a kind of imprisonment had given him ironic pleasure. Now the counting of days a simple statement of fact. The riddle of that first day had resolved itself. The message that Cangrande had been conveying was now painfully, exhaustingly, terribly clear. Cesco was just another red hawk, and Cangrande was an expert falconer.

Each day began with a ride into some unknown part of the territory. Early on they'd traveled in company, usually a knight intent on teaching Cesco some lesson. Sword practice was the most common, in various styles – on foot, on horseback, in concert, alone, with shield, without, in armour, in shirtsleeves. He'd been taught spear-work, different from his lessons with a staff, just as his lessons with a club differed from his training in mace or flail.

Sometimes he excelled, having been taught the rudiments of this or that by Uncle Pietro and the Moor. But those two were amateurs compared to the men instructing him now. Each teacher was chosen for extreme competence if not outright mastery of the lesson of the day. Cesco was often humiliated at his own lack of ability.

Hardest of all were the wrestling matches. Small and lithe, Cesco could often twist away from any teacher's grasp, but he lacked the strength to pin an opponent for any duration. Without fail those lessons ended with his face in the muck, pinioned while a friendly voice told him what he had done wrong.

But even more humiliating were the horse lessons. His skill in a saddle was beyond compare, but not in armour, nor in strictly regimented martial moves. He preferred to improvise, resulting in a serious chastisement regardless of whether he succeeded or not. His choices quickly became fail and learn, or succeed and be punished.

All under Cangrande's critical eye.

Not that Cesco begrudged the training. Far from it. His hunger to learn was equal to the number of lessons. And he was learning to ignore his ego. It was only his body that couldn't match the pace. Each night, when the rest of the palace was asleep, Cesco was made to show what he had learned that day in private for the Scaliger. When the lesson called for them to spar, the Scaliger – older, stronger, and rested – always won.

Cangrande was not neglecting the court, or himself. Handing Cesco off to a new tutor with strict instructions as to the day's schedule, the Scaliger would oft disappear for a few hours with Tullio or Castelbarco, or simply to his chamber for some much-needed slumber.

Cesco's one respite, his single interlude of peace with Antonia three weeks before, had been repaid in the worst way. Cangrande had cancelled all their plans and taken him up into the mountains, the foothills of the Alps. Though it was summer, they went high enough to feel the chill. Then Cangrande insisted on teaching Cesco how to climb. Three days later Cesco's fingers were ripped raw and he had a gash down his forearm from a nearly fatal slip. He hadn't visited Antonia since.

Surprisingly, last week one of Cesco's instructors had been Nico da Lozzo. The lesson that day was knife-fighting, and it made Cesco wonder where the ex-Paduan had learned such low skills.

That wasn't all he wondered. Nico had come from Vicenza, where Uncle Pietro was staying. Yet no matter how Cesco pressed and goaded, Nico wouldn't tell him what Pietro was really doing there.

"Come on, you can tell me," said Cesco, leaning away from a knife-stroke.

"Nothing, really. Law. Boring stuff. Pour the wine." This was not an instruction regarding actual wine, but a memory device Nico used to teach the unarmed Cesco where to place his hands to fend off his attacker's next thrust.

Cesco raised one hand to the level of his forehead, leaving the other at his beltline. As the knife came in, Cesco's high arm came down on Nico's elbow, while the low hand gripped the wrist and drove the knife up towards Nico's own chin.

They stopped, disengaged, and reset themselves. "You left with him, so you're party to whatever he's doing."

"Since he's not doing anything, that's what I'm a part of – nothing. Offer the platter."

This time Nico was stabbing downwards. Cesco's goal was to catch Nico's wrist with the left hand, step behind Nico's right leg with his own and force Nico's knee to buckle, and use the right hand to sweep Nico's left shoulder, knocking him off balance. It was the last part that Nico referred to as 'offering the platter.'

But Cesco took it a step further. Once Nico was on the ground, he stripped the knife away. Sitting on Nico's chest, he held the knife loosely over the Paduan's breastbone. "What is he doing?"

Nico ignored the knife. "Nothing. Making judgments, hearing cases – you know, like assault, and murder by idiocy." With a sudden twist, Nico had Cesco pinned to the ground and eating dirt yet again.

The next day Nico had gone, which told Cesco the Paduan had come on Cangrande's business. Business that involved Uncle Pietro.

Uncle Pietro was an ideal judge. That wasn't the point. Pietro would never have left Verona if there weren't something going on. Cesco suspected that it had to do with him, probably trying to track down the guiding hand behind the poison. Cesco was glad someone had time to do it. He certainly didn't.

*Focus!* This kept happening to him, these sudden bouts of self-pity. It wasn't the hunger or the fatigue alone, but his awareness of them that was eating up his mind. *If only I had more of those sticky chews that Tharwat gave me! But he's gone, and they're gone with him. I'll just have to manage on my own.*

Today it was just him and his master, having ridden out from some old castle called San Bonifacio to a clearing that Cesco had never seen before, and was sure he wouldn't see again for weeks. This whole last week Cangrande had been Cesco's sole tutor. Cesco was sure there was a reason, but couldn't muster up the energy to care.

Dismounting, Cangrande laid aside his sword. "Today, we begin with falls."

Cesco had to laugh. "Prat-falls are for fools."

"Every man falls. Not every man can rise again."

"Oh goody, metaphors," sulked Cesco.

Cangrande's leg shot out and buckled Cesco's knees from behind, sending the boy to the ground. "That's no metaphor."

On his back, Cesco said, "I think I prefer metaphor."

"Again, your fostering does you no favours. Poetry is for the salon. Are you ready?"

"Ready and eager!" Giving no sign that remaining on the ground was his fondest wish, Cesco leapt to his feet and took on a wrestling stance, reciting:

> *Charon the demon, with eyes of glowing coals*
> *Beckons to them, herds them all aboard,*
> *Striking anyone who slackens with his oar.*
>
> *Just as in autumn the leaves fall away,*
> *One, and then another, until the bough*
> *Sees all its spoil upon the ground,*
>
> *So the wicked seed of Adam fling themselves*
> *One by one from the shore, at his signal,*
> *As does a falcon at its summons.*

Cangrande began to circle him, looking for an opening. "And here I thought my eyes were blue."

Cesco countered, sliding each foot across the dirt, never more than a half-inch from the ground. "My point was that in Hell, the damned are eager to get on with their torment."

"Are you telling me that you're in Hell?" asked Cangrande.

"Nothing so prosaic. Purgatory, perhaps."

Cangrande changed direction. "We can end your training at any time. You need only ask."

"Beg, you mean."

"Ask. Just ask."

"Then I guess I'm truly damned. Let's get on with this." Leaping forward, Cesco was instantly knocked flat on his back again.

Cangrande helped him up, laughing. "Never tell your enemy your intention, not even for dramatic emphasis!"

Cesco wanted to use the pause to close his eyes and rest. Instead he threw himself into a cartwheel and renewed his former stance. "Again."

♦   ◊   ♦

## Padua

Marsilio da Carrara had a headache, and that headache's name was Niccolo da Carrara. His cousin was on him at first light, badgering relentlessly about this or that. The German cavalry were complaining that Niccolo had taken one of their horses without paying. It was a damned lie, he'd won that piece of horseflesh in a bet. And the members of the Smith's Guild were grousing about the extra tax Niccolo had seen fit to levy when they were insolent to his son Giacomo. And then there was Marsilio's sister, Cutinize, who was making eyes at the stable boy. Niccolo insisted Marsilio do something about that. And when was Marsilio going to recall Ubertino?

Who would have dreamed it would come to this? Six years ago, when Marsilio's uncle had been invested with supreme power in Padua, who could have guessed the stress would kill him? Who would have imagined that, inheriting his uncle's power, Marsilio would find it a paper power – impressive sounding but effectively meaningless. He'd had to beg for foreign troops to keep Verona out, thus declaring his impotence to the world.

At last Marsilio understood his late uncle's admiration for the Scaliger. Far from loathing Cangrande, Marsilio longed to know his secret. *How does he do it? How does he hold sway over a whole nation?* A growing nation, with disparate peoples, all bound by a single man's will. Were the Veronese less ornery than Paduans? Or was Cangrande simply a better man? That thought kept Marsilio awake at night.

Walking from his palace to the city offices, surrounded by guards, clients, and other licker-fish, Marsilio felt very alone. But he made certain he looked impassive, controlled. He even waved to the commoners, who received his greetings with their own impassivity. *I don't need them to love me, but for God's sake, don't let them despise me!*

Still waving, his own sleeve caught his eye. Embroidered on it was the Carro, four spoked wheels on a tripod, the Carrara family crest. *I should have it changed to a single wheel. The Scaliger has only one ladder. He is the be-all and the end-all. Whereas I am what my crest makes me – just another cog in the family machine.*

Reaching the center of the public square, Marsilio waited as his guards cleared a crowd of petitioners out of the way. In the crush of people, someone brushed hard against Marsilio. It was the kind of thing that people in Padua died for these days. But in the throng Marsilio couldn't quite see who had done it.

There was something in his hand. The fellow must have put it there. Marsilio held up his hand and saw a scrap of paper with writing on it.

The hairs at the base of Carrara's neck began to prickle. It wasn't idle curiosity that made him read the note there and then. It was the instinct of a man who had read his history. Caesar had been handed a note and declined to promptly read it. Ten minutes later, Caesar was lying on the floor of the Pompey's theatre, pouring forth blood. The lesson was clear.

Marsilio da Carrara unfolded the note and read:

> *Arm. Dente is coming.*

Scrawled at the bottom was a rude symbol.

"Niccolo, we'd better —" He heard the sound of thunder low to the ground. He'd heard it once before, long ago, in Vicenza. That day he had barely kept his life, losing instead a great deal of pride. Forgetting the order on his lips, Marsilio began shoving men aside to run for his life. He didn't pause until he reached the mouth of an alley. Glancing back he saw the armed Dente on horseback, bearing a flag with a red cross on white field. It was a banner Marsilio had carried a hundred times, the banner of Padua. Behind Paolo and Vitaliano Dente were other faces – Giovanni Camposampiero, Schinello, Maltraverso, Abbot Gualpertino and his sons. All were shouting the same refrain: "Death to the House of Carrara!"

As his men engaged the traitors, Marsilio ran down the alley and out the other side. At first he was afraid they had cut off the square before entering it, but no, this was not a military maneuver. This was civil revolt. They were trying to murder him and rally the people in one fell swoop.

In his hand he clutched the four word note that had saved his life. *Thanks and God keep you, unknown author!* He didn't know what to think of the symbol, and didn't have time to care. Tucking the note into his shirt, he ran down the street to the first friendly house he could find.

Ironically, the first one he came to belonged to another Schinello – or rather, Schinella. But this one was a Carrara confederate. Leaping, Marsilio propelled himself headfirst over the wall and ran into the house. There he found Schinella da Dotto rising from breakfast.

"Schinella, quick, I need a horse!"

# THIRTY-NINE

THINGS WERE GOING WELL for the Dente faction. In Padua's central *piazza*, the Carrarese guards had fallen back under the surprise onslaught. Dente horsemen had broken the knot of Carrara's men, and the foot had taken them apart, disarming those who didn't insist on dying. Best of all were the cheers of the citizens, who had taken up Paolo Dente's cry, "Death to Carrara!" The coup seemed to be fact already.

Pietro and Nico cracked a few skulls, then looked about for another target, but there was no one left. "Cowards!" Nico grinned at the blood on Pietro's sword. "Thank God you aren't your brother." Poco had been a squire under da Lozzo's tutelage, and had failed spectacularly in his duty.

Pietro hadn't lost sight of their purpose. "Where's Marsilio? Did they get him?"

Nico shrugged, looking around for Marsilio's body. "Don't see him." As Gualpertino galloped past them, his mace spotted with gore, Nico hailed him. "Carrara?"

"Escaped, damn him!"

The abbot's dismay was justified. The goal had been to kill Marsilio da Carrara in the first moments of the revolt. Alive, Marsilio could rally his men. Immediately Nico said, "Which way?"

"We don't know! His cousin Niccolo ran down there," he pointed to a side street, "but Marsilio wasn't with him!"

Nico cursed and Pietro said, "Where's Dente?"

"Chasing Niccolo! You two help secure the square! We'll spread out from here. Marsilio can't be far. If he leaves the city, it's as good as ours! God knows, he has to fight now or lose it forever!"

There was a commotion down the alley where Dente had gone, and they heard the ugly music of swords meeting swords. Instantly Gualpertino swung his horse's head around towards the sound. Pietro and Nico took off after him on foot.

The mouth of the alley was a slaughter, far bloodier than the square. The Dente and their fellow knights were hacking away at someone on foot. Pietro couldn't see past the horses, but it had to be Marsilio's cousin making a stand with whatever men he had left.

Pietro had an idea. Tugging Nico's arm, he dashed right, away from the alley. Opening the first door he found, he swung his sword inside to clear anyone in his path, then barreled into the building.

Nico trotted along beside him. "Where are we going?"

"Thermopylae!"

Nico nodded. The Persians at Thermopylae had used goat-paths to get behind the defending Spartans. In this case Pietro and Nico would find the rear door to this building and come at Niccolo da Carrara from behind.

It was some sort of civic office, peopled with clerks and scribes. One brave soul came forward to protest something and Nico cracked him on the skull with his staff. That ended any attempt at intervention.

Pietro saw a large shuttered window at the back. "There!" Prying it open, Pietro stuck his head out and looked left towards the back end of the alley. Niccolo da Carrara was fighting hard, furiously swinging a stolen a pike at Dente faces. He alone had the fortitude to stand, but his men-at-arms refused to leave him.

"Come on! Let's go!" Nico pushed Pietro forward.

Pietro had one leg over the windowsill when he heard hoofbeats from his right and turned in time to see a dozen men riding for the alley's mouth. At their head was Marsilio da Carrara.

Pietro yanked his leg back inside a second before the horses crashed by. Had he been in the street, he would have been trampled under foot.

Marsilio's cousin saw the reinforcements and dove to one side, allowing the Dente forces into the open just as Marsilio's men arrived. The two sides fell upon each other's necks with screams and orders.

Pietro took another look right. Ten loyal Carrarese foot soldiers were racing up to swell Marsilio's numbers. Pietro and Nico hopped over the sill and they took up a stand.

"What was that about Thermopylae?" asked Nico lightly, then let out a war-whoop and began swinging his staff, forcing the Paduans back.

Pietro took a defensive stance to Nico's right, protecting the more exposed side as Nico used his staff to good effect. Tip and butt twirled in blurring arcs, rattling skulls and sweeping legs.

Like Nico, Pietro knew the wisdom of circular motion, and kept his sword moving in repeated *molinelli*, arcing twists and turns, the blade never stopping. By not using the tip he was less likely to kill, but outnumbered it was better to wound several than kill one and be exposed.

Engaged, Pietro couldn't look behind him. If any one of Marsilio's horsemen disengaged from the scrum at the alley, he and Nico would be easy pickings. But that was out of his hands. He had to prevent these men from aiding Marsilio. "Come on, then! Come on!"

◆ ◊ ◆

## San Bonifacio

"*Molinelli* are pretty," instructed Cangrande. "But they aren't threatening unless you can hide your intent, where the blow will finally fall."

They had moved on to swordplay, the Scaliger teasing Cesco by simply stepping back from his attacks. Cesco had responded by advancing fast, whipping his blade in circles. "So no dramatic flourishes, you mean."

"Precis—"The Scaliger was cut off mid-word by the fall of Cesco's blade towards his neck. Cangrande fended it off, and the next, and the next, before stepping out of reach. "Better. Your arm-strength is improving. Keep at it and you may be able someday to cut through something thicker than air." He wasn't allowing practice with a short gladius anymore. Cesco was now using a real longsword, as his aching shoulders testified. "Define the *molinello*, please."

"Literally, like a windmill," answered Cesco dutifully, still on guard. "It's a pivot of the blade from shoulder, elbow, or wrist, creating a circular motion, over the head, or either inside or outside the lines of attack. See?"

"Yes, you're very good at making circles in the air. Now why don't you try naming the Thirteen Guards." Without any more warning that that, Cangrande swung his own blade, bringing it across hard towards Cesco's leg.

Cesco blocked, the blow rattling all the way up his arms to his head. Obediently he named the position his hands were in. "*Porta Ferra!*" The Iron Door.

The next blow was already falling towards his exposed neck. Keeping the point low, Cesco twisted his wrists and brought the weapon up and over his right shoulder. "*Donna sovrana!*" The Queen.

Expecting another attack, Cesco wasn't prepared for his teacher to back away. Cangrande kept his blade moving, performing his own series of malign *molinelli*. "What would you say is man's greatest ambition?"

Once Cesco might have said, *Immortality.* Now his answer was quite different. "A full belly."

Circling his pupil, Cangrande looked amused. "Not a full head?"

"A stuffed head is nothing if you cannot use it for something. A stuffed belly comes—" He parried the blow before he even knew the blade was snaking towards him. "*Dente di cinghiale.*" The Wild Boar's Teeth. "As I was saying, a stuffed belly comes first."

The Scaliger's *molinelli* continued as if the blow had never happened. "I think your present existence is colouring your perspective. Man must aspire to things greater than mere survival."

"Without survival, there is nothing else."

"Does that mean that there is nothing—"

"*Breve!*" The Short Guard.

"— nothing worth dying for? This, in an age when men dream of the right kind of death."

"Is that what you dream of, death? I'm sure there are many who would be willing to oblige."

"Doubtless. But only a fool ignores death."

"Call me a fool—" began Cesco.

Cangrande lunged, but as Cesco made to guard pulled his weapon back. "Fool."

"—but I've never seen the point. Death is the necessary end, it comes when it comes."

"Ah, but when it does," countered Cangrande, "what kind of death will it be? Will it be a good death, or a bad one?" As if to demonstrate, he lunged again.

"*Coda lunga e distesa!*" Long and Stretched-Out Tail. Cesco adopted an admonishing tone. "You've been reading one of the *Ars Moriendi.*" These were the popular instruction guides on ways to die, and how to face the end when it came.

"Actually I've been thinking of penning one. But since you're the poet's pet, perhaps I'll have you write it in my name."

"I wouldn't know where to begin," said Cesco lightly. "Since I have no intention at all of dying."

"Ah, the cocksureness of youth. I once had no thought for death. But its shadow falls across every man at some time. Even you."

Now it was Cangrande who was unable to resist dramatic emphasis. The cold steel of his blade sliced the air, and Cesco was driven down to one knee as he caught the blow in a parry over his head. "*Falcone!*" He angled his blade and let Cangrande's slide down his back, then took a small swipe at the Scaliger's legs. "Falcon guard. Are you trying to tell me something?"

♦ ◊ ♦

## *Padua*

The irony was greater than Cesco knew, for at that moment Pietro was using the Falcon Guard to fend off a blow from above.

He and Nico had fared well, wounding all but three of the foot reinforcements. But the thing he had feared had come about. One of Marsilio's horsemen had seen the fighting up the street and had come to dispatch the two fools in Dente livery.

Pietro heard the clatter of hooves an instant before the sword came at his head. His own sword flicked up, a rising wall of steel. He pushed off the horseman's blade, but didn't have the reach to unseat the bastard.

To his right, Nico was fending off the remaining trio with a flurry of blows from both ends of his staff. Pietro shouted, "Nico! Trade!"

Without hesitation, Nico rolled around Pietro's back and swung his quarterstaff at the horseman's head. Pietro stepped into Nico's place and cut across one man's arm with a brutal stroke. Both the others attacked, but one seemed to fall of his own volition. Pietro parried the other's strike and stepped in close, *corps à corps*, swords joined at the hilt.

The Paduan who had tripped wasn't rising, but the one with the wounded arm laughed and raised his sword to cleave Pietro's skull. Left-handed, Pietro grabbed the arm of the nearer one and twisted it upwards, raising his own sword at the same time, so that their combined blades formed a V that neatly trapped the third man's descending blade in its crook.

Pietro hooked a knee, wresting the sword away as he fell, then spun around, swinging both swords at the last man standing. The Paduan managed to block the first strike, but the second shattered his leg.

He couldn't leave an uninjured man at their backs. Unwilling to kill a fallen foe, Pietro cracked the least injured man on the skull with the flat of his blade, then stepped on the other's broken leg. The Paduan screamed. Pietro thought he deserved thanks for his mercy.

Spinning, he saw Nico was now in the saddle, its former occupant on the ground, still. "He just fell! Not a horseman, I guess. I've always said I'd rather be lucky than good."

"Helps to be both," observed Pietro, breathing hard.

The *mêlée* in the alley's mouth was still contested, neither side winning. "Shall we?" Nico kicked his spurless heels.

Hobbling after in the best run he could manage, Pietro could only watch as Nico smashed his stolen horse sidelong into two Carrarese, clubbing one from behind, striking the other full in the throat.

Pietro felt a surge of excitement when he spied Marsilio, who wasn't even fully armoured. Nor was his horse. Damning his leg, Pietro forced himself to run harder.

♦    ◊    ♦

In the middle of the swelling, tumbling crush of men and horses, Marsilio da Carrara was hacking and slashing away, a sword in his right hand, an axe in his left. Standing in the stirrups, he fought now for more than his country. He fought for his life, his name, his honour. He fought like the Devil himself was breathing down his neck.

That sensation took on an added urgency when he heard a scream from behind him. Someone was attacking their rear. *Oh no, you won't!* he thought, wheeling his horse about to face the backstabber.

It was a limping man in Dente's livery. The fellow obviously had delusions of grandeur. He wasn't even a knight! Marsilio stabbed, twisting the blade as he did so to open a deeper hole in the idiot.

To his surprise, his thrust was easily parried and he found himself unexpectedly defending a slice at his leg. *So, you think you know something!* Marsilio brought the axe into play, beating the other's sword aside while his own sword drove in for the kill.

But the man on the ground was clever, evading the thrust. Suddenly the horse under Marsilio trembled, and he felt a painful pressure on his thigh. Looking down, he saw a sword piercing his thigh. He shouted in horror.

But his leg hadn't been the target. The sword had driven straight into a lung of the horse that carried him. *"Patavinitas!"* cried his limping attacker, twisting and tearing his blade free. Marsilio cried again, staring at the foot-soldier with angry brown eyes that looked somehow familiar.

There was no time to place those eyes now. Marsilio was injured, his horse dying. Swiping down with his sword, he dropped the axe and gathered the reins to force the injured beast's head around. "To the Piazza delle Biave! We'll slaughter them in the execution square! Everyone, follow me!"

The Carrarese turned and fled after their master, the Dente in hot pursuit.

♦    ◊    ♦

"Don't let him get away!" shouted Pietro, grimly satisfied. *Now he has a scar to match the one he gave me.* It had been a crossbow bolt fired by Carrara that had injured Pietro's leg.

Dente's mounted forces were already giving chase with sixty or seventy foot-soldiers streaming out of the open alley mouth behind them. Pietro knew he should join them, but distances were not for him, he'd get there too late. *To Hell with this!* Pietro grabbed the reins of a riderless horse and clambered into the saddle. "Let's go finish the job!" Spurless as he was, he managed to kick the steed into a gallop.

Nico pulled alongside him. "I'm glad the Scaliger insisted I bring you along!"

The world seemed to stop with Pietro's heart. "What did you say?"

Nico was full of pride. "He didn't want to order you, but he said that whatever happened, you and I had to be a part of this fight. And he was right! You almost had the bastard!" Seeing Pietro's stricken look, he added, "Don't worry! You'll get him yet!"

That wasn't Pietro's worry. *Cangrande sent me here, on purpose. Why? To kill Marsilio? Or to die myself? Which would suit him more?*

There was no time to curse or wonder. Carrara had decided to make a stand in the Piazza delle Biave, Padua's traditional spot for executions. One way or another, Pietro was suddenly sure it would live up to its name.

◆   ◊   ◆

## San Bonifacio

Cesco dashed at Cangrande, attempting to throw the Scaliger off-balance with his speed. But Cangrande did a pirouette, spinning aside and smacking Cesco on the behind with the flat of his sword. "Impatience is frowned upon."

"Here, or in the *ars moriendi?*" retorted Cesco, rubbing his backside.

"In facing a foe or facing death itself, patience is always a virtue."

"'Slow but steady wins the race?' I am horrified that you have sunk to aphorisms."

"I never said slow. I said patient. Choose your moment, let it come, then strike with all the speed you have."

Cesco's arms were almost as tired as the rest of him. "So do you aspire to a tame death, in bed, surrounded by family?"

"Having met my family," said Cangrande, "I'd rather die alone."

"What, don't we measure up?"

"You barely measure up to my breastbone." The *ting-ting* of a half-hearted pair of strikes marked a growing boredom. "No, when I die, I hope it will be in a battle of steel. Not an orderly battle, but a desperate fray in which more than life and death hang in the balance. A battle for country, or for God. Something memorable. That's the best kind of death."

"Except your death will probably damn your side to failure. Not so good, neh?"

Their sparring had taken on the aspect of a dance. In constant motion, giving and receiving light blows, it became a test of never letting the blade come to rest. They circled and spun around each other to a rhythm only they could hear, a dizzying flow of martial music they composed together at this time, in this place.

The dialogue was important as well. The second level of this trial was to continue a philosophical discussion while slinging steel. Given the subject of their talk, their impromptu ballet qualified as a true *Danse Macabre*.

"I'll tell you how I don't want to go," said Cangrande, looping his blade across his back to switch hands. "Disease. Illness strips a man of his dignity. An invisible foe that causes internal imbalance. No, if I show signs of succumbing to a pest, you have my permission to stab me right through the breast." He emphasized the statement with a left-handed thrust.

Cesco parried, then performed a pair of his own spins, the first to knock away Cangrande's blade, the second to slice at his ear. "That would be an amazing grant of trust, were anyone here to hear it. Tell me, do you feel the same about poison?"

"I would," said Cangrande, ducking, "except that you've shown that one can come out the other side. Besides, with poison, there must be a poisoner. If it was my last act, I would have them exposed and hanged."

Cesco kept the patter of swords and words alive. "'Vengeance is mine,' sayeth the Lord. What about starvation?"

"As a means of dying, it goes both ways. Self-starvation is a good death, enforced starvation a bad one."

"None of these sound appealing."

Cangrande laughed. "So don't die."

Cesco heard more than challenge in that laugh – he heard disdain. Hardly aware of what he was doing, Cesco brought both swords to a crashing halt and pressed in so that his guard locked with Cangrande's. With unexpected venom he hooked Cangrande's right knee just as Nico had shown him and pressed fiercely forward with his sword. The Scaliger lost balance, and Cesco rode the grown man to the ground.

Sitting atop Cangrande's chest, the swords bound tight, Cesco's anger dissolved as quickly as it had come. "Now may we eat?"

◆    ◊    ◆

## Padua

Marsilio's horse died just as he reached the Piazza delle Biave. Leaping from the saddle to keep from being crushed, Carrara pressed himself against a wall as the fighting spilled out into the open square. A man wearing his own colours staggered past him, bleeding from a dent in his skull. Grabbing the dying foot soldier, he used the knife at his belt to slice a rent in the man's tunic, tearing the cloth into strips to bind his wounded leg, all the while using the dying man for cover. Once the blood-flow was staunched, he left the man to die while he looked for a new horse. He had a revolt to put down.

The Piazza delle Biave was not the widest public square on Padua, but it was the most commonly used, possessing a high wide dais, an excellent place to carry out executions. Public executions were as popular here as anywhere else, and in this lawless time there were no shortage of victims. Unlike lawful Verona, which imported foreign criminals just to satisfy the crowd's lust for blood.

Limping up onto the dais, Marsilio surveyed the melee. All his enemies wore helmets, hiding their coward faces.

He spied a young red-headed Paduan atop a massive war-horse, old but sturdy, and fully barded. In fact, the beast looked far more prosperous than its owner, who wore half-armour pieced together from battlefield remnants. The impoverished red-head killed one of Dente's men, his horse biting the arm of another, leaving the man momentarily unopposed. Limping to the edge of the dais, Marsilio shouted, "You!"

The red-headed man spurred closer. "My lord? Are you hurt?"

Marsilio leaned in. Oddly, the horse looked familiar, though the man did not. "Your horse! Now!"

"My – my horse?" the red-head echoed reluctantly.

"Now!" Marsilio shoved the bastard out of the saddle and climbed into his place.

"Take care of him!" cried the red-head in desperation. "He's my only horse!"

But Marsilio didn't hear him, already looking around for the Dente. Seeing Paolo, he gave the mount the heel of his boot and it started off. Only looking down at its fine neck armour did he recognize the beast – it had once belonged to Vinciguerra, Count of San Bonifacio. How bizarre that Carrara should be riding it now against another traitor.

"My name is Benedick!" shouted the red-head, running alongside. "I live by San Tommaso! You can return it there—"

"Get away from me!" shouted Carrara as he plunged into his enemies. He blocked the sword of one, then another. Someone stabbed a spear at the horse's chest. Benedick threw himself forward and grasped it. Wrenching it free, he reversed it and began swinging it wildly before him. "Stay away from my horse!"

Two men fell, and several more backed away. Benedick's fighting impressed Marsilio, but his ferocity had the counter-productive effect of keeping enemies away from Marsilio's blade. Whichever way he moved, Benedick would counter, putting himself between his beloved horse and danger, in effect keeping Marsilio out of the fray.

Frustrated, Marsilio swung out and smacked Benedick's head with the flat of his blade. Benedick crumpled to the ground and Marsilio rejoined the fighting.

Once engaged, Marsilio became a rallying point for the Carrarese. They clustered around him, fighting hard. His cousin Marsilietto Papafava appeared on his right. Further off to the left was his cousin Niccolo da Carrara with his son Giacomo, fighting as hard as any of them. *Family. A wretched nuisance, but at least I can rely on them to fight.*

Marsilio risked a glance up at the walls. Heinrich's German soldiers stood unmoving, watching the fighting unfold in the streets. *Damn your hides!* Marsilio vowed that if he survived, he'd make every one of them pay.

But survival was becoming less likely each second. Cousin Marsilietto had just screamed as a sword had caught him full in the teeth, shattering them and breaking his jaw.

Distracted by his cousin's broken mouth, he missed the spear-thrust that caught his borrowed horse in the breast. The foot-soldier drove the haft in hard and deep, killing the beast at once. Marsilio fell to the earth for a second time. Sensing victory, the rebel forces cheered.

Using the bodies of the dead and wounded to protect his flanks, Marsilio da Carrara stabbed and hacked upwards, sword glued to his naked hand with gore. He heard a scream behind him, but couldn't break off to look. His cousin Niccolo was screaming, "My nose! My nose!" Absurdly, Marsilio laughed. *Typical Niccolo, to earn so ridiculous a wound. Imagine losing a nose!*

Then Marsilio heard Niccolo's son shouting, "Father, stay! If you quit this fight, you will never return to Padua!"

That was the truth. They had to hold. But the spirits of Dente's men were swelling, while Carrara's side was faltering. Dente's forces were closing around them, encircling them, cutting them off from any possibility of retreat. Paolo Dente himself came into view, screaming with joy, his vengeance nigh.

Throwing away his helmet, Marsilio gave a full-throated roar. "Dente! Come and face me! I dare you! Come on! Take the chance of hate!"

Hearing his name, Dente grinned and gave Marsilio a mocking salute with his sword. Spurring his horse closer, the two men fell to fighting, one high, one low.

Carrara's men closed in beside him. They sensed that this was the end for them, and were determined to bring down the man behind their doom before the eternal night felled them all.

Marsilio parried a blow from Dente's sword, then used his guard to punch Dente's horse in the mouth. The beast reared and Marsilio felt himself being flung backwards, caught by one of the spiked hooves. He landed on his side, and as he started to rise he was stepped on by one of his own men.

Lying on the ground, Carrara was reminded of a duel long ago. When he'd fought Dante's son, he'd knocked the impudent shit to the ground just like this. Marsilio wondered if that bastard Alaghieri had felt the same fatalistic certainty, the sure knowledge that his life was finished.

Alaghieri had been saved by Cangrande's intervention. Unlike now, when there was no hope of salvation. *This is not how I was meant to die! I should die at the hands of foreign foes, not my own people! What's the matter with us? Padua, you are your own worst enemy!*

*At least Cangrande isn't here to see this. How he will laugh when he hears!* Marsilio imagined the sound of Cangrande's profane laughter…

But that wasn't the sound in his ears. It was a trumpet. Whose? Over the screaming and the clash of metal, Marsilio couldn't tell. Was it the Germans, moved to help at last? Or more of Dente's men, riding in to mop up?

A hand clasped his arm, hauling him up to stand. Giacomo. There were tears in the young man's eyes. "Peraga! It's Peraga!"

Fighting mightily against the crush, Marsilio struggled to his feet. Looking around, he saw the Dente had turned to face a new threat. The loyal Giacomino da Peraga and his men-at-arms were riding into the square and mauling Dente's forces from the rear.

Marsilio threw himself forward in renewed attack, but the rebels were already pulling off to the side, out of reach. Moments later Peraga was close at hand, smiling down through the cheek-pieces of his helmet. "Sorry it took so long," said Peraga. "I only got your message after dawn."

Marsilio frowned. "My message?"

"That Dente was attacking this morning. I armed my men at once, but it took time to get here."

Young Giacomo rounded on his cousin in incredulous rage. "You knew?"

"No!" said a bewildered Marsilio. "I sent no note. It seems we have an unknown benefactor." The young man opened his mouth. "No time for that now! Peraga, can you lend me a horse? I want to be in the thick of it when we crush Dente and all his followers!"

◆        ◊        ◆

From immanent victory, the Dente faction was suddenly fighting for their lives. Paolo still tried to snatch victory, but the fresh Peraga soldiers were too much, and both he and Vitaliano were swept away from Marsilio.

Pietro and Nico had been working their way towards where Marsilio had fallen when suddenly came the rush of mounted Paduans and they became part of a full retreat. *So close!* Pietro raked his eyes over the spot where Marsilio had fallen, but couldn't tell in the throng who was still living.

A Paduan came screaming at Pietro, swinging a long-chained morning star. Pietro ducked low, letting the horrible spiked ball pass hissing and rattling overhead. At the same moment he stabbed, his sword piercing the man's hip. The Paduan screamed and reeled away.

Pietro's relief was shattered by a war cry from his other side, and he turned to see a blade driving at his breast. Gasping, Pietro froze, already imagining the blade entering his body. But the attacker faltered. Slowly lowering his sword, the Paduan took his left hand from its grip and touched his breast. Raising his hand to the light, he saw blood on his fingertips. Then he keeled over, dead.

There was an arrow protruding from the man's chest, the back end of the shaft pointing towards Pietro. He saw the fletching and felt a thrill. Black duck feathers. The fletching used by the Moor.

Pietro spun around as another man fell, dropped by the Moor's second arrow. "Tharwat!" He scanned the rooftops but there was no sign of al-Dhaamin.

Suddenly Nico was dragging on Pietro's reins as well as his own. "Let's go!"

"But Tharwat—"

"Stay and we die!"

Nico was right, Carrara's men were attacking on all sides. Pietro grasped his reins and joined Paolo Dente's remaining forces as they retreated in good order to the walls. From there they scattered, Dente in the lead.

Riding away, Pietro realized he was fleeing a battle for the first time in his life. Covered in sweat, he made certain his helmet was in place and prayed no one had recognized him.

Two thoughts kept rattling around his brain, one comforting, the other infuriating.

It was a comfort to know Tharwat had been there, watching over him. He remembered the Paduan who'd seemed to trip and not risen. And how Nico's foe seemed to just fall out of his saddle. How many other times had the Moor stepped in to rescue them without their knowledge?

But that comforting thought was drowned out by the image of the Paduans riding to Marsilio's rescue at the end. Those men had been fully armed. But they hadn't had time to arm that well unless they were warned.

*Which means we were betrayed.*

And Pietro knew by whom.

◆    ◊    ◆

## San Bonifacio

"I suppose I'm lucky," said Cangrande, cracking his mutton-bone and sucking at the marrow. "Has no one ever taught you the meaning of sparring? The goal is not to kill your partner, but to learn."

"You mean sword-fighting isn't about killing? I have so much to learn…" Cesco gnawed on a small slice of his master's mutton.

Cangrande continued as if Cesco hadn't spoken. "Still, it's a good thing your fit of temper didn't take my life. You'd have a hard time explaining that. Nor is it how I'd like to pass from this world."

"Not a good death?"

"At your hands? Definitely not. Accidental deaths are all well and good, but only in a noble cause. I'm not sure training you is noble enough."

"So an accidental death in battle is good, in regular life it's not?"

"In life it's laughable." Cangrande threw his bare bone over a shoulder. "War is the high point of human endeavor, it earns a man eternal glory."

"I think the artists might object," observed Cesco wryly.

"Really? One poet in a generation may last the test of time. The same is true of painters, musicians, sculptors. Philosophers come and go like women's fashions. And no one remembers lawyers."

"There is always *l'amour.*"

Cangrande scoffed. "Lovers are remembered only if their love is doomed – Guinevere and Lancelot, Antony and Cleopatra, Pyramus and Thisbe, Troilus and Cressida – the list is nearly endless, and again, they're remembered for how they died, not what they died for." Cangrande stood. "Which returns us to my earlier question. What is it Man desires most?"

Rising as well, Cesco chose to speak his innermost answer. "Not to die."

"A specious reply, given the impossibility."

"Let me rephrase," said Cesco. "To gain immortality."

"Yes! Now you've hit on it. And to gain it, one must start as a warrior. No, not just a warrior – a conqueror, a destroyer. A human scythe, taking down the chaff of an age."

Cesco was dubious. "Is that something to aspire to? It's that thinking led Heliostratus to his horrendous act."

"That you remember his name says it all. The Greeks outlawed it from being spoken, and in so doing they insured it would outlive them all."

Cesco considered. "So fame is the pillar of life? No matter how terrible the deed that achieves that end?"

"Fame is not immortality. Heliostratus chose an easy way – simple destruction, the cheap route to eternity. He didn't have it in him to spend a lifetime building after he destroyed. Building better than he had found. That's the real way, a man's way. To strive. Achievement matters less than the trials. Immortality is reputation, and that is not gained cheaply. I will be remembered alongside Caesar, Alexander, Arthur, Charlemagne. Men who destroyed so they could build."

Though genuinely moved, Cesco couldn't resist poking. "All those men had someone else's shadow cast over them. Their real struggle was to free themselves from that shadow. Once they emerged into the light, their own excellence could shine."

Cangrande gazed down at him. "That's very astute, monkey."

"Which means the way to immortality is to have a foe as grand as yourself, and to free yourself from their clutches." Cesco raised his eyebrows at his master. "I know whose shadow I need to emerge from. But who do you have, to strive against?"

The question gave Cangrande pause, not as if he was seeking an answer but fighting one. "I? I have one of the greatest foes in the history of man. I have myth. I must emerge from the shadow of the Greyhound if I am ever to make my name known."

"But you *are* the Greyhound!"

Cangrande was very still. "The Greyhound is a myth. He is not a man. He is legend. I am no legend, merely human. If great men are defined by what they struggle against, then I am defined by the Greyhound. For I have fought that myth all my life."

"That makes no sense at all! Everything you do is attributed to the myth, not to —" The breath hissed out from between Cesco's teeth as understanding came. "Oh, that's rich! You're right, it's horrible! You're forever denied the grandeur of your own deeds, because they will always be ascribed to your mythic stature!"

Cangrande reached across and ruffled Cesco's hair. "Now you grasp the evil shadow I live under. The Greyhound is my true nemesis. One that I mean to conquer. But enough! Come, we must resume your training."

◆　◊　◆

## Padua

It was at the end of that victorious, vindicating day that Marsilio da Carrara at last had the chance to look again at the warning note. He compared it to the one Peraga had received. The writing was identical. But Peraga's bore the scribbled crest of the Carrara family. Only Marsilio's note showed the symbol of the ladder. The sign of Cangrande.

*But how did Cangrande know about this coup? And, more important, why did he write? Why did the Scaliger save my life?*

*To put me in his debt, of course.* The answer was probably more complex, but in the end it was all that mattered. Marsilio had been saved from death at the hands of his fellow Paduans by his worst enemy. Now Marsilio owed the lord of Verona a debt of honour. He felt a thrill of dread, sure that someday soon the debt would be called due.

◆　◊　◆

## Outside Mirano

Hiding in an abandoned farmhouse while his horse took water and rested, Pietro wrote to his sister. Hands shaking as he formed the coded words, he laid before her the bald facts of the battle and its aftermath:

> *Nico and I parted company as soon as we emerged from the city. I imagine he's headed for his estates, and Paolo Dente has gone to Treville. Myself, I rode east, away from both Carrara and Cangrande.*

*I grasp now that this was Cangrande's true plan to be rid of me. He instructed Nico to bring me to the battle, having already sent a warning to Marsilio. By ensuring that Dente lost, Cangrande has earned Marsilio's good will while at the same time placing me in a cleft stick. If I return to Verona now, Carrara will mysteriously learn just who it was fighting alongside Dente. It's why I was made to pass judgment in the law case, to tie me to Dente. Cangrande will be 'forced' to denounce me to keep the terms of the truce. I'll be on the run with another price on my head.*

*He's maneuvered me like a master. Oh, he'll keep his promise to the letter – I'm welcome in Verona. But returning is a death sentence. My fault. In my wildest imaginings, I never thought that Cangrande would deliberately lose this chance to snatch Padua.*

*The one pleasing piece in all this is that Marsilio has aged. Being the head of his family is not sitting well on him. He's fatter, his hair is routed, and at thirty he looks forty. But then I haven't seen my reflection lately – I'm sure this summer has aged me past all recognition.*

*I plan to hide for a few days. If my name doesn't come up, I'll take ship south to Ravenna, and from there to Bologna to resume my studies as if nothing were amiss.*

*Take care, and be wary. Even knowing a trap was being set, I fell right into it. Stay low, don't give him cause to remember you're even alive. You and the doctor are the only ones left to look after our boy. At least we now know what Tharwat's been doing – shadowing me. I owe him my life yet again. More than I deserve.*

*Send me any news, and let Cesco know I'm well.*

*—P.*

Sealing the note and tucking it in his pack, Pietro wondered where he should go to send it. Mounting, he gave his horse its head, letting chance dictate.

The animal followed the road to a fork and there paused. Looking at the signpost, Pietro realized the answer was before him.

*Perhaps my exile can benefit us.*

# FORTY

## Venice

THE ISLANDS of the Venetian lagoon were first settled during barbarian incursions when the people of the Feltro sought refuge in the marshes. These refugees built watery villages on rafts of wooden posts, unknowingly laying the foundations for floating palaces. Exciting and exotic, Venice was a city like no other on earth.

Everywhere one encountered the seal of San Marco. The device was engraved on a dozen walls, flapping on a hundred flags and banners, and atop a pillar in the main square a stone lion held a shield bearing the Cross. Venice had forever linked its name with San Marco when the apostle's earthly remains were spirited out of Alexandria four hundred years before to rest in the aptly named Basilica di San Marco.

The Rivo Alto – or as it was commonly called, the Rialto – was the highest point in the lagoon and the natural focus for settlement. Just off the Rialto, Pietro rented a room under an assumed name. He had funds, thanks to a local Jew, cousin to Cangrande's jester. All of Cangrande's clandestine banking was done through the Jew, whose name Pietro had never been able to pronounce. But the fellow knew Pietro's credit was good, and wasn't likely to tattle – he'd lose too much business if he did.

It was the Jew who dispatched Pietro's letter to Antonia, and it was through him that Pietro received her reply:

*So far you are safe. News of the Paduan revolt spread quickly, but with no real urgency. Another squabble between the Paduans? Ho-hum.*

There were those among the Veronese who pressed
Cangrande to strike now while things were still unsettled. But
the Capitano declined, citing several reasons:

First, he said, Heinrich's Germans haven't gone
anywhere.

Second, Verona and Padua are still under a truce. He
says he needs a Just Cause to go to war and until they make
some move against Verona, he is content to let them stew.

Third, he says he has better sport in the offing. Everyone
thinks he means the coming trouble between Bologna and
Mantua - Lord Bonaccolsi is amassing some Ghibelline armies
in the south, and the rumour is that Cangrande will join him
there sometime next month. Not a very pleasant wedding present for Passerino's bride!

I confess I interpret his 'better sport' comment differ-
ently. I think he means Cesco's hawking.

I understand about you going to earth, but shouldn't
you be in Vicenza? Won't it be easy for Marsilio to note that,
after you condemned him at law, you disappeared just before
the attack?

I'm worried for you. Almost as worried as I am for
Cesco. Because you're wrong. He doesn't have two protectors left, only one — me. Esta's illness has taken a turn, and
Morsicato has taken her back to Vicenza. He's even hired a
nurse to live with them. He's wracked with guilt, of course, but
he feels he's done his part for Cesco and the least he can do
for Esta is to move her back home while she recovers.

I hear your thoughts even as I write this. But, Pietro,
Cangrande is not Satan Incarnate. Of all people, Morsicato
would be the first one to detect poison. Sometimes an illness
is just an illness.

I won't write again unless I have some vital news. As it
is, I have very little to impart. I don't see Cesco much. Though
I think life will ease for him next month when he goes with
Cangrande to Passerino's wedding. Then, if the rumours are
true and Cangrande means to field his army, he'll take up the
real duties of a squire.

All this I hear by the way. I'm taking your advice and
keeping my head down. The only gossip I've heard is about
your friend Capulletto. He's behaving strangely, not at all like
I expected the new doting father to act. He's absenting himself
from court a lot, in favour of his country estates. It's beginning

*to be said that he has a mistress there. Which, I must confess,*
*I hope he does. As long as that mistress is someone other then*
*Gianozza, it can do nothing but good.*

*Oh, stop your laughing. I'm no longer a girl, and though*
*I have no experience, I have lived long enough to see the*
*world as it is, thank you. And no, it isn't Gianozza he's*
*running around with. She's far too consumed with her son*
*to even consider a dalliance – thank God. Because I think*
*that, bored enough, she might entertain the idea just to stir*
*the pot. Not very charitable, coming from her friend. But I*
*have never ascribed to the maxim that friendly eyes don't see*
*faults. Rather we must rely on our friends to curb our faults.*
*As you have always done for Cesco, and Tharwat has always*
*done for you.*

*Take care of yourself. Don't fret about Tharwat. The*
*fact that he was there when you needed him says everything.*
*Trust him, and let him trust you again. That's all I can think*
*to say.*

*Write me a note back so that I won't worry. Without*
*you, all I'd have is Poco. You wouldn't wish that on me, would*
*you?*

— *cA.*

Pietro used the taper beside his bed to burn the letter, making sure
even the ash was destroyed. Then he lay in his bed, considering.

*She's right, I should be in Vicenza, passing judgments as if nothing*
*happened.* But being in Vicenza didn't help Cesco at all. In Venice, Pietro
could do something constructive. He could find the house of the courtesan Borachio had described, the one with the three faces.

That same day news arrived of a great Ghibelline victory in
Tuscany. On the twenty-third of September, Castruccio Castracane had
led an army against the Florentines and beat them soundly. Pietro had
no love for Castracane, the current lord of Lucca. He'd gained that title
by deposing Pietro's friend, the late Uguccione de Faggiuola. Uguccione
had been the first to welcome Dante and young Pietro back to Italy after
their sojourn in Paris. A gregarious man, he'd died six years before in
Vicenza, where he'd stayed after his ignominious exile from a land he'd
once ruled. Thus Pietro had nothing but ill will for Castracane.

But Castracane was one of the few Ghibelline leaders that could
challenge Cangrande's pre-eminence. That at least was something. While
Pietro wanted Cangrande to conquer far and wide for Cesco's sake, he
also didn't want it to be easy, and welcomed anything that pricked the

Scaliger's pride, as this victory surely would.

The Venetians seemed bored by the Guelph-Ghibelline wars, deeming themselves above such concerns. Nor were they much interested in the young man with the slight limp who wandered the streets of Venice, looking for a tripartite face carved above a palace door. It was a frustrating search. He'd expected to succeed in the first few days. But a week went by, then two, and nothing.

While so far he'd failed to find the three faces, he had succeeded in finding the tavern that Borachio had mentioned. Paradiso Perduto was a famous tavern where it was said the drinks were so sinfully good, a man wouldn't miss Heaven. It made sense that some witty fellow would open a rival tavern in the seedier part of the city that played off the fame of the other. So Pietro returned each night to Paradiso Trovato, thinking that if this was Paradise Found, he should remain excommunicated.

But there was no help to be had in the tavern. The men who had abducted Borachio were hardly likely to be here now. And asking questions would give away more answers than they received. So he was content each night to sit, sip, and watch. He saw a seedier side of life than he'd experienced until now, receiving more than a few offers by the infamous wives of Venice. Even had he been so inclined, the tales of sailor's diseases would have stopped him.

As requested, Pietro penned a brief note to his sister to let her know he was well. He followed it with a similar note the next week, and the next. Each consisted of a line of their father's poetry, but with the words rearranged in what he hoped was an amusing fashion.

In frustration one afternoon in mid-October, Pietro stopped his search long enough to browse the contents of a bookseller's shop. Naturally he drifted first to his father's works, and was pleased to see the hefty price attached. Next, on a whim, he asked to see any works by Albertino Mussato. To his amazement, the shopkeeper returned with a pristine copy of *Ecerinis*. Pietro bought it in a trice.

After his purchase, he looked at the meager remains of his purse. His funds were definitely beginning to lag. So instead of his usual fruitless afternoon prowl through the streets, he made his way towards the small section of the Rialto known as the Yellow Crescent to talk the Jew into advancing him more money.

The Yellow Crescent was a curved street only two blocks long, so called because it was where Jews plied their trade. Navigating it, Pietro couldn't help recalling Tharwat's words — *I have been the other, the alien, through all my adult years.* That was certainly as true of Jews as it was Moors.

Pietro's opinion of Jews was not that of most the world. Church doctrine clearly proclaimed them tools of Satan, far worse than even pagan unbelievers, because they had denied Christ as the savior and helped bring about his death. But since he'd been denied access to the Church, Pietro had spent a great deal of time reading the gospels and studying the writings of San Giovanni, whom the Romans called Iohannes. Nowhere could he find it written anywhere that the Jews as a people had betrayed Christ. It was Caiaphas and Judas, two men. *And we must remember that Christ, too, was a Jew.*

When he was about Cesco's age, Pietro had seen a family of Jews herded down a cobblestone street, being pelted with filth and offal. There were only two men in the huddle of Hebrews, the rest had been women, one a girl of no more than five. Pietro remembered wondering, *How can that child be guilty of Christ's murder?*

Now as he approached the tall, thin casa, he knew from experience that whatever sympathy he felt towards Jews was about to be tested. But if it wasn't fair to judge them all by Caiaphas, nor was it fair to judge them by the man he sought. Pietro mused that it would be like judging all Romans by Caligula.

There were sounds of habitation within, but no one answered the door. The master was probably on the street here, somewhere. Pietro would have to ask around. The only problem with that was that Pietro couldn't pronounce the name. According to Manuel, it was the Hebrew word for cormorant, a bird of prey unfit for food. Whether that was the case or Manuel was once again having fun at Pietro's expense, it didn't matter. It was the man's name, and couldn't be avoided.

Approaching one of the residents of the Crescent, Pietro tried once again to wrap his tongue around it. "Pardon me, *signore*. I'm looking for Shalakh."

The man flinched, though if it was the mangling of the name or being accosted by a Christian, Pietro couldn't tell. The fellow merely pointed, bowing and giving Pietro a closer look at the imposed horns Hebrews had to wear on their hats.

Following the man's outstretched finger, Pietro saw the person he was looking for. Like his cousin the jester, Shalakh was short, barely as tall as Pietro's chin. But he owned an impressive forehead over his wedge of a nose. He was well-muscled in arm and leg, slim and somewhat forbidding. Dressed in the mandatory pointed cap and well-tailored gabardine clothes, wearing a trim mouth-beard beneath his scythed nose, he was everything one imagined a money-lender to be. Only there was a humour about the eyes that entirely removed the element of villainy such men were reputed to have. He looked like a kindly older gentleman in a ridiculous hat.

Not wanting to mispronounce the man's name to his face, Pietro cleared his throat as he approached. Looking up, Shalakh's lively eyes radiated a slow amusement. "My my! Run through your funds already? Dear me, but you are a shining example of Christian charity!" He dropped his pitch a little as Pietro drew nearer. "It is a shame you must travel incognito, or else all of Venice would be singing peans to your largesse, since you are keeping so many ale-house keepers in work."

The tenor of the sarcasm was light, but Pietro was aware that the scorn was real. "I didn't know my movements were generally known."

Shalakh smiled broadly. "Are they? I merely assumed it was so. Reveling seems to be the nation's pass-time. Venice is a city overrun with publicans," he mused, playing off the word for both tavern-keeper and tax-collector.

"I will attempt to be more frugal," said Pietro.

"O, don't bother for my sake! Your credit is more than sufficient. I can draw on your funds here, or in Verona. Which would you prefer?"

"Verona, please," said Pietro softly. "It would be better if I can avoid leaving a trail."

"Nothing easier. I will draw on your master's funds, and let the banks of Verona repay me at leisure. He has more than enough lodged with me. There are not many Christians who use us as their bankers – we are more often a last resort. But then, your master is hardly average. An exceptionally practical man, the Capitano. Don't fret," said Shalakh, seeing Pietro's furrowed brow. "We are among friends. It is not the practice of my tribe to overhear the business dealings of our fellows. If we do, we are honour-bound to close our ears. Come."

They walked back along the street to Shalakh's house, where the Jew produced a ring of keys and opened the massive oak door with a hearty push. The door was deceptively heavy, Pietro knew, having been to the Jew's house twice before – once ten years before, and again on his recent arrival.

The interior was as spare as the façade, though Pietro understood that this reflected more the owner's personality than necessity. Entering, Pietro was amazed to hear the echoing sound of feminine laughter, out of place in such an austere establishment.

At once Shalakh's face grew grim. "Jessica!"

The laughter instantly stopped and footfalls sounded on the stairs. A moment later a young woman entered. Pietro had seen Shalakh's daughter on that first visit long ago, but then she'd been a child of four. Now nearly fifteen, she was a beauty. Hair as dark as a raven's down, skin an exotic olive, she was dressed as modestly as the furnishings. Yet there was something sensual in the way she moved that made Pietro blush.

Behind Jessica there ambled a young man dressed as a servant. He was as ugly as she was beautiful, covered in pimples and blemishes. He bore none of the marks of a Jew, either in his clothes or his person. Shalakh had a gentile servant? Fascinating!

Shalakh looked at them both was distaste. "Jessica, this is a client. Fetch him some refreshment. Launcelot, since you are so fond of entertaining that you shirk your duties, you may stay with him while I see to his business." To Pietro he said, "The same amount as last time?" Pietro assented, and Shalakh stumped up the stairs, not needing to hold onto the rail. Vigourous for his age, though what age Pietro couldn't guess. He'd looked just the same ten years ago.

Because her father had not named him, Jessica did not ask for an introduction. She merely curtsied and headed for the back of the house, leaving Pietro facing the servant. When he thought the old Jew was out of earshot, Pietro said, "I hope my visit hasn't fouled your day. I didn't mean to trouble you."

The servant shrugged. "No trouble. My mistress is fond of wordplay, and I amuse her while I go about my duties. Though my name is Launcelot, I have no pretensions to being a great lover. I believe my master hired me for my features, and has since repented that a mind came with it."

Already Pietro felt himself warming to the lad. "Launcelot?"

"Launcelot Gobbo, after my father, who is Old Gobbo."

Ah, that explained it. Being the son of a cripple, this Launcelot had to take ignominious work. *Gobbo*, of course, meant hunchback. On an impulse, Pietro said, "Perhaps you can aid me. I'm looking for a house – a certain house I have heard of."

The servant's eyes twinkled under the folds of pock-marked skin. "Would this be a woman's house?"

Pietro had no trouble looking embarrassed. "It would. The only mark I know it by is a three-faced masque, over the door." Pietro described it as well as he could. "I have spent two weeks wearing out my boots looking for it, but without any luck at all."

Launcelot tilted his head, quivered, and Pietro thought the fellow was about to sneeze until he burst out laughing. "Oh my lord, you do not understand Venice! You are looking at doors leading out onto our paved streets? I confess, in any other city that would be the logical kind of door to examine. But not in Venice! Here in the Serenissima, the most serene city, the real streets are the canals! The doorway you're looking for most probably leads to the water, not to the pavement."

Launcelot had not come right out and said Pietro was a fool, but the implication was there. And he was right! Hadn't Borachio said his abductors had trundled him into a gondola and punted to the courtesan's house?

Pietro thanked Launcelot just as Jessica returned with a cup of wine – rather good, Pietro noted. At once he changed the topic, asking politely after Jessica's mother.

The girl dipped her head, and Launcelot supplied the answer for her. "The lady Leah died two years gone. A tremendous sadness for us all."

Pietro offered his condolences. He'd met Shalakh's wife long ago, and knew that Jessica inherited her looks from her mother. Certainly she looked nothing like her father – except about the eyes, bright with intelligence and scorn. But where Shalakh's guile was obvious to anyone, Jessica worked hard to tamp hers down. Probably why she spent so much time with her head lowered.

Shalakh returned with a draft for a hundred Venetian ducats. Given the current exchange, this was slightly better than the same number of Florins, but not much. Pietro knew that he wouldn't cash the draft in gold, but in silver, a more every-day coinage. Yellow money was extravagant, memorable. Black money, copper or bronze, was next to useless, only good for gratuity or cheap labour. White money – silver – was the most generally accepted.

But it wasn't the banker's draft tucked in his doublet that had Pietro whistling as he departed the Yellow Crescent. It was the thought that he had a new avenue of inquiry. Or rather, new canals.

After withdrawing enough white money to survive without becoming a target for theft, he leapt into the nearest gondola for hire. "Show me all the famous courtesan houses of Venice!"

The driver grinned, tugged his forelock, and used his long pole to shove. He was bemused by the fact that his passenger only wanted to look, not stop at any of them. To each his own!

On the second day he saw it, just as Borachio had described. On a narrow twisting side 'street' was a small quay with three stone steps leading up to a door. Above the door were three faces, all attached. One laughed, one screamed, one wept. The shutters on the windows looked oriental, and on the house just next to this one was a trellis covered in pink roses.

Pietro turned to his gondolier, a different fellow from the day before. "Whose house is that?"

"Ah!" cried the driver, leaning on his punting stick to slow their progress. "That is the casa of Donna Dolfino. Unless you are a rich man, she is not for you. And perhaps not even then!"

"Exclusive, is she?"

The driver misinterpreted Pietro's suppressed excitement. "It is said that perhaps God has enough gold to tempt her, but not for more than an hour."

Tipping the gondolier well, Pietro returned to his lodgings and paid the due. He then returned to that curved canal and hired a new room just across from Donna Dolfino's house. He made sure his window faced the short flight of steps that led to the door under the three faces – the same door Borachio had been ushered through three months before.

Setting up station in that window, he wrote a quick note to Antonia describing both his discovery and intention:

> Simply, I mean to wait. If the man who blackmailed Borachio is indeed Venetian, he will likely visit here at some point. Especially if the place is as exclusive as my gondolier hinted. If that plan doesn't work, I will pretend to be a client, though I don't think I am adept enough at dissembling to maintain the guise for long (Oh, are you blushing? Your own fault! You set the tone!)

The letter sent off to Shalakh for posting, Pietro opened his single saddlebag and removed the manuscript of Maestro Mussato's play. Sitting beside the window so he could see the comings and goings of the courtesan's casa, he settled in, looking up at every gondola that passed. It made for choppy reading, but also ensured that he would not finish the famous screed against Cangrande too soon. He was determined to enjoy it.

The story began with a mother talking to her two sons, describing the hour of their conceptions:

ADELHEITA
Was there a mighty, blood-stained star ascendant
In the north, whose baleful rays struck me alone
When I conceived you wretched boys in that
Accursed marriage-bed? Now shall I reveal
The wiles of your deceitful sire, distraught
Mother that I am. The earth refuses
To hide for long a crime. Secrets will out.
Now hear your lineage never to be denied,
Children of doom...

Adelheita then began to relate how, sleeping beside her husband, Satan came and impregnated her. But she fainted in the middle of the telling, and her older son, Ezzelino da Romano, demanded she awaken and finish the tale. Ezzelino's eagerness to hear the Devil's part in his heritage damned him from the outset.

In keeping with the Senecan style, Mussato's description of Adelheita's rape was vividly explicit. It wasn't just the graphic nature of the violation of Ezzelino's mother that disturbed Pietro. The description of an earthly upheaval, of an angry sky echoing the roar of a growing sulfurous chasm below, brought to Pietro's mind another night.

He had not been present, nor had he ever heard a full account. But the night Cesco had been born there had been several portents – the greatest being two stars descending and crossing in the night sky. One boded ill, the other good. Unconsciously the play evoked a picture of that fateful night. Was it indeed a mighty, blood-stained star ascendant? Or was the second star more powerful?

Pietro read at the window all through the day. At night, when a light would make him conspicuous, he closed the manuscript and sat in the darkness, watching the rainbow procession of painted gondolas below. He went to bed at dawn, hoping that the customer he waited for was not an early riser. *Early riser.* Dropping into sleep, he chuckled. *A pun worthy of Cesco.*

The next afternoon, the sixteenth of October, Pietro was in his perch with the second act of the play, reading a really delicious description of Verona as Hell-on-Earth, the enemy of Peace. Most of the story was told through messengers and the chorus, not through action. Pietro was amused to see several references to Mariotto's family, the Montecchi – though, in the text, it was Monticulti. And there was the heroic Count of San Bonifacio, grandfather to the Count that Pietro had struggled against long ago.

His eyes never left the quay for very long, but he was so engrossed in one passage that he almost missed a gondola angling towards the quay. This was only the second visitor of the day, and the first had not matched Borachio's description. Setting aside *Ecerinis*, Pietro squinted across the canal. Nor did this one. He was certainly fashionable, and the masque he wore to protect his identity was obviously expensive. But not even in his boots could he be called tall.

Pietro returned eagerly to the play. Ezzelino and his brother were rapacious conquerors, quite unrepentant. Indeed, in just about every speech Mussato had them reveling in their lineage, claiming it to be higher than Mars, the father of Romulus and Remus. In one shocking passage, Ezzelino himself repudiated Christ. A few pages later he claimed to be God's instrument to bring divine justice to the earth. Pietro could see why Cangrande had been so upset by this play. As an allegory for his own person, it was quite vicious.

In the late afternoon light, things began to unravel for Ezzelino. Amusingly, his undoing began in Venice, where a great force marched out to meet him. One of Ezzelino's soldiers, Ansediusis, arrived with ill tidings delivered in a series of short, staccato lines, powerful in the plain Latin:

> ANSEDIUSIS
>> Padua's lost. Our enemies hold it.

> EZZELINO
>> Lost by force?

> ANSEDIUSIS
>> Lost by force.

> EZZELINO
>> What force?

> ANSEDIUSIS
>> The sword, and flight, and fire. The way all cities fall.

> EZZELINO
>> But you survived? Your face, unscarred,
>> Shows me an enemy! It demonstrates
>> Your guilt. Away with you! To punish you
>> With death would be too easy a penalty!

This section resonated, perhaps because the punishment was exile. An exile himself, Pietro understood the pain of never returning home. Feeling a tear welling up, he winked it away. *You're ridiculous! Imagine, weeping over a play!*

Just then he noticed another gondola poling up to the steps of the courtesan's palace. This one had several men in it, and for a moment Pietro was shamefully speculative. But only one alighted. He was tall and graceful. And though his masque hid his hair as well as his face, Pietro recognized him at once. *That bastard!*

Ducking, Pietro waited until he was sure Donna Dolfino's customer was within doors. Then he bolted from his perch and out of the house.

He had to run three blocks before he found an arched bridge that would take him over the thin canal. He'd spent his evening hours considering how to enter the casa unseen. The only sure way, he'd decided, was to climb up the rose trellis on the next building over and from there leap into a window. Fortunately Venetian houses were jammed in beside their fellows, sometimes with hardly shoulder-width between them.

Reaching the rose trellis, he pretended to stop and smell the flowers, glancing covertly around. No one was watching. Ignoring the thorns, he gripped the wooden slats. Sturdy enough. Abandoning caution, he planted a foot into one square opening and began the ascent.

Venetian architecture was much influenced by the returning Crusaders of the last few centuries. Eastern ornaments and pediments adorned many houses. Donna Dolfino's windows bore the onion-top, the small crown favoured in places such as Constantinople and Jerusalem. Though thin, there was more than enough room for a man to pass, the onion-top being the right size for a man's head to pass through.

It was a cool day, but not cold – the oriental shutters were open. Reaching the right level of the trellis, Pietro didn't hesitate. He stepped onto the sill, turned his body sideways, and slipped through the window into the courtesan's house.

Crouching low, he listened. Kitchen sounds from below, the usual background hum of a busy household. Then he heard a rich feminine burble of something like laughter, only more musical. A man's voice answered it. A voice Pietro knew. *I was right. It is* him.

The voices came from the next floor. Pietro crept up the nearby staircase, pushing through wafting curtains to reach it. On the landing he paused again, looking at the area above. A double-door of delicately carved wood stood ajar, leading to a room that faced the canal.

Blood pounding away with a combination of exultation and anger, Pietro ascended to the top of the stairs. *Now what? Listen at the keyhole? Hide and wait? What would Cangrande do?*

The answer was obvious. Steeling himself, Pietro rose from his crouch, pushing the doors wide, strode into the room in his best imitation of nonchalance.

On a canopied couch-area were two figures. One, the lady of the house, was in a state of undress. She was atop her visitor, her long blonde hair falling down the length of her back, all the way to her bare buttocks. Her head came around and she frowned, though she showed no sign of embarrassment. "And who might you be?"

Ignoring her was difficult, but Pietro fixed his eyes on the man beneath her. He still wore shirt and doublet, though both were unlaced. His points were all undone and his hose lay pooled at his ankles. The *bauta* masque lay on the couch beside him, leaving the face of Francesco Dandolo as bare as his mistress' backside.

Breathless, Pietro smiled darkly. "Ambassador. Is this a bad time?"

Then the world went dark.

# FORTY-ONE

San Bonifacio
Friday, 1 November
1325

"WE WILL HAVE to take a brief hiatus from your hawking," Cangrande informed his young charge. Fingers stained with ink, the Scaliger had clearly been occupied with legal matters.

Exhausted from a day of riding with Lord Montecchio, attacking targets from horseback, Cesco clumsily fetched a bowl of water for Cangrande to wash in. "Do you mean my training, or the rearing of my own little hawk?"

"Both. Tomorrow we go to Mantua. Passerino is marrying the Estensi girl, and we must honour him. And it looks like the Bolognese might come out of their shell to fight for Modena once again. It won't be much of a battle, but just the right thing to cut your teeth on, my little puppy. Whoops! Forgive me, I forget – no dog nicknames for you."

Dead on his feet, Cesco was in no condition to match Cangrande's verbal sparring. Instead he asked a practical question. "Who is Bologna fighting against?"

"Really, us. But technically Ferrara owns Modena – the leading man in Modena is the father of the Lord of Ferrara, Rainaldo d'Este. Though no friend to me, Rainaldo is an ally of Verona and about to be tied in marriage to Passerino, another ally. I'm related to them both, through marriage."

Cesco had been trying to learn the family tree. "Your eldest sister, Costanza, was married to the bride's grand-father, and then later to the groom's brother." Reciting this gave him an excuse to close his eyes.

"Well summed! But what matters most is that the city of Ferrara is marrying the city of Mantua. Now go and pack my bags. We're due there tomorrow to take part in the obverse and reverse of life — wedding and warring. Now, show me what you learned today."

Cesco kept his sigh within himself. *So tired. I should fly. At the wedding, when he's not looking, I should slip away and run to Venice, or Ravenna, or Rome, or Paris, or even London. Even hawks get aired and have the choice of flying off or returning to the falconer.*

*But the master only airs the bird when he's sure it will come back. Cangrande won't let me out of his sight until he's broken me. Which means I haven't broken yet.*

*Nor shall I.* Opening his eyes, Cesco picked up his sword.

◆        ◊        ◆

## Venice

Midnight. Pietro could hear the tolling of church bells. They were the only way to mark time. His cell had no window, not even a slat in the door to see light by. Total darkness.

Not that he was alone. There was a barred opening in the center of the floor, the canal's water flowing just a hand span beneath. Too small to admit a man, the gaps in the grating were just large enough for rats to squeeze through. They swam along in the water and came up to visit several times a day. Pietro wondered if it was the same set of rats, or new ones every time.

The bells were the only sound he could hear above the lap of the water, echoing around the small stone chamber. Worst of all, the sucking and rushing sounds just below him gave rise to horrible imaginings. In his mind's eye he pictured the city's water rising, flooding his cell and drowning him. He wondered if that was what Dandolo was waiting for.

He'd been in this eternal darkness for — what, fifteen days? Sixteen? Ever since his rash attempt to surprise Dandolo *in flagrante*. He hadn't known the lady had her own set of guards, nor that he'd been seen watching the house on the first day.

*What was I thinking? What I should have done was write a letter to Antonia. To Cangrande, even.*

His interview with Dandolo had been brief. The day of his arrest, the Venetian ambassador had asked if anyone knew where Pietro was. Pietro had lied, saying that soon it would be all over the Feltro. Immediately Dandolo had ordered Pietro clapped in irons and smuggled into the prison beneath the Doge's palace in San Marco's square.

Solitude gave him time to think. At first he had wrestled with the problems at hand, and the greater question of betrayals and politics. Huddled in cool darkness, he had considered every fact he knew about the poisoning, turning each one over in his mind like pieces of a puzzle. And he had made some startling shapes out of those pieces, until something like a mosaic appeared before mind's eye. The mosaic was of a human face, a man that Pietro knew and liked. He had no proof, of course, only inference. But he was certain he was right.

And there was nothing he could do about it.

Worse, there was time to consider his own part in the drama of the last few months. Slowly, inexorably, his disgust in himself grew. Thinking of the threat to Fra Lorenzo, he felt shame. Remembering his dealings with Borachio, he wanted to weep. His part in the Paduan uprising, viewed in hindsight, was wholly shameful.

Cangrande liked to mock Pietro for his unerring morality. But that morality seemed to have left him. Or else, been perverted.

*I am my own man,* thought Pietro bitterly. *And I do not like the man I have become. Nor can I blame Cangrande. If he opened the door, I didn't have to walk through it. A man is responsible for his actions, if not his stars.*

The most damning part was the attempt to surprise Dandolo. Ill-conceived, impulsive, foolish, yes. But the worst part was that, when looking for a model of behavior, he'd chosen to emulate a man he reviled.

*And why do I revile him? What was it Abbot Gualpertino said? 'No man is just one thing.' Maybe the truest words I've ever heard. Cangrande is not a monster — he is a man. With flaws, yes, but also strengths. And I? I am not the ideal knight everyone says I am. I became so obsessed with the Scaliger, I started to behave as he does, think as he thinks. Would a true knight behave as I have?*

The answer was as painful as it was certain.

Pietro was startled by the sound of a heavy bolt being slipped. His cell door swung open on its creaky metal hinges and he was ushered out, blinking even at the dim light of the stone corridor. Hands shackled before him, Pietro was marched between four of the Doge's guards out of the basement prison and up the stairs to the palace proper.

He was shoved to his knees in the middle of a room paneled in carved wood. The thick panels were not only decorative, they deadened sound. This well-appointed room was for secrets and interrogation.

There wasn't a stick of furniture by him, not even a stool. He was meant to answer questions from his knees.

Across the room the occupant of the Doge's high-backed wooden throne ordered the guards to depart. Francesco Dandolo had forsaken the doublet for this interview, wearing instead the long rust-coloured *gonella* of the senator, with his gold senator's ring flashing in the candlelight.

Dandolo waited for the doors to close before speaking. "Ser

Alaghieri, the Doge has consented that I be the one to interrogate you."

Pietro tested the waters. "I would prefer to speak to the Doge himself."

The Venetian shook his head sadly. "Impossible, I'm afraid. He is otherwise engaged."

"Does that mean the Doge doesn't know you ordered the death of a child? Or does he not care?"

"Do not bait me, Ser Alaghieri," said Dandolo with an air of resigned patience, as if speaking to a disobedient dog. "We are already off to a poor start, you and I. You lied to me. No one knows where you are."

"Of course they do," said Pietro, too quickly.

"It has been two weeks. No one has come for you. No, please do not continue the lie. It is truly not to your benefit."

At that, Pietro winced, though not for any reason Dandolo might think. *Continue to lie. Is that how a knight behaves?* Still, he forced himself to speak. "Why is that?"

"Because I have issued orders that the moment inquiries are made about Pietro Alaghieri, you are to be executed. So you see it is far better for you if no one comes."

Pietro raised his head defiantly. "I've been charged with no crime, let alone been accorded a trial."

"Oh," said Dandolo airily, "there was a trial. Guilty, *in absentia*."

The lawyer in Pietro was appalled. "You have no authority to charge me – especially without representation!"

"But we do. You've heard, perhaps, of our newest governing body? The Council of Ten? Established to, and I quote, '*preserve the liberty and peace of the subjects of the Republic and to protect them from the abuses of personal power.*' Only fifteen years old, yet infinitely more capable than either the *Maggior Consiglio* or the *Pregadi*, by which I mean the Senate. Those bodies are good for making the people feel a part of their government, but it is difficult for a body of fifteen hundred men to move at more than a tortoise pace. Even the Senate with six score men has trouble deliberating. Whereas ten men – well, seventeen, really, because the Doge and six *signoria* sit in, but you take my point – they move like the wind! Such an efficient little body."

Pietro's chill of fear turned to rage at this glib recitation. "What was the charge?"

"Heresy." Dandolo said the word slowly, letting the elegance of Pietro's plight sink it. "You are an excommunicant. Venice has a long memory, and our own communal excommunication is too recent to cherish the idea of keeping a heretic alive." The ambassador leaned forward in the throne, fingers steepled. "Please understand, I bear you no ill will. In fact, I feel I owe you a debt for the way your father perished."

"Let me free and we'll be quits," said Pietro at once.

"Amusing. But then the son of a poet should be adept at word-play."

"I wasn't the recipient of that gift. That went to the boy you tried to murder."

Dandolo's face became momentarily pinched. "As I indicated before, I did not have you brought here so that I might be baited."

"Then give me an unbated weapon, I'll use that instead."

The ambassador sighed heavily, wearied by this conversation. "No, Ser Alaghieri, you will not. Nor will you batter me with your blunt wits. Nor will you insult me further. I have explained to my fellow council members that you are marginally more valuable to us alive than dead. You are known to be a partisan of the lord of Verona. You raised his son in secrecy. You may know more of his secrets. Which, by the by, is what they believe we are speaking of at this moment. I am pressuring you to betray your master, the Scaliger."

First Shalakh, now Dandolo. It was beginning to rankle, and Pietro said so. "He's not my master."

The elegant eyebrow arched. "No? You are his knight, entrusted with his most valuable possession – his heir."

"I have no love for Cangrande della Scala." Pietro's declaration bore the unmistakable ring of truth.

"Indeed? Then perhaps you actually *are* willing to betray his secrets? If I were able to show the council that you were cooperating, they might consent to better accommodations, perhaps even a servant to tend to you."

"You misunderstand me. I am not Cangrande's creature. But I will never betray Verona. And I will certainly never help *you*."

"Oh?"

"Ambassador, you ordered the death of the one person I hold dearer than any other. Cangrande may be his sire, but make no mistake, it is an enraged father you are facing."

"Yes, I see. The heir. Forgive me, I was indeed being obtuse. Of course you will not betray Verona's secrets, for those very secrets may matter at some future date. It also explains your brash and headstrong behavior that led to your apprehension. Whatever the cause, I am grateful for it. It means no awkward questions. You were living under an assumed identity. No one knew you were here. There will be no questions if you simply vanish. Which, for all intents and purposes, you have."

Pietro allowed Dandolo his feeling of superiority. Truth be told, he wasn't feeling too much concern for his own skin. He was more interested in exposing Dandolo as the would-be child-killer that he was. But even more than that, he wanted to confirm the conclusion he'd come to. "I have one question. Did Passerino come to you, or did you seek him out?"

It was well done. That Dandolo hadn't been expecting the question was obvious, for he blinked. His recovery was instantaneous, but in that moment Pietro knew he'd guessed right. *Damn. Passerino.*

"I don't know what you mean," said Dandolo in his best ambassadorial tones.

"But you do. You hired Borachio days *before* the rumour of Cangrande's death. Someone had to have passed that information to you. Fool that I am, I believed it was Cangrande himself. But if not, then only one other man could have done it. Lord Bonaccolsi. Cangrande must have explained the raw facts to Bonaccolsi – that his heir had been secretly fostered out, and that only his death could lure the boy out of hiding. Bonaccolsi was entrusted with disseminating the rumour. But before he did, he came to you and gave you a vital piece of information – that there was an heir."

"Even if what you say is so, and I'm speculating just as you are, why would Lord Bonaccolsi wish Cangrande's heir dead?"

"He's been eclipsed. Cangrande shines like the sun, blotting out other men." Pietro was guessing, but it was an easy guess. "Perhaps Bonaccolsi could bear it when he saw that it would end someday. He's had years to get the measure of Mastino and Alberto, he knows he could run roughshod over them. All he had to do was wait for Cangrande's death. Verona would be thrown into chaos, and Mantua would step into the void."

"For a lawyer, you are assuming a great deal of evidence not entered into fact."

Pietro shrugged. "You're right, I may be wildly off the mark. Perhaps Passerino doesn't want Cesco dead at all. Maybe he just wanted your help with something. What could you give him that he couldn't get from Cangrande?" Pietro let the question hang in the air. Then he saw the answer. "The marriage. He's marrying into a rival family, thus solidifying his power. And if that family is an enemy of Cangrande's, well, it's always good to have a foot in both camps." Pietro smiled thinly. "It doesn't matter why he did it, really. It's enough that he's the only one who could have done it."

Pietro watched Dandolo for a reaction, but the diplomat had taken firm control of his features. The Venetian merely examined a curve in the polished wooden arm of the throne. "You have no evidence of any of this."

"Of Passerino's involvement, no. But I have more than enough to hang you, my lord. I don't think your exalted position could protect you from a charge of hiring an assassin to poison a child."

Dandolo was amused. "Because I visit a courtesan, you think you can connect me to such an act? Trust me, Ser Alaghieri, there are few in Venice who do not indulge."

Pietro saw the riposte, the perfect reply. *I have Borachio.* But it was another lie. Thus the lawyer in Pietro changed the words so they did not contradict his honour. "We caught Borachio. How else did I find the house?"

Dandolo said nothing. There was nothing to say, really. He could protest that there was no way Borachio could identify him, but then he'd be admitting he was indeed the man behind the screen. Dandolo could deny knowing Borachio, but as there was no other audience to posture for, he didn't bother. Instead he rose and crossed to a sideboard laden with fruit and sweets, popped a date into his mouth, and chewed. Pietro's mouth begin to move as he imagined tasting that date.

"Ser Alaghieri," said Dandolo, filling a small dish with a variety of treats, "this situation distresses me more than I can express. I respect and admire you, for both your family and for yourself. But you have chosen to ally yourself with Verona, which puts us at odds. Verona is a threat to Venice. One we take quite seriously. Here." Dandolo placed the dish in on the floor in front of Pietro.

With real regret, Pietro ignored it. "Ambassador, as far as I am concerned, you may threaten and chastise the Scaliger as much as you please. But do anything that threatens Cesco's future and you will answer to me."

"You forget, the boy is also a Scaliger, not an Alaghieri."

"He is both," declared Pietro. "I will do whatever I can to ensure his future."

"At the present moment, there is nothing you can achieve. Do try the candied figs, at least. They are a rare treat."

Pietro looked down at the bowl offered him, then up into Dandolo's face. "You first."

Dandolo chose to be amused rather than angry. He bent over and pointed to a fig. Pietro nodded, and Dandolo popped the fruit into his own mouth. For an instant Dandolo was close enough that Pietro could try some desperate move. But he was weak, and the guards were just outside. *You've done enough stupid things already.*

"Actually, the stars favoured you more than you know," said Dandolo, seemingly agreeable to confessing his sins. "There was also a trap laid for you on the road to Vicenza. But the retreating Paduan army confused matters, allowing you to slip by."

"Saved by the Paduans," observed Pietro. "Carrara will be furious."

Dandolo smiled at the irony. "If we had known that you were in

Ravenna, rest assured, things would not have been handled in such a slipshod manner. But that was a fact Passerino did not possess."

"I'm right about the rest of it?" asked Pietro.

"For the most part." Dandolo resumed his seat, steepling his fingers
and leaning against the throne's high back as if discussing nothing of consequence. "Lord Bonaccolsi has long wished to step out of the Scaliger's
shadow. We've had an arrangement with him for nearly a year wherein,
if the opportunity arose to betray the Scaliger, he would do so, provided
no suspicion would alight on him. It is my understanding that once, some
years ago, he tried to remove the Greyhound. Perhaps you've heard about
Ponte Corbo, where Cangrande was wounded and fled, leaving behind
fourteen of Verona's standards. What the Scaliger did not know, does
not know to this day, is that the men who fell on him so viciously were
not Paduan. They were mercenaries in the employ of none other than
Cangrande's best friend in the world, Lord Passerino Bonaccolsi."

*Ponte Corbo.* The event had changed Cangrande, shaken his confidence, dimmed the light of his valour. All because of Passerino, privy to
Cangrande's plans and so able to place the perfect ambush. *Damn.*

Dandolo continued on to more recent events. "This summer,
when Cangrande began his little charade and took refuge with the friars,
he told Passerino to go spread the rumour of his untimely death. And as
you surmised, he explained about his son, but only in the vaguest details,
and without mentioning where the boy had been reared. Passerino took
horse straight to me. We then put in motion several plans. The first was to
waylay the child before he reached Vicenza, which Passerino was certain
would be his first stop. The second was Borachio."

"How did you choose him?"

"The Council of Ten routinely collects evidence against men, even
when we have no intention of prosecuting. We have often found it useful
to have leverage over those who come to the Serenissima. The drunkard was chosen because he had no conceivable connection to either the
Senate of Venice or Lord Bonaccolsi. He was dispatched to Verona in the
event the child did not go to Vicenza. And the final plot was a band of
loyal soldiers sent to the monastery where Cangrande was hiding."

"You tried to murder Cangrande?" Pietro wasn't surprised at the
idea, only that he hadn't heard about it.

Dandolo smiled. "That would have been the real coup – while
the Scaliger pretends to die, we oblige him with a real demise. Alas, he
did not remain at the monastery, choosing instead to play the woman
and ride along the road to see his son. Passerino told me of it afterwards.
We'd sent him back to Cangrande, of course, to lull any suspicions the
Scaliger might have had. Bonaccolsi did his level best, but he was unable

to convince your master – forgive me, the Scaliger – to remain at the monastery long enough to die in truth." Dandolo favoured Pietro with a wry look. "As I said, slipshod. It was all arranged in a matter of hours. I'm astonished that of all our plans, Borachio came the closest to succeeding."

Tamping down his fury, a new question occurred to Pietro. "Why send Borachio to Mantua to acquire the poison?"

"Quite the lawyer's mind! It occurred to me that, should Borachio's connection with Venice be exposed, it behooved us to have him tied to Mantua as well. That way Lord Bonaccolsi had as much reason to protect – or silence – Borachio as we did. A little insurance."

"What did Bonaccolsi get in return?"

"Several things." That Dandolo had lost any vestige of reluctance made Pietro worry. "Money, of course. Some trade rights. And, most important, we were able to help the Este family with some longstanding debts. Your beloved lord of Verona has kept them impoverished ever since he helped them regain control of their city. Not overtly, but he calls upon them to field a larger army than they can maintain, and so they are forced to borrow money from him to pay the mercenaries he demands of them. It is a simple, common, and effective means of keeping vassals in line. But thanks to us, Ferrara is solvent for the first time in eight years. We bought their debts, then lost them. Shoddy book-keeping. But it was done in Lord Bonaccolsi's name, which opened up the way to his coming marriage."

"No wonder Cangrande looked unhappy about the match," observed Pietro. "Tell me, did you actually burn the debts, or are you holding on to them?"

Dandolo's smile was extravagant. "It is a long game, and as I have already said, it is prudent to have insurance for all contingences."

Pietro was growing tired of politeness. "So what happens to me?"

"Well, I clearly cannot allow you to leave here with ruinous infor-mation."

"Ruinous for whom?"

"For me. Doge Soranzo is old. I intend to be the next Doge. You can expose me. Even without evidence, you can damage my standing, my *dignitas*. That, I cannot allow. I owe your family a debt of honour, but not so great a debt that I am willing to dash myself on the shoals of personal ruin. Here is what I will do. I will keep you alive, incommunicado with the outside world, until I am elected Doge. After that, nothing you could say can harm me. Doge is a lifetime appointment. So you will remain under lock and key until such time as Doge Soranzo resigns or leaves behind our mortal cares. Be it a month of days, a month of weeks, or a month of months. If you attempt to escape or communicate with the outside world, I will have the order for execution carried out." Dandolo picked an imaginary piece of lint from his *gonella*. "Or, if I choose not to be accused of murdering the son as well as causing the death of the father, I can simply hand you over to the Florentines. There is a man named Donati who has been quite vocal of late in demanding your death. Is something funny?"

"Nothing." *Oh Cesco. Whatever would I do without you to keep life interesting?*

"I see. Well, those are my plans for you, Ser Alaghieri. However, if you give me your word of honour that you won't try to escape or contact your friends, your confinement could be of greater comfort than you are presently afforded. I could even hold you in my own palace. You could write, study, play music, however you wish to pass the time. Continue your study of Law, perhaps? I might even be convinced to allow you a feminine visitor or two. And, let me add, I would take great pleasure in your company. O, the debates we could have! You could lead me through your father's works with an eye towards his original intent! I promise, I would be a most willing pupil."

Pietro had stopped listening. The lawyer in him saw a chance. Dandolo had been careless in his wording. According to the oath, if Pietro swore, he couldn't contact his friends. But there was nothing in the vow to stop him from contacting an enemy. And, as he had already told Dandolo, Cangrande was no friend to Pietro.

But the knight in him saw the dishonour in quibbling over the details to an oath. Dandolo's intent was clear. If Pietro were to swear, he would be honour-bound to refrain from contacting anyone. *A knight obeys the spirit as well as the letter of the law.*

"Well, Ser Alaghieri," pressed Dandolo, "what do you say? May I have your word of honour?" Pietro shook his head, and Dandolo heaved a great sigh. "Very well. Then we have nothing left to discuss."

Before Dandolo could ring his bell to summon the guards, Pietro said, "I have a counter-offer. Let me expose Passerino. In return, I give you my word that Venice will not be implicated."

Dandolo looked pained. "I must sadly decline. Bonaccolsi may do the thing himself, which would be as ruinous as if you shouted it from the rooftops."

"Then I won't expose him," said Pietro. "I'll kill him. Pick a duel."

"You could lose," said Dandolo.

"True. But Cesco would know to be wary of Bonaccolsi. It would be enough."

"Your paternal devotion is touching." Dandolo was thoughtful for a time. "What about dear Borachio?"

"He cannot identify you."

"You said he could."

"I implied it," corrected Pietro.

Dandolo gave him a wispy smile. "Ever the lawyer. Either you were lying then or you are now. No, I choose not to take the risk. Besides, even if you mean what you say, he provided you with the means to find me out. He could do so again, to others who have not given their word."

Dandolo was trying to close the interview. Pietro grew desperate. "So publish the information you have on him, but hold off on pronouncing a sentence. I'll see to it that he flees Italy."

Dandolo sat in state, considering. "No. It is more to my liking to have the Scaligeri wiped out, Verona crippled, and the triumphant Bonaccolsi in my debt. I understand your feelings for the boy, but my grief at your father's death extends only to your family, and Cangrande's heir is not, strictly speaking, an Alaghieri."

"Wait," said Pietro, again forestalling the ringing of the bell. "You sound very sure. This isn't some hypothetical threat. You know something."

Dandolo paused, then shrugged lightly. "It will make no difference. It is my understanding that one of the Scaligeri has joined with Lord Bonaccolsi against the rest of the family. I do not know which. Could it possibly be your young squire?"

"No," said Pietro with certainty. "Even if it was in his nature, which it isn't, Cangrande keeps him close. Passerino couldn't have subverted his loyalty without Cangrande knowing."

"Then alas, he will most likely not survive. There will be a battle soon between the forces of Verona, Mantua, and Ferrara on one side, and Bologna and Pisa on the other. The object will be the city of Modena, which has always been contested land between Ferrara and Bologna. During the battle a signal will be given, and certain Veronese lords who have been bribed or blackmailed into aiding Bonaccolsi will turn their swords away from the Bolognese and lodge them in the backs of the Scaligeri."

"Not just Cangrande," said Pietro, voice leaden.

"No. Mastino will fall, and his brother. And sadly I am certain that your foster-son will meet his end, as well as Lord Nogarola and his elder son, who are Scaligeri by marriage and sympathy. No one will be left to inherit except the traitor within the Scaligeri ranks. Before you ask, no, I don't know who, but there are a score of Scaligeri bastards occupying places in Cangrande's court, from clergy to clerks. Though none of Cangrande's own making that I know of, besides your young Cesco. And Verona has just recently shown its willingness to be led by a child from the wrong side of the sheets."

"Do the Estensi know what Passerino intends?"

"I doubt it," said Dandolo. "Rainaldo d'Este may be chafing under the penury imposed by Cangrande, but he is an honourable man and owes his lordship of Ferrara to the Scaliger. No, I believe Lord Bonaccolsi is gripping the dice quite tightly. If he didn't require our financial aid to bribe certain Veronese, I doubt we would know anything of this."

Sick at heart, Pietro was turning these facts over in his mind. Cesco was in Mantuan lands, with Cangrande, Mastino, Alberto, Detto, Bailardino and the rest. Paride was probably there, too, though Dandolo hadn't mentioned him. And one of them was a traitor, plotting the deaths of his kin. Someone who didn't believe in the family curse. Someone who would see Cangrande dead, and Cesco with him.

Pietro threw his dignity to the wind. "Lord Dandolo, I beg of you, do not let this happen! Whatever you may think of Cangrande, his son matters. Not just to me and mine, but to the future! There is a secret – so important, even, that the boy himself doesn't know it!"

"I take it you will share this secret with me, so that I will spare his life? Please. I am all agog."

"Moments ago you referred to Cangrande as the Greyhound. It's a title that fits with his name, and certainly my father had him in mind when he made reference to the Greyhound in *L'Inferno*. But Cangrande is not the Greyhound of legend. That title belongs to Cesco. If you let Cesco die, then Italy will be denied a new golden age, a renewed greatness."

Pietro waited expectantly while Dandolo digested this revelation. *Surely he sees that this is more important than Verona or Venice. This is about ushering in a new age, a rebirth of greatness in this land! He* must *see it!*

Looking down his long patrician nose, Dandolo said levelly, "Ser Alaghieri, there is nothing you could have said that would have made me more firm in my resolve. If your Cesco is indeed the Greyhound, it is all the more reason to see him destroyed."

Pietro threw out his hands in supplication. "Please! Surely you see—!"

Dandolo rang the small bell, and the guards came in to lift Pietro off the ground. Pietro kept pleading all the way to the door, shouting the names of Bonaccolsi and Borachio in the hopes of betraying to some random auditor some details of the plot. But Dandolo had arranged it so there was no one in the palace at this hour who was not his creature.

Pietro was thrown sprawling into his cell. The door was barred and bolted, leaving him once again in darkness. Rubbing his bruised shoulder, Pietro couldn't help thinking that Cesco would have pulled the interview off with more style. Or at least eaten the offered food.

# FORTY-TWO

Venice
Friday, 8 November
1325

GIUSEPPE MORSICATO wrapped his cloak more tightly about him. It was a chilly evening, foggy, with that sense of moisture in the air that makes one believe one is drinking rather than breathing. It misted on his forked beard, making it damp and limp.

The fog also added to an annoyance that had grown with each minute he spent navigating the walkways of Venice. Like Mantua, there were no names to any of the streets! Oh, there was an occasional sign pointing to this church or that palace, but Pietro's letter to Antonia had named a street. He kept having to ask natives for directions, which was frustrating as well as dangerous.

Morsicato wasn't actually concerned for Pietro's well-being. The lad was capable enough. But he hadn't written to his sister in over three weeks. That, combined with the revelation that Cangrande was behind Pietro being condemned by Paduan law, was distressing. They'd expected some kind of trick, but damn if the Scaliger hadn't placed them in check anyway.

Antonia had been insistent about accompanying the doctor to Venice, and he'd wasted over an hour talking her out of it. Stubborn girl, that Alaghieri. Just like her father. It had taken pure good sense, laid out in the frankest terms, that got her to agree to stay behind.

"If you come to Venice, you'll be abandoning your post. With me, Pietro, and that damned Moor all out of the way, Cesco has to have you to run to. Not that he will, of course, but you've got to be there." Finally she had consented to remain in Verona, extracting a series of promises from him to write the moment he found her brother.

It wasn't just concern for Pietro that made the doctor journey to Venice. Part of him was shamefully glad to get away from his wife's sickroom, if only for a day. Esta's condition was only made worse by his frustrating inability to diagnose it. During August she had lost weight in her face and limbs with horrible rapidity, while her belly had become bloated and sore. In September she'd recovered a little, gaining back some of the weight, but she was still not wholly well. Maddening! All those years in Ravenna she had longed to return home, and this was her reward?

Though in truth, the return held little reward for any of them. *Damn Cangrande, damn him straight to Hell.*

Finding the boarding house at last, Morsicato knocked and was received with a wary look. His jourdan had that effect. No one liked to see a doctor at their door, it was often the prelude to bad news. "There's a pest going around, you've probably got it already, either you'll die or lose all your hair or both." There were times he hated his brethren. So many were fools.

Still, there were advantages to the common fear of medicos, and he was not averse to exploiting them. "Madam, I am looking for a patient of mine. It is my understanding that he's staying here."

"I don't have any lodgers at the moment," she replied, trying to close the door on him.

"A little taller than me, thinner, with brown hair and a slight hook to his nose. Crooked smile. He looks a little like that poet fellow, Dante," he added, as if in afterthought.

"Oh him! He was staying here, but right in the middle of the month he left."

"Left the city?"

"No idea. Just went out in the middle of the afternoon and never came back. My guess is that he was robbed and murdered. Poor fellow."

"I see." Morsicato chewed his lower lip, feeling his first real stab of concern. Antonia was right, something had happened to Pietro.

"He was a patient, you say?"

"Mmm? Oh, yes."

"What he had – is it catching?"

Morsicato was loathe to frighten her further, but he needed more information. "It could be. May I see his room?"

She frowned, but the answer was never in doubt. "He was only here a couple of days," she explained as she led him upstairs, "though he was paid to the end of the week. Quiet. Had a good appetite." She opened the door to her guest room. It was small and tidy. "He just spent his time sitting in that window, reading and watching the boats go by."

Morsicato went to the window. Yes, there was the courtesan's house, the three-faced stone head, pink flowers and all. "He went out, you say? Did he leave anything behind?"

"Oh, yes. I still have his belongings," said the landlady. "Shall I fetch them?"

She was gone only a moment, hardly enough time for Morsicato to gather his thoughts. She came back with a wrapped bundle. It was remarkable that she had held onto these things, though, truth be told, they were not likely to demand a high price. The clothes were fairly non-descript, probably bought here in Venice. There was one book, a play. "Did he have any papers?"

"Blank sheets, and some ink." She opened a drawer in the small desk in the corner. "Could they carry his disease?"

"Maybe," said Morsicato. "I should take them."

"Do! Get them out of here, please! I don't want to be holding onto a sick man's things!"

"Did he have a sword?"

"Aye, but it wasn't here. He must've been wearing it when he left."

She might have been lying, but there was no use pressing it. "I need a place to stay while I look for him."

The landlady shook her head vehemently. "Not here! I don't want any sickies coming in and out of here. I run a clean house! No, I mean it! Get out, and don't come back! My neighbours will already be talking! Go!"

Back on the street, Pietro's things under his arm, Morsicato fretted about what to do next. His hackles were up – Antonia was correct, something had happened to Pietro. *Feminine intuition. Never discount it.* Night was falling and he had to find a place to sleep. But he decided to first find the local constable and make inquiries.

It took another hour of wandering the fog-shrouded streets before he found the constable's house. Poised to knock, he was framing his questions in his mind when suddenly a large hand clamped down over his mouth. He struggled, but his assailant was powerful, dragging Morsicato away from the misty light of the burning lamp beside the door, into the shadows of the underside of a nearby bridge.

"Don't cry out," rasped a familiar voice. "You will endanger Ser Alaghieri more than you already have."

*Tharwat!* A horrible suspicion came over the doctor. The Assassin had killed Pietro to keep his secret, and now the bastard was about to murder him too!

As the grip on Morsicato's jaw was released, the doctor shoved himself away from the tall shadow amongst the shadows. He wanted to shout, cry for help. But before he could do either he was enveloped in the folds of a cloak and thrown hard against the ground. Something struck him a mighty blow and he lost all sense.

♦          ◊          ♦

He awakened in a dingy little room filled with litter and very little furniture. Touching his aching head, he blinked in the dim candlelight. The Moor was seated across the room, between himself and the door, idly going through Pietro's belongings.

Morsicato sat up, gently caressing his scalp. "Why are people always hitting me on the head?"

"The exposed skin makes an excellent target," said the Moor.

"Quips? From you? Now I know I'm going to die."

"Someday, doctor. But not at my hand, nor by my will." Tharwat al-Dhaamin laid aside the satchel and fixed the doctor with his gaze. "I apologize for striking you. It was necessary, as you will learn."

"Is Pietro alive?"

"He is, but in grave danger."

"Where are we?"

"My rooms, not far from the Yellow Crescent."

"What the devil are you doing in Venice? And how did you know I was here?"

"I was only made aware of your arrival in Venice this hour, and it took me some time to find you."

How could he have known Morsicato was in Venice? The only person he'd spoken with at length was...

Irritatingly, the Moor knew his thoughts. "The housekeeper has been well paid to keep me informed if anyone came looking for Ser Alaghieri. That is why she kept his belongings, so that she might have an excuse to leave the company of an inquisitive guest and send word to me. Sadly, her message did not reach me until after you had departed the lady's house."

"Where is Pietro?"

"In the Doge's prison."

"Prison?" gawked the doctor.

"Yes. It was imperative that I keep you from making official inquiries about him. His gaolers are under instructions that if anyone comes looking for him, he is to be executed at once."

"Executed!"

"Please lower your voice," said Tharwat softly. "My neighbours are inquisitive. Yes, executed. I do not know what the truth of his imprisonment is, only that it is quite suspicious."

Morsicato's voice became softer though no less urgent. "We have to free him."

"I was working on a plan to do just that. With you here, matters become simpler. Follow me." Lifting the candle before him, Tharwat led the way to a single back room.

Morsicato rose and followed. In the candlelight, the doctor could see now that Tharwat was dressed in rags. His medical eye took in a few puffing blotches on the older man's face. The Moor had been beaten, and recently. "You're hurt."

"It is nothing," said Tharwat, gingerly seating himself on a stool. "The price of being a Moor in Venice. It has nothing at all to do with our present trouble."

Morsicato recalled what risk Tharwat was taking in being present in the city at all. "What is your guise these days?"

"A blind poet. I am kicked and spit upon, but generally ignored. And I hear everything."

"I'm surprised the landlady was willing to work for you."

"She thinks she is working for a rich nobleman, and I am a mere go-between. She has made her distaste known."

"You say Pietro had been condemned," said Morsicato. "For what crime?"

"Heresy. He is an excommunicant. That is all the cause they require."

"Why hasn't anyone heard of this?"

"It is a close-held secret. I believe they do not wish to kill him, but have placed themselves in a position where they may. It is why I have not written. If the Scaliger or anyone of note were to demand his freedom, they would find out that, sadly, he had been executed that very day. I tempted fortune by asking about him myself. Fortunately, no one pays me much heed."

"I thought you were well loved in Venice," said Morsicato.

"As myself, I am known at the Doge's court. But I thought it best to remain unknown. If I present myself to the Doge, I will be watched thereafter. This way I may move freely. I have lived this life before. It is no hardship."

The Moor was obviously glossing over very real dangers, all undertaken for Pietro's sake. Morsicato wondered if the roiling in his gut was hunger or shame. "You said you were working on a rescue?"

"Yes. The reason I was unavailable to find you sooner was that I was procuring this." Tharwat fished into his loose shirt and handed across three small packets. Morsicato opened one, sniffing the contents. His nose was assaulted by the sweet scent of Dog's Mercury. He hissed out a breath and dropped the packets to the floor. "I do not deal in poisons! I am no Assassin!"

"Please doctor, lower your voice, or we shall find ourselves in the cell adjoining Pietro's. It was my hope that I could fashion a drug that would cause illness, not death. But as you pointed out to me some months ago, I am no expert in pharmacology. My training was in the Hashish, and in fatal poisons. With you here, we can devise a less lethal dose. Enough to sicken the guards, make them vomit their hearts out of their mouths, turn their bowels to water, just long enough for us to free Ser Alaghieri."

That mollified Morsicato. It was not something he'd ever done, but he knew of generals who dosed the water of a besieged city. It was dishonourable to kill, but a common practice to sicken the defenders long enough to take the walls.

His face must have betrayed him, for the Moor pressed him further. "You can make certain no one dies. If I attempt it, I may cause more injury than necessary."

Morsicato chewed the bit of his beard that jutted out below his lip. "Do you want a powder, or a paste?"

"Whichever you think easiest to use. But nothing that will cause harm to the one who delivers it."

Morsicato was still chewing, but thoughtfully. "Powder, then. We just have to be sure we don't inhale it."

"Thank you, doctor." Tharwat rose and began preparations to depart.

"It won't be ready for a few hours," protested Morsicato.

"Take as much time as you require. I have an errand, one that will take the better part of a day. Please, once your task is finished, stay within doors. No one will come knocking. Despite its appearance, this room is clean. There is food, so there will be no need to go out. Use the window for your nightsoil. It faces the water. I will return tomorrow, late."

In utter consternation, Morsicato put his hands on his hips. "Where are you going?"

The Moor sighed. "I can get us both into the palace. But I do not think either you or I could enter the kitchens. We require a master of pranks. And I do not think he will be averse to a brief holiday from the Scaliger's care, do you?"

# FORTY-THREE

THE WEDDING FEAST for Lord Passerino Bonaccolsi and Ailisa d'Este was a lavish affair. "Not much by Veronese standards," confided the groom to his best man. "But it will do, don't you think?"

"Rather," replied Cangrande wryly, looking at the banquet being laid out on table after table in the open square. Horses were making the *entrée*, bearing wagons heaped with meats, cheeses, breads, fish, and the inevitable Golden Morsels, the choice delicacy of the moment.

The ceremony had been equally lavish. Ailisa's brothers, delighted with the match and newly swimming in funds, had spared no expense. Ferrara and Mantua were now united in blood as well as politics, much the way Vicenza and Verona were tied by the union of Cangrande's sister to Bailardino Nogarola. And as Cangrande had told Cesco, there were ties between Verona, Ferrara, and Mantua – Cangrande's sister had been married into both the families being united this day.

The guests cheerfully settled in to feast. Castelbarco wasn't present – he was in charge of Verona in Cangrande's absence – but Nico da Lozzo was there, free of any suspicion of having taken part in the Paduan uprising. Montecchio and Capulletto were both in attendance, though without their wives – a blessing, as no one wanted to witness Antony yet again mooning over Mari's wife. It had long ago ceased to be amusing. As an additional precaution, they were seated quite far from one another.

In fact, there were no Veronese wives in attendance. Petruchio Bonaventura had left his Katerina at home with their children, and Bailardino had likewise left *his* Katerina in Vicenza. The moment these celebrations were finished, the men were off to war. So the wedding feast was a noticeably masculine affair.

Alblivious was laughing with Jacopo Alaghieri, while Mastino sat in the corner with Fuchs. Mastino felt a growing excitement about the coming battle. Of all the jibes thrown at him back in July, one had been painfully on the mark. Mastino had never been in a serious battle. Worse, he'd been made a fool on horseback by the imp, leading to knowing looks and whispers about his lack of martial prowess.

For this reason Mastino had decided not to challenge the child directly – there was no honour in besting a boy – but instead throw himself into war. When not otherwise engaged, he and Fuchs had spent the last three months training, riding, jousting, sparring. If there was an uprising that Cangrande needed put down, Mastino was the first to volunteer. He was never allowed to lead such an effort, but under the orders of such men as Castelbarco, Bonaventura, or Nogarola, he learned much.

Skirmishes and strikes were not battles, however. The coming battle would be his first, and while the little bastard was forced to ride behind Cangrande, carrying the great man's spurs, Mastino would be in the thick of it, building his reputation. All of which put him in fairly good cheer during the feast.

Cesco was buoyant as well, reunited with Detto at last. Both squires stood dutifully behind their masters, Cesco at the head table, Detto at a further one. But Bailardino kept gesturing his son over to tease him, and Petruchio didn't seem much to care, so Detto finally fell in beside his friend to share whispered jokes and stories.

"You know," said Cangrande to Passerino as he quaffed yet another cup of wine, "I feel rather useless. Time was the best man would watch the horses and hold off the girl's family while the groom stole her away."

"Yes," replied Passerino, chucking his new wife under the chin, "we are quite civilized these days."

"I don't know," said Rainaldo d'Este, the bride's brother. "I like the idea of fighting the girl's relations. It would spice up an otherwise boring day."

"Since you are those relations," said Cangrande, "you'd be fighting yourself."

"At last!" cried Rainaldo. "A battle I can win!"

"One you can't lose, as least," replied Cangrande.

"I wonder what our friend Carrara thinks of this match," said Bail idly. "The Paduans can't be pleased that Verona, Vicenza, Mantua, and Ferrara are drawing even closer together."

Passerino shook his head. "He's still counting his lucky stars that he's among the living. That coup nearly did away with him!'"

All innocence, Nico chimed in. "I wish it had! Now, if I'd been there…"

Passerino popped a Golden Morsel in his mouth. "From what I hear, he was warned. Dente must've had a spy in his camp."

"Or else Carrara is just a prudent man," observed Cangrande. "His paranoia doesn't mean there aren't people after his head."

Nico lifted a cup. "True enough!"

Cangrande drained his own cup and held it out to be refilled, but Cesco missed the signal, busy snickering with Detto. The Scaliger had to turn in his seat and cough. "You have something you'd rather be doing?"

"Training my hawk," said Cesco lightly, pouring the wine. He winked at Bonaccolsi. "I've been getting such expert instruction, I'm hungry – to try it on her, I mean. She's almost ready to air."

"Your first bird?" asked Rainaldo d'Este. "And how is she coming along?"

"Wonderfully!" enthused Cesco. "She's still in flack, but we're beyond the darkened room and the partial starving. We're venturing into the city at night to get her used to strange sounds and smells."

"He hasn't even named her yet," observed Cangrande.

"Make certain you praise her excessively." Rainaldo turned to his new brother-in-law. "Women need constant praising."

Bonaccolsi stroked his wife's hair. "You're very pretty." Ailisa blushed and giggled.

Rainaldo laughed in triumph. "See?"

Cangrande used the opportunity to wave Cesco away before he became the focus in the conversation. To Cangrande's great consternation, Cesco had become the fascination of the entire Mantuan court. By day the boy performed acrobatic feats that defied the Devil, while at night he provided heart-wrenching music, capping off each performance with a string of cantos from Dante's *Commedia* in so perfect an imitation of the poet that those who'd known him laughed and wept at once.

Cesco obeyed Cangrande's dismissive wave, returning to stand beside Detto. Rainaldo d'Este turned to Cangrande and jerked his thumb over his shoulder at the boy. "You know, my grandfather had himself legitimized by the papacy."

"My sister could not have married him else."

"I'm saying, why don't you do the same for your son? Apply to Avignon, have him declared legitimate!"

As many heads turned, Cangrande made certain to speak loudly enough for every eavesdropper to hear. "Firstly, there is the matter of the mother. She is presently anonymous, and wishes to remain so. The

Pope will not likely grant Cesco legitimacy without me supplying her name. Secondly, the present Pope is no partisan of mine, I don't think he'd be interested in accommodating an excommunicant. And finally," Cangrande leaned back placidly under the sea of stares, "I am quite content the way things stand."

"Well I'm not," said Passerino, standing. "There's too much wine on the table, and not enough in me. I'm going to make room for more."

Cangrande rose as well, meaning Cesco had to follow, hoping the Capitano wouldn't ask his squire to unlace the points for him.

Thankfully, he did no such thing. At the side of a bridge, the two men paused. Cesco stayed a good distance back. Being who he was, Cangrande was through with his business and relacing before Passerino had even begun to make a splash in the flowing river. "See you back there!"

"Leave some wine for me, you old drunk!" Passerino waved over his shoulder and almost lost his balance.

It was only two city blocks back to the festivities, but before Cangrande and Cesco reached the well-lit square, they saw a figure emerge from the shadows of a wall. "My lord?"

"Antony!" Cangrande clapped Capulletto on the shoulder. "How do you like Mantua?"

"Lovely," answered Antony shortly, a furrow across his brow. "My lord, there's something I wish to speak to you about—"

"Can it possibly wait? My head is swimming a bit, and the only cure is to flood it with more wine."

"It's important."

"Well, if it can't wait, it can't wait," sighed the Scaliger. "Tell me the worst!"

"Well, my lord—"

Capulletto was cut off by the arrival of Passerino, still fiddling with his wedding finery as he stumbled back. "Now what are you two talking about? He's not proposing another marriage alliance, is he? It's all he talks about! Is that it, Antony? Has my wedding made you hear little bells for yourself and this lad here?" Passerino pointed at Cesco.

"No." Antony began to retreat, looking guilty.

"No?" pressed Passerino. "Then it probably has to do with Montecchio's bride. O Antony! You mustn't bore us with the tales of your affairs! In love, remember, *audi, vide, tace*. Come on, let's get back to the feast!" He threw one arm around Capulletto's shoulders and dragged him back to the square.

"I wonder where Lord Bonaccolsi studied," murmured Cesco.

Cangrande turned to smile. "Because he got the quote wrong?"

"He cut it short, at least. It wasn't the full quote, and it's most definitely not a reference to love."

Cangrande closed his eyes to recite. "*Audi, vide, tace, si tu vis vivere.* Hear, see, be silent, if you wish to be alive. Interesting. Though I suppose it as easily refers to love as to war. After all," said Cangrande with a wink, "they are two sides to the same coin."

"So you keep telling me. I am perfectly patient to discover the truth."

They returned to the square to find several men on their feet, and many more looking anxious. It didn't take long to see why. Capulletto was shaking a fist at Montecchio and shouting. Montecchio, for his part, looked equal parts surprised and enraged.

"I don't know what you think I did," Mariotto was saying, his hands held wide, "but I didn't do it!"

"That's just the kind of answer I'd expect from such a noted coward!" sneered Antony.

Mariotto coloured. "Coward?!"

"Montecchio, you couldn't guard a woman's virtue in a house of Greek actors!"

"O Christ," sighed Petruchio to the heavens. "Here they go!"

As Cangrande waded through the crowd, Cesco stepped nearer to Detto. "What happened?"

"No idea! One minute everything was light and fun. The next, Capulletto was claiming that Montecchio had bumped him or something. I didn't see it, but he's making quite a fuss."

"I can see that." Cesco enjoyed the sight of Capulletto spewing venom and Montecchio protesting his valour.

"I've never shied away from fighting! Unlike some I could mention!" Montecchio was being restrained by Benvenito Lenoti.

"Then why are your men always at the back of the fighting? You don't see the Scaliger cowering behind the front lines! He's always in the lead, his best men acting as his personal bodyguard! And those men are going to be mine, you toad. The house of Capulletto knows more of valour than any Montecchi!"

Shaking off the hands of his brother-in-law, Mariotto flourished the dagger that still carried a hunk of his dinner meat. "My lord Cangrande, I demand the right to shove those words down his throat!"

Cangrande's answer was frigid. "Though we are in Mantua, Veronese law applies. Duels are forbidden, as you both have cause to know."

"Then I request the right to prove him a liar! I crave the honour of being your personal guard during the battle!"

"That, you shall have," said Cangrande impatiently. "If it will get you both to stand down and stop spoiling Lord Bonaccolsi's nuptials!"

Glaring at each other, both men subsided. Capulletto was drawn off by Nico da Lozzo to get drunk, while Petruchio sat and bent a sympathetic ear to Mariotto's justifiable complaints. For the Mantuans and the Ferrarese it was the height of the evening's entertainments, and the feast began to pall.

Sensing this, Rainaldo d'Este turned to Cangrande. "My lord Capitano, this feast needs a bit of livening. Why don't you send that boy of yours to fetch his lute and play for us?"

Unable to think of a reason to deny the request, Cangrande sent Cesco back to their rooms to fetch his instrument. With Petruchio and Benvenito tending Montecchio's wounded ego, Detto took a chance and followed in Cesco's wake. They raced each other up the steps and through the hall, Cesco losing only because Detto shoved him at the last moment into a wall. Detto's victory dance was stopped by a retaliatory shove that sent him sprawling across one of the beds, and a wrestling contest ensued, both boys employing what they'd learned – Cesco from Cangrande, Detto from Petruchio's rough-and-tumble sons.

Entangled and breathing hard, they heard the door close and were stunned to see Tharwat appear from behind the open door.

"Gah!" Detto pointed. "What's he doing here?"

Feigning unsurprise, Cesco strode to pick up his lute from the dark corner. In Arabic he said, "If thou didst not come bearing gifts, thou should depart again unwelcomed."

"Thou hadst means sufficient to last months. If it is gone, thou wast incautious."

"I used as needed," protested Cesco.

"As *wanted*," corrected Tharwat. "First lesson of the drug – master it, or be mastered."

Cesco bowed in the Arabic fashion. "O, very wise! I bow to thy wisdom! Surely thou knowst what mine body requires better than I, its humble inhabitant." He let his hands drop with scorn.

Looking back and forth between them, Detto repeated his cry of old. "Speak a language I know!"

Tharwat was studying Cesco. "I see he has not broken you."

"Not for lack of trying. If you don't mind, I was ordered to play, and that's an order I plan to obey." Cesco started for the door.

Tharwat blocked his path. "Dress for the road. We leave at once."

Cesco stared, probing, divining. "Who is in danger? Me or Detto?"

"Danger?" demanded Detto. "What are you talking about?"

Gazing at Cesco, Tharwat gave him a careful answer, once again in

Arabic. "Thy foster-father."

Mocking demeanor vanished, Cesco turned. "Pack a bag, Detto. We're leaving."

◆     ◊     ◆

Sneaking away was not difficult. Tharwat had horses waiting for them a short distance from the gate and a forged pass ordering him every consideration, including the opening of the city gates after nightfall.

On the road, Cesco said, "You had three horses. You knew I'd bring Detto?"

"I considered it possible. Better to have three and need two than to have two and need three."

"You're rather intelligent for a heathen blackamoor. Now tell us, what's wrong with Pietro?"

Tharwat explained as much as he knew. He spoke in clear Occitan, so that Detto could follow along, and was rewarded by that young man's expression of horrified concern. Cesco's only expression, however, was furrowed brow. "So they don't want him dead, but they've sentenced him to die. That makes sense."

"It does?" asked Detto.

"No," replied Cesco. "What are they really after?"

Tharwat said, "You are the lover of puzzles. Solve it."

"A puzzle usually has pieces."

"As does this. We just cannot see them. Until we do, we ride in silence. Come." They kicked their horses into a gallop.

# FORTY-FOUR

*Venice*
*Sunday, 10 November*
*1325*

THE FOG HAD RETURNED, hanging miasmatically in the air. Morsicato was grateful for it, except that it felt strange on his naked face. Walking up to the Doge's palace with Tharwat and the boys, he once again reached up a hand to stroke the unfamiliar territory of his chin.

"Stop that," murmured the Moor.

"I'm not used to it," growled the doctor.

"By persisting, you are telling the world that this is unusual, this depriving the disguise of its value."

"Fine!" Morsicato dropped his hand, grumbling. "Don't see why I had to shave in the first place."

"You are a recognizable figure," said Tharwat, devoid of amusement. This could not be said of Cesco and Detto, who stared at the doctor and sniggered behind their hands. The Moor ignored them. "It is possible, even likely, that the ambassador would recognize you."

Morsicato eyed al-Dhaamin's fine robes suspiciously. "Won't he recognize *you?*"

"He is supposed to."

"But didn't he see you in Verona as well, standing with Cesco?"

"That is easily explained. I am known to work for Donna Nogarola, the Scaliger's sister. She employed me to take the auspices of that day. He will not know that I am Ser Alaghieri's partisan. But if we two came together, as ourselves, he would grow suspicious. A disguise is your price of admission to our little drama."

The original plan was for the Moor and the boys to go in alone.

But Morsicato had argued persuasively that, if something went wrong, it was good to have an extra pair of hands to fight. Hence the disguise. It was the first time in twenty years that he'd bared his face to the world, and Morsicato couldn't resist running the back of his hand across his jaw one more time.

"He's doing it again!" cried Detto.

"Tattletale," retorted Morsicato.

Cesco nudged Detto. "Watch out! He's as touchy as a new hatched viper."

"He looks like the egg, not the snake," snickered Detto.

"You two stop as well," warned Tharwat as they drew near the palace. "If he doesn't expose himself, we can't have you doing it for him."

"I certainly hope he doesn't expose himself," said Cesco. "Unless he shaved down there as well." Again the boys fell about laughing. Free from Cangrande's watchful eye, Cesco's spirit was light as air. He had slept, he had eaten, and there was a game to play. That the stakes were mortal only made the game more delightful.

Tharwat stopped to give the boys an evil glare, and Cesco threw up his hands. "No, no! We'll be good. We promise."

"We need one of you," said Tharwat. "I could leave the other outside, with the doctor."

"We're all going," said Cesco.

"I certainly am," said the doctor, refusing to be left behind after making such a sacrifice. "Though why we're putting Cesco at risk, I don't know. He must have seen Cesco the day we came to Verona."

"At a distance," said the Moor. "And he hardly looks the same boy."

That was true. Cesco had never been fat, but now was positively wiry. And his hair was so short that none of the curls showed. "As long as he hides his dubious wit under a bushel, we should be well."

Morsicato decided to add a warning of his own. "You boys remember to be careful with that phial—"

"We know!" said Cesco in exasperation. "Don't get it on our fingers, don't breathe it in, don't add it to anything that hasn't already been cooked, heat ruins its efficacy, burble burble burble!"

"I don't know about burble burble," said the shaven doctor, ruffled. "But at least you've got the rest of it down. I only ask because you seem to have a problem with rules."

"Arbitrary rules," replied Cesco. "Nature's rules I am much more interested in. Having been poisoned once, I don't mean to dose myself by accident."

"We are here," said the Moor, which brought all conversation to a halt.

Having written ahead, Tharwat was expected. Barely concealing their dislike, the palace guards escorted the quartet to the Doge's receiving room. Before entering, Tharwat addressed the chief guard. "I doubt the Doge wishes to receive my pages. They must wait outside."

Cesco and Detto made a show of looking disappointed, shuffling their feet as they took up their servile stance outside the double doors as Tharwat and Morsicato entered.

Inside, the Doge was seated in his throne of state. An old man, jowl upon jowl hung loosely from his face. Morsicato's medical eye perceived at once the broken veins and the rosacea that spoke of several illnesses – none fatal, all debilitating.

Behind the throne stood Francesco Dandolo, ambassador and statesman. His gaze was as probing as the Doge's was placid. Morsicato followed al-Dhaamin's lead, lowering his head and bowing deeply.

"Your magnificence, Doge Soranzo," rumbled the Moor. "I am your humble servant."

Soranzo clapped in pleasure. "Theodoro of Cadiz, it *is* you! Praise be to God you've come! We've been bereft of anyone with any skill since you and your master left us!" The Doge's face grew grave. "I understand that Maestro Ignazzio is no longer with us?"

"This is so. He died nine years ago, in Sicily. Murdered."

"I suppose it was too much to expect him to foresee that," observed Dandolo wryly.

"All his arts could not prevent the hour of his passing," intoned Tharwat. "Nor can any man deny his stars."

"We heard you were in Verona," said the Doge petulantly. "Why has it taken you so long to call on us?"

"My deepest regrets," replied Tharwat in an apologetic tone, just the sort of voice a servant would use. "I have been engaged in study, unaware of your desire to converse with my humble self."

"I had asked Mastino della Scala to find you. Alas, it must have slipped his mind." Dandolo nodded to Morsicato. "And who is this?"

"This is my new master, Focarile da Trento. Master," he said to Morsicato, "allow me to present *il Serenissimo Principe*, Giovanni Soranzo, Doge of Venice."

Morsicato made another leg. "Your highness."

The Doge gave Morsicato a phlegmatic smile. "Maestro Focarile, you are most welcome. Are you an astrologer as well?"

"I hope to be, my lord," said Morsicato, bowing humbly. "I have bought this slave in the hopes of furthering my art."

"Enough," chided Dandolo, stepping out from behind the Doge's throne. "There is no more need for disguises."

Morsicato felt himself pale. He made to bite his beard hairs, remembering too late they weren't there.

Tharwat seemed unperturbed. "Disguises? Whatever do you mean, my lord?"

"It has not escaped the Doge's notice, Maestro Theodoro, that your broken throat is always the source of the true predictions. He understands why, in traveling our world, you might feel the need to play the role of a servant. But here, within these walls, you are safe. So admit to us the truth – *you* are the true astrologer. You hire men to play your masters, while you take on the role of slave. Ingenious, but hardly necessary among friends."

Tharwat bowed his head. "The noble Doge is most perspicacious. He has seen through our charade. Here, within these walls, I confess that I am the author of our predictions."

Looking immensely pleased, the Doge beckoned Tharwat and Morsicato closer. "Come, come, sit with us and crush a cup of wine! Then we shall have a candid discussion, and you can display your art as you would among friends."

Tharwat bowed again. "You honour me, my lord."

◆      ◊      ◆

Outside the heavy doors, Detto was kneeling to make friends with one of the palace hounds as Cesco approached the chief of the palace guards. "Please," he began, eyes wide and pleading, "the devil, my master – he does not let us eat but once a day, and only to taste his food for him. I beg you, while he is engaged – might we have a bite to eat? Some gruel, something small? Please! Oh, he's a cruel master, the Moor!"

There was no mistaking Cesco's skeletal looks, though the other boy seemed well-fed enough. Feeling the pull of pity, the guard glanced at the closed double door at his shoulder.

"They'll be hours," said Cesco. "He's planning to give them a full reading in hopes of gaining a permanent post. But you and I know there's no chance the noble and wise Doge Soranzo would ever keep a Moorish magician in the palace! So my master will be in a foul mood tonight, which he'll take out upon us!"

"We're willing to work for our food," added Detto, his voice even more plaintive as he scruffed the hounds neck. "We'll scrub the plates, fetch and carry, anything!"

The temptation to help fellow Christians outwit a heathen blacka-moor was too strong. "Off to the kitchens with you," said the head guard. "Tell them Nardo sent you, and they'll see you fed." He gave directions and they went running off with a look of gratitude that warmed the guards' hearts.

"That was the right thing to do," said one of his fellows.

"Damn Moor," said the head guard, shaking his head. "How does he end up owning decent Christian lads like that?"

Around the corner, Cesco was palming the small phial of powder, having already passed an identical one to Detto. The only trouble was that the dog was following them.

◆     ◊     ◆

The reading did indeed go on for hours. Tharwat used every trapping of his art, from incense to pendulum, from charts to knucklebones with sigils carved in them. He performed palmistry and phrenology, feeling the bumps on the Doge's head with great care. For his part, the Doge was excitedly fascinated. Dandolo, too, looked interested in how long Soranzo might have to live.

Morsicato sat in relative silence, grateful that Tharwat had been named the astrologer, thereby relieving him of the need to play anything more than what he was, an imposter. He did manage not to touch his face more than once, but he couldn't keep himself from glancing at the door and wondering what was happening outside. Had the boys made it as far as the kitchens? Had they used the powders? Would the dishes even reach the gaol below? How long could the Moor drag this out? Would it be long enough?

◆     ◊     ◆

Crouched in darkness, blocking out the sounds of rats and water, Pietro listened for footfalls outside the door, determined to escape. Cesco's life depended on it!

Each time footsteps echoed in the stone corridor, he would rise to his haunches and ready himself to pounce on the opening door. But the door never opened. Twice a day a slat in the bottom would open and a bowl of slop was shoved through it, followed by a cup of water. But they never opened the door to remove the bowls. He had quite a collection now, and he'd started using them to trap and kill the rats. Not that it did any good. There were always more rats.

He was growing faint from hunger. The slop kept him alive, but barely. If he was going to escape he would need strength. He wondered how long he would last before he tasted a raw rat. But he kept putting off that adventure until tomorrow. And tomorrow, and tomorrow. *I'm not that desperate yet.*

He'd caught one rat the other day as it gnawed his heel. He'd torn it apart, hoping to find a bone that he could either dig with or use as a weapon. But there was no bone large enough. At least he'd been able to wash himself clean of the blood through the grating in the floor.

Footsteps! *I've already had my supper tonight – what could this mean?* Another interview with Dandolo? Wincing, Pietro crept from his corner and took up a position just in front of the door. It opened outwards, so the moment he heard the hitch of the latch he would throw himself against it, praying to catch his gaoler off-balance.

There was only one set of steps, which was good. And they were lighter than usual. If it was a small fellow, even better. The steps came near, then stopped. There was a pause, then the sliding bolt echoed around the cell.

Pulse pounding, Pietro launched himself forward, hitting the door hard. It sprung wide, striking the body behind it and knocking it to the ground. Pietro dove around the door and leapt on top of the prone figure.

His hands were on the throat before he saw whose it was. "*Cesco!?*" Releasing his grip, he fell sideways off the boy. "Are you all right?"

"No, Nuncle." Cesco coughed, ruefully lifting himself from the stone floor. "But I'm glad to see you so eager."

Amazement and joy battled for dominance. "Thank God! But how—?"

"No time." Cesco glanced down the corridor. Detto was there, keeping watch, a hound by his side. "No telling how devoted the gaoler is. Once he's done vomiting up his shoes, he may come back. Come on."

Pietro didn't need telling twice. In the tattered remains of his hose and shirt, he followed Cesco down the hall, wincing as he left bloody footprints behind him. "You've lost weight."

"You and I are on the same diet," replied Cesco, inspecting Pietro's lean figure. Suddenly the boy's mouth broke into a wide grin. "I'm betting that at this moment the guards are all wishing they could say the same. We dosed their food with Dog's Mercury, and for good measure their drinks as well."

"Dog's Mercury? What, is Fra Lorenzo with you?"

"Should he be?" asked Cesco quizzically.

"Someone's coming," hissed Detto.

Ducking back around the corner, the trio listened. There were a few quick footfalls down the steps leading to the cells, then two slower ones before the sound stopped altogether. Then there was an odd noise, like the low rumble of a geyser, and a groan of, "O dear lord!" Running now, the footsteps came closer. Pietro tensed, but before the guard turned the corner they heard the opening of a cell door and the quick removal of clothes. Then an outpouring of liquid, drowned out by the sigh of relief.

The man was using the grate in an empty cell as an emergency latrine.

With a twinkle in his eye, Cesco edged past Detto. Peeking around the corner, he darted and threw closed the cell door, slipping the bolt in place. From within a voice cried, "Oi! Oi, don't play the fool! It's me! Let me out!"

"Hope you feel better soon!" said Cesco. "Because in a couple hours, you'll have another reason to shit yourself!"

Detto laughed and even Pietro was grinning as they headed for the end of the hall and began edging up the stairs into the main palace. Here there were many windows, unbarred but so heavily shuttered that they might as well be walls. The only difference was that bars could not be opened from within, while shutters could.

Opening the one set, Cesco motioned for Pietro and Detto to drop out. They obeyed, Detto patting the hound farewell. "Wish you could come with us, but you wouldn't like the water."

Pietro landed on the stones, wincing and crouching low between the wall and the water. Detto was beside him in a moment, and Cesco began closing the shutters. "Detto, get him to the boat. I'll give the signal."

*Boat?* Clearly there was a plan in place. Not wasting time, Pietro allowed himself to be led down an alley, away from the Doge's palace to vanish into the foggy evening.

◆    ◊    ◆

Morsicato was beginning to wonder if the wine he was drinking had been dosed with Dog's Mercury by mistake. His bowels were certainly fluid, and he kept burping up little bubbles of gas. *Nerves.* How could it be taking this long?

Suddenly a messenger entered, looking queasy. The Doge broke off his conversation with Tharwat to chastise the man. "It's about time! Where is our meal?"

The man explained apologetically that there was something wrong with the garrison's food. "The men are sick. A reaction to bad meat or something very like. It's not at all fatal, only – well, embarrassing. We don't wish to risk your majesty's health, so we have sent for food from another kitchen, in another quarter. That is the delay. Our deepest regrets." He bowed and scurried off, his own belly groaning audibly.

Morsicato made certain his face was grim. "Maestro, perhaps we should depart. Our presence only adds to the Doge's troubles."

"Certainly not!" cried Doge Soranzo. "Perhaps you could go to the kitchens and divine the cause of the illness!" He laughed, expecting everyone to join in. Dandolo, however, was worryingly pensive.

Tharwat bowed deeply. "If *Sua Serenità* wishes it so, it shall be done."

"No, no, I'm only joking," said Soranzo. "Please stay! I promise, what we eat will be tasted long before it passes our lips."

"Yes, do stay," said Dandolo. "I have not heard enough yet about your new apprentice. Tell us about him – where he hails from, how he came to be in your service. I am fascinated! Where did you say you were from, Signore Focarile?" The way he was eyeing Morsicato was unsettling. Had he recognized the beardless doctor? Was his sensitive nose finally smelling out a rat?

Morsicato opened his mouth to answer, but was interrupted by a slight tapping on the door. It opened, and Cesco came through. His hat was pushed to the back of his head, exposing his face entirely. There was a faint blueness to his lips and some vomit on his sleeve. He clutched his stomach painfully. Had the idiot eaten some of the tainted food himself?

"Master, beware! We are poisoned! Angelo is barely able to stand, and I am vomiting blood!" There was no sign of blood, but Cesco did certainly look poorly.

"Still your tongue, boy," snapped Tharwat in anger. "Do not presume to accuse our host of such a thing! It is not you alone who suffers. Something wrong in the meat, as we have already heard. Everyone in these walls has been affected." He turned quickly to the Doge. "Forgive my page, your majesty. He is overly dramatic." Tharwat gave Morsicato a nod. "Go, see to this one and Angelo. Take them back to our lodgings. I will be along."

Morsicato left with Cesco leaning heavily on his arm. The doctor felt Dandolo's eyes on him all the way out. Tharwat must have sensed Dandolo's suspicions, and was remaining behind to allay suspicions. *Sacrificing himself to save Pietro. Hardly the act of a devilish Assassin.*

The guards at the palace doors were too busy fighting off their own queasiness to ask where the second boy had gotten to. If they wondered, they probably assumed he was still attending the Moor.

As soon as they were out of the palace, Morsicato said, "You didn't actually ingest any of it, did you?"

Cesco straightened at once. "Of course not! But it had to look good, so I held my breath as long as I could, several times in a row, then stuck my finger down my throat. Convincing?"

"Very. Where is Pietro? Did you get him out?"

"He and Detto should be at the ship by now."

"The ship," said Morsicato with a heavy sigh.

"That's right!" cried Cesco brightly. "You don't like being on the water, do you? In all our years at Ravenna, I never saw you go swimming or even take a pleasure cruise."

Morsicato didn't rise to the imp's bait. It was true, he was a very poor sailor – the largest ship in the calmest sea had the ability to churn his stomach worse that Dog's Mercury. But it was the best plan of escape, so he had acceded.

The hired gondola was waiting for them, and they shoved off at once. "What about my Shadow?" asked Cesco in real concern.

"We can't delay." Morsicato's glance conveyed the unspoken, *Or we might all be caught.* "If he's there when we set sail, he's there. If not, well…"

In twenty minutes they were climbing up the short ladder to the ship, already bobbing between San Marco's Basin and the Arsenale, far off the quays. It was a long, low, single-decked cutter, hired by Tharwat in his servile guise. The crew was well-paid, the captain moreso, on the condition that he deliver his passengers to their destination with all haste. Moreover, he was Genoese by descent, and hardly inclined to tattle to Venetian authorities.

By arrangement, the ship had already cleared the customs officers and moved out into the lane. But now, thanks to a handy bit of chicanery, there was a fouling of the lines, which brought a sail whipping free. It was rigged to do so, and could be back up in a moment, but from the shore it looked as if the crew were simply incompetent.

The gondola angled as if to head for San Marco's basin. At the last moment it whipped left and pulled up alongside the waiting vessel. Cesco scrambled up the ladder, the doctor practically throwing himself after. The gondola, having wasted only fifteen seconds, continued on towards the basin as if nothing had chanced.

The captain was there to greet them. "Well done. And this mist is a real blessing. Otherwise all this coming and going might bring that customs bastard back."

"So the others have arrived?" demanded Morsicato anxiously.

"Another boy, and some poor beggar," said the captain. "Came in a couple minutes ago. I sent them below and gave him some new clothes. Looks like he's been gnawed by rats!"

"Then he should be right at home on board," said Cesco. The captain stumped off, grumbling.

"We have to tell him to shove off right now," said Morsicato.

"We'll wait ten minutes," said Cesco firmly. "I understand your concerns, but we didn't save one to lose the other." He descended to the cabin, and Morsicato followed, grumbling. Cesco had that effect.

◆        ◊        ◆

Down in the cabin, Pietro was shirtless, scrubbing himself with a stone over a basin of water. He glanced up as the door opened. "Cesco! Thank God. Who is that with – Morsicato? Is it you? What the devil happened to your face?" gaped Pietro, causing both Cesco and Detto to titter like girls.

Before the doctor could reply they heard a commotion outside and ran up to the deck, Pietro throwing on a borrowed sailor's shirt as he went.

Idle sailors clustered along the starboard side, gazing through the mist at some excitement on the quay. Several torches illumed the mist, their light reflecting on steel weapons in the near distance.

"S'a fight," observed a sailor, squinting hard.

"Who's that tall fellow they're after?" asked his mate. "Looks like he's burned."

"He's a black, fool!" said a third.

"A negro?"

"A Moor." Cesco elbowed his way to the rail, craning to see.

On the quay Tharwat al-Dhaamin was swinging a polearm at his attackers, who jabbed back at him with sword and spears and oars. Even as he parried and feinted, one of the weapons connected and the Moor toppled backwards over the edge into the water.

"No," breathed Pietro.

"Poor bastard," said Morsicato.

"He's not done yet," insisted Cesco.

At once several attackers rushed to the edge to throw spears into the disturbed water. There was a lighter mark in the water where the Moor's fine outer wrap came floating to the top.

Amid the mutters of the sailors, Morsicato said, "Do you see him?"

"No," replied Pietro, watching closely.

"He's there," said Cesco with certainty.

The men at the quay's edge moved aside for a tall figure in a flowing gonella – Dandolo. The Venetian Ambassador was cursing every one of the men surrounding him. The fine patrician head then came up to stare out into the lanes. It seemed that for a moment he was staring right at Alaghieri. Pietro didn't move, lest he draw more attention to himself. Then it occurred to him that the presence of two boys might be just as revealing.

But Cesco was now on the higher deck, hidden from view as he stood beside the vessel's master. "Captain?"

Reluctantly, the captain tore his eyes away from the quayside excitement. "What is it, boy?"

"My master is in a hurry," murmured Cesco, nodding towards

Morsicato. "He feels that if we stay, we may be caught up in a general search of vessels. Those bastard customs agents," he added, shaking a fist.

If the captain made a connection between fighting on the docks and his eager passengers, he said nothing of it. Perhaps thinking of his promised fee, he gave orders to set out at once. The 'fallen' sail was righted, the oars were manned, and in moments they were underway.

"Now you want to leave?" demanded Morsicato in Cesco's ear. "*Now?*"

"He'll be fine," said Cesco tranquilly.

Pietro watched the place where Tharwat had dived. *He better not be dead. I didn't have a chance to apologize.*

Cesco was on the poop of the ship, fiddling with a length of rope. He began to whistle, until he was told to stop by the sailors who kept mistaking his whistles for orders. Instead he took up singing a childish ditty, one that was commonly sung in conjunction with a game – throwing stones or mock-jousting on another boy's shoulders at an apple on a string.

> *Can'st thou not hit it, my good man?*
> *Can'st thou not hit it, hit it, hit it?*
> *Yes, I can hit it, yes, I can,*
> *Yes, I can hit it, hit it, hit it!*
>
> *Thou can'st not hit it, hit it, hit it,*
> *Thou can'st not hit it, my good man.*
> *And I cannot, cannot, cannot,*
> *And I cannot, another can!*

After singing it through once, Cesco substituted other words for hit. At first the words were common synonyms for hit – *strike, cuff, beat.* Then he moved on to more titillating replacements – *whack, pinch, slap* – and from there to words with strong double meanings – *stroke, spear, pierce.*

By this point all the sailors were singing the answering part of the song, chortling as they did. Was the boy even aware of what he was singing?

Cesco remained sitting on the poop, looking aft, tying knots around a loose plank. But he soon had them all howling when he proved he knew what he was about, substituting the verb 'hump.' The sailors sang with gusto, "*Yes, I can hump it, yes I can! Yes, I can hump it, hump it, hump it!*"

Expecting Cesco to tease them with the reply of "Thou canst not hump it, hump it, hump it," they were surprised when he leapt out of his seat. "Man overboard! Man overboard!" Immediately he threw his plank into the water, the rope trailing after it.

The sails were hauled in and the idlers clustered around the poop deck, staring aft into those fog-shrouded waters. One said, "I didn't hear a splash."

"We was singin' too loud," said another.

"Poor devil," exclaimed a third. "Look at this fog! He's a goner for certes!"

None of them dived in, for none could swim. Instead a lamp was brought to peer into the water just in case by some miracle the poor devil had learned to paddle.

Cesco's rope went suddenly taught and a cheer went up from the crew – the man in the water had clutched at the plank! Then a gust of wind cleared the nearby fog. "He's a Moor!" The man instantly drew his knife, raising it to hack the heathen's lifeline.

Cesco grasped the man's arm at the elbow and wrist. A simple twist and the man's hand was empty, the knife skittering down the deck. "He's with us."

Pietro and Morsicato hauled the rope to pull the Moor aboard. A magnificent feat of strength and will, to swim under the water until out of sight of the quay, then to carry on to intercept the ship. Pietro realized that Cesco had used a slow rhythm to his song, keeping the oars moving with less power, so that the Moor could have a chance. In fact, the song served a double purpose, also leading Tharwat to the right ship. *Clever!*

They got the sodden Tharwat below decks to dry him. Barely had he sat before Cesco was demanding, "What happened! Tell us everything!"

"Dandolo suspected," croaked the Moor, rubbing his shivering limbs to life again. "He sent to the gaols. Before the answer returned, I struck Dandolo cold and told the Doge he would be cursed forever if he raised the alarum. I departed. They pursued."

"We saw the rest." Pietro laid a hand on Tharwat's shoulder. "I am very glad to see you."

Tharwat actually smiled. "I am equally pleased you still live."

"Thanks to you," replied Pietro feelingly, "here and in Padua both. How did you know I'd need you more than Cesco?"

"I *am* an astrologer." In spite of his chattering teeth, the Moor's note of real mirth had them all laughing. "But were I not, nothing could prevent Cesco's treatment at the Scaliger's hands. It seemed assured that, as long as he was with Cangrande, he was safe. Whereas you were alone, part of a scheme none of us saw until too late."

"I'm thankful. Cesco told me about dosing the Doge's guards. Is that the kind of thing you were trained to do?"

Tharwat's eyes veiled, but he sensed Pietro was reaching out, trying to understand. "An ounce of humiliation is worth a pound of poison."

"What are you two talking about?" demanded Cesco. "Trained for what?"

"Never you mind." To Tharwat, Pietro said, "I wish I'd seen you strike Dandolo."

The ship caught a fresh wind and lurched, sending the doctor to his knees. "Ooooch…"

"Why, what's the matter?" asked Cesco.

"Hate boats," growled the doctor to no one. "Hate 'em."

Pietro said, "Where are we heading?"

Tharwat answered. "They'll be searching for us on the road east to Verona, and in the waterways south. So the captain has orders to feint south, then move north and put us off somewhere close. We'll be heading inland by midnight."

"Right, but wrong," said Pietro firmly. "They know you have me with you, and I'd be telling you to head for Modena. That's where Cangrande is, isn't it?"

Cesco nodded with a frown. "How did you know?"

"Ooooooh!" The doctor clutched at the wall as they entered the larger waterways and the chop increased.

"Do not close your eyes," suggested Tharwat helpfully. "Lock your gaze on a fixed point."

"Doesn't help!" Morsicato gagged.

"Ew!" cried Detto.

"Yes, ew! Go outside, if you're going to heave!" Grinning, Cesco turned back to Pietro. "How do you know he's at Modena? You've been imprisoned!"

"What's the date?" Pietro was answered with quizzical glances. "Today's date, what is it?"

"The tenth of November," said Tharwat, always aware of dates and moon and stars.

"Then we're not too late." In a few brief words, Pietro explained all the elements of the failed plot between Passerino and Dandolo, and of Bonaccolsi's current enterprise with the unknown Scaligeri. He concluded by saying, "Dandolo will think I'll convince you all to head for Modena to warn Cangrande."

"That's too bad," said Cesco. "Because that's just what we have to do."

"No, we go –Vicenza, maybe? Or back to Ravenna. Guido Novello is a friend, he'll hide you until this is all over." He saw the bewilderment in the boy's face. "Don't you see? Whoever the plotter is, as long as you stay alive, his plan has failed."

Cesco held up a hand. "Wait. I just found out who I am, who my father is. Are you saying I should now turn tail and let him be murdered?"

"Not at all," snapped Pietro, though in his soul he recognized the question's fairness. Acutely aware of his recent deficit of morality, he was determined to save the Scaliger's life. On the day he was knighted, Pietro had sworn to serve the Scaliger, and that oath bound him tightly.

None of which obscured Pietro's paramount responsibility. "But *you* have to stay alive. You're more important than anything."

"How could I live with myself knowing I did nothing while my father was stabbed in the back?"

"He won't be. We'll put in and I'll ride inland. The rest of you, hide."

Cesco gave a soundless laugh. "How do you think that's better? Letting you risk your life while I play the hare and hide in a hole? No, I'm going with you."

"I'm going with Cesco," said Detto instantly.

Pietro's voice grew sterner by the moment. "Talk all you like, neither one of you is going back to Modena. When the battle happens, you're not going to be there. No – Cesco, I don't care what you want, as long as you're alive to want it."

"I'm sorry I saved you!"

"I'm grateful. Now let me save you."

Cesco glowered at Pietro, who stared back unrepentantly. The moment was broken by the sound of Morsicato swallowing down his own gorge. Cesco clucked his tongue. "I'm astonished you're such a poor sailor, doctor! You have such a natural rolling gait – it goes back and forth, back and forth..."

"Stop! Stop!" begged Morsicato.

"Yes, do," said Pietro. "However mad you are at me, we don't need him vomiting like one of those Venetians."

"At least if he does, he now has no beard to catch it," observed Cesco.

"I have a potential solution," said the Moor, referring not to the doctor's suffering but their general dilemma. "We land and find shelter, and at the same time send someone innocuous to Cangrande, someone who cannot be stopped without the whole world coming to an end."

"Not Antonia," said Pietro.

"I was thinking of someone else." He explained and they agreed. In five minutes the plans were laid and Tharwat went to issue the captain new instructions.

# FORTY-FIVE

*Modena*
*Monday, 11 November*
*1325*

"TWO DAYS! Two days!" The Scaliger was pacing like a hungry beast in a kennel. "I'll skin him alive."

"There hasn't been any sign of them?" inquired Passerino Bonaccolsi, sipping a cup of honeyed water.

"No," fretted Bailardino. "Not of either of them."

"Why not organize a search?" suggested Passerino.

Cangrande scowled. "If I had the time, I'd set my hound after him."

"You aren't concerned?"

Cangrande wagged an angry finger. "This was no kidnapping. He took his cloak and some gold I had lying about. At this moment our heirs are gallivanting around the city laughing their fool heads off. He thinks it was bad before? O, I'll *flay* him!"

"Well, allow me to supply you with a squire until he turns up," offered Passerino. They had set up camp near Modena, and the battle would commence in the next day or so. Cangrande would indeed be needing a squire, whose duty was to ride beside his master all the way up to the moment combat was engaged and aid his master in any way possible. If the knight was unhorsed, the squire fetched another *destrier* or offered up his own mount. When his knight was hurt, the squire brought him from the field and bound the wounds, burning them closed with a red-hot dagger if necessary. And if a knight died in battle, it was the squire's duty to see to the burial arrangements.

Cangrande thanked Passerino for his concern. "But I've already spoken to Montecchio, my personal bodyguard for the coming battle, and he's agreed to lend me one of his. Another relative, actually, but far more reliable. Young Paride."

Shrugging, Passerino rose to go. "Excellent. Well, I'll see you both at noon. May I wish you the best of the day?" Saluting, the Mantuan lord left the tent.

Bailardino clapped a hand on his brother-in-law's shoulder. "We were young once, and I daresay we got up to more trouble than those two ever will."

"*I* was young," corrected Cangrande. "You were always ancient."

"Whelp! Fine. But today is an important day for you and me, and we can't be slack. Dress for the feast. Meanwhile, I'm sending out searchers. You're likely right, they've scarpered. But Cesco was poisoned, remember. I want to be sure my son is safe."

"Do as you please," replied Cangrande. "But they'll turn up all grins and insolence. See you at the feast. "

It was San Martino's day, the anniversary of their knighting, and the soldiers were planning a midday celebration for the Capitano di Verona and the Podestà of Vicenza. Of course, the real hosts were the officers and nobles like Nico da Lozzo, Montecchio, Bonaventura, and Capulletto. But the ranker soldiers were invited to cheer their lord and gorge themselves in his honour.

Mastino and Fuchs were present, carousing with the ranker soldiers. Alblivious was more subdued, being deprived of his boon companion – being unmartial to the point of ridiculousness, Poco had returned to Verona directly following the wedding.

Mingling with the poorer knights and low soldiers, Mastino hid his resentment behind an easy smile. He hated the need, but as the Scaliger's heir had wooed all the nobility with his golden tongue and silver tonsils, there was little left for the Mastiff to take but the scraps. He had to build a faction, something he'd never paid attention to before. Before this summer he had simply assumed he would inherit all of Cangrande's followers and rule Verona. Cesco had changed everything.

Tomorrow he had to be seen to be brave, brave enough to earn a knighthood. Verona's knighthood was called the Order of the Mastiff, yet here was Mastino, sans knighthood, sans honour, sans anything.

Fuchs could read his master's thoughts. He murmured, "At least the bastard won't be getting knighted ahead of you. He isn't even here."

Mastino grunted. "Wonder where the little shitheel has got himself. Whatever he's doing, I'll wager it steals the Capitano's thunder. Wouldn't that be nice?"

At the head of the main table, Cangrande was deflecting the inevitable questions about his heir with such humour that only a trained watcher could discern the ember burning in his eye. That Scaligeri temper, so much closer to the surface since Ponte Corbo, was on the verge of spewing forth.

All around him the celebration went on, becoming sloppier as such events invariably did. After the salutes and drinks there were songs and games, and a man could sit near the Scaliger without drawing much attention. Cangrande was surprised to feel a light touch at his elbow. Turning, he found himself nose to nose with Antony Capulletto. "My lord, I need to speak to you."

Passerino appeared as if by magic at Antony's side. "Capulletto! There you are! There's a bet that Montecchio can juggle four knives at once. He says you've seen him do it. Will you testify? Or are you busy bothering the Scaliger again?" He turned to Cangrande. "I keep telling him your son is too young to marry his daughter! Not everyone enjoys a child-bride!"

Capulletto didn't colour, as one might have expected. Instead he looked pale. "My lord, a moment of your time—"

But at that moment a page came struggling through the throng to Cangrande's side. "You have a visitor, my lord. She is in your tents."

Cangrande grinned at Passerino. "A gift?"

Passerino shook his head, smiling also. "Not from me. If you don't want her, be sure to pass her along."

"For shame! Aren't you recently married?"

"In the field, no man is married"

"Well said. No, wait – you stole that from me! I declare, Passerino, one of these days you're going to have to have an original thought. You can't trod in my footsteps forever!"

"True," said Passerino evenly. "But until you stumble, I don't see why I shouldn't follow the trail you blaze."

Capulletto had already slipped away, so Cangrande left the feast and ducked inside his tent in the nearby camp. The smell of lavender girded him even before he laid eyes on her. But Cangrande still threw up his hands in mock surprise. "Katerina! What a pleasure! Are you here to help honour us valiant knights? Or do you mean to don men's clothes once more and fight beside us? If you think your health can manage, I'll let you lead a division. No matter their superior numbers, the enemy would not be able to prevail. I know I never could. We'd win before noon."

His sister was seated on his camp stool, hands folded in her lap, the picture of patience, her fixed smile polite and bored at once. "Are you quite through?"

"I am well lubricated," said Cangrande, pouring himself more wine from his private stock, "meaning I may start again at any moment. You'd best get in while there's a lull."

"Well, brother dear, as tempting as your martial invitation is, I am afraid I must decline. If this army wins, it shall do so without my help. Or yours," she added.

Cangrande set his wine aside. "Oh? Why, pray?"

"First things first. Cesco is in Vicenza. So is Detto." Katerina's voice was neither furtive nor low, simply crisp as she relayed facts. "This battle is a trap for you. Our own beloved Ser Alaghieri uncovered a plot, though he required some little assistance in relaying it. The crux of it is that in the midst of the battle you will be cut down by men pretending to be allies. And not just you. Mastino, Alberto, Paride. And Cesco, were he here. My husband and son, too, just for good measure. All slain in combat. If it's any comfort, it would be a good death. That is, if you do not object to your whole line being stamped out at once. Myself, I have some qualms."

Sitting at the edge of his camp bed, Cangrande showed no surprise. "Tell me more."

Katerina was equally composed. "Pietro, Cesco, Detto, and company all appeared at the palace in the early hours this morning. They relayed their news, with all the details Pietro had gathered while a prisoner in Venice. Did you know he has been in a cell in the Doge's palace for the last month?"

"No." Cangrande raised an eyebrow. "That must have been uncomfortable."

"He seems whole, if thin. Almost as thin as Cesco," she added.

Cangrande waved that away. "This is no time to discuss my hobbies. Did Pietro say who was the author of my impending misfortune?"

"Authors," she corrected. "He only knows two names. Dandolo and Bonaccolsi."

"Passerino." Cangrande's eyes became veiled as he sat, turning the name over. All at once he brightened. "Trying to step out my shadow. Good for him!"

Katerina evinced no surprise at his lack of anger. "There is also a member of our family working to take your place."

Cangrande's eyes twinkled. "Is it you?"

"No. If I wished you dead, Francesco —"

"I would be long in my grave. Well I know it."

"What do you mean to do?"

"What can I do? I cannot call Bonaccolsi out without tangible proof – letters, whatnot. Besides, even a whisper of this might cause a rift between our two armies, who may take it upon themselves to sort the matter out. Then, while we're biting each other's necks, the Bolognese will fall on us and tear us to pieces. No, this cannot be made public. Not yet."

"Don't rely too heavily on the loyalty of your own men," warned Katerina. "Pietro's information is that Passerino has turned at least one of your nobles."

Cangrande snapped his fingers. "Capulletto! Fool that I am, I should have seen it. He's been trying to get me on my own. I thought it was more of his idiot marriage alliances, so I deflected him."

"There's an easy way to find out — call him here. You will have your proof to break with Mantua."

Cangrande shook his head. "Too obvious. Besides, he must be under duress. Who knows what sword is hanging over his head? It could be that if he speaks out openly, something dire will befall him and his. He won't thank me for putting him at risk."

"Then what will you do? Ride into battle and sacrifice yourself? Noble, certainly, and you can die content knowing your heir will live to take your place, with me there to guide him. But I didn't believe you were so altruistic. Or stupid."

"You paint a compelling fresco. But your baiting jibes are only a tithe of what awaits me."

"In the afterlife?"

"Here, in Modena. My allies are about to be terribly put out."

"Because?"

A slow smile spread. Not his famous *allegria*, but something more feral. "Because I plan to take umbrage. I will indulge myself in a monumental snit over some trifle and remove my armies. During our retreat I will have a little chat with Capulletto. But not before. Knowing that a plot exists is enough to act. I can learn the details later."

Katerina rose. "You know, brother, he may try your temper, but having Cesco has restored you. You have a *purpose* again. Even if I don't approve of the purpose, I applaud the results."

If her compliment wounded him, he was far too skilled to ever show it. "I'm surprised my little heir is not here with you. Afraid of my wrath?"

Katerina smiled, the left side of her face drooping only slightly. "Embarrassingly, I don't believe he's even conscious of it. He has been forced to remain behind, having sworn a solemn oath not to try to come to Modena or meet you anywhere. Why are you laughing?"

"Because *that*, sweet sister, is a very carefully worded oath."

♦ ◊ ♦

### Vicenza

In the atrium of the Nogarola palace, Pietro, Tharwat, and Morsicato were resting on stone benches. It had been a hard ride through the night hours, and the boys were sent directly to bed just as the sun was rising. Informed, Donna Katerina had shown she was well enough to ride by galloping off to Modena.

The three men now sat, Morsicato tending to Pietro's many bites and scrapes, while they speculated which della Scala was party to Passerino's plan.

"My money is on Mastino," said Morsicato, pressing a hot coal quickly against a bite.

"*Ah!* Stop that." Pietro shook off the quick pain. "We're forgetting Pathino. As a bastard Scaliger, he has as much claim as Cesco."

"How on earth would he get Passerino's support?" demanded the doctor, smearing a salve over the burn. "He's entirely unknown to the people. No, it's Mastino."

Pietro turned to the Moor. "What do you think, Tharwat?"

The Moor sat perfectly still, his eyes closed. "Federigo."

*Federigo!* Pietro saw it at once. Used, slighted, banished, Federigo was the prime candidate for a Venetian plot. Passerino had even been assigned to escort the exiled della Scala away from Verona. They could have hatched this plot that very day.

Morsicato also saw sense in that accusation. "I wonder where he is at this moment?"

"Somewhere near Verona, probably," guessed Pietro. "If his plan works, he needs to be close to take advantage and declare himself the new Capitano."

Finished, Morsicato set aside his tools. "Should we try to find him? He's an exile, we could arrest him."

"Where do we start? North, south? In the city, in the countryside? Not a clue."

"We should turn it over to Cesco," said Morsicato with a laugh. "Just the kind of puzzle to appeal to him. In fact, I'm surprised he hasn't figured it all out already—"

Pietro sat bolt upright, sharing a startled look with Tharwat. Both men leapt to their feet and started to run, Pietro's injured feet bursting open again.

"What?" demanded Morsicato in their wake. "What did I say?"

They pounded up the stairs and down the corridor, past the sentry outside Detto's room, and threw wide the doors.

The beds were empty.

"Damn it!" cried Pietro, rounding on the sentry. "You were supposed to make sure they stayed put!"

"I was told to guard them," said the man, peering into the room. "I thought that meant—"

"You let them sneak by you! Idiot!" Pietro's anger was not for the guard. Once again the two boys had disappeared, just as they used to slip away into the stews and alleys of Ravenna. But this situation was far more dire.

"How did he have the strength? He looked as exhausted as I feel."

Tharwat bowed his head gravely. "The fault is mine. Before we went to Venice, I supplied him with a few doses of that herb we discussed. It endows one with renewed energy, for a time."

Though reconciled to the Moor's past, Pietro was furious to hear that Cesco had again been given hashish. Seeing the conflicted feelings written on Pietro's face, the Moor said, "It is not evil that he has another resource, when so many of us had abandoned him. But that is an argument for another day. We must divine where they're headed."

"Got a pendulum handy? That's the only way we'll trace them."

"Maybe he left a note," said the puffing doctor, just catching up.

"Yes." Tharwat strode into the room to examine the beds. "If he was concerned with fooling us, he would have stuffed the beds with bolsters, make it look like they were still in them. He wants us to follow him. He just doesn't want to be stopped."

Pietro joined the Moor by the beds. There was no note on either. In fact, the only object other than bedding was a cap. Not a brimmed hat, but a night-cap, floppy and loose.

Tharwat picked it up, turning it over in his fingers. "Cesco never wears such things."

"A clue," said Pietro. "But what does a night-cap..?" His mind leapt to a family crest, one he knew well. "Dammit! I know where he's gone!" *But why there?*

♦        ◊        ♦

The retreat order was not popular among Verona's soldiers, but Cangrande was proud of how he had engineered it. He'd returned to the feast and, feigning drunkenness, had indulged in a monumental fit of pique. As the inciting cause, he first singled out one of the foreign generals, a Visconti, whose father Cangrande had never liked. "Your father is a secret Guelph, I know it, I. And I own no desire to fight alongside the scion of such a man!"

He'd been interested in how Passerino would respond. Sure

enough, the lord of Mantua intervened on Cangrande's side, demanding the Visconti to take his troops off a ways and wait until needed – he was to have no hand in the coming battle. Bonaccolsi had done his damnedest to keep Cangrande from renouncing the battle.

The Scaliger next went after the Imperial standards. Passerino had understandably given his new brother-in-law, Rainaldo d'Este, the honour of carrying them in to the coming battle. But by strict protocol they belonged to Cangrande as leader of the Lombard Ghibellines. He'd demanded them, and at the slightest hesitation had launched into a tirade over being insulted on his most honoured day. Before Passerino could intervene again, he'd issued orders for his army to pull up stakes and leave within the hour.

Having indulged his love of playacting, the Scaliger was now racing back to Verona in the company of anyone who could keep up. It was forty miles to Verona and he couldn't let his army's slower pace hold him back. Instead he left Bailardino in charge of the army, with Katerina in tow – she had already ridden hard enough just to reach them. *Interesting, dear sister, how the stroke effects come and go...*

Those who had a nose for such things scented a rat. The Scaliger had been drunk – until in his saddle, when he had spurred like the Devil was nipping his heels. Something was in the wind!

Mastino was among those who kept pace, and he used his status as family to demand an explanation. "This was going to be my first big battle! Why are we running away?"

Because he couldn't be sure which of his family was in Passerino's purse, Cangrande chose the reply that would most annoy Mastino. "Thank your cousin Cesco."

Mastino cursed. "What's he done now?"

"Mischief, is all I know. Don't worry, you'll have a decent battle next year. Now be a good boy and tell Capulletto to get his lazy arse up here."

Seething, Mastino dropped back into the knot of riders and relayed the message. Capulletto left his groom and retainers and pulled level with the Scaliger. One look at the big face under the sandy hair and Cangrande knew he was correct. He gave no preamble. "I don't blame you. Whatever you've done, you were clearly unwilling."

Blood rushed into Antony's unusually pale face. "Thank God! O, thank God! When you gave the order I was so relieved! I kept trying to warn you, but—"

"Who's behind it, Antony?"

"Bonaccolsi, I think."

"You're not certain?"

"He's the one who always steered me away from you, and his men were camped around mine. A neat trick."

"But he never said anything outright?" pressed Cangrande.

"No. No, it was Federigo who contacted me."

The breath hissed from between Cangrande's teeth. "Of course. The last Scaliger standing. It's almost clever, except that Verona will never follow him. What did he say to you, Antony? How did he think he could manage it?"

"With my support. He…" Capulletto tried to speak more, but his words came out in an exasperated sigh.

Cangrande thought he understood. "Extortion, obviously. Whatever it is, Antony, I pardon you. Though I might not have if you hadn't goaded Montecchio into being my personal guard. What made you do that?"

It is difficult to shrug while riding a horse, but Antony managed something like it. "You needed protection. If I volunteered to guard you, the conspirators would have ordered me to do the deed myself. Federigo is in my house at this moment, holding my family hostage."

"And using your house as a base," said Cangrande, thinking aloud. "Not bad. A stone's throw from the palaces, and your home is so walled in, he and a dozen men might go unnoticed." Cangrande saw Capulletto's expression and smiled reassuringly. "Don't worry, we'll free them. How did it start? What was their toehold?"

Colouring again, Antony spoke in fits and starts that had nothing to do with the rhythm of the horse. "Some – business dealings. With Padua. Before the truce." He took the plunge. "Arms. I sold arms to Padua."

Cangrande chose to laugh. "No wonder they moved on you! Technically, that's treason. How did they learn of it?"

Antony's voice was almost inhuman. "I imagine my in-laws let something slip. It's how they forced me to marry their daughter."

Cangrande's eyebrows shot up. "Another riddle solved! It's shaping into quite a day."

Capulletto cleared his throat. "I am at fault for not braving all and coming right to you. If I have to die, you'll get no argument."

"O Antony, do not beg your death of me! We are all guilty of a little treason, now and again. I've done far worse, I assure you. And you quite made up for it by making sure I was protected. Though I'm surprised you chose Mariotto as my champion."

"He's the only one I could have baited into it. And he'd die to protect a friend in battle. I know."

"That's very honest, Antony, as well as clever. I like you the more for it. Should we tell Mariotto your high opinion of him?" Before Antony could protest, the Scaliger swept on. "No, we couldn't without mentioning the extortion. A shame! It might soften his heart towards you. It's far past time the two of you made up!"

"Maybe," allowed Capulletto. "But not this minute."

"Quite right. First and foremost, we have to get back to Verona and make certain your family is safe. And put down cousin Federigo's little revolt!"

◆　◇　◆

### Verona

Cesco and Detto arrived in Verona about three hours past midday. The city was in the midst of celebrating San Martino's day, and there were roars of cheers for Castelbarco, being feasted in the Piazza della Signoria with his wife and grown son. Like Cangrande and Bailardino, he had been knighted on this day, and here in Verona he had the celebrations all to himself.

The boys avoided the central square. Nor were they headed for Capulletto's house, which Cesco had said was their ultimate destination. Instead they skirted the eastern edge of the Adige.

"How do you know Federigo's at Capulletto's house?" demanded Detto again. "Or even that it's him?"

"I have powers and abilities far beyond those of mortal men," replied Cesco mysteriously. "Also I'm a good guesser. Federigo is the only Scaliger who won't be at Modena, and Capulletto was anxiously trying to tell Cangrande something the other night. Bonaccolsi stopped him with a very heavy-handed quote. I'm surprised I didn't see it all then. Keep your hat on, and your head low. If we're recognized, our ship is sunk. This way."

Detto followed Cesco down a winding sidestreet. "Why not go to Castelbarco"

Cesco was already turning at the next bend. "First, if I'm wrong — don't look so shocked, it happens!"

"I'm just shocked you're admitting it!"

Cesco blew a raspberry. "Figs. If I'm wrong, which I'm not, and Federigo is somewhere else, which he isn't, we'll have let him know we're looking for him. Also we will have scared all the nice people in the Capulletti household. On the other hand, if I'm right and Castelbarco breaks down the front gate, there's no telling what a bunch of desperate men trapped in that house will do. Again, women and servants suffer.

Better to sneak in and find the lay of the land." Cesco beamed at Detto. "Besides, who do you trust more – the adults, or us?"

"Us, definitely." Detto grinned. "We just broke someone out of a Venetian prison!"

"Out of the Doge's Palace," corrected Cesco. "Has a grander ring to it. Here we are." He reined in half a block from the gate to the convent of Santa Maria in Organo. "Go and ask for Suor Beatrice."

"Why don't you?" demanded Detto.

Cesco rolled his eyes. "Because, dunce, we're on a secret mission. If I go, they'll recognize me for sure. They might not you. Even if they do, it won't cause as much of a stir."

"Don't call me dunce, you moron. What should I tell her?"

"Exactly what I told you. Then ask if she's willing to take a risk and go call on the household. We're going to need a distraction." Cesco produced a small sticky wafer and popped a piece of it into his mouth. "If she says yes, tell her to go now. If she says no, leave as quick as you can. She'll run right to Castelbarco, and we won't have much time."

"What's that you're eating?"

"Nothing," said Cesco, stuffing the sticky remnants into the leather case on his belt.

Detto held out his hand. "I'm hungry. Give me some."

"It's medicine," said Cesco. "For the poisoning, the after-effects."

"Oh." Detto withdrew his hand. "Where are you going to be?"

"I'll wait at the Torre dei Lamberti. From there we can climb to the roof overlooking the Capulletti house. Meet me there, no matter what she says. Go on!" Cesco turned the horse's head and rode off.

Detto watched his friend go, then rang the convent's bell.

# FORTY-SIX

THIBAULT CAPULLETTO lay on the floor of his cousin Giulietta's nursery, trussed like a Christmas hog, a rag stuffed in his mouth in place of an apple. He watched the comings and goings of the household servants with what he hoped were withering looks. He'd been allowed the same freedom until he had tried to stab their captor's neck. That had earned him a beating. When he'd tried again, he'd been bound hand and foot and tossed into Giulietta's room, high in the tower. When he hadn't stopped yelling, even after a repeated kicking, he'd been gagged. So now there was nothing to do but glare at the servants who weren't fighting back, weren't even trying to do anything but stay alive. *Cowards!*

It was loud in the nursery. Babies are sensitive to their environs, and the tension in the air caused a great deal of wailing. Angelica was singing softly to the infant at her breast. But every few minutes one of the mercenaries would come in and tell her to keep it quiet, or else. Thibault tried to do with his eyes what he wanted to do with his dagger.

The most recent time the order had come, Thibault had waited for the mercenary to leave, then writhed and kicked until Angelica noticed him. "I'm sorry, my lovie!" she told him. "If I let you loose and you get caught, they'll know who did it, and they might hurt the girls. O, if only you weren't such a hothead, you might have slipped away and spread word!"

Run? Was she insane? It would just the thing his uncle could use to keep him from his birthright – an accusation of cowardice. And clearly this was Uncle Antony's fault. He wasn't a real man, to have let his home be taken over in secret like this!

A bell rung below, meaning someone was at the gate. *Spread the alarum!* thought Thibault fiercely. *Take the risk!* But he knew the porter was a coward. It was infuriating for ten year-old Thibault to know he was the only real man in the house.

He imagined what was happening in the tunnel three floors below: the porter shambling to the small door in the large wooden gate, a knife at his back. The courtyard was filled with a dozen mercenaries, surrounding the household staff. Meanwhile the leader would climb to threaten his best hostages.

On cue, Federigo della Scala arose from the open staircase into the highest room of the house. Behind him was a mercenary, dragging Tessa by the arm. Even in distress, she was beautiful. Generally Thibault had little use for women, but his feelings for her had only grown. Motherhood had endowed her with a kind of steel he hadn't seen in her before.

It was evident now. Her eyes didn't go to Angelica or to her child, but to Thibault. *This would never have happened if you were* my *wife!* He imagined the same thought in her eyes as she was tossed into a corner chair.

Federigo strode to the window overlooking the street. His henchman asked, "Can you see who it is?"

Federigo craned his neck. "A nun, I think. Alone. Who is she?" Tessa shrugged defiantly and Federigo slapped her across the cheek. Thibault writhed while Angelica gasped, burying her face in the suckling baby's neck. "Who is she?"

Still a few months shy of her thirteenth birthday, Tessa's steel only went so far. "Suor Beatrice. A friend of my husband's."

"Will she want to come in? What does she want?"

Angelica answered for her mistress. "She's here to ask after the little ones, that's all. A courtesy."

"And if she's told to go away?" asked Federigo.

"She'll go, and come back tomorrow."

Federigo considered, still peeking out of the tower window. "Go, make sure she's gotten rid of." The henchman trotted down the stairs, leaving Federigo alone with Thibault, the women, and the children. As a precaution the traitor drew his long dagger, letting it hang loosely by his side, a passive threat.

No one said anything. The tension was as thick as it had been when the armed men had first arrived the day before, under cover of darkness.

Federigo was leaning out the window. "Good. She's going. Lucky for all of you."

Thibault heard light footfalls on the stair. Still watching the nun suspiciously, Federigo said, "What did she want?"

"She bore a sad message, cos," replied a laconic young voice from the lip of the stairwell. "No *coup d'état*, I'm afraid. Just a *coupé*."

Gasping, Federigo whirled about. Had his mouth been clear, Thibault too would have gasped. The Scaliger's heir was leaning against the rail of the stair he had just ascended. Thin and wild-eyed, when he saw Thibault lying trussed on the floor his features became darkly amused. "O mighty Ratcatcher, how low have we fallen?"

"What are you doing here?" demanded Federigo breathlessly.

"A family reunion, of course! I got your invitation and decided I couldn't refuse! Ah ah!" he said, wagging an admonishing finger. "Don't call for your men. Before they arrived, I'd have your guts out for my lute strings." He showed his own dagger, just as long and wickedly sharp as Federigo's. "I'm young and much faster than you. Besides, by now our sweet Suor Beatrice has informed Lord Castelbarco and the city militia is descending upon this place in droves. So your men will have other concerns."

Federigo's mouth was working on soundless protests as Cesco swept into the room, taking in his surroundings. "Really, cos, I must commend your choice of bolt-holes. Enclosed, and thus invisible to prying eyes, yet within a shout of the palace. The only mistake is something you couldn't possibly have guessed. You see, I'm very familiar with the rooftops hereabouts. Getting in was no problem – a cat once showed me the way." He sent the ghost of a wink Thibault's way.

Federigo held his knife towards Tessa. "Don't come any closer, I'll kill her!"

"Lord Capulletto will be devastated. He'll have to find another child to warm his sheets. Maybe one of Petruchio's girls this time?" But Cesco stopped walking.

Federigo stared at Cesco as if the boy could be killed by willpower alone. "How did you know where to find me?"

"Oh really, it was bound to come out, one way or another! What a shabby, bungled, hole-in-the-wall affair! I'm stunned you've lasted as long has you have. The Venetians know, Passerino knows, Capulletto knows. One of them was bound to talk. Cangrande is outside the city walls, waiting to hear you're dead. Passerino is deposed, Capulletto in chains, Dandolo in disgrace. They're all talking to save their necks. You know the old saying – two men can keep a secret, when one is dead."

Cesco took a lazy step forward, coming within striking distance of Federigo. The older man seemed frozen, fascinated by the way those feverish green eyes were boring into him. "Here's what I say – don't give the Scaliger the satisfaction. He's far too smug in his certainty that you'll die, either by Castelbarco's hand or your own. That's why I snuck in here, to tell you to give up. Publicly. Demand a trial. Air every bit of dirty laundry you know. Don't give the Capitano the joy of seeing you dead. Make him squirm in the best way possible – hurt his pride, wound his vanity, make it bleed."

"You're lying." The words were barely a whisper. "He's in Modena, he's going to die in the battle."

"Sorry, that's one battle that will never be fought. To forestall it, he took it upon himself to negotiate a peace. Bologna gets Modena, in return for some money and a few smaller castles further north. A bad bargain, but it got him back here in time to deal with you."

"I am going to be Capitano," protested Federigo feebly.

"Tch! You barely escaped with your life last time. The *condottieri* will never support you now that Cangrande is back – he pays their contracts, not you. The real Veronese soldiers despise you, while the people believe you were responsible for the summer's chaos. Now, you and I both know that mess was Mastino's fault. If you give up, the Anziani will be forced to give you a real trial, during which you can speak the truth, explain how you were used, how betrayed, how cast aside."

Caught in the grip of those bright eyes, Federigo was wavering.

Thibault took his chance. Kicking out with both legs, he put his heels into the back of Federigo's knees. Cesco instantly lunged forward to strike the killing blow, but Federigo's doublet was thick and Cesco's long dagger caught the fabric, dragging the point aside before it could pierce flesh.

Angelica tried to run past the stumbling Federigo. His flailing hand grasped her mantle and he gave her head a clout with his dagger's pommel. As she fell to the ground Federigo snatched the baby from her arms and put his back to the wall, his knife at the infant girl's throat.

"Giulietta!" shrieked Tessa. The infant's answering wail was almost soundless except when she gasped for breath.

Thibault twisted around, trying to see what was happening. Cesco was standing entirely still, staring at the knife against the infant's throat. Federigo grasped the squirming, screaming baby tight. "I'll kill her!"

A pounding on the gates below made them all jump. The next moment they heard a clatter as city soldiers emerged from the neighbouring buildings, spears threatening the mercenaries below.

"It's over," said Cesco looking even more wild-eyed, shivering and sweating all at once. *What's wrong with him?* thought Thibault. *Attack, attack now, while he's dazed!*

But Cesco's only move was to lower his dagger a fraction, taking it off the line of attack. "Don't hurt the child. Don't."

It wasn't a threat. It was a plea. Thibault wanted to spit in disgust.

Hearing footsteps below, Federigo shouted, "Stay back or Capulletto's girl dies!" Instantly the footsteps stilled, replaced by murmurings that drifted up to them.

Cesco roused from whatever trance he'd been in. "You're a fool, Federigo. So far you haven't killed anyone, they might let you live. If the child dies, you're sure to hang. Tortured, flogged, racked, unhanded, castrated, and hanged. They'll let the father take his choice of revenges and then the women will pluck out your eyes and your tongue and make you eat them."

Thibault twisted again in frustration. *Stop talking at him, you idiot, and attack!* In his struggles, Thibault's feet made a thumping sound on the tile floor.

Federigo thought it was a foot on the stair. "Don't come up here!"

Thinking to frighten the traitor, Thibault thumped his feet again. Several things happened at once. Federigo threw the baby at Cesco. Tessa screamed as Cesco dropped his blade to catch the little girl, who had ceased her low wail. Cesco had to fall to his knees to catch her, and in so doing he escaped Federigo's desperate lunge by an inch. Tessa was out of her chair, screaming with all the power in her twelve year old lungs. The other infant in far the crib echoed her, and their combined screams roused the nurse where she lay dazed on the floor.

Federigo leapt desperately past them all and fled down the stairs. There were shouts from below and the sounds of a struggle. Cesco ignored the noise, yanking the rag from Thibault's mouth and pressing it against the baby's neck. Instantly the cloth went from white to a blossoming crimson. Federigo's knife had done its work.

"Tessa!" croaked Thibault. "Tessa, untie me!"

Tessa was staring at the baby, whose mouth was beginning to show little pink bubbles, despite Cesco's efforts to bind the cut closed. Blood pooled on the tiled floor.

Angelica rose to her knees, shaking her head like a dog. Then she saw the baby and screamed. Thibault struggled against his bonds, calling out her name and Tessa's. But everyone was focused on the bleeding baby.

The room flooded with men. There was a bald man and a blackamoor and someone who looked like a young Dante, plus several soldiers, all packing themselves into this cramped little room.

Tessa knelt down, hands fluttering, tears racing down her cheeks. "Giulietta, Giulietta!" Then she leaned in closer, looked into the tiny face. "Blue," she said, shaking her head. "My daughter has blue eyes." She turned to the nurse. "Angelica..."

It took several moments for the dazed Angelica to comprehend these words. When she did, her face became grotesque in anguish. "Suzanna!?" Angelica rushed forward to pull the limp body from Cesco's arms. "No! No, oh my sweet girl, *no!*" Again and again the nurse pressed the bloody mouth to her exposed nipple, but little Suzanna failed to latch on.

Finally untied, Thibault leapt to his feet and pointed at Cesco. "It's his fault! He was trying to play the hero. It's *his* fault!" But an evil look from the blackamoor stilled Thibault's voice in his throat.

Blinking several times, Cesco slowly crossed the room to the crib. Making a soft shushing noise, he lifted the wailing Giulietta from where she lay. Turning towards Angelica, he gave a gesturing nod to thin young Dante, who gently removed the dead baby from the nurse's arms. The short bald man turned her by the shoulders, and before she knew what was happening Cesco had pressed the living girl to the nurse's breast. The thin knight wrapped Suzanna's body in a blanket and laid her in Giulietta's place.

Tessa fell sobbing into Thibault's arms. He held her, weeping too, shameful hot tears of rage and loss and anguish. *This is Uncle Antonio's fault! And Cesco's. This is not my fault, it's not…*

Shamed, he looked around.

Cesco had gone.

♦     ◊     ♦

Cangrande's party arrived after dark. Informed of the events, Capulletto had to break the news to his groom, Andriolo, that little Suzanna had been murdered. The huge man went at once to comfort his wife, an act that did not occur to Antony to emulate.

The household was bundled off, servants and all, to Capulletto's country estates. Suor Beatrice offered to journey with them and give what comfort she could. It was appreciated, and accepted.

Antony told his groom to forget his duties and go with his wife, but the man requested the right to stay. "I want to see that bastard hang, my lord."

"Of course." Antony ordered the departing staff not to speak of these events to anyone. They left in a hurry, and no one could be blamed if they failed to count heads.

Detto had been kept in the convent until everything was over. Hearing his news, Antonia had ordered him locked up and raced directly to Castelbarco. As they worked out what to do, Pietro, Tharwat, and Morsicato had arrived, all breathless. Unable to find Cesco, they suggested she follow the boy's original instructions – knock on the door to Antony's house and create a diversion, during which Castelbarco's men would gather in the neighbouring buildings.

Things had unfolded quickly, and the insurrection was put down, with the single bloody tragedy as the only loss. Somewhere in all the confusion that followed, Cesco had disappeared. Searching high and low to no avail, Pietro sent for Detto, hoping to lure Cesco into the open where he could be chastised and consoled.

But somehow the reverse happened. The moment their backs were turned, Detto too vanished without a trace. Frantic, wondering what punishment Cesco would put himself through for his failure, Pietro took a measure of solace in the thought that Detto would keep him from any real harm.

Federigo was locked in a middle room in the Capulletti tower, two floors above the arch. The only window faced the inner courtyard. Pietro watched as Cangrande dismissed guards and strode in, closing the door behind him. Walking gingerly on his injured feet, Pietro took up station upon the balcony, scant feet away from the window. *Keeper of Keyholes*, Cangrande had said. But Pietro saw no dishonour in standing here in the open air, with open ears.

Cangrande's words were clear enough. "A child-killer. What honour you've brought the family name."

"What else was I supposed to do?" came Federigo's voice in heated reply. "You stripped me of everything!"

"Not that I imagine it was difficult," said Cangrande, "but what did Passerino say to make you betray me?

"That he was afraid of you. That if you could feed me to your hounds, you could betray anyone. He feared the day when you would turn and sink your teeth into him."

"Sadly, cousin, he was toying with you. He'd already betrayed me once by then. He was behind the poisoning of my heir. You both are excellent company – infanticides both. Though I suppose you deserve more credit. You succeeded."

Federigo's voice was low, almost inaudible. "It was a mistake. I was desperate. You shouldn't have banished me!"

"You shouldn't have proved me right to do it!" Cangrande lowered his voice. "In a couple of years I could have had you recalled. You were too valuable to lose forever. You don't know how to run an army, but no man defends a fixed position with more skill. Yet today I am ashamed to know you, cousin, let alone admit a blood-tie."

"Poor Cangrande. I weep for you."

"You will when I'm through." Pietro heard the click of the latch, and Cangrande exited the chamber, locking the door behind him with a key that he slipped into his belt. He noticed Pietro. "These family affairs are so scintillating."

"Yes. First Pathino, now Federigo. Once again one of the Scaligeri tries to be the instrument of the others' destruction."

Cangrande cocked his head, the folds around his eyes creasing in contemplation. "Hadn't thought of it that way. It does make one wonder if the whole family isn't a little mad." He shrugged. "Still, genius often looks like madness."

"Federigo is no genius. Just a man filled with envy and resentment."

"Like me, you imply." Entering the house, Cangrande descended the stairs. "Do I own envy for our red hawk? Do you see a green-eyed monster on my shoulder? Where is my impetuous little falcon, by the way? Trying to wash that little girl's blood from his hands?"

"Wherever he is, Detto's with him."

"Then I will assume he is safe in form though bruised in spirit. Perfect fodder for a resumed hawking. But that will have to wait, as here come Bailardino and my doting sister to give me council."

Cangrande ordered guards back up to Federigo's door, then gestured for Pietro and the new arrivals to join him in Capulletto's office across the empty yard.

It was already occupied, as Castelbarco, Tharwat, Morsicato, and Antony shared a flagon of wine. The Scaliger took the patron's seat behind Capulletto's massive carved desk. "An interesting assembly." Without servants to tend them, they were forced to serve themselves as Cangrande enlightened the newcomers of the day's ugly events.

Katerina's first response was to repeat her brother's question. "Ser Alaghieri, where is Cesco now?"

"Resting, I hope," replied Pietro. "Detto's with him, so he shouldn't get into any trouble. He's sick over what happened."

"He should be," said Cangrande coldly.

"He saved my Giulietta," interjected Antony. "Federigo might've murdered my whole family if not for him."

"Cesco's rash rescue aside," said Cangrande, "I need to decide how to deal with Federigo and, by extension, Bonaccolsi. You all share the information, but retain your own unique perspectives." Cangrande gave a wry nod to both his sister and Pietro. "I would value your counsel. Truly," he added.

"Federigo may be family," said Katerina at once, "but he is also an exile who has returned without permission. For that act alone you are within your rights execute him."

Pietro looked dubious. "Without a trial? Is that legal?"

"No," said Castelbarco. "It isn't."

"We must do it regardless," said Bailardino, taking his wife's part.

"Lord Nogarola is correct," agreed Tharwat unexpectedly. "Federigo must die, at once."

Cangrande seemed surprised. "Your reason?"

"If he is allowed a defense," said the Moor, "he will use Passerino's name."

Morsicato was nodding. "If it leaks out that the lord of Mantua was conspiring against you, the people will demand his head. The last thing Verona wants is open war with Mantua."

"It's a single tree that knocks down a forest," said Pietro.

"I don't see that," said Castelbarco.

"Federigo at trial condemns Bonaccolsi. If we then take Passerino to trial, he'll expose Dandolo's hand in all this. Mantua and Venice – Verona will be at war with them both."

"Are you advocating no trial?" asked Cangrande.

Pietro shook his head firmly. "Absolutely not. Every man deserves a trial. I'm saying there are consequences, small and large. Think of Antony. Can his role be kept out of it?"

Antony's voice was grave. "If my evidence is what condemns both Federigo and Bonaccolsi, I will take my punishment. Verona matters more."

"Antony, you are full of the most astonishing depth today." Cangrande faced the others. "Capulletto has my full pardon. If necessary, I will swear that he was working under my orders to expose the traitors." This was clearly a relief to Antony, who took in a long breath.

"Perhaps you could try Federigo in secret," suggested Castelbarco, "and wait to expose Bonaccolsi until matters are better suited."

"Oh, worse and worse!" cried Bailardino, smacking his hands together. "Now we have to delay squashing that traitorous bug?"

"Dear," replied Katerina, "think. Pietro's point about toppling trees is well made. If Venice and Mantua rise against us, Padua will surely break the truce and join them. Ferrara will stand by its new brother-in-law, Bonaccolsi. Add to that tally Treviso and Cremona, and we are surrounded by foes. It will be Verona and Vicenza against the whole world." She turned her gaze upon her brother. "He must die."

"You make a strong case," said Cangrande. "But Federigo is blood of my blood. I cannot kill him outright."

"The curse," muttered Pietro.

Bailardino stood. "I'll do it, then."

Antony was on his feet in an instant. "Allow me!"

Cangrande held up a restraining hand at them both. "That's no better. I ascribe to the Greek manner of thinking. A murder I order is on my head as much as on the man who carries it out. I cannot order the death of a kinsman without a trial. It must be an act of state. That I can tolerate. Nothing else."

"Then it's war," said Katerina.

"A war we can't possibly win," added Castelbarco.

Cangrande was firm. "I refuse to shed the blood of my blood without the weight of law behind me."

"I think our father would forgive you this lapse," said Katerina.

Cangrande's laugh was tinged with darkness. "I think you're forgetting what kind of man our father was. He burned some friends along with the Paterenes. We are not to shed family blood – unless we choose to defy our stars. I don't think even little Cesco is that reckless."

His words drifted up through the open window and out into the night. There they were caught at the rooftop's edge by Cesco's keen hearing. He was stationed at the very spot where three months ago he had struggled with Thibault, the perfect vantage for eavesdropping on Capulletto's office.

Detto was nearby, listening as well. Summoned to the house, he'd been in the yard when he heard a hiss from above. When no one was looking, Detto had clambered up a doorframe and onto the rooftop.

At first he'd been angry at Cesco for undertaking the adventure alone. One look at Cesco's face and bloodied clothes and Detto's indignation died in his throat. Now he waited as Cesco just sat there staring into the growing shadows, shivering. Detto didn't think it was from the cold.

Nor was it. Cesco was reliving the events in the tower over and over. Tharwat had warned him against over-indulgence in the drug, how to measure his weight and fatigue against the dose. Cesco had taken just enough after leaving Vicenza to propel him through the day. But on the verge of entering the house, he'd consumed a second dose, thinking it would heighten his energy and clarity. Instead, things had become horribly twisted.

That Cesco had always had bad dreams was common knowledge among the people who had raised him. But he'd never told anyone what those dreams were. Not even Detto. For he knew, even as a little child, that there was something evil about his dreams. They were dreams of death, of each kind of torture Dante had devised for his depiction of Hell, along with several others from Cesco's own pure brain. He dreamt, too, of humiliations. Broken spirits, broken hearts, broken dreams. For Cesco, sleep was a necessary horror.

The moment Federigo had placed the knife against Suzanna's throat, Cesco's world had turned into a waking dream. A reddish-brown fog had descended, and Suzanna's face had vanished to be replaced by his own. He knew it was him from the coin of Mercury hanging at his neck. Just below the knife.

Federigo had grown and stretched in Cesco's eyes until he was a distorted shadow. Their surroundings changed to the lowest part of Hell, near Lucifer's upturned legs. Federigo's head swam up and became a hound's, snapping and snarling.

That was when Cesco willed himself back to the real world. The whole episode only lasted seconds, but it was burned into Cesco's thoughts as if by a brand. He'd come back too late, hesitating for the moment it took to stop that little baby's heart.

His impulse now was to throw away the rest of the sticky chews. But the fault was not in the drug. It was in himself.

Cesco hiccoughed, swallowing a sob. At once Detto laid a hand on his best friend's shoulder. "Blame Federigo. He did it, not you."

"Oh no," said Cesco bitterly. "There's enough blame for all. Blame me, blame Bonaccolsi, blame Federigo, blame Capulletto. And save some blame for the king of cats." With an air of decision, he rose and dusted his hands. "Come on."

"Where are we off to now?"

"We're off to offer the damned a chance to give God the fig."

# FORTY-SEVEN

FEDERIGO DELLA SCALA sat head down, arms bound to his chair. The sun through the sole window was down, casting him into darkness. There was a candle on a desk in front of the window, but it wasn't lit. Perhaps they were afraid he would start a fire. He'd already proven himself capable of the unthinkable.

A little girl. What had he become?

He heard a slight commotion outside, the sound of running feet. For a moment his hopes lifted. But the door did not open. No rescue came.

Staring intently through the darkness towards the door, he did not notice the shape at the window until the flint sparked and a candle was lit. It cast light on the face of Cangrande's little bastard heir, the cause of all Federigo's sorrows. He must have leapt from the long balcony across to the window.

Holding the candle, Cesco put a finger to his lips. "Don't shout, cos."

The boy was still covered in the infant's blood, and Federigo felt a knot of shame and defiance at once. "What do you want?"

"To offer you a chance to clean part of the mess you've made."

"It's not my mess," answered Federigo. "That belongs to you and your sire. I'm just playing my part."

"As am I," replied Cesco. "We are both mere players. But you've started working from a different script."

"So much like him," said Federigo in disgust. "Always taunting, never a genuine word out of your mouths."

"You judge me based on two afternoons, three months apart. That's hardly fair, don't you think? I may be a delicate flower, with only one or two prickly thorns."

"You're just proving my point. Why have you come?"

Cesco turned back to the window, fiddling with something. "I have a question. You planned for all of us to be cut down. Aren't you afraid of this family curse I've heard so much about?"

Federigo's laugh was sour. "*Sanguis meus?* A dying man's attempt to keep his sons in check after he was gone. And it worked! They believed it, the more fool they. I have no use for superstition."

"Nor do I."

Federigo felt a chill pass over him. Despite his words, he did believe in the curse. It was actually Federigo's great hope. In spite of all, Cangrande would not kill him.

But the boy hadn't been raised to fear the curse, didn't respect its power. Swallowing, Federigo tried to sound defiant. "Have you come to kill me, boy?"

"No," answered Cesco. "I've come to watch you die." As the boy moved away from the windowsill, Federigo saw in the dim light that what he had been fiddling with – a rope, firmly knotted to the foot of the heavy desk.

"You don't mean to hang me," said Federigo. "You're too small, you could never manage it."

"You're right," said Cesco agreeably. "Besides, you've already hanged yourself."

Federigo noticed the rope was moving. It shifted again, as if a great weight were hanging from it. Or rather, a weighty man ascending.

Eyes fixed on the rope, Federigo didn't notice how close Cesco was until the boy shoved a rag into his mouth. Federigo tried to yell, but that only allowed Cesco to press the cloth in further. Leaning close, the boy whispered in Federigo's ear. "Choke on the blood of the girl you murdered."

Federigo flailed, trying to fight the bonds. Cesco prevented the chair from toppling, eyes fixed on the window. From the darkness a hand reached up to grasp the sill. An elbow followed, and a huge rough man in workaday clothes hauled himself up and into the room. His shirt bore the Capulletti crest.

Cesco spoke in a low whisper. "Federigo, this is Andriolo. You murdered his daughter today. He's here to repay you in kind."

The massive groom was normally a merry man, but now his genial face was blank, raw – primal. To Cesco he said, "How?"

Cesco answered in gentle tones. "First I must offer you the chance to turn back. The deed is appealing today, and tomorrow. But in a month or a year, you may regret it."

Andriolo gazed hard at Federigo. "Never."

"Then it needs to look like suicide or, better, an accident while he was trying to free himself. There can be no marks on the body. Much as you might wish to beat him, it would betray our presence. And we must hurry – Detto cannot distract the guards much longer."

Federigo saw Andriolo's attention go at once towards the edge of the fine wooden bed just to Federigo's back. Craning his neck, Federigo saw that the corners had fine solid squares of wood supporting them.

Again Federigo struggled futilely against his bonds. Cesco stepped away as Andriolo grasped the chair and twisted it around. The massive groom took hold of Federigo's flailing head and leaned close. "For Suzanna." Then he drove the base of Federigo's neck down towards the hard corner of the bed.

Federigo felt a sharp pain, then nothing. Nothing at all. He could still see, still hear, but it was as if he were floating. Nothing held him down.

Suddenly he couldn't breathe. As the groom laid his broken body on the ground, chair and all, Federigo tried to speak. His mouth might have moved, but no sound issued from it beside a strange gurgle. That was the moment he knew his life was over.

Cesco knelt down to gaze into Federigo's dying face.

*You did it*, thought Federigo, trying to communicate with his eyes alone. *You killed me. Sanguis Meus, boy. Blood of my blood, you had me killed. It doesn't matter that it wasn't by your own hand. You've invoked the curse!*

But as light faded, Federigo could see from the expression in those wide green eyes that the boy understood all this. And did not care.

Removing the bloody cloth from Federigo's slack mouth, Cesco murmured softly, "You are a sore and sorry ass."

♦   ◊   ♦

It was another hour before they found Federigo's cooling body. Cangrande had come upstairs in the company of Castelbarco and Bailardino. Still without a course, their intent was to question Federigo further in the hope that his answers would light their way.

Unlocking the door, the room was just the same as the Scaliger had left it, but for the chair on the floor and the immobile figure in it. There was a pool of liquid where the dead man's bowels had loosened.

Morsicato was called at once to study the dead man. "He must have struggled to free himself and hit his head." His tone was dubious, though, and the look he gave to Pietro bespoke his doubts.

But Pietro knew Federigo had been alive when Cangrande had locked the door, and there was no other way into the room. This unlikely explanation had to be the truth.

"Perhaps this was deliberate self-slaughter," suggested Castelbarco.

"I doubt that Federigo took his own life," said the Scaliger woodenly. "He was too much the survivor. He even murdered a child to prolong his existence."

"But to stop a family scandal? Spare us the wars ahead? Mightn't he have—?"

"This was definitely not to benefit us," said Katerina, taking in the scene from the doorway. "An act of defiance, perhaps. A final statement of contempt."

Cangrande rose from beside his cousin's corpse. "Or it could be as the doctor says, and he fell the wrong way in his struggles to be free. Whatever the cause, this has solved our troubles."

"For the moment," he added.

◆      ◊      ◆

Cesco did not join Andriolo on his return to the stables, rope coiled over his arm. Instead he waited on the L-shaped rooftop for Detto to return from distracting the guards. He appeared just before the body was found, grinning all over his face.

"What did you tell them?" asked Cesco, helping him descend from this end of the balcony onto the roof a floor below.

"I said I was looking for you," beamed Detto, "and that they had to help me find you before you did something rash. They searched high and low, then ordered me home. They'll swear you weren't anywhere in the tower when Federigo was... when it happened." His face was frightened and eager. "*Did* it happen?"

"Did what happen?" asked Cesco lightly. When Detto frowned in protest, Cesco said, "What you do not know cannot hurt you. If there is a curse, let it fall on my head, not yours. You are, after all, of Scaligeri blood as well. Come on. Let's get back to the palace and wait for the tongue-lashing I'm sure to get for all my idiotic risk-taking."

They crept over to the short stairs on the roof, meaning to leave over the wall. Suddenly a figure stepped out from beneath one of the supporting arches. The stars caught the white-blonde hair in a seeming halo. But the reflected light from the dagger was more arresting.

Cesco sounded more resigned than wry. "Ah, Monsignor

Ratcatcher! How well you can see."

"You got her killed," hissed Thibault. "It was your fault!"

For once Cesco's face was empty. "It's true that if I hadn't come, she might still be alive. But we'll never know, will we?"

"You killed her!" insisted Thibault.

"So you want to fight me?"

"Yes!" said Thibault, keeping his voice low so the adults in the house wouldn't interfere. "To prove I'm no coward!"

"Prove to whom?" asked Cesco tiredly. "I'm certainly convinced. You are no coward. A fool? Yes, definitely. But no coward."

"It's your fault she died!"

"You keep saying that," answered Cesco in scorn, "as if it might become true. We both know what happened up there, mouse-breath. The more you mew, the guiltier you sound. Now put the knife away. I am not going to fight you, but I have some friendly advice to offer, one rancorous child to another."

Face wary, Thibault didn't lower his blade. "What's that?"

"If you intend to ruin your uncle, at least be wise about it. You're lucky that his in-laws are such obvious suspects, otherwise he'd be on you in a heartbeat. If you're mistreated now, how would everyone react to the knowledge that Federigo wouldn't have even been in the house without you?"

Thibault blanched. "What – what are you talking about?"

"The question is, what were *you* talking about on the night of our little scuffle? I may have been a little worse for wear by evening's end, but I had eyes enough to see you and Passerino tucked into a corner of the yard below. Was he chatting you up? Did you happen to mention how you hated your uncle? Did Passerino offer to help you ruin him? Did you pass him some incriminating papers? Are you the cause of the blackmail that brought Federigo to your door?"

Thibault was shaking. "You can't prove it!"

"Nor would I want to. There's no point. I get nothing from exposing you. Not even satisfaction. I only wanted to say this: be wary, oh King of Cats. You have just used one of your lives. Don't waste the rest. You may need them someday." With a bow, Cesco leapt up and climbed over the wall. Detto followed, leaving Thibault quaking with fearful wrath.

◆　◊　◆

At Cangrande's request, Pietro stood with the Capitano at the door to Santa Maria Antica as the litter bearing Federigo's body was brought in. The servants departed, leaving the two men alone.

"Come inside with me," said Cangrande, crossing the threshold to the Scaligeri chapel. "We can speak in private."

"I cannot," said Pietro.

"I respect your piety. But this is a private chapel. It will not offend God if you enter at the invitation of the chapel's owner."

Pietro considered. Cesco had turned up safely in the palace and now had both Tharwat and Morsicato sitting watch over him. If this was a ploy or trap, the boy would be safe. Pietro entered.

At once he smelled the familiar incense, the expensive candles. Bands of light-coloured marble made up the walls and pillars, while high windows provided ventilation. He knew this chapel well, had prayed here the morning of his knighting. It was here Cesco had been baptized.

Pietro went through the rituals he had missed, touching the font and crossing himself, genuflecting, and praying for a time. Then he joined Cangrande beside the altar where Federigo had been laid out.

"In a way I pity him," said the Scaliger. "He played his game and lost."

"But instead of accepting the consequences," said Pietro, voice full of meaning, "he injured a child for no reason other than that he was afraid."

Cangrande heaved a sigh. "You insist on drawing parallels that do not apply. I have not lost, nor have I murdered the boy. I may treat him roughly, but as you now know, I have not tried to kill him or even place him in harm's way. Few people could claim as much – not even my darling sister."

"Allow him to be someone else's squire. You've had your fun."

Cangrande shook his head with a blossoming smile. "O no! I'm not done taming my little hawk. Besides, who could I give him to? Not you! You won't be here long enough to teach him more than to pack."

"Yes," said Pietro bitterly, "I've noticed the Paduan sword you placed over my head."

"*I* placed?" asked Cangrande with convincing surprise.

"You ordered Nico to make sure I fought."

Cangrande had the good grace to look chagrinned. "Told you that, did he?"

"Yes. Sorry to disappoint you, but I'm willing to take my chances here. Where else am I supposed to go? I'm under a death sentence in both Florence and Venice, with a price on my head. Meanwhile you're threatening to turn me over to Carrara."

"Admirably summed up. Though I needs must add another straw to your load. One that, in all seriousness, is not of my bale. It is wheat plucked from the chaff of circumstance."

Pietro steeled himself. "Go on."

"Thanks to the intercession of our Ravennese friend, Lord Guido Novello, the Bolognese have for years been willing to overlook your status as a Florentine exile. I think you may find them reconsidering this at present. With Mantua nipping at their heels, they need to solidify their standing with their friend and ally to the south. They won't go so far as to hand Pietro di Dante over to the Florentines for execution – they like you too much. But—"

"—but I can't go back to Bologna," said Pietro hollowly.

"I'm afraid not." Cangrande was almost sympathetic. "Rather than a university degree at law, you must be satisfied with a universal degree in practicality. Both Lombardy and Tuscany are rife with danger for you. So what is an Alaghieri to do? I advise a little trip further afield."

Cangrande passed something over, and Pietro found himself holding a packet of papers bound up in a leather satchel. "These are?"

"Documents I had Tullio draw up just now. Travel orders, with guarantees of safe conduct."

"To where?"

"Why, to Avignon!" said the Scaliger triumphantly. "I hope your feet are quite healed, though you'll spend a fair amount of time on your knees as well. It took some mighty persuading and not a little bit of bribery, but the papal court has consented to hear an appeal of your excommunication. You will have to grovel a bit, say some nauseating things, but I think you'll find them kindly disposed towards your plight. And mine," he added, almost as an afterthought.

Pietro knew the Scaliger far too well to believe the final addition to be anything but deliberate. "Yours?"

"Oh, didn't I say? You are going as my representative, to have my own status returned to that of the saved, rather than damned. You will plead for us both, as our cases are now linked."

"Linked how?"

Cangrande smiled pleasantly. "I have informed the papal court that while you were in Ravenna, you were still acting under my orders as a Knight of the Mastiff. I have said that it was as my delegate that you refused to over-tax the Ravennese. The fact that you were entrusted with my heir proves this beyond all doubt."

"Thus making my cause your own. Either I get us both reinstated, or neither of us are saved."

"Quite. It also has the added benefit of making me beloved in Ravenna."

"Glad to be of help," said Pietro with a bitter laugh.

"Oh, there's something more in it for you. By removing the interdiction, you will effectively end the Venetian death sentence. They only condemned you for being a heretic. No more heresy, no more charges."

"Speaking of Venice and Dandolo, what do you plan to do about them?"

Cangrande glowed with dark amusement. "In due time, I will unleash Cesco on them."

That elicited a half-smile from Pietro. But with the Scaliger's grip tightening on him once more, he felt the need to strike back. As it happened, the perfect weapon was at hand. "I have a fact for you that you're not going to like."

"I'm certain of that! Your face, my puppy, is like a book. If you mean to beguile juries and advocates, you'd best learn not to let your looks put on your purposes. What is it you have to impart that I will be so unhappy to hear?"

"Bonaccolsi was responsible for Ponte Corbo. Those were his men, supplied not to aid Padua but to kill you."

Cangrande stood in silence, perhaps recalling that day when he had broken, when he had fled the field of battle. Yet when he spoke, his voice held no trace of that defeat. "Thank you, Ser Alaghieri. I did not know quite what a debt I owed my dear Passerino."

"What does it say, my lord, when even your best friend on this earth wants you dead?"

"I don't know what it says to you. To me it says that I am on the way to being another Caesar. But, unlike the great Julius, I plan to listen to the auguries."

"Does that make Cesco Augustus?"

"Unlikely. He has the mind, but lacks the patience."

Pietro looked down at the papers in his hand. "Why is it that whenever we meet, you're sending me into exile?"

"You're far too pretty. I can't be trusted around you."

Revolted at this badinage inside a chapel, Pietro said, "I read Mussato's play. There's a line that sticks in my head. Something the mother said – 'Secrets will out.'"

At the mention of *Ecerinis*, Cangrande's face closed. "I remember it well."

"It's true, you know. Cesco will learn the truth soon enough."

Cangrande studied the large cross suspended before the wall. "What truth? In this life we are often faced with facts, but rarely with truths. Let alone *the* truth."

"The truth about who he is."

Expecting an eruption, or scorn, or an angry laugh, Pietro was not prepared for the naked thing that emerged and spread across Cangrande's features. "Who is he, Pietro? Tell me, who is he? Do you know? Do I?" The long-fingered hands came up to scrub across the Scaliger's face. "He is himself. What he is cannot be known from a star-chart or a prophecy. A man may control his actions, but not his stars, remember? Destiny is only known in the fullness of time. If even then."

Though suspicious of Cangrande's skill at play-acting, Pietro could not help but be moved. Again he recalled Abbot Gualpertino's words. "No man is just one thing,"

Cangrande turned to face him, a keen look in his eye. "Just so. A great warrior may be a poor father or a worse husband. A respectable cleric might hide a youthful crime in a lifetime of good deeds. Most often a man is remembered for the evils he commits. But there is no man who ever lived that did nothing worthwhile through the course of his life."

Pietro glanced down at the corpse on the altar. "What will he be remembered for, do you think?"

"If I have anything to say, for his magnificent defense of the city, years ago." Cangrande paused. "I think I owe both Passerino and Dandolo a kindness. They have softened your opinion of me, a little."

"Have they?"

"You once believed I was a god, a mythic figure. Then I allowed you to see my feet of clay – yes, *allowed*, Pietro. Ever since that day, you have deemed me a monster. But now you behold me as a monster in a world of monsters, and you are beginning to wonder which is the lesser evil?"

"Better the devil I know."

"Just so. Who knows? Perhaps someday we will meet as equals. Friends, even. I hope for no less." The nakedness vanished, replaced by something more controlled, less animal. "Come along and say farewell to our lad. I will grant you both this one night of fellowship before you depart on your mission. For tonight, you may make believe he is your son." Cangrande's eyes narrowed. "Tomorrow, he's mine."

Before leaving the chapel, Pietro received Cangrande's permission to pray.

# EPILOGUE

*Illasi*
*Thursday, 21 November*
*1325*

"BE CAREFUL NOW," warned the Scaliger, his breath misting in the morning air. "Many men have gone to great lengths to keep my heir alive. It would be a shame to return with him bled out like a hoisted carcass."

"Nag nag nag. I'm not frightened of a pretty girl like this."

"Perhaps not. But you should be respectful. Especially of the pretty ones."

They stood together in the predawn light on a grassy sward, far from any city or hamlet. With them was Cesco's hawk, who felt the excitement of her master even if she couldn't see his luminous green eyes. Cesco was fidgeting, hence the rebuke. But his left arm was still, held perfectly rigid as his little hawk perched upon it, fanning her wings and bating slightly. She wanted the blindfold removed so that she might soar, fly free.

Cesco slipped the jess off the loop on the long glove and stroked the bird's head once. His fingers stopped at the knot on the leather blindfold. He clicked his tongue twice, the signal to the bird that food was near.

Then, without properly warning the bird, Cesco yanked the blindfold off and threw his arm high.

Cangrande started forward. "No!"

"I know what I'm doing!" cried Cesco, ducking as one of the flailing pounces whisked by his left eye.

The bird shrieked, startled at the sudden freedom. She flapped frantically at the air as Cesco snatched his arm away, removing the perch from under the pounces. Falling, she almost hit the ground. But she beat hard and at the ultimate moment caught an updraft. Spreading her majestic wings, she took flight.

Cangrande cuffed the boy on the ear. "What did you think you were doing? You've spent weeks building her trust. Why scare her that way?"

Cesco's response was cruel. "I don't want to possess any creature that's entirely dependant on me. What good is that? I want her loyal, but she's got to know that in the end it's all up to her."

"I sense an allegory."

"What, you're the only one who can teach by metaphor?"

"I have no idea what you mean."

"Of course you don't."

Above them the dark-eyed falcon ringed, gliding on the faint wind. It watched for movement in the tall grass of the field, at the edge of the nearby forest.

In an idle tone, Cesco said, "Lord Bonaccolsi's army won without you."

"A resounding victory," agreed Cangrande, "for which Passerino received all the credit, while I am covered in shame."

"Do you think Passerino suspects your real reason for abandoning him?"

"You mean, do I suspect that he suspects that I suspect him of betraying me?" Cangrande laughed. "All this cross-biting is a bit confusing. Yes, he probably does. But he'll never know for certain until the moment I pull the blade across his throat. The real shame of it is that Mastino will never know that he owes his life, in part, to you."

Cesco's eyes were still on his bird. "By the by, I know why the merlin."

Cangrande raised his eyebrows at the seeming non sequitur. "Oh?"

"Yes. Arthurian myth. King Arthur's wizard was called the Merlin. There's a legend that states the Greyhound prophecy originated with him. So you fly a merlin, which is beneath you, to show your affinity to the prophecy."

"Hm. That would be very cunning of me."

"A subtle cunning. A careful crafting of an aura around yourself. Makes you more than human."

Cangrande grinned wolfishly, showing his perfect teeth. "Are you awed?"

"A little. I certainly haven't met your like before."

"Except in a looking glass."

"I don't own one." Cesco nodded towards his bird. "She's got a high pitch."

"That she does. Pray she doesn't fly too high."

"Another allegory." Cesco sighed, then brightened. "By the by, I never did thank you."

"For?"

"It was quite considerate of you to let me meet my mother."

Cangrande shot his heir a sidelong glance. "Shame on Pietro. He promised not to tell you."

"Ah. Thank you again."

"For?"

"Confirming my suspicions. I wasn't sure if Pietro knew who she really was."

"Damn me. Well, there's a good lesson for you. Never answer more than is asked. So who was it told you? My sister?"

"She knows as well? It seems a secret very loosely kept. Was she your mistress? Is that your type?"

"I have no types – except, perhaps, not stupid. Yes, I do prefer my women to have a little something to bite back with."

"No toothless women, then. I quite agree." Cesco jerked his head in his falcon's direction. "Though if *she* bites back, I'll probably regret it."

"Probably." The bird pulled away in a wider and wider circle. "She may be raking out."

"No. She's just hunting. You'll see."

The dark smear in the sky darted suddenly down towards the ground, picking up speed as it changed angles to come up behind some prey. Something in the air must have alerted the quarry, for there was a quick rustle of grass beneath her. Moments later the falcon rose again, sailing just above the level of the grass.

Cangrande took a short step back, leaving the boy alone to complete the exercise. Petruchio had taught the boy well. This time everything was done properly, from the vocal cooing to the single click of the tongue, to the rigidly held left arm. Just before she settled into her perch the beautiful falcon dropped the pelt at the boy's feet. Apparently he had won the bird's complete trust, despite his shenanigans. Or because of them.

The dead animal was a hare, eyes wide and unseeing, its neck crushed by the falcon's pounces. "The skin's barely broken, there's very little blood to stain the fur," remarked Cangrande, impressed.

Cesco stroked the bird's cere, the naked wax-like skin above the beak. "She's a good footer, a natural born gamer." He had adopted Petruchio's phrases as his own.

The hare was bagged and the falcon treated with a bit of older meat. Then she was flown again, this time with greater care.

"Ser Alaghieri leaves today for France."

"We've said our good-byes," said Cesco tranquilly.

"Actually," said Cangrande slowly, "I was wondering if you wanted to go with him."

That gave the boy a start. Cangrande was pleased to see he was still capable of surprises.

Cesco looked wary. "You'd let me leave?"

"Despite your late foolishness, you have earned a choice. I give you the greatest gift one man can bestow upon another. I give you liberty. You are free to fly away."

Cesco smiled a little. "This is my airing?"

"If you like."

"So you deem me broken?"

"Quite the opposite. But I tell you – if you choose to stay, I will break you. Nothing surer."

Cesco stood looking at his bird, dragging out the silence. Finally he answered. "Thank you, but no. I accept no gifts, need no favours. And you will *not* break me."

"Believe what you like," said Cangrande. "But if you remain, it will happen."

Cesco's smile became a wide grin. "Well, one of us will break, surely."

"You believe you are hawking me?"

"In my fashion."

"I will die before you break me."

"Funny. That's just what I was going to say."

Prince and princeling watched the bird fly across rising sun. Above it, further north, the moon still hung high in the morning sky. A partial moon, unfulfilled. Soon the sun would obliterate the moon entirely with its light.

"Have you named her?" asked Cangrande.

"Yes. Her name is Susanna."

◆　◊　◆

Based on prior experience, Pietro had eschewed hiring Veronese servants. So the morning sun found him riding his horse Canis alone through the Porta Palio. He'd planned on leaving even earlier, but even with Cesco absent, his goodbyes in the city had taken longer than he'd expected. He'd not teared up until he took leave of his hounds, now a part of the Scaliger's menagerie.

Pietro hadn't gone a mile before he spied a familiar figure off to the side of the road. Pietro kicked and guided Canis over to where the Moor waited. "I looked for you to say farewell."

"I had other business. Your sister is well?"

"She is, thank you." Pietro detested the formality that had sprung up between them, but couldn't find a way to break it.

Tharwat pulled his horse's head around, ranging his mount alongside Pietro's.

"Are you going with me?"

"No."

"A shame. I'd like to see the Pope's face when he met you." It was the type of glib reply that Cesco could have pulled off. From Pietro it sounded boorish and insulting.

They rode in silence for another quarter mile. Then Tharwat turned his mount down a track, leading Pietro down into a glen. "Where are you taking me?"

"To a cabin in the valley."

It occurred to Pietro that he should be afraid. But in his heart he knew Tharwat was no Assassin. He may have been trained in their arts, but that was not the man he had become. The man who had risked his life to free Pietro from prison was the same soul Pietro had known and trusted these last ten years.

Their destination was only a shack at the bottom of a deep ravine, nestled up against the rocky wall. Isolated, with no cover, no trees or shrubs, it would have been impossible to creep up upon unseen.

But it was clearly deserted. More, it had been burned. For some reason the fire had not caught well, and only one wall was blackened and charred. The rest of the cabin was whole.

"What is this place?" asked Pietro.

The Moor turned to face him. "I traced Donna Maria to this valley. Too late. This is where she was taken, but she is not here now."

Pietro became instantly more alert. "Who brought her here?"

"I do not know. More than one man. Despite the smoke, there are still traces of blood on the floor. Not much. She was not killed here. Only—"

*Only tortured.* Hardening himself for what lay ahead, Pietro tried not to conjure the image of the vibrant woman with the lilting accent, the one who had received just moments of her son's life, and had now paid dearly for them. *Damn.*

"I would have spared you this. But there is something you must see." Dismounting, the Moor led Pietro into the shack. It was sturdier inside that it appeared, the walls of thick-cut wood. Tharwat struck a light. "Over here. You'd be best off kneeling."

Pietro did as he was told, and in the light of the Moor's candle he saw the blood in question. But he also saw something else. Beneath the dried blood, fifteen letters were scratched into the floor. They didn't make a word. Instead they were divided in sets of three – up, across, down, across, up, across, down. The whole jumble looked like the letter 'M':

| M | R | C | | T | S | M |
|---|---|---|---|---|---|---|
| A | | A | | T | | A |
| B | | V | X | D | | B |

"What does it mean?"

Tharwat closed his eyes to picture the scene. "She sat here, bleeding, her back to the wall. Tortured, injured, both, she used her wit to leave this behind. I can only assume her hands were tied behind her. She scratched this."

"Does it identify her attackers, do you think?"

The Moor shook his head. "I believe this is not a dying declaration demanding salvation or revenge. I believe it is something more important."

Pietro studied the letters. "I can't make heads or tails of it. Can you?"

"I have been struggling with it since I found this place." Tharwat produced a small, flat bundle. Unwrapping it gingerly, he revealed a piece of slate with chalk markings on it. In the center was an exact copy of the letters on the floor, in their same relative positions.

"I have, I think, worked out a small piece. The letters are Roman, so I believe the code is in part in Latin. I have nothing to base that upon, other than this." He pointed to a chalked scrawl at the bottom. Next to the letters CAV, he had added a small E, and a legend:

*CAVe - beware.*

"It *is* a warning," said Pietro. "It could be about her attackers."

"I may be wrong in my interpretation, but I believe this was not meant for us. This is for Cesco. A puzzle. In her limited time with him, the mother in her saw his nature. She knew the trick to engaging him."

Pietro considered for a long time. "Should he be told?"

"That question has plagued me. It is why I came to you. What do you think?"

Warmed as he was by Tharwat's trust, Pietro's mind did not stray far from the question at hand. *His mother left this message for him. Would he conceive it his duty to find her? Or would he shrug it off, pretend that it didn't matter? Would it matter to him? Having gained Cangrande's grudging respect, would the mother who abandoned him even enter his thoughts?*

Pietro took the slate board and re-wrapped it in the Moor's cloak, careful not to smudge the chalk. "Let's try to solve it ourselves. And we have to find her, if she's still alive. Meantime we make certain no one else finds this code."

Together they finished the job the lamp had failed to do. In minutes the whole cabin was ablaze.

Pietro squinted at the growing fire. "I'm for Avignon. You have to stay by him as long as Cangrande allows. Please."

"The Scaliger will find a way to be rid of me," said Tharwat. "When he does, I will find you. Until then, I will protect the boy. And search for his mother."

"Tharwat, I want you to know something. There's no one I trust more than you."

A long moment passed, the only sound the crackling of the flames. Then, at long last, the Moor nodded. "It is an honour to have the trust of the best knight in Christendom," rumbled Tharwat al-Dhaamin from out of his broken throat. "An honour I strive every day to earn."

They stayed until the darkness fell, the first stars appearing overhead. Flames licked at the sky, reaching to their utmost height, yet unable to touch those damning harbingers of future history. Instead they distorted them from view, making them seem to dance and writhe before Pietro's eyes. There was no telling what they held in store.

# AFTERWORD

## HISTORICAL APOLOGIES AND ADDENDUMS

The fate of poor Dante's bones have been the cause of much speculation, almost as much as the events of his life. Immediately following his burial in the Church of the Frati Minori in Ravenna, the city of Florence demanded his remains. The Ravennese refused. Now, there is no evidence of an attempt to steal the poet's body, that's a fiction on my part. But a century later the Florentines enlisted Pope Leone X to their cause, and Dante's bones were ordered back to Florence by papal authority. The Ravennese Prior, Antonio Santi, submitted, but when he opened the tomb he was shocked – *shocked!* – to find it empty. He proclaimed it a miracle, saying the poet who had walked with the dead had risen again to continue his travels. Since they had nowhere else to look, the Pope and the Florentines had to accept this adorable story. How could a pope deny the reincarnation of the soul in the body?

In 1865 Italy was preparing to celebrate the sixth centenary of the poet's birth when a worker, opening a hole between the two chapels Rasponi and Braccioforte, found by chance a long wooden box half-decomposed by the damp. Inside it was an almost complete skeleton and a letter in which Antonio Santi, now long-dead, testified that those were Dante's bones, quickly saved from Florentine arrogance.

But that doesn't end the story. Some dust was taken from the box and placed in six leather bags, which were taken God knows where. The contents of one of these bags was somehow transferred to an envelope, which was found in the 20th century by a very excited clerk who claimed he'd found the poet's true ashes in a library in Florence. Truth is definitely stranger than fiction.

Meantime, a fine tomb was built in Ravenna, and there the poet's bones rested undisturbed until World War II, when they were hurriedly exhumed and buried in a mound of earth to protect them from bombing. After the war they were reinterred in the tomb, where, I hope, they remain to this day.

Above his sarcophagus hangs an eternal lamp whose oil is still provided by the city of Florence in penance for having exiled Dante seven hundred years ago. As far as I know, Venice bears no share in that particular penance.

♦ ◊ ♦

Speaking, as we are, of corpses...

On February 12th, 2004, Cangrande della Scala's body was exhumed. This was the second time the great man's remains were disinterred. The first was in 1921, when the main intent was to find a rumored copy of Dante's *Paradiso* written in the poet's own hand. This was, alas, only myth. But the recent unearthing of the Scaliger, replete with scientists and historians from several fields of study, led to some wonderful discoveries. My favorite was the noting of Cangrande's perfect teeth. No wonder his smile was famous – he lived his whole life without a single cavity. And died with a liver destroyed by alcoholism.

On Good Friday, 2004, I received a copy of the initial findings thanks to my friend Antonella Leonardo, who has facilitated every important meeting I've had in the city. I truly cannot thank her enough, both for her encouragement and for the many wonderful people she has introduced me to.

♦ ◊ ♦

Once more, all of my initial ideas for this book came from Shakespeare. As we draw a little nearer to the events of the week of July 12, 1339 (Juliet dies two weeks away from her 14th birthday – again in my life I am betrayed by math), I get to add in more characters from his Italian plays. Shylock, Jessica, and Launcelot Gobbo are all, of course, from *Merchant*. Valentine, a featured player in *Two Gents*, has also gotten a place in Mercutio's roster, since the invitation to the Capulet ball reads 'Mercutio and his brother, Valentine.' The closest Cesco has to brothers are the two Nogarola boys. Petruchio, Kate, and their children I brought up in the last book, but now I've added Grumio, whom I only mentioned in passing, as well as mentions of Baptista, Lucentio, Hortensio, and Bianca, all from *Shrew*. Borachio and Corrado (Conrade) are now added to list of *Much Ado* members I've used – Don Pedro, Don John, & Benedick. More of these and other plays to come.

For those keeping score, the minor treason at the heart of Antony's troubles was born in my short story VARNISHED FACES, where he and his uncle crash a Paduan wedding reception in masks and make a shady business deal with an old man named Gremio, another character from Shrew.

In answer to the obvious query – yes, this series will indeed end with events laid out in Shakespeare's play *Romeo & Juliet* (I do have an idea for a coda novella, but it's hard when most of your leads are dead!). Because these books were born out of that play, I have no plans to contradict anything said in that show. Rest assured, everything that happens on the stage will be treated as Gospel.

Which doesn't mean I don't have some surprises in store, both historical and literary. Knowing that I'm playing a long game, be assured that, as Mussato says in *Ecerinis*, 'secrets will out.' Living with *R&J* the way I have, I know it better than I know most people, and still it has the power to astonish me. Such is the might of Shakespeare's pen.

Nevertheless, there are many books between now and then. Plenty of time to build the expectations I intend to flout.

Names, names, names. I resisted the name Paris as hard as I could, intending to use the title as a mocking nickname later in life. But re-reading *R&J*, I decided there was no way around it being his baptismal name. It's the young men who so address him, but Capulet, Lady Cap, Friar Lawrence – people not accustomed to using nicknames. Therefore, much as I changed Tybalt to Thibault, I turned Paris into Paride, the modern Italian version of the name. This is contrary to Dante, who uses *Paris* when referencing the Trojan lover. But I like Paride. I find it easier to create if I vary character names a trifle – Montecchio, not Montague, and so on. A failing, perhaps, but one that I hope in no way diminishes the story. And now I have painted myself into the corner with Cesco, who won't be called Cesco too much longer...

Corrado, as mentioned above, is the Italian version of Conrade.

The Nurse being named Angelica is from Shakespeare. Lord Cap says the name once towards the end of the show. He could be addressing a servant or Lady Cap, but it's the Nurse who answers him. Her husband's name, Andriolo, is my own invention – I saw it in a book of Italian names and it reminded me of *Androcles and the Lion*. I did that show once, too, a long time ago (I was the lion). Their daughter, Suzanna, is simply from the Nurse's mention that 'Susan and she – God rest all Christian souls – were of an age. Well, Susan is with God; She was too good for me.' (*R&J, Act I, Scene iii*)

Tessa for Lady Cap has no literary or historical origin. I read off a list of Italian names to my wife, who has played Lady Cap more times than she'd like to remember. That's the one she chose. Done and done.

While I'm discussing Giulietta's mother, I feel the need to address her childhood sexual encounter with Thibault, and her becoming a mother at the age of twelve. Starting with the latter, in the play she tells her daughter, "I was your mother much upon these years that you are now a maid." (also *Act I, Scene iii*). So she was already a mother by the time she was Juliet's age, and Juliet, remember, is *thirteen*. Now there's always a possibility that she's lying about her age – I've seen it played that way many times. But it does me little good to assume that Shakespeare's characters lie – usually when they do, they tell the audience the truth first. And there's quite a bit of dramatic tension created in Tessa marrying a man nearly three times her age.

Choosing to be hemmed in by her age, I still needed to establish the bond between Tessa and Thibault. We know from the play that the Nurse is rather, shall we say, frank about her sexuality. With that as an example, how could children not be curious? Small children often sate their curiosity by playing doctor, and that's the scene I wrote. Like all premarital sex in Shakespeare (and, indeed, almost all sex), it does not turn out well for anyone involved.

◆   ◊   ◆

Staying with the Capulletti, I must confess a (minor) heresy. I have used the Veronese building currently labeled 'Juliet's House' as the basis for the Capulletti household. While it was indeed built in the late 13th century, *La Casa Di Giulietta* was actually bought by the city in 1905 and turned into a tourist attraction.

(Digression: The balcony that you can see in this yard was glued on to the building around the time they started billing the place as the setting for the famous scene. There is an actual period balcony a floor above the fake that runs the length of the building, and looks down not only on the courtyard, but also on the rooftop of the neighbouring building. Interesting, that. So I mention the higher running balcony, but not the fake one.)

(Further digression: I have qualms about using a balcony at all. Shakespeare never mentions a balcony. *Never*. He says window, and he says it several times. But I have years before I get there to make up my mind. I mean, it's the Balcony Scene, right? It's gotta have a balcony! Who cares what Shakespeare actually *wrote?*)

Similarly, I have kept the name of the street outside the house as the modern *via Cappello,* rather than the accurate *via di San Bastiàn,* from the name of a church built in 932 AD at one end of the street. I actually prefer the latter, but I think the modern makes more sense for the overall story.

In an effort to be totally inconsistent, I have taken the location marked as Juliet's tomb and returned it to its proper owners, the Franciscan friars of the Capuchin. My reasoning is simple – in the play, the Capulet family vault is accessible from the open air, not through a church (though the line "stony entrance to this sepulcher" does give me pause). Besides, I have difficulty putting the Capulletto tomb inside the city walls at all. Space was at a premium and, from Roman times, family vaults were outside the proper walls. What did the dead need of that stony protection? The only exceptions, of course, were the tombs of the Scaligeri, and those few knights like Castelbarco who had ties to certain churches. So San Francesco al Corso has been restored to the Order that needed it, the Franciscans.

As to our beloved (if rather callow) Franciscan, Friar Lorenzo, the blackmailing of him is from one of Shakespeare's sources, Luigi da Porto. In that version of the tale, young Romeo has some dirt on the good friar, and Lorenzo is arm-twisted into helping the lovers. But that doesn't jive with the relationship that Shakespeare's Romeo has with the friar, so I've transferred the idea, giving it to Pietro. Which meant, of course, I had to come up with something to blackmail him with…

Oh, and I do know that Franciscan friars dwell in convents, not monasteries. But in the modern shorthand, convents are for women, monasteries for men. I didn't want to be confusing (or confused), so I have used the common rather than proper term.

While I'm speaking of proper terms: I've been reliably informed that *Signore* isn't the most correct mode of address, that *Messer* would be far more suitable. I tried it, read it, and finally realized why I didn't like it. In Shakespeare's Italian plays, men are always calling each other *Signior*. So as this series is based as much on Shakespeare as upon history, and as I'm writing for a primarily English-speaking audience, I ask my Italian readers to forgive me my foible. It's hardly the only one, but this time it's not due to ignorance, but stubbornness.

The same applies to Ser Alaghieri and the like. In Italian, as in English, it should be Ser Pietro – Sir Peter. We don't say Sir Stewart or Sir McKellen – it's Sir Patrick and Sir Ian (Sir Ian, Sir Ian). But Ser Alaghieri helps tremendously in the story-telling. I'm making up my own rules here, people. It's wild!

To prove I'm utterly hopeless even in the face of facts, I've kept to calling the main square the Piazza della Signoria when both my Veronese friends and AM Allen's maps clearly call it the *Piazza dei Signori*. Why? Because that's what it says in my guidebook, dammit. And I think it rolls off the tongue. I'm sure it will be fixed in the Italian edition.

Knowing the anguish I caused last time, there are again two Shakespeare-related anagrams hidden in the text. But this time, hints: one is an anagram for *William Shakespeare*, the other for *Romeo and Juliet*. Please, don't hurt me.

◆　◇　◆

Away from Literature and Language, on to History.

The major events of Cangrande's life are fairly undisputed, only the minutiae are murky. So all the feats I attribute to him are based in as much fact as we have. Even diminished from his youthful glory, he is a man made for fiction. For example, Cangrande's fake death and miraculous return is perfectly true – the rumor of his death, the panic, the rise of Mastino, the sudden return, the banishment of Federigo. I wish I were creative enough to make that kind of thing up but, I assure you, it's all history. Only Cesco and the motives are mine.

Motives. I received a good deal of guff from several of my Veronese friends for the final chapter of THE MASTER OF VERONA, and I'll confess I ended up vilifying Cangrande far more than I'd originally planned (though I think Mastino deserves everything I give him – read Petrarch's excoriation of him). Part of the problem was that I was falling into hero-worship with the character I was writing – always dangerous. So feet of clay for him! But also, the more I looked for patterns, the more scheming I found on Cangrande's part. Many are the reports of his growing pride in the last years of his life. What was good for Verona became entangled with what was good for him, and what was good for him was hard on personal relationships, as witnessed by his falling out with Bonaccolsi.

On the other hand, I'm the first that I know of to suggest that Bonaccolsi was equally culpable in the deterioration of their relationship. Not everything can be laid at Cangrande's door, as Pietro learns. Thus while I have made him a villain in so many areas, I've actually exonerated Cangrande for the one deed he was condemned for in life – his turning against Passerino. It's astonishing where fiction can lead.

As I've kept Katerina della Scala artificially (if, I hope, artfully) alive an extra twenty years, what's a few more? Even crippled, the machinations of the Scaligeri matriarch are wonderful fun to write. And like a Shakespeare play, there are far too few women in this tale. I refuse to lose one of the most interesting.

Small note to ward off the obvious objection – Venetian gondolas used to be multi-colored, not black as they are today.

◆　◇　◆

Regarding Cesco's horsemanship: I know of no child who can do what I ascribe to eleven year-old Cesco. Yet the skills of the Jighitovka are well established in the modern world and have their roots in the 6th Century. Like modern gymnasts, training began quite young. Cesco is admittedly self-taught, but the possibility exists. And if it's only improbable, not impossible, Cesco will work until the job is done. To quote the saint that shares his name: 'Start by doing what is necessary. Then do what's possible. And suddenly you're doing the impossible.'

Yet another disclaimer, a personal one: when I finished the first draft of this novel, my son was two years old. His name is Dashiell, after Dashiell Hammet, whose works I love. At the time of publication, his sister Evelyn is just a touch older. I want to put it into writing that they were marvelous infants and toddlers. We couldn't wish for better tempered, more ingenious, curious, adventurous, charming, devilish children. I say this because when Dash and Evie are grown, I will have to explain to them in no uncertain terms that, no, I had nothing against them as babies. With so many young characters, I am invariably going to harm one or two in the process. I swear, next book, no baby danger (though things get dicey for a couple of teens).

◆    ◊    ◆

A.M. Allen's A HISTORY OF VERONA is still my primary source, along with PADUA UNDER THE CARRARA by Benjamin J. Kohl. For the history of Dante's family I again used Emanuele Carli's DANTE E GLI ALLIGHIERI A VERONA, a volume containing some contentious information but that I nonetheless quite enjoy. Lastly, the Italian version of GLI SCALIGERI, 1277-1387, edited by Arnaldo Mondadori, is chock full of facts and contains photos of just about every Scaligeri artifact a body could want.

The conversation of excellent ways to die is pure theft. Frances Stonor Saunders begins her marvelous history of the period, THE DEVIL'S BROKER, with just this discussion (she also mentions the Scaligeri, always pleasing.). And it echoes the conversation Julius Caesar had the night before his assassination, which was the basis for my play *Eve Of Ides*.

For *Ecerinis*, I must thank Joseph R. Berrigan, whose 1975 translation is the only copy I could find in English (though it seems quite popular in German). Hailing from an age that saw the rise of Dante, Petrarch, and Boccaccio, the poet Albertino Mussato has been all but forgotten. His play is not, perhaps, great theatre, but it is great art in the Senecan style. Just prior to 1300, the Paduan literati came into possession of several of the Roman playwright Seneca's manuscripts, and Mussato embraced the form. He meant this particular play as more than art — he was ringing the alarum bell, warning Padua of another tyrant of Verona who was bearing down upon them. But civil strife proved a greater threat to Paduan peace than Cangrande ever was.

As in MoV, the translations of select Italian poems comes from an anthology by Marc A. Cirigliano.

I am also indebted to Dale Antony Girard's privately published volume, THE FIGHT ARRANGER'S COMPANION. Girard has taken centuries of French, Italian, English, and Spanish sword terminology and created a unified dictionary. I hope he has plans for a wider publication in the future, as it has proven even more useful to me as an author than as a fight director, and other writers and scholars should have access to it.

Like the last one, this novel could not have been fully formed without the internet. Halfway through a paragraph I'd come up with a question that I'd go online to answer. What were the makes of saddles in 1325? Who was ruling Aragon, or Egypt? What was the date of Easter Sunday, 1329? Fully half of my research happened on the web, sifting through incomplete and conflicting data. It is perhaps sinful of me not to note herein the sources of my information, but this is fiction, not journalism (though I did try to double-source everything). If any reader has questions, I encourage them to go hunting – there are more details out there than I could possibly render here. But a note to the website asking for further sources will be answered as best I'm able: WWW.DAVIDBLIXT.COM, or the blog at WWW. THEMASTEROFVERONA.COM. Or else my Facebook author page. Or else on Twitter. It's a brave new world.

♦     ◊     ♦

Thanks to Tara Sullivan for reading it piecemeal as it was written, and for forgiving what I was doing to characters she loves (the texts I got were very angry). Thanks to Scott Kennedy for being another early reader, and Chris Walsh for his kind encouragement. Thanks to Breon Bliss for reimagining Friar Lawrence's physicality for me. To all the Patches, past and present, thanks for playing.

Big thanks to Michael Denneny, *editor extraordinaire*, for his ability to slice away the fat and leave the lean.

Grazie to Judith Testa and Marina Bonomi for fixing my many, many Italian infelicities. Thanks too to Constance Cedras for hunting down the pesky and persistant typos as this was prepared for print. They all tried valiantly to correct my blunders, and any remaining errors are entirely mine.

The best question to ask an author is, "Who do you read?" I'm fortunate enough to have rubbed shoulders with some of my favorite authors, among them Sharon Kay Penman, C. W. Gortner, MJ Rose, and

Michelle Moran, to whom I owe incalculable debts, both for their words and for their kindness. If you haven't read them, do yourself a favor and pick up their books now. For earlier influences, check out Dorothy Dunnett, Bernard Cornwell, Colleen McCullough, Patrick O'Brian, and Raphael Sabatini.

My parents, who gave every kind of help imaginable during the writing of this book and the one before it, I cannot thank enough — it simply isn't possible (my mother designed the maps, too). Much love to my brother Andrew, the soul of patience.

Dash and Evie are the light of my days and the bane of my nights.

But not my inspiration. To inspire means to breathe in. The person I breathe in is my wife. Janice, *cara mia*, every day is new, every face is you.

The next novel is entitled *Fortune's Fool*.

*Ave,*
*DB*

MORE DAVID BLIXT NOVELS
FROM SORDELET INK

---

The Star-Cross'd Series

THE MASTER OF VERONA
VOICE OF THE FALCONER
FORTUNE'S FOOL

*and coming Summer 2013*

THE PRINCE'S DOOM

---

The Colossus Series

COLOSSUS: STONE & STEEL
COLOSSUS: THE FOUR EMPERORS

*and coming Fall 2013*

COLOSSUS: WAIL OF THE FALLEN
COLOSSUS: TRIUMPH OF THE JEWS

---

HER MAJESTY'S WILL

Visit
WWW.DAVIDBLIXT.COM
for more information.

Made in the USA
Charleston, SC
03 November 2013